*Forthcoming in hardcover from DAW Books

ALTERNATE REALITIES

PORT ETERNITY

VOYAGER IN NIGHT

WAVE WITHOUT A SHORE

C.J. CHERRYH

DAW BOOKS, INC.

DONALD A. WOLLHEIM, FOUNDER

375 Hudson Street, New York, NY 10014

ELIZABETH R. WOLLHEIM
SHEILA E. GILBERT
PUBLISHERS

www.dawbooks.com

A fast forward from the author. . . .

These books are special . . . and thanks to Betsy Wollheim for carrying on the tradition of a kind of science fiction publishing that's not a spinoff, not a copy of a TV show—in fact, not "just like" much else you'll meet. In her decision to put these books out in a modern format she's guaranteed they're findable. Trust me: colored lights and sfx aren't the "real stuff" of science fiction, that branch of writing we fondly called "the literature of ideas" long before NASA flew. No, the "real stuff" is extrapolation—that twelve-letter word for taking a concept and running with it as far and as fast as a lively mind can follow, be it into whimsy or down a scary slip on thin ice. Extrapolative tales require a rarer kind of reader, a mind that enjoys hopping from ice floe to ice floe to get to . . . well, you just can't predict, and that's the point, isn't it?

It's very certain you don't get rich writing or publishing what Betsy Wollheim and I call the "magic cookie books," but there's the special reward of putting these hard-to-place books out where the right readers can find them.

PORT
ETERNITY

I was lucky in my first publisher and lucky in the era in which I wrote my earliest books; Donald Wollheim of DAW Books, owning his own publishing house, gave me free rein to experiment, and to write the outrageous, and to exercise a set of muscles a writer ideally needs. Ever seen a butterfly come out of the chrysalis? The wings are small and shriveled. But the wings begin to beat, and to expand, and they stretch out and show their patterns as life flows into them. The relationship of a writer to someone who gives them the chance to do that imagination-stretch is precious.

My original title for this was Involutions, because it spirals in upon itself. Reality starts down a whirlpool ride into dream and into fiction, and the fictional world becomes more real than surrounding space, at least for a time . . .

Or isn't it, after all, that all fiction is the backyard of the house we live in, our release from the four-walled constraint of daily chores we do just to eat and have a place to sleep? And while we're there . . . it's real.

Stories are what we all work to have. Oh, how destitute are those who don't have access to stories at all, or who don't realize that stories are the prize in the box, and that daily life without them is so much less!

Stories aren't escape. They're the living of an active mind. Making money and acquiring things can scratch a few itches, too, but give me a man who loves the companionship of human beings and animals, who appreciates good stories and good food at his fireside, and who'll bestir himself considerably to get them around him.

Well, Don and I discussed the book, but Don said it was science fiction, not a philosophy text, and I needed a better title. So he came up with **Port Eternity**, and so it is.

And where did this particular idea come from? Well, I've loved the Arthurian legends since I played at castles and knights, and

I think they'll have immediacy so long as the English culture survives in any of its farflung children.

That's the other thing stories teach us: that we extend farther than our own lifespan, and that there's unsuspected greatness in the least of us.

When we believe that for a starting fact, everything we do, we do in a different light.

I

. . . Fairy Queens have built the city, son;
. . . And as thou sayest it is enchanted, son,
For there is nothing in it as it seems
Saving the King; tho' some there be that hold
The King a shadow, and the city real. . . .

She was a beautiful ship, the *Maid of Astolat*, beautiful in the way ships can be when cost means nothing, and money certainly meant nothing except the comfort and the pleasure of my lady Dela Kirn. I had seen the *Maid* from the outside, but her crew had not, at least not since the day they boarded her. She was beautiful outside and in, sleek, with raking lines to her vanes which meant nothing at all in space, but pleased the eye and let everyone know that this was no merchanter, no; and inside, inside she was luxury and comfort, which I appreciated too, more than I appreciated the engineering. Where lady Dela went, I went, along with the other servants lady Dela had for her personal comfort; but the *Maid* was the best of the places Dela Kirn lived, and I was happiest when she gave the order that packed up the household for the winter season and took us up to station, for whatever destination pleased her.

Usually this move coincided with some new lover, and some of these were good and some were not—more disagreeable than pleasant, truth be told; but we managed, usually, to enjoy ourselves by avoiding them at their worst. Often enough the *Maid* had no really binding course, more duration than destination. She just set out and toured this station and another, and because Dela loved to travel, and grew bored with this and that climate, we were a great deal on the move. Dela Kirn, be it understood, was one of the Founders of Brahman, not that she herself had founded a world, but her predecessors had, so Dela Kirn inherited money and power and in short, whatever she had ever fancied to have or do.

My name is Elaine, which amused my lady Dela, who gave the name to me. I have a number on my right hand, very tiny and tasteful, in blue; and the same number on my shoulder, 68767-876-998, which I *am*, if anyone asked, and not Elaine. *Elaine* was Dela Kirn's amusement. I was *made* 68767-876-998. *Born* isn't the right word, being what I am, which is a distinction I don't fully understand, only that my beginning was in a way different than birth, and that I was planned. I've never had any other name than Elaine, I think, because before Dela I have no clear memory where I was, except that it was nowhere—one of the farms. On the farms they lock you up and you spend a lot of time doing repeat work and a lot of time exercising and a lot of time under deepteach or just blanked, and none of it is pleasant to think back on. When I have nightmares they tend to be of that, of being locked up alone, with just my own mind for company.

They worked over my genes in planning me, me, 68767-876-998, so that I'm beautiful and intelligent, which isn't vanity to say, because I had nothing at all to do with it. And probably there are hundreds of me, because I was a successful combination, and a lot aren't. I cost my lady a lot of money, like the *Maid*, but then, she wouldn't have wanted me if I hadn't.

And Lancelot and Vivien were beautiful too, which they were made to be . . . Dela gave them their names from the same source she got mine, having this fancy for an old poem-tape. I knew. I had heard it. The story made me sad, especially since that Elaine, the lily maid, died very young. I knew of course that I would too, which happens to our type . . . they take us when we get a little beyond forty and put us down, unless we have learned by then to be very clever or unless we have somehow become very important, which few of us do.—But they made us on tape, feeding knowledge into our heads by that means, while they grew our bodies, so I suppose they have the right to do that, like throwing out tape when it gets worn—or when we wear out, beyond use.

Lance—for him I felt sorriest of all when I first heard the tape, because of what he was and because of the story too, that it came out just as badly for him. It was a terrible story, and a grand one at the same time. I heard it over and over again, whenever I had the chance, loving it, because in a way it was me, a

me I would never be, except in my dreams. Only I never wanted
to give it to Lance to hear, or even to Viv, because their part in
it was crueler than mine; and somehow I was afraid it might
come true, even if we have no love the way born-men do.

Dying—that, of course, we do, all of us. But what it was to
love . . . I only dreamed.

I was still young, having served my lady Dela just five years.
Vivien was older; and so was Lance, who was trained for other
things than keeping the household in order, I may add, and very
handsome, more than any of Dela's other lovers that she had for
other reasons. Dela was good to Lance when she was between
lovers, and as far as we could love, I think Lance loved her very
much. He had to. That was what *his* taped psych-set made him
good for, and mostly it was what he thought about, besides being
beautiful. He was older than any of us, being thirty-six—and
forty frightened him.

I was, precisely, twenty-one, after five years' service; because
really my mind was better than the training they put into it—and
I was sold out at sixteen, finished two years younger than most
leave the farms. I read; I wrote; I sang; I knew how to dress and
how to do my lady's hair and how to make love and do simplest
math, all of which recommended me, I suppose. But mostly I
was innocent, which pleased my lady Dela. She liked the look
of me, she would say, holding my face in her two hands and
smiling. I have chestnut hair and greenish eyes, and I blush
quickly, which would make her laugh; besides that I have, she
would say, a face like in the old romance, my eyes being very
large for my face and my skin decidedly pale. I have a romantical sad look—not that I am sad a great deal of the time, but I
have the look. So I was Elaine, the lily maid, like the ship. Elaine
loved Lancelot and died for love, Elaine my namesake in the
poem, but love was very far from me.

Actually, if I had something to make me melancholy, it was
that I had that name which meant dying young, and I had been
out of the farms so short a time that death, however romantical,
hardly appealed to me. I had never thought much about death
before that tape—but I did think of it afterward.

Vivien—Vivien now: she was different, all sharpness and wit,
and that was *her* function, not being beautiful, although she was,
in a dark and elegant fashion. The Vivien of the story was a cold

and intelligent woman; and so was ours, who managed the accounts and all the things that Dela found too tedious, the really complicated things. Age had no terror for Vivien—she was sure to go on past forty: without *her*, my lady Dela would hardly have known what to do about her taxes.

Mostly Viv kept to herself. She was of course older, but she looked down not just on me, but on Lance—which she had a right to do, being the most likely of us all to be given rejuv and to live as long as Dela herself. Viv did sleep with us in the servants' quarters, and she talked to us without spite, but she was not like us. I bored her; and Lance did, entirely, because Viv had no sex drive at all and made no sense of Lance. Attractive and elegant as she was, she got all her pleasure from her account-keeping and from organizing things and telling us what to do, which is as good a way to get pleasure as any other, I suppose, if it works, which it seemed to do for Vivien.

Then there was the crew, who were like us all, made for what they did. Their pleasures were mostly of Vivien's sort—taking care of the ship and seeing that everything aboard was in order. Only sometimes they did have sex when the *Maid* was in dock, at least three of them, because there was nothing else for them to do. They lived all their lives waiting on Dela's whim to travel.

The men were Percivale, Gawain, and Modred. Modred was a joke of kinds, because he was one of the really cold ones who mostly cared for his computers and his machines; and there was Lynette, who was the other pilot besides Gawain. None of them could make anyone pregnant and Lynette couldn't get pregnant, so it was all safe enough, whatever they did; but they had that kind of psych-set that made them go off sex the moment they were set on duty. The moment the ship activated, the ship became mistress to all of them: they served the *Maid* in a kind of perpetual chastity in flight, except a few times when my lady had guests aboard and lent them out.

That was the way we lived.

On this particular voyage there was just one guest, and my lady Dela was busy with him from the time we all came aboard. He was her favorite kind of lover, very rich and better still—young. He had not yet gone into rejuv; was golden and blond and very serious. His name was Griffin, and it might have been one of Dela's own conceits, but it really was his name. It meant a kind of beast which was neither one thing nor the other, and that was very much like Griffin. He read a great deal and had a hand in everything; he spent a lot of his off time enjoying tape dramas, to my great delight . . . for with that store of them which had come aboard the *Maid* because of him, I was going to have a great many of them to spend time with, as I had had constantly during the time he had been at the country estates at Brahmani Dali. Born-man dramas were a kind of deepteach I dearly loved, stories where you could just stretch out and let your mind go, and *be* those people. (But several of his tapes I had not liked at all, and they gave me nightmares: This was also Griffin. They were about hurting people, and about wars, and I hated that, but there never was a way to tell what kind of stories they were when I was sneaking them out of library, no way at all to tell what I was going to get until I took the drug and turned the machine on, and then, of course, it was too late to back out.) All of this was Griffin, who came from neighboring Sita, and who visited for business and stayed for pleasure. He surprised us at first by staying longer than a week, and then a month, and four, and lastly by getting invited to the *Maid*. He was, truth be known, half Dela's real age, although she never looked the difference . . . she was seventy, and looked thirty, because Dela hated the thought of getting old, and started her rejuv at that age, for vanity's sake, and also I think because she had no desire for children, which holds most born-men off it another decade. At thirty-odd Griffin had not yet needed it, although he was getting to that stage when he might soon think of it. He attended on Dela. He slept with no one else; his vices were secret and invisible—austere by comparison to some of Dela's companions. By the stories Griffin liked, I suspected he was one of those who didn't mind being hurt, and my lady was certainly capable of obliging him.

Dela herself. Dela was, as I say, thirtyish looking, though over twice that, and she dyed the silver that rejuv made of her hair, so that it was palest blonde and she wore it in great beautiful braids. She was elegant, she was pink and gold and quite, quite small. She never liked figures and accounting; but she loved planning things and having things built. She built four cities on Brahman, with all their parks and shops, and owned them. All the inside of the *Maid* was Dela's planning, down to the light fixtures, and the sheets on the beds. She had built the *Maid* a long time ago—the *Maid* was getting old inside, just like Dela (but still beautiful) and she was something worth seeing, though few ever did. She was a fairytale; and special to Dela. Deep inside Dela I think there was something that hated life as it was, and hated her expensive safety, and the guards and the precautions that were all about her on Brahman. She hated these things and loved the stories until she began to shape them about her—and shaping them, she shaped the *Maid*.

I thought by that strange fancy I could understand Dela, who lived stories that were long ago and only maybe so, whose life came down to tapes, just like mine.

Tapes and new lovers. Like Lance, she was desperately frightened of getting old. So I always knew how to please her, which was to make her believe she was young. When Dela was happy she could be kind and thoughtful; but when things went badly, they went badly for all of us, and we mourned her lost lovers with earnest grief—all of us, that is, except Lance, whose psychset drove him inevitably to comfort her, so Lance always had the worst of it. If there was ever a face that life *made* sad—Dela always favored the storybook looks—it was surely Lance's, beautiful as he was; and somehow he had gotten caught in it all unawares, because she had never given him the old story tapes I had heard. I always thought he would have understood that other Lancelot, who lost whenever he seemed to win.

Maybe Dela was a little crazy. Some of her peers said so, in my hearing, when I was making myself a part of the furniture. It is true that we lived in a kind of dream, who lived with Dela Kirn; but only those who entered the *Maid* ever saw the heart of it, the real depth of her fancy. The ship was decorated in a strange mix of old fables and shipboard modern, with swords, real swords and hand-stitched banners fixed on the walls, and old-looking beams masking the structural joinings, and lamps that mimicked live flame in some of the rooms like the beautiful dining hall or her own private compartments. And those who became her lovers and played her game for a while—they seemed to enjoy it.

It struck me increasingly strange, me, who had nothing of property, and was instead owned and made, that for Dela Kirn who could buy thousands of my kind and even have us made to order . . . the greatest joy in her life was to pretend. All my existence was pretense, the pretense of the tapes which fed into my skull what my makers and my owner wanted me to know and believe; and until I was sold to Dela and until I saw Dela's secret fancies, I thought that the difference between us and born-men was that born-men lead real lives, and see what really is, and that this was the power born-men have over the likes of us. But all Dela wanted with all her power was to unmake what was, and to shape what the story tapes told her until she lived and moved in it. So then I was no longer sure what was true and what was false, or what was best in living, to be me, or to be Dela Kirn.

Until the end, of course, when they would put me down because I had no more usefulness, while Dela went on and on living on rejuv, which our kind almost never got. Seventy. I could not, from twenty-one, imagine seventy. She had already lived nearly twice as long as I ever could, and she had seen more and done more, living all of it, and not having the first fifteen years on tape.

Maybe, I thought, in seventy years she had worn out what there was to know; and that might be why she turned to her fables.

Or she was mad.

If one has most of the wealth of a world at one's disposal, if one has built whole cities and filled them with people and gotten bored with them, one can be mad, I suppose, and not be put down for it . . . especially if one owns the hospitals and the labs. And while far away there was a government which sent warnings to Dela Kirn, she laughed them off as she did most unpleasant things and said that they would have to come and do something about it, but that they were busy doing other things, and that they needed Brahman's good will. About such things I hardly know, but it did seem to work that way. No one came from the government but one angry man, and a little time in Dela's country house at Brahmani Dali under our care, and some promises of philanthropy, sent him back happier than he had come.

This much I understood of it, that Dela had bought her way out of that problem as she had bought off other people who stood in her way; and if ever Dela could not buy her way through a difficulty, then she threatened and frightened people with her money and what it could do. If Dela felt anything about such contests, I think it was pleasure, after it was all over—pleasure at the first, and then a consuming melancholy, as if winning had not been enough for her.

But the *Maid* was her true pleasure, and her real life, and she only brought her favorite lovers to it.

So she brought Griffin . . . all gaiety, all happiness as we hurried about the *Maid*'s rich corridors settling everyone in our parting from Brahmani Station—but there was a foreboding about it all which my lady understood and perhaps Griffin did not; it was months that she would love a man before she thought it enough to bring him to the *Maid*, and after that, it was all downhill, and she had no more to give him. The dream would end for him, because no one could live in Dela's story forever.

Only we, Elaine and Lancelot and Vivien; and Percy and Wayne and Modred . . . we were always there when it ended; and Lance would be hurt as he always was; and I would comfort him—but he never loved me . . . he was fixed on Dela.

So we set off on holiday, to play out the old game and to revel while we could, and to make Dela happy a time, which was why we existed at all.

II

Then ran across her memory the strange rhyme
Of bygone Merlin, "Where is he who knows?
From the great deep to the great deep he goes."

Griffin, as I say, was one of the strange ones my lady Dela picked up from time to time, not easy to fix which of his several natures was the real one, no. I had found him frightening from the start, truth be told. He didn't laugh often, but much when he did, and he could be mortally stubborn and provoke Dela to rages which came down on all of us and darkened the house at Brahmani Dali for days. He interfered with Dela's business and talked to Vivien about the books, which ordinarily Dela would never allow—but Griffin did, and had his way about it, amid storms in the country house which would have disposed of less appealing lovers. He wound himself in tighter and tighter with my lady's business, and that disturbed us all.

He was an athletic sort, who looked rather more like one of us than he did like a born-man; but then, they play games even with born-man genes when women are rich, and Griffin certainly came from wealthy beginnings. Like Lance, Griffin seemed to fill whatever room he was in. He was very tall and slim in the hips and wide in the shoulders . . . and he had an interesting, strong-boned face—not so fine as Lance, who was dark-haired and handsome and had meltingly dark eyes, but Griffin was bronzed and blond like one of the knights in the storybook tape. That answered, physically, why Dela had been attracted at the outset.

But Griffin was not, like most of her previous lovers, empty-headed; and he had not gotten pretty by spending all his time taking care of that beautiful body. He was just that way, which left the rest of his time to be doing something else—and in Griffin's case, that something else was meddling with Dela's business or lying lost in the tapes. He was one of the few men I ever did know who looked merely asleep under the tapes, and not lackwitted: Griffin did not know how to be ungraceful, I think it was muscle. He just did not collapse when he slept the deep-sleep. And when he was awake, he was imposing. He tended to stare through the likes of me, or at very most remembered and thanked me for doing some small extra service for him—a courtesy far greater than I had gotten from most of my lady's associations, and at the same time, far less, because he could still look through me while he was thanking me. He never bedded with me, and he was the first of Dela's lovers who had never done that. He stayed to Dela. That fact upset me at first, but he bedded with none of the estate servants male or female either, so I understood it was not my failing: he simply wanted Dela, uniquely and uninterrupted by others—quite, quite different from the usual. I saw them together, matched, blond and blonde, story-book knight and storybook lady, a man full of ideas, a man my lady let into more than the bedchamber. He was change; and he frightened us in strange and subtle ways.

What, we wondered, when she should tire of him?

We had set out from station that morning, and Dela was taking a nap, because we had been up too many hours getting up from the world and getting settled in, and we had gone through a time change. We were, of course, under acceleration and moving a little cautiously when we walked, but nothing uncomfortable: the *Maid* rarely hurried. Griffin was still up and about, typical of the man, to be meddling with charts and tapes and comp in his cabin; and he wanted a little of my lady's imported brandy. I brought it to his cabin, which was next to Dela's own, and since he had not dismissed me I stood there while he sipped the brandy and fussed with his papers.

This time? I wondered. It would spoil all my reckonings of him if he asked me to bed with him now. I stood thinking about it, watching his broad back, no little distressed, thinking of all those tapes he listened to, about murdering and pain. He was altogether imposing under those circumstances. Dela was abed, drugged down; perhaps he felt he needed someone. A lot of people get nervous before jump. I waited. I blanked, finally, went null as my knees locked up, and I was in some pain; blinked alert as he stood up and looked down at me.

"I'm sorry," was all he said. "Go. Go on. That's all."

"Thank you, sir," I said, wondering now if it would have pleased him had I been forward with him: some expected that. I looked back from the doorway. But Griffin had snugged down on the bed on his belly, head on his arms, and looked genuinely content enough: the brandy seemed to have had its effect. So he was happy; Dela would be. That was all I wanted. I went back and took the empty glass, set it on the tray, and left.

It might not be, I was thinking then, so bad a voyage, Griffin simply remaining Griffin: some men changed aboard, becoming bizarre in their fancies and their demands, but he did not. I diverted myself through the library, a simple jog from the corridor that joined his and Dela's cabin and the outer hall, into the library/deepsleep lab, with its double couch. A touch of a button, the unsealing of a clear-faced cabinet, neat tucking of a tape cassette into my coveralls pocket and off and out the other door, into the same hall and out into the main corridor. Dela never minded, but then, Dela had whims: I kept my borrowings neat and quiet.

The galley then, on lowermost level, and up again to our own quarters, midway in the ship, very nice, very comfortable, after the fashion of things aboard the *Maid*. Deep, fine beds, the finest sheets, fine as Dela's own—she never scanted us. Beautiful thick carpet, all the colors rust and brown and cream, a fine curved couch wrapped all the way around the corner, one level behind the other, with multiple deepstudy outlets, and the screens above, on the ceiling. Lance was there, not deepstudying, just sitting on the couch, arms on his knees, looking downhearted and tragic as he usually did at such settings-forth. I had had some thought of using my tapes; I gave it up, and sat down by Lance and took his hand in my lap and simply went into blank again. For us too, it had been too many time changes, and it would be better for Lance when he was rested.

Vivien came in from attending whatever business had occupied her with the station and the undocking, accounts and charges all squared, presumably. Not the least drooping, not a sleekly chignoned hair mussed, but Viv was on our schedule: she had a brittleness to her movements, all the same. And came Percy and Lynette, of the crew, who were on ship's time and who looked like business as they usually did when we saw them. Percy was a youngish man with red hair and a delightful beard, all very close and delicately trimmed, his great vanity. And Lynn, Lynn was a flat and ethereal sort with an aquiline nose and freckles that had never seen much of any sun, brown hair trimmed as close as Percy's.

"What sort have we got this trip?" Percy asked, reclining on the nearest bed, his booted ankles crossed. He propped himself up sidelong on his elbow. This was our haven, this room. We could say what we liked with no one listening, so it was safe for him to ask. Lynette had settled sidelong the other way, leaning against him, not flirting, but because we all like touching when we relax, which is the way we are, sexed or not. Percy and Lynn, being crew, and busy all this while, had not yet met Griffin.

I shrugged. That was the kind of impression I had to give about Griffin, that I didn't have a clear impression, even after all this time. We had gotten used to him down at Brahmani Dali, as much as one could get used to Griffin—which meant we accepted that he would be up to something constantly, and alternately upsetting my lady and pleasing her.

"I don't like him," Lance said suddenly. Four months of silence, and: "I don't like him." He had never said that before, not even with some of my lady's absolute worst, who had abused him and any others of us accessible. "I wish she would get rid of him."

That frankness upset me. It was one thing to think it, but it was another to say it out like that, even here.

"This one," said Vivien, "this one is different than the others. I think she might *marry* this one."

"No," I exclaimed, and put my hand over my mouth, guilty as Lance.

"Why else does she have me going over her accounts and letting him into them, and why does she have spies going over *his?* She said once she might marry him. I don't think it was a joke. I think she's really thinking about it. It has to do with that government business last year. This Griffin's family has influence. And the worlds, Brahman and Sita—position for a natural alliance. The government has other concerns at the moment, can't afford prolonged trouble in this direction. And besides—she seems to enjoy him."

Viv looked satisfied. *Her* position wasn't threatened. No one said anything for a while. This move seemed then to have monetary reasons behind it, which we understood: everything my lady did seriously tended to have such reasons in it, so this frightened me more and more. "He's not so bad," I said, not that I really believed it, but Lance was beside me and his hand was sweating in mine. "And she'll get cooler toward him someday. If he stays—it'll still happen that way, won't it? And he's never done anything to any of us, not like that Robert she took up with."

There was a general muttering, a reflexive jerk of Lance's hand. Robert had been the worst.

"Maybe she'll get some favor out of him or his family," Lynette said, "and then it'll be like the others."

"But she talked about marrying," Vivien persisted, unstoppable. "And she's never considered that. Ever. Griffin's intelligent, she says. Someone who could run things in years to come. She's never talked like that about the others. He's *young*."

More silence and heavier, even from Percy and Lynette, who were generally not bothered with estate finances and problems of that sort. After all, if another owner came into the picture, if Griffin began to involve himself permanently and changed Dela's way of operating—then the *Maid* might not go on making such trips as she did now. So the crew faced uncertainties too.

The *Maid* might—the thought came washing over me—might even be *sold*, and so might we all, being part of a fancy Dela might tire of if she changed her life and stopped taking lovers. Being sold was . . . I could not imagine it. I had heard dread whispers that it meant being taken back into the labs for retraining, and that meant they took your mind apart. It was effectively like dying. I didn't say that aloud. We had enough troubles, all of us. And Lance . . . he was old for retraining. Lance could be put down.

I was never inclined to sudden panics, but I had one. I sat there and blanked, and when I came out of it, Lance was tugging at my hand to shake me out of it.

"Elaine?" he said.

I clenched his hand in mine and said nothing.

"We're going to make jump sooner than usual," Lynn said. "She's told us to keep up acceleration all the way. It has to do with *him*, maybe. Ask Wayne and Modred about particulars: but it's Delhi."

The regional capital. The kind of place her ladyship had stayed out of, with her wealth which she had no desire thus far to flaunt near the government.

"Griffin has property on Delhi," Vivien said.

"What kind?" I asked, heart pounding, because I had heard of establishments on Delhi where a lot of our kind came from. Percivale was one of Delhi's breeding, so he said; and I knew that Modred was.

"Farms," Vivien said tautly. "And training centers. Labs. They've been talking about taking an interest in that. In shifting assets—Griffin's wealth and our lady's can pull hard weight in Delhi Council if they start playing games with banks. Those kind of maneuvers . . . Griffin can do. All he has to do is free up some currency. His farms there—"

Then they all seemed to think of selling and being sold, and Percy blanked, and Lynn too, for a moment, like two statues reclining there.

"I think we should get some sleep," Vivien said, with a stretch of her back. She had spent all *she* had to say, and in our matters, that was as far as Vivien's interest went. She got up and left. Sleep seemed a good idea, because there was certainly nothing pleasant to think of awake. We moved to our beds, all of which were close together, and began to get undressed. Only Lance still sat there, and I felt sorry for him. They psych-set me so that I can't stand to see someone suffering. Born-men feel; we react; so the difference runs. And Lance was reacting to everything, and especially to this most frightening of the lady's affairs. I think maybe he would rather have had Robert aboard again. Any of them. It had already been hard on him, this involvement with Griffin, lasting now for four months and promising to go on *long*—but *marry* him . . . and all this maneuvering, this trip to Delhi which seemed to make it all more and more like the truth. . . . All this had surely struck poor Lance to the gut. He wasn't blanked, and it would have been healthier if he were. He just sat there like he was bleeding inside.

"Come on," I said, walking back over to tug at his hand. "I want you"—which was a lie. I was tired, but it was his psych-set, and it gave him something to react to that would take his mind off Dela and off his own future at least for the moment. He undressed and we got between the sheets. He made love to me . . . he *was* good. What handsome blond Griffin was like I had no idea, but if it were me, or if I were lady Dela, I would have preferred Lance, who was very beautiful and who did sex very well and with endless invention, which was what he was made for.

Only his eyes were sadder than ever and he was not, this time, as good as he could be. His body reacted to his psych set; and that was that, tired or not, up to reasonable limits. But there were times when Lance was *there* and times when he was not, and this time he was not. Worry, like everything else, every other disturbance in his patterns, he channeled into his psych-set outlet the way he was healthily supposed to, so he was not breaking down and he didn't panic, but it was as close to panic as I had ever seen him.

I held him close for a long time afterward and tried to keep his mind on me—which it had never been, all the while be-cause I *liked* him, in a different way than I liked anyone else. I would have called it love, but love—was for the likes of the lady Dela, who could fall into and out of grand and glorious passions, sighing and suffering and flying into rages. We just blank when we're upset. The least anguish of an emotional sort turns us off like a light going out unless we're directly ordered to stay around, or unless we're occupied about some duty. We have better sense than to cause ourselves such pains, and we have better manners than to tease one another too seriously—which, besides, would be interfering with Dela's property, and rather like vandalism, which we could not do either.

Pilferage now . . . borrowing . . . that we could do. I got up and got the tape I had pilfered out of the library and set the hookups over by the couch for Lance and me, figuring that he needed an escape just now. He wanted only to lie there staring at the ceiling, but I took him by the hand and pulled at him until he stirred out of bed and came; and then he put the sensors on himself and took the drug gladly enough when I gave it to him. I got a blanket and my own rigging fixed, drugged out and settled in, hoping for something good.

It was a story tape: I had thought so from where I pilfered it; but it was one of *those*, one of Griffin's, that could almost kill you with fright. I knew when I was still sliding into it what it was going to bc, and I tricd to opcn my mouth to yell out to

Percy or someone to help, get it off us, pull us out of it, but I
must have been too far gone. No one came.

Only the story got better. Lance and I were in it together, and
while it was more bloody than I liked, I found myself enjoying
it after all. That was it: once you give your mind to one of these
things, especially if you're down, that means the drugs have got
your threshold flat and you're locked into the tape, so that you'll
agree to whatever happens. I lived it. Lance did, to whatever degree he could, according to his own pre-programming. Probably
he was what I was, which was a hero, and very strong and extraordinarily brave and angry. Griffin had a passion for such stories, of angry men. For a little while I could handle anything at
all: I was a born-man; and I fought a great deal and sometimes
made love to a very beautiful blonde lady who reminded me of
Dela. Lance would have loved *that*. And I'll bet the men he fought
were all Griffin; but for me they were Robert, that I killed a
dozen times and enjoyed it more thoroughly than I liked to think
about when I finally woke out of it.

But when I did wake up I knew for sure it was not the kind
of tape that we were ever supposed to have, not at all, because
it was violent, and bloody, and all my psych-sets were disturbed.
Lance was that way about it too, and avoided my eyes and seemed
to be thinking about something. So I figured I had better get this
one back into that library before it was missed.

We *can* deceive, at least I could, and Lance could, and probably all of us. Vivien and Lynette and Modred were too cold to
play games . . . or to talk much with born-men, a silence which
was deception of another kind, when they had reason to use it.
At least that trio wouldn't get up and sneak about some project
for their own personal pleasure.

But Modred, now. . . .

Modred was the one I went to when I wanted a tape back in
the library undetected, a ride up in the lift toward the bow, up
to the bridge where duties were still going on. No one suspected
Modred of nonsense like tape-pilfering; and he *would* take my
orders, because the operational crew maintained the library and
were always pulling references to this and that through the computer. If I wanted a tape for my own use for a while, it was nothing for him to spin a tape through and record it, and then do

things with the records of its use. It was even less for him to
play with the records and drop a tape into the chute for the au-
tomated sorting to whisk back to its slot in the rack back in library. He could do that and never miss a beat in what else he
was doing, and I think he really preferred the more complicated
larcenies: they were problems, and this was not.

Modred and Gawain. Wayne, we called the one, for short: he
had long brown hair, and was very handsome—but he was all
business whenever I would see him, given to working himself
very hard. He was the mainday pilot, as Lynn ran things on alterday shift, and Percy was alterday comp. Gawain had a work
compulsion, which tended to make Gawain lose weight when we
were on long trips, but he really enjoyed what he did, and smiled
a lot when he was working. Me, with my psych-set to worry
about other's pain, I always carried him his dinners when he forgot them and when I happened to be awake on the same schedule; and I did the same for Modred, who shared his shift and
also worked too much and got too thin, but who never showed
exuberance about it. Modred was the only one but me whose
name we never shortened to something sensible, because when
we did it came out Dread, and that was just too much like him
to be clever. Modred had a beard as black as Percy's was red,
one of those jawline-following thin ones, but very heavy despite
how close he cut it, and while Gawain let his hair go down to
his shoulders for vanity's sake, Modred had his cut very short—
Lynn and Percy played barber, among other skills—and he cut it
square across his brow, which made his dark eyes very sinister.
That was why my lady Dela named him Modred, and I think
why she bought him, because she was fascinated by dangerous-
looking men. Even born-men moved out of Modred's way, and
that was a useful thing with some of the guests Dela had had.
Not that Modred would *hurt* anyone, being like us, psych-set
against it, but he looked like he would, and people reacted to
that. Actually, he seemed to enjoy doing me small favors I asked,
and getting small attentions from me and from Lynn when she
was in the mood. Mostly that grim face—handsome, because my
lady would not have had him about otherwise—seemed to me to
conceal a very blank sort, who did his duty, who thought and
calculated constantly, and who liked, like the rest of us, to sleep
close at night, with someone close enough to let him feel com-

panied. Vivien avoided sleeping next to him, somewhat scared of him, truth be told—and I always preferred Lance. So mostly Modred, really sexless, slept with his crewmates, who were also sexless during the voyages, and they kept each other company. Likely those four were neither concerned nor jealous about the freedom Lance and Viv and I had to come and go with my lady, to be in attendance on her, to share her luxuries, and in my case, to share her lovers—because they four were psych-fixed to the *Maid*, and when Modred or the others handled her controls, I think it was really like touching the body of a lover. It was a sort of grim joke, the stainless steel *Maid* and her crew doomed to love her with a chaste and forever devotion.

I preferred Lance.

But I flirted with Modred because it was pleasant. I always suspected he liked my touching him . . . at least that killer's face of his acquired a certain placidity like a pet being stroked by a familiar hand. He was not immune to sensation; it was just sex that was missing in him.

"Thank you," I whispered in his ear, leaning close, when he settled back into his place at the console, from disposing of the tape for me. I was not supposed to be on the bridge, any more than Modred was supposed to be doing things to the library records, but *supposed* was often a very lax word in my lady Dela's world: Dela cared nothing about laws or limitations in anyone. As long as the *Maid* served well as what she was, an abode of utmost luxury, and an extravagantly expensive toy, then what her living toys did in their off hours was of no concern. We could have held orgies on the bridge and abstracted the whole library to the crew quarters had we liked, and if my lady was in one of her relaxed moods, she would notice nothing.

There were, of course, other moods. Remembering those, we always kept the record purified.

"They'll be wanting you," Modred said in his flat way, staring at his screens to find out where things stood at the moment. Gawain was at the main console. I had my hands on Modred's shoulders and leaned to deposit a kiss on the side of his neck, which, he took about like the touch of my hands, as something relaxingly pleasant. "I think my lady is awake."

He could do that, never missing the thread of the conversation when I teased him, which was the difference between him and Gawain or Percy, who at least grew bothered.

"I'll see to it," I said, and patted his shoulder. Actually Modred fascinated me because he *couldn't* be moved, and it was my function to move people. I hadn't seen him in months, and it was a new chance to try.

I had once tried more direct approaches, in the crew quarters. I think Modred wanted, with some dim curiosity, to do what others did, but it was only curiosity. "Let him alone," Lynn had said when she saw it, with a frown that meant business.

So you play the same game with him, I had thought then, but likewise Lynette was not one to cross lightly; and when it occurred to me that I might hurt someone my psych-set intervened and cooled me down at once. I confined myself after that to small games that Modred himself found pleasant.

"We're going to make jump in another hour," Gawain said from his post.

I wrinkled my nose. That meant getting my lady and the rest of us prepped with the drugs to endure jump. That was what she wanted, then. Jump always scared me, even drugged. It was the part of voyages that I hated.

And then: "*Modred*—" Gawain said in a plaintive voice I had never heard him use. It frightened me. Modred's reaction did, because he flung off my hand and reached for another board in a hurry, and alarms were going off, shrieking.

"Out!" he shouted, and Modred never shouted. I scrambled toward the exit, staggering as the whole ship heeled, and then vocal alarms were going, the *take-hold*, which means wherever you are, whatever is closest, regardless. I never made the door. I grabbed the nearest emergency securing and got the belt round me, while already the *Maid* was swinging in a roll so that we came under *G* like coming off a world.

"We're losing it," Gawain shouted into com. "We're losing it—Modred—"

"I don't know what it is," Modred yelled back. "Instruments . . . instruments are going crazy. . . ."

I looked up from my position crouched against the bulkhead, looked at the screens, and there was nothing but black on them. We were in the safe area of our own home star and with traffic around us. There was no way anything ought to be going wrong, but *G* was pulling us and making the lights all over the boards blink red, red, red.

Then it was as if whatever was holding us had just stopped existing, no jolt, but like sliding on oil, like a horrible falling where there *is* no falling.

And jump. Falling, falling, falling forever as we hurtled into subspace. I screamed and maybe even Modred did—I heard Gawain's voice for sure, and it became space and color. There was no ship, but naked chaos all around me, that stayed and stayed and stayed.

III

. . . and from them rose
A cry that shivered to the tingling stars,
And, as it were one voice, an agony
Of lamentation, like a wind that shrills
All night in a waste land, where no one comes,
Or hath come, since the making of the world.

I don't like to think of that time, and it was a long, long while before it dawned on me that I could move, and draw myself back from the void where I was. Things were all distorted. It seemed I could see through the hull, and through myself. Sometimes the chaos was red and sometimes the red became black and red spots crawled here and there like spiders. I cried, and there were other sounds that might be other voices, or the *Maid* herself still screaming.

Then like in the time before I left that white place where I was made, I had to have something to look at, to control the images, to sort truth from illusion, and I concentrated simply on getting my hand in front of my face. Knowing what it ought to look like, I could begin to make it out, bones and veins and muscles and skin. Not red. Not black. My own true color. I concentrated on it until it took the shape and texture it ought to have, and then I was able to see shadows of other things too, like the deck, and the rest of my own body lying there.

"Gawain," I cried, and by concentrating on shapes I could see the controls, and Gawain, who looked dead hanging in the straps; and Modred, who lay on the floor . . . his restraint had given way, as mine must have, and it should have broken my ribs, but it had not . . . there was, at least, no pain. Modred was trying to move too, like something inky writhing there on the deck, but I knew who it was, and I crawled across the floor which was neither warm nor cold nor rough nor smooth . . . I made it and got his hand, and hoped for help, because Modred was frightened by nothing, and if there was any of us who had a cold enough mind up here to be able to see what to do, I had most hope of Modred.

"Hung in the between," he said. "I think we're hung up in the between."

His voice did strange things in my head, echoed round and round as if my brains had been some vast room. For a moment I didn't want to look down, because there *was* a Down and we were still falling into it. Gawain had to get us out of this; that was all I could think of, and somehow Modred was pulling himself to his feet and heading in Gawain's direction. I scrambled up to follow him, and stood swaying with one foot on one side of a chasm and the other foot on the other side, stars between, the whole flowing like a river in born-men's Hell, all fire and glowing with the stars like brighter coals. *Don't move*, my brain kept telling my body, and I didn't for a moment. I stood there and shut my eyes.

But there is an advantage in being what we are, which is that wherever we are, that's what *is*, and we don't have such problems as some do, trying to relate it to anywhere else. I was upright. I set one foot out and insisted to feel what was under it, and after that I knew that I could walk. I moved after Modred, though the room kept shrinking and expanding insanely, and sometimes Gawain was very far away and sometimes just out of reach, but two-dimensional, so that he seemed pressed between two pieces of glass, and his beautiful hair hanging down at an unconscious angle seemed afire like the river of stars, streaming and flowing like light.

"Gawain!" Modred shouted, all distorted.

"Gawain!" I shouted too.

Gawain finally began to move, slow reaching of an arm which was at the moment two-dimensional and stretched all out of proportion. He tried to sit upright, and reached for the boards or what looked like an analogue of them in this distortion of senses, a puddle of lights which flowed and ran in swirling streams of fire.

He's there, I insisted to my rebel senses, and he began to be solid, within reach, as I knew he had to be. I grasped Modred's arm and reached for Gawain's, and Gawain twisted around and held onto both of us, painfully tight. "What you want to see, you *can* see," I said. "Don't imagine, Gawain. *Don't imagine*."

He was there, all right. I could feel him heaving for breath, and I was breathing in the same hoarse gulps, and so was that third part of us, Modred.

"We've been malfunctioned into jump," Modred said, carefully, softly between gasps for breath. Voices distorted in my ears, and maybe in his too. "I think we're hung up somewhere in subspace and there's no knowing what happened back there. We could have dragged mass with us into this place. We could have dragged at the sun itself. I don't know. The instruments aren't making sense."

"Lady Dela," I said, thinking about her caught in this disaster, Dela, who was the reason for all of us existing at all.

"No drugs," Gawain murmured. "We're in this with no drugs."

That frightened me. We drug down to cope with the between of jump, that nowhere between here and there. But we were doing it without, if that was where we were . . . and like walking a tightrope across that abyss, the only hope was not to look down and not to lose our balance to it. One necessity at a time. "I'm going for lady Dela," I said.

"You'll get lost," Gawain protested, because the floors were still going in and out on us, taming reds and blacks and showing stars in the middle. "Don't. If we ripped something loose back there, if those corridors aren't sound. . . ."

"Use com." That was Modred, clearer headed than either of us. Modred passed me like a great black spider, and reached into the pool of lights, perhaps able to see them better because he knew what ought to be there. "Lady Dela," he said. "Lady Dela, this is Modred on the bridge. Do you hear me?"

"*Modred!*" a voice wailed back like crystal chimes. "Help!"

"Lady Dela!" I said. "Make up your mind to see . . . can you see? Look at something familiar until it makes sense."

"Help me," she cried.

"Do you see anything?" Gawain asked her. "Modred says we've had a jump malfunction. I agree. I think we're hung up in the between, but what I have on instruments looks like the ship is intact. Do you understand me, Lady Dela?"

"Get us out!" she screamed.

"I'm trying, lady. First I have to know where we are."

And to anyone who was thinking, that answered it, because

even I knew enough to know we weren't anywhere at all that our instruments were ever going to make sense of.

Com was open. There were voices in from all over, like tiny wailings. I could make out either Lynette or Vivien, and Percivale and Lancelot. And Griffin, giving orders.

"I can't," Gawain was saying. It was to his credit that he didn't blank, nor did Modred; but this was not an emotional crisis, this was business, and we were in dire trouble with things to do—if we could do them under these conditions.

I shivered, thinking that I had to navigate the corridors and somehow get to lady Dela. I clung to something solid on the bridge, trying to remember what the hallways looked like down to the last doorway, the last bolt in the walls, because if I forgot, I could get very, very lost.

"We may have been here a while," Modred's voice came to me out of the surges of color that filled my vision, and I made him out, black and slim, in front of the pool of lights. "Our senses are adjusting to interpret by new rules. If we're very careful, we should be able to keep our balance and find our way about."

"How long?" I asked. "How long can we have been here?"

"We play games with time and space both," Gawain's near-far voice returned, loud and soft by turns. "Jump . . . does that. Only we haven't come out of it. We're somewhere in subspace. And in the between, *haven't* is as good a prediction as we can make."

"Time," said Modred, "is the motion of matter; and relatively speaking, we're in a great deal of trouble. We don't know how long. It means nothing."

I grasped that. Not that I understood jump, but I knew that when ships crossed lightyears of distance by blinking here and there through jump, there had to be some kind of state in between, and that was why we took the drugs, not to have to remember that. But of course we were remembering it now: we were sitting in it, or moving through it, and whether time was stretched and we were living all this in seconds or whether we were really what Modred and Gawain said—hung—my mind balked from such paradoxes *They* juggled such things, Gawain and Modred and Percy and Lynn, but I had no desire to.

All at once Lynette came wading through the red and black

toward us, stained with the glow that was everywhere, and walking steadily. It was a marvelous feat, that she had gotten from the lower decks up here, and gotten to her post, but there she was, and she pushed me out of the way and sat down in the phantom of a chair, reached into the pool of lights and started trying to make sense of things.

"Percy's coming," she said. And he was. I could see him too, like a ghost striding across the distances which behaved themselves better than they had been doing a moment ago. Everyone was getting to their posts, and I knew mine. I stood up and reached out my hands so that I wouldn't crack my skull and I walked, having less trouble about it than I feared. Spatial relationships were still giving me trouble, so that things looked flat one moment and far away the next, but I kept my arms out for balance and touched the sides of the corridors when I could, shutting my eyes whenever the chaos got too bad.

It meant going far back through the ship, and the corridor writhed like a transparent snake with a row of lights down its spine. At times I shut my eyes and felt my way, but the nerves in my hands kept going numb from time to time and the walls I couldn't see felt sticking-cold and burning hot if I let them.

But they were only feelings, lies my senses tried to tell me, and once and long ago I had lived in that white place where only the tapes are real—where I got so good at seeing that I could make pictures crawl across the walls of my cell just as if the tapes were really running. Reality—that doubtful commodity that I had learned to play games with a long time ago, because my own reality was dubious: I knew how to make up what I liked; and I had flown and flashed from world to world with my lady Dela; and I had sat in country meadows under blue skies at Brahmani Dali and talked to simpler-trained servants who thought the blue was all there was, and who patted the ground and said that *that* was real—but I knew it wasn't. Their up and down was all relative, and their sitting still was really moving, because their world was moving and their sun was moving and the whole relational space of stars was spinning out in the whirlpool eddy of *this* galaxy in the scattering of all galaxies in the flinging-forth that was time.

But their time, these servants' time, was the slow ticking away of decay in their cells, and in the motion of a clock toward the date that they would be put down, and their reality would end.

They would have gone crazy here, walking down a heaving belly of a snake in that place which somehow bucked the flinging-outward that made all they knew; and *I* did not break down, being sensible, and having an idea from the beginning that it was all like the tapes back in the labs, that told our senses what to feel and do and pay attention to. There was no sense being emotional over it: new tapes, new information.

So I kept telling myself, but my nerves still would not obey the new rules and my brain kept trying to tell me I was falling and my stomach wanted to tell me I was upside down.

I sent strong orders to my eyes. The wall straightened itself marvelously well when I really bore down on it, but shadow was really shadow, like holes into nothing. Like snippets cut out of the universe. I saw space crawling there, with hints of chaos.

Left turn. I felt for a doorswitch, wondering if anything was going to work with the ship where it was, but com had worked; and the instruments back in controls were still working, even if they picked up nothing sensible. And the door did open.

I kept going, down a corridor which seemed nightmarishly lengthened. The door at my right was open, and these were my lady's compartments. I held out my hands and walked along quite rapidly now, felt my way through the misshapen door.

Someone was sobbing, a throaty, hoarse sound that moaned through the walls: that guided me. I tripped over something that went away like chimes, over and over again, caught myself on something else I could not recognize and tried to get my bearings. There were points of light, shimmers of metal—the artificial flame lamps and the old weapons that Dela loved. That puddle of color up/down? was one of the banners, a lion in gold and red and blue. And beyond that puddle was a doorway I knew. I went to it, and through the corridor inside, to the open door of her bedroom . . . a lake of blue, a great midnight blue bed, and a cluster of shapes amid it.

My companions . . . they had reached her. Lance sat there holding my lady in his arms, and Viv huddled next to him.

"Who is it?" my lady wailed.

I came and joined myself to the others, and we held and comforted her. "It's all right," Lance kept saying. "It's all right." And

I: "You know our faces. *Look* at us and everything will be what you tell it to be. It's Elaine. Elaine. Tell your eyes what they should see, and make them believe it."

"Elaine." Her hands found my face, felt for it, as if to be sure. "Go. Go help Griffin. Where is Griffin?"

"He's well," I said. "I heard him giving Wayne orders."

"Go," she pleaded, so abjectly I knew she was upsetting herself. I gathered myself up and steadied my own nerves, felt Lance's hand clinging to mine. I pulled loose of it, reached out my own toward the doorway and found it—better, much better now that I had walked this way once. I forced the room into shape and got to the corridor, felt my way along it past the library doors on the left and toward Griffin's door at the end. I got it open and a voice bellowed out at me, echoing round and round in my head.

Griffin was sick, blind sick and raving. I found the bed, found him, and stripped sheets to do what I could to comfort him. He lay on the mattress and writhed, and when I tried to make him be still he fetched me a blow that flung me rolling. It was some few moments before I could clear the haze from my eyes again, with the floor going in and out of touch with my hands, but I made it behave itself, felt the carpet, made myself see the texture of it. When I could sit up and rub the starbursts from my eyes, Griffin was sitting up and complaining; and demanding Gawain get us out of this place.

"Can't, sir," I said, hanging on the back of a chair. "We're in the between and we don't know where we are."

"Get away from me," he said. I couldn't, because my lady had told me to stay, but I pulled myself around to the front of the chair and sat down there with my knees tucked up in my arms, listening to Griffin swear and watching him stumble about the room knocking into furniture.

Eventually he discovered what we had discovered already, that he could control his stomach, and see things, and he finally seemed to get his bearings. He stood there the longest time, holding onto the dressing counter and looking at me with an expression on his face that clearly said he had not known I was there. He straightened back, stood up, felt with spidery moves of his hands toward the wall close by him. Ashamed. That was clear. And that surprised me despite everything else, because it was the first time

Griffin had ever looked at me, really seemed to notice whether I existed. He turned away, groped after the bed and threw the remnant of the bedclothes over the side. Then he sat down and leaned his head into his hands, in brittle control of things. I think it took Griffin longest of all of us because he was used to having his own way, and when the whole world stopped being what suited him, it really frightened him. But our lady Dela, who lived in fantasies, she was mobile enough to attack the corridors, and showed up unexpectedly, using Lance for her help, and with Vivien trailing anxiously after.

"Worthless," lady Dela snapped at me, finding me still perched on a chair and her precious Griffin evidently neglected, sitting on the bed. I started to warn my lady when she swept down on Griffin, but at least he refrained from hitting her. He cursed and shook her hand off . . . her precious Griffin, I thought, who had never once asked about Dela.

"Out," Dela ordered me, so I got up and left her to her ministries and her lover, finding the floor a great deal plainer than it had been and the walls at least solid. I walked out, and she cursed Lance and Viv too, telling them they ought to be about their proper business, so I waited for them outside, and caught Lance's hand and held onto it for comfort when they came outside the door. What we were supposed to be doing, what our business was now, I had no least idea. Lance looked vastly shaken. Vivien looked worse than that, her eyes like one vast bruise, her hair disheveled, her fingers locked like claws on Lance's other arm, as if she were afraid he would dissolve at any moment. I reckoned that Vivien, who was so very good at books and figures, really had the least concept of all what had happened to the *Maid* and to her; she was narrow, was Viv, and so long as her accounts balanced, that was enough. Now they did not.

"I think maybe we should get Viv to bed," I said, and Lance pried her fingers loose and took her hand. We put our arms about her and guided her between us, all the long confusing way back to the lift; and that was the worst, that little loss of vertical stability after all the rest had been ripped away from us. Viv simply moaned, too dignified to scream, and leaned on us. We got her out again at the bottom and back to the crew quarters. She was better when we had put her into bed, not troubling to undress her. I tucked the sheet up over her and Lance patted her

forehead and got her a drink, holding her head with great tenderness despite all his own distress. It seemed strange how Lance
and I managed better than Dela and Griffin and even Vivien, who
until now had managed our lives and told us what to do. But we
didn't have to cope with the whys and the what-nows, just do
little things like walk the halls and keep ourselves on our feet.
The ones I least envied in this calamity were the *Maid*'s crew,
who were up in controls trying to figure where we were and even
when—with no reference points.

IV

―――――――

. . . but Arthur with a hundred spears
Rode far, till o'er the illimitable reed,
And many a glancing plash and sallowy isle,
The wide-wing'd sunset of the misty marsh
Glared on a huge machicolated tower. . . .

Hour by hour, if that was really a word we could use any longer, the world grew clearer, and Vivien confessed she would live. Then came peevish orders from my lady, who complained she was deserted by the whole staff: she wanted Lance—which meant Griffin was better, I reckoned, since she sounded more angry than hysterical.

Lance went off in his pained despair, called up there to be near Griffin, which he hated, and with Dela, which was all he ever wanted. That left us with Vivien in the crew quarters then, in disfavor, I suspected. Vivien had drifted into quiet, exhausted, and we had given her a little sedative we had had ready for jump, belatedly, but it let Viv rest, not quite out, not really tracking on much either. And in a ship the walls of which were none too stable yet in my senses . . . the lonely quiet seemed to put me all too far from everyone else. I was also conscious suddenly that my stomach was terribly empty. If time had gone as wrong as we thought it might have, then it might have been a long while that we had not wanted food or water, but now it hit me all of a sudden, so that I found my limbs shaking, as if all the demands of some long deprivation were coming due.

And sure enough about the same time came Lynette's voice ordering one of us to get food up to the bridge as quickly as we could, claiming they felt faint. I was not sure that my lady Dela and particularly Griffin or Viv wanted to see food yet, but I staggered down to the lift and out on the lowermost level to the galley, and tried to put food for all of us together, out of the shambles our wild careering into jump had made of the place.

Then Vivien showed up in the doorway, a little frayed about the edges, it was true, muzzy with the drug, but moving along without touching the walls. She said nothing. Her face was set and determined with more fortitude than I had reckoned existed in Viv, and she had put most of the strands of her hair back into place so that she looked more herself. She was hungry, that was what: discomfort had gotten her moving again the same way it had sent her to bed, and without a by-your-leave she started into one of the trays. So had I, truth to tell. I had been stealing a bite and a drink while I was making the rest, because I wanted to stay on my feet to do it.

"Do they know anything yet?" she asked.

"No," I said. I refrained from adding that they weren't going to, not to pull the props out from under Viv a second time. The intercom came on: "My lady Dela wants a breakfast sent up," Lynette advised me, from the bridge, and I frowned: it was a lunch I had just put together. "If she wants it quick," I said back, "she can have a lunch that is ready. She'd have to wait ten minutes for the breakfast."

A delay. "She wants it now," Lynette relayed back. "Anything."

"It's coming." I stacked up the trays in a carrier, along with the coffee, looked up at the sound of a step in the corridor. Lance showed up and leaned there in the doorway, a shadow of himself. "Tray for you too," I said. "Here."

"She's sent for breakfast."

"I got the call. She takes what she can. Here." I put a hot roll into his hand and he ate that while I finished stacking the other carrier for the crew. I gave Dela and Griffin's carrier to Lance.

"I'll go," Vivien said, swallowing down her milk. She dried her hands, wiped possible wrinkles from her clothing. "I'll go with you."

Lance nodded, the carrier in one hand. He left, and Vivien went with her arm locked in his . . . up where Dela was. I might have gone. I might be where there was Dela to make sense of things. But I remembered the other carrier and Lynette, the whole crew up there, and then I realized what Vivien had done, leaving the work all to me.

I picked it up, grabbed another roll for myself and carried the box to the lift, rode it up, swallowing a mouthful of the roll and trying to keep my stomach down as well.

They were anxious for the food when I arrived, shadow-eyed and miserable. Percivale came and took the carrier from me and passed it round, looked puzzled at me when there were not enough. "I had a roll down below," I said, settling on a counter edge, still chewing the last of it and knowing it must sound as if I had fed myself first of all. "While it was in the oven."

They said nothing, but peeled back the covers and drank out of cups that shook in their hands . . . working harder than the rest of us and using up their reserves far faster, I thought, wishing I could have hurried it. As for me, I could go now to my lady, find what comfort there was now in her—but that was none, I thought. The screens all looked full of the same bad news. "Where are we?" I asked, after lingering there a moment, after they had at least had a chance to get a few swallows of the food down. "What's happening? Can you tell anything?" I thought—if there was any hope, I would like to take it to Dela. But they would have done that: they would have called her at once, if there were.

"We're nowhere," Lynette said sourly.

"But moving," said Modred.

The idea made me queasy. "Where?"

Modred waved a hand at the screen nearest Percy. It showed nothing I could read, but there were a lot of numbers ticking along on it.

"We've tried the engines," said Gawain. "We're moving, but we don't get anything. You understand? We've tried to affect our movement, but what works in realspace won't work here at all, wherever here is. We've tried the jump field and it won't generate. We don't know whether there's something the matter with the vanes or whether we just can't generate a field while we're in this space. Nothing works. We're without motive power. No one's ever been here before. No one knows the rules. Jumpships only skim this place. We're *in* it."

I nodded, sick at my stomach, having gotten the bad news I had bargained for.

"But there's something out there," Percivale said. "That—" He indicated the same screen Modred had. "That's a reading coming in, relative motion; and it's getting stronger."

I thought of black holes and other disquieting things, all impossible considering the fact that we were still alive and functioning, and kept arguing with myself that we had been safe where nothing like this should have happened, in the trafficked vicinity of a very normal star—which might or might not be normal now, the nasty thought kept recurring. And what about all the rest of the traffic which had been out there with us when we went popping unexpectedly into jump, presumably with some kind of field involved, which could tear ships apart and disrupt all kinds of material existence. Like planets. Like stars. If it were big enough.

"How—fast—are we moving?" I asked.

"Can't get any meaningful referents. None. Something's there, in relation to which we're moving, but the numbers jump crazily. The size of it, whether the thing we're picking up is even solid in any sense . . . or just some ghost . . . we don't know. We get readings that hold up a while and then they fall apart."

"Are we—falling into something?"

"Can't tell," said Modred, with the same calm he would have used ordering another cup of coffee.

I sat there a long time, letting the fright and the food settle. By now to my eyes the ship interior had taken on normal aspects, and my companions looked like themselves again. I reckoned that the same sort of thing must be happening with all of us, that about the time our bodies began to trouble us for normal things like food, our sensory perceptions were beginning to arrange themselves into some kind of order too.

We wouldn't starve, I thought, not—quickly. The lockers down there had the finest food, everything for every whim of my lady. The best wines and delicacies imported from faraway worlds. An enormous amount of it. We wouldn't run out of air. The interior systems were getting along just fine and nothing had shut down, or we would have had alarms sounding by now. Bad air or starving would be easiest, at least for us, who would simply blank and die.

I was terrified of the thing rushing up at us, or that we were rushing down into, or drifting slowly, whatever it was that those figures meant . . . because we had just had a bad taste of being where we were not designed to be, and another fall of any length did not sit well with my stomach.

But we could take a long time to hit and it seemed there was nothing to be done about the situation. I stood up, brushed my suit out of wrinkles. "I'm going to see my lady," I said. "Is there anything I can tell her?"

"Tell her," Gawain said, "we're trying to keep the ship intact."

I stared at him half a beat, chilled cold, then left the bridge and walked back out through the corridors which now looked like corridors . . . back to my lady's compartments.

Griffin was there when I arrived. They had gotten him up and mobile at least, into the blue bedroom, to sit at a small table and pick at the food. My lady sat across from him. I could see them through the open door. And Viv and Lance waited outside the bedroom doors, Vivien sitting on a small straight chair which had ridden through the calamity in its transit bolts. Lance was picking up bits of something which had shattered on the carpet, and some of the tapestries were crooked in their hangings.

I sat down too, in a chair which offered some comfort to my shivery limbs. Lance finished his cleaning up and took the pieces out, came back and paced the floor. I did not. I sat rigidly still, my fingers clenched on the upholstery. I was thinking about falling into some worse hole in space than we had already met, feeling that imagined motion of those figures on the bridge screen as if it were a hurtling rush.

"Where are we?" Vivien asked, my former question. Her voice was hushed and hoarse.

"In strange space," I said. And then, because it had to be said: "The crew doesn't really expect we're going to get out of it."

It was strange who came apart and who did not. Lance, who was always so vain and so worried about his appearance and his favor with my lady—he just stood there. But Vivien sat and shivered and finally blanked on us, which was the best state for her, considering her upset, and we did not move to rouse her.

"I think," Lance said, looking on her sitting frozen in her chair, "that Vivien planned to live a long, long time."

Of course that was true. Poor Vivien, I thought. All her plans. All her work. She stayed blanked, and kept at it, and finally Lance went over to her and patted her shoulder, so that she came out of it. But she slipped back again at once.

"It's a ship," Percivale's voice broke over the intercom uninvited. "It's another ship we're headed for."

That brought my lady and Griffin out of their bedroom refuge, all in a rush of moved chairs. "Signal it!" my lady ordered, looking up at the sitting room speaker panel as if it could show her something. "Contact it!"

Evidently they were doing something on the bridge, because there was silence after, and the lot of us stood there—all of us on our feet in the sitting room but Viv. Lance was shaking her shoulder and trying to get through her blankness to tell her there was some hope.

"We're not sure about the range," Modred reported finally. "We'll keep trying as we get nearer."

Griffin and lady Dela settled on a couch there near us, and we turned from Vivien to try to make them comfortable. Lady Dela looked very pale and drawn, which with her flaxen hair was pale indeed, like one of the ladies in the fantasies she loved; and Griffin too looked very shaken. "Get wine," I said, and Lance did that. We even poured a little for ourselves, Lance and I, out of their way, and got some down Vivien, holding the glass in her hand for her.

"We don't seem to be moving rapidly in relation to it," came one of Modred's calm reports, in the aching long time that passed.

"We are in Hell," my lady said after yet another long time, speaking in a hoarse, distant voice. This frightened me on the instant, because I had heard about Hell in the books, and it meant somewhere after dying. "It's all something we're dreaming while we fall, that's what it is."

I thought about it: it flatly terrified me.

"A jump accident," Griffin said. "We are *somewhere*. It's not the between. Our instruments are off, that's all. We should fix on some star and go to it. We can't have lost ourselves that far."

There were no stars in the instruments I had seen on the bridge. I swallowed, recalling that, not daring to say it.

"We have *died*," my lady said primly, calmly, evidently having made up her mind to that effect, and perhaps after the shock and the wine she was numb. "We're all dead from the moment of the accident. Brains perhaps function wildly when one dies . . . like a long dream, that takes in everything in a lifetime and stretches a few seconds into forever . . . Or this is Hell and we're in it."

I shivered where I sat. There were a lot of things that tapes had not told me, and one of them was how to cope with thoughts like that. My lady was terrifying in her fantasies.

"We're alive," Lance said, unasked. "And we're more comfortable than we were."

"Who asked you?" Dela snapped, and Lance bowed his head. We don't talk uninvited, not in company, and Griffin was company. Griffin seemed to be intensely bothered, and got up and paced the floor.

It did not help. It did not hasten the time, which crept past at a deadly slow pace, and finally Griffin spun about and strode out the door.

"Griffin?" my lady Dela quavered.

I stood up; Dela had; and Lance. "He mustn't give orders," I said, thinking at least where I would be going if I were Griffin, and we heard the door to the outside corridor open, not that to his own rooms. "Lady Dela, he's going to the bridge. He mustn't give them orders."

My lady stared at me and I think if she had been close enough she might have hit me. But then her face grew afraid. "They wouldn't pay any attention to him. They wouldn't."

"No, lady Dela, but he's strong and quick and I'm not sure they could stop him."

Dela stirred herself then and made some haste. Lance and I seized up Viv and drew her along in Dela's wake, out into the corridors and down them to the bridge. It was all, all too late if Griffin had had something definite in mind; but it was still peaceful when we arrived, Griffin standing there in the center of the bridge and the crew with their backs to him and working at their posts. Griffin was ominous looking where he was, in the center of things, hands on hips. None of the crew was particularly big . . . only Lance was that, the two of them like mirrors, dark and gold, the lady's taste running remarkably similar in this instance. And Lance made a casual move that took himself between Griffin and Gawain and Lynn at main controls, just standing there, in case.

"Well?" Dela asked.

"We don't have contact," Percivale said, beside Modred. "We keep sending, but the object doesn't respond. We were asked about range: we don't know that either. Everything has failed."

"Where *is* this thing we're talking about?" Dela asked, and Modred reached and punched a button. It came up on the big screen, a kind of a cloud on the scope, all gridded and false, just patches of something solid the computer was trying to show us.

"I think we're getting vid," Percivale said, and that image went off, replaced with another, in all the flare of strange colors and shapes that drifted where there ought to be stars, in between blackness measled with red spots like dapples that might be stars or just the cameras trying to pick up something that made no sense. And against that backdrop was something that might be a misshapen world in silhouette, or a big rock irregularly shaped, or something far vaster than we wanted to think, no knowing. It was flattened at its poles and it bristled with strange shapes in prickly complexity.

"We've been getting nearer steadily," Modred said. "It could be our size or star-sized. We don't know."

"You've got the scan on it," Griffin snapped at him. "You've got that readout for timing."

"Time is a questionable constant here," Modred said without turning about, keeping at his work. "I refrained from making unjustified assumptions. This is new input on the main screen. I am getting a size estimate.—Take impact precautions. Now."

Near . . . we were coming at it. It was getting closer and closer on the screen. My lady caught at Griffin, evidently having given up her theory of being dead. "Use the engines," Griffin yelled at Gawain and Lynn, furious. "If we're coming up against some mass they may react off that . . . use the engines!"

"We are," Gawain said calmly.

We grabbed at both Dela and Griffin, Lance and I, and pulled them to the cushioned corner and got the bar down and the straps round them, then dragged Vivien, who was paralyzed and nearly blanked, with us to the remaining pad. The crew was putting the safety bars in place too, all very cool. That we couldn't feel the engines . . . no feel to them at all . . . when normally they should have been kicking us hard in some direction. . . .

Screens broke up. We were just too close to it. It had filled all our forward view and the last detail we got was huge. Something interfered with the pickup. I wrapped the restraints about myself while Lance did his, and all the while expected the impact, to be flung like some toy across a breached compartment on a puff of crystalizing air. . . . I didn't know what was out there, but the most horrible fate of all seemed to me to be blown out of here, to be set adrift naked in *that*, whatever that stuff was out there. This little ship that held our lives also held whatever sanity we had been able to trick our eyes into seeing, and what was out there—I wondered how long it took to die in that stuff. Or whether one ever did.

The last buckle jammed. I refitted it, in sudden tape-taught calm. I was with the ship and my lady. I had my referents. My back was to the wall and my most favorite comrades were with me. I didn't want to end, but there was comfort in company—far better, I conned myself, than what waited for us by our natures, to be taken separately by the law and coldly done away. This was like born-men, this was—

"Repulse is working," Gawain said, about the instant my stomach felt the slam of the engines. "Stop rotation."

Don't! I thought irrationally, because I trusted nothing to start working again once it had been shut down in this mad place, and if rotation stopped working the way it did when we would go into a dock at station, we would end up null G in this stuff, subject to its laws. We were not, for mercy's sake, coming in at a safe dock with crews waiting to assist, and there was no place to put the *Maid*'s delicate noseprobe, all exposed out there.

G started going away. We were locking into station-docking position, the crew going through their motions with heart-breaking calm, doing all the right things in this terrible place; and the poor unsecured *Maid* was going to be chaos in her station-topside decks.

A touch came at my fingers. It was Lancelot's hand seeking mine. I closed on it, and reached beside me for Vivien's, which was very cold.

She had, Lance had said it, planned to live, and everything was wrong for her. No hope for Vivien, whose accounts and knowledge were useless now. I understood suddenly, that Vivien's function was simply gone for her; and she had already begun to die, in a way as terrible as being dumped out in the chaos-stuff.

"The lady will need you," I hissed at Viv, gripping her nerveless hand till I ground the bones together. "She needs us all."

That might have helped. There was a little jerk from Viv's hand, a little resistance; and I winced, for Lance closed down hard on mine. My lady and Griffin screamed—we hit, ground with a sound like someone was shredding the *Maid*'s metal body, and our soft bodies hit the restraints as the ship's mass stopped a little before that of our poor flesh. I blanked half an instant, came out of it realizing pain, and that somehow we had not been going as fast as I feared a ship might in this place (which estimate ranged past C and posed interesting physics for collision) or what we had hit was going the same general direction as we were, at an angle. Mass, I thought, if that had any meaning in this place/time . . . a monstrous mass, to have pulled us into it, if that was what it had done. Our motion had not stopped in collision. The noise had not. We grated, hit, hung, grated, a shock that seemed to tear my heart and stomach loose.

"We're up against it," Modred's cool voice came to me. "We'd better grapple or we'll go on with this instability."

Instability. A groaning and scraping, and a horrifying series of jolts, as if we were being dragged across something. The *Maid* shifted again, her dragging force of engines like a hand pushing us.

Clang and thump. I heard the grapples lock and felt the whole ship steady, a slow suspicion of stable G that crawled through the clothes I wore and settled my hair down and caressed my abused joints and stomach and said that there was indeed up and down again. It was a kilo or so light, but we had G. Whatever we were fixed to had spin and we had gotten our right orientation to *it*.

The crew was still exchanging quiet information, doing a shutdown, no cheers, no exuberance in their manner. That huge main screen cleared again, to show us ruby-spotted blackness and our own battered nose with the grapples locked onto something. Strong floods were playing from our hull onto the surface we faced, a green, pitted surface which was flaring with colors into the violets and dotted with little instabilities like black stars. It made me sick to look at it; but it was indeed our nose probe, badly abraded and with stuff coming out of it like trailing cable or black snakes, and there was our grapple locked into something that looked like metal wreckage. The lights swung further and it was wreckage, all right, some other ship all dark and scarred and crumpled. The lights and camera kept traveling and there was still another ship, of some delicate kind I had never imagined. It was dark too, like spiderweb in silhouette, twisted wreckage at its heart with its filament guts hanging out into the red measled void.

My lady Dela swore and wept, a throaty, loud sound in the stillness about us now. She freed herself of the restraints and crossed the deck to Gawain and Lynn, and Griffin came at her heels. I loosed myself, and Lance did, while Dela leaned there on the back of Gawain's chair, looking up at the screen in terror. Griffin set his big hands on her shoulders. "Keep trying," Griffin asked of the crew, who kept the beam and the cameras moving, turning up more sights as desolate. Aft, through the silhouette of the *Maid*'s raking vanes, there was far perspective, chaos-stuff with violet tints into the red. More wreckage then. The cameras stopped. "There," Modred said. "There."

It was a curve, lit in the queasy flarings, a vast sweep, a symmetry in the wreckage, as if the thing we were fixed to were some vast ring. Ship bodies were gathered to it like parasites, like fungus growth, with red and black beyond, and the wrecks themselves all spotted with holes as if they were eaten up with acid light illusion of the chaos-stuff, or something showing through their metal wounds, like glowing blood.

"Whatever we've hit," Percy said quietly, "a lot have gone before us. It's some large mass, maybe a station, maybe a huge ship—once. Old . . . old. Others might fall through the pile into us the same way we've hit them."

"Then get us out of here," my lady said. "Get us out!"

Gawain and Lynette stirred in their seats. Wayne powered his about to look up at her. "My lady Dela, it's not possible." He spoke with the stillest patience. "We can wallow about the surface, batter ourselves into junk against it. If we loose those grapples we'll do that."

I thought she would hit him. She lifted her hand. It fell. "Well, what are you going to do?"

Gawain had no answer. Griffin set his hands on my lady's arms, just stood there. I looked at Lance and he was white; I looked at Vivien and she plainly blanked, standing vacant-eyed in her restraints. I undid them, patted her face hard until I got a flicker in her eyes, put my arms about her and held her. She wrapped her arms about me and held on.

"The hull is sound," Modred said. "Our only breach is *G*-34. I've sealed that compartment."

"Get us out of here," Dela said. "Fix what's wrong with us

and get us out of here, you hear that? You find out how to move in this stuff and get us away."

The crew slowly stopped their operations, confronted with an impossibility. I held to Viv, and Lance just stood there, his hand clenched on one of the safety holds. I felt a profound cold, as if it were our shared fault, this disaster. We had failed and the *Maid* was damaged—more than damaged. All the crew's skill, that had stopped our falling, that had docked us here neatly as if it was Brahmani Station . . . in this terrible, terrible place. . . .

"We're fixed here," Lynette said. "There's no way. There's no repair that can make the engines work against this. The *Maid* won't move again. Can't."

There was stark silence, from us, from Dela, no sound at all over the ship but the fans and the necessary machinery.

"How long will we survive?" Griffin asked. He kept his steadying hold on my lady. His handsome face was less arrogant than I had ever seen it; and he came up with the only sensible question. "What's a reasonable estimate?"

"No immediate difficulty," Gawain said. He unfastened his restraints and stood up, jerking his head so that his long hair fell behind his shoulders. "Modred?"

"The ship is virtually intact," Modred said. "We're not faced with shutdown. The lifesupport and recycling will go on operating. Our food is sufficient for several years. And for the percentage of inefficiency in the recycling, there are emergency supplies, frozen cultures, hydroponics. It should be indefinite."

"You're talking about living here," Dela said in a faint voice.

"Yes, my lady."

"In *this*?"

Modred turned back to his boards, without answer.

Dela stood there a moment, slowly brought her hands up in front of her lips. "Well," she said in a tremulous voice, with a sudden pivot and look at Griffin, at all of us. "Well, so we do what we can, don't we?" She looked at the crew. "Who knows anything about the hydroponics?"

"There's a training tape," Percy said, "in library. It's a complicated operation. When the ship is secured—"

"I can do that." Vivien stirred at my side, muscles tensing. "Lady Dela, I'll do that."

Dela looked at her, waved her hand. "See to it." Viv shivered, with what joy Dela surely had no concept. Sniffed and straightened her back. Dela paced the deck, distracted, with that look in her eyes—panic. It was surely panic. She laughed a faint and brittle laugh and came back and laced her fingers into Griffin's hand. "So we make the best of it," she said, looking up at him. "You and I."

He stood looking at the screens and the horror outside, while my lady Dela put her arms about him. Maybe she was building her fantasies back again, but it was a different look I saw on Griffin's face, which was not resigned, which was set in a kind of desperation. My jaw still ached where he had hit me in his panic, and I was afraid of this man as I would have been afraid of one of my own kind who had had such a lapse—for which one of *us* might have been put down. But born-men were entitled to stupidities, and to be forgiven for them.

What was outside our hull didn't forgive. We were snugged by some attraction up against a huge mass. Even if the big generation vanes were to work in this vicinity as the repulse had— from what little I knew of jump, I knew we dared not try, not unless we wanted to string our components and bits of that mass into some kind of fluxing soup . . . half to stay here and half to fly off elsewhere. That mass was going to serve to keep us here, one way or the other.

A wandering instability, a knot in time and space, a ripple in the between that came wandering through our safe solar system and sucked us up. And with who knew what other ships? I almost opened my mouth on that sudden thought—that perhaps we should try to see if we had company in this disaster, if others had been sucked through too; material things seemed to work here, and maybe the com would. And then I thought of some big passenger carrier, short of food and water in relation to its number of passengers, and what that might mean for *us*, if they did make contact.

No. Old—Percy had said it. Perhaps—the thought went shivering through my flesh while I stared at the screens—others had faced similar moments, had lived out their lives until they decayed, the light eating through them. From what we had seen of the mass, from the insane way in which the ships were fused, one upon the other, they must all be very old, if age meant anything at all here, and that was not the quick eating away of matter by the chaos-stuff.

"Go," my lady said suddenly, waving her hands at us. "See what's damaged. Start putting things in order. See to it. Are you going to stand like you've lost your wits?"

I looked desperately at Lance and Vivien, turned and went, a last backward look at the screens, and then I hurried out to check the halls and the compartments. My lady now talked as if she had given up her premise that we were dead, and I took some comfort in that while I walked the corridors back to her compartment—only mild damage there. The wine bottle had been mostly empty, the dew had been so generally distributed in null-G that there remained no visible trace of it except on the table-tops and the steel doors. The rest had soaked into the carpet and covered the woodwork, beyond helping. And the glasses were unbreakable, lying where returning G had dropped them. I wiped surfaces, straightened the bed, gathered up fallen towels in the bath. At least there had been no furniture out of its braces. Not so bad. I walked outside, confronted suddenly with the chill corridors, the light G that made my stomach queasy. It came back to me again what my lady had said about eternity being compassed in dying, about the brain spilling all it contained in random firings—but then, if that were so, then we should not be sharing the dream, unless all that I had touched, the ship, the lady, Lance, everyone—was illusion, and I had never seen or touched at all.

Perhaps I had built it all out of the chaos-stuff as I had built my hand when I willed to see it. Perhaps I had just gone too far in my building, and what the lady said about dying was my own brain talking to itself, trying to convince me by logic that the dream had to end and that I should be decently dead.

And I would not listen, but went on dreaming.

No, I thought, and shuddered, because there had just crept a touch of red into the shadows in the hall, the old way of looking at things coming back again, and if I could not stop it my eyes would begin to see the chaos-stuff through the walls.

They had experimented, so my lady's pilfered tapes had told me, with living human senses; and the brain could be re-educated. Eyes could learn to see rightside up or upside down. Somewhere in the waves of energy that impinged the nerves, the brain constructed its own fantasies of matter and blue skies and green grass and solidity, screening out the irrational and random.

A reality existed within us too, tides of particles that were themselves nodes in chaos, all strung together to make this reality of ours. And in this place the structure of matter gaped wide and I could see it . . . miniature tides like the tides of the moving galaxies in one rhythm with them, and us spread like a material veil between, midway of one reality and the other.

No, I thought again, and leaned against the veil/wall in my chosen viewpoint of what was, was, was . . . don't look down. One was advised not to look at such things and never to know that all of us were dreaming, dreaming even when we were sure we were alive, because what the brain always did was dream, and what difference whether it built its dreams from the energy affecting it from outside or whether it traced its own independent fancies, making its own patterns on the veil. Don't lean too hard. Don't look.

I slid down onto the corridor floor and heaved up my insides, which was my body's way of telling me it had had enough nonsense. It wanted the old dream back, insisted to have it. I lay there dry-heaving until I dismissed my ideas of dreams and eternities, because I hurt inside and wanted to die, and if I could have waked and died at once I would have gladly done it.

So a pair of slippered feet came up to me; and my lady Dela, all tearful, cursed me for useless and kicked me besides, in my sore stomach. That helped, actually, because when my lady had gone on in and shut the door, I was angry, which was better than hurting. And before I had gotten up on my own, Percy came after me, saying she had sent him. Gentle Percy cleaned the hall up and cleaned me up and carried me to the crew quarters. There, when he had gone back to his duties, I took care of myself and changed and felt better, if somewhat hollow at the gut.

So much for fighting it. I moved meekly about the reality of the *Maid*, loving her poor battered self as I did my own body, and doing all I could to get her into order again. So did we all, I think with the same reason, that if the *Maid* had been precious to us before, she was ten thousand times so now.

V

Then to her tower she climb'd, and took the shield,
There kept it, and so lived in fantasy.

It seemed a long time that we worked. The clocks said one thing and our bodies told us something else, and they were never in agreement, so that some hours flew past as if we had been daydreaming and others dragged on and on while we ached and got thirsty and hungry. I kept thinking of the way the walls had come and gone at first, and that hours were doing the same thing, or our bodies were. Whatever happened to matter, Lynn said, would happen to us; and if there were phases in this place, I reckoned, where things just went slower, then we and the clocks ought to agree, but it didn't work out that way. It was one of the small horrors that worked at our nerves and urged us that just blanking out might be better. Likewise Modred and Percy said comp went out on them: it dumped program at times, and at others behaved itself. The crew stayed on the bridge or back at the monitor station—worried, I gathered, about the power plant that kept us going—but it did go, the fans kept turning and the air kept recycling and, Gawain said when I brought them another meal, there was no real need for them to stay by controls, because what was automatic was working tolerably well and what was not automatic was not doing well at all and they couldn't fix anything, just live with it and be patient when comp dumped.

Gawain was tired. His eyes were terrible. So were Modred's, like black pits. They had been in their day cycle and had been through more than a day now. They ended by deciding perhaps they should stay up in controls after all, all of them—in case the alarms didn't function dependably. "Until we see," Modred said. So I brought up mats and pillows and blankets for the four of them and they bedded down up there.

Vivien—Viv was asleep too, busy deepstudying, locked into that tape that would make her useful again, after which time she would likely have a thousand orders to give us all. Lance was somewhere repairing damages and cleaning up, where unsecured items had smashed into walls, or unbraced chairs made wreckage of themselves. Not technical things, but such things as we could do.

Griffin called me, wanting two suppers in my lady's quarters, so I went to the galley and fixed all he asked for . . . he and my lady, who consoled each other, who had been consoling each other all afternoon of that quick/slow day. Well enough. It put no demands on us, tired as we were. I carried the trays up in a carrier and walked in with them, very quietly, into the sitting room.

I walked farther, cautiously, and I could see the big blue bed and them tangled in the middle of it, golden blond Griffin and my pale blonde lady, pink to his gold, and white, and her braids all undone in a net about them. They made love. I waited, waited longer, finally put the carrier on the mobile table and quietly as I could I eased it through the door, just to leave it where they could have it when they wanted. They never noticed my being there, or they ignored it, lost in each other, and very quietly I left and closed all the doors behind me, downcast with my own aches and pains and where we were and what hopelessness we had of doing something about it.

Sleep, I thought. I was due my rest, finally; and overdue.

And I was right outside the library.

I came in very quietly. Viv was on the couch, limp in deepsleep. She chose to do her deepstudy in the library, maybe not to bother those of us who wanted to talk in the crew quarters, but such extreme consideration was not Viv's style. It was more, I figured, out of fear of being supplanted; she wanted no rivals who could do what she could do, and she didn't want that tape in our hands.

The lights were low. I could have slapped her face and not roused her, but all the same I kept very quiet picking out the tape *I* wanted. I slipped it into my jacket and went out again, trusting Modred would cover for me when he must. Ah! I wanted the deepsleep.

I walked down the corridor to the main hall, and the lift and so down to the crew quarters with my treasure. I undressed and bathed and in my robe set up the unit on the couch, attached the

sensor leads, took the drug—thinking with melancholy that we
would run out, someday—not of the tapes but of the drug that
made them more intense; that when my lady thought of that . . .
we would lose our supply, and she would not be long in thinking of it. It was only fair, perhaps, because we could sink into
the tapes and the dreams so much more easily than born-men. I
felt a guilt that had nothing to do with my tape-pilfering: I stole
my lady's dreams. It was selfish, and bothered my psych-sets;
but I rationalized it, that she had *not* forbidden it, and sank back
with my tape, in it, part of it.

> Elaine the fair, Elaine the loveable,
> Elaine the lily maid of Astolat,
> High in her chamber up a tower to the east
> Guarded the sacred shield of Lancelot. . . .

It was my dream, my own, my world better than the real: my
lady Dela's world; and mine. We were made, we who served,
never born; we were perfect, and needed no dreams to make us
more than we were created by the labs to be. We were not intended to love . . . but it was seeing born-men's sharing love that
made me lonely, and made me think of my tape—

> I know not if I know what true love is,
> But, if I know, then, if I love not him,
> I know there is none other I can love. . . .

I thought of Lancelot. Probably I cried; and we don't do that
generally, not like born-men, because where they would cry, we
go blank. Only in the taped dreams, then we might, because
there's no blanking out on them. While the tape was running, I
loved, and had a soul, and believed in the born-men's God; and
when it would stop I was all hollow and frightened for a moment: that was the price, I knew, of pilfering tapes not meant for
us. But then my other tapes, those deep in my mind, would take
over and bring me back to sense.

> Then while Sir Lancelot leant, in half disdain
> At love, life, all things, on the window ledge,
> Close underneath his eyes, and right across

Where these had fallen, slowly past the barge
Whereon the lily maid of Astolat
Lay smiling, like a star in blackest night.

I waked for real. Arms held me. I thought it was part of the
tape at first, because sensations in them were that real, called out
of the mind; but the sound had stopped, and I was still lapped
in someone's arms, and comforted. I would have gone on into
normal sleep except for that; I was conscious enough now to
fight out of it, pull the piece from my ear and the other attachments from my temples and my body, sweeps of a half-numb
hand. My eyes cleared enough that I saw who slept with me, that
it was Lance. Like a thief he had slipped into my dream, to share
the tape while it was running . . . the tape that he was never supposed to have. His face was sadder than it had ever been. His
eyes were closed, tears running from under his lashes. More than
mine, the tape was his, and his part was sadder than mine by far.
I loved and lost *him*, young and only half knowing love at all;
but he, older, having more, lost everything.

And that was always true for him.

I hurt, and maybe it was more than my psych-set that grieved
me. I was still in the haze of the tape's realities. I swept the tiny
sensors away from his brow and his heart, and wiped the tears
away for him. I kissed him, not for sex, as my tapes are, but because it was what the real Elaine would have done, a kind of
tenderness like touching, like lying close at night, that kind of
comfort.

He waked then and embraced me purposefully, and I shifted
over, getting rid of other sensor connections, because I was willing. I reckoned it was the best thing for him, to occupy his mind
and body both after going through that dream.

But he couldn't. It was the first time he ever outright couldn't,
and it shook him. He blanked, then, which froze my heart—because blanking out from something beyond your limits is one thing;
but blanking on your training, on your whole reason for being at
all—He stayed that way a moment, and then he came out of it
and rolled over and lay there with his eyes open and a terrible sorrow on his face. He shivered now and then, and I put my arms
about him and pulled the sheets up about us.

"I'm sorry," he said finally without ever looking at me. I might have been anyone.

"We're all awfully tired," I said. And in my heart: O Lance, you should never have heard it, and I should never have used it here—because he had one thing that he did and that was it, and maybe he had just seen something else, yearning after that other Lancelot as I did after that other Elaine, who was absolute in love, and who was so much that I was not made to be. What was Lance's other self that *he* was not? Much, that no lab-born was ever made to be.

I wiped the last trace of tears from off his face and he did not blink. I leaned close and kissed him again.

"It does no good," he said.

"I didn't mean it that way," I said, and I didn't. I just held him and hurt for him like my own heart was breaking, because they made me that way, my psych-set was involved, and I couldn't help him. "It's a very old story," I whispered, prattling on because I knew his whole reality was upset and I had to make it make sense to him or he was in trouble. "It's the lady's fancy, that tape; and so she named us what she did when she bought us, and maybe there's a little truth in the names—because she did think about which she gave to whom, after all, and *she's* read our psych-sets— But it's a joke, Lance, it's our lady's joke, a play, a thing from very long ago and some world with nothing to do with ours. You understand that? It's not *ours*. The *Maid* is just a dream Dela takes up when she's bored. You've always known that, and it's always true. How long have you been with her?"

"Twenty years."

And me with my five, I was going to tell him what truth was. That long he had belonged to her: I had had no idea it could have been so many years, or I had never added it up and thought. Thirty-six. He had been sixteen when he came to her. That long he had been fixed on her, and Dela was all his life . . . always Dela, Dela, like some guidance star his whole self was locked onto. Lover after lover she took—but Lance was always waiting when love was done.

Love—not us. Ours was a tape-fixed complex of compulsions and avoidances; pain if we turned away from our duty . . . pain, and guilt; and this horrible twisting inside, at any thought of losing what we were fixed to, and created to do.

And there was deep irony in it all, because Elaine—the real Elaine, the one realer than I—had destroyed herself trying to turn Lancelot's love to herself, when it was fixed on Guinevere: she had to try, because in the story Elaine was fixed on him and he on his lady, and that made sense within my frame of reference. I was not supposed to fix on him, but pain always went straight to my gut and made me try to stop it; and he had the most pain of anyone aboard.

That was what had happened to me when I saw him hurting like this. And because I had done this to him myself, that settled a horrible guilt on me. I lay there thinking desperately that maybe I ought to get up and go to our lady and tell her what I had done, but that was bound to bring down one of her rages, and I didn't see how it could help Lance either. The last thing he wanted, I was sure, was for Dela to find out how much he knew or that he had failed with me just now.

I had a sense of empathy: it was my training; and I put myself in Lance's place, who had always to endure these voyages in which the rest of us took pleasure, endure them and wait for Dela to tire of her new lovers and to come back to him, which she always had. But there was no coming back from this voyage; and Griffin was not getting off the ship, ever. Where that led in Lance's poor mind, I was afraid to follow. I remembered how strong he was, and I knew how desperate he was, and I knew that Griffin was both strong himself and could get desperate as this place fretted at him—and that scared me beyond wanting to think about it. One of us could never raise a hand to a born-man. An avoidance was built into us which would send us hurtling into blank long before the hand left our side.

But Griffin was dangerous. My lady had always fancied dangerous men, because there was very little in this world she could not control or predict, and she liked her games wild and enjoyed a certain feeling of risk.

It had never occurred to me before that Lance himself was dangerous. He had been there too long, too quietly, was too much one of us, bowing his head, taking even blows, accepting the worst that ever my lady's associates chose to do—

My lady chose dangerous men, and this one had been with her for twenty years, pretty as he was, and while it was always Modred strangers stepped aside for, with his dark and cold face—

Something had snapped in Lance. Maybe it would heal. Maybe like Vivien, who had gone in a single day from managing my lady's accounts to being in charge of the hydroponics which were going to keep us all alive, he would do some kind of transference and pull himself out of it. He still shivered now and again, and the look on his face stopped being pain and became a lock-jawed stare at the ceiling. He blinked sometimes, so it was not a blank; and the eyes were lively, so he was thinking, in that place inside his skull to which he had gone. But his face that had always been sad was something else now, as if there had been some harsh wind blowing that he was staring into, and I was not even there.

I never was, for him. That part of the story was true.

And finally he decided he would stop thinking about what-ever it was, and he got up and got dressed, while I decided I had better take the tape and hide it somewhere until I could get it to Modred, before something worse happened.

"Don't," Lance said, holding my hand with the tape in it.

"It's got to go back. I'll take it to Modred."

"He can run a copy. Can't he?" He took the tape from me. *He* put it away, in his locker. I stood watching and reckoning that he was caught in it now like I was. He would listen to it again, and it would become his as it was mine. I shared it now, like it or not.

"I wish you'd asked before coming in on me," I said.

He turned and lifted his hand to my face, touched my cheek. It was a strange gesture, for him. I could see him doing it to Dela. Then he hugged me against him like the old friend I was to him. "Don't tell her I couldn't," he asked of me.

"Of course I won't," I said. "Bed with me and sleep a while. It'll be different. You're tired, that's all."

But it wasn't different, and then I was really frightened for him; and I knew that he was scared. There began to be an even worse look on his face, that was not merely sadness, but torment, and worse still for the likes of us—anger.

He was gone the next morning, after breakfast. The whole ship was about such routine as existed in such circumstances, the crew trying to get their own equipment into order, checking out things that they knew how to do, and there had been no emer-

gencies. Dela took to her bed again, and Griffin stayed mostly
about the sitting room, what time he was not poking into things
about the control room, the monitor station, and the observation
dome, bedeviling the crew with worry over what he might do—
grim and scowling all the while, with Dela taking pills for her
nerves. A second day in this place, all too much as novel as the
first, any time anyone wanted to look at the horror on the screens,
and watch the acid light eating through our neighbors, or to look
out on that vast dead wheel which held us all to its mass. Dela
called for *that tape*, and my heart stopped; but the original, at
least, was back where it belonged: Lance had seen to that, so we
were safe. And soon my lady slept the deepsleep, lost in the
dream.

Vivien was up and about her new business, keeping Percivale
busy finding this and that for her out of storage. She had appropriated a large space topside, a private queendom into which
she had brought loads of stored tanks and pipe and electronics
over which Percivale sweated. So all of us were accounted for.

Except Lance, to Vivien's extreme pique.

There was no one else who had reason to think anything might
be amiss. He might even be off about the lady's instructions. And
Modred or others of the crew might know where he was, since
he must have been on the bridge getting that duplicate tape run
sometime around breakfast . . . but I was afraid to ask questions
and make much of his absence.

I searched . . . quietly, between duties I had to do, between
fetching Vivien this and that. And I found him finally, in almost
the last place I thought to look before starting on the topside
holds . . . in the gym that lay bow-ward of the galley, all by himself, drenched in sweat despite the cold in there.

I stood there in the open doorway with my heart beating hard
with relief. He saw me. He said nothing, only walked on over
to another of the machines and meddled with it, by which I decided he didn't want to say anything, or see anyone. He started
up his exercise again as if he could force his body to do what
it ought by making it stronger. Or maybe that wasn't his reason.
In any event he should hardly be here when others had duties . . .
but I was far from saying so.

I closed the door again, walked away to the galley, figuring
that the crew might appreciate something hot to drink about now.

I tried to do something useful—and all the while Lance's look kept gnawing at me, dark and sullen.

The lift worked, not far away from the galley. I heard someone come down, and went to the door, expecting maybe Percy, who was coming and going on Viv's errands. It was a man's tread.

I met Griffin.

Maybe fright showed. He looked at me and frowned, and I vacated the doorway, letting him in. "Have you seen Lancelot?" he asked, setting my heart pounding afresh. "They said he might be around the gym."

I cursed them all, the crew—who had sent Griffin down here, to get him off their necks up there, I reckoned. I even tried to think of a lie; but he was a born-man and his frown turned my bones to jelly. I nodded meekly, found a tray and some cups to occupy my sight and my hands. "I was going to make a snack, sir. Would you like?"

"You think we have enough to be making up meals off-schedule?"

I looked at him, already unnerved; and yes, I had thought of it, but the crew had needs, and the lady had given no orders. Griffin couldn't tell me what to do. He was a guest, not giving orders for my lady. But he had that kind of voice that made muscles flinch whether they wanted to or not. "They've been working hard up there," I said, "by your leave, sir. Would you like some?"

"No. They're not working up there. Except doing the hydroponics setup. That." His eyes raked around the galley as if he were hunting for fault. "I'll be in the gym," he said then. "If Dela asks."

"Sir," I murmured, eyes lowered, a quick turn toward him. He left. I leaned on the counter a moment, not wanting now to do what I had set out to do as an excuse; but I was afraid to follow him.

I busied myself after a moment, not hearing him come back, made the coffee and took it up. It was what master Griffin had said, that there was not much going on about the bridge. The hateful screens stayed the same. Gawain was there alone. Modred and Lynn were out in the observation bubble—strange to have everyone on the same shift, but when I thought about it, it was not as if we would be needing the mainday/alterday rotation. Not here. Gawain called the others, and they were glad of the coffee; Percy and Viv came too, Percy in sweat-stained coveralls and Viv in a neat beige suit.

"Is Lance *fixing* something down there?" Viv asked, and then I knew who might have told Griffin, if she had found it out to tell. I frowned. "He was working over the machines," I said without a flicker. Lance had problems enough without being dragooned into Viv's merciless service. "I think he's busy."

"Huh," Vivien said, and sipped her coffee.

"What did Griffin want?" I asked. "To use the gym?"

"He asked where Lance was," Percy said.

"I'd been looking for him," I said.

"Griffin?"

"Lance."

"Could have asked," Modred said.

I fretted, sipped my own coffee. "I'd think he'd have come back by now."

"Griffin? He's been everywhere this morning. Insisted to have us explain controls to him."

"He's handled insystem craft," Gawain said tartly. "He says. Elaine—drop a word to my lady. The *Maid* isn't in a position we can afford difficulties. You understand."

"I'll try," I said, looking at my coffee instead of at the screens, with their terrible red images. "I'll do it when she wakes up."

It made me cold, that worry of Gawain's, and this restlessness of Griffin's. Griffin, who was down in the gym; with Lance— in his frame of mind.—Why aren't you working? I could, hear Griffin asking Lance, meddling-wise. What are you doing down here? And I could see Lance with that sullenness in his expression, that hurt that was there, exploding—

I put my cup empty onto the tray. Gawain did. The others lingered drinking theirs, so I had no excuse to go. "I think I may have left a switch on in the galley," I said.

"Comp can check it," Percy said.

I abandoned excuses and left the bridge, forgetting the tray, hurried to the lift and rode it back down to the lowermost level, walked quickly down the dim corridor forward.

The gym door was open. I walked into that echoing place with its exercise machines and its padded walls, hearing grunts and crashes, and my heart stopped in me, seeing the two of them, Lance and Griffin, locked in fighting. And then I saw them more clearly, that they were wrestling, stripped down. They grappled and shifted for advantage. It was sport, a game.

—and not. They struggled, bled where fingers gripped, strained and heaved strength against strength. Muscles shivered and shifted blinding quick. They broke, panting, eye to eye, shifted and charged again, seeking new advantage, making the echoes ring. Both were sleek with sweat, both matched height for height and reach for reach, in weight and width of shoulder and length of arm and leg. Dark head beside bright, olive skin next golden, they turned and moved and strained, locked in a grip that neither one would give up, and I ached watching it, turned half away, for it seemed that bones and joints must crack . . . looked again, and they seemed blind to all else, still locked, glassy-eyed, each trying to make the other yield. A born-man, in contest with one of us. And that one of us could fight a born-man, even in sport—

I knew why Lance wrestled, and what he fought, and I was cold inside.

Lance, O Lance, it's not a game.

Not for either of them.

"Griffin," I cried. "Master Griffin!—I think you should see my lady. She's been locked away too long. Please come."

They broke. Griffin looked toward me. I ran away, but I waited in the crosspassage outside until I knew Griffin had believed my lie and was gone from there, sweaty as he was, carrying his shirt over his arm and headed for the lift.

Lance came, later. He didn't see me. I stayed to the shadows and watched him pass, walking with shoulders bowed, showered and cleaned and bearing no mark on him.

I could have bit my tongue for the lie I'd chosen, that Dela had had need of Griffin—and not of him.

At least I had stopped it. That much. What was more, it worked—at least for Dela, who got Griffin back; and for Griffin, who at least found himself welcome. No more of them that afternoon, no more intrusions on the crew, no more of Griffin's frettings.

Lance . . . helped Viv and Percy set up the lab, unnaturally patient.

*   *   *

That evening—evening, as we had declared the time to be—my lady decided to throw a private party—a party in Hell, she declared it, with that terrible born-man humor of hers; and we had to serve the dinner and serve as guests as well . . . to fill up the table.

Griffin fell in with this humor in reluctant grace, and dressed. It was Lance who had to attend him, Lance that Dela appointed his servant. Better me, oh, better me; but that was how it was. I dressed my lady Dela in her best, a beautiful blue gown, and did her hair, and fixed the dinner, and in betweentimes I saw to myself, and to Viv and to the crew.

The crew, for their part, was not enthusiastic. They were still on their duty fix.

"They're to enjoy themselves," was Dela's order, which I relayed. It was a kind of absolution, and that wrought a little change (at least I imagined one) in Lynn and Wayne and Percy, once they did off their plain duty clothes and changed into their best.

Vivien now preened and became her chignoned, elegant self again, fit for the halls at Brahmani Dali. It's not precisely so that Vivien couldn't love: she adored her own handsomeness. "Bring me my gown," it was; and "Careful with that," as if she were Dela. As if her clinging to me and Lance during the catastrophe embarrassed her now, so she put more feeling than usual into giving orders, and took more fussing-over than all the rest of us put together.

No fussing at all for Modred. He stayed himself, and came in black, like what he wore on duty. My lady said in seeing him that it matched his soul—but that was figurative, I took it, souls being a born-man attribute.

Griffin came; and Lance—Griffin in blue and Lance in darker blue, a color almost as grim as Modred's. We saw Griffin and Dela seated and served the wine, and hurried below to bring up the feast, Lance and I; and Percy, who was not too proud to help—smiling and chattering with easy cheerfulness. Lance put on a smile, if you didn't look at the eyes—and Percivale used the wit in that handsome skull of his and chattered blithely away while we arranged things, with a tact I think he learned on his own. Certainly his duties never included filling awkward silences.

I squeezed Percy's arm when we passed the door, a thank you, and Percy pursed his lips and put on a blankness that would have done Modred credit. He knew—at least he reasoned that there was trouble; Percivale was good at thinking, duty fix or no.

We came topside, into that huge formal dining room with the weapons and the real wooden beams and the flickering lights like live flame. All of them who had sat down at table got up again to help serve, excepting Griffin and Dela of course, who sat together at the head of the table. It was a scandalous profusion of food, when we were only then setting up the lab that was, at best, never going to give us delicacies such as this: but Dela was never one to scant herself while the commodity held out—be it lovers or wines or the food we had to live on. Maybe it pleased her vanity to feed her servants so extravagantly; she had brought us to appreciate such things—even Modred was not immune to such pleasures. Perhaps it was humor. Or perhaps it was something more complicated, like flinging her money about like a challenge—even here. Here—because Griffin was here to be impressed.

"Sit, sit down," Dela bade us with a grand wave of her hand, and we did. She had saved Lance the place at her left hand, and me the one at Griffin's right; and then came Gawain and Lynette, Percivale at the end; Vivien and Modred next to Lance. We ate, serving ourselves further helpings. Dela chattered away quite gaily—so beautiful she was, with her pale braids done up beside her face, and her gown cut low to show off her fine fair complexion; and Griffin, blond and handsome beside her . . . they talked of times they had had in the mountains near Brahmani Dali, and of what a bizarre occurrence this was, and how Griffin thought she took it all marvelously well and was very brave.

Nonsense, I thought. Neither one of them was taking it that calmly: *we* saw.

"I have good company," she said. And she patted Griffin's hand on the tabletop and patted Lance's, and I swallowed hard at my wine, having about as much as I could stomach. I unfocused my eyes and looked at the plate. I knew that I ought not to look on Lance's face just then; I gave him that grace.

"Lancelot, and I," Griffin said, "passed time in the gym today. We should meet again tomorrow. It's been a long time since I found a match my size."

"Sir," Lance murmured.

"Not sir," Griffin said. "Not down there. You don't hold back. You really fight. I like that."

"Yes, sir," Lance whispered back.

"Be there tomorrow," Griffin said, "same time."

"Yes, sir," he said again.

Dela looked at Lance suddenly. She was frivolous at times, our lady, but she was not stupid; and she surely knew Lance better than she knew any of us. A frown came over her face and I knew what did it, that meek softness in Lance, that quiet, quiet voice.

There was a little silence in the party, over the taped music, in which Gawain's letting a knife slip against his plate rang devastatingly loud.

"We can't let it get us down," Griffin said. "We're here, that's all; and there's no getting out again; and we're going to live for years."

"Years and years," Dela said, winding her fingers with his. "All of us." She looked on us. "We're—very glad not to be quite alone. You understand that, all of you? I'm very glad to be able to trust my staff. However long we stay here—there's no law here; we've talked about that, Griffin and I: there's no law——no fortieth year. Even if we reach it here. You understand me? We're together in this."

It took a moment, this declaration. It hit my stomach like a fist even when I felt happy about it. A shift like that in the whole expected outcome of my life—it was a change as bizarre as dropping through the hole in space, and demanded its own sensory adjustments. Not to be put down. To live to be old. *Old* was not a territory I had mapped out for myself. I looked at Lance, who looked somewhat as dazed as I, and at the others—at Vivien, who had wanted this for herself and thought she was exclusive in her privilege; at Modred, whose face never yet showed any great excitement, only a flickering about the eyes; at Gawain and Lynette and Percy, who looked back at me in shock.

Of course, I thought, of course my lady needed us. It was insanity for them to put any of us down. They'd be alone then. It made sense.

"Thank you," I said, finding my voice first, and the others murmured something like. It was an eerie thing to say thank you for. Dela smiled benevolently and lifted her glass at us. She was,

I think, a little drunk; and so perhaps was Griffin, who had started on the wine when Dela had. Both their faces were flushed. They drank, and we did, to living.

And something hit the ship.

Not hard. It was a tap that rang through the hull and stopped us all, like the stroke of midnight in one of Dela's stories, that froze us where we sat, enchantment ended.

And it came again. Tap. Tap-tap. Tap-tap-tap. Tap-tap-tap-tap.

"O my God," Dela said.

VI

He names himself the Night, and oftener Death,
And wears a helmet mounted with a skull,
And bears a skeleton figured on his arms,
To show that who may slay or scape the three
Slain by himself shall enter endless night.

We ran to the bridge, all of us in a rush, Gawain and Percy first, being nearest the door, and the rest of us on their heels, out of breath and frightened out of our minds. The hammering kept up. Gawain and Lynn slid in at controls, Percy and Modred took their places down the boards, and the rest of us— the rest of us just hovered there holding on to each other and looking at the screens, which showed nothing different that I could tell.

Modred started doing something at his board, and com came on very loud, distantly echoing the tapping.

"What are you doing?" Dela asked sharply.

"Listening," Lynette said as the sounds shifted. Other pickups were coming into play. "Trying to figure out just where they are on the hull."

Dela nodded, giving belated permission, and we all stayed very quiet while Modred kept sorting through the various pickups through the ship.

It got loud of a sudden, and very loud. I flinched and tried not to. It went quiet of a sudden, then loud again, and my lady Dela swore at Modred.

"Somewhere forward," Modred said with a calm reach that did something to lower the sound. "About where we touch the mass."

"Trying to break through," Gawain muttered, "possibly."

"Wayne," Percivale said abruptly, urgently. "I'm getting a pulse on com; same pattern. Response?"

"*No!*" Dela cried, before ever Gawain could say anything. "*No*, you don't answer it."

"Lady Dela, they may breach us."

"They. They. We don't know what it is."

"He's right," Griffin said. "That *they* out there counts, Dela; and they're trying a contact. If they don't know we're alive in here, they could breach that hull and kill us all—at the least, damage the ship, section by section. And then what do we do?— That area forward," he said to the crew. "Put the emergency seals onto it."

"Presently engaged," Lynn said.

"Don't you give orders," Dela snapped. "Don't you interfere with my crew."

Griffin no more than frowned, but he was doing that already. My lady pushed away from his arm, crossed the deck to stand behind Gawain and Lynn. "Are there arms aboard?" Griffin asked.

"*Stop meddling.*"

"Tapes never prepared your crew for this. How much do you expect of them? Are there weapons aboard? Have they got a block against using them?"

Dela looked about at him, wild. She seemed then to go smaller, as if it were all coming at her too fast. I had never imagined a born-man blanking, but Dela looked close to it. "There aren't any weapons," she said.

The hammering stopped, a dire and thickish silence.

"Are we still getting that signal?" Griffin asked.

"Yes," Percy said after a moment, answering Griffin. It made me shiver, this yes-no of our lady's, standing there, looking like she wanted to forbid, and not. Percy brought the sound from the com up so we could hear it, and it was a timed pulse of static. One. One-two. One-two-three.

"Maybe—" Dela found her voice. "Maybe it's something natural."

"In this place?" Griffin asked. "I think we'd better answer that call. Make it clear we're in here.—Dela, they know, they *know* this ship's inhabited if it's whole: what *are* ships but inhabited? And the question isn't whether they breach that hull; it's how they do it. Silence could be taken for unfriendly intentions. Or for our being dead already, and then they might not be careful at all."

Dela just stared. The static pulses kept on. I held to Lance's arm and felt him shivering too.

"Answer it," Griffin said to Percivale.

"No," Dela said, and Griffin stared at her, frowning, until she made a spidery, resigning motion of her hand.

"Go on," Griffin said to Percivale. "Can you fine it down, get something clearer out of that?"

The whole crew looked round at their places, in Dela's silence. And finally she nodded and shrugged and looked away, an I-don't-care. But she did care, desperately; and I felt sick inside.

"Get to it," Griffin snapped at them. "Before we lose it."

Backs turned. Percy and Modred worked steadily for a few moments, and we started getting a clear tone.

"Answer," Griffin said again, and this time Percy looked around at Dela, and Modred did, slowly and refusing to be hurried.

"Do whatever he says," Dela murmured, her arms wrapped about her as if she were shivering herself. She rolled her eyes up at the screens, but the screens showed us nothing new.

And all of a sudden the com that had been giving out steady tones snapped and sputtered with static. It started gabbling and clicking, not a static kind of click, but a ticking that started in the bass register like boulders rolling together and rumbled up into higher tones until it became a shriek. We all jerked from the last notes, put our hands over our ears: it was that kind of sound. And it rumbled back down again—softer—someone had gotten the volume adjusted—and kept rumbling, slow, slow ticks.

"Not human," Griffin said. "Not anything like it. But then what did we expect? *Send.* Answer in their pattern. See if it changes."

Hands moved on the boards.

"Nothing," Percy said.

Then the com stopped, dead silent.

"Did you cut it?" Griffin asked, ready to be angry.

"It's gone," Modred said. "No pickup now. We're still sending."

The silence continued, eerie after the noise. The ventilation fans seemed loud.

"Kill our signal," Griffin said.

Percy moved his hand on the board, and the whole crew sat

still then, with their backs to us, no one moving. I felt Lance's hand tighten on mine and I held hard on to his. We were all scared. We stood there a long time waiting for something . . . anything.

Dela unclasped her arms and turned, flinging them wide in a desperately cheerful gesture. "Well," she said, "they're thinking it over, aren't they? I think we ought to go back down and finish off the drinks."

Her cheer fell flat on the air. "You go on back," Griffin said.

"What more can you do here? It's their move, isn't it? There's no sense all of us standing around up here. Gawain and Modred can keep watch on it. Come on. I want a drink, Griffin."

He looked at her, and he was scared too, was master Griffin. Dela had let him give us orders, and now whatever-it-was knew about us in here. I felt sick at my stomach and probably the rest of us did. Griffin didn't move; and Dela came close to him, which made me tense; and Lance—Griffin might hit her; he had hit me when he was afraid. But she slipped her white arm into his and tugged at him and got him moving, off the bridge. He looked back once. Maybe he sensed our distress with him. But he went with her. Percy and Lynette got up from their places and Lance and Viv and I trailed first after Griffin and my lady, getting them back to the dining hall.

They sat down and drank. We had no invitation, and we cleaned up around them, even Lynette and Vivien, ordinarily above such things, while my lady made a few jokes about what had happened and tried to lighten things. Griffin smiled, but the humor overall was very thin.

"Let's go to bed," my lady suggested finally. "That's the way to take our minds off things."

Griffin thought it over a moment, finally nodded and took her hand.

"The wine," Dela said. "Bring that."

Viv and I brought it, while Lance took the dishes down and Percy and Lynn went elsewhere. My lady and Griffin went to the sitting room to drink, but I went in to turn down the bed, and then collected Vivien and left. We were free to go, because my lady was not as formal with us as she had us be with her guests. Whenever *she* left us standing unnoticed, that meant go.

Especially when she had a man with her. And especially now, I thought. Especially now.

We went back to our quarters, where Lynn and Percy and Lance had gathered, all sitting silent, Lynn and Percy at a game, Lance watching the moves. There was no cheer there.

"Go a round?" I asked Lance. He shook his head, content to watch. I looked at Vivien, who was doing off her clothes and putting them away. No interest there either. I went to the locker and undressed and put on a robe for comfort, and came and sat by Lance, watching Lynn and Percy play. Viv sat down and read—we did have books, of our own type, for idle moments, something to do with the hands and minds, but they were all dull, tame things compared to the tapes, and they were homilies which were supposed to play off our psych-sets and make us feel good. Me, I felt bored with them, and hollow when I read them.

We would live. That change in our fortunes still rose up and jolted me from time to time. No more thought of being put down, no more thinking of white rooms and going to sleep forever; but it was strange—it had no comfort. It gave us something to fear the same as born-men. Maybe we should have danced about the quarters in celebration; but no one mentioned it. Maybe some had forgotten. I think the only thing really clear in our minds was the dread that the horrid banging might start up again at any moment—at least that was the clearest thought in mine: that the hammering might start and the hull might be breached, and we might be face to face with what lived out there. I watched the game board, riveting my whole mind on the silences and the position of the pieces and the sometime moves Lynn and Percy made, predicting what they would do, figuring it out when expectation went amiss. It was far better occupation than the thoughts that gnawed round the edges of my mind, making that safe center smaller and smaller.

The game went to stalemate. We all sat there staring blankly at a problem that could not be resolved—like the one outside—and feeling the certainty settling tighter and tighter over the game, were cheated by it of having *some* sort of answer, to something. Lynn swore, mildly, an affectation aped from born-men. It seemed overall to be fit.

So the game was done. The evening was. Lance got up, undressed and went to bed ahead of the rest of us, while Viv sat in her lighted corner reading. I came and shoved my bed over on its tracks until it was up against his. Lance paid no attention, lying on his side with his back to me until I edged into his bed and up against his back.

He turned over then. "No," he said, very quiet, just the motion of his lips in the light we had left from Viv's reading, and the light from the bathroom door. Not a fierce no, as it might have been. There was pain; and I smoothed his curling hair and kissed his cheek.

"It's all right," I said. "just keep me warm."

He shifted over and his arms went about me with a fervent strength; and mine about him; and maybe the others thought we made love: it was like that, for a long time, long after all the lights but Viv's were out. Finally that one went. And then when we lay apart but not without our arms about each other, came a giving of the mattress from across Lance's side, and Vivien lay down and snuggled up to him, not because she was interested in Lance, but just that we did that sometimes, lying close, when things were uncertain. It goes back to the farms; to our beginnings; to nightmares of being alone, to good memories of lying all close together, and touching, and being touched. It was comfort. It put no demands on Lance. In a moment more Percivale and Lynette moved a bed up and lay down there, crowding in on us, so that if someone had to get up in the night it was going to wake everyone. But all of us, I think, wanted closeness more than we wanted sleep.

I know I didn't sleep much, and sometimes, in that kind of glow the ceiling let off when eyes had gotten used to the dark, I could make out Lance's face. He lay on his back, and I think he stared at the ceiling, but I could not be sure. I kept my arm about his; and Percy was at my right keeping me warm on that side, with Lynette all tangled up with him; and Viv sleeping on Lance's shoulder on the other side. No sex. Not at all. All I could think of was that sound: we had fallen into something that was never going to let us go; we clung like a parasite to something that maybe didn't want us attached to it at all; and out there . . . out there beyond the hull, if I let my senses go, was still that terrible chaos-stuff.

If this was death, I kept thinking, remembering my lady's mad hypothesis, if this was death, I could wish we had not tangled some other creature up in our dying dream. But I believed now it was no dream, because I could never have imagined that sound out of my direst nightmares.

It came again in the night, that rumbling over com: Gawain came on the intercom telling Percy and Lynn so; and all of us scrambled out of bed and ran for the lift.

So had Griffin come running from my lady's bedroom. He stood there in his robe and his bare feet like the rest of us; but no word from my lady, nothing. It left us with Griffin alone, and that rumbling and squealing came over the com fit to drive us all blank.

"Have you answered it?" Griffin asked of Gawain and Modred, who sat at controls still in their party clothes; and Percy and Lynn took their places in their chairs wearing just the robes they had thrown on. "No," Modred replied. He turned in his place, calm as ever, with dark circles under his eyes. "I'm composing a transmission tape in pulses, to see if we can establish a common ground in mathematics."

"Use it," Griffin said. "If the beginning's complete, use it."

Modred hesitated. I stood there with my arms wrapped about me and thinking, no, he wouldn't, not with my lady not here. But Modred gave one of those short, curious nods of his and pushed a button.

The transmission went out. At least after a moment the transmission from the other side stopped. "I should see to my lady," I said.

"No," Griffin said. "She's resting. She took a pill."

I stood there as either/or as Modred, clenched my arms about me and let this born-man tell me I wasn't to go . . . because I knew if my lady had taken a pill she wouldn't want the disturbance. This terrible thing started up again and the crew asked help and Dela took a pill.

An arm went about me. It was Lance. Viv sat near us, on one of the benches near the door.

"You'd better trade off shifts," Griffin said to the crew, marking, surely, how direly tired Gawain and Modred looked.

"Yes," Gawain agreed. He would have sat there all the watch if Griffin hadn't thought of that, which was one of the considerate things I had seen Griffin do . . . but it gave me no comfort, and no comfort to any of the rest of us, I think. It was Dela who should have thought of that; Dela who should be here; and it was Griffin instead, who started acting as if he owned us and the *Maid*. Until now he had looked through us all and ignored us; and now he saw us and we were alone with him.

"We'll dress," Lynn said, "and come up and relieve you."

"Get back to sleep," Griffin said to those of us who were staff. "No need of your being here."

We went back to the crew quarters and got in bed again, except Lynn and Percy, who dressed and went topside again. Then Gawain and Modred came down and undressed and lay down with us as Lynn and Percy had—I think they were glad of the company, and worked themselves up against us, cold and tense until they began to take our warmth, and until they fell asleep with the suddenness of exhaustion.

What went on out there, that noise, that thing outside our hull—it might go on again and again. It might not need to sleep.

VII

The huge pavilion slowly yielded up,
Thro' those black foldings, that which housed therein.
High on a nightblack horse, in nightblack arms,
With white breastbone, and barren ribs of Death,
And crowned with fleshless laughter—some ten steps—
Into the half-light—thro' the dim dawn—advanced
The monster, and then paused, and spake no word.

We went about in the morning on soft feet and small steps, listening. We stayed to our duties, what little of them there were. Even the makeshift lab was quiet, where Vivien was setting things up . . . running tests, that took time, and we could do nothing there. Griffin and Dela stayed together in her bed, and I walked and paced feeling like a ghost in the *Maid*'s corridors, all too conscious how vast it was outside and how small we were and how huge that rumbling voice had sounded.

"It's probably trapped here too," Dela said when I came finally to do her hair, "and maybe it's as scared as we are."

"Maybe it is," I said, thinking that scared beasts bit; and I feared this one might have guns. On the *Maid* we had only the ancient weapons which decorated her dining hall and the lady's quarters and some of the corridors. Precious good *those* were against this thing. I thought about knights and dragons and reckoned that they must have been insane.

I finished my lady's hair . . . made it beautiful, elaborate with braids, and dressed her in her green gown with the pale green trim. It encouraged me, that she was up and sober again, no longer lying in her chambers prostrate with fear: if my lady could face this day, then things might be better. If there was an answer to this, then born-men could find it; and she was our born-man, ours, who dictated all the world.

"Where's Griffin?" she asked.

"It's eleven hundred hours. Master Griffin—asked Lance—"

"I remember." She waved her hand, robbed me of the excuse I had hoped for to stop all of that, dismissing it all.

"Shall I go?" I asked.

Again a wave of the hand. My lady walked out into the sitting room and sat down at the console there, started calling up something on the comp unit—all the log reports, I reckoned, of all the time she had slept; or maybe the supply inventories. My lady was herself again; and let Griffin beware.

I padded out, ever so quietly, closed the door and wiped my hands and headed down the corridor to the lift as fast as I could walk. I went down and toward the gym in the notion that I had to be quiet, but quiet did no good at all: the gym rang with the impact of feet and bodies. They were at it again, Griffin and Lance, trying to throw each other.

It was crazy. They were. I had thought of lying again, saying that Dela wanted this or that, but she was paying sharp attention today, and the lie would not pass. I stood there in the doorway and watched.

They were at it this time, I reckoned, because there had been no decision the last encounter, thanks to me. No winner; and Griffin wanted to win—had to win, because Lance was lab-born, and shouldn't win, shouldn't even be able to contest with the likes of Griffin.

They went back and forth a great deal, muscles straining, skin slick with sweat that dampened their hair and made their hands slip. Neither one could get the advantage standing; and they hit the floor with a thud and neither one could get the other stopped. They didn't see me, I don't think. I stood there biting my lip until it hurt. And suddenly it was Lance on the bottom, and Griffin slowly let him up.

I turned away, fled the doorway for the corridor, because I was ashamed, and hurt, and I didn't want to admit to myself why, but it was as if I had lost too, like it was my pain, that Lance after all proved what we were made to be, and that we always had to give way. Even when he did what none of the rest of us could do, something so reckless as to fight with Griffin—he was beaten.

Lance came up to the crew quarters finally, where I sat playing solitaire. He was undamaged on the outside, and I tried to act as if I had no idea anything was wrong, as if I had never been in that doorway or seen what I had seen. But I reckoned that he wanted to have his privacy now, so downcast his look was, and I could hardly walk out without seeming to avoid him, so I curled up on the couch and pretended to be tired of my game, to sleep awhile.

But I watched him through my lashes, as he rummaged in his locker, and found a tape, and set up the machine. He took the drug, and lay down in deepsleep, lost in that; and all the while I had begun to know what tape it was, and what he was doing, and what was into him. The understanding sent cold through me.

He should not be alone. I was sure of that. The lady had deserted him and his having the tape in the first place was my fault. I took the drug and set up the connections, and lay down beside him in his dream—lay down with my fingers laced in his limp ones and began to slip toward it.

The story ran to its end and stopped, letting us out of its grip; and whether he felt me there or not, he just lay there with tears streaming from his closed eyes. Finally I couldn't stand it any longer and took the sensors off him and me and put my arms about him.

But he mistook what I wanted and pushed me away, stared at the ceiling and blanked awhile.

It was that bad.

And when he came out of it he said nothing, but got up, went to the bath and washed his face and left. Me, who was so long his friend, he left without a word. I heard the lift go down again; and it was the galley or the gym down there, so I had no difficulty finding him.

It was the gym. From the door I watched him ... doing pushups until I thought his arms must break, as if it could drive the weakness out of him.

Now, Beast, I thought toward the voice that had terrorized our night. Now, if ever you have something to say. But it stayed mute. Lance struggled against his own self; and I wished with all my heart that someone would discover some duty for him, some use that would get him busy.

He saw me there, turning suddenly. I knew he did by his scowl when he got to his feet, and I turned and fled down the corridor, to the lift, to the upper level, as far from the gym as I could excepting Viv's domain.

And came Percivale, down the corridor from the bridge, looking as dispirited as I felt.

"Percy," I said, catching at his arm. "Percy, I want you to do something for me."

"What?" he asked, blinking at my intense assault; and I explained I wanted him to go down to the gym and fight with Lance. "It's good for you," I said, "because we don't know what's out there trying to get in, do we? and you might have to fight, to protect the ship and the lady. I think it's a good idea to be ready. Griffin's been working out with Lance. I'm sure it would be good for all of you."

Percy thought about that, ran a hand over his red hair. "I'll talk to Gawain and Modred," he said. "But Lance is much stronger than we are."

"But you should try," I said, "at least try. Lance did, with Griffin, with a born-man, after all; and can't you, with him?"

Percivale went down there first, and later that afternoon the three of them were looking the worse for wear and there was a little brighter look in Lance's eyes when I saw him at dinner. I smiled smugly across the table in the great hall, next Griffin and my lady, with all the table set as it had been the evening before, and all of us again in our party best.

"I think it's given up," my lady said, quite cheerful, lifting her glass.

It was true. There had been silence all day. Modred was glum. His carefully constructed tapes had failed. Gawain said so . . . and my lady laughed, a brave, lonely sound.

Griffin smiled a faint, small quirk of the lips, more courtesy than belief. And drank his wine. Before dinner was done something did ring against the hull, a vague kind of thump; and the crew started from their places, and Griffin did.

"*No!*" my lady snapped, stopping the crew on the instant, and Griffin, half out of his chair, hesitated. "We can't be running at every shift and settling," Dela said. "Sit down! The lot of you sit down. It's nothing."

My heart felt it would break my ribs. But no further sound came to us, and the crew settled back into their places and Griffin sat back down.

"We would have felt a settling," Griffin said.

"Enough of it. Enough."

There was silence for a moment, no movement, all down the table; but my lady set to work on her dessert, and Griffin did, and so did we all. My lady talked, and Griffin laughed, and soon we all talked again, even Lance, idle dinner chatter. I took it for a sign of health in Lance, that I might have done some good, and I felt my own spirits higher for it. Dela and master Griffin finished their meal, we took the dishes down, and Lance remained tolerably cheerful when we were in the galley together. He was smiling, if not overly talkative.

But it didn't help that night. Lance was sore and full of bruises, and he wanted to be let alone. He didn't object to my moving my bed over or getting in with him, but he turned his back on me, and I patted his shoulder. Finally he turned an anguished look on me in the light there was left in the room, with the others lying in their beds. He started to say something. He didn't need to. I just lay still and took his hand in mine, and he put his arm about me and stroked my hair, with that old sadness in his eyes, stripped of anger. I could hear noises from farther over toward the wall, where Lynn slept. Either Gawain or Percy had come somewhat off the duty fix, and presumably so had Lynette.

Misery, I thought. And Lance just lay there in the dark looking at me.

"It happens to born-men too," I said. I knew that, and maybe he didn't. He had been more sheltered, in his way. "They're more complicated than we are, and they get this a lot, this trouble; but they get over it."

He shivered, and I knew he was caught somewhere in his own psych-sets, where I couldn't truly help him, and he wasn't about to discuss it. There was no *reason* for Lance, I thought. The lady and Griffin, and when it turned out that this voyage wasn't ending, ever, then that was it for Lancelot, done, over. He cared for nothing else in all existence but my lady; and when he was shut away from her, that was when he—

—heard the story in the tape, and learned what the meaning of my lady's fancy was, and what he was named for, and he began to dream of being that dream of hers. That thought came to me while we lay there in the dark. And there was a great hollowness in me, knowing that. Lance had found himself a kind of purpose, but I had nothing like his, that touched his central psych-sets. Being just Elaine, a minor player in the tape, I was meant to do nothing but keep Lance entertained when my lady was otherwise occupied, and to do my lady's hair and to look decorative, and nothing more, nothing more.

Our purposes are always small. We're small people, pale copies, filled with tapes and erasable. But something had begun to burn in Lance that had more complicated reasons; and I was afraid—not for myself, not really for myself, I kept reasoning in my heart, although that was part of my general terror. We should live as long as we liked. The lady had promised us, ignoring that thing out there, ignoring the uncertainties which had settled on us . . . like growing old. Like our minds growing more and more complicated just by living, until we grew confused beyond remedy. We were promised life. The thing out there in the dark, the chaos waiting whenever we might grow confused enough to let our senses slip back into the old way of seeing—this living with death so close to us, was that different than our lives ever were? And didn't born-men themselves live that way, when they deliberately took chances?

It was just that our death talked to us through the hull, had called us on com, had tapped the hull this evening just to let us know that he was still there. *Death*, not an erasing; not the white room where they take you at the end.

We're already dying, my lady had insisted once; and my mind kept wandering back to that. I looked into Lance's troubled eyes and sniffed, thinking that at least we were going to die like born-men, and have ourselves a fight with our Death, like in the fables.

Thermopylae. Roland at the pass. When it got to us we would blow the horns and meet it head on. But that was in the fables.

I began to think of other parts of the story, Lancelot's part, how he had to be brave and be the strongest of all.

And of what the rest of us must be.

Lance slept for a while, and I snuggled up under his chin and slept too, happy for a while, although I couldn't have said why . . . something as inexplicable as psych-set, except that it was a nice place to be, and I found it strange that even in his sleep he held onto me, not the closeness we take for warmth, and far from sex too . . . just that it was nice, and it was something—

—like in the tape, I thought. I wondered who I was to him.

I reckoned I knew. And being only Elaine, I took what small things I could get. Even that gave me courage. I slept.

Then the hammering started again on the hull.

I tensed, waking. Lance sat up, and we held onto each other, while all about us the others were waking too. It wasn't the patterned hammering we had heard before. It came randomly and loud.

Gawain piled out of bed and the rest of us were hardly slower, excepting Vivien, who sat there clutching her sheet to her chest in the semidark and looking when the lights came on as if it was all going to be too much for her.

But she moved, grabbed for her clothes and started dressing. Modred was out the door first, and Percy after him; and Gawain and Lynette right behind them. Lance and I stopped at least to throw our clothes on and then ran for it, leaving Viv to follow as she could.

We ran, the last bit from the lift, breathless, down the corridor to the bridge. The crew had found their places. My lady and Griffin were there, both in their robes, and my lady at least looked grateful that we two had shown up. I went and gave her my hand, and Lance stood near me—not that presumptuous, not with one of my lady's lovers holding the other.

"They say it's the same place as before," Dela informed us as Vivien showed up and delayed by the door. "But it doesn't sound like a signal."

It sounded like someone working on the other side of the hull, to me. Tap. Bang. And long pauses.

The crew was talking frantically among themselves—Modred and Percy answering questions from Lynn and Gawain, making protests. Griffin let go my lady's hand and walked into that half U near them, leaning on the back of Percy's chair.

Only my lady Dela stood there shivering, and went over to a bench and sat down. I sat down and put my arms about her, and Lance hovered helplessly by while I tried to keep her warm in her nightgown. She was crying. I had never seen Dela cry like this. She was scared and trembling and it was contagious.

"Give us vid," Griffin was saying. "Let's see if we can't figure out what happened to the rest of the ships around us. See if they're breached in some way."

Vid came on, all measled red and glare, shading off to greens

and purples where some object was. "Forward floods," Modred
said "Wayne."

"Just let it alone," Dela snapped. "Let it be. If we start turning the lights on and looking round out there we'll encourage it."

Modred stopped. So did Gawain.

"Do it," Griffin said. And when they did nothing: "Dela, what
are we going to do, wait for it?"

"That's all we can do, isn't it?"'

"It's not all I choose to do. We're going to fight that thing if
it has to be."

"For what good?"

"Because I'm not sitting here waiting for it."

"And you encourage it and it gets to us—"

"We still have a chance when we know it's coming.—Put the
floods on," he said to Gawain.

Gawain looked at Dela. "We think the sound is coming from
inside the wheel . . . not one of the smaller ships: from where we
contact the torus."

Dela just shivered where she sat, between us; and Viv hovered near the door, frozen.

"Dela," Griffin said, "go on back to bed. Give the order and
go back to bed. Nothing's going to happen. We look and get
some clear images of where it's coming from, that's all."

Dela gave the order, a wave of her hand. The floods went on
and played over blacknesses that were other ships. We sat staring into that black and red chaos, at ships bleeding light through
their wounds. Dela turned her face into my shoulder and I locked
my arms about her as tightly as I could, stared helplessly into
that place that I remembered of a sudden, that chaos senses had
to forget the moment it stopped. I turned my face away from it,
looked up at Lance's face which was as chaos-lost as I felt; and
Viv, Vivien holding on to the door. It was hard to look back
again, and harder not to. Griffin was still giving orders—had the
cameras sweep this way and that, and there was that ship next
to us, the delicate one like spiderweb; and a strange one on our
other side, that we had slid up against when we were grappling
on; we couldn't see all of it. And mostly the view dissolved in
that red bleeding light. But when the cameras centered on our
own bow, we could almost see detail, like it was lost in a wash
of light across the lens, something that was like machinery. A

cold feeling was running through my veins. "I don't remember our nose like that" I said. No one paid attention to me.

"See if you can fine it down now," Griffin said. "What happened to your last setup on that?"

"Everything's shifted," Modred said. I hoped he meant the figures.

Griffin swore and turned away, paced the floor. Maybe it was hard for him to stare at the screens for any length of time. I know it got to my stomach; and even the crew looked uncomfortable, jolted out of sleep, with that terrible banging never ceasing. Tap. Bang. Bang. Tap-tap-tap.

Lynette turned around at her place. "We might ungrapple," she offered, looking at Dela, not Griffin. "We can push off and disrupt whatever they're doing on the other side."

"*Do* it," Dela said, snatched at that with all the force in her. Griffin looked like he wanted to say something and shut his mouth instead. Lynn turned about again, all coolly done. She touched switches and boards came alight.

"Take hold," Percy warned us. We hurried and got Dela and Griffin to the emergency cushions, got ourselves snugged in, Viv first, and Lance and myself together, holding hands for comfort.

Moving would delay things. It would give us time. But maybe the thing out there had guns, I thought; maybe when we moved it would just start shooting and all we would have of life would be just the next moment, when the fragile *Maid* was blown apart.

Did Lynn and the others think of that? Was that what Griffin had almost said? Maybe my listening to his tapes, all those things about wars and killing people, let me think such things. I felt like I was sweating all the way to my insides.

The crew talked to each other. It took them forever . . . judging, I guessed, how hard and how far and what we were going to grab to next that might make it harder for whatever was trying to hammer through our bow. Finally: "Stand by," Lynette said.

VIII

And Vivien answer'd frowning yet in wrath:
"O ay; what say ye to Sir Lancelot, friend,
Traitor or true? that commerce with the Queen,
I ask you. . . ."

It came simultaneously, the clang of the grapples disconnecting, the shudder that might be our engines working.

"Shut it down," Percy cried. "Shut it down!"

"No," Lynn said, and the shuddering kept up, like out-of-tune notes quavering through metal frame and living bone. Lynn reached suddenly across the board. The harmonies stopped. Gawain, beside her, made a move and the grapples slammed on again.

"We didn't move," Dela said softly; and louder: "We didn't move."

Lynn swung her chair about. "No." There was thorough anguish on her freckled face. "Something's got a grapple on us. We can't break it loose."

"Do it!" Dela was unbuckling the restraints. She got them undone as the rest of us got out of ours. She stood up and thrust Griffin's hand off when he got up and tried to put his hand on her shoulder. "You find a way to do it."

"Lady Dela, we already took a chance with it."

"Listen to your captains," Griffin said, taking Dela's shoulders and refusing this time to be shaken off. "Listen. Will you listen to what she's trying to tell you?"

"We didn't move at all," Lynn said, with soft, implacable precision. "Our own grapples went back on right where they had been, to the millimeter. We gave it repulse straight on and angled and we didn't shake it even that much. That's a solid hold they've got on us."

"Well, why did you let them get it on us?" Dela's voice went brittle. "Why did you play games with it and let this happen?"

"Last night at dinner," Modred said in his ordinary, flat voice, "we should have investigated. But it was probably too late."

Only Modred was that nerveless, to turn something back at Dela. She cursed him, and all of us, and Griffin, and told him to let her go. He didn't and Modred never flinched.

"They've told you the truth," Griffin said, making her look at him: there was no one but Lance could fight back against a strength like Griffin had; but he let her go when she struck at his arms, and stood there when she hit him hard in the chest in her temper. And we stood there—I, and Lance—even Lance, watching this man put hands on Dela, because somehow he had gotten round to Lynn's side, and Modred's and the ship's, and we were standing with him, not understanding how it was happening to us.

Maybe Dela realized it too. She made a throwaway gesture, turned aside, not looking at anyone. "Go on," she said. "Go on. Do what you like. You have all the answers."

She stayed that way, facing no one, her hands locked in front of her. Griffin stared at her as if she had set him at a loss, like all of us were. Then he looked over at us. "Get her out," he said quietly. "All of you who don't have to be here, out. Crew too: offshift crew, go back to sleep. This may go on into the next watch. We have to put up with it."

I didn't know what to do for the moment. I wasn't supposed to take his orders about my lady Dela, but then, Dela was fit to say something if she wanted to say something. I hesitated. Lance did, not included in that order, things being as they were. "Come," I said then, and went and hugged Dela against me. "Come on."

Dela put her arms about me, seeming suddenly small and uncertain, and I put mine about her and led her back through the corridor to her own rooms. Then she walked on her own, in her own safe sitting-room, but I held her hand, because she seemed to want that, and led her back into her own bedroom and did off her shoes and her robe and tucked her into that big soft blue bed. She was still shivering . . . my brave, my strong-minded lady. Just last evening she had put courage into us, had talked to us and made us sit down and almost made us believe it would all turn out. She had made herself believe it too, I think; and it was all unraveling.

Vivien had followed us . . . not Lance. He had not felt permitted, or he would have. "Get her a drink," I told Viv—when she could hardly round on me and tell me to do it myself; she gave me a black hysterical look and went over to the sideboard. I sat with my lady and kept my arm about her behind the pillow. The banging at the hull began again, and Dela's hands were clenched whitely on the bedclothes.

"It can't get in," I offered, not believing it myself any longer. "Or it would have done it already. It's just wishing, that's all."

Vivien brought the wine. Dela took it in both hands and drank, and seemed to feel better after half a glass. Vivien sat down on the other side of the wide mattress and I stayed where I was, just being near Dela. For a long time Dela drank in small sips, and stared with detached interest at some place before her, while the hammering kept up.

"Go on," my lady said finally, to Vivien. "Go on." But she didn't look at me when she said it, and when Vivien got up and left, I stayed. "Get me another drink," she asked quite calmly. "I can't stand that noise."

I did so, and took one for myself, because alone, we were not on formalities.

And I sat there beside her while she was on her second glass, my hand locked in hers. Psych-set: Dela was hurting, above and beyond the fear; I could sense that. A frown creased her brow. Her blonde hair fell about her lace-gowned shoulders and she leaned there among the lacy pillows drinking the wine and looking oddly young.

"Why doesn't he come back?" she asked of me, as if I should know what born-men thought. "We're stuck here. Why can't he accept that?"

"Maybe he thinks he could beat it."

She shook her head, a cascade of pale blonde among the pillows. "No. He doesn't." She freed her hand of mine and changed hands with the wineglass, patted Griffin's accustomed place in the huge bed. "He's so good to me. He tried so hard to be brave, and I know he's scared, because he's young—that's not rejuv: that's his real age. He doesn't know much. Oh, he's traveled a bit, but not like this." A soft, desperate laugh, as if she had realized her own bad joke. A reknitting of the brows. "He's scared. And he doesn't have to be nice, but he is, and I do love him, Elaine. He's the first one of all of them who ever didn't have to be nice to me, and he is, and I hate that it has to be him in this mess with us."

I looked desperately at my lap, at my fingers laced there, not liking this business of being dragged into born-man confidence. But we're like the walls. Born-men can talk to us and know our opinion's nothing, so it's rather like talking to themselves. Sold on, we're erased; and here—here where we were, there was no selling, and no gossiping elsewhere, that was certain.

"He's good," Dela said. "You understand that? He's just a good man."

I remembered that he had hit me, but maybe he hadn't seen me right, and he had been scared then. Hitting made no difference to me. Others had hit me. I held no grudges; that wasn't in my psych-set either.

"I'm seventy," Dela said, still talking to me and the walls at once. "And do you know why he's with me? Because we started out as allies to do a little bending of government rules . . . because the government . . . but it doesn't matter. Nothing back there matters. His family; my estates—it doesn't matter at all. There's just that *thing* out there, and I wish he'd leave it alone, let it take its time.—Does dying frighten you, Elaine? Do you ever think about things like that?"

I nodded, though I didn't know if I thought of it the way she meant. She changed hands again and reached and stroked my hair. "Griffin and I . . . you know there are people who don't think you ought to exist at all—that the whole system that made you is wrong. But you value your life, don't you?"

"Yes."

"Griffin and I talked about it. Once. When it mattered. It doesn't now. I meant what I said. We share everything, Griffin and I and all of you, all the food, everything, as long as there's anything. That's the way it is."

"Thank you," I said. What could I say? She had frightened me badly and healed it all at once, and I put my arms about her, really grateful—but I knew better than to think they wouldn't think on it again sometime that things really did run short. I knew my lady Dela, that she had high purposes, and she meant to be good, but as with her lovers and her hopes, sometimes she and her high purposes had fallings-out.

The hammering, dim a moment, suddenly crashed out louder

and louder. Dela rolled her eyes at the wooden beams overhead
and looked as if she could not bear it. She slammed the empty
glass down on the bedside table and scrambled out of bed in a
flurry of gowns and blonde hair, on her way back to the intercom in the sitting-room.

"Griffin," I heard her say over the hammering on the hull. I
took up her wineglass and refilled it, trembling somewhat, expecting temper when Griffin was Griffin and refused.

"Dela," he answered after a time.

"Griffin, stop it up there and let it alone and come back down
here."

"Dela," I heard, standing stock-still and holding my breath.
"Dela, there's no waiting for this thing, Modred and I have something. There're *tubes*, Dela, tubes going to all those ships we can
see. We don't know what or why, but we're trying to get them
a little clearer."

"What good is it to see it? *Modred*, Modred, let it all be, shut
it down and let it be."

"Let them alone!" Griffin snapped back. "They're doing a job
up here. Do you want me to come down there and explain it all
or do you trust me? I thought we had this out. I thought we had
an agreement, Dela."

There was long silence, and I clenched my hands together,
because there was no one born who talked to Dela Kirn that way,
no one.

"All right," Dela said in an unhappy voice. There was a sudden silence, then another tap, very soft, that ran from the hull
through my nerves. "All right Modred, help him. All of you,
work with Griffin."

She came back into the bedroom then, and for a moment instead of the youth the rejuv preserved, I saw age, in the slump
of her shoulders and the gesture that reached for the doorway as
if she had trouble seeing it. I started to go and help her; and then
I froze, because I felt wrong in seeing such a thing. She was
wounded and sometimes in her wounds she was dangerous. She
might hit me. I resigned myself to that when she let go the door
and came near, her hand stretched out for me. I took it and set
her down on the bedside.

No violence. She began to crawl beneath the covers and I
tucked her in and sat down again on the bed, because she had

not yet dismissed me. She lifted a hand and patted my cheek, with a mournful look in her blue eyes.

"You'll do what Griffin says too," she said.

"Yes," I said, "if you ask me to."

"I do." She stroked the side of my cheek with her finger as if she were touching statuary. "You're special, you know that. Special, and beautiful, and maybe I shouldn't tangle up your minds the way I have, but you're people, aren't you? You understand loyalty. Or is it all programming?"

"I don't know how to answer," I said, and I was afraid, because it was a terrible kind of question, having my lady delve into my programming and my logic. There were buttons she could push, oh, not physical ones, but real all the same, keys she had that could turn me frozen or, I suspected, hurt me beyond all telling—the key instructions to all my psych-sets. "I could never know if I felt what you feel. But I know I want to take care of you. And I'm very glad it's you and not someone else, lady Dela."

"You think so?"

"I've met others and their owners, and I know how good you really are to us. And if it doesn't offend you, thank you for being good to us all our lives."

Her lips trembled. Outside the hull the hammering still continued, like someone fixing pipes, and she pulled me to her, my face between her hands, and kissed me on the brow.

It touched me in a strange way, like pulling strings that were connected to something deep and connected to everything else. Psych-sets. It's a very pleasurable thing to fulfill a Duty, one of the really implanted ones. And this made me feel I had.

I sat back and she just stared at me a time and kept her hand on mine, as if my being there mattered to her.

"Griffin is a *good man*," she insisted when I had never argued; and there was that frightened look in her eyes.

I reckoned then for once Dela was up against something she just didn't want to think about, just as she tried to believe us all dead when it began to go wrong. This wasn't like the Dela who ran the house on Brahman, who built cities. Then she was all business and hard-minded and no one could say no to her; but now she had no inclination to go running up to the bridge to take command. She might have fought. She abdicated. Griffin showed himself more competent with the ship . . . at least knowing how to talk to the crew. We hadn't defended her. I think that hurt her deeply.

Watch yourself, said I to Griffin, absent. Watch yourself, bornman, when you begin to take the *Maid* away from my lady.— But she had already lost it; and maybe it was that which had so broken Dela's spirit, that the *Maid* which had been so beautiful and so free, which had been Dela Kirn herself in some strange metaphysical connection . . . was held here and smashed and broken, and now threatened with further erosions. I perceived pain, and held to Dela's hand, minded to go on pouring her drinks and to stay here until she could sleep, whatever the infernal hammering meant out there.

I mean, Dela had never cared for the running of the ship, just that it did run, and she had bought Gawain and the others and they were good, the very best: that was her pride. Her money bought the best and it worked and she gave the orders and the ship ran . . . all magical. She had not the least idea how it all worked, far less idea than I did, who lived with the crew. And now Griffin, who claimed to do a little piloting himself insystem . . . just walked in and took them over; and Dela couldn't fight any longer. We were pinned here . . . I think that was the most horrible thing to her, that whatever we did, however we fought, there was never any hope, and while that was true, she had no spirit left at all.

"Call Lance," she said.

My heart stopped. I opened my mouth to babble some excuse on his behalf: he can't, he can't, I thought; but there was no excuse that would hide the truth, and perhaps—perhaps with her— I nodded, rose and went out to the com, pushed 21, the crew quarters. "Lance," I said. "Lance."

"Yes?" the answer came.

"My lady wants you in her quarters."

A silence. "Yes," he said plainly. It was all that had to be said. And very quietly I slipped away out the door, because all that I could do was done.

O Griffin, I thought, you never walk out on my lady; you didn't know that. But you will. And more than that, you're doing things your own way, and she'll never bear with that, not where it touches the *Maid*. Not in that.

But for Lance—for him I was mortally afraid.

I didn't want to go down the lift. I might meet Lance there, coming up, and that was not a meeting I wanted. The knell still rang against the hull, insane hammering that grew loud and soft by turns. I avoided the lift, kept to the main corridor, that took me back to the vicinity of the bridge, where I was not supposed to be, by Griffin's order.

Viv was there, just standing, where she could see in the open door, her hands locked together in an attitude of worry. I startled her, being there, and she scowled and looked back to the bridge.

"What are they up to?" I asked.

"What would you know?" she said. That was Viv. Her old self, worried as she was.

I edged up into the doorway. The main screen was off, but they had a clear image on some. I stood there and stared at our neighbors.

Tubes. Tubes, Griffin had said, and there were, everywhere. At every point a wreck contacted the wheel, the station, whatever it was that had snared us . . . tubes like some kind of obscene parasites that sucked the life from them. Tubes between the ships, as if the growth had pierced them and kept going. The wounds I had thought to have seen, holes in the ships themselves through which the light bled . . . some of those were not: some of those holes had been the arch of those tubes, against the chaos-stuff that was measled black in the still picture. They were huge, those structures, big enough for access, and irregular in their shapes, like many-branched snakes, like veins and arteries growing out of this thing we had snuggled up to and growing us to its body.

It didn't take much guesswork now to know what was proceeding out there with all those noises. Or why we were stuck fast. There's a thing I'd seen on vid, an access box, and they use it when there's some emergency . . . Hobson's Bridge, I had heard it named. It's a tube and two very powerful pressure gates; and they use it in shipboard disasters when ships have to be boarded and suits aren't sufficient to get people off. You rig it at one side and ride it across; you lock on with the magnetic grapple and you make the seal. You cut through. You're in.

Sometimes I wished I listened to fewer tapes.

Griffin had looked around. He caught me in the doorway, fixed me with that mad blue-eyed stare of his. "Elaine. Did Dela send you?"

"She dismissed me, sir."

He nodded, in a way that more or less accepted my presence there. I took a tentative step inside. Noticed by a born-man, one doesn't vanish when his back is turned. Griffin walked the length of the U at controls, stopped by Modred and looked back again at me. "You understand what we've got here?"

I swallowed against the tightness in my throat and nodded. "Yes, sir."

"How's Dela taking this?"

She had told me to take Griffin's orders, even if she really didn't want me to; and I stood confused, not knowing what I owed where; but I'm high-order, and I don't blank in choices. "I think she's scared, sir; and I don't think she wants to think about it for a while."

That at least was the truth; and it kept Lance out of it. I didn't want Griffin dashing back there to comfort Dela, not now, no.

Griffin ran a hand through his pretty golden hair, and he leaned standing against the chair absent Percy used, looking mortally tired. I felt sorry for him then, and I was not in the habit of feeling sorry for Griffin. He was trying. He had sent Lynn and Percy to rest; and Lance and Viv . . . even if no one was able to. He tried to solve this thing. So did the crew . . . fighting for the *Maid*, even if Dela saw no hope in it.

"You know what a Bridge is?" he asked. "Ship to ship?"

I nodded.

"And Dela—what does she say?"

"Nothing," I said. "But she would understand if she saw that."

He looked still very tired. Looked around at all of us, Gawain and Modred, and back to me. "You're good," he said. "You're very good."

I made a kind of bow of the head, pleased to be told that, even by a stranger. We knew our worth; but it was still good to hear.

"What they're doing," Griffin said, and all at once I was conscious that the hammering had stilled for a while, "is linking into all those ships. That means that something's been alive and doing that a long, long time."

"Yes, sir," I said, contemplating the age of those ships that

had come here before us. I looked round the control center, a
nervous gesture, missing the sound. "It doesn't take long to set
up a Bridge, does it?"

"No," Griffin said. "But I daresay they're jury-rigging. They.
It. We have to do something to stop it. You understand that. When
you talk to Dela—" He spoke very, very softly, in conspiracy.
"When you talk to her, believe that. Protest it in her ear. For her
sake. It's your duty, isn't it?—Where's Lance?"

I must have flinched. "Below, sir." We can lie, in duty. He
looked at me—he could not have suspected when he asked that
question; me, with my face—he had to suspect something behind
that flinching, had to think, and know why one of us would lie,
and for whom.

"When you see him," he said, ever so quietly, only that tired
look on his face, "tell him I'll see the whole staff up here at
1000 this morning. I want to talk to all of you at once. And keep
it quiet. I don't want to frighten Dela. You understand that."

I nodded. He walked away himself, his hands locked behind
him, and stopped and looked at the screens. I stood there, while
Modred and Gawain consulted and did things with the comp that
showed up in the image on the screens.

It looked uglier and uglier, defined, where before the bleeding smears of light had masked all detail. It took on colors, greens
and blues. Finally Griffin walked over to the side and looked at
Gawain and Modred. "You've got that inventory search run."

"Yes," Modred said, and reached and picked up a handful of
printout. Griffin took it. The hammering started again, and even
Modred reacted to it, a human glance at the walls about us. Griffin swore, shook his head.

"Go get some rest," he told them. "I'm doing the same."

He started away then, and I moved out of the doorway, to
show respect when a born-man wanted past. My heart was beating very fast: com, I was thinking, I could get to com before
Griffin could get to Dela's rooms; I could think of something casual to say—something; but Griffin delayed, fixed me with a
strangely sad look. "I'm going back to *my* quarters," Griffin said.

I felt my face go hot. I stood there, he walked out, and I
didn't make the call. I walked down the corridor after him,
headed my own way, for the lift that would take me down to
the crew quarters.

Vivien trailed after me, maybe the others too; but I watched Griffin's broad back, his shoulders bowed as if he were very tired, his head down, and for a moment he looked so like Lance in one of his sorrows that I found myself hurting for him.

I knew pain when I saw it. Remember . . . it's my function.

I wished I might go to him, might balance things, set it all right by magic. I walked faster, to overtake him; but my nerve failed me, with the thought that I had no instruction from Dela, and I could not side against her. Not twice. I stopped, close by the lift, and Viv pushed the button, opening the door.

Tap, the sound came against the hull. Tap-bang.

IX

In love, if love be love, if love be ours,
Faith and unfaith can ne'er be equal powers:
Unfaith in aught is want of faith in all.

We fled into the crew quarters, Gawain and Modred, Vivien and I . . . quietly as we could, but Lynn and Percy lifted their heads from their pillows all the same. We started taking off boots, settling down for a little rest.

"Where's Lance?" Gawain asked, all innocent.

"Dela called," I said, from my cot where I had lain down next Lance's vacant one; and Gawain's face took on an instant apprehension of things. Viv looked up from taking off her stockings. I closed my eyes and folded my hands on my middle, uncommunicative, trying to shut out the sound from the hull. It was down to a familiar pattern now . . . tap-tap-tap. It grew fainter. I thought of the tubes like branching arteries. Maybe they were working somewhere farther up, at some branching. I imagined such a thing growing over the *Maid*, a basketry of veins, wrapping us about. I shuddered and tried to think of something pleasant. About the dinner table with the artificial candles aglow up and down it, dark wood set with lace and crystal and loaded with fine food and wines. I would like a glass right now, I thought. There were times when I would have gone to the gallery and stolen a bottle. I didn't feel I should. Share and share alike, my lady had said; and the good wine was a thing we would run out of.

Supposing we lasted long enough.

There was silence. I opened my eyes.

"It stopped," Percy said, very hushed.

"Whatever they're doing," Modred said, "they'll have it done sooner or later. I'm only surprised it's taken this long."

"Stop it," Vivien said, very sharp, sitting upright on her bed, and I rolled over to face them, distressed by Viv's temper. "If you'd done your jobs," Viv said, "we wouldn't be in this mess. And if you did something instead of sit and talk about it we might get out."

"Someone," Lynn said, "might go out on the hull with a cutter."

"In *that*?" Percy asked. That was my thought; my stomach heaved at the idea.

"I could try it," Lynn said.

"You're valuable," Modred said. "The gain would be short term and the risk is out of proportion to the gain."

Like that: Modred's voice never varied . . . like Viv's sums and accounts. I had had another way of putting it all dammed up behind my teeth. But the crew wasn't my business, any more than it was Viv's.

"What are you going to do?" Viv asked. "What are you doing about this thing? Our lady depends on you to do something."

"Let them be," I said, and Viv looked at me, at me, Elaine, who did my lady's hair and had no authority to talk to Vivien. "If it was your job to run the ship you could tell them what to do, but they've done everything right so far or we'd none of us be alive."

"They left us grappled to this thing. Was *that* right? They *talked* to that thing instead of breaking us loose on the instant. Was that right?"

"Grappling on," Modred said, unstoppable in locating an inaccuracy, "was correct. We would have damaged the hull had we kept drifting."

"And talking to it?"

"Let them be," I said, because that argument had bit them: I saw that it had. "Maybe it was right to do. Wasn't that our lady's to decide, and didn't she?"

"*Griffin,*" Viv said. "Griffin decides things. And he wouldn't be deciding them if the crew's incompetency hadn't dropped us into this. We were in the middle of the system. You can't jump from the middle of the system. And they did it to us, getting us into this."

"We were pulled in," Gawain said. "There wasn't any warning. No evasion possible."

"For *you*. Maybe if you were competent there'd have been another answer."

That was Vivien at her old self again: she did it in the house at Brahmani Dali and sent some of the servants into blank. Now she tried it on the crew. I sat up, shivering inside. "Maybe if Viv's hydroponics don't work out, *she* can go out on the hull," I said. It was cruel. Deliberately. It left me shivering worse than ever, all my psych-sets in disarray. But it shut Viv down. Her face went white. "I think," I said between waves of nausea my psych-sets gave me, "you've done all the right things. So it breaks through. It would do it anyway; and so you've talked to it: would it be different if we hadn't? And so it's got us; would we be better off if we'd slid around over the surface until we made a dozen holes it could get in, and it grappled us anyway?"

They looked at me like so many flowers to the sun. Percy and Gawain and Lynn looked grateful. "No," Modred said neatly, "the situation would be much the same."

Viv could scare them. She could scare anyone. She had my lady's ear . . . at least she had had it when she did the accounts; and she had that reputation. But so did I have Dela's ear. And I would say things if Vivien did. I had that much courage. Dela's temper could *make* the crew make mistakes. She could order them to do things that might endanger all of us. She could order Lynn out on the hull. Or other dangerous things.

"We're supposed to be resting," I said. "It's against orders to be disturbing the crew."

"Oh. Orders," Viv said. "Orders . . . from someone who skulks about stealing. I know who gets tapes they're not supposed to have. Born-man tapes. I suppose you think that gives you license to tell us all how it is."

"They might do you good. *Imagination*, Viv. Not everything comes in sums."

That capped it. I saw the look she gave me. O misery, I thought. We don't hate like born-men, perhaps, but we know about protecting ourselves. And perhaps she couldn't harm me: her psych-set would stop that. But she would undermine me at the first chance. I was never good at that kind of politics. But Viv was.

It didn't help my sleep. I was licensed to have that tape, I thought; I was justified. My lady *knew*, at least in general, that I pilfered the library. It was all tacit. But if Vivien made an issue, got that cut off—

I had something else to be scared of, though I persuaded myself it was all empty. Bluff and bluster. Viv could not go at that angle; knew already it would never work.

But she would suggest me for every miserable duty my lady thought of. She would do that, beyond a doubt.

The hammering started up again, tap, tap, tap, and that hardly helped my peace of mind either. We quarreled over blame, and *it* meanwhile just worked away. I rolled my eyes at the ceiling, shut them with a deliberate effort.

Everyone settled down then, even Vivien, but I reckoned there was not much sleeping done, but perhaps by Modred, who lacked nerves as he lacked sex.

I drowsed a little finally, on and off between the hammerings. And eventually Lance came back—quietly, respecting our supposed sleep, not brightening the lights. He went to his locker, undressed, went to the bath, and when he had come back in his robe he lay down on his bed next to me and stared at the ceiling.

I turned over to face him. He turned his head and looked at me. The pain was gone. It could not then have gone so badly; and that hurt, in some vague way, atop everything else.

I got up and came around and sat on the side of his bed. He gave me his hand and squeezed my fingers, seeming more at peace with himself than he had been. "I was not," he said, "what I was, but I was all right. I was all right, Elaine."

Someone else stirred; his eyes went to that. I bent down and kissed him on the brow, and his eyes came back to me. His hand pressed mine again, innocent of his difficulties.

"Griffin knows," I warned him. I don't know why it slipped out then, then of all times, when it could have waited, but my mind was full of Griffin and dangers and all our troubles, and it just spilled. He looked up at me with his eyes suddenly full of shock. And hurt. I shivered, that I had done such a thing, hurt someone for the second time, and this time in the haste of the hour.

"They quarreled," I said, walking deeper into it. "Lance, we're supposed to help him . . . you understand . . . with the ship. Lady Dela says so. That we're to help. She's afraid, and there's something going on—" The hammering stopped again. This time the silence oppressed me, and a cold breeze from the vents poured over my skin. I put my hands on Lance's sides, and he put his on my shoulders, for comfort. There was dread in his face now, like a contagion. "Bridges," I said. "Whatever-it-is means to use a Bridge to get to us. All the other ships . . . have tubes going in and out of them. They've seen it . . . the crew . . . when they fined down the pictures on the bridge. That's what that hammering is out there."

He absorbed that a moment, saying nothing.

"Lady Dela's not to know yet," I said. "Griffin doesn't want to frighten her."

Lance nodded slightly. "I understand that." He lay there thinking and staring through me, and what his thoughts were I tried to guess—I reckoned they moved somewhere between what was working at us out there and what small happiness I had destroyed for him.

"What are we going to do about it?" he asked finally.

"We're supposed to be back up on the bridge at 1000. All of us. I think Griffin's got something in mind. I hope so."

"It's after 0800, isn't it?"

I turned around and looked at the clock. It was 0836. "I think I should have gotten everybody breakfast. There's still time."

"I don't want it. Others might."

"Lance, you should. Please, you should."

He stayed quiet a moment, then got up on his elbow. "You go start it, I'll come and help."

I got up and started throwing on my clothes again. There was time, indeed there was time; and it was on my shoulders, to see that everyone was fed. Everyone would think of it soon, and maybe our spirits wanted that, even if our stomachs were not so willing.

It took all kinds of strength to face that thing out there, and in my mind, schedules were part of it, insisting that our world went on.

But I kept thinking all the while I rode the lift down to the galley and especially before Lance came to help me, that it was very lonely down there. The hammering was stopped now; and I was in the outermost shell of the *Maid*, so that the void was out there, just one level under my feet while I was making plates of toast and cups of coffee. I felt like I had when I had first to walk the invisible floor and teach my eyes to see—that maybe our Beast didn't see things at all the way our senses did, and maybe it just looked through us whenever it wanted, part and parcel of the chaos-stuff.

Lance came, patted me on the shoulder and picked up the ready trays to take them where they had to go. "I'll take those topside," I said purposefully, meaning Dela, meaning Griffin; and I took them away from him.

He said nothing to that. Possibly he was grateful. Possibly his mind was somewhere else entirely now, on the ship, and not on Dela; but I doubted that: his psych-set didn't make that likely.

Dela was abed, where I looked to find her. She stirred when I touched her bare shoulder, and poked her head up through a curtain of blonde hair, pushing it back to discover breakfast. "Oh," she said, not sounding displeased. She turned over and plumped the pillows up to take it in bed. 'Is everything all right then? It's quiet.'"

"I think it's given up for a while," I lied, straight-faced and cheerfully. "I'm taking breakfasts round. May I go?"

"Go." She waved a dismissing hand, and I went.

Griffin I found asleep too—all bent over his desk in his quarters, the comp unit still going, the papers strewn under him on the surface. "Sir," I said, tray in hand, not touching him: I was wary of Griffin. "Sir."

He lifted his head then, and saw me; and his eyes looked his want of sleep. I set the tray down for him and uncovered it, uncapped the coffee and gave that into his hands.

"It's stopped," he said.

I nodded. "Yes, sir, off and on. It's been quiet about half an hour so far. It's 0935, sir."

He turned with a frown and dug into the marmalade. I took that for a dismissal on this occasion and started away.

"Have you slept, Elaine?"

I stopped. "Much as I could, sir."

"The others?"

"Much as they could, sir." My heart started pounding for fear he would ask about Lance or discuss my lady, and I didn't want that. "They'll be eating now. They'll be on the bridge soon."

He nodded and ate his breakfast

So we came topside at the appointed time, to the bridge. The crew took their posts; Lance and Viv and I stood. The quiet about the hull continued, the longest lapse in hours. And that quiet might mean anything . . . that whatever-it-was had finished out there, that the Bridge was built and we had very little time . . . or that it really had given up. But none of us believed the latter.

1005. Griffin delayed, and we waited patiently, no one saying anything about the delay, because a born-man could do what he liked when he had set the schedule. Viv found herself a place on the cushion by the door, alone, because I wasn't about to sit by her; and Lance stood by me.

"Nothing more has come in," Modred said after checking the records from the night. "Everything's as it was."

Transmissions, he meant. All around us the screens showed the old images, the unrefined images, just the glare and the light, the slow creep of measled red and black shading off to purples and greens.

There were footsteps in the corridor outside. Griffin arrived, and Dela was with him, in her lacy nightclothes, her hair twisted up and pinned the way she would do when I wasn't convenient to do it in its braids.

She looked us all up and down, and looked round the bridge, and Viv and the crew rose from their places and stood respect-fully—as if she had just come aboard, as if she had just come here for the first time. As if—I don't know why. Neither, perhaps, did the others, only it was a respect, a kind of tenderness.

She looked around a moment at things I knew she couldn't read, at instruments she didn't know, at screens that showed only bad news, but not the worst. And she kept her hands clasped in front of her, fingers locked, and looked again at all of us. All of us. And Lance: her eyes lingered on him; and then on Gawain. "Griffin has talked to me," she said after a moment. "And he wants to fight this thing, whatever it is. And he wants you to help him. You have to. I see that . . . that if it tries to get in, someday it's going to. And that means fighting it. Do you think you can?"

We nodded, all of us. We had no real compunction about it, at least I didn't, small damage that I could do anything because it threatened our lady; and it wasn't its feelings we were asked to hurt.

"You do that," Dela said, and walked away.

And out the door, past Viv. Very small and sad, and fright-ened.

I wanted to run after her; I looked at Griffin instead, because we had our orders, and on Griffin's face too there was such an expression of pain for our lady—I looked at Lance, and it was the same. And Gawain and Percy and Lynn. Only Vivien scowled; and Modred had no expression at all.

Griffin made a move of his hand, walked to the counter where he could face all of us at once. "Here it is," Griffin said. "They *are* going to get in. Maybe they'll come in suits and blow our lifesupport entirely, and rearrange it all, because they need something else. They could be some other ship who's trying to survive here and doesn't mind killing us. But I don't think so. The tunnels are general; they're everywhere. And that points to the wheel itself. The station. Whatever it is we're attached to. I've talked to Dela about it. There's no gun aboard; but we're going to have to set up some kind of a defense. If they blow one compartment, we can seal it off, so we'll just redraw the line of defense. But they're going at it so slowly . . . I think it's more deliberate than that. They've done it—to all the ships. And maybe time isn't important to it. To them. Whatever." He looked from one to the other of us. "What we can't have is someone panicking and blanking out at the wrong time. If you don't think you *can* fight, tell me now. Even if you're not sure."

No one spoke.

"Can you, then?" he asked.

"We're high order," Gawain said, "and we don't tend to panic, sir. We haven't yet."

"You haven't had to kill anything. You haven't come under attack."

That posed things to think about.

"We can," Lynette said.

Griffin nodded. "You find weapons," he said. "Cutting torches and anything that could do damage. Knives. If any of those decorations in the dining hall have sound metal in them—those. Whatever we've got that can keep something a little farther away from us."

So we went, scouring the ship.

X

. . . but in all the listening eyes
Of these tall knights, that ranged about the throne,
Clear honor shining like the dewy star
Of dawn, and faith in their great King, with pure
Affection, and the light of victory,
And glory gain'd, and evermore to gain.

It was one of those *long* days. We scoured about the ship in paranoid fancy, cataloguing this and that item that might be sufficiently deadly.

Of course, the galley. That place proved full of horrors.

And the machine shop, I reckoned: the crew spent a long time down there making lists.

And of course the weapons in the dining hall and Dela's rooms. They were real. And it was time to take them down.

That was Viv and I. I stood on the chairs and unscrewed brackets and braces while Viv criticized the operation and received the spears and the swords below. And my lady sat abed, so that I earnestly tried to muffle any rattle of metal against the woodwork, moving very slowly when I would turn and hand a piece to Viv, who was likewise quiet setting it down.

I thought about the banners, whether we should have them; the great red and blue and gold lion; the bright yellow one with green moons; the blue one with the white tree; and all the others. And I thought of the stories, and it seemed important, if we had the one we should have the other—at least the lion, that was so gaudy brave.

"That's not part of it," Vivien said when I attacked the braces.

"Oh, but it is," I said. I knew. And Viv stood there scowling. I handed it toward her.

"It's *stupid*. It doesn't do anything."

"Just take it."

"I'm not under your orders."

"Quiet."

"*Who's* quiet? Put that back and get down off the chair."

"I'm not going to put it back. At least get out of my way so I can get down."

"*Elaine?*"

Dela's voice. "See?" I said. It was stupid, the whole business. I turned the cumbersome standard with its pole so that I could gather the banner to me, and stepped down from the chair, having almost to step on Viv. We can be petty. That too. And Viv was. Too good for menial work. It was me my lady called and we don't call out loud like born-men, shouting from place to place. I hurried across to the bedroom door and through, with my silly banner still clutched to me and all the while I expected Viv was right.

"Elaine, what's that you've got?" My lady sat abed among her lace pillows, all cream lace herself, and blue ribbons.

"The lion, lady."

"For what?" my lady asked.

"I thought it should make us braver."

A moment Dela looked at all of me, my silly notions, my other self, *that* Elaine. Her eyes went strange and gentle all at once. "Oh my Elaine," she said. "Oh child—"

No one had ever called me that. It was only in the tapes. "Lady," I said very small. "Shall I put it back?"

"No. No." Dela flung off the covers, a flurry of lace and ribbons, and crossed the floor; I stepped aside, and she went through into the sitting room, where we had made a heap of the weapons, where Viv stood. And she bent down all in her nightthings and gathered up the prettiest of the swords. "Where are these to go?" She was crying, our lady, just a discreet tremor of the lips. I just stood there a heartbeat, still holding the lion in my arms.

"Out to the dining hall," I said. "Master Griffin said we should bring all the things there because it was a big place and central so—"

—so it wouldn't get to our weapons store when it got in; that was the way Griffin put it. But I bit that back.

"Let's go, then," said Dela.

"Lady," Vivien said, shocked. But Dela nodded toward the door.

"Now," Dela said, taking up another of the swords and an-

other, and leaving Vivien to gather up the heavy things. Me, I
had the lion banner, and that was an armful. Dela headed out the
door and I followed my lace-and-ribboned lady—not without a
look back at Vivien, who was sulking and loading her arms with
spears and swords.

So we came into the dining hall turned armory, and I unfurled
the lion and set him conspicuously in the center of the wall, to
preside over all our preparations. There was kitchen cutlery and
there were pipes and hammers and cutters, and the makings of
more terrible things, in separate containers—

"What are those?" Dela asked.

I had no wish to answer, but I was asked. "Chemicals. Gawain
says we can put them in pipes and they'll blow up."

Dela's face went strange. "With us in here?"

"I think they mean to carry them down to the bow and not
make them up till then. They're working down there—Master
Griffin and the others. They don't mean they should get through
at all."

"What else is there to do?"

I thought then that she *wanted* something. I understood that.
I wanted to work myself, to work until there was no time to think
about what was going on outside. From time to time the hammering stopped out there and then started again. And I dreaded
the time that it would stop for good, announcing that they/it/our
Beast might be ready for us. "There's all of that to carry and
more lists to make; we're supposed to know where all the weapons
are; and food to make and to store in here and the refrigeration
to set up—in the case," I finished lamely, "we should lose the
lower deck."

Viv had arrived, struggling with her load, and dumped it all.
"Careful," my lady said sharply, and Viv's head came up—all
bland, our Viv, but that was the face she gave my lady.

"And they're welding down below," I finished. "They're cutting panels and welding them in, so if they think they've gotten
through the hull, they've only got as much to go again.

"We should all help," my lady concluded. "All."

"I have my work upstairs," Viv said; she could get away with
that often enough, could Viv. I have my books; I have accounts
to do; and Go do that, my lady would say.

Not now. "You can help at this," my lady said, very sharp and frowning. "Make yourself useful. You're not indispensable up there."

Oh, that stung. "Yes, lady," Vivien said, and lowered her head.

"I'll get the rest of the weapons," I offered.

"No," my lady said, "Vivien can start with that. Get the galley things in order."

"Yes," I said. It was no prize, that duty, but it was the one I well understood.

"I'll be down to help," my lady said.

"Yes, lady," I murmured, astonished at the thought, and thinking that I would have one more duty to care for, which was Dela herself, who really wanted to be comforted. I left, passed Vivien on my way out the door and hurried on to the lift, wiping my hands on my coveralls.

I took the lift down. The ship resounded down there not alone with the crashes and thumps of the thing outside, but with the sounds of Griffin and the others working, trying to put a brace between ourselves and the outside.

The galley was close enough to hear that, constantly, and it reminded me like a pulsebeat how the time was slipping away, and how we had so little time and they had all the time that ever might be in this dreadful place.

Other ships must have fought back. Nothing we had seen gave us any true hope. But I went about the galley reckoning how we could store water—we have to have water in containers, Griffin had said, because they might find a way to cut us off from the tanks. And we have to have the oxygen up there; the tanks and the suits. The whole ship had to be replanned. We had to think like those would think who wanted to kill us; and I was never trained for such things—except in my dreams. I set my mind to devious things, and reckoned that we must take all the knives and dangerous things out; and my lady's good silver too, because they should not have that, nor the crystal. And all our medical supplies must come up.

And the portable refrigeration. That came first. We had it in the pantry, and I got down with a pliers I had from upstairs, and on my hands and knees I worked the bottom transit braces loose. Then I climbed up on the counter and attacked the upper braces.

So Dela found me, sweating and panting and having barked my fingers more than once—but I had gotten it free. "Elaine, call

Percy," she said: it was always Percy we called for things like this.

"Lady, Percy's helping Master Griffin. They all are. I can manage."

My lady looked at it uncertainly; but when I pushed from the back she wrestled it from the front, and the two of us got it out. I looked at her after, Dela panting with maybe the first work but sport she had ever done; her eyes were bright and her face flushed. "To the lift?" she asked.

I nodded, dazed. And she set her hands to it, so there was nothing to do but push . . . through the galley and over the rough spot of the seal track, down the corridor toward the lift. And all the while that frenetic banging away toward the bow of the ship, toward which Dela turned her head distractedly now and again as we pushed the unit up to the lift door. But she said nothing of it.

We took it up; we wrestled it down the corridors and over section seal tracks and into the dining hall pantry where we decided was the best place to put it. "We have to brace it again," I said. It was too heavy to have rolling about if the ship should shift or the like. So my lady and I contrived to get it hooked up and then to get it fastened into a pair of bottom braces.

And we sat there in the floor, my lady and I, and looked at each other. She reached over and put a hand behind my neck, hugged me with a strange fervor; but I understood: it was good to work, to do something together when it was so easy to feel alone in that dinning against our hull, and in our smallness against *that* outside.

We got up then, because there was the food to fetch up, and the water tanks. It was down again in the lift, and filling carts with frozen food and taking it up again; and hunting the tanks out of storage.

"The good wine," Dela said. "We should save that."

"And the coffee," I said. My knees were shaking with all this pushing and climbing and carrying. I wiped my face and felt grit. "My lady, I think everyone might like to have something to eat."

She thought about that and nodded. "Do that," she said. "We can take something to Griffin."

"I can do that," I said, thinking how grim it was forward, where they were building our defenses.

But Dela was determined. So I made up as many lunches as I knew there were workers forward, which was everyone but Vivien; and we took the trays into that territory of welding stench and hammering, where the crew and Lance worked with Griffin.

They stopped their work, where the hallway had suddenly shortened itself in a new welded bulkhead improvised of a section seal and some braces. They were scorched and hot—the temperature here was far too high for comfort. And eyes widened at the sight of Dela: people stood up from their work in shock, Griffin not least of them, and took the trays Dela brought, and looked at her in a way that showed he was sad and pleased at once.

"We've got a lot of the upstairs work done," Dela said, "Elaine and I."

Griffin kissed her: we had washed, my lady and I, and were more palatable than they—a tender gesture, and then the They across the division boomed out with a great hammering that made us all flinch, even Griffin. "No need for you to stay here," Griffin said.

But my lady took a tray and sat right down on the floor, and I did; so all the rest settled with theirs. I saw the crew dart furtive disturbed glances Dela's way: she shook their world, and even Modred, who was too close-clipped to be disheveled ever, still looked disarranged, sweating as we all began to, and with exhaustion making lines about his eyes. Percy had hurt his hand, an ugly burn; and Gawain had his beautiful hair tied back in a halfhearted braid, and some of it flying about his face; and Lynette, close-clipped as Modred, had her freckled face drowned in sweat that gathered at the tip of her nose and in the channels of her eyes. Lance—Lance looked so tired, never lifting his eyes, but eating his sandwich and drinking with hardly a glance at us . . . or at Dela sitting next to Griffin.

"We're going to make braces for sealing more than one point in the ship," Griffin said. "Lower deck; and the middecks. If they get to top—they've got everything. Only the topmost deck and the hydroponics . . . we draw our final defense around that, if it has to be."

"One of us might still go out there," Lynette said. "Might still try to see what they're up to."

"No," Griffin said.

"We could try." Lance lifted his head for the first time. "Lady Dela, if one of us went out and tried to get into the thing—"

"No," Dela said, with finality.

"They could learn us," Griffin said. "It's not a good idea. With one of us in their hands. . . . No. We can't afford that. But we'll see; it's possible—they have rescue in mind. One can hope that."

It was a thought to cherish. But I remembered that voice on the com, and how little it was like us. And the ships, pierced by the tubes like veins, bleeding light through their wounds.

Perhaps everyone else thought of that. The surmise generated no cheer at all, not even from my lady.

And time, as time did in this place, weighed heavy on us, so that it felt as if we had been all day at work instead of only half. Maybe it was the battering at our hull, that went on and on; and maybe it was a slow ebbing of the hope that we tricked ourselves with, that wrung so much struggle out of us, when a little thought on the scale of things was sufficient to persuade us we were hopeless.

I longed for the plains of my dreams, I did, and the horns blowing and the beautiful colors and the fine brave horses Brahman had never seen. But here we sat dirty and scorched with the welding heat and with the hammering battering at our minds; and never room or chance for a good run at our Beast. I looked up at Lance, wondering if he longed the same. I saw his eyes lifted that once, but it was a furtive glance toward Dela with all that pain on his face that might have been exhaustion. Might have been. Was not.

That was never changed.

"We'd better get to work," Griffin said.

So we gathered up our used trays and weary bones; and we carried them back to the galley, Dela and I, while the others set themselves to their business.

There was food to be carried up; and we filled tanks and ran them up; trip after trip in the lift, until my lady was staggering with the loads. And we broke a bottle of the wine, glass all over the corridor, which I hastened to mop up, picking up all the glass. It was like blood spilled there, everywhere, running along the channels of the decking: I thought of that, with our clothes stained with it from the spatter, and the hammering that never stopped. My lady looked distracted at the sight—so, so small a thing threatened her composure, when larger things had not. We were tired, both of us.

"Where's Vivien?" Dela wondered sharply, with that tone in her voice that boded ill for the subject. "Where's Vivien all this time?"

"Probably at inventory," I offered, not really thinking so. "I'll go find her."

"I will," my lady said, with that look in her eye.

I kept working. That was safest.

And it was not until my next trip topside that I found Viv, who was busy storing items in the freezer. Immaculate Vivien. No hair out of place. At least she was working.

I added my own cart to the lot and began to help. "Did my lady go to rest?" I asked: it was evident Dela had found her— very plain in Viv's sullen enthusiasm for work. But Dela was nowhere about the dining hall.

"She went to take a bath," Viv said, all brittle. "You might, you know."

"I'm sure you haven't worked up a sweat."

Viv rounded on me, with such a look in her eyes, on her elegant oval face, that I had never seen. *"You,"* she said. Just *you*, as if that were all the fault. Her lips trembled; her eyes brimmed.

"Viv," I said, contrite, and reached out a hand: I was greatly shaken, not having seen that coming.

She struck my hand down and turned her face away, went on about her work. My lady must have been very hard with Viv. And now and again while we worked she would wipe fiercely at her eyes.

"Viv, I'm sorry."

"Oh, was it *your* doing?" She looked at me again. It would have made me laugh, because I had never seen Viv's face like that with the mascara smeared like soot. But I was far from laughter. It was like seeing wreckage. Viv started to cry; and I put my arms about her, just held on to her until she had gotten her breath and shoved me hard.

That was all right. Viv was afraid as well as mad and tired. I knew what that felt like. "It's all stupid," she said. "It's none of it going to work."

Viv indeed had a mind.

"Griffin says they might be trying a rescue after all," I offered.

"They're not," Vivien judged, and turned her shoulder to me. I emptied the cart and took it down for another load.

So my lady had had her fling at work and bravely at that, and now she had exhausted herself enough to rest; but I had things yet to do. And Griffin and those with him—they were only now bringing their equipment up the corridor to lift it to middecks, clatter and bang.

It was lonely down there after they had gone; I worked there by myself, loaded up two carts with the last that we had to bring up.

What if it should break through of a sudden, I thought. What if it should be now? I pushed my carts into the lift and rode it up into safer levels, the hammering distant up here and easier to forget.

So we fought, with our wits and our small resources; and the deadliest things we had found in all the ship were the welders that Griffin used to fortify our poor shattered bow.

Viv was not talkative. It was not a good day for her, not in any sense. She sulked about the things we had to do together, and her hands shook when the pounding from belowdecks would get loud. She complained of headache; doubtless that was true. I thought that I might have one if I slowed down and let it have its way.

But Dela came out of her retreat again, bathed and fresh, and helped us, which I think scandalized Viv, and which Viv blamed me for. All the same the working comforted Dela, and she smiled sometimes, braver than we when she had a task under her hands: only sometime the facade cracked and I could see how nervous she was, how her eyes would dart to small sounds. Viv hardly knew how to react to this: I think it was the first time my lady had ever gotten to watch Viv work, which was, excepting Viv's trained functions, dilatory and involved much motion over little result. And Viv was trying to reform this tendency under that witness, but habit was strong. It would have been funny except that poor Viv was so distracted and so unhinged I remembered the tears.

We knew, when we were finished, how much of everything

we had, and we had taken a great deal of it into storage on main level, including bedding enough for us all if we had to sleep here; and we had filled the huge tanks for Vivien's domain topside. Vats and pipes everywhere up there; but there was a lot of water involved, and we felt the more secure for that. That was another thing that gnawed at Viv, because my lady insisted on Viv telling her what it all did while I was there to hear it—because, my lady said, something might happen to one of us. Poor Viv. That was not the thing she wanted to think about.

But came the time that all of us had run out of strength, and Griffin's party came up to the dining hall, all dirty as they were, to the dinner we fixed on the last of our strength—even Viv's. And Lynn looked ready to fall over on the table, sitting there stirring her soup about without the strength to get it to her mouth, and Modred was as down as I had ever seen him, not mentioning the others, who had burns and cuts from the metal and who looked as if a dinner at table was only further torment. They would probably rather a sandwich in solitude, and maybe not that. Griffin was drawn as the rest of them . . . as worn, as miserable; but he smiled for Dela, and made a joke about frustrating our attackers.

Then there was a signal from the bridge, which meant that something had happened, and we staggered away from our supper, all of us.

It knew, I thought, it *knew* that we were trying to rest: our hammering had stopped, and maybe it picked up that silence inside. So we stood shivering on the bridge, under the images of the dead ships and the bleeding space outside, and listened to that nonsensical sound that rumbled and roared like a force of nature. Even Dela was there to hear, and Viv—Viv just blanked, frozen in the center of the room.

"Respond?" Modred asked.

"No," Griffin said.

"I might point out—"

"No," Griffin said. "No more reaction to it. They know too much about us already, I'm afraid."

Modred cast a look toward my lady, not real defiance; but there was that manner to it. "I might point out we have defenses. But they're worth nothing in the long term. We should talk while we have something to talk with. I have a program—"

"No," Dela said, ending that. Modred only looked tired, and turned back to the board.

"Leave it," Griffin said. "All of you—go below and sleep. All of us can use it. Hear?"

We heard. Modred shut down; Gawain left his place, and Lynn and Percy did. Myself, I wanted nothing more than to go down to my own bed and rest. I saw my lady go off arm in arm with Griffin; and remembered the dishes with an ache in my bones and a wish to leave them and go curl up somewhere.

No Viv. Percy had gotten her by the arm and they were on their way out the door. Only Lance stayed, looking like death and all but undone.

"Can't come," I said. "I've got the dishes."

"I'll help," he said. We worked like that, Lance and I, both of us staff and responsible for our born-man and for the things not in anyone else's province. So he came with me. I don't know which of us was more tired, but I reckoned it was Lance: his poor hands were burned and the china rattled in them—I reckoned that water would hurt on the burns so I did all the washing.

And after that, we went to see to our born-men, who were together: nothing to do there. Dela and Griffin were locked in each other's arms and fast asleep. I looked back at Lance who had come closer to the door, made a sign for quiet—but he only stood there, and a great sadness was on his face.

I dimmed the lights they had forgotten or not cared about. "Come on," I whispered, and took him by the arm, walked with him outside and closed the door.

"Go on down," he said. "I'll stay hereabouts."

"Lance, you shouldn't. You're not supposed to."

"He's good to me—you know that? He knows, like you said. And he loves her. And all of today—he never had any spite. Nothing of the kind. And he might have. Anyone else would have. But he treats me no different for it."

"He's all right," I said finally. "Better than any of the others."

"Not like any of the others," Lance said. He shook his head, walked away with his head bowed—the way Griffin had walked away that night, as sad. Not like the others. Not someone Dela would tire of. Not someone to put aside. And kind. Maybe he wished for Robert back. But Lance was in the trap. He had so

little selfishness himself—he opened to generosity. He was made
that way.

"Lance." I caught up with him, took his arm. "Lance—I don't
want to be alone." I said it, because he had too much pride. He
let me take his hand. "Come downstairs," I asked him.

He yielded, never saying anything, but he walked with me to
the lift, and I was all but shaking with relief, for pulling him out
of that. We should have a little comfort, we two, a night lying
close, among our friends.

We came in ever so quietly, Lance and I, into the mostly dark
sleeping quarters . . . stood there a moment for our eyes to adjust, not making any noise. Everyone was on the couches, and a
tape was running; the screen flickered. I was sorry that we had
missed the start, because it was maybe the best thing to do with
the night, to be sure of quiet dreams. We could still hear the
hammering.

We might slip in on the dream, I thought: when my eyes had
adjusted enough that I reckoned not to bump into anything, I
crossed the room and looked up at the screen to know what sort
it was.

And then my heart froze in me, and I flew back across the
room to my locker, and Lance's. I felt there, on the shelf, but
the tape was gone; was in the machine; running, and they were
locked into it—*all* of them.

Maybe my face showed my terror. Lance had seen; he looked
only half disturbed until he looked at me, and reached out his
hand for mine. "Viv," I said, reckoning who would have stolen.
"O Lance, we're ruined, we're lost, they shouldn't—"

"We can't stop it," he said, half a whisper. "We daren't stop
it halfway—not that one. They'd never sort it out."

"It's my fault," I mourned. "Mine." But he put his arms about
me and held, which was comfort so thorough I had no good sense
left and held to him, which was all I wanted.

"We might use it too," he said. "If it's beyond stopping. I
want it, Elaine."

So did I, for twisted, desperate reasons—even if I lost him
again. So we joined them, helpless in the dream that had gotten
loose on the ship, that filled the *Maid* and told us what we might
have been.

But for some of us it was cruel.

XI

Then that same day there past into the hall
A damsel of high lineage, and a brow
May-blossom, and a cheek of apple-blossom,
Hawk-eyes; and lightly was her slender nose
Tip-tilted like the petal of a flower;
She into hall past with her page and cried,
". . . Why sit ye there?
Rest I would not, Sir King, an I were king,
Till ev'n the lonest hold were all as free
From cursed bloodshed, as thine altar-cloth
From that best blood it is a sin to spill.
My name? . . .
Lynette my name."

It was a good way to have passed that aching night—if it had been any other tape. We were free for a time; we knew nothing about the terrible place where we were.

I loved and lost again. But I knew the terms. And there was Lance with me, who had learned the tape under his own terms, and who had made his peace with what he was. He was trapped, the same as I was. And not afraid anymore. His world made sense to him, like mine to me.

But when we woke, with the hammering still going on the same as before—when we stirred about with the light slowly brightening to tell us it was another morning in this place—it was hard to look at one another. Everyone—crew and staff—moved about dressing, and no one looked anyone else in the eye.

That was what it did to us.

I went over and took the tape myself, and no one said anything; I stored it in my locker again. But they all knew where, and I reckoned so long as we lasted in this place, they would not let it alone. Could not let it alone. Lance came and laid his hand on mine on the locker door, and pressed my fingers. He was afraid too, I thought. Of the others. Of what now we knew we were.

Only there was Percy, who came to us, his face all distressed. Who just came, and stopped and stared. Gentle Percivale.

"It's a tape," I said out loud, so they all could hear. "It's an old story, an amusement. Lady Dela owns it and let me borrow it. You have to understand."

But there was no easy understanding. Not for that.

"Viv said—" Percivale began, and dropped it.

Vivien. I looked her way; and Vivien met my eyes by accident. She was just putting her jacket on; and her head came up. It was not a good look, that. She turned away and began sweeping her hair back, to put it up again in its usual immaculate order.

"We had better get to the bridge," Gawain said then quietly, "and see how the night went." He started to the door, looked back. Percivale had joined him. And Lynn. "Modred?"

Everyone looked. Modred had been sitting on the couch getting his boots on—and still sat there, inward as ever. And when Gawain called him he got up and went for the door, as silent, as quiet as ever.

But we got up afraid of him, as we had never been. And it was wrong. I felt it wrong. I intercepted him on his way, took his arm.

"It's amusement," I said. But Modred had always been innocent of understandings —without sex, without nerves. "It's a thing that happened a long time ago, if it ever happened."

His dark eyes fixed on mine, and I saw something in the depth of them . . . I couldn't tell what. It might have been pain; or just analysis—something that for a moment quickened him. But he had nothing to say. *Our* Modred could make jokes, the lift of a shoulder, the rhythm of his moves; but this morning he was— quiet. Without this language. He used the quieter story tapes; mostly I suspect they bored him, and the more violent ones were outside his understanding. But when one is tired, when one's defenses are down to begin with—

"Yes," Modred said, agreeing with me, the way we agree with born-men, to make peace and smooth things over. And he went away with the others.

"Vivien," I said, turning around. "Vivien, you've done this."

She went on pinning up her hair.

"Let be," Lance said, taking me by the shoulders.

She was dangerous, I thought to myself, and she ran all our lifesupport up there; and our future food supply; all the technical things in the loft.

But maybe—I tried to persuade myself—that was what we were all doing this morning: maybe we had all learned to look at each other askew; and, we were cursed to know how others saw us.

"Modred," I mourned. "O Modred."

"It should never have happened," Lance said. "It was my fault, not yours."

"How do we prepare against a thief?" I asked, meaning Viv. But Viv had finished her dressing and swept past us without a look.

"My fault," Lance repeated doggedly.

"They'll sort it out," I insisted, turning round to look at him. "You did. I have."

"I'm not so sure," he said, "of either of us."

"You know better than that."

"I don't." He put his hands in his pockets. "Aren't we—whatever tapes they put in?"

I had no answer for that. It was too much like what I feared.

"Elaine," he said sadly. Touched my face as he would have touched Dela's. "Elaine."

And he walked away too.

My fault, I echoed in myself. When they all had gone away, I knew who was to blame, who had been selfish enough to bring that tape where it never should have been.

"What's wrong?" Dela asked at the breakfast table, and sent my heart plunging. We sat, all of us silent: had sat that way. "Is something wrong no one's saying?"

"We're tired," Griffin said, and patted her hand atop the table. "All of us." He laughed desperately. "What else *could* be wrong?"

It got a laugh from Dela. And a silence then, because some of us had humor enough to have laughed with her if we had had the heart.

O my lady, I wanted to say, flinging the truth out, we've heard what we never should; I stole what I never ought; we know what we *are* . . . and that was the terror of it, that we were and were not, locked together in this place apart from what was real.

"Elaine?" she asked, and touched my face, lifted my chin so that I had to look her in the eyes. "Elaine, don't be frightened."

"No," I said. It did her good perhaps, to comfort *us*. The lion banner looked down on us where we sat at breakfast at the long table among all the deadly things we had gathered. I heard the trumpets blowing when my lady looked at us like that. But louder was the hammering that had never ceased.

Dela smiled at me, a grin broad as she wore for new lovers. But there was only Griffin. It was the banner; it was her fancy moving about her. She smiled at me because I understood her fancy, if Griffin did not—She had her courage back. She had found her footing in this strange place, and there was a look in her eyes that challenge set there.

"I wish there were more to do," I said.

"There *is* more," Lynette said, suddenly from down the table. "Let us go outside. Let us breach *them* and see what they are before they come at us. We've got the exterior lock—"

"No," Dela said.

"I've been up in the observation deck," she said. "I've seen— if you look very hard through the stuff you can *see*—"

"Stay out of there," Griffin said. "It's not healthy."

"Neither," Modred muttered, "is sitting here."

It was insubordinate. I think my heart stopped. There was dead silence.

"What's your idea?" Griffin asked.

"Lynn's got one idea," Modred said. "I have another. First. If you'd listen to me, sir—my lady Dela. We take the assumption that it's not hostile. We feed it information. It's going to stop to analyze what we give it."

"We feed it information and then what?"

"We try the constants. We establish a dialogue."

"And in the end we give away the last secrets we have from it. What we breathe, who we are, whether we have things of value to it—I don't see that at this point. I don't see it at all."

Modred remained very quiet. "Yes, sir," he agreed at last, with that tiniest edge of irony that Modred could put in his flattest voice.

"Modred," Dela said, tight and sharp.

His face never varied. "My lady," he said precisely. And then: "I was working on something I'd like to finish. By your leave.

My heart was racing. I would never have dared. But Modred *had* no nerves. I hoped he had not. He simply got up from his chair. "Gawain," he said, summoning his partner.

"I need Gawain," Griffin said in a level tone, and Gawain stayed. There was apprehension in Gawain's face . . . on all our faces, I think, but Modred's, who simply walked out.

"He's very good," Dela said.

Oh, he was. That was so. That's why they made him that way, nerveless.

"I'd like," Griffin said, "monitoring set up below. Shouldn't be too hard."

"No, sir," Percy said quietly. "Not hard at all."

We dispersed from the table; we cleaned the dishes; we found things that wanted doing, my lady and I; and Vivien. There was the cleaning up of other kinds; there was Vivien's station—

Oh, mostly, mostly after yesterday, after working so hard we ached . . . it was waiting now; and we had so little to do that we found things.

We were scared if we stopped working. And Vivien was in one of her silences, and my lady was being brave; and Lance went down to the gym with Griffin as if there had been nothing uncommon in this dreadful day, the both of them to batter themselves beyond thinking about our Beast.

Might Lynn, I wondered, envying that exhaustion—care for a wrestling round? But no. I had not the nerve to ask. It was not Lynn's style; or mine; and the crew really did find things to do.

Lynn went out in the bubble . . . sat there, hour upon hour, as close to the chaos-stuff as we could get inside the ship. She did things with the lenses there. I took her her lunch up there, trying to keep my back to the view.

"You can see," Lynette advised me softly, "you can see if you want to see."

I knew what she meant. I wasn't about to look.

"I could make it across," she said. Her thin freckled face and close-clipped skull looked strange in the green light from the screens; but out there was red, red, and red. "I could see."

"I know you could," I whispered, hoping only to get out of

here without looking at the sights Lynn chose for company. "I'm sure you could. But I know the lady doesn't want to lose you."

"What am I?" Lynn asked. "One of the pilots. And what good is that—here?"

"I think a great deal of good." I rolled up my eyes, staring at the overhead a moment, because something was snaking along out there and I didn't want to see. "O Lynn, what is that out there?"

"A trick of the eyes. A shifting."

"Lynn," I said, because I felt very queasy indeed. "Lynette?"

"Elaine?" Of a sudden something was wrong. Lynn rose half out of her chair, pushed me aside; and then—

Take-hold, take-hold, the alarm was sounding: and Modred's voice: *"Brace, we're going—"*

I yelled for very terror. "Let me out of here," I remembered screaming, and flinging myself for the hole that led to the bridge. But: *"No!"* Lynn yelled, and grabbed me in her arms, hugged me to her and I hugged her and the chair and anything else solid my fingers could reach, because we were losing ourselves—

—back again, a blackness; a crawling redness. I held to something that writhed and mewed like the winter winds round Dali peaks, and hissed like breathing, and grew and shrank—

"—another jump," I heard a distant voice like brazen bells.

"Modred?" another called.

"Griffin?" That was my lady, like crystal breaking.

My eyes might be open. I was not sure. Such terrible things could live in one's skull, eyeless and unaided in this place. "We've jumped again," the thing holding me said, the voice like wind.

"Are we free?" I cried. "Are we free?" That was the greatest hope that came to me. But then I got my eyes cleared again and I saw the familiar red chaos crawling with black spiders of spots. And the veins, all purple and green, and the thing to which we were fixed. That was unchanged.

"We're not free." It was Percivale's voice, thin and clear. "It jumped again; but we're not free."

There was a moment of silence all over the ship, while we understood the terms of our captivity. Like all the ships before us.

"O God," Dela's voice moaned. "O dear God."

"We're all right." Griffin's voice, on the edge of fright. "We're all right; we're still intact."

"Situation stable," Modred's cold clear tones rang through the ship. "Nothing changed."

Nothing changed. O Modred. Nothing changed. I clutched the cushion/Lynn's arm so tight my fingers were paralyzed.

"You might have been out there," I said. It was what we had been talking of, a moment/a year ago. "You could have been outside in that."

Lynn said nothing. I felt a tremor, realized the grip she had on me. "We're stable," Lynn echoed. "It must happen many times."

"The hammering's stopped," I whispered. It was so. The silence was awesome. I could hear my heart beating, hear the movement of the blood in my veins. We were so fragile here.

"That's so," Lynn said. She let me go and pushed me back, leaned forward to reach the console. "Modred, I get nothing different on visual."

I managed to get my feet under me while those two exchanged observations. I stared at familiar things and they were normal. And almost I wished for that horrid dislocation back again, that chaos ordinary minds would feel. We were no longer ordinary. We had learned how to live here. For a moment we had been *out* of this place, and that was the horror we felt; that drop into normal space again. And comfort was breaking surface again in Hell.

"We're traveling," I said. Lynn looked at me, bewildered a moment. "We're traveling," I said again. "This place *moves*, goes on moving; we must have reached a star and left again."

"Yes," Lynn said with one of her abstracted frowns. "That's very probable.—Do you copy that, Modred? I think it's likely."

"Yes," Modred agreed. "Considerable speed and age. I think that's very much what we're dealing with. We're a sizable instability. And we grow. I wonder what we might have acquired this time."

"Don't." Dela's voice shivered through the com.

"We're old hands," came Griffin's. A feeble laugh. "We know the rules. Don't we?"

"O dear God," Dela murmured.

Silence then, a long space.

And about us in the bubble, the chaos-stuff swirled and crawled and blotched the same as before.

"Is everyone all right?" Percivale asked then. "Do we hear everyone?"

I heard other voices, my comrades. Lance was there with Griffin; and Gawain. "Elaine's with me," Lynn said. "Vivien?"

Silence.

"She's blanked," I said. "I'm going."

"Vivien," I heard over com, again and again. I felt my way, hand-over-handed my way from the bubble to the ladder and to the bridge . . . across it, through the U where Modred and Percivale were at work. "I'm after Vivien," I said.

"Gawain's on the same track," Percivale said, half rising. "She was at her station when it hit—"

I ran, staggered, breaking rules . . . but Viv was weakest of us, the most frightened. I had to wait on the lift because Gawain had gotten there first; I rode it up to the uppermost corridors, floors/ceilings with dual orientation, dual switches, that crazy place where the *Maid*'s geometries were most alien, where Vivien worked in her solitary makeshift lab. I made the inner doors, and there was Lancelot and there was Gawain before me. They knelt over Viv, who lay on the floor in a tuck, her eyes open, her hair immaculate, her suit impeccable; her hands were clenched before her mouth and her eyes just stared as if they saw something indescribable.

They were afraid to touch her. I was. It was not like blanking, this. It was like the wombs. It was —not; because what Viv saw, she went on seeing, endlessly, like a tape frozen-framed.

"Viv," Lance said, looked at me as if I should have some hope neither of them did. I sank down. I touched her, and all her muscles were hard.

"It's your fault," Gawain said, a strained voice. "It's your fault. That tape of yours—that tape—"

It was Lance he meant. Gawain's face was the color of Viv's. His eyes flickered, jerked, searched for something as if he could not get enough air.

"It was my tape," I said. "Mine. And Viv that stole it. Wasn't it? But it's nonsense. It's not important. It's—"

"Viv is *lost*," Gawain said.

"Lance. Lance, pick her up. I'll find a blanket."

He took Viv's wrist, but there was no relaxing her arms. He lifted her by that limb, got his arms under her, his other arm beneath her knees, and gathered her to him. I scrambled up. "Just get her out of here," Gawain said. "Let's just get her *out*."

"How is she?" That was Percivale, on com. "Is she all right?"

"She's blanked out," I said, looking up at the pickup, above all the eerie tubes and lines and vats and tanks and glare of lights. "We've got her. We're coming down."

And then the hammering started again.

Not where it had been. But close.

Up here. Above.

"Oh no," I said, above the chaos of com throughout the ship. "Oh no."

It was more than here. It was at our side. It was at our bow. We were attacked at all points of the ship.

"Something might have come loose," Lance murmured, standing, holding Viv's rigid body in his arms.

"No," Gawain said, calmly enough. "No. I don't think so. Get her to quarters, Lance. Let's get out of here and seal the door."

XII

. . . Why, Gawain, when he came
With Modred hither in the summertime
Ask'd me to tilt with him, the proven knight.
Modred for want of worthier was the judge.
Then I so shook him in the saddle, he said
"Thou has half prevail'd against me," said so—he—
Tho' Modred biting his thin lips was mute,
For he is always sullen: what care I?

So we came down to main level and got out to take the down-side lift—Gawain and I, and Lance carrying Vivien's rigid weight. Not a flicker from Viv. I stroked her hair and talked to her the while, and Gawain talked to her, but there was nothing.

Only when we had come out into the corridor, lady Dela was there to meet us, on her feet and about as if we had not been hurled who-knew-where. "Bring her to my rooms," Dela said. "I won't have her wake alone down there."

So we brought her to Dela's own apartments, to lay her down on one of the couches in the sitting room; but:

"The bed," Dela insisted, to our shock. "That's easiest for her."

Surely, I thought, when Lance had let Vivien down there amid the satin sheets, surely if there was a place Vivien would come out of her blank, this was it—in such utmost luxury, in such re-newed favor. I knelt down there at the bedside and patted Viv's face and chafed her stiff hands. "Vivien," I said, "Viv, it's Elaine. You're in my lady's quarters and my lady's asking after you. You're in her own bed and it's safe, you understand me?"

I doubted that anything reached her. Her eyes kept staring, and that was not good. They would be damaged. I closed them, as if she were dead. In a moment more they opened again.

"Vivien," I said, "you're in Dela's bedroom."

A blink. I got that much out of her, which was much, considering—but nothing more. Outside, from many points of the ship now, I could hear the hammering.

And Vivien had chosen her refuge from it.

I got up from my knees and looked back toward the door into the sitting room, where a door had opened. Griffin had come in; I heard his voice; and Gawain had gone out there. Lance waited for me, and I went with him to join the others—my lady, and Griffin.

"She won't respond," I said very quietly when my lady looked to me for a report, "but her reflexes are back. —It takes time, sometimes."

"I don't understand you," Dela said in distress. *Us*, she meant, compared to born-men. "Why do you *do* that?"

"We aren't supposed to—" I started to say, and the words locked up in my throat the way things would that weren't supposed to be talked about. —We aren't supposed to do things for ourselves, I wanted to say; and blanking's all that's left. She had wanted to do something, Vivien had, but she was made, not born, so she had no way out. Alone. Viv was always alone, even with us.

"Don't any of the rest of you do that," Dela said. "You hear me? Don't you do that."

"No, lady," Lance said with such absolute assurance it seemed to touch both our born-men, while all about us the hammering continued.

On all sides of us now. So all the preparations we had made, every defense Griffin had planned—all of that was hopeless now.

"Call the others to the dining hall," Griffin said. "I want to talk to them."

"Yes, sir," Gawain said, and went.

So Griffin thought that there was reassurance to give us. O born-man, I thought, we aren't like Vivien. We'll go on working now we know the rules, because we know we have work to do for you. You don't have to reach so far to find us hope.

But seeing Vivien cave in as she had done, Griffin believed he had to come up with something for the rest of us. He looked so distressed himself that it touched me to the heart. It was Dela that went to him and held his hand. And Lance just stood there.

"*Ah!*"

Vivien's voice. A terrible sound, a shriek.

I spun about and flew into the bedroom. There was Vivien wide awake and sitting up as if from some nightmare, the covers clutched to her breast and that same stark horror in her eyes, but waking now.

"It's all right," I lied to her fervently, coming through the door. I ran to her and caught her hands which held the sheets and I shook at her. "Viv, come out of it. You're in Dela's room, you're safe. It can't come here."

"Can't it?" Her teeth chattered. Her hair was mussed, trailing about her face. She gave a wrench to get away from me and I let go. Then she looked beyond me at the others who had come in. I looked around. My lady was there, foremost, and Griffin and Lance. "It's coming through up there," Vivien said. "Right into the lifesupport."

"Maybe we could move the equipment down," Dela said.

Griffin said nothing. Nor did Lance or I, probably all thinking the same.

"It's making those things all around us," Vivien said. "Until it has its tendrils into us and we're done. Nothing we do is working."

"We lose the tanks if it gets in there," Griffin said.

"And then we lose everything," Dela said. "We have to move the lab."

"No," Griffin said. "Come on. Let's go talk to the others."

He took Dela with him. I delayed, with Lance, to see to Vivien, who sat amid the bed with her head fallen into her hands. She swept her hair back, then, adjusted pins, beginning to fuss over herself, which was one of her profoundest reflexes. She could be dying, I thought, and still she would do that. For a moment I felt deeply sorry for Viv.

"Shut up," she said then, when I had said nothing. "Let me alone." She had a way of rewarding sympathy.

"Vivien," Lance said, "get up and come with us."

That was asking for it, giving Viv orders.

"Or we leave you here," I added.

Alone. Vivien got out of bed then, fussed with her suit and brushed at imaginary dirt. Lance held out his hand for her arm, but she pointedly ignored that and walked out ahead of us.

"We're due in the dining hall," I said, being kind, because Viv would have no idea where we were supposed to go and would have had to wait on us otherwise, outside, a damage to her dignity. So she went on ahead of us without a thank you, click, click, click of the trim heels and sway of the elegant posterior and still fussing about her hairpins.

O Viv, I thought with deepest pity, because Lance gave me his strong hand and we walked together; but Viv walked all alone. She was made that way. There was none of us as solitary as Vivien.

Or as narrow. Not even Modred.

We came last into the dining hall, Lance and I and Vivien, but not by much. It was our stronghold, our safe place, the long table under the lion banner, amid the weapons. We could hear the hammering, but more faintly here than elsewhere. We knew our proper seats and settled into them.

"Have we got a location, on the attack?" Griffin was asking.

"Middecks after section," Modred said, "portside. And topside forward. That's main storage and the hydroponics. As well as the action at the bow."

"They're slow about it," Griffin said.

No one said anything to that. We were only glad it was so.

"We look forward," Griffin said then, "to more traveling. To going on and on with this thing. This ship. Whatever it is. But if it travels, it leaves this space from time to time. If we could somehow break loose . . ."

"If you'll pardon me," Modred said, "sir, the crew has been working on that possibility. It won't work."

Griffin's face remained remarkably patient. "I didn't much reckon that it would, but spell it out. Mass?"

"Mass, sir. It's growing with every acquisition, not only the ships, but debris. Mass, and something that just confirmed itself. We're moving. We have an acquired velocity in relation to real-space and there's no means to shed it. This mass has been sling-shotted as many times as there are ships gathered out there; if we could hazard an unfounded presumption, and even factoring it conservatively, the acquired velocity would itself increase our mass beyond any reasonable limit. We're a traveling discontinuity, an infinitude, a local disturbance in spacetime. We *are* the disturbance and our own matter is the problem."

I blinked, my hands knotted in my lap under the table, understanding more of what Modred said than I usually did; but Modred was talking down to us. To Griffin.

"If I could reconstruct what happened," Gawain said, "something a long time ago either kicked or pulled the original core object into subspace. And either it never had control or it lost it. So it careens along being attracted by the gravity wells of stars and accelerating all kinds of debris into its grasp. It hasn't got a course. Just velocity. It picks up velocity at the interface and it never gets rid of it. It's no part of our universe any longer."

"We *are* in Hell," Dela murmured, shaking her head.

"Wherever we are," Griffin said, "we have company. And if we can't hope to get out of it, then we have to do something about it. Lynette, you had an idea—to breach the core object itself."

Lynn looked up, eyes aglitter in her thin face.

"I've seen a place," she said, "not so far from the emergency lock starboard. I think we could get into it there."

"And create what kind of difficulty inside the wheel," Griffin asked, "if you breach their lifesupport?"

"We'll rig a Bridge from our own side. Pressure seal. We can do it."

Our eyes went from one face to another—seeing hope, seeing doubt, one and then the other.

"We could save time," Modred said dryly, "by opening our own forward hatch and using theirs."

"We can control matters," Lynn said, "by building our own lock. By having a way round *behind* their position. We could attach to our upper airlock and have a way to attach either to a tube they might build to our upper section or to attach to the wheel itself and have an access we control so we don't get trapped."

"And then they move behind *us*, don't they? And we don't know what we're going to meet in weapons. No. It won't work."

"Lynn could be lost out there," Dela said, adding her force to Modred's.

"No, lady," Lynn said. There was that kind of look on Lynn's face that had to be believed while she was saying it. "I can *do* it. Give me the chance. It's all that can stop us being trapped."

"It's worth the try," Griffin said.

"Lady," Modred said.

"I can do it," Lynn said again.

She wanted to so badly: she said it herself, how it hurt to be useless. We all had this compulsion to serve. And Lynn's, I thought, might well be the end of her.

"All right," Dela said.

"Lady—" Modred objected.

"Let her try," Dela said. "Someone has to do something that works."

Modred subsided. His face—I had never seen him so out of countenance—He looked like murder.

"Let's find what we have to use," Griffin said then. But he sat there a moment, as if some of the strength had drained out of him, while our Beast—we knew now for sure it was more than one—battered at the hull on all sides of us.

"We don't really have any choice," Dela said. "We have to do something, and that's all there is left to do, isn't it?"

"That's all there is to do," Griffin agreed.

"Isn't—" Viv asked, breaking the silence she had kept in our councils, "isn't there the shuttle? Couldn't we get off in that?"

Faces turned toward her. "We could use it," Gawain said, "not for that—but to get up against their hull. Without breaching our own."

"And getting back again?" Griffin asked.

"That," Gawain admitted, "not so likely."

"The shuttle might end up anywhere," Lynn said. "It might swing off against the hull somewhere else and we couldn't control it. The only answer has to be a kind of Bridge. That's all that has a chance of working."

"We could get off from the ship," Viv protested.

"No," Lance said patiently, having understood things a long time ago, "we can't. You don't understand, Viv. The shuttle engines are less powerful than the *Maid*'s. And engines only work here, up against the mass."

"Where matter exists at all," Modred added.

Viv simply shut her eyes.

"Don't," Dela said. "Vivien, it's all right."

Vivien didn't understand. She simply didn't want to understand. I think we all knew that much, even Dela, who understood us least of all.

And Vivien opened her eyes again, but she kept her mind sealed, I was sure of that.

"What do you reckon to do?" Griffin asked Lynn. "Do you have it mapped out?"

"There's equipment and parts in storage," Lynn said.

"Let's find it," Griffin said.

So Griffin launched himself—wherever we were now, and whatever had changed since that leap through space we had made. Dela still sat at table after the others had left, and I did, and Vivien did.

"Might I get you something?" I asked Dela.

"No," Dela said hoarsely, her hands locked before her on the table. And so we sat for a while. "He has to do something. That's Griffin's nature. I couldn't let him not do something, could I? But we're in danger of losing Lynn."

"Yes," I said. "I'm afraid we might."

"It's awful, that place out there. It's a terrible way to die."

"Lynn's not that afraid," I said.

Vivien got up from the table and fled, out the door.

"But some of us are," I added.

"Vivien's worthless," Dela said. "Worthless."

"Don't say that. Please don't say that."

"Isn't she?"

"She was very good, with the books. They're just not here, now."

Dela looked up at me, puzzled-seeming. So hard she could be, my lady; but she looked straight at me, not into me, not through me, as sometimes she would. It was as if I had gotten solid enough for her to see. "Do you care?" she asked. "Vivien doesn't care about anyone at all but Vivien."

"She can't," I said, thinking of that tape, *the* tape, and what wounds *that* Vivien had suffered that our own Viv had shared. Like Modred. Like the rest of us. And Lynn. O Lynette, who had to be brave and brash and find a way to *be* that other self if it killed her. My lips trembled. "My lady—" I almost told her. But I couldn't face the rage. "Some of us don't have our sets arranged like that," I said. "Some of us have other priorities."

"I know Vivien's," Dela said. Of course, she knew us all.

"She's Vivien," I said, afraid. "And she would be happy if she weren't."

'That's a strange things to say."

"Like I'm Elaine," I said. "And Lance is Lance."

Dela said nothing at all, not understanding, perhaps, the thing I tried to creep up on, to tell her. She gave me no help. I found the silence heavier and heavier.

"We should *do* something," Dela said. "It would be healthier if we did something." She dropped her head into her hands. I patted her shoulder, hating to see her that way.

"We could go help them," I said. "We can fetch things."

It was unthinkable, that impertinent *we*. But that was the way it had come to be. Dela lifted her head, nodded, got up, and we went to find the others.

We, my lady and I, as if she were one of us, or as if I had been born.

Finding them was another matter. They had disappeared quite thoroughly when we called to them from the lift on one and the other level.

"The holds," Dela said, "if they're going to be hunting supplies."

So we went to the bridge to track them down, because the *Maid* had a great many nooks and dark places where it was difficult to go and no little dangerous.

Especially now.

So we came to the bridge, and found one of them after all, because Modred was at his post, talking to them, running catalogue for them, as it seemed. We walked in, my lady and I, and waited, not to interrupt. After a moment Modred seemed to feel our presence and turned around.

"Where are they?" my lady asked.

"Middecks hold number one section," Modred said. "It's not a good idea," he added then, with never a flicker. "This operation. But no one argues with master Griffin."

"Do what he told you to do," my lady said sharply, and turned and walked out. She had no wish to be told it was hopeless. Neither did I, but I lingered half a breath and looked back at Modred, who had not yet turned back to his post.

"Lynn will die," Modred said, "if she has her own way."

"What can we do?" I asked.

"Be glad it will take them days to be ready."

"And then what?" I asked. "In the meanwhile, what?"

Modred shrugged, looking insouciant. Or dead of feeling. He turned his back on me, which hurt, because I thought us friends, and he might have tried to answer. If there were answers at all.

"Elaine," my lady called, impatient, somewhere down the corridor outside, and I turned and fled after her.

So we found the rest of them, all but Vivien.

They were on middecks, down the corridors from the crew quarters, and bringing parts out of storage by now, out of that section of the *Maid* that was so cold they had to use suits to go retrieve it; the stuff they set out, a big canister, and metal parts, was so cold it drank the warmth out of the air, making us shiver. "We make a Bridge," Griffin explained to us. "We've got the rigging for it if we improvise. We use our own emergency lock on our side, and grip onto whatever surface we choose with a pressure seal, so we can sample their atmosphere before we break through."

Dela said nothing to this. I knew she was not sanguine. But Griffin was so earnest, and so was Lynn, and it was what we had to do.

It was a matter of finding everything and then of carrying it all up the difficult areas of the *Maid*, into places our present orientation made almost inaccessible. We had weight to contend with—and Gawain and Percy got up on juryrigged ladders in the impossible angles of passages we were never supposed to use in dock as we were, in places where the hammering outside the hull rang fit to drive us mad. We added to it the sound of drills and hammering of our own, making a rig of ropes that would let us lift loads up the slanting deck and get it settled.

We worked, all that day, fit to break our hearts, and most all we had done was just moving the materials into place and making sure that the area just behind the lock was pressure-tight, and that everything they would need was there. Modred never came, nor did Vivien.

It was, I knew, I think more than one of us knew, only another one of Griffin's schemes, that Lynn had been convenient to lend him; and if it had not been this, it would have been another. But it kept us moving; and when we had worked all the day, we went to our quarters exhausted, aching in our arms and elsewhere.

Even Lynn—even she looked hollowed out, as if she had finally gotten the measure of what she had proposed doing, and being tired and full of bruises had beaten the mettle out of her. But she had said no word of giving it up. And no one told Lynn it was hopeless.

Not until we met Vivien.

I suppose that Vivien had been in our quarters most of the day; or in some comfortable hole of her own devising. She was there to meet us when we came in, sitting robed and cross-legged on the couch with one of the study tapes running, a soft murmur that drowned out the tappings from outside. I was glad when I saw her, relieved that she was no longer sick: this was the reflex my psych-set gave me, to be so naive.

But Viv knew where to put a shot.

"You know he'll believe anything now," she said right off, in that low and proper voice of hers. "So now everyone's working to build something to kill the lot of us. It's one project today, and that's not going to work; and what new one tomorrow? It's only worse, and he never knew what he was doing. No more than you do."

We all stood and stared at her, bereft of anything reasonable to say. She got up from the couch like a fire going up, all full of heat and smoke, and we were all disarranged.

"You shouldn't talk like that," I said.

"So she gave him the crew and the ship because it's broken. And the best idea you come up with is going out there with it."

"It's all we *can* do," Lynn said, defending herself.

"Of course, like you didn't move us until it was too late. That was all your idea too. And now you want to make a way for them to get in as if it weren't happening fast enough. You never knew what you were doing."

"Shut up," I said. But Lynn just sat down, elbows on her knees—not staff, Lynette, not prepared against lies that we who dealt with born-men knew how to deal with. The crew was innocent and told the truth. Vivien worked at them in painful ways. "It was all your doing, Viv," I said, "that tape, everything—I know who would have taken it. I know who could be a thief in our quarters. I should stop feeling sorry for you. Everything that ever happened to you, you brought on yourself."

"I took that tape," Percy said in a faint voice, very loud in that quiet. "I did, Elaine. I never expected—*that* . . . I never . . ."

I felt cold all over. I just stood there, wishing that someone would say something, even Viv. Percy's voice trembled into silence, asking answers, and I had never meant to hurt him, not Percy, not any of them.

"We're none of us right," Percy said, looking at me, at Lance. "If we weren't supposed to have it—what is it? And why?"

How do you make sense of a whole life in a why? I shook my head, looked at all the pain I had made, at Lynn who was trying to kill herself, at Gawain who had lost all his cheerfulness and gone sullen; at Vivien who had turned on us; at Percy that I had named a thief, when there was no one more kind and gentle, not even Lance. "The why won't make sense," I said. "But there were people like us a long time ago. Born-men. We can't be what they were. Or maybe never were.'"

"They were ourselves," Gawain said, finding his voice.

"No."

"I never saw myself that way," Gawain said distressedly, far from hearing anything I said. And it was so: that Elaine, myself, me, I—there was no sorting it. She was far more live than I: she loved.

And what did their images—but love, and want, and struggle—things far more live than they? I knew the Lancelot who stood behind me now, who gently put his big hands on my shoulders. And oh, what was Vivien's pettiness to *that* Vivien's malice; or Percy's kindness to *that* Percivale's goodness; or Lynn's bravery to Lynette's? We tried to live, that was what; we caught sight of something brighter and more vivid than ourselves and we wanted that.

Even Vivien—who wanted power, who was made and not born, and who knew nothing about love in either case. She struggled to be more than she was and narrow as she was, it threatened her sanity.

"Oh Viv," I said aloud, pitying.

"Oh Viv," she mimicked me, and turned away, playing the only role she knew how to play, the only one her psych-set and her name fit her for. I stood there trembling.

"Don't listen to her," Lancelot said, his fingers pressing my shoulders.

"She's not to blame," I said. "It's all she can see."

"So what do we do?" Percy asked. "Elaine?"

"We do what we see to do."

"Where's Modred?" Lance asked suddenly.

A silence among us.

"It's not right," I said, "to think about him the way the tape is. Modred's not changed. It can't have affected him, not *him*. We can't all walk off from him. And we can't treat him like that."

"He won't say anything about it," Percy said. "He won't talk."

"He wouldn't," Gawain said.

"He's still working up there," Lynn said, from where she sat, her arms about her thin knees. "He's convinced about his program. He still hopes for that."

"He *wouldn't* do that," Percy said. "Against orders. Not on his own."

Lance's hands were heavy on my shoulders. "Maybe somebody ought to see about him."

"Let him be," Gawain said sharply.

"What's he up to?" Lance asked. And when Gawain stood there staring back at us: "Gawain, what's going on up there?"

Still no answer. Lance let go my shoulders and turned for the door. Gawain started after him and I spun about, "Lance," I cried. "Gawain—"

Gawain overtook him at the door, but there was no stopping Lance when he was in a hurry: he shrugged off Gawain's hand with one thrust of his arm and kept going.

I heard laughter at my back; and not laughter at all, but a very bitter sound, unlike us. I looked back past Percy and Lynn, at Vivien.

"Percy," I pleaded, "Lynn, come on—someone stop them." I headed for the door, knowing everything amiss.

XIII

This night a rumor wildly blown about
Came, that Sir Modred had usurp'd the realm
And leagued him with the heathen. . . .

. . . Gawain, surnamed The Courteous, fair and strong,
And after Lancelot, . . . a good knight, but therewithal
Sir Modred's brother, and the child of Lot,
Nor often loyal to his word . . .

I ran, and was too late for the lift. But Gawain was not: he and
Lance were headed topside together, in what state I hated to
imagine. Percy and Lynn came running after, and caught me up
by the time the lift, empty, had come down again.

"Modred's his partner," Percy said, meaning Gawain's, meaning where loyalties lay. Lynette said nothing; it was like that between them, I thought, while the lift shot us up topside: that Percy
and Lynette worked together, were together, that while it was
Gawain most often Lynette bedded with—blithe and light
Gawain—it was Percivale who worked with her, close, close as
ever we could be; like Modred and Gawain.

The door opened and let us out: I ran, but Lynette and Percy
ran faster, for the doors where already we heard shouting.

The doors were closed. Locked. Of course, locked. Modred
knew his defenses.

"Open up," Lance shouted, and slammed the sealed door with
his fist. But he was staff: he had no right to command the crew.
And Gawain stood there doing nothing to help until Lynn and
Percy came running up ahead of me. "Order him to open," Lance
asked of them, and Lynn: "Modred," she called. "Modred—" But
gently, reasonably.

From inside, no answer.

"Ask him," Percivale asked of Gawain. "He'll listen to you.

"I doubt it," Gawain said. And so there we stood, the several of us—oh, it was terrible the look of us, of Lance and Gawain face to face and glaring at each other—

"It can't happen," I said, tugging at Lance's arm. "O Lance, go and fetch my lady. He'll listen to *her*. Please. We're what we always were. We can't have changed; and he can't. O run, run and tell her. Modred's not well."

He yielded backward to my tugging at him—like tugging at a rock, it was; but I put myself between the two of them—him and Gawain. Too proud to back very far: I saw Lance's eyes. "Percy," I said, "go."

And Percy ran. The lift had worked again, down the corridor. Vivien was there, and I could see she was satisfied . . . O the malice, the bitter, bitter malice that her makers never put into her, but the place had given her, and the ruin of all she was.

"What," she said, "has he shut you out then?"

"Be quiet," Gawain said. "We don't need you here."

"Modred," Lynette called, gently, using the com by the door. "Modred, are you all right in there?"

"He's gone over the brink," Lance said. "Modred, come out of there. We've sent for my lady. She won't be amused."

Silence from the other side.

"Maybe something *has* happened to him," I said, fearing more and more. "We aren't right to think the worst of him."

"He hears us," Lance said. "His partner knows what he's doing. I'd bet on it."

I looked at Gawain, whose beautiful face was flushed with anger, whose eyes had no little of fear: Lance could beat him, and there was no doubt of that.

"Wayne," Lynette said, "you covered for him? You *knew?*"

"Should I let you kill yourself and the rest of us?"

Lance reached out very deliberately and took Gawain's arm, brushed me aside as if I had not been there. "We have orders," Lance said.

And might have said more, but Percy came hurrying back to our relief. "She's coming," Percy said, "my lady and Griffin—" He stopped, transfixed at this sight we made, this laying on of hands that we had never done to each other. But we had nerved ourselves to fight, and had nothing of substance to fight but each other. Lance let Gawain go, further argument abided. And down the hall came Griffin and my lady, in their nightrobes, Griffin with his hair wet from the bath, my lady all a flurry of loose blonde hair and laces and her eyes—oh, my lady's eyes, so full of fright. She knew, *she* knew how wrong we had gone: but Griffin's face was ominous, all threat and anger. He came right through us, punched the com button, slammed his great fist on the door.

"Modred," he said. "Enough of this nonsense. Get this door open."

And more silence. I found myself with my hands clasped before my mouth, like praying. O Modred, I thought, Modred, you can't, you can't defy him. O Lance, O Gawain, do something.

"Modred!" Griffin yelled, another slam of his fist.

And my lady slipped past and leaned up to the com. "Modred. You know my voice."

A delay. "Yes, lady Dela." Like himself, it was, all quiet and untroubled as Pass the salt, please.

"Modred, I want this door open."

"In a moment, my lady."

In a moment. O Modred. Something shivered through me. We had all gotten very still, even Griffin. My lady looked distraught and then gathered herself.

"What are you doing, Modred?"

Silence.

"Modred, what do you think you're doing?"

Silence. A long silence. "That *program* of his—" Griffin said. "That program he wanted to use—"

"Modred," lady Dela said. "I want this door open right now. I want you to shut down what you're doing and come out here. No argument."

A longer silence.

"We'll have to get the cutters," Griffin said.

"Modred. Did you hear that? Are we going to have to do the *Maid* damage on account of you? Open the door."

It opened, so unexpected it jolted all of us—whisk! and he was standing there facing us across the bridge, a black figure against the comp lights and the screens that showed nothing they had not showed before.

"Get him out of there," Griffin said, and Lance and Percy moved in, took Modred's arms—nothing. No countermove. Modred gave way to them and would have let them take him out now, but Griffin barred the way, and the rest of us, and lady Dela.

Griffin put his hand in the middle of Modred's chest and stopped him face to face. "What have you done?" Griffin asked.

"Discover that," Modred said, "sir."

"Modred," Dela said—not angry, not anything but stunned. Modred looked at her then, and even he had to feel something: we're made that way. It had to be pain all the way to the gut, every psych-set torn. But Modred had no nerves. His expression hardly varied. "My lady Dela," he said equably, "I've sent it out, all of it."

"Contacting that thing?"

"It's done."

"And what did you get from it," Griffin asked. "Anything?"

"I was working on that. If you'll let me continue—"

I don't think he even understood it was effrontery.

"Not likely," Griffin said.

"How could you do a thing like this?" Dela asked. "Who gave you leave? Did I?"

"No," Modred said.

"And what have you sent out? *What* have you told it?"

"Mathematics. Chemistry. Our chemistry . . . in symbolic terms."

"Then it knows what we are," Griffin said.

"As well as I could state it."

"Get him out of here," Griffin said. "Lock him somewhere."

"Sir," Lance said. "Gawain knew."

Griffin looked at Gawain, and Gawain's face went white.

"Then we'll be talking to you as well," Griffin said.

"Sir," Gawain breathed and bowed his head.

Griffin looked about at all of us then, and I felt my bones go cold. "Get him out," Griffin said then and Lance and Percivale took Modred past me without argument from Modred. I stood, close to blanking, knowing what I had done.

"Staff's dismissed," Griffin said. "Go about your business. We'll straighten this mess up. Now. Out. Crew stays."

I fled, down the corridor after Vivien, disheveled as I was. My bones ached, somewhere inside the terror and the confusion: we had worked ourselves until we staggered with exhaustion, and now this—this, that was somewhere at the bottom of it my doing.

I went down and washed and put on clean clothes, because I knew there was no hope of sleep, Our night was over before it had started.

"See," Vivien said, "how organized it all is. No one knows what's afoot." She looked up and about her, where the noise continued, maddening, lifted her hands to her ears as if that could give a moment's relief. "They lost all our chances days ago."

"Shut up," I said, zipping my clean jacket and pulling my hair from the collar. "If you're so efficient, go back to your lab."

Oh. Cruel. Viv turned such a look on me that was hate and terror at once.

"Or do something outside *yourself*, Viv. Be something larger than you are. Think how to protect that lab of yours. Come up with something. Help us, for once."

"Elaine the fair."

"Don't be trapped by it. By the tape. You don't have to be. Oh, Viv—"

"Percy talks about God," she said. Gleaming behind the hate in her eyes was outright terror. " '*He* found God,' our Percy says. And what kind of thing is that for one of us? What's for *me*? You've all gone mad . . . and Percivale's gone and Modred—What of this wouldn't have happened without you? I think it's funny. Oh, it's a fine joke, Elaine."

"Hush, be still."

"What, be still? *Me*, who could work miracles in that stupid tape . . . Let me do one enchantment and I'd be out of here, let me tell you, sweet Elaine."

"Couldn't it be *we*?" I asked. "It's always I, isn't it?" I went for the door. Stopped, hearing uncharacteristic silence at my back.

She might have been upset, I had thought. But there was that terrible anger on her face, a sullenness unlike Modred's nerveless quiet.

"He talks about *God*," she said. "We're all rather above ourselves, aren't we? Like Modred."

She had stopped caring for living. That was the way she had coped with the shocks. I saw that suddenly, and it made me cold. She jumped from attacking Lynn to attacking Modred, to Griffin, to whoever had tried to do anything to change what was. Most of all she had me to blame, when the threat had gotten to the lab and the tape had gotten to her: that was twice she had

had her functions shaken apart—and now there was just the tape, and her own defenses.

Percy talking about God and Modred turning on us—and Lance and Gawain at odds. . . .

O God help us, I thought, which was unintended irony. We're all lost in Dela's dream.

And in it we faced our war.

They were busy on the bridge, Percy and Gawain and Lynette and Griffin and my lady Dela—there was nothing I could do there. They were busy trying to figure out what Modred had done on the bridge; but Modred was very good and I doubted they could find it at all if Modred had taken pains to hide it.

And Lance guarded the small room down the corridor which was a small cabin we had used on other voyages, where he had found to put Modred, I reckoned. Lance stood there, against the wall by the door, not moving, and looked tired beyond reckoning. "I can get a chair for you," I offered. "Is there anything I can do?"

"I'm well enough," he said, "but I'd like the chair, thanks."

I brought it, out of Dela's rooms, and set it down for him. He sank into it, with shadows round his eyes, with his big shoulders bowed. There was nothing anywhere to be happy about . . . and still that hammering continued.

I knelt down, took Lance's hand and looked up at him, which was the only way I could have his attention on me. It was focused elsewhere until then—somewhere insubstantial, maybe, on my lady, on our prospects. On what craziness brought him to lay hands on Gawain. I had no idea. His thoughts had grown complex, and they had never been that before. But he saw *me* because he had to, and his fingers tightened a little on my hand, cold and loose in mine until that.

"We've done all we can do," I said. "Lance—it's still all right. He can't have done us that much harm. Let me talk to him, can I? I always could talk to him. I might make sense of him."

"You don't know what might be in his head."

"I know you'll be right outside," I said in all confidence. His eyes flickered—it was a touch of pride, of what his shadow was. He wanted so much—so many things. For him a little praise was much.

"I think," he said, "he got nothing at all to eat or drink yesterday: he might want that."

Break Modred's neck he might; but cruelty was not in Lance. He thought of such things. I nodded.

"I think he might," I said, and got up and went off about that, while Lance kept his watch at the door.

So I came back from the dininghall stores with a sandwich and a cup of coffee, and Lance got up and let me through the door. Just a moment he stayed there, while Modred got up from the bed where he had been sitting, but Lance said nothing, and Modred said nothing, until Lance had closed the door.

"You haven't had anything to eat," I said.

"Thank you."

As quiet as before, as precise and proper, his thin hands clasped before him.

"Modred, why did you do a thing like that?"

He shrugged. "Thank you for the food," he said. I had not set it down. He meant I should leave, that was clear.

"Doesn't it hurt?" I asked. "Haven't you got any nerves at all?"

"If they make the bridge across, they might be right or wrong. But they don't *know*. And it's reckless."

Modred—to talk about recklessness, after what he had done. I set the tray down. "Then why won't you talk to them, tell them what you've done?"

"I don't see that it makes any difference."

"*You* don't see. When did you see everything?"

Another shrug. No one attacked Modred. I stared into that dark-bearded face that frightened born-men and tried not to think of the tape, of that *other* Modred.

"Modred, *please* talk to them."

"The program isn't locked," he said. "They'll have had no trouble accessing it."

"You could have asked permission."

"I did."

It was so. I knew that he had done that again and again.

"And if I'm wrong," he said, "there's Lynette's way; but if she's wrong—there's nothing left, is there?"

"You might be *right*. And if you are, come back, beg their pardons, talk to them."

He shook his head, walked over matter of factly and investigated the tray I had brought. "Thanks for the food. I hadn't time yesterday."

"*Why* won't you talk to them?"

He looked up at me. There was a hint of pain, but he looked down again and unwrapped the sandwich, looking only tired.

"Modred."

A second time he looked up at me. "They will never listen—to *me*—even when they should. Reason won't work, will it—not against what a born-man wants to believe. I've seen that before now."

"Do you understand—what it was in that tape Percy found in the locker?"

"Entertainment. A fancy. The logic on which this ship exists."

And the *Maid* was for him—the reason he existed. So it had gotten through to him. There was no reason in it. Modred had not even the nerves to be afraid: he was only trying to think it through and coming out with odd sums. He took a bite of his sandwich, a sip of the coffee. "It was kind of you to come," he said.

"If you could explain to them—"

"I have explained to master Griffin. I don't think he really understands. Or he looks at my face and stops listening." His brow furrowed. "I've exhausted reason. There's nothing else but what I did." A second sip of coffee, and absently he turned his back on me and walked away.

"Modred, look at me. Don't be like that."

He turned back again. "I don't precisely understand what kind of reasoning it is. Only that I'm not trusted. And that Griffin commands this ship."

"He's a good man."

"But do you think he's *right?*"

That was the logic that divided us . . . We went by other things; and Modred only on his reckonings.

"I'm still following original instructions," Modred said. "To get us out of this. Vivien has the right idea and none of you will listen to her either."

"You said it can't be done."

"I said there was no escaping the mass. I said other things no one heard."

"You mean talking to that thing."

"It's not attractive. It's dangerous. You don't like things like that. I know."

"You left Gawain in trouble on your account."

"Gawain did as Gawain chose to do."

"Then you're not alone. You can't say no one believes in you."

"Or the tape chose for him. He's my . . . brother . . . in the dream. It's a very dangerous thing, to see one's whole existence, from beginning to end, isn't it? I'm Modred. And not to be trusted. Even if I have the right idea."

The door opened, abruptly. Born-men do such things, without a by your leave. It was Griffin.

"I'll see you now," Griffin said, "in the dining hall. Now."

And Griffin left, like that, leaving the door open and Lance standing there.

I was afraid suddenly, seeing the look on Modred's face, that was stark frustration—a born-man could do terrible things to us; there were all our psych-sets. There was all of that.

Modred set the tray and cup down, click, mostly untasted, and straightened his shoulders and walked out, past Lance without a look or a word. Lance followed him directly. I hurried after— knowing nothing else to do and nowhere else to go.

So we all came—not alone Lance and I, but all of us on the ship, the rest of them already gathered there, in that hall beneath the embroidered lion. My lady Dela was at the head of the table along with Griffin, and my place and Lance's and Modred's were vacant. We went to our places, Lance and I having to pass all that long distance down the table—and Modred took his after a moment, understanding that was what was wanted of him. Gawain was there, his hands clenched before him on the table, not look- ing up. Percy sat there equally pale, beside Lynette. And Vivien, whose bright eyes missed nothing.

"We'll have an account, if you please," Dela said, "Modred."

"Lady, I think you'll have had access by now to the tape I used. I'm sure Percy can understand it."

"I don't care to go through it all. I want to know why you did such a thing."

Dela had not learned what had happened to us—my heart leapt and sank again in guilty relief—no one had told her about the stolen tape. I should, and had not the courage. And then I thought what that would do for Modred, how Dela would never trust him if she knew what he had heard. Or Lance. Or look at any of us the same.

And Modred as likely might tell her—having no nerves; and no knowledge of born-men.

"I explained," Modred said, "that there was a chance of contacting it."

"He—" I said aloud, my heart beating against my ribs, "Modred told me, lady Dela, that he had it figured—that if his plan failed, then—then there was Lynn's, wasn't there? But if Lynn's failed—then—"

"How many of you consulted on this?" Dela asked sharply. "Gawain? Elaine?"

"I never—" I said. "I—"

But all of a sudden I was having trouble concentrating, because something had stopped, the noise forward stilled, and that diminished a great deal the noise that had been constant with us for days.

"I—" I tried to continue, thinking I ought, trying to gather a denial, to explain, but Griffin held up his hand for quiet.

"It's stopped out there," Griffin said.

"It's—" Dela said.

And then that Sound was back again, our Beast talking to us over com. It had *heard.* None of us moved for the moment, and then Modred got out of his seat, and Griffin did, and the rest of us, as Modred headed out of the room.

We knew where he was going.

"Modred!" my lady cried.

But that did no good either.

XIV

. . . but she saw,
Wet with the mists and smitten by the lights,
The Dragon of the great Pendragonship
Blaze, making all the night a steam of fire.
And even then he turn'd; and more and more
The moony vapor rolling round the King,
Who seemed the phantom of a Giant in it,
Enwound him fold by fold and made him gray
And grayer, till himself became as mist
Before her, moving ghostlike to his doom.

Our Beast snarled at us, whispered to us, a low ticking that rose and assaulted our ears as we came—shaking us with the power of its voice. Vivien had come: she clung to the doorway with a kind of demented fixation on the sound. She had become entranced with her destruction, but that noise got to the bones and put shivers into the flesh, and Viv was right now close to sanity, in sheer fright. The crew headed for their places, but Lance laid hands on Modred to stop him.

"Let him go," Griffin said, and Lance looked at Dela, and did what he was told. I stood by shivering, physically shivering in the horrid sound. But we were better than we had been, and braver: my lady stood there with her fingers clenched on the back of Modred's chair and wanted answers from him—at once, now, immediately.

"We're getting screen transmission," Percy said, and it came up, a nonsense of dots and static breakup.

"That's an answer," Modred said calmly. He half turned, looking at my lady at his back, but receiving no instruction, he turned back again.

"What's it saying?" Griffin asked.

Modred ignored the question, busy with a flood of beeps that came through, and Griffin allowed it, because Modred was doing *something*, and Percy was, and then Lynn and Wayne came over from their posts to watch. It was craziness; the bass clicking stopped and became a maddening loud series of pulses. I wrapped my arms about myself, standing there and not understanding any of it. Griffin and Dela didn't understand: that also I came to believe. But they let the crew work with the computer.

"Equipment's not compatible," Modred said finally, the only word he gave us in all that time. "Stand by: we're getting it worked through comp."

"So it can hear us," Dela murmured. She moved back, shaking her head, and Griffin put his arm about her shoulders.

Lance and I and Viv, we just stood there, not understanding anything—until of a sudden lines began to come across one of the screens and it began to build itself downward into a picture. I wasn't sure I wanted to see—whatever it was. "We can clean that up," Gawain said. The crew began to work, and Percy sweated over the computer in greatest concentration, while Modred intervened with small gestures, an indication of this and that, quiet words. And then Modred reached for another control. Lynn reached out instantly and checked his hand from that. "No," Lynn said.

"My lady." Modred half turned in his seat. "We have to transmit and give it something back to keep its interest. This is going to take us time."

"Give it—what?" Griffin asked.

"The same thing as before," Modred said. "Repeating it. Giving it the notion we're still working."

"All right," Dela said quietly, and Lynette took her hand away, so whatever Modred wanted to send went out.

It went on a long while, this consultation, this meddling with the computer, and sometimes the lines on the screen grew clearer, and sometimes more confused. My knees ached, and my back and shoulders, so that finally I went over to that bench near the door where Vivien had sat down. After a moment more Lance came and took the place by me, silent company, image of other terrible nights trying to cope with this place.

But my heart was tired of beating overtime, and my limbs were all out of shivers. Terror had acquired a kind of mundanity, had become an atmosphere, a medium in which we just went on functioning, and did what we were supposed to do until somehow our Death would get to us. I reckoned that tired as I was it might not even hurt much. Maybe Vivien reckoned that way, sitting by me with her hands clasped in her lap—not blanked at all, but following this; and maybe Lance felt the same—who had Dela and Griffin in front of him, their arms about each other. Only the crew went on driving themselves because they had something left to do.

Our born-men—they had no least idea, I reckoned, what made sense to do, but they stood there, while the voice of our Beast rumbled away over the distant sound of hammering. At last Dela turned away as if she would leave—having had enough, I thought: this might wear on for hours. Almost I got to my feet, thinking she might need me—but no, she went only as far as the bench on the other side of the door, drawing Griffin with her, and they sat down there to wait it all out while the crew kept on at their work.

The image came clear finally, and it made no sense, being only dots. "Get the other one up," Modred said, and they started it all over again.

So the crew kept at their work, still getting something, and whatever-it-was kept up its noise. And my lady, who once would have gone to her rooms and shut out the sound—stayed, not even nodding into sleep, but watching every move Modred made.

Not trusting him. Modred had said it. It was very clear why all of us were here, why this one night the lady stayed to witness, and therefore all the rest of us stayed. Modred had to know that.

There had been a time, when the *Maid* had made tame voyages ferrying lovers from star to star, that my lady had liked Modred in contrast at her banquets, with his dark dour ways. He was the shadow in her fancy, the skeleton at the feast, the memento mori—a dangerous-looking sort whose impudence amused her, whose outrages she forgave. But that was before things had passed out of control, and we all had to rely on him. O my lady was afraid of him now, for all the wrong reasons—a grim face, an insolence which had taken matters into his own hands. And a name that had stopped being a joke. He was Modred: she had always had a place for him in her fancy. And so she stopped trusting him.

Me, with my little understanding—I watched him work, the

fevered concentration, the sometime flagging of his strength, and the cold, cold patience of his face; and I heard his voice, always quiet, cutting through Percy's dismay at something or Gawain's and Lynn's frustration—like ice it was, beyond disturbance . . . and I knew what it was I feared. I was afraid of his *reasoning*. Modred dealt with our Beast because it was there to be dealt with like the chaos outside, like the numbers that came up on the machinery, a part of this universe and no more alien to his understanding than I was.

But Modred understood now he was not trusted, and he was threatened somehow by that. One little emotion had to be gnawing at him, who could feel nothing else. He had been jolted through a host of sensations in that tape, things his nerves had never felt before. It must have been like a dip in boiling water, leaving no clear impression what the water had been like because the heat was everything.

And what he wanted now, what drove him so, I had no least idea.

The work continued. As with our general terror, information wore us out and left us without reaction—one could only look at so many lines and dots and listen to so much talk that made no particular sense. I found my head nodding, and leaned on Lance, who was more comfortable than the wall; Lance leaned back then and his head bowed over against mine—I went plummeting down a long dark, just too tired to make sense of anything, and the voice of our Beast and the hammering at the hull sang me to sleep.

I came out of it aware of an ache in my neck and of a set of voices in hushed debate.

"No," one said, and: "It's been quiet all this time," the other—Lynn and Modred. "No." Percy's voice. "There's no way—" Gawain's, rising above the level of the others. "Modred, no."

"Lady Dela," Modred said.

I waked thoroughly, sat up as Lance did, as all of us who had been drowsing came awake. Modred looked like death—no sleep, no food or drink but what I had brought him: it showed.

"Lady Dela, it's answered. The transmissions—there's an urgency—" He turned and started touching controls, bringing up a sequence of images, that was all dots and squiggles and lines and circles. "We've rationalized its number system, gotten its chemistry—it's methane. There are all kinds of systems on the wheel—" He brought up another diagram, that was all a jumble of lines, and he pointed to it as my lady and Griffin got to their feet. "There, see—"

"I don't make any sense of it," Dela said.

"There." Modred's hand described a circle: I could see it among the lines when I looked for it, among the other shapes that radiated out from it. And then it made sense—the wheel and the ships appended to it, and the network of tubes that wove them all so that the whole looked like a crown seen from above, with rays and braidings going out in all directions. Modred's thin finger lighted on a single point of this. "This is the *Maid*. Here. Oxygen." His finger underlined a series of dots, and swept to another, impossibly complicated series of dots inside the wheel. "That's methane out there. But here—" His finger swept the torus. "See, there's oxygen, just beyond that partition out there; and a line going that way, from our bow, to that partition. We docked in the wrong segment, and they've corrected that. The torus—has seven divisions. Water, here: they must melt ice. And process other things. Here's a different mix of oxygen; methane/ammonia and sulphur . . ."

"You profess to read this thing's language?"

"A dot code, lady." Modred never looked back, went on showing us his construction—its construction, whosoever it might be. "It's compartmented, various pressures, I'd guess, various temperatures for all its inhabitants. But these—" His hand went to the network of veins. "Methane. All methane. And we may be dealing with a time difference . . . in thought. The creature talking to us sends the images very slowly. But put them together and they animate. Percy—"

Percy ran it back again to earlier images, and we watched, watched the torus naked of ships; and then ships arriving. We watched the network actually grow, watched the lines start from one ship and penetrate the torus, then penetrate the neighboring ship-figure. The dots in it—I had not noticed, but suddenly there were a lot of them.

"Do you see?" Modred asked. "The atmosphere in that ship went to methane. It changed."

But now the lines were going in both directions. New masses popped up, more ships arriving; or asteroids and whole plane-

toids swept in, docked like ships, because some of the shapes
were tiny and some were unaccountably lumpy. Some acquired
lines crossing the torus to other sections. I watched, and I felt
cold, so that when Lance put his arm about me, I was grateful.
Maybe he was cold too. I reached out for Vivien, while the thing
went on building, took her cold hand, but she simply stood there
with her eyes fixed on the screen and no response at all to my
touching her.

So the lines advanced, like blind worms, nodding about and
leeching onto a ship-form or a bit of rock; and generally the ships
went to that complicated pattern that meant methane. So Modred
had said. He watched it grow and grow until the network was
mostly about the torus. Until Modred pointed to a ship that suddenly appeared amid the net.

"Ourselves," he said, and the course of it was all but finished
except for the waving of the tubes that attached themselves—so,
so sinister those thin lines, and the line that appeared leading in
another section, and the arrival of another bit of debris far across
the wheel . . . something our last jump had swept in, I reckoned.

And Modred looked back at us then. "It's shown us our way
out," he said. "We've got to open our forward hatch and go to
it."

"O dear God," Dela said with a shake of the head.

"No," Lynette said. "I don't think that's a thing to do that
quickly."

"You persist," Modred said, "against the evidence."

"Which can be read other ways," Griffin said. "No."

"Lady Dela," Modred said. Patiently, stone-faced as ever, but
his voice was hoarse. "It's a question of profitability. Some of
those ships on the ring didn't change. At some points that intrusion failed. And others directly next to them changed. So some
do drive it off. There's the tubes, and separately—the wheel itself. It's made an access out to the point where we touch the
wheel. We're very close to an oxygen section. Very close to where
we should have docked. It can let us through where we have to
go."

"Has it occurred to anyone," Vivien asked out of turn, "that
however complicated—however attractive and rational and difficult the logical jump it's put us through to reach it—that the thing
might *lie*?"

A chill went through me. We looked at one another and for a moment no one had anything to say.

"It's a born-man," Percy said in his soft voice. "Or creature. And so it might lie."

I felt myself paralyzed. And Modred stood there for a moment with a confusion in his eyes, because he was never set up to understand such things—lies, and structures of untruth.

Then he turned and walked toward the main board, just a natural kind of movement, but suddenly everyone seemed to think of it and the crew grabbed for him as Lance and Griffin moved all in the same moment

Modred lunged, too near to be stopped: his hand hit a control and there was a sound of hydraulics forward before Lance reached past Gawain and Percy and Lynn who pinned Modred to the counter. Lance hauled Modred out and swung him about and hit him hard before Griffin could hinder his arm. Modred hit the floor and slid over under the edge of Gawain's vacant seat, lying sprawled and limp, but Lance would have gone after him, if not for Griffin—And meanwhile Lynette was working frantically at the board, but there had not been a sound of the hydraulics working again.

Our lock was open. Modred had opened us up. The realization got through to Dela and she flew across the deck to Griffin and Lance and the rest of them. "Close it—for God's sake, close it," Dela cried, and I just stood there with my hands to my mouth because it was clear it was not happening.

"It's not working," Lynn said. "Lady Dela, there's something in the doorway and the safety's on—"

"Override," Griffin said.

"There might be someone in the way—"

"*Override.*"

Lynn jabbed the button; and all my nerves flinched from the sound that should have come, maybe cutting some living thing in half—But it failed.

"They've got it braced wide open," Gawain said. "Percy—get cameras down there—"

Percy swung about, and reached the keyboard. All of a sudden we had picture and sound, this hideous babble, this conglomeration of serpent bodies in clear focus—serpents and other things as unlovely, a heaving mass within the *Maid*'s airlock. The second door still held firm, and there was our barrier beyond—there was still that.

"We've got to get down there," Griffin said.

"They can't get through so quickly," Dela said. Her teeth were chattering.

"They don't have to be delicate now they've got that outer lock braced open." Griffin was distraught, his hands on Dela's shoulders. He looked around at all of us. "Suit up. Now. We don't know what they may do. Dela, get to the dining hall and just stay there. And get him out of here—" The latter for Modred, who lay unmoving. "Get him out, locked up, out of our way."

Lance bent down and dragged Modred up. I started to help, took Modred's arm, which was totally limp, as if that great blow had broken him—as if all the fire and drive had just burned him out and Lance's blow had shattered him. For that moment I pitied him, for he never meant to betray us, but he was Modred, made that way and named for it. "Let me," Percivale said, who was much stronger, and who would treat him gently. So I surrendered him to Percivale, to take away, to lock up where he could do us no more harm.

"He'd fight for us," I said to Griffin, thinking that we could hardly spare Modred's wit and his strength, whatever there was left to do now.

"We can't rely on that," Griffin said. He laid his hand on my shoulder, with Dela right there in his other arm. "Elaine—all of you. We do what we planned. All right?"

"Yes, sir," I said, and Gawain the same. A silence from Vivien.

"Come on," Griffin said.

So we went, and now over com we could hear the sound of what had gotten into the ship. I imagined them calling for cutters in their hisses and their squeals, and scaly dragon bodies pressing forward—oh, it could happen quickly now, and my skin drew as if there had been a cold wind blowing.

No sound of trumpets. No brave charge. We had armor, but it was all too fragile, and swords, but they had lasers, all too likely; and all the history of this place was theirs, not ours.

XV

A land of old upheaven from the abyss
By fire, to sink into the abyss again;
Where fragments of forgotten peoples dwelt,
And the long mountains ended in a coast
Of ever-shifting sand, and far away
The phantom circle of a moaning sea.
. . . And there, that day when the great light of heaven
Burned at his lowest in the rolling year,
On the waste sand by the waste sea they closed.
Nor yet had Arthur fought a fight
Like this last, dim, weird battle of the west.
A deathwhite mist slept over sand and sea:
Whereof the chill, to him who breathed it, drew
Down with his blood, till all his heart was cold
With formless fear; and ev'n on Arthur fell
Confusion, since he saw not whom he fought.
For friend and foe were shadows in the mist,
And friend slew friend not knowing whom he slew.

We had put the suits all in the dining room, all piled in the corner like so many bodies; and the breathing units were by them in a stack; and the helmets by those. . . . "Shouldn't we," I said, taking my lady's suit from Percy, who was distributing pieces. I turned to my lady. "—shouldn't we take Modred's to him—in case?"

"No," Griffin said behind me, and firmly. "He'll be safe enough only so he stays put."

I doubted that. I doubted it for all of us, and it seemed cruel to me. But I helped my lady with her suit, which she had never put on before, and which I had never tried. Lance was helping Griffin with his; but Lynn and Gawain had to intervene with both of us to help because they knew the fittings and where things should go and we did not.

Griffin was first done, knowing himself something about suits and getting into them. He had his helmet in his hand and waved off assistance from Gawain. "Dela," he said then, "you stay here. You can't help down there, you hear me?"

"I hear you," she said, "but I'm coming down there anyway."

"Dela—"

"I'll stay back," she said, "but I'll be behind you."

Griffin looked distraught. He wanted to say no again, that was sure; but he turned then and took one of the swords in hand, his helmet tucked under his arm. "There'll be no using the beam cutters or the explosives," he said. "If that's methane out there. Modred did us that much service. So the swords and spears are all we've got. Dela—" Maybe he had something more to say and changed his mind. He lost it, whatever it had been, and walked off and out the door while we worked frantically at my lady's fastenings.

"Hurry," Dela insisted, and Lynette got the last clip fastened.

"Done," Lynn said, and my lady, moving carefully in the weight, took her helmet from my hands and tucked that up, then gathered up several of the spears.

"Vivien," my lady said sharply, and fixed Viv with her eye, because Viv was standing against the wall with never a move to do anything. "You want to wait here until they come slithering up the halls, Vivien?"

"No, lady," Vivien said, and went and took the suit that Percy offered her.

"Help me," Viv said to us. She meant it as an order. But my lady was already headed out the door, and Lance and I were in no frame of mind to wait on Vivien.

"Get us ready," I said to Lynn and Gawain. "Hurry. Hurry. They're alone down there."

But Percivale delayed his own suiting to attend to Vivien, who was all but shivering with fright. I heard the lift work a second time and knew my lady had gone without us . . . and still we had that sound everywhere. Lynn batted my overanxious hands from the fastenings and did them the way they should be done, and settled the weight of the lifesupport on me so that I felt my knees buckle; and fastened that with snaps of catches. "Go," she said then, and I bent gingerly to get my helmet and took another several of the spears. But Lance took a sword the same as Griffin's, and a spear besides. He moved as if that great weight of the suit were nothing to him. He strode out and down the corridor, and I followed after him as best I could, panting and trying not to catch a spearpoint on the lighting fixtures of the walls.

I had no intention that he should wait; if he could get to the lift and get down there the faster, so much the better, but he held the lift for me and shouted at me to hurry, so I came, with the shuffling haste I could manage, and I got myself and my un-wieldly load into the lift and leaned against the wall as he hit the button with his gloved knuckles. It dropped us down that two deck distance and the door opened on a hideous din of thumps and bangs, but remoter than I had feared.

My lady was there, and Griffin. They stood hand in hand in front of the welded barrier, their weapons set aside, and they looked glad to see us as we came.

"Elaine," Griffin said right off, "your job is to protect your lady, you understand. You stay beside her whatever happens."

"Yes, sir," I said.

"And Lance," he said, "I need you."

"Yes, sir," Lance said without quibble, because it meant being up front beyond a doubt, with all our hopes in defense of all of us.

"They're not through the airlock yet," Dela said. "They're working at it."

"When our atmospheres mix," Griffin said, "we're in danger of blowing everything. At least they know. I imagine they'll use some kind of a pressure gate and do the cut in an oxygen mix. If they've got suits, and I'm betting they do."

"We could set up a defense on next level," Lance said.

"Same danger there; they convert this level to their own at-mosphere, then we've got it all over again. Our whole lifesup-port bled out into all that methane would diffuse too much for any danger; but if they let all that methane in here—it could blow the ship apart. A quick way out. There's that. We could al-ways touch it off ourselves."

"Griffin," Dela said.

"If we had to."

I felt cold, that was all, cold all the way inside, despite that carrying the suit made me sweat.

The lift worked. Vivien came, alone, walking with difficulty, and she had gotten herself one of the spears, carrying that in one hand, and her helmet under the other arm. She joined us.

And the lift went up and came down again with Gawain and Lynn and Percy, who moved better with their suits than the rest of us. They had swords and spears, and some of the knives with them.

"We wait," Griffin said.

So we got down on our knees, that being the only way to sit down in the suits, and I only hoped we should have a great deal of warning, when the attack came, because even the strongest of us were clumsy, down on one knee and then the other, and then sitting more or less sideways. I was all but panting, and I felt sweat run under the suit, but my legs felt the relief, and finding a way to rest the corner of the lifesupport unit against the deck gave me delirious relief from the weight.

Bang. Thump.

Be careful, Beast, I thought at it, imagining all its minions and ourselves blown to atoms, to drift and swirl out there amongst the chaos-stuff. In one part of my mind—I think it was listening to the wrong kind of tapes—I was glad of a chance like that, that we might do some terrible damage to our attackers and maybe put a hole in the side of the wheel that they would remember . . . all, all those scaly bodies going hurtling out amongst our fragments.

But in the saner part of my mind I did not want to die.

And oh, if they should get their hands on us. . . . Hands. If they had hands at all. If they thought anything close to what we thought.

If, if, and if. Bang. Thump. Griffin and my lady told stories— recollected a day at Brahmani Dali, and smiled at each other. "I love you," Griffin said then to Dela, a sober, afterthinking kind of voice, meaning it. I knew. I focused beyond them at Lance, and his face looked only troubled as all our faces did. It was no news to him, not now.

So we sat, and shifted our weight because the waiting grew long.

"They could take days about it," Dela said.

"I doubt it," Griffin said.

"They'll suit up," Gawain said. "They'll have that weight to carry, just like us."

"I wish they'd get on about it." That plaintive voice from Vivien. Her eyes were very large in the dim light of the corridor, where the makeshift bulkhead had cut off some of the lighting. "What can they be doing out there?"

"Likely assuring their own safety."

"They can't come at us with firearms," Lynn said. "If we can't use them, they daren't."

"That's so," Dela breathed.

"Not at close range," Griffin said. He laughed. "Maybe they're hunting up weapons like ours."

That would be a wonder, I thought. I was encouraged by the thought—until I reckoned that the odds were still likely theirs and not ours. And then the realization settled on me darker and heavier than before, for that little breath of hope, that we really had no hope at all, and that we only did this for—

When I thought of it, I couldn't answer why we tried. For our born-men, that was very simple . . . and not so simple, if there was no hope. It was not in our tapes—to fight. But here was even Vivien, clutching a spear across her knees, when I *knew* her tapes were hardly set that way. They made us out of born-man material, and perhaps, the thought occurred to me, that somewhere at base they and we were not so different—that born-men would do things because it leapt into their minds to do them, like instincts inherent in the flesh.

Or the tapes we had stolen had muddled us beyond recall.

The sound stopped again, close to us, though it kept on above. "They've arranged something, maybe," Dela said. "God help us."

"Easy," Griffin said. And: "When it comes—understand, Dela, you and Elaine and Vivien take your position back just ahead of the crosspassage. If anything gets past us you take care of it."

"Right," Dela said.

If. It seemed to me a very likely if, recalling that flood of bodies I had seen within our lock.

But the silence went on.

"Lady Dela," Percy said then, very softly.

Dela looked toward him.

"Lady Dela, you being a born-man—do you talk to God?"

My heart turned over in me. Viv's head came up, and Lance's and Gawain's and Lynn's. We all froze.

"God?" Dela asked.

"Could you explain," Percivale went on doggedly, stammering on so dreadful an impertinence, "could you say—whether if we die we have souls? Or if God can find them here."

"Percy," Viv said sharply. "Somebody   Percy—"

Shut him up, she meant—right for once; and I put out my hand and tugged at his arm, and Lance pulled at him, but Percy was not to be stopped in this. "My lady—" he said.

My lady had the strangest look on her face—thinking, looking at all of us—and we all stopped moving, almost stopped breathing for Percy's sake. She would hurt him, I thought; I was sure. But she only looked perplexed. "Who put that into your head?" she asked.

No one said, least of all Percy, whose face was very pale. No one said anything for a very long time.

"Do you know, lady?" Percy asked.

"Dear God, what's happened to you?"

"I—" Percy said. But it got no further than that.

"He took a tape," Vivien said. "He's never been the same since."

"It was me," I said, because she left me nothing more to say. "It was the tape—The tape." I knew she understood me then, and her eyes had turned to me. "It was never Percy's fault. He only borrowed it from me, not knowing he should never have it. We—all . . . had it. It was an accident, lady Dela. But my fault."

Her eyes were still fixed on me, in such stark dismay—and then she looked from me to Lance, and Gawain and Lynette and Vivien and Griffin and last to Percivale, as if she were seeing us for the first time, as if suddenly she knew us. The dream settled about us then, wrapped her and Griffin too.

"Percivale," she said, with a strange gentleness, "I've no doubt of you."

I would have given much for such a look from my lady. I know that Lance would have. And perhaps even Vivien. We were forgiven, I thought. And it was if a great weight left us all at once, and we were free.

Vivien, whose spite had spilled it all—looked taken aback, as if she had run out of venom, as if she found a kind of dismay in what she was made to be. Maybe she grew a little then. At least she had nothing more to say.

And then a new sound, a groaning of machinery, that clanked and rattled and of a sudden a horrid rending of metal.

"O my God," Dela breathed.

"Steady. All of you."

"They've got the lock," Lynn surmised. And a moment more and we knew that, because there was a rumbling and clanking closer and closer to the makeshift bulkhead behind which we sat. I clenched my handful of spears, ready when Griffin should say the word.

"Helmets," he said, reaching for his.

I dropped the spears and picked up my lady's, to help her, small skill that I had. But Percy took it from my hands, quick and sure, and helped her, as Lynn helped me. The helmet frightened me—cutting me off from the world, like that white place of my nightmares. But the air flowed and it was cooler than the air outside, and Lynn took my hand and pressed it on a control at my chest so that I could hear her voice.

". . . your com," she said. "Keep it on."

I heard other voices, Lance's and Griffin's as they got their helmets on and got to their feet. Griffin helped Dela stand and Percy got me on my feet so that I could lean on my spears and stay there. Everything was very distant: the helmet which had seemed for a moment to cut off all the familiar world from me now seemed instead to contain it, the cooling air, the voices of my comrades. It was insulation from the horrid sounds of them advancing against our last fortification, so that we went surrounded in peace.

"Get back," Griffin said; and Dela reached out her hand for his and leaned against him only the moment—two white-suited ungainly figures, one very tall and the other more suit and lifepack than woman. "Take care of her," Griffin wished us, all calm in the stillness that went about us.

"Yes, sir," I said. "We will." We meaning Viv and I. And Dela came with us, a slow retreat down the corridor, so as not to tire ourselves, the three of us armed with spears. Dela kept delaying to turn and look back again, but I didn't look, not until we had reached the place where we should stand, and then I maneuvered my thickly booted feet about and saw Lance and Griffin and the crew who had determined where *they* would stand, not far behind the bulkhead. Their backs were to us. They had their swords and a few weighted pipes that Gawain and Lynn had brought down, and a spear or two. They stood two and three, Lance and Griffin to the fore and the crew behind. And I felt vibration through my boots, and heard their voices discussing it through the suit com, because they had felt it too.

"It won't be long," Griffin said. "We go forward if we can. We push them out the lock and get it sealed."

"They may have prevented that," Gawain said, "if they jammed something into the track."

"We do what we can," Griffin said.

Myself, I thought how those creatures had gotten up against us, and wrenched the second door apart with the sound of metal rending, a lock that was meant to withstand fearful stress. Modred's had been a small betrayal; it lost us little. They could easily have torn us open—when they wished, when they were absolutely ready.

"Feel it?" Dela asked.

"Yes," I said, knowing she meant the shuddering through the floor.

"They can't stop them," Viv said.

"Then it's our job," I said, "isn't it?"

The whole floor quivered, and we *felt* the sound, as suddenly there was a squeal of tearing metal that got even through the insulating helmets. Light glared round the edges of the bulkhead where it met the overhead, and widened, irregularly, all with this wrenching protest of bending metal, until all at once the bulkhead gave way on other sides, and drew back, showing a glare of white light beyond. The bulkhead was being dragged back and back with a terrible rumbling, a jolting and uncertainty until it dropped and fell flat with a jarring boom. A head on a long neck loomed in its place. For a moment I thought it alive; and so I think did Griffin and the rest, who stood there in what was now an open access—but it was machinery silhouetted against the glare of floods, our longnecked dragon nothing but a thing like a piston pulling backward, contracting into itself, so that now we saw the ruined lock, and the flare of lights in smoke or fog beyond that.

"Machinery," I heard Lance say.

But what came then was not—a sinuous plunge of bodies through the haze of light and fog, like a cresting wave of serpent-shadows hurling themselves forward into the space the machinery had left.

My comrades shouted, a din in my ears: "*Come on!*" That was Griffin: he took what ground there was to gain, he and Lance—and Gawain and Lynn and Percy behind them, two and then three more human shadows heading into the wreckage and the fog, tangling themselves with the coming flood.

"Come *on*," my lady said, and meant to keep our interval: I came, hearing the others' sounds of breath and fighting—heard Griffin's voice and Lance's, and Lynn who swore like a born-man and yelled at Gawain to watch out. We ran forward as best we could, behind the others. "No!" I heard Viv wail, but I paid no attention, staying with my lady.

And oh, my comrades bought us ground. Shadows in the mist, they cut and hewed their way with sobs for breath that we could hear, and no creature got by them, but none died either. We crossed the threshold of the rained bulkhead, and now Griffin pushed the fight into the lock itself, still driving them back. "Wait," I heard, Viv's voice. "Wait for me." But Dela and I kept on, picking our way over the wreckage of the fallen bulkhead, then past the jagged edges of the torn inner lock.

And then they carried the fight beyond the lock, in a battle we could not see . . . driving the serpent-shapes outside.

But when we had come into the lock, my lady and I, and Vivien panting behind us—it was all changed, everything. I knew what we *should* see—an access tube, a walkway, something the like of which we had known at stations; but we stared into lights, and steam or some milky stuff roiled about, making shadows of our folk and the serpents, and taller, upright shapes behind, like a war against giants, all within a ribbed and translucent tube that stretched on and on in violet haze. "Look out!" I heard Lance cry, and then, "Percy!"

And from Lynette: "He's down—"

"Dela—" Griffin's voice. "Dela—"

"I'm here," she said, wanting to go forward, but I held her arm. They had all they could handle, Griffin and the rest.

"Fall back," I heard him say. "We can't go this—Get Percy up; get back."

They were retreating of a sudden as the other, taller shapes pressed on them like an advancing wall. I heard Gawain urging

Percy up; saw the retreat of two figures, and the slower retreat of three. "Back up," Griffin ordered, out of breath, and then: "Watch it!"

Suddenly I lost sight of them in a press of bodies. I heard confused shouting, not least of it Dela's voice crying out after Griffin; and Gawain and Percy were yelling after Lance and Griffin both.

But still Griffin's voice, swearing and panting at once, and then: "You can't—Lance, get back, get back.—*Dela!*—Dela, I'm in trouble. I can't get loose—Modred—Get Modred—"

"Modred," Dela said. She turned on me and seized my arm and shook at me so that I swung round and looked into her eyes through the double transparency of the helmets. "Let him loose— let Modred loose, hear?"

I understood. I gave her my spear and I plunged back past Viv, back through the lock again and over the debris—no questioning; and still in my suit com I could hear my comrades' anguished breaths and sometimes what I thought was Lance, a kind of a sobbing that was like a man swinging a weight, a sword, and again and fainter still . . . Griffin's voice, and louder—Dela's.

"Get them back," I heard. That was Lance for sure; and an oath: that was Lynette.

I had the awful sights in my eyes even while I was feeling my overweighted way over the debris in the corridors; and then my own breath was sobbing so loud and my heart pounding so with my struggle to run that the sounds dimmed in my ears. I reached the open corridor; I ran in shuffling steps; I made the lift and I punched the buttons with thick gloved fingers, knees buckling under the thrust of the car as it rose, one level, another. Up here too I could hear a sound . . . a steady sound through the walls, that was another attack at us, another breaching of the *Maid*'s defense.

Get Modred. There was no one else who might defend the inner ship, and that was all we had left. I knew, the same as my lady knew, and I got out into the corridor topside and shuffled my clumsy way down it with my comrades' voices dimmed altogether now, and only my own breaths for company.

I pushed the button, opening it. Modred had heard me coming—how could he not? He was standing there, a black figure, just waiting for me, and when I gestured toward the bridge he

ALTERNATE REALITIES 167

cut me off with a shove that thrust me out of the way . . . ran, the direction of the bridge, free to do what he liked.

"Go," his voice reached me over com, in short order, but I was already doing that, knowing where I belonged. "Elaine . . . get everyone out of the corridors."

"Modred," Dela said, far away and faint. "We're holding here . . . at the lock. We've lost Griffin—"

"Get out of the corridors," he said. "Quickly."

I made the lift. I rode it down, into the depths and the glare of lights beyond the ruined corridor. They might have taken it by now, I was thinking . . . I might meet the serpent shapes the instant the door should open; but that would mean all my friends were gone, and I rushed out the door with all the force I could muster, seeing then a cluster of human shapes beyond the debris, three standing, two kneeling, and I heard nothing over com.

"My lady," I breathed, coming as quickly as I could.

"Elaine," I heard . . . her voice. And one of the figures by her was very tall, who turned beside my lady as I reached them.

Lance and my lady and Vivien; and Gawain and Lynette kneeling over Percivale, who had one arm clamped tight to his chest, his right. But of Griffin there was no sign; and in the distance the ranks of the enemy heaved and surged, shadows beyond the floods they had set up in the tube.

"Modred's at controls," I said, asking no questions. "He'll do what he can." And because I had to: "I think they're about to break through up there."

My lady said nothing. No one had anything to say.

Modred would do what was reasonable. Of that I had no least doubt. If there was anything left to do. We were defeated. We knew that, when we had lost Griffin. And so Dela let Modred loose, the other force among us.

"Lady Dela," Modred's voice came then. "I suggest you come inside and seal yourselves into a compartment."

"I suggest you do something," Dela said shortly. "That's what you're there for."

"Yes, my lady," Modred said after a moment, and there was a squealing in the background. "But we're losing pressure in the topside lab. I think they're venting our lifesupport. I'd really suggest you take what precautions you can, immediately."

"We hold the airlock," Dela said.

"No," Modred said. "You can't." A second squealing, whether of metal or some other sound was uncertain.

And then the com went out.

"Modred?" Dela said. "Modred, answer me."

"We've lost the ship," Lynette said.

"Lady Dela—" Lance said quietly. "They're moving again."

They were. Toward us. A wall of serpents and taller shapes like giants, lumpish, in what might be suits or the strangeness of their own bodies.

Dela stopped and gathered up a spear, leaned on it, cumbersome in her suit. "Get me up," Percy was saying. "Get me on my feet."

"If they want the ship," Dela said then in a voice that came close to trembling, "well, so they have it. We fall aside and if we can we go right past their backs. We go the direction they took Griffin, hear?"

"Yes," Lance said. Gawain got Percy on his feet. He managed to stay there. Lynette stood up with me and Vivien. Out of Vivien, not a word, but she still held her spear, and it struck me then that she had not blanked: for once in a crisis Vivien was still around, still functioning. Born-man tapes had done that much for her.

The lines advanced, more and more rapidly, a surge of serpent bodies, a waddle of those behind, beyond the hulking shape of the machinery they had used to breach us, past the glare of the floods.

XVI

But now farewell. I am going a long way
With those thou seest—if indeed I go—
For all my mind is clouded with a doubt—
To the island-valley of Avilion.

So we stood. In front of us was that machine like a ram, and
that was a formidable thing in itself; but it was frozen dead.
And about it was a fog, a mist that made it hard to see—I thought
it must be of their devising, to mask how many they were, or
what they did, or prepared to do. Within the mist we could see
red serpent shapes shifting position, weaving their bodies together
like restless braiding, like grass in a sideways wind, like cours-
ers held at a starting mark, eager and restrained. It was pecu-
liarly horrible, that constant action; and broadbodied giants stood
behind, purplish shadows less distinct, an immobile hedge like a
fortification.

"You understand," said my lady Dela, "that when they come,
we only seem to hold; and fall aside and lie low until we can
get behind their lines. Don't try more than that. Does everyone
understand?"

We avowed that we did, each answering.

And then a clearer, different voice, that was from the *Maid*'s
powerful system. "My lady Dela." Modred. And a sound behind
his voice like groaning metal, like—when the lock had given
way. "I've sealed upper decks. They're breaking through the seal.
I suggest you withdraw inside. Now."

"My orders stand," Dela said.

"There's danger of explosion, lady Dela. Come inside *now*. I
am in contact with the alien. It instructs we give access."

"Protect the ship."

"I'm doing that."

"You take your orders from me, Modred."

A silence. A squeal of metal.

"Modred?"

"They're in. We've lost all upper deck. Withdraw into the ship."

And now it began. In front of us. The serpents were loosed, and they came, looping and heaving forward like the breaking of a reddish wave. The giants behind them moved like a living wall.

"Stand still," Dela said, paying no more heed to Modred. Lance and Lynette put themselves in front of her, and Percy and Gawain stood to either side. Myself, I gripped my spear in thick gloved hands and left Viv behind us, moved up to Percy's side, because his one arm was useless now.

Oh, there was not enough time, no time at all to get used to this idea. I had never hit anything. I had a sudden queasiness in my stomach like psych-sets amiss, but it was raw fear, a doubt of what I was doing, to fall under that alien mass—but that was what our lady had said we must do.

"They're hard to cut," I heard Lance tell us; very calm, Lance, my lady's sometime lover and never meant for more. "But hit them. They do feel it."

They. I could see them clearly now. The serpents had legs and used them, poured forward overrunning their own slower members, like the rolling of a sea, all soundless in the insulation of my helmet, and time slowed down as my mind began to take in all of this detail, as my heart beat and my hands realized a weapon in them. The tide reached Lance and Lynette and boiled about them, hip-high until they felt Lance's blows. One reared up, and others, and those behind overran, climbing the rearing bodies, with blind nodding heads, and flung themselves aside and poured past. One came at me, a snaky, legged body whose hide was a slick membrane of purples and reds. I swallowed bile and jabbed at it with all my strength: the point of the spear made a dent in its muscle and scored its slickish hide: it nodded its head this way and that in eyeless pain: a small *O* of a mouth opened and its screaming reached me past my comrades, amplified sobs for breath and my lady's curses. I had no idea what became of that beast or where it went: there was another and I struck at that, and went on jabbing and beating at them until my joints ached, until finally one slithered behind my legs and another slid off an attacking body and came down in my face, huge and heavy and horridly alive.

I was buried in such bodies. I yelled out for horror, bruised, aghast at the writhing under and over me as I became flotsam in that alien tide. "My lady!" I cried, and heard someone cry out in great pain—O Percy! I thought then, with his arm already torn; and where my comrades were in this or where my lady was I could not see. Even the light was cut off, as a body pressed over my faceplate, and then my com went out, so that I had only my own voice inside my helmet, and the murmuring rush from outside.

Then the mass above flowed off me, and I saw light—saw—the giants passing near, next in the alien ranks. One almost trod on me, indifferent, and I clawed my way aside, scrambled atop that heaving mass of dragon-shapes, tumbled then, borne toward the *Maid*'s gaping lock. I remembered the com control on my chest, pressed the button and had sound again, Lance's deep voice calling out a warning: "Look *out*!"

And oh—the giants were not the worst, them with their broad violet bodies like gnarled trees come to life—There was a shape that shuffled along as if it herded them all, a lumpish thing larger even than they, and puffed with delicate veined bladders about its face, its—I could not see that it had limbs in its fluttering membranous folds. It seemed brown; but the membranes shaded off to greens, to—blues about its center and golds about its extremities. It rippled as it moved. There was a wholeness and power about it that—in all its horror—was symmetry.

I saw one of us gain his feet, sword in both his hands. It was Lance: I heard his voice calling after help even while he swung at it to drive it off. Its membranes fluttered with the cuts. I scrambled over bodies to gain my feet; I saw another of us closer, trying to help; but it came on, and on—just spread itself wider and gathered Lance in sword and all; and that other, who must be Gawain—it got him too, and it kept coming, at me. I couldn't find my spear; but of a sudden my feet met bare decking, the serpents all fled as the fleshy webs spread about me, all dusky now: more limbs/segments—I saw the floods glow like murky suns through the folds as it swept about me. I felt—horror—muscle within those folds, a solid center. I heard one of my friends cry out; I heard someone curse.

And it *spoke* to us—our Beast: it was nothing else but that. It rumbled deep within and moaned and ticked at us, a sound that quivered through my frame until it was beyond bearing. I yelled back at it—*I* screamed at it, till my throat hurt and my voice broke. I heard nothing. The sound pierced my teeth and marrow, too deep for hearing.

I hit the flooring on my back suddenly, which for all my life-support and padding hardly more than jolted me. The veil of its limbs swept on, the sound was gone, and it passed, leaving me lying amid the litter of our weapons. I flailed about getting over on my knees so that I could begin to get up. I heard Viv making a strange lost sound, but she was there. And my lady—"Lady Dela," I called, trying to reach her to help; but Lance was first, pulling her to her feet. A hand helped me, and steadied me, and that was Gawain. Percy—I looked about, and he was on his feet, with Lynette. I found my spear, or someone's, and gathered it up. Our Beast lumbered on, into the *Maid*'s open airlock, as all the rest had done, leaving us alone.

"Modred," Gawain cried, and he would have gone after, but Lance caught his arm. And Lynette:

"My lady," she said then, and pointed with her sword the way toward the machine, the way down the passage, that we had hoped to go.

And there amid the smokes stood another rank of giants, no less than the first.

Dela swayed on her feet. The weight we all carried seemed suddenly too much for her. "We've lost," she said. "Haven't we?" And slowly she turned toward us. I couldn't see her face: our faceplates only reflected each other, featureless. "Percivale," she said, "is the arm broken?"

"My lady," he said, "I think it is."

She was silent for a moment. "So we've nowhere to go."

She bent down. I thought she meant to sit down. But she picked up a spear from off the ground and stood up and faced toward the giants.

So did we all then. It was that simple. It occurred to me finally that my knees hurt and I was bruised and sore from that battering, when my heart had settled down, when the minutes wore on. One of us sat down, slow settling to the deck. We looked; and that was Viv, sitting there, but not blanked . . . "Vivien," my lady asked, "are you all right?"

"Yes, lady," Viv said, a small thin voice. She was with us.

She had her spear in both her hands. She was just never very strong, except in will. She wanted to live. She fought for that, perhaps. Perhaps it was something less noble. With Vivien I never knew.

But she was there.

It was a strange thing, that none of the rest of us sat down, when it was so much more reasonable to do. When giving up, I suppose, was reasonable. But getting up took so long a time, and we had seen how fast the enemy could move. Besides—besides, there was a sense in us that it was not a thing to do, facing this thing. My hands clenched tight about the spear and while I had no strength to go charging at them, I wished they would come on so that I could do something with this frustration that was boiling in me . . . in *me*, who could feel such a thing.

We should have the banner here, I thought. We should have the bright true colors, which was what we *were*, in this place of violet murk and white mist and glaring floods. It might be they would understand us then—what we meant, standing here. Maybe others besides humans used such symbols. Maybe it would only puzzle them. Or maybe they would think it a message where voices meant nothing at all, one side to the other.

But we had nothing. We had no faces to them; and they had none for us, standing like a wall of trees.

And silent.

"Ah!" Vivien cried, a sudden gasp of horror from behind us. I jerked about, nextmost to her—a serpent was among us, loping from out the lock. Vivien hurled herself aside from it, and I did, thoroughly startled; but as I turned to see it pass, Gawain hit it with his sword. It writhed aside and scuttled through with all its speed, evading Lance and my lady and Lynette, running as hard as it could go toward the cover of the machine and its waiting giant comrades.

"A messenger," Dela said. "We should have stopped it."

"My lady—" A faint voice, static-riddled.

"Modred," Dela exclaimed. "Modred, we hear you."

"It . . . inside . . . the tubes . . . I don't . . ."

"Modred?"

". . . broken through . . ."

"Modred."

". . . tried . . ."

And then static overwhelmed the voice.

"I think," said Lynette, "that's a suit com."

"Modred," Dela said, "keep talking."

But we got nothing but static back.

"If he's still near controls," Percy said, his voice very thin and strained, "he may be communicating with the other side."

I cast an encumbered look toward the line of giants, fearing *that* coming at our backs. "My lady," I said, "they're closer."

Others looked as I looked back; and then—"The lock!" Percy exclaimed.

It was back, our Beast. It filled the doorway, having to deflate some of its bladders to pass the door; and in leathery limbs like an animal's limbs it had something white clutched against it and buried in its membranes.

"Modred," Dela exclaimed in horror.

He looked dead, crushed and still. And the bladders inflated again, in all their murky shades of blue, taking him from view. But then the limbs unfolded and it squatted and let him to the decking, a sprawl of a white-suited figure out of that dreadful alien shape. It spoke to us, a loud rumbling that vibrated from the deck into our bones; and oh, what it was to be held inside it when it spoke, with the sound shaking brain and marrow. It stood over Modred, partly covering him with its membranes. It quivered and rumbled and wailed and ticked, and Lance came at it, not really an attack, but making it know he would. I moved, and the others did; and the giants were a shadow very close to us, coming at our side.

Then our Beast retreated, a flowing away from us toward the giants, a nodding, slow withdrawal, and rumbling and ticking all the while. A loping serpent, murky red, came out of the lock and ran along beside it as it went.

And Modred stirred, alive and making small motions toward getting up. "Oh, help him," I asked my friends, but I was closest besides Lance, and I bent and went down to one knee as best I could, so that Modred found my other knee and levered himself up. He touched his chest, got his com working, but his head was turned toward the Beast in its slow retreat toward the giants, who had stopped in their advance. I only heard Modred's breathing, that came in gasps. And somehow the hinder view of the Beast looked more humanlike in shadow, like a slump-shouldered giant shuffling away, its monster serpent looping along beside it like some fawning pet, ignored in its master's melancholy.

"It's the oldest," Modred said. "The captain of the core object . . . first here. Unique."

"You called it here," my lady said, accusing him. "You brought this on, all of it."

"No," Modred said. "It had to come. There were the tubes."

Sometimes Modred failed to make sense. And sometimes I feared I understood him after all.

"They took Griffin," Dela cried, with a sweep of her hand in the direction of the retreating Beast. "They took him away with them."

A lift of Modred's head. "I think I know where."

That struck my lady silent. I looked up, past her, past Lance, where this creature, this shuffling monster passed behind the giant ranks and disappeared. *They* stayed, beside the giant ram, indistinct in the fog they had made. But they came no nearer.

"The tubes," Modred said indistinctly. "They had to get us out of the way . . . the *Maid*'s filled with methane now, where they can carry the fight into the tubes themselves; but we're to follow the passage to the next sector. That's where they'll have taken him, most probably."

"Did they tell you that?" My lady's voice was still and careful, edged and hard. "Do you carry on dialogues, you and that thing?"

"It was in the map," Modred said.

A silence then. My heart hurt, from fear. From—I had no notion what. I was shivering. Maybe Modred was mad. Or maybe we had all lost ourselves in a dream, and we had forgotten what he was.

"He did the best he knew," I said for him. "He tried not to be Modred, lady Dela. He really tried. He did."

"Down the passage," Dela said then. "So we hand ourselves over to them?"

We thought about that.

"I'll go," Lance said quietly. "And come back again if I can."

"No," Dela said. "We'll all go.—Modred, can you walk?"

He pressed hard on my knee trying to get up. Gawain helped him, steadying him with an arm; and then Lynette had to help me, because I just hadn't the strength left to straighten my leg and lift the weight of my suit. She held me on my feet a moment until I had my breath and got my feet braced. What held Percy on his feet—he was not large or so strong as Lance—I had no idea. And Lynette helped Vivien up next.

"We can't go through that," Vivien protested, meaning the giants, who stood like a murky wall in front of us. Her voice shook. I took her hand that still held the spear and pressed her gloved fingers about the shaft, set the butt of it firmly on the decking.

I said nothing. With Viv that was usually safest. "Come on," Dela said, and so we went, all of us, with what strength we had.

XVII

Then from the dawn it seemed there came, but faint
As from beyond the limit of the world,
Like the last echo born of a great cry,
Sounds, as if some fair city were one voice
Around a king returning from his wars.

There was no suddenness in this encounter. The giants stood, and we—we came as best we could, at the little pace that the least of us could manage. Lance was first of us, strongest, and Vivien trailed last. Breath sounded loud in my ears, mine, my comrades', while the giants loomed closer still; and over us as we passed by the huge machinery, amid the smoke.

"Stay together," Dela said, because for that moment we couldn't see at all, except the white mist about us, with the glare of lights, and sometimes a shadow that might be one of us or the movement of some creature in ambush there.

A shape came clear to me, like a pillar in the murk and going up and up; and this was the leg of one of the giants, armored by nature or wearing some kind of suit different than ours. I shied from it and shied the other way at once, about to collide with another. I had lost my comrades. In the helmet I had no sense of direction. I plunged ahead the way that I thought I had been going, blind, among these monstrous shapes.

And they ignored us as we passed, never stirred, unless those vast heads looked down with slight curiosity and wondered what we were. We passed through the mist and I saw my lady and Lance and Lynette; looked back and I saw Gawain and Modred coming out from the mist; then another that was Vivien, by the size.

"Percy," I called.

"I'm here," he answered me, hoarse and faint. I saw one more of us clear the mist and follow, and I let Viv pass me, delayed to walk with Percy, not to lose him again.

"I'll make it," he said, but that was only to keep me happy: none of us knew where we were going or how far . . . except maybe Modred, who limped along in our midst.

And ahead of us stretched more and more of the passage, which bent gently rightward, and the way was dim, violet shadowed, once we were past the floods and the mist. "My lady," Lynette said from up ahead, "we could use the suit lights, but I don't think we should."

"No," Dela agreed, hard-breathing. "We don't need more attention than we have."

"They don't care," Modred said faintly. "They could have stopped us if they had."

No one answered. No one had Modred's confidence. And even his sounded shaken.

The shadows deepened. The way branched left, toward a vast sealed hatch; and right, toward more passageway. We walked toward that choice, saying nothing, only breathing in one breath, a unison of exhaustion, mine, my lady's, everyone's. Lance and Lynette stopped there, stood and looked back until we had come closer.

"Bear right," Modred said, between his breaths, and gestured toward the open passage.

"Go right," my lady said after a moment, and herself began to walk again. So we all did, getting our weighted bodies into reluctant motion. I saw Vivien falter; she used her spear like a staff now, to keep herself steady, and leaned on it and kept moving. We walked slower and slower through the murk.

Until the second door, that closed off the way ahead, another hatch vast as the first, everything on giant scale.

We caught up to one another, and Lynn turned on a light that she played over the huge machinery of the lock, but I saw no control, no panel, nothing in our reach.

Lance struck it a blow with his sword, frustration if nothing else.

And it shot apart, two sideways jaws gaping with a rumble that shook the deck under us, showing murky dark inside, a second steel door. My heart stopped and started again, faltering; my lady called on God; and someone had cried out. Then:

"Come on," my lady said, and the first of us went in. Vivien delayed, in front of Percivale and me. "Move, Viv," I said, and

Percivale just took Viv's arm in his good hand, and I took the other, so we kept up.

I knew that those doors would close again with us inside. They must. It was a lock. And they did, when we were barely across the threshold, a thunder at our heels, a shock that swayed us on our feet, and a machine-sound after, like pumps working. I flinched, and Viv jerked, but kept her feet.

Then the inner doors thundered back, and we blinked in brighter light, in light like sunshine, and an impression of green.

"Oh," my lady said, very quietly, and I shivered where I stood, because it was a world we faced, a land, an upward-curving horizon hazing into misty distances, with a vast central lake that disappeared in an overhead glare of lighting far above.

That was not all. Things moved here, from either side of us at once—tall creatures, gangling, clothed, some brown skinned and some azure-blue, some red-furred; and all armed, taking up a defensive line.

And they had Griffin with them—suitless, unrestrained.

"Griffin," my lady cried. And threw down her spear and went to him, trying all the while to rid herself of the helmet.

He knew her at once. There was none of us so small as she was; he flung his arms about her, and helped her with the helmet then, so we all knew it was safe.

The crew knew how; it took Gawain's help for my helmet and Lance's and Viv's. We stood there, having let our weapons fall, while my lady and master Griffin were lost in what they had to say to each other. We were drenched in sweat; even Viv was. My legs wanted to shake, the while we stood with our born-men forgetting us and so many strange creatures—a few were beautiful, but most were fierce—looking at us and wondering.

Dela shed her pack and dropped that with the helmet, and Griffin, who was dressed in clothes he must have gotten here—blue and green, they were, and not at all like ours—Griffin drew her over to a rocky place that thrust up out of the soil amid plants like vines that covered what must be decking under our feet. Among the rocks stranger growth had taken hold in soil heaped up about them. He gave her that mossy place to sit, and sat down himself, holding her gloved hands.

And Lance—he stood watching this, and finally gathered more courage than any of us, and walked up to them and knelt down there. So we all drifted closer. Griffin bent and hugged Lance against him, a great fierce hug that warmed us all and I think near broke Lance's heart.

"It's all right," Griffin said, looking worn and with tears running down his face. And to Modred: "You were right."

"Yes, sir," Modred said, in that way of his. "I knew I was."

We settled there, too tired to do more than that, and listened.

"I thought I was dead," Griffin said, "when they brought me through the doors and took the helmet off. But it's what you see here—I wanted to go back then and bring you here, but I couldn't make them understand. Or trust me if they did."

"They came through the ship," Dela said. "Modred saw."

"I think they went right on going," Modred said, "into the tubes, after what lives there. What that is, I had no chance to see. But they meant to stop it, and I think they have."

"We're safe," Griffin said, and took Dela's hand. "We can rest here. Like the others."

A creature came to us—one so pale and delicate it seemed more spirit than substance—and brought a flask of something clear and a bit of what could only be bread. It cheered us immeasurably, the more that it was pure water, clean and cold and food that spoke worlds of likeness between us and these. We were near and sibs to whatever creatures drank water and breathed this air; our skins could touch; our eyes could look at other eyes without a faceplate between. We smiled, we laughed, we cried, even we.

And then we shed the suits which were our last protection. For Percy, we gave him all the ease we could, binding up his arm, giving him what help we carried in our kits, so that he had relief from pain. And after, one by one, we settled down ourselves to sleep, absolutely undone. Griffin watched over us, his arms about our lady, who slept against him. And creatures watched us strange as any heraldic beasts of our dream, but wise-eyed and armed and patient.

We thought we should never see the *Maid* again . . . but after what might have been two days, they opened up that great lock and showed us through, suitless themselves, so we knew it was safe.

And we went where they guided us, to visit our damaged

home. They had sealed up the holes in the upper decks. It was all oxygen again.

But after some few days my lady missed the green wide expanses. So we came back to the huge lock bringing our baggage and whatever we could carry. And they opened for us——I think expected us, having come that way themselves.

It was not the last trip. They gave us stone, stones that like the soil were the fragments of wandering asteroids, and we understood, because there were all sorts of shelters if one wandered about the place. It was surely the strangest of human houses that we made, a simple place at first, a room for Griffin and my lady, with huge open windows, because the weather never varied and there was nothing there to fear. We carried the great dining table out when we had made another room, and set the banners there; there was the crystal and the fine plates. We dined together, and learned all manner of things grew here good to eat—of what source we only guessed, that some ships had brought plants in, some for food and some for air and more perhaps exotic things that were only beautiful.

And we became a wonder, having all kinds of visitors, some horrific and some very shy and beautiful. With some we learned to speak, or to make signs.

They came in a kind of respect. I think it was the banners, the bright brave colors, the shining crystal and the lovely things my lady Dela brought from the *Maid*. They took Griffin and my lady for very important, because we did; and because—in some strange fashion they loved the color we had brought.

So we settled there.

And lived.

Time . . . is different here. The Captain is very old . . . no one knows how old, perhaps not even he. But we don't age.

And we fight his war, whenever he has need: Griffin and Lancelot and Gawain and Lynn . . . they've gotten very wise, and the Captain calls on them when it's a question of some ship in our sector—because more come. Our voyage is forever, and while the builders round our rim seldom win a ship, they always try. Like with us. They're methane-breathers; a plague; a determined folk . . . oh, very dangerous; but our air would kill them, so it's only ships they try, ships and sometimes great and terrible battles in methane sectors of the wheel where they can break through. And once there was a great battle, where all of us were called who could go—in our suits, and armed with terrible weapons.

There might be such again. We know.

But the time passes, and we gather others, who come whenever Griffin calls.

And we . . . we come, at such time: Modred from his berth on the *Maid*, where he spends endless time in talking with all sorts of living things and devising new ideas; and Vivien keeps him company, making meticulous records and accounts.

Percivale has a place up in the heights of the curve. We see him least of all; but very old and wise creatures visit him to talk philosophy, and when he comes to visit us his voice is quiet and makes one very warm.

And Gawain and Lynette—they travel about the land, even into the strange passages that lead elsewhere, so of all of us they have seen most and come with the strangest tales to tell.

And Lance—

"I love them both," he said once and long ago. And so he left the hall where Dela and Griffin lived, first of all to leave.

And that was the worst pain of any I had ever had.

"Where's Lance?" my lady asked that next day; and I was afraid for him. I ran.

But Griffin found me, all the same, there back of the house, where I thought that I was hidden.

"Where's Lance?" he said.

"He went away," I said, just that. But Griffin had always had a way of looking through me.

"Why?"

"For love," I said, which was a word so strange for me to be saying I was terrified. But it was so. It was nothing else but that.

"He shouldn't be alone," Griffin said. "Elaine—can you find him?"

"Yes," I said.

And he: "Go where you have to go."

So it was not so much trouble to track one of us, when every creature everywhere knew us. And I found Lance sitting on the shore of that huge lake which lies central to our world . . . itself a strange place and full of thinking creatures.

"Elaine," he said.

"They sent me," I said to him. And he made a place for me beside him.

So we live, Lance and I, in a tower on that shore, a long time in the building, but of time we have no end.

And from one window we look out on that vast lake; and from the other we look toward our Camelot.

Whether we dream, still falling forever, or whether the dream has shaped itself about us, we love . . . at least we dream we do.

And whenever the call goes out, echoing clear and brazen through the air, we take up our arms again and go.

VOYAGER
IN NIGHT

This book was one of those odd experiments aside from my works of wider appeal. Don and I discussed the outcome of the story—often. We absolutely disagreed on what happened. I find that a wonderful, whimsical kind of situation. Both of us certainly read the same book—well, he edited it and I wrote it—but both of us saw a different story at the end and both of us believed in what we saw.

Think of this as the kind of science fiction some writer might create who lived (or will live) at some time in the next half millennium, after we've gone to the stars. And will we still write science fiction then? I see no reason we won't—Homer wrote science fiction, didn't he? So did Dante. And Jules Verne. So do we. Why shouldn't our descendants?

My job as a science fiction writer is only half about technology, the what-if and the what-next? Homer wrote about traveling beyond the rim of known seas, and meeting strange people. Dante used his science fiction writing for a political medium. Verne explored the future. And I've done a bit of each. But throughout all the meeting and the voyaging and the politicking and the imagining—I do the other thing those others did: I hold up a mirror to ourselves.

What would you do if you could live your life over—and over—and over?

What would you be if there were no end in sight?

Ever?

I

1,000,000 rise of terrene hominids
75,000 terrene ice age
35,000 hunter-gatherers
BC 9000 Jericho built
BC 3000 Sumer thriving
BC 1288 Reign of Rameses in Egypt
BC 753 founding of Rome

Trishanamarandu-kepta was, <>'s name, of shape subject to change and configurations of consciousness likewise mutable. But *Trishanamarandu-kepta* within-the-shell kept alert against the threat of subversive alterations, for some of the guests aboard were unreliable in disposition and in sanity.

Concerning <>'s own mental stability, <> was reasonably certain. <> had a longer perspective than most and consequently held a different view of events. The chronometers which might, after so many incidents and so frequent transits into jumpspace, be subject to creeping inaccuracies, reported that the voyage had lasted more than 100,000 subjective ship-years thus far. This agreed with <>'s memory. Aberrations in both records were possible, but <> thought otherwise.

AD 1066 Battle of Hastings
AD 1492 Columbus
AD 1790 early Machine Age
AD 1800 Napoleonic Wars
AD 1903 Kitty Hawk
AD 1969 man on the moon

<> never slept. Some of the minds aboard might have seized control, given that opportunity, so <> managed <>'s body constantly, sometimes at a high level of mental activity, sometimes at marginal awareness, but <> never quite slept. Closest analogue to dreamstate, <> felt a slight giddiness during jumpspace transits. That was to be expected in a mind, even after long and frequent experience of such passages. <> leapt interstellar distances with something like sensual pleasure in the experience, whether the feeling came from the unsettling of <>'s mind or <>'s physical substance. Fear, after all, was a potent sensation; and all sensations were precious after so long a span of life.

<> traveled, that was what <> did.

<> set <>'s sights on whatever star was next and pursued it.

AD 2300: discovery of FTL

AD 2354: The Treaty of Pell

       End of the Company Wars

       Founding of the Alliance

1/10/55: colonization of Gehenna

       Building of Endeavor

Another voyage began. Little *Lindy* moved up in the immense skeletal clutch of a Fargone loader into the cargo sling of the can-hauler *Rightwise*, while *Rightwise*'s lateral and terminal clamps moved slowly to fix *Lindy* in next to a canister of foodstuffs. She actually massed less than most of the constant-temp canisters *Rightwise* had slung under her belly, less than the chemicals and the manufacturing components destined for station use.

She was in fact nothing but a shell with engines, an unlovely, jerry-rigged construction; and the Lukowskis, the Viking-based merchanter family which owned *Rightwise*, having only moderate larceny in their hearts and a genuine spacers' sympathy for *Lindy*'s young owners, settled for the bonus Endeavor Station offered for the delivery of such ships and crews in lieu of *Lindy*'s freight, and took labor for the passage of the Murray-Gaineses themselves. *Rightwise* had muscle to spare, and *Lindy*'s bonus would clear two percent above the mass charge: the owners were desperate.

So *Rightwise* checked *Lindy*'s mass by Fargone records, double checked the dented, unshielded tanks that they were indeed empty for the haul, grappled her on and took her through jump to Endeavor—unlikely reprieve for that bit of scrap and spit which should long since have been sent to recycling.

AD 3/23/55

The Murrays and Paul Gaines arrived at Endeavor with the same hopes as the rest of the out-of-luck spacers incoming. Endeavor was a starstation in the process of building, sited in the current direction of Union expansion, in a rich (if unexportable) aggregation of ores. But trade would come, extending outward to new routes. Combines and companies would grow here. And the desperate and the ambitious flocked in. There were insystem haulers, freighted in on jumpships, among them a pair of moduled giant oreships, hauled in by half a dozen longhaulers in pieces, reassembled at Endeavor, of too great mass to have come in any other way. They were combine ships out of Viking, those two leviathans, and they collected the bulk of the advertised bonus for ships coming to Endeavor. There was a tanker from Cyteen; a freighter from Fargone, major ships—while most of the independent cold-haulers that labored the short station-belt run were far smaller, patched antiquities that gave Endeavor System the eerie ambiance of a hundred-year backstep in time. They were owned by their crews, those ancient craft, some family ships, most the association of non-kin who had gambled all their funds together on war surplus and ingenuity.

And smallest and least came ships like the Murray-Gaineses' *Lindy*, an aged pusher-ship once designed for nothing more complex than boosting or slowing down a construction span or sweeping debris from Fargone Station's peripheries, half a hundred years ago. They had blistered her small hull with longterm life-support. A human form jutted out of her portside like a decoration: an EVA-pod made of an old suit. Storage compartments bulged outward at odd angles almost as fanciful as the pod. Tanks were likewise jury-rigged on the ventral surface, and a skein of hazardously exposed conduits led to the war-salvage main engine and the chancy directionals.

No established station would have allowed *Lindy* registry even before the alterations. She had been scheduled for junk at Fargone, and so had many of her parts, taken individually. But at Endeavor *Lindy* was no worse than others of her size. She was rigged for light prospecting in those several rings of ore-laden rock which belted Endeavor System, feeding the refiner-oreships, which would send their recovered materials in girder-form and bulk to Station, where belt ores and ice became structure, decks, machine parts and solar cells, fuel and oxygen. *Lindy* would haul only between belt and oreship, taking the richest small bits in her sling, tagging any larger finds for abler ships on a one-tenth split. She even had an advantage in her size: she could go gnat-like into stretches of the belt no larger ship would risk and, supplied by those larger ships, attach limpets to boost a worthwhile prize within reach: *that* kind of risk was negotiable.

And if she broke down in Endeavor's belt and killed her crew, well, that was the chance the Murray-Gaineses took, like all the rest who gambled on a future at Endeavor, on the hope of piling up credits in the station's bank faster than they needed to consume them, credits and stock which would increase in worth as the station grew, which was how marginal operators like the Murray Gaineses hoped to get a lease on a safer ship and link into some forming Endeavor combine.

There was Endeavor Station: that was the first step. *Rightwise* let go the clamps; the Murray-Gaineses sweated through the unpowered docking and the checkout, enjoyed one modest round of drinks at the cheapest of Endeavor Station's four cheap bars, and opened their station account in Endeavor's cubbyhole of a docking office, red-eyed and exhausted and anxious to pay off *Rightwise* and get *Lindy* clear and away before they accumulated any additional dock charge.

So they applied for their papers and local number, paid their freight and registered their ship forthwith with hardly more formality than a clerical stamp, because *Lindy* was so ridiculously small there was no question of illicit weaponry or criminal record. She became *STARSTATION ENDEAVOR INSYSTEM SHIP 243 Lindy*, attached to SSEIS 1, the oreship/smelter *Ajax*. She had a home.

And the Murrays and Paul Gaines, free and clear of debt, went off arm in arm to *Lindy*'s obscure berth just under the maindawn limit which would have logged them a second day's dock charge. They boarded and settled into that cramped interior, ran their checks of the charging that the station had done in their absence, and put her out under her own power without further ado, headed for Endeavor's belt.

For a little while they had an aftward single G, in the acceleration which boosted them to their passage velocity; but after that small push they went inertial and null, in which condition they would live and work three to six months at a stretch.

They had bought three bottles of Downer wine for their stores. Those were for their first tour's completion. They expected success. They were high on the anticipation of it. Rafe Murray, his sister Jillan, merchanter brats; Paul Gaines, of Fargone's deepminers, unlikely friendship, war-flotsam that they were. But there was no doubt in them, no division, when playmates had grown up and married: and Rafe was well content. "It's tight quarters," Jillan had said to her brother when they talked about Endeavor and their partnership. "It's a long time out there, Rafe; it's going to be real long; and real lonely."

Paul Gaines had said much the same, in the way Paul could, because he and Rafe were close as brothers. "So, well," Rafe had answered, "I'll turn my back."

They called Rafe, half-joking, half-not, their Old Man, at twenty-two. That meant captain, on a larger ship. And they *were* his. Jillan planned on children in a merchanter-woman's way. They were life, and she could get them, with any man; but, unmerchanter-like, she married Paul, for good, for permanent, not to lose him, and snared him in their dream. Their children would be Murrays; would grow up to the Name that the War had robbed of a ship and almost killed out entire . . . and he dreamed with desperate fervor, did Rafe Murray, of holding Murray offspring in his arms, of a ship filled with youngsters—being himself a merchanter-man and incapable of pregnancy, which was how, after all, children got on ships: merchanter-women made them, and merchanter-women got his and took them to other ships which did not need them half so desperately.

He had had his partnerings with the women of *Rightwise* and bade all that good-bye—"Go sleepover," Paul had advised him on Endeavor dock. "Do you good."

"Money," he had said, meaning they could not spare the cost of a room, or the time. "Had my time on *Rightwise*. That's enough. I'm tired."

Paul had just looked at him, with pity in his eyes.

"What do you want?" he had answered then. "Had it last night. Three *Rightwisers*. Wore me out." And Jillan walked up just then, so there was no more argument.

"We'll have a ship," Rafe had sworn to Jillan once, when they were nine and eight., and their mother and their uncle died, last of old freighter *Lindy*'s crew, both at once, in Fargone's belt. Getting to deep space again had been *their* dream; it was all the legacy they left, except a pair of silver crew-pins and a Name without a ship.

So Rafe held Jillan by him—*Don't leave me, don't go stationer on me. You take your men; give me kids—give me that, and I'll give you—all I've got, all I'll ever have.*

Don't you leave me, Jillan had said back, equally dogged. *You be the Old Man, that's what you'll be. Don't you leave me and go forget your name. Don't you do that, ever.* And she worked with him and sweated and lived poor to bank every credit that came their way.

Most, she got him Paul Gaines, lured a miner-orphan to work with them, to risk his neck, to throw his money into it, Paul's station-share, every credit they three could gain by work from scrubbing deck to serving hire-on crew to miners when they could get a berth.

Having children waited. Waited for the ship.

And Endeavor and a dilapidated pusher-ship were the purchase of all they had.

Rafe took first watch. He caught a reflection on the leftmost screen of Jillan and Paul in their sleeping web behind his chair, fallen asleep despite their attempt to keep him company, singing and joking. They had been quite a handful of minutes and there they drifted, collapsed together, like times the three of them had hidden to sleep, three kids on Fargone, making a ship out of a shipping canister, all tucked up in the dark and secret inside, dreaming they were exploring and that stars and infinity surrounded their little shell.

3/23/55

Mass.

<> came fully alert, feeling that certain tug at <>'s substance which meant something large disturbing the continuum.

Trishanamarandu-kepta could have overjumped the hazard, of course, adjusting course in mid-jump with the facility of vast power and a sentience which treated the mindcrippling between of jumps like some strange ocean which <> swam with native skill. But curiosity was the rule of <>'s existence. <> skipped *down,* if such a term had relevance, an insouciant hairbreadth from disaster.

It was a bit of debris, a lump of congealed material which to the questing eye of *Trishanamarandu-kepta* appeared as a blackness, a disruption, a point of great mass.

It was a failed star, an overambitious planet, a wanderer in the wide dark which had given up almost all its heat to the void and meant nothing any longer but a pockmark in spacetime.

It was a bit of the history of this region, telling <> something of the formational past. It was nothing remarkable in itself. The remarkable time for it had long since passed, the violent death of some far greater star hereabouts. *That* would have been a sight.

<> journeyed, pursuing that thread of thought with some pleasure, charted the point of mass in <>'s indelible memory in the process.

The inevitable babble of curiosity had begun among the passengers. <>'s wakings were of interest to them. <> answered them curtly and leaped out into the deep again, heading simply to the next star, as <> did, having both eternity *and* jump capacity at <>'s disposal.

There was no hurry. There was nowhere in particular to go; and everywhere, of course. <> was now awake, lazily considering galactic motion and the likely center of that ancient supernova.

Such star-deaths begat descendants.

II

The Downer wine was opened, nullstopped and passed hand to hand in celebration. Music poured from *Lindy*'s comsystem. There was food in the freezer, water in the tanks, and a start to the fortunes of the Murray-Gaineses, a respectable number of credits logged on the orehauler *Ajax*, from what they had delivered and a share of what others had brought in with their beeper tags. They were bathed, shaved and fresh-scented from a docking and sleepover on *Ajax*. Even *Lindy* herself had a mint-new antiseptic tang to her air from the purging she had gotten during the hours of her stay.

"None of them," Jillan said, drifting free, "none of them believed we could have come in filled that fast. No savvy at all, these so-named miners."

"Baths," Paul Gaines murmured, and took the wine in both hands for his turn, smug bliss on his square face when he had drunk. "We're civilized again."

"Drink to that," Rafe agreed. "Here's to the next load. How long's it going to take us?"

"Under two months," Jillan proposed. "Thirty tags and a full sling."

"We can do it." Rafe was extravagant. He felt a surge of warmth, thinking on an *Ajax* woman who had opened her cabin to him in his onship time. He was feeling at ease with everything and everyone. He gave a quirk of a smile at Jillan and Paul, whose privacy was one of the storage pods when they were down on supplies, but they were full stocked now, with solid credit to their account, stock bought in Endeavor itself. "Someday," he said, "when we're very old we can tell this to our kids and they won't believe it."

"Drink to someday," Paul said, hugging Jillan with one arm, the bottle in the other. The motion started a drift and spin. Rafe snagged the bottle from Paul's hand as they passed, laughing at them as the hug became a tumble, the two of them lost in each other and not needing that bottle in the least.

I love them, Rafe thought with an unaccustomed pang, with tears in his eyes he had no shame for. His sister and his best friend. His whole life was neatly knitted up together; and maybe next year they could build old *Lindy* a little larger. Jillan could look to family-getting then, lie up on *Ajax* for the first baby; be with them thereafter—close quarters, but merchanter youngsters learned touch and not-touch, scramble and take-hold before they were steady on their feet.

And even for himself—for his own comfort—Endeavor was a haven for the orphaned, the displaced of the War, people like themselves, taking a last-ditch chance. There might be some woman someday, somehow, willing to take the kind of risk they posed.

Someone rare, like Paul.

"Drink up," Jillan insisted, drifting down with Paul. The embrace opened . . . a little frown had crossed Jillan's face at the sight of his; and Paul's expression mirrored the same concern. For that, for a thousand, thousand things, he loved them.

He grinned, and drank, and sent their bottle their way.

Trishanamarandu-kepta was in pursuit of delicate reckonings, had chased plottings round and round and busily gathered data in observation of the region. <> might have missed the ship entirely otherwise.

<> detected it in the Between, a meeting of which the ship might or might not be aware. It was small and slow, a bare ripple of presence.

It too was a consequence of that ancient stardeath . . . or came here because of it. Weak as it seemed, it might well use mass like that which <> had recently visited as an anchor, a navigation fix when the distance between stars was too great for it. <> diverted <>'s self from <>'s previous heading and followed the ship, eager and intent, coming *down* at another such pockmark in the continuum, where <>'s small quarry had surfaced and paused.

(!), <> sent at once, in pulses along the whole range of <>'s transmitters. *(!!!) (!!!!!)* It was an ancient pattern, useful where there was no possibility of linguistic similarity and no reasonable guarantee of a similar range of perceptions. <> waited for response on any wavelength.

Waited.

Waited.

Even delays in response were informational. This might be recovery time, for senses severely disorganized by jumpspace. Some species were particularly affected by the experience. It might be slow consideration of the pulse message. The length of time to decide on reply, the manner of answer, whether echo or addition, whether linear or pyramidal . . . species varied in their apprehension of the question.

The small ship remained some time at residual velocity, though headed toward the hazard of the dark mass by which it steered. Presumably it was aware of the danger of its course.

<> remained wary, having seen many variations on such meetings, some proceeding to sudden attack; some to approach; some to headlong flight; some even to suicide, which might be what was in progress as a result of that unchecked velocity.

Or possibly, remotely, the ship had suffered some malfunction. <> retained corresponding velocity and kept the same interval, confident in <>'s own agility and wondering whether the ship under observation could still escape.

<> observed, which was <>'s only present interest.

The little ship suddenly flicked out again into jump. <> followed, ignoring the babble from the passengers, which had been building and now broke into chaos.

Quiet, <> wished them all, afire with the passion of a new interest in existence.

The pursuit came *down* again as <> had hoped, at a star teeming with activity on a broad range of wavelengths.

Life.

A whole spacefaring civilization.

It was like rain after ages-long drought; repletion after famine.

<> stretched, enlivened capacities dormant for centuries, power like a great silent shout going through <>'s body.

Withdraw, some of the passengers wished <>. *You'll get us all killed.*

There was humor in that. <> laughed. <> could, after <>'s fashion.

Attack, others raved, that being their natures.

Hush, <> said. *Just watch.*

We trusted you, <^> mourned.

<> ignored all the voices and stayed on course.

1/12/56

The intruder and its quarry went unnoticed for a time in Endeavor Station Central. Boards still showed clear. The trouble at the instant of its arrival was still a long, lightbound way out.

Ships closer to that arrival point picked up the situation and started relaying the signal as they moved in panic.

Three hours after arrival, Central longscan picked up a blip just above the ecliptic and beeped, routinely calling a human operator's attention to that seldom active screen, which might register an arrival once or twice a month.

But not headed into central system plane, where no incoming ship belonged, vectored at jumpship velocities toward the precise area of the belt that was worked by Endeavor miners. Comp plotted a colored fan of possible courses, and someone swore, with feeling.

A second beep an instant later froze the several techs in their seats; and *"Lord!"* a scan tech breathed, because that second blip was *close* to the first one.

"Check your pickup," the supervisor said, walking near that station in the general murmur of dismay.

That had nearly been collision out there three lightbound hours ago. The odds against two unscheduled merchanters coinciding in Endeavor's vast untrafficked space, illegally in system plane, were out of all reason.

"Tandem jump?" the tech wondered, pushing buttons to reset.

Tandem jumping was a military maneuver. It required hairbreadth accuracy. No merchanter risked it as routine.

"Pirate," a second tech surmised, which they were all thinking by now. There were still war troubles left, from the bad days. "Mazianni, maybe."

The supervisor hesitated from one foot to the other, wiped his face. The stationmaster was offshift, asleep. It was hours into maindark. The supervisor was alterday chief, second highest on the station. The red-alert button was in front of him on the board, unused for all of Endeavor's existence.

". . . it's *behind* us," he heard next, the merchanter frequency, from out in the range. "Endeavor Station, do you read, do you read? This is merchanter *John Liles* out of Viking. We've met a bogey out there . . . it's dragged us off mark . . . Met . . ."

Another signal was incoming. (!) (!!!) (!!!!!)

". . . out there at Charlie Point," the transmission from *John Liles* went on. An echo had started, *John Liles*' message relayed ship to ship from every prospector and orehauler in the system. Everyone's ears were pricked. *Bogey* was a nightmare word, a bad joke, a thing which happened to jumpspace pilots who were due for a long, long rest. But there *were* two images on scan, and a signal was incoming which made no sense. At that moment Endeavor Station seemed twice as far from the rest of mankind and twice as lonely as before.

". . . It signaled us out there and we jumped on with no proper trank. Got sick kids aboard, people shaken up. We're afraid to dump velocity; we may need what we've got. Station, get us help out here. It keeps signaling us. It's solid. We got a vid image and it's not one of ours, do you copy? *Not one of ours or anybody's.* What are we supposed to *do*, Endeavor Station?"

Everywhere that message had reached, all along the time sequence of that incoming message, ships reacted, shorthaulers and orehaulers and prospectors changing course, exchanging a babble of intership communication as they aimed for eventual refuge out of the line of events. What interval incoming jumpships could cross in mere seconds, the insystem haulers plotted in days and weeks and months: they had no hope in speed, but in their turn-tail signal of noncombatancy.

In station central, the supervisor roused out the stationmaster by intercom. The thready voice from *John Liles* went on and on, the speaker having tried to jam all the information he could into all the time he had, a little under three hours ago. Longscan techs in Endeavor Central were taking the hours-old course of the incoming vessels and making projections on the master screen, lines colored by degree of probability, along with reckonings of present position and courses of all the ships and objects everywhere in the system. Longscan was supposed to work because human logic and human body/human stress capacities were calculable, given original position, velocity, situation, ship class, and heading.

But one of those ships out there was another matter.

And *John Liles* was not dumping velocity, was hurtling in toward the station on the tightest possible bend, the exact tightness of which had to do with how that ship was rigged inside, and what its capacity, load, and capabilities were. Computers were hunting such details frantically as longscan demanded data. The projections were cone-shaped flares of color, as yet unrefined. Com was ordering some small prospectors to head their ships nadir at once because they lay within those cones.

But those longscan projections suddenly revised themselves into a second hindcast, that those miners had started moving nadir on their own initiative the moment they picked up *John Liles'* distress call the better part of three hours ago. Data began to confirm that hypothesis, communication coming in from *SSEIS I Ajax*, which was now a fraction nadir of original projection.

Lindy had run early in those three hours, such as *Lindy* could . . . dumped the sling and spent all she had, trying to gather velocity. Rafe plotted frantically, trying to hold a line which used the inertia they had and still would not take them into the collision hazard of the deep belt if they had to overspend. Jillan ran counterchecks on the figures and Paul was set at com, keeping a steady flow of *John Liles'* transmission.

If *Lindy* overspent and had nothing left for braking, if they survived the belt, there were three ships which might match them and snag them down before they passed out of the system and died adrift . . . if they did not hit a rock their weak directionals could not avoid . . . if the station itself survived what was coming in at them. They could all die here. Everyone. There were two military ships at Endeavor Station and *Lindy* had no hope of help from them: the military's priority in this situation was not to come after some minuscule dying miner, but to run, warning other stars so Paul said, who had served in Fargone militia, and they had no doubt of it. It was a question of priorities, and *Lindy* was no one's priority but their own.

"How are we doing?" Rafe asked his sister, who had her eyes on other readouts. The curves were all but touching on the comp screen, one promising them collision, and one offering escape.

"Got a chance," Jillan said, "if that merchanter gives us just a hair."

Paul was transmitting, calmly, advising *John Liles* they were in its path. On the E-channel, *Lindy*'s, autowarning screamed collision alert: the wave of that message should have reached *John Liles* by now.

"Rafe," Jillan said, "recommend you take all the margin. Now."

"Right." Rafe asked no questions, having too much input from the boards to do anything but take it as he was told. He squeezed out the last safety margin they had before overspending, shut down on the mark, watching the computer replot the curves. In one ear, Paul was quietly, rationally advising *John Liles* that they were ten minutes from impact; in the other ear came the com flow from *John Liles* itself, babble which still pleaded with station, wanting help, advising station that they were innocent of provocation toward the bogey. "Instruction," *John Liles* begged again and again, ignoring communications from others. It was a tape playing. Possibly their medical emergency or their attention to the bogey behind them took all their wits.

"Come *on*," Rafe muttered, flashing their docking floods in the distress code, into the diminishing interval of their light-speed message impacting the 3/4 C time-frame of *John Liles*' Doppler receivers. He was not panicked. They were all too busy for panic. The calculations flashed tighter and tighter.

"We've got to destruct," Paul said at last in a thin, strained voice. "Three of us—a thousand on that ship—O God, we've got to do it—"

Sudden static disrupted all their scan and com, blinding them. *"She's dumping,"* Jillan yelled. *John Liles* had cycled in the generation vanes, shedding velocity in pulses. They were getting the wash, like a storm passing, with a flaring of every alarm in the ship. It dissipated. *"We're all right,"* Paul yelled prematurely. In the next instant scan cleared and showed them a vast shape coming dead on. Rafe froze, braced, frail human reaction against what impact was coming at them at a mind-bending 1/10 C.

It dumped speed again, another storm of blackout. Rafe moved, trembled in the wake of it, fired directionals to correct a yaw that had added itself to their motion. Scan cleared again.

"Clear that," Rafe said. "Scan's fouled." The blip showed itself larger than *Ajax*, large as infant Endeavor Station itself.

"No," Paul said. *"Rafe, that's not the merchanter."*

"Vid," Rafe said. Paul was already flicking switches. The camera swept, a blur of stars, onscreen. It targeted, swung back, locked.

The ship in view was like nothing human-built, a disc cradled in a frame warted with bubbles of no sensible geometry, in massive extrusions on frame and disc like some bizarre cratering from within. The generation vanes, if that was what those projections were, stretched about it in a tangle of webbing as if some mad spider had been at work, veiling that toadish lump in gossamer. Lightnings flickered multicolor in the webs, and reflected off the warted body, a repeated sequence of pulses.

It had exited C and actually gone negative, so that their relative speeds were a narrowing slow drift.

"Twenty meters-second," Jillan read the difference. "Plus ten, plus five-five, plus five-seven K."

There were no maneuvering options. *Lindy* was already at the edge of her safety reserve, and a ship which could shift course and stop like that—could overhaul them with the merest twitch of an effort. Rafe flexed his fingers on the main throttle and let it go.

"Maybe it's curious," Jillan said under her breath. *"Liles* never said it fired."

"Got their signal," Paul said, and punched it in for both of them . . . *(!) (!!!) (!!!!!)*.

"Echo it," Rafe said. They were still getting signal from *John Liles*, a screen now Dopplered in retreat, echoed from other ships. Station might be aware by now that something was amiss; but there was still the lagtime of reply to go. As yet there was only *Ajax* sending out her longscan and her frantic instruction to *John Liles*.

Lindy, on her own, facing Leviathan, sent out a tentative pulse.

(!) (!!!) (!!!!!)

Scan beeped, instant at their interval. "Bogey's moving," Jillan said in a still, calm voice. It was. "Cut the signal," Rafe said at once; and on inspiration: "Reverse the sequence and send."

(!!!!!), Paul sent. *(!!!) (!)*

No. Negative. Reverse. Keep away from us.

The bogey kept coming, but slower, feather-soft for something of its power, as if it drifted. "10.2 meters-second," Jillan read off. "Steady."

"It could shed us like dust if it wanted to," Paul said. "It's being careful."

"So we ride it out," Rafe said. A hand closed on his arm, Jillan's. He never took his eyes from the screens and instruments. Neither did she.

The bogey filled all their vid now, monstrous and flashing with strange lights, a sudden and rapid flare.

"It's braking," Jillan said. "4 . . 3 . . . relative stop."

"Station," Paul sent, "this is *SSEIS 243 Lindy*, with the bogey in full sight. It's looking us over. We're transmitting vid; all ships relay."

There was no chance of reply from station, a long timeline away. *"Relaying,"* a human ship broke in, someone calling dangerous attention to themselves by that sole and human comfort.

"Thank you," Paul said, and kept the vid going, still sending.

The surface of the bogey had detail now. The warts were complex and overlapping, the smallest of the extrusions as large as *Lindy* herself. The camera swept the intruder, finding no marking, no sign of any identifiable structure which might be scanning them in turn.

Suddenly scan and vid broke up.

And space did.

III

Capture.
    Trishanamarandu-kepta reached for the mote with <>'s jump field.
    <> left the star, dragging the captured mote along.

Rafe had time to feel it happening. He screamed—a long, outraged *"No!"*—at the utter stupidity of dying, perhaps; at everything he lost. His voice wound strangely material through the chaos of the between, entwined with the substance and the terrified voices of Jillan and Paul. He was still screaming when the jump came, the giddy insideout pulse into *here* and *when*, falling unchecked out of infinity into substance that could be harmed. He reached out, groping wildly after controls as the instruments flashed alarm. Orientation was gone. They were moving, his body persuaded him, though he felt no G. He pushed autopilot: red lights flared at him, a bloody haze of lights and blur.

Lindy's autopilot kicked in, and it was wrong . . . he felt it, the beginning of a roll, a braking insufficient for their velocity. The wobble *Lindy* had always had with the directionals betrayed her now. He tried to shut it down, while G was whipping blood to his head, rupturing vessels in his nose, a coppery taste at one with the bloody lights and the screams.

Paul and Jillan.

"Jillan!"

Paul's voice.

Tumble went on and on. Instruments broke up again, and another motion complicated the spin: autopilot malfunction. They had been dragged through jump, boosted to velocity a good part of C, and *Lindy* was helpless, uninstrumented for this kind of speed. Every move the autopilot made was wrong, complicating *Lindy*'s motion.

He fought to get his hand to the board, to do something, a long red tunnel narrowing black edges between him and the lights.

Someone screamed his name. His eyes were pressing at their sockets and his brain at his skull, his gut crawling up his rib cage to press his lungs and heart and spew its contents in a choking flood that might be hemorrhage. The tunnel narrowed and the pressure acquired a rhythm in his ears. Vision went in bursts of gray and red, and mind tumbled after.

<> maneuvered carefully to secure the ship: field seized it, stabilized it from its spinning, snugged it close. Getting it inside once stable was no problem at all.

Getting inside *it* . . . was another matter altogether.

Kill it, some advised.

</> moved to do that. <> blocked that attempt with brutal force. An extensor probe drifted along a track and reached down, punched through the hull with very precise laser bursts and bled off an atmosphere sample from the innermost cavity.

Nitrogen, argon, carbon dioxide, oxygen . . . *Trishanamarandu-kepta* had no internal atmosphere. <> started acquiring one, here and in other sections.

<> had no need of gravity; but <> began to acquire it, basing calculations on the diameter and rotation of the structure back at the star.

<> extended other probes and surveyed the small ship's hull, locating the major access.

The interior was, once <> had gotten a probe inside to see, messy. The occupants, stained with red fluids, stirred only feebly, and more and more extensors cooperated in freeing the occupants from their restraints, in moving them outside, while other extensors intruded into every portion of the diminutive ship, testing the instrumentation, sampling the consumables. <> flurried through incoming data in a general way, relating that and what it discovered in the tiny ship's computers, simple mathematical instruments adequate only for the most basic operations.

The subjects offered resistance, though weakly, at being containered and moved a great and rapid distance through *Trishana-marandu-kepta*'s twisting interior. One was very active: it thrashed about at intervals, losing strength and smearing the transparent case with red fluids at every outburst, which indicated rapidly diminishing returns, whether this motion was voluntary or not. It screamed intermittently, and whether this was communication remained to be judged.

It screamed a very long scream when it was positioned in the apparatus and the recorder came on and played through its nervous system. So did the other two. Most vocal organisms would.

Each collapsed after the initial spasm. Vital signs continued in a series of wild fluctuations which seemed to indicate profound shock. <> maintained them within the recorder-field and realigned them with the hologrammatic impression <> had taken.

<> took cell samples, fluid samples, analyzed the physical structures from the whole to the microscopic and chemical while the entities remained conscious. <> was careful, well aware that some of the procedures might cause pain. <> reduced what wild response <> could, elicited occasional murmurings from the subjects. <> recorded those sounds and played them back; played back all response it had ever gotten from this species, here and from the other ship and from the star system in general.

The subjects responded. Sympathetically, on both recorded words and answers, the holo images <> had constructed . . . reacted.

<> used lights and sounds and other stimuli, and mapped reflexes in the hologrammatic brains, obtaining sensory reactions from the imprints along the appropriate pathways. <> discovered what seemed to be a rest state and maintained the organisms close to sleep, yet able to react and speak, prolonging this interrogation in words and sensations.

The two weakest sank deeper, refusing when prodded to come out of this state, eventually deteriorating so that it required more and more stimulus to keep them functioning. At last decomposition set in.

The third subject remained in sleep-state. <> questioned it further and it reacted in dazed compliance.

The simulacra still reacted . . . all three of them.

The surviving organism fell into deeper and deeper sleep and <> let it rest.

<> further examined the remains of the other two, analyzed them in their failure, finally committed them to cryostorage.

<> wasted nothing that <> took in.

Rafe moved, and knew that he moved. He felt no pain. His limbs seemed adrift in void, and when he opened his eyes he thought that he was blind.

"Jillan!" he cried, struggling to stand, reaching out with his hands. "Paul, Jillan!"

"Rafe—!" Jillan's voice came back; and she was there, coming toward him in the starless void. Paul followed. They were naked, both; so was he; and their bodies glowed like lamps in the utter dark, as if they were their own light, and all the light there was. They began to run toward him, and he ran, caught Jillan in his arms, and Paul, ashamed for his nakedness and theirs and not caring, not caring anything but to hug their warmth against him. He felt the texture of their skin, their hands on him, their arms about him.

He wept, shamelessly. There was a great deal of tears, that first, that most important and human thing. "You're here," Jillan kept saying; "you're all right, we've got you, oh Rafe, we've got you—hold on."

—Because the fainting-feeling was on him, and they all three seemed to drift, to whirl, to travel in this dark. There were sounds, far wails, like wind. Something brushed past them through the dark, vast and impersonal, like the whisper of a draft.

"Where have we got to?" Paul wondered, and Rafe looked at Paul and looked at Jillan as they stood disengaged, in this dark nowhere.

"I don't know," he said, ashamed for his helplessness to tell them. *I'm scared.* He kept that behind his teeth. He looked about him, into nothing at all, and kept remembering jump, and the sinuous wave of arms.

"There was something—" Jillan said, her teeth chattering. "Oh God, God—" She stood there, shivering in her nakedness, and Paul hugged her against him. "Don't," he said, "don't. Don't think, don't—"

"We're through jump," Rafe said as firmly as he could, filling the void, the dark about them all with words to listen to, making them fix on him. "There was that bogey; it's got us. Remember? That's where we are. It's got us in the dark, and we can't come undone, you hear me, both of you. Let's think our way out of this. It's kept us alive and together. That's something, isn't it?"

They said nothing. Their faces were dreadful, full of shadows within their glowing flesh.

"Why no light?" Jillan asked.

"Maybe they don't have eyes," Paul said.

She looked at her glowing hands, at him, at Paul, with a whole dreadful range of surmises in that glance.

"It's some kind of effect," Rafe said, searching for any plausible thing, "some light trick. That's all."

"Sure," said Paul, attempting cheerfulness, "sure. Who knows what kind of thing." But his voice was thin. He walked a little distance away and distances themselves played tricks, so that he became small rapidly, as if he strode meters at a time. "Come back," Rafe said, and Paul turned, looking small and frightened.

"God, what is this place?"

"I'm cold," Jillan said, hugging herself; but the air was not cold at all; it was nothing. It was the nakedness that diminished all of them, that made them vulnerable, the dark that made them blind.

"Look," Rafe said, "let's not go off crazy. We can't ask questions. You have to know something to ask questions and we don't. We've got no referents. We're just alive, that's all—" *They hurt us,* his memory insisted, and he fought that down. "Nothing matters but now and facts, and facts we're short of. Calm down."

"What do we do?" Jillan asked.

"We stay close together," he said, "and we try not to lose each other. Let's try to find a wall, a door, somewhere in this place." He took her hand and walked to Paul in those curious several-meter steps that were the law here, while Paul stared at them with nightmare in his eyes that showed dark as the dark about them. "We're having trouble with our senses," Rafe said to them both, and even his voice seemed lost in void. "Maybe it isn't even dark. Jump can do things to you. We weren't tranked."

"You mean we're crazy," Paul said. "All three of us at once. Or do I imagine you? Or you us? Or what?"

"I'm saying our eyes aren't working right."

"What about the floor?" Paul said, sinking to one knee, touching what felt like air underfoot. "I don't feel anything. I don't feel *anything!* I don't even feel my breathing. Like it isn't air."

"We'll come out of it," Jillan said, and drew Paul to his feet.

"Paul, we'll make it. Rafe's right; it's the jump; it's done something to us. We're not getting sense out of it."

"Between?" Paul asked, blinking as if he had just thought of that. "You mean we're still in hyperspace? Could that be it?"

"Maybe," Rafe said, clinging to that hope.

"O God," Paul murmured, shaking his head, and looked up and about again—hopeless to ask how long, how far, where there was no reference. "That makes sense."

Then light began to grow about them, white and green. It took on shadows of shapes.

It became a nightmare, bits and pieces of *Lindy* rooted in a noded, serpentine hallway fuzzed in gossamer like spiderweb over carpet. There stood the seats, part of the control console, the EVA-pod standing at attention like some humanoid monster grown from the wall at an angle. A row of luminants snaked like a chain of warts down the center of the noded ceiling, giving what light there was.

And Rafe saw himself lying there naked on the floor.

"That's *you*," Jillan moaned. "Rafe, what's happening to us?"

The lights went dim again. Rafe strode forward, desperate, recalling how the dying saw their bodies from some other vantage. He felt the cold, felt a vast love of that poor wounded flesh that was himself, wanting it back again.

"Rafe!" Jillan called, and the horror dawned on him, that they were dead, that Jillan and Paul were bodiless, and he almost was. *"Rafe!"*

The dark closed about him and he fought it, trying to get back to the light. He felt their hands like claws, clutching at him to drag him back to death with them.

"Let me go," he cried, "let me go!"—cursing their selfishness.

Rafe moved, and knew that he moved. He felt other things, pain, and chill, and G holding him supine against a cloth surface. He opened his eyes and kept them open, on a graygreen arched ceiling of warts and white fuzz, like what his fingers and body felt under him, soft and rough like carpet. He felt a draft on all his skin so that he knew he was naked. His heart started speeding, his mind sorting. *"Jillan—Jillan, Paul?"* He rolled over, wincing from torn muscles, from a sudden lancing pain from eyes to the back of his skull.

Dim distance, warts and cobwebby stuff snaked on and on as far as he could see, graygreen to white in an irregular corridor, lumpish and winding as if the place abhorred a straight line.

He scrambled to his knees, trembling, and stopped cold. His blurred eyes fixed on nightmare. Bits and pieces of *Lindy* were rooted in the tunnel, the seats, part of the control console, the EVApod standing there like some humanoid monster rising out of the warted, gossamer wall at an angle. The sanitary compartment stood intact, enveloped in graygreen moss and cobweb above and below. The storage cabinets thrust up from the floor like angled teeth.

He pressed his hands to his face and rubbed his eyes, felt days-old stubble on his jaw. He staggered erect, his muscles gone weak from those lost days. The corridor went on and on in that direction too, beyond the point where *Lindy*'s parts gave out, mossy and cobwebbed, all lit from luminous warts in the ceiling, irregularly placed, a line of lights winding with the serpentine turns.

"Jillan," he called aloud. "Paul?" His voice was terrible in that stillness. He turned, looked all about him, down two ways of the corridor equally desolate and strange and vanishing into turns and dark.

"Jillan," he shouted suddenly, desperate. "Jillan, Paul, do you hear me?"

Silence.

He searched for other sleepers, staggered among the nightmare remnants of *Lindy* until there were no more, and he faced only the warted corridor ahead. He went back and opened all the doors of the cabinets and the cases, even looked into the dark faceplate of the EVApod, fearing what he might find.

All empty. There were *Lindy*'s stores, food, supplies, clothing in the lockers . . . his, Paul's, Jillan's, all as it ought to be. He looked up in the panicked imagination of someone watching him. Nothing. No indication of any living soul.

He took clothes from his locker, dressed painfully, pulling seams past sore joints. He found his watch, his soft-soled boots, his tags . . . the pin that was from the old, the first *Lindy*, that had been his uncle's. He sat down on the floor and put on the boots and the rest of it. His hands shook. His heart was doubling its beats. He went through mundane motions in this insane place and tried to go on functioning while flashes of memory came back, disjointed. He remembered the surface of the alien vessel and saw the same architecture everywhere about him. He had no doubt where he was. He remembered jumpspace . . . and no trank; remembered (he had thought) dying—

And worse things. Far worse than the nightmare of *Lindy*'s dissected portions at his side. Arms. Arms snaking into the ship. Machinery. Pain.

Pain.

"Jillan . . . Paul . . . " He staggered up, hesitated between forward and back, the two ways from this place being alike. *"Who are you?"* he screamed at the ceiling.

There was no answer.

He walked the direction his mind sorted as *ahead*, treading around the hummocks of the floor. The wall evolved to white instead of graygreen; he touched it, but it felt like the other had felt . . . gossamer silk to a light touch, but rough to a harder one, like cobweb over stiff carpet, resisting compaction. The walls went on in alternate color changes, areas of graygreen, areas of white, all warted and noded and twisting and cobwebbed, and he tried to think what manner of inhabitant might call this home.

They were across jump: that memory was solid. Other recollections came, of confinement like a coffin; of pain running through all his nerves at once, of pain so intense it was sight and hearing and being burned alive and clawed apart from inside; of pain that still ached through joints and bone and made his muscles shake. All the voices of the other ships had rung in his skull at once, over and over; Jillan's voice and Paul's voice and the voice of *John Liles* all wound together, pleading for help and rescue.

They had been in this place with him. He remembered them screaming, amid the pain. Remembered Paul's voice calling his name.

There was no knowing where they had been brought, how far, how long. The intruder had simply dragged them off in its field, off into the dark, as if Endeavor star had been the firelight and this beast had just bounded into the light to snatch a victim . . . to take it where it could do what it liked, at its leisure. There was no hope of help. They could be taken apart piece by piece and the whole procedure transmitted to Endeavor on vid, and there was nothing Endeavor could do about it. There was nothing here, not even human sympathy.

"Jillan," he called from time to time. It grew harder and harder to challenge that silence, which was greater and deeper than any he had known in his stationbound, shipbound life. He felt a pulse somewhere too deep for proper hearing, the working of some constant machinery . . . but no sound of fans, no ping of heating and cooling or sound of hydraulics. No feeling of being on a ship under acceleration. Just more and more corridor, cobwebbed, warted silence.

His knees grew weak in walking. He thought that it might be shock catching up to him. He realized he had no idea where he was going or why, and that his walking itself was reasonless. He sat down to rest and dropped his head into his arms.

The lights went out.

He sprang up in alarm, facing what light remained, far down the corridor. He went for the lighted section, stumbling over the nodes, hurrying until his ribs hurt—and those lights went out as he reached them as lights further on flared into life.

He understood the game then, that he was watched, that it/they wanted him to come—to them, to something. He moved helplessly toward the light that beckoned, afraid of dark and blindness in this place. They threatened to shut him off from his primary sense and he reacted in animal instinct, knowing what they were doing to him and how simply; and hoping somewhere at gut level that doing what they wanted might bring him to where Jillan and Paul were. He ran, even hurting, slowed only as his strength gave out and he fell farther and farther behind the lights until they stayed on at the limit of his sight, in one fixed sector, beyond which was unremedied dark. He reached that place as the lights dimmed and moved on into vastness where the walls were walls and were farther and farther apart.

Sweat chilled his face. What had been a limp became a stagger. He tended more and more toward the right-hand wall as the left-hand one strayed off into black, as the whole corridor opened into the likeness of a vast cavern, one with low knobbed points to the ceiling like a cavern of warts, whose farther reaches were wrapped in deepening shadow.

A sudden bright light speared from the ceiling in front of him. He flung an arm across his eyes. "Who are you?" he asked the light and the darkness, irrational as cursing: there had been no answers and he expected none.

"I don't know," a voice came back to him, and *he* was standing there, a naked man at one heartbeat strange and then—like recognizing a mirror where one had expected none—altogether familiar. He was staring at himself, at what might have been a mirror in its expression of shock and fear—he knew that look, was startled when it lifted a hand he had not lifted and opposed itself to him.

"Damn you," he cried to the invisible, the manipulater. *"Damn you,* use your own shape!"

"I am," the doppelganger said. Tears glistened in his/its eyes. "O God, don't—don't look like that. Help me. I don't know where I am."

"Liar," he told himself.

"Rafe." The voice drifted from the lips, his own, uncertain and lost and vague. "Please. Listen to me. You're awake. I'm you. I think I am. I don't know. Please—" The doppelganger walked, sat down above a node, not quite phasing with it. It tucked its bare knees up, locked its arms about them, looked up at him with eyes full of shadow, as if the image were breaking down. "Please sit and talk with me."

He watched his own face shape words. The lips trembled, quirks in the chin that he knew and felt in his own gut, as if it were himself fighting tears, fighting for his dignity. It hurt to watch. He was trembling as if the tears were his, and they began to be. "Where's Jillan? Where's Paul? Can you tell me that?"

"Sit down. Please, sit down."

He found a place and sat, hugged his knees up until he realized he had taken the mirror pose, clothed version and naked one. His gut heaved, and he swallowed hard. "What's your name?" he asked.

"Rafe. You have to call me something. I'm you. Or something like. I can see you—there. I guess you can see me. Do I look like you?"

"Where's Jillan and Paul? The people with me—where are they?"

"They're—" The doppelganger pointed off toward the dark outside the light. "They're somewhere about. Not speaking to me. Please—let me try to explain this. I don't know where their bodies are. I found you. Me. Lying there. I thought—you know, the way you can see yourself—they say you can see yourself when you die. You float up near the ceiling and look down and see yourself lying there, and you can hear, and you don't want to go back—But I wanted to. I tried. Jillan and Paul—they're like me. They're with me. I think they are."

"You're talking nonsense." He hugged himself, trying not to shiver, but the thought kept circling him that it was not an alien in front of him. He wanted it to be. He wanted it to change into something else, anything else. "Evaporate, why don't you?"

"Please." The doppelganger seemed to shiver. Tears ran down its face. "I think I might. I don't know. Maybe I'm you, a part of you, and we got separated somehow."

"Maybe I'm dreaming this."

"Or I am. But I don't think so. There's this dark place. I come and go out of it and I don't know how. You walk and you cover so much ground you can get lost. Maybe you can lose yourself and not get back. I'm afraid that's what's happened to Jillan and Paul. I think they're off looking—looking for their own selves. Like you. They're not taking this well. I'm scared. Please don't look like that."

"God, what do you expect me to look like?"

"I know. I know. I feel it like we were still connected when you look like that."

"You read my mind. Is that it? You're the alien. You just pick up on what I think, what I'd think—"

"Don't." The doppelganger shook its head, wiped a fist across its mouth in an expression which was his own. "Don't do that. I know I'm not. I know. I wouldn't choose to feel like this if I had a choice. I don't remember being anything else. I was born at Fargone; Jillan's my sister; our kin all died—"

"Cut it!"

"It's all I know. It's all I know, and—Rafe—I remember the jump, remember this place we were in—"

He remembered too, the terror, the waving arms, the pain, the ungodly pain. . . .

"I woke up in the dark," the doppelganger said. "And they were with me, Jillan was, and Paul. And somehow I found you. You were lying on the floor. I tried to get to you. I thought—I thought we were dying then. That I had to get back."

"I don't know why I'm talking to you." Rafe put his head down, ran his hand through his hair, looked up again in the earnest hope the apparition would have gone. It had not. It stared at him, a mirror image of despair.

"I'm afraid," it said. "O God, I'm scared."

"Where are they?"

"I don't know."

He drew a deep breath and got to his feet, came closer and saw the image lose its coherency at close range. "I can see through you."

"Can you?"

"You're an image. That's all you are." He kept walking till the image lost all its coherency and he moved into it. He saw it projected around his outstretched hand. "Fake!"

"But I'm here," the voice persisted, forlorn, with an edge of panic. "Don't. Don't do that. Back off. Please back off."

He swept his arm about as if that could scatter it, like vapor. "You're *nothing*, hear?"

There was no answer. The image reconstituted itself a little way away, naked and frightened looking. Tears still glistened on its face.

"I think," it said, "I think—somehow they made me. I don't know how. While you were asleep. O God, hold onto me. Please hold onto me."

"How?" The terror in the voice was real. It hurt him, so that at once he wanted to deal it hurt and heal it. "I can't touch you. You're not *here*, do you hear me? Wherever you are, it's not here."

"I think—think they made me out of you. Up to—I don't know how long ago—we have the same memories, because I was you." The doppelganger folded his hands over his nakedness, wistful, lost-looking, in a dreadful calm. "I'm really scared. But I guess I haven't got title to be. All I am—I guess—is you."

"Look—" he said to himself, hurting for himself, feeling half mad. "Look, where are you? Can you tell that?"

"Here. Just here. There's that other place. But it's only dark. I don't want to go back there."

"I think—I think they've made some kind of android."

"I might be."

"The Jillan and Paul with you—they're like you?"

"I don't know."

"What do you mean you don't know? Bring them here."

"I don't know how to look."

"Liar." He flung his arm at the doppelganger, somewhere between hate and pity. "Go try."

"It's dark out there."

He wanted to laugh, to curse, to weep. He did none of them, feeling a shaking in his knees, a mounting terror. He had never liked dark confined spaces. Crawlways, like Fargone mines. "Go on," he said. "Come back when you know something."

And that too was mad.

"Will you—" his double asked, in a faint thin voice, "will you find something to call me—so I have a name?"

"Name yourself."

"*You* name me," the other said, and sent chills up his spine.

"Rafe," Rafe said. He could not commit that ultimate robbery. "That's what you are, isn't it?"

The shoulders straightened, the head came up, touching a chord in him, as if he had discovered courage in himself he had never seen. "That's what I am," the doppelganger said. "Brother."

And it walked away.

What it had said chilled him, that it had said a thing he had not dreamed to say.

He sat down where he was, locked his arms over his head, thinking that he might have witnesses.

He looked up when he had got his breath back.

"If you've built that thing," he said to the walls, able to think of it as *thing* when he was not staring at it face to face, "you've got some way to interpret it. Haven't you? You understand? Why are you doing this?"

There was no answer. He sat there until the strength had returned to his legs and then he began carefully to retrace his way back to the small horror that was his, the place stocked with food that he could use.

Habitat, he thought. *As if I were an animal.* He nursed hope, all the same, that if he had come through it, if the pain was done, then their captors were only being careful. It did not guarantee that they were benign. There were darknesses in his mind that refused to come into the light, the memory of the ship that had done what no ship ought to do; of pain—but they might have been ignorant, or in a hurry to save them.

So he built up his hope. The lights came on ahead of him, at an easy pace. He went, looking over his shoulder from time to time, and quickly forward, fearing ambushes.

He remembered the bogey's size, like the starstation itself. Hurling that into jump took more power than any engine had a right to use; and for the rest, for technology that could tear a mind apart and reconstitute it inside an android—that was the stuff of suppositions and what-ifs, spacers' yarns and books. No one did such things.

No one jumped a station-sized mass. By the laws he knew, nothing could, that did not conform to the conditions of a black hole. And it did it from virtual standstill.

He did not run when he had home in sight; he restrained himself, but his knees were shaking.

He sat down when he had gotten there, in the chair before the disjointed console, in the insane debris of *Lindy*'s corpse, and bowed his head onto his arms, because it ached.

Ached as if something were rent away from him.

He wiped his eyes and idly flipped a switch, jumped when a screen flared to life and gave him star-view.

He tried the controls, and there was nothing.

Com, he thought, and spun the chair about flipping switches, opening a channel, hoping it went somewhere. "Hello," he said to it, to whatever was listening. "Hello—hello."

"Aaaiiiiiiiiiiieeeeeeee!"

"Damn." he yelled back at it, reaction; and trembled after he had cut it off.

He went on, shaking, trying not to think at all, putting himself through insane routine of instrument checkout, as if he were still on *Lindy*'s bridge and not managing her pieces in this madness.

Com was connected to something—what, he had no wish to know. Vid gave him starfield, but he had no referent. The computer still worked, at least in areas the board had not lost. The lights still worked; one of the fans did, insanely; their tapes were still there, but the music would break his heart.

He slumped over finally and hid the sight of it from his eyes, suspecting worse ahead. It played games with him. He already knew that they were cruel.

IV

There was the dark, forever the void, and Rafe moved in it, calling sometimes—"Jillan, Paul—" but no one answered.

He should have been cold, he thought; but he had no more sense of the air about him than he had of the floor underfoot.

He turned in different directions, in which he found himself making slower and slower progress, as if he walked against a wind and then found himself facing (he thought) entirely a different direction than before.

"Aaaiiiiiiiii!" something howled at him, went rushing past with a glow and a wail like nothing he had ever heard, and he scrambled back, braced for an attack.

It went away, just sped off insanely howling into the dark, and he sank down and crouched there in his nakedness, protecting himself in the only way he had, which was simply to hug his knees close and sit and tremble, totally blind except for the view of his own limbs.

"Jillan," he whispered to the void, terrified of making any noise, any sound that would bring the howler back. His own gold-glowing flesh seemed all too conspicuous, beacon to any predator.

Android. He reminded himself what he was, that he could not be harmed; but his memories insisted he was Rafe Murray. It was all he knew how to be. And he knew now that they were not alone in this dark place.

At last he got himself to his feet and moved again, no longer sure in what direction he had been going, no longer sure but what the darkness concealed traps ahead, or that he was not being stalked behind.

"Jillan," he called aloud. "Paul."

Had that been one of the aliens—that passing, mindless wail, or some other victim fleeing God-knew-what ahead?

What is this place?

They were androids. That was what they were, what he had

been when he had met his living body—met Rafe. Something had projected him into that green-noded corridor.

But then, he reasoned, Rafe ought to have been a projection sent in turn to him, and he had not been. Viewpoint troubled him, how he had seen through hologrammatic eyes. How that Rafe had thrust his hand into the heart of him and cursed him—*Evaporate, why don't you?*

Why not? a small voice said. *If I'm an android they can make me what they like. Can't they?*

Maybe they have.

Fake, that other Rafe had said, screaming at him his outrage at self-robbery.

That Rafe Murray had the scars, the bruises, the pain that proved his title to flesh and life.

Where are we? Where are Jillan and Paul? What will they do to us? What have they done already and what am I?

"Jillan," he screamed with all his force. "Paul! Answer me! *Answer me . . .*" with the terror that he would never find them, that they had been taken away to some final disposition, and that it would take him soon, questions all unanswered.

Why did they make us?

He feared truths, that whoever had made him could throw some switch and bring him somewhere else, back where they had made him, back to that place with the machinery and the blood; perhaps would unmake him then. He feared death—that it was still possible for him.

"Aaaaaaaaaaaauiiiii!" Another thing passed him, roaring like some machine out of control, and he stopped, stood trembling until it had faded into the distance.

"Stop playing games with me," he said quietly, trusting of a sudden that something heard him better than it would hear that other, living Rafe. *"Do you hear me? I'm not impressed."*

Could it speak any human tongue? Had it learned, was it learning now?

"Damn you," he said conversationally, shrugged and kept walking, pretending indifference inside and out. But the cold that was not truly in the air had lodged beneath the heart. *God,* he appealed to the invisible—he was Catholic, at least the Murrays had always been; but God—God was for something that had the attributes of life.

Rafe One had God; he had Them. It. Whatever had made him. It might flip a switch, speak a word, reach into him and turn him inside out for a joke. That was power enough.

"Jillan!" he yelled, angry—He could still feel rage, proving—proving what? he wondered. The contradictions multiplied into howling panic. *"Jillan!"*

"Rafe?"

He turned, no more anywhere than before, in the all-encompassing dark. He saw a light coming to him, that wafted as if a wind blew it. It was Paul, and Jillan came running in his wake.

"Rafe," Jillan cried, and met him and hugged him, warm, naked flesh that reminded him flesh existed here—*synthetic?* he remembered. Paul hugged him too; and his mind went hurtling back to that howling thing in the dark, remembering that here it would be palpable and true, He shivered in their arms.

"There are *things* in here," Jillan said.

"I know, I know. I heard them," he said, holding her, being held, until the shivers went away.

"Don't go off from us again," Paul said. "Dammit, Rafe, we could get lost in here."

He broke into laughter, sobbed instead. He touched Jillan's earnest, offended face and saw her fear. "Did you find what you were looking for?"

"Dark, "Jillan said. "Just dark. No way out."

"I met someone," he said to them, and let the words sink in, watching their faces as the sense of it got through. "I *met* someone."

"Who?" Jillan asked, carefully, ever so carefully, as if she feared his mind had gone.

"Myself. The body that we saw. There in the corridor. He wants to talk to you."

"You mean you went back," said Paul.

"I talked to him."

"Him?"

"Myself. He's alive, you understand that? I met him—face to face. Jillan—" he said, for she began to turn to Paul. "Jillan—we're not—not the real ones. They've made us. The memories, our bodies—We're not real."

There was devastated silence.

"If we could get back," said Paul.

"It's not a question of getting back," Rafe said, catching at Paul's arm. *"Paul, we're constructs."*

"You're out of your mind."

Rafe laughed, a sickly, sorrowful mirth. "Yes," he said. "Out of his. The way you came out of Paul's; and Jillan's out of her. Constructs, hear? Androids. Robots. Our senses—aren't reliable. We got only what the ones who made us want. God knows where we really are."

"Stop, it!" Jillan cried, shaking at his arms. "Rafe, stop it, you hear me?"

He seized her and hugged her close, felt her trembling—Could an android grieve? But it was Jillan's grief, Jillan's terror. His sister's. Paul's. It was unbearable, this pain; and like the other it did not look to stop.

"Rafe," Paul said, and pulling him away into his arms, pressed his head against his shoulder and tried to soothe him as if he had gone stark mad. There was the smell of their flesh, cool and human in this sterility; the touch of their hands; the texture of their hair—Real, his senses told him. Someone was playing with their minds; that was the answer. *That's why Rafe's solid to me and I'm not that way to him.*

"Please," he said, pushing away from them. "Come with me. Let me take you to him. Talk with him."

"We've got to get out of here." Jillan's eyes had all space and void in their depths. "Rafe, pull yourself together. Don't go off like this. They're tricks. They're all just tricks. They're working on our minds, that's what's happening. That's why none of this makes sense."

"Get out of it, how, Jillan? We came through jump. *Lindy's* in pieces, back there in that hall."

"It's illusion. They want us to think it is. They're lying, you understand?"

"Jump wasn't a lie."

"We've got to do something to get out of here."

"Jillan—" He wanted to believe her. He wanted it with all his mind. But he suspected a dreadful thing, staring into her eyes. He suspected a whole spectrum of dreadful truths, and did not know how to tell her. "Jillan," he said as gently as he could. "Jillan, he wants to talk to you and Paul, he wants it very much."

"There is no *he*!" Paul shouted.

"Then come with me and prove it."

"There's no proving it. There's no proving anything about an illusion, except you put your hand into it and it isn't there."

"He did that to me. Put his hand through me. I wasn't there."

"You're talking crazy," Paul said.

"All you have to do is come with me. Talk to him."

"It's one of them. That's what it is."

"Maybe it is," Rafe said. He felt cold, as if a wind had blown over his soul. "But prove it to me. I'll do anything you want if you can prove it to me. Come and make me believe it. I want to believe you're right."

"Rafe," Jillan said.

"Come with me," he said, and when they seemed disposed to refuse: "Where else can we find anything out for sure?"

"All right," Jillan said, though Paul muttered otherwise. "All right. I'm coming. Come on, Paul."

She took his hand. Paul came up on his other side. He turned back the way he had come, as near he could remember, walking with two-meter strides, not knowing even if he could find that place again. But the moment he started to move it began to be about him again, the light, the noded, green-gossamer corridor, *Lindy*'s wreckage like flotsam on a reef.

And the other Rafe, the living one, sat on the floor against the wall. That Rafe looked up in startlement and scrambled stiffly to his feet, wincing with the pain.

"Rafe," Rafe said, for it had been a long and lonely time, how long he did not know, only he had had time to meddle uselessly with the console, to shave and wash, and sleep. And now the doppelganger was back, in the shadows where his image showed best, naked as before.

And on either side of him arrived Jillan and Paul, naked, pitiful in their fear.

At least their images—whose eyes rested on him in horror, and warned him by that of their fragility. He could not hurt them. His own doppelganger—that was himself, but Jillan and Paul drove a wedge into his heart. "He found you," he said to them, patient of cruel illusion, of anything that gave him their likenesses, even if it mocked him in the gift.

"What *are* you?" Jillan said, driving the dagger deeper. There was panic in her voice.

"Don't be afraid," Rafe said. But Paul went out—*out*, like the extinguishing of a light, and Jillan backed away, shaking her head at his offered hand.

"No," she said. "No." And fled, raced ghostlike through the wall.

His own doppelganger still stood there, naked, hands empty at his sides, with anguish in his eyes.

"I tried," the doppelganger said with a motion of his hand. "I tried. Rafe—they'll come back. Sooner or later they'll have to come back. There's nowhere else to go."

Rafe sank down where he stood, where a node made a sitting-place against the wall. He ached in every bone and muscle, and looked up at the doppelganger in unadulterated misery.

"Rafe," the doppelganger said. "I think they're dead. You understand me? They haven't found anything of themselves. I'm not sure there's anything left to find."

Rafe shut his eyes, willing it all away; but the doppelganger had come closer when he opened them. It knelt in front of him, waiting, his own face projecting grief and sympathy back at him.

"You understand?" the doppelganger said. "They're copies. That's all I found. They're like me."

He wanted to scream at it to go away, to be silent, but a strange self-courtesy held him still to listen, to sit calmly with his hands on his knees and stare into his own face, knowing the doppelganger's pain, knowing it to the height and depth, what it cost and how it hurt. *Jillan dead. And Paul.* He had known it in his heart for hours, that this place, this graveyard caricature of *Lindy* had all the important pieces in it. The console. The EVA-pod. Himself. All the working salvage that was left. "Do they know?" he asked, half insane himself.

"I can't tell." The image remained kneeling there. "On the one hand they could be right; they thought—they thought this was illusion. Maybe it is. But it was too strong a one for them."

"It's not illusion."

"I don't think so either."

"God, this is mad!"

"I know. I know it is. But I think you're right. We split—I

remember all this pain. I remember—these arms waving about. It hurt, I never remember any pain like that—"

"Cut it out.!"

"I think—that was where they died."

"Shut up!"

That Rafe tucked up his knees, rested his forehead on his arms—grief incarnate, mirror of his own, mirror until it hurt to look at himself, knowing what he felt, seeing it mimed in front of him. Rafe Two lifted his head at last, stared at him with ineffable bleakness, and he began to shiver himself in long slow tremors.

"Cry," the soft voice came to him. "I did, awhile, for what it's worth. I cried a lot. But it can't change what is. Don't you think I want to believe you're not real? That we're all of us all right? I wish I could believe that. You wish you could get rid of me. But you can't. And we aren't."

"Damn you!" He leaped up, ran to the console, seized on the first thing he could find and flung it at the doppelganger. It was one of his music tapes, which passed through the image and hit the wall, falling harmless as the curse; and the doppelganger just sat there, breathing, doing everything it should not. Its breath came hard, one long heave of its naked shoulders, its head bowed as if it fought for self-control. It mastered itself, better than he; or having fewer options. It was resignation that looked back at him with his own face, out of bruised and weary eyes, and he could not bear that defeat. He sank down at the console and gasped for air that seemed too thin, with thoughts that seemed too rarified to hold without suffocating. Things swirled about him: *Dead, dead, dead—*

Die too, why can't you?

He did not cry. Sitting there, he shivered until his muscles ached and cramped, until lack of air brought him to bow his head on the console.

"He's real," he heard his own voice say; and Jillan's then: "No," so that he opened his eyes and found them standing there, all of them, his dead, his living self—

"O God," he said, "God, Jillan, Paul—don't go, don't go this time." He levered himself up, unsteady on his feet, offered them his hand, even knowing they could not touch it. "Stay here. Don't run."

His doppelganger walked to him, stood close by him, ghostly thin, standing where he stood in parodied embrace. There was no sensation from it, only a confusion of image, as if it had superimposed itself deliberately.

"Don't go," it echoed him. "Don't you see—we're the illusion. Projected here. We're androids. That's all we are. Made out of him, his mind, Jillan's, Paul's. We're the shadows. He's the real one."

They stood there, the two of them, staring at him. "It doesn't make sense," Jillan said in a small voice. "Rafe—we can't be dead. Can we?"

Rafe himself sank down to his knees on the gossamer-covered carpet, squeezed his eyes shut and shook his head to clear it of all the accumulated lunacy.

"I think," said the other Rafe, standing over him, about him, a moving pale shimmer—"I think it's very likely, if we can't find the bodies. I think you are."

"Then what are we?" Paul yelled.

"Androids," said Rafe Two. "Something like that, at least. They made us. And the originals are gone." He walked over near the console, touched the edges of the seats with insubstantial fingers. "We never rigged *Lindy* for much stress."

"Something that they made," Jillan said. "is that what you're saying?"

"Yes," Rafe said, himself, looking up at her from where he knelt. She was still in every particular his sister, that look, that quiet steady sense. It shattered him. "Yes. Something that they made."

She stared in his direction a moment, then shrugged and laughed, taking a step away. "I don't *feel* dead." A second step, so that she began to fade out at the wall. "I'm going out of focus, aren't I?" Soberly, with horror beneath the surface. "It's a pretty good copy. Aren't I?"

"Stop it!" Paul said.

"Jillan's right," Rafe Two said, by the EVApod. "It was the seats, understand? We never rigged for more than two or three G at most. We got a lot more than that. It flung us off. Remember? Autopilot went crazy. My fault, maybe. But I couldn't stop us. Nothing could, our tanks depleted—Couldn't if we'd had *Lindy* at max. *Lindy* couldn't cope with it."

"We're not dead," Paul said.

"Whatever we are," Rafe Two said, folding his insubstantial arms, "I guess we don't have that problem. Not anymore we don't."

"We aren't dead!"

"Let be," Rafe said, hating his own tendencies to push a thing. Paul hated to be pushed.

"We're us-prime," Jillan said. "That's what we are." She came and squatted near him, looking at him closely for the first time, her hands clasped together on her knees, her knees drawn up. "I wish you could lend me a blanket, brother."

"I wish I could," he said. "Are you cold?" That she should be cold seemed to him the last, unbearably cruelty.

She shook her head. "Just the indignity of the thing. I tell you, when we meet what did this to us, when we meet them, I'll sure insist on my clothes back."

"I'll insist on more than that," he said.

"You've already met it!" Paul shouted, over by the wall. "*That's* Rafe—the one like us! Ask it where we are. Ask it what kind of jokes it likes to play, what it's up to, where it came from, what it wants from us!"

"I'm alive," Rafe said.

"He's the one that bleeds," said his doppelganger, from close by. "Look at his face. He's the one that survived the wreck. Not a mark on any of the rest of us—is there?" Rafe Two squatted down nearby, elbows on his knees. "At least," he said to Jillan's wraith, "you've got title to a name. Rafe and I—we aren't the same anymore, not quite. We split. He's been alone and I've been chasing you, and on that reckoning we get less and less in step, while you—you *are* his sister, much as mine; you took up where the other left off—permanently. And so did you, Paul. That's why it seems to you you're still alive. But I can tell myself apart from him. I'm Rafe who found that one lying unconscious on the floor; and he's the one who met himself face to face awake. Different perspectives. Dead's meaningless to you. You're not that Jillan Murray; you're her hypothesis, you're what she would have done—being met with that place where we woke up. You're not that Paul Gaines. You're just living your present on his memories—the way I split off from his, and did things different than he did."

Paul came slowly away from the wall, stood there and shook his head. "I won't give in to this. You're wrong."

"At least," Rafe said, "sit down. Sit down. Please."

"It's dark out there," said Paul, as if it were a matter of petulant complaint.

"Rafe said," Rafe answered him. "Stay here. Please."

Paul came and joined them, farthest away, crouched on the floor and plucked disinterestedly at a shred of gossamer he failed even to touch.

"We're interested in the same things, aren't we?" Rafe said. "We're still partners. We need to find out where we are. And I love you," he added, because it was so, and he had not said it often enough. He remembered what he was talking to, but it was as close as he could come. "I do love you two. . . ."—To convince himself, he thought.

"I know," Jillan said. Her eyes were dreadful, as if they saw too much. "I know that, Rafe."

"Nothing for me," said Rafe Two, who sat by him mirrorlike, arms about naked knees. "You see what it is to be surplus? Better to be dead. At least there's appreciation."

"Shut it up," Rafe said. "I always had a bad sense of timing. I won't put up with it from you."

"Stop it!" Paul said.

"It's like being schizophrenic," Rafe said, looking at the floor, pulling with his fingers at another loose bit of gossamer that refused to tear. "It's really strong, this stuff."

"What are we going to do?" Jillan asked.

"I don't see any profit in sitting still," Paul said. "Do you?"

"What do you suggest? It—they—whatever—whatever, runs this place knows where *we* are. When it gets bored, it'll find us."

Paul glared at him.

"I don't want to sit here," Jillan said.

"There's the corridors," said Rafe Two. "We could try to go as far as we can. As far as we can stay with each other."

"We could try that," Rafe said.

The outsiders moved slowly down the corridor which had been allotted to them and there was, immediately, throughout the ship, a focusing, of attention.

"They're a hazard," [] said. [] had tried them once, but <>

had interfered in no uncertain terms and [] kept respectful distance.

"Let them go," said <^>. <^> was constantly disposed to gentleness. It was part of <^>'s madness, forgetting <^>'s heredity.

But </> ranged all about the perimeters, gathering others of </>'s disposition: there were many such aboard. There were two or three fiercer, but none more devious, except maybe the segments of = <–> = = <+> = that grew longer with every cannibalistic acquisition. = <–> = = <+> lg = had fifteen other segments, currently at liberty, and it was a question where these were or what the whole matrix thought, breaking apart and sending segments of itself everywhere in search of information.

</> laughed to </>self, loving chaos, seeing opportunity.

Trishanamarandu-kepta devoted only a part of <> 's mind to this maneuvering. There were other things to occupy <>'s mind, a wealth of things the little ship had given up, records, names.

Of the simulacra themselves, three templates existed, which were deliberately dissociated in fragments.

From those templates <> integrated three temporary copies.

Rafe waked, aware of nakedness, of dark, of Paul and Jillan close beside him.

He wept, recalling pain, got to his knees and shook at Jillan's bare shoulder. "Jillan," he said.

The eyes opened, fixed. Jillan began to tremble, to convulse in spasms, to scream long tearing screams.

"Jillan!" Rafe yelled, trying to hold her. Paul was awake too, trying to restrain her and evade her blows.

These were temporary copies, easily erased, and served as comparison against which <>'s own symbol systems could be examined.

<> tried one on. It proved difficult, and retreated into gibberish; <> shut it down.

There remained Rafe and Jillan. The one called Rafe seemed the easiest of entry. The most stable seemed Jillan, and <> shut Rafe-mind down for the moment, to consider Jillan's, which bent and flexed and made defensive mazes of its workings—giving way quickly and then proving vastly resilient.

*   *   *

"Rafe," Jillan cried as they waked together in this dark place, and Rafe stared at her, leaning backward on his arms, seeming unable to do more than shiver. "There was—" he said, started to say, and cried out and fell back.

"Rafe!" she cried, and shook at him, but he was loose as if someone had broken him, and then he went away, just vanished, as if he had never been.

"Rafe!" she screamed at the vacant air, at the ceiling, and the dark. *"Paul!"* She scrambled up and threatened the invisible with empty hands and great violence.

It would fight, this Jillan-mind. <> learned that. The passengers who hovered near to witness this were profoundly disturbed.

"<> is taking risks again," </> whispered in far recesses of the ship. "One day <> will miscalculate. Remember = = = = before = = = = turned cannibal? <> did not foresee that either."

<> ignored these whispers, being occupied with <>'s insertion into the Jillan-mind.

Who are you? Jillan-mind asked <>. She wept; she fought the intrusions and when she no longer could do that she took in the flood with the peculiar strength she had and started trying to bend it to her shape.

She looked at </>, which had come to hover near, and bent <>'s thoughts to notice the observer in the dark.

"I don't trust that one," she declared, and <> laughed for startlement, in the rest of <>'s mind, which went on seeing things from outside, and managing <>'s body, and doing the other things <> did in the normal course of <>'s existence.

Then <> moved in Jillan-mind abruptly and without gentleness. <> brushed aside defenses and began to take what <> wanted. Jillan screamed at <> in anger and in pain and finally, because <> filled all the pathways of her mind at once and ran out of storage, the scream changed character and reason.

<> meddled with this state for a moment, adjusting this, tampering with that. <> had known already that the storage was not adequate and now <> formed strategies, knowing the dimensions of what <> had. The pain went on, while <> probed connections and relationships.

Jillan stabilized again, regarded the dark and welcomed it with fierce enthusiasm and hunger.

<> erased her then abruptly, for she had gotten far from the template, and ceased to be instructive. Or safe. In any sense.

<> made a second, fresher copy. <> could do that endlessly, in possession of the templates <> had made.

<> began again, with a surer, more knowing touch.

"Is it worth it?" <∗> asked, straying close. "Let this creature go."

<> turned the Jillan-face toward <∗>'s undisguised self and felt a jolt of horror and of sound.

"That was unkind," <> said, and destroyed her yet again.

"You'll have to wait," Rafe said, in their trek through endless corridors of endless green-gossamer and lumpish contours. Nothing had changed. They discovered nothing but endless sameness. He sank down, resting his back against the wall, and shut his eyes—opened them again for fear of finding himself alone, but the images stayed with him. They had sat down as if they needed to, Rafe Two foremost, always closest to him. He heaved a breath, felt his bruised ribs creak, felt thirst and hunger. Tears leaked unwanted from his eyes, simple exhaustion, and horror at the sameness and the sight that kept staring back at him.

Ghosts. Solemn Rafe; Jillan being nonchalant; Paul glowering—they frightened him. He could not touch them. He could not hug them to him, ever again. He knew those looks—Paul's when he had an idea and would not let it go, Jillan's when she was on the edge, and tottering.

"Come on," he said, "Jillan. Swear. Do something. Don't be cheerful at me."

Her face settled into something true and dour. She looked up at him, thinking

—thinking what? he wondered. Seeing aliens behind his eyes? Or feeling her own death again?

"You all right?" he asked.

"Sure, sure I'm all right," Jillan said, and looked about, redirecting what got uncomfortable. "Whatever designed this place was crazy, you know that?"

"Whatever keeps us here sure is," Rafe Two said.

"It's kept me alive," Rafe answered the doppelganger. He wiped at his mouth, looked up and down the windings of the corridor—they had gone down this time, if the large chamber had been up. "That it leaves me alone, you know, is something encouraging."

"There's another place," said Rafe Two. "It's dark, and nothing, and if that's its normal condition, that thing's nothing like us at all."

"It's playing games," Paul said; and Rafe looked at him with some little hope—*it*, then; Paul had stopped throwing that *it* at him, had perhaps reconceived his situation. "There's no guarantee it has a logic, you figure that?"

"It's got math; math's logic," Jillan said.

"A lunatic can add," Paul said, gnawing at his lip. "I don't get tired. You're sweating and I don't get tired."

"Dead has advantages, it seems," Rafe Two said.

"Shut up!"

"Try thinking," Rafe said, shifting to thrust a leg between his doppelganger and Paul's image. "Try thinking—how we go about talking to this thing. It tried to talk to us. Back there—at Endeavor, it made an approach. Maybe taking us was a mistake in the first place."

"Come on," said Jillan harshly. "It knew we were there, knew how small we were. We couldn't support jump engines. It damn well knew."

He blinked at his sister, felt the sweat running in his eyes, mortality that she was beyond feeling. "I'll find a way to ask it," he said. Of a sudden he wanted to cry, right there in front of them, as if the jolt had just gotten through to him, but all he managed was a little trickle from his eyes and a painful jerk of breath. "I'll tell you this. If it turns out the way you think and you can't get your hands on it, I'll get it. I'll go for it. You can believe I will."

"I've thought of something else," said Rafe Two.

"What's that?"

"That offending it might turn us off. That it can do that anyway when it wants."

"What he's saying," Jillan said, "is that it has us for hostages. And maybe it's not being whimsical with us. Maybe it's looking to learn—oh, basic things. Like how we build; what our logic's like—"

"—from *Lindy*'s wire and bolts," Rafe scoffed. "Lord, it'll wonder how we got to space at all."

"—our language; our little computer, simple as it is—"

"—how our minds work," said Paul. "They'll start prodding at us. They've kept us too—you figure that, Rafe? They've gone to a lot of trouble."

"It still could be," Rafe said, "what you might say . . . humanitarian concern. Maybe they panicked and bolted and we were an unwanted attachment."

"How long were you awake?" Paul asked. "I *died*." His voice went faint; the muscles of his insubstantial face shook and jerked with such semblance of life it jarred. "*I am dead.* Isn't that what you've been insisting? I remember what it did. I remember the pain, Rafe. And it wasn't any damn humanitarian concern."

Rafe sat and stared at him, looked away finally, for Paul had begun to cry and to wipe his eyes, and finally faded out on them.

Jillan went after that, just winked out.

"How do you do that?" Rafe asked his double, hollow to the heart. "Where do you go when you go out? That dark place?"

"Don't get superstitious about it. It's just a place, that's all. You think hard about it—I think we've got a simple off-on with a transmitter somewhere."

"It wouldn't be simple."

"Bad choice of words."

"Dammit, I don't like arguing with you. It gives me the shakes."

"You ever wonder how I found you," Rafe Two asked, waving a hand toward the vastness of the hall, "in all this? Coincidence?"

"Something's pushing the buttons."

"Don't put it that way," Rafe Two said and hunched his bare shoulders, hands tucked between his knees. "You make me nervous, twin."

"You scared of dying?"

Rafe Two nodded, slowly, simply. "So are they, I think. Jillan and Paul. They've got experience."

"I'm hungry. My knees ache. Do yours?"

"No body left—brother. Got nothing like that left to bother me." The eyes were his own, and worried. "I'm going to go after them."

"Don't leave me here!"

Rafe Two looked at him. "It'll see we get back together. Won't it?"

"I have to go back to the ship. I have to. We're gaining nothing out here wandering these passages. Get them back. Come back yourself. To the ship. When you can."

"The ship." The doppelganger gave a dry and bitter laugh. "It won't let you lose that either, will it?"

"I'm afraid for them."

"So am I."

The doppelganger left, a winking-out more abrupt than Paul's.

So there had been violent parting of the ways; one fled: two gave chase; the living one pursued a painful trek back, <> surmised, to origins.

</> is gathering malcontents," said = (+) =, on leave from its cannibalistic whole.

<> was amused, with that part of <>'s attention it had to spare. *Trishanamarandu-kepta* rode inertia at the moment. <> had figured (accurately thus far) that this carbon-life, having ships capable of FTL, having the tendency to cluster together as they seemed to do, would not disperse themselves in long solitary voyages in between the stars and points of mass, so this vacancy seemed a likely place to coast undisturbed. <> preferred a few problems at a time: there were the passengers, after all, who were disturbed enough at three outsiders in their midst. So <> did not court attack from this carbon-life at large. The species might, <> judged, with the example of Jillan-mind, be very quick to attack if it had the chance.

<> was learning things. Jillan-mind and Rafe-mind in particular were responsive to the logic <> discovered in the primitive machinery, while Paul-mind refused focus, being a flood of strong responses on every level. They were not structurally the same, but there were strong similarities. Conclusions suggested themselves, but <> did not rush headlong into judgment, having wide experience which made surmise both slow and elaborate.

Throughout the ship other passengers were waking, more and more of them during this interlude, some of which had not waked in a very long time. Often they blundered into the barriers <> had made. But nothing got into the area where the visitors were at liberty.

This defense <> managed with one part of <>'s mind, and used another small probe on the Jillan-consciousness.

<> erased one temporary image, which began to disintegrate in subtle ways; but it was no effort now to enter the Jillan-mind on the level <> had already achieved, and <> integrated another.

Trishanamarandu-kepta had found a large bit of debris, meanwhile, and stored it for conversion, as it dealt with dust and interstellar hydrogen. <> constantly attended such things.

<> called up the Rafe-mind, and probed him with some sophistication, seeking out the differences, both physical and otherwise.

Rafe was, <> decided, less resilient but more stubborn. His barriers lasted longer, and snapped with a suddenness and disintegration that made <> suspect for a moment <> had met some clever trap, so disorienting and painful the reaction.

It was shock, <> decided. Rafe-mind had simply no experience with losing on that level, and he had met defeat without expectation, absolute and devastating, when he had planned to endure pain and outwait it.

From this collapse, Rafe-mind did not reintegrate, though <> observed him patiently and gave him every chance. So he would perish, ultimately. <> destroyed him and recreated him afresh.

It was paradoxical defense at best. It hinted irrationalities, capacities that would be augmented by physical systems in the living one, and Rafe himself had been, <> thought, stunned by his own failure.

<> suspected then why this one had survived in physical form, and why <> had so quickly broken him.

<> had robbed him of motives, that was what. That was why Rafe-mind had come apart, in solitude, without the other two.

<> did not intend Rafe-mind to learn this about himself; not yet.

Distress continued among the three newcomers. The simulacra which had gotten loose ran at hazard through their confinement, emitting terror as they went.

Paul, <> thought; it would of course be Paul in the lead, and <> was right in <>'s assessment, <> discovered, reaching out to prevent him from a meeting with = = = =, which lurked in anticipation.

= = = = was outraged. But <> pent Paul Gaines safely out of

harm's way, diverted Jillan elsewhere, and established barriers in haste, having <>'s mind on a dozen other matters.

"Robber!" = = = = hissed.

"Out," said <>. And = = = = went, calling in = = = ='s segments that were still at large. Most howled in protest. But they came. And the idle curious scattered.

Trishanamarandu-kepta found a second bit of rock, and sucked that down as well, while automata attended small repairs.

<> considered *Lindy* with another part of <>'s large mind, its structures, its simplicity, for <> had not yet sent the mote to feed *Trishanamarandu-kepta*'s needs. It might. But <> thus far refrained, finding interest in it.

Then because Paul continued to batter himself unreasoningly at the barriers, <> gave Paul a Rafe-simulacrum to keep him calm and let him wonder why that Rafe should be difficult to wake. Paul shook at him and wept and cursed. That, <> judged, would keep him out of mischief.

For more immediate purposes <> chose the Jillan-face.

V

Rafe went striding through the dark, calling Jillan and Paul by name, tireless in his pace and wishing desperately that endurance made some difference—for they would not grow tired here any more than he would, and he could not overtake them by all the laws he knew of this place. He could never overtake them until one of them came to his senses and stopped.

Paul was running; that was what Rafe guessed, running in hurt and fear. Paul had always been the gentle one, the little boy who had played at explorer and shuddered at the dark—

—*Space frightens me,* Paul had confessed to him once. *I'm all right in ships; just keep walls around me. When I have to go EVA, I just keep looking at the ship, the rock, whatever. Give me boundaries.*

Paul was station-born. He had a stationer's way of looking at things, and large concepts got to him, like the idea of staring time in the face when he looked out at the stars. The inside-out of jump frightened him. There were dimensions of time and space Paul staunchly refused to believe in, or at least to think of, even while he used and traveled through them.

I'm not dead, Paul had insisted; Paul Gaines could not die; no stationer could be so much alone as that. The universe would not permit so gross a violence to the devoutly nonviolent.

"Paul," Rafe called, aching for him. His own ill-timed joking, his bloody sense of humor, the other Rafe's—Paul did not support the contradictions. "Paul! Jillan, come back!"

Eventually a light came toward him, looking like a star at first, then a figure walking with that gliding, too-rapid stride that was the law within this place.

It was Jillan, by herself.

"Where's Paul?" he shouted at her, but Jillan kept coming without answering, and that silence chilled him, intimating that something dire had happened—Jillan, without Paul.

Her face was dreadful when they met, her eyes vast and shadowed, and again the illogicity of themselves overwhelmed him, that whatever they were could suffer—*Have we flesh of a kind,* he wondered, *bodies somewhere, beyond this dark? Metal bodies standing in a row or going through pointless motions? O Paul, Jillan—*

"Where's Paul?" he asked his sister.

"R-r-r-aaa-ffe," the lips shaped, a hoarse, rasping effort with Jillan's voice. It reached for him.

"O God. God, no!" He flung himself back and ran with all his might.

He hit a barrier, not a hard one, but a slowing of his force until he could not move more than a few feet in any direction. He felt a touch on his shoulders. He turned and met Jillan's eyes, encountered its embrace.

It was strong, stronger than he was by far. "Let me go," he cried, and struck at this thing, beyond any fear of harming Jillan. *"Let her go, damn you!"*

It hugged him to its heart. *"R-r-raaa-ffffe,"* it said, handling him with irresistible force, as if he had been a child in Jillan's arms.

He screamed, yelled out names—his own was one—*"Rafe!"*— as if his other self could hear him, help him, at least know that he was lost.

Jillan carried him some distance and stopped at last, just stopped, and let him go. *Free,* he thought, having wild hope of escape. He flung himself away as she winked out, but he came up against a barrier, solid as a wall.

Pain hit, and he screamed and went on screaming, from shock at first, and then because he could not stop.

"Rafe," he heard Jillan say out of a vast void darkness; and he waked again, blind and numb at first, lying on nothing, face up? face down?

Then Jillan was by him, kneeling there bright with gold-green glow, with seeming tears glistening in her eyes and spilling down her face. He felt her hands as she shook at him. "Come on, Rafe, wake up, you've got to wake up, hear me?"

He moved: he could, and writhed out of her reach, sat there shivering and staring back at her.

"Paul's lost," she said in a hoarse and hollow voice.

He shivered then, not for Paul, whose fate seemed a thousand years ago to him; but for himself, for the inexplicable that happened to him and went on happening in this blind dark.

"We've got to get back," he said at last, for it was truly Jillan. He convinced himself it was. He forced sense past numb lips, going on living, desperately ignoring memory as something unmanageable. "We've got to get back to the ship, tell *him*—" as if his living half would know what to do, would have some holistic view he lacked. He no longer trusted himself or anything he saw. He had dreamed his kidnapping. He had dreamed the pain. He wanted to believe in none of it. "Jillan—how did you find me?"

"I just kept walking back," she said. "Paul's *lost.* He's out there somewhere and he's not answering or something's happened to him—"

Something happened to me, he started to tell her, facing her hysteria; and some reticence held the truth dammed up. It was Jillan. He kept looking for flaws and cracks, but it was indeed his sister. He had to believe it was. "Let's get out of here," he said, not wanting to be touched by her, not wanting to look in her eyes. *Have you met something too?* he wanted to ask. *Have you already met it?*

Is it somewhere still inside you?

Is it alive in me?

"I've tried to get out," she said.

"What do you mean, tried to get out?"

She nodded toward the dark in general, or in a particular direction. "A few paces off—there's just a wall." She hugged her knees against her, tight, muscles rigid in her arms. "It's got us penned here. That's what."

He stood up and tried, all round, but it was like hitting some painless wall of force, insubstantial and absolute at once. He battered it with his fist, and his arm simply stopped short, impotent and forceless.

"*Aaaaaaiiiiiieeeeeee!*" something wailed, just the other side.

"God!" he said, and staggered back, crouched down in primate tuck, shoulders hunched, facing the barrier with Jillan at his back. He felt vulnerable so, deliberately kept staring into the dark, determined to believe in her, that it *was* Jillan behind him.

Sister, he thought, *sister.* They had called him the Old Man, she had. Paul had. The thinker, captain, planner, head-of-family, for all he was only twenty-two. He had outright failed them, all down the line; and he saw it now, how they had looked to him, Paul in his way, Jillan in hers, because he told her he could do it all for her and Paul, and she trusted that he could. She handed her life and future to him—*Here, brother, I've got what I need; I've got Paul: you take us, and do something, make something of yourself and us——*

—merchanter-man, who was nothing without his ship, his sister to give it children—

He was not sure of Jillan now. He was not sure of Paul. If Jillan was truly gone nothing mattered, not even Paul.

But he would, he discovered, go on fighting, as long as it was not Jillan herself who struck the blow. Being a merchanter brat, he had a certain stubbornness: that was all he could call it at this point, a certain rock-hardness at the center that did not know where to quit.

Not revenge. That was nothing. It was Murray-stubbornness, that lasted through the War, the mines, *Lindy*'s making, the Belt. He had always wondered if there was anything in him but Jillan.

Now he knew.

And he was, he thought with a jolt that ached, only the merest shadow of the man. The real substance of him was back in the lighted corridor, waiting for him, depending on him.

Two of us, he thought, and it occurred to him that, being Old Man, he still had one living crewman to protect. He was father to one at least. Himself.

"Rafe's our business," he said to Jillan at his back. "You understand me. Not me-Rafe. The other one. They can still hurt him. We've got to do something."

"You got an idea?" she asked. No protest. That other Rafe was her brother too, the living one. "You got an idea?"

"No," he said, "just a priority. Paul's no worse off than we are. No better either. But our brother—" It was easier to think of Rafe that way. "They're going to some trouble in his case. They saw to it that we found him. Didn't they? That wasn't accident."

"There's still the outside chance, like Rafe says—they're not altogether hostile. Maybe we can't figure the way they think. Maybe they're too different."

He twisted on his knees and looked back at her, snatching up a hope from that innocence of events. "I met one," he said. "It wore your shape."

Jillan blinked rapidly in shock, stared at him, seeming then to put things together.

"I figure you'd better know that," he said, "so you don't trust everything you see. It hurt. Quite a bit. Like at the beginning. It's still got us here, wherever here is."

The shock was real in her eyes. He saw that.

"Paul and Rafe," she said, putting that together too. "It can get at them that way."

<> was pleased in <>'s acquisition. It had been a question whether to shock Rafe Two with any kind of contact, any apprehension at all of his circumstances before securing his template, but <> had decided in the affirmative. The second Rafe-mind's difference was precisely, after all, its knowledge, its adjustment to the environment more extensive than Rafe One's. And the Jillan-face provided a certain insulation in the contact.

<> tried out what <> had gained, this Rafe with a little bit of knowledge where he was and what he was. The flexibility was greater. <> had hoped for that.

The solitude was worst, the long, gnawing away of expectations until the loss of the most dreadful fear seemed like the parting of a cherished possession, leaving increasingly remote and strange possibilities.

One could only pace so much, eat so often, meddle with the few active circuits *Lindy* had left just so many hours, and bathe and sleep and bathe and sleep and make-work at the console, like the visual analysis of stars, the infinite working of infinite problems, calculation of space and acceleration and distances given things that would never, from his vantage, ever be true. But those hypotheses filled the mind and kept it focused, for a little while, on sane outcomes.

Rafe worked at guesses, had pegged several high-magnitude stars, two of which were conspicuous, almost touching. He tried one and another theoretical perspective on them, tormented himself with hopeful and despairing suppositions.

"Hey!" he shouted at the winding corridor more than once, frustrated and desperate. But no sound came back, from either direction.

He called the others' names; he called his own, and had nothing but silence.

"You can't take them away," he muttered to himself, to God, to whatever ran this place, and bowed his head on the console. Finally, which he had never yet done, he truly mourned his dead and sobbed hysterically.

Even that wore thin. There was only so much grief, so much anger, not even so much as when he and Jillan were orphaned. Then there had been guilt—a child's kind of guilt—*Maybe if I'd been good they'd be alive—*

It's my fault. I should have loved them more—

There was no guilt here. Not with Jillan and Paul. He sat there with the last of the tears still cold on his face and judged that whatever mistakes they had made, they were paying for all of it together; Jillan and Paul's being dead was not final but drawn-out, shared, a life-in-death which still could make jokes about its state, shed tears for itself, know fears for the future. The same thing waited for him, he reckoned, when whatever-it-was got around to his case.

It's going to do that soon; they don't want to watch what happens to me.

Or maybe they're just gone. Turned off, of no more use.

No pain that way, at least.

And at last, all but sobbing in self-pity, he thought: *But Rafe's afraid to die.*

He shuddered away from that entanglement and wiped his face with both his hands until the tears went down.

He thought of taking another long, long walk. His bruises had gone to livid green by now. He was stronger. He might take food, fill his pockets with it, use a plastic bag for a canteen—just walk, walk until he ran out of everything and those in charge had to do something about him, either meet him face to face or let him die.

But: *Come to the ship,* he had told his doppelganger. Perhaps their time sense was different. Maybe for them it was only a little while. If he left they might come and he would never know.

He flung himself down against the wall where he often sat and just stared at *Lindy*'s remains, not looking down the corridors which led into the dark.

"Rafe," his own voice said.

He started half to his feet, braced against the wall, levered himself the rest of the way up. "Where have *you* been?" It came out harsh. He had not meant that. He was all but shaking, facing his naked self, which stood over against the dark of the corridor. "Did you find them?"

"Were you worried?"

"Was I worried? Don't joke with me, man. I'm not laughing. Where are they?"

The doppelganger pointed, vaguely up and off beyond the walls. "There."

"They won't come?"

"Paul's not coping well with this."

He let go his breath, found his hands shaking, walked over to the console and sat down, firmly, in a place he knew. "Not coping well."

"Not at all."

"Jillan?"

"Better. She's all right."

"She's with him."

The doppelganger shook his head. "No. She's not."

"Cut the riddles. Where's Jillan?"

"You're upset."

"God, what's wrong—*wrong with you?*"

"Nothing's wrong."

"I know what it's like—talking to myself; I do know; and you don't follow my lead, not half right—" He put himself on his feet, leaning on *Lindy*'s board. "*What are you?*"

The doppelganger winked out.

"*What are you?*" Rafe screamed after it. He hit the useless board. "*Jil-lan!*"

And he sat down again, fell into his seat, trembling from head to foot.

"Clever," said the doppelganger voice, off to his side.

He spun the chair, faced it where he sat. It stood over by the EVApod, dimmer, for the light was brighter there.

"You," he said to it, gathering up his mind, "you're the one I've been wanting to get in reach. Why don't you come in here in person?"

"You want to kill me."

"Maybe." He sucked in a copper-edged breath and stood up. "Where's my sister? Where's Paul?"

"The physical entities? Dead. I tried to hold them. They died."

"Dead. And their copies—" He did not want to admit how much it meant, but his knees were weak. He held onto the counter. "Do they still exist?"

"Oh, yes."

"Bring them here."

"I'll let them loose again. Soon. I came to talk with you."

"Why?" he asked, staring at the mirrored face before the blank visage of the EVApod. "To say what? What shape is Rafe going to be in? Do I get my own doppelganger back?"

"Yes. He's safe. Is that a concern to you?"

He did not answer. It already knew weaknesses enough in him; it wore his doppelganger like a skin. He straightened his back and moved back to the console, turned around again. "Why not your own shape?"

"It would distress you."

"You think this doesn't?"

"A question of degree."

"You're not very like us."

"No. I'm not."

"You're fluent."

The image blinked. "It did take time."

"How did you do it? How did you learn?"

"It would distress you. Say that I know you pretty well. From inside. I have a lot of your character right now."

"And my memories?"

"That too."

Rafe sank again into the chair, wiped a hand across his mouth to still the tic that plagued him. "And the way I think about things. I don't suppose you've got that too."

"There is a great deal of congruency at present. I've walled off some of myself; that's the nearest analogue. I'm larger. Smarter. Far more educated."

"Modest too."

The doppelganger grinned.

"God," Rafe said, "a sense of humor." It sent a chill up his back, lent him other thoughts. "You can feel anything I'd feel. Do you?"

"Everything."

"Like—loving them. Like that."

"I do."

He sat silent a moment, trying not to shiver.

"While I'm you," it said. "In my full mind there are other considerations, I assure you. But within this configuration, I do love them. I understand perfectly what you mean."

"You hurt us. Do you know that?"

"You can assume I remember. You don't have to ask. You're concerned about your safety, about the others. Let me destroy your illusions—"

"Don't. Please. Don't."

"Not those." The mouth twisted in a smile that left no residue of humor. "Not physically. . . ."

</> had made a move. In the rest of <>'s mind, extended elsewhere in the ship, <> was well aware of this. </> gained access to apparatus </> could not otherwise have touched, and </> grew suddenly knowledgeable. It was the file on the intruders </> had gotten. </> gained sudden capability.

"Help," (#) cried, rushing through the ship. "Help, help!"

"I told you so," said <^>.

". . . but I won't tell you any more than you really have to know, if you'd rather not. I do mean to take you back."

"Where?"

"To the star where I found you."

"Is this a game?" Rafe's heart was beating hard. "Why? Why do that?"

"A capsule with a beacon. They'll pick you up, so this mind believes."

"Why go to the trouble?"

"Why not? Harm to me? I don't think they could."

"You're lying."

There was long silence. "I understand your caution. Believe me. I do understand."

"More humor."

The mouth—his own—quirked up in a touch of mirth. "It doesn't depend on your belief anyway."

"You mean you'll do what you like."

"Aaaaiiiiiiiiii!" The sound began from far away; it roared closer and closer, speakers coming alive right overhead and fading away again, lightning-fast, blinding pain that hit and left: Rafe leaped up, trembling in its wake.

"Is that for effect?"

"That one's mad," the doppelganger said. "And a little upset right now. Don't let it trouble you."

"Sure. Sure I won't. Cheap trick, hear? Like all the rest. Real cheap."

"I'll leave now. Something wants my attention. A minor thing. But I'll put in somewhere soon at a human port and drop you off. Don't worry for the jump drugs. I don't know the composition of what you take. You don't. But I can make you sleep; that should be enough."

"Why does it matter? You've killed two people, damn you! Why does it matter now?"

"Because it's easy," the doppelganger said, and faded out altogether.

"Why?" he yelled after it until his voice cracked. He fell down into the chair, being alone again, in the silence. "Rafe?" he said aloud, querulously, hoping for the old one, the friendly one. "Jillan." And last and with least hope: "Paul?"

No one answered. No one came. He was scared finally, finally terrified for himself, sitting and staring at nothing at all.

Going home, he thought. With human beings. Living ones. He did not believe it. He did not believe it loved. He did not believe it told the truth at all, or that it cared.

But there remained the possibility.

There remained the greater likelihood it had other motives. And it wore a human shape and used a human mind.

*   *   *

"Paul," </> said, having penetrated the barriers <> had imposed about the stranger, having, momentarily, seized control of that territory. "Paul."

And </> took the Rafe-image on </> self.

"You're awake," Paul said. "You're awake."

"Paul," </> said, getting to </>'s human feet. "Paul." </> had that word down pat. </> snatched Paul in </>'s borrowed arms and carried him rapidly out through barriers, along passages.

Paul screamed, and stopped screaming, simply clinging to what he feared, a logic that </>, in Rafe's mind, understood with curious poignancy.

<> was too late to prevent the theft.

<> simply recreated the Paul-simulacrum of which <> had been robbed and left him asleep in a safer place, far inside <>'s boundaries.

Paul was not a serious loss. Paul had never adjusted and likely never would, but <> was still nettled.

"<> wish you success," <> taunted </>, for <> had shed the Rafe-mind and felt differently about many things.

There was a division in *Trishanamarandu-kepta*. It had happened long ago. There was a place where </> did very much as </> pleased; and another where <> was the law. This was an agreement they had, one which made diversions, and <> cherished those.

Slowly, as <>'s humor improved, <> found a sense of ironical amusement in the theft, for the Paul-entity was unstable, and the Rafe one had been unwaked and was now vastly disturbed. One did not intrude into a simulacrum and leave it intact.

"Do something," <^> mourned.

"<> have," <> said, for <> was still controlling the moves: </> had, being flawed, acquired two flawed entities, one flawed by nature, the other by invasion.

The important two were safe.

<> was awake again. All the way.

And the passengers scurried this way and that in panic, examining old alliances and likely advantage.

Only ((())) ranged the passages, wailing in ((()))'s madness. Perhaps only ((()))'s lower mind was left; perhaps some memory remained, what side $((()))$ had taken once. "Aaaaiiiieeeee," $((()))$ cried. "Help us, help us all! O strangers, rescue us!"

"Paul," Rafe said, who was not-Rafe, and something very strong.

Paul lay still and stared, heaving for breath in the all-enveloping dark while Rafe changed into something huge and slightly blurred. Paul flinched at this transformation and started to twist away, but Rafe's touch was gentle, very easy, on his shoulder.

"You're not him," Paul said, and his own voice seemed very distant in his ears, as if he had been drugged. Everything seemed far.

"You're safe," it told him, which he wanted now desperately to hear. "You're safe with me." The strangeness had gotten to the all-enveloping point and battered at his mind; and just when it was at its worst, it promised him safety and protection. He was ready to believe.

"I have you," the blurred shape said. The voice was Rafe's, but strange and deep, like a motor running. "You're very safe in my company. You don't have to worry while I'm here."

He let it hold him like a child. The voice sank to be one vast burr that filled everything, replaced everything. It touched him, mother-gentle, spoke to him in a language eloquent of protection; and he shut his eyes, trusting finally, because he could only sustain the fear so long in such closeness, in an existence in which he could not tire or sleep: the voice went on and on.

"Let go," it hummed, "listen to me. You're safe."

"I'm dead," he said. "What's safe in that?"

"Not dead. Not truly. Not at all. You exist. You can come and go at will. You have long life ahead of you; and a comfortable one, with me. Be still, be quiet, rest. Nothing can reach you in my heart."

"We don't get hungry," Jillan said. "I could wish we got hungry. I miss—" She shook her head and stopped, wisely.

Rafe stared at her bleakly, remembering many things he missed. At length he got up and tried the barrier again. It still held and he came and sat down again, letting his shoulders fall. There was no pretending with Jillan. Finally they had passed all embarrassment, all other pretenses; he was naked inside and out with Rafe and stopped minding: now he could be that way with Jillan, at least in most things.

"Beats station life," he said, which was an old joke with them, that anything did. Even dying.

"Got ourselves a ship," she said, rising to it valiantly, but the grief never left her eyes. *Paul, Paul, Paul,* they said, wrath and divided loyalties.

"Got ourselves a big one," he said.

"What we have to do," she said, "we find our way to controls— in our android shapes—and then we take this thing."

"Deal," he said.

But they sat there, with a barrier about them. With Paul missing, and neither of them made guesses about Paul.

He'll find a way to rescue us, Rafe thought, trying to convince himself. *He's still loose, he's smart—So's Rafe—*without modesty. *But Paul can move through the ship. . . .*

Maybe it's taking Paul apart now.

"Idea," said Jillan.

"What?"

"Rafe. They're keeping Rafe locked up. That means he could do damage."

"They're keeping us locked up, too," he said, and they turned that thought over separately for a moment.

"Huh," she said, his Ma'am; his number One, his crew.

"I'll make you a present of this ship," he said.

"That's the Old Man talking," she said, seeming to take heart. "You do that, Rafe. Let's find something to break, when we get out of here."

"No way," he said. "It's our ship, remember. We want this thing intact."

The chittering came back, the wailing thing passed, as it had passed before. He refused to wince, refused even to acknowledge it.

When we get out of here.

Then, in a blink, Paul was lying a dozen feet beyond them.

Jillan moved, scrambled to Paul's side with a soft, frightened oath.

Rafe moved up and knelt again, cautious of such gifts. "Paul," he said.

Paul opened his eyes to pale slits, shuddered and came suddenly wide-eyed, lurching up on his arm.

"Where are we?" Paul asked. "O God, where are we? Jillan—?" He sat upright, looked down at his own body, at theirs—panicked, darting glances. *"What is this place?"*

"The same as it's ever been," Rafe said.

"What do you mean, the same?" Paul's voice rode close to breaking. "Where are we? Where's the ship?"

"He doesn't remember," Rafe said, at Jillan's frightened glance his way. "He's lost it all."

"Lost what?" asked Paul. *"What* don't I remember?"

Rafe put out a hand and held it on his shoulder. "This place— you've lost a little time, Paul. Just take it easy. We're all right. Take it easy. We'll fill you in."

Paul was scared again, mortally scared. So was Jillan; he could read it in that thin-lipped calm.

"It's all right," Jillan said. "It's all right, we've got you back. We lost you for a while. You scared us; Paul."

<> listened for a time. <> had debated with <>self, how much interference was wise, whether to restore Paul to the set at all. And then it occurred to <> that a different waking experience might change the Paul-mind to some advantage.

So <> had restored him to the others, this copy fresh from its death experience.

</> would know that, of course. There remained the very strong likelihood </> would attempt a substitution the moment </> had a chance.

But <> took the risk. Perhaps Jillan or Rafe-mind had left its influence on <>. <> was not sure. Many entities had tried; but their desire to keep that set intact was strong.

There was also, native to <>self and them—curiosity.

<> took up the Rafe-image again and visited the corridor, finding Rafe asleep.

<> squatted there, just watching, running through the feelings Rafe-mind had about himself and his living original. Then:

"Wake up," Rafe heard. "Wake up, Rafe."

He opened his eyes, knowing the voice, braced himself back

on his hands in a scramble for the wall, for it was close, until he had gotten his thoughts together.

"Which one are you?"

His own face smiled back at him, answering that question. Rafe Two would have been puzzled at the least.

"Stay back," Rafe said.

"You know I can't touch you."

He let go his breath, still pressed as close against the wall as he could get. "Like hell. You promised me the others back. Where are they?"

"Plotting together. They want to take the ship."

"Good for them."

The alien grinned, squatted there with his elbows on naked knees, went sober once again. "It's not too likely a threat."

"I want to see them."

"Ship's important to you, isn't it? I think about this star where I found you; this mind doesn't care. I think of others. But when I think of ship, it reacts. Like love. Like need. It feels strong as sex-drive. Stronger, maybe. But *Lindy*'s finished, I'm afraid. It was, you'll pardon me, not much of a ship to start with."

"Shut up."

"On the other hand," the doppelganger said, "—I love that idea, you know? The other hand. I understand a number of things: you'd want to be dropped as far away from Endeavor as you could get. They'd ask questions there at Endeavor, years of questions. There and at Cyteen. I could drop you, oh, say, Paradise. There'd be questions there, too; but maybe less anxiety. Less chance of your being—confined. Wouldn't you say?"

He sat and listened to this prattle, roused out of sleep to listen, tucked up against the wall. He ignored most of it, let it drift through his mind and out again, refusing to let it stick. "Stop playing this game. I don't care where you drop me."

"I want to prepare a canister for you. This takes a little time. I won't stay long at all at Paradise, not to make a stir."

"What's your name?"

"My name?"

"You've got a name of your own the way I presume you've got a shape. What is it?"

It seemed to think a moment. "Kepta, if you like."

"Kepta. What are you really up to?"

"Right now," the doppelganger. said, "I'm merely clearing decks. I'll take another impression before I turn you out; this will put me up to date with all you've gotten here. I've put that off; it is stressful. But that's the only thing I want of you."

"The others. What will happen to them?"

"I won't turn them off, if that's what you mean. That's the last thing I'd do."

"Meaning what?"

"They're mine," Kepta said.

"What do you mean, yours? You mean you're taking them somewhere?"

"They can hardly leave the ship with you—can they? No, there's nothing really to worry about at all. I could put some of this business off; but on the other hand—I'd like to get you to the lab, just to make sure, well, of having that copy. It's my only condition." The image got to its feet, held out a hand. "Come on, get up. I'd like you to walk there."

"Meaning there are other choices?"

"There are other ways."

Rafe thought that over, staring up into his own face, hating the mock-regretful look on it. He put his hands on the gossamer-carpeted floor and shoved himself up, straightened and glared at the image eye to eye, but it refused the confrontation, walked off a way and held out its hand, beckoning.

"Come on."

"Why should I believe this, when you haven't come through with the other promise? I want to see the others, hear?"

"Afterward. I promise. Come on, now, Rafe. Let's not be difficult."

"Let's," he echoed sourly. "What is my choice?"

"I really don't want to do that."

"What?"

"I could send something in here to bring you. I'd have it carry you and spare you the long walk; but walking makes it your choice, that's why I want you to do it. I really think that's valuable."

"You know, I never noticed it; I don't like the way I talk."

"Humor?"

Rafe said nothing, but started walking; looked back again, at home, at *Lindy*'s jumbled fragments, then fell in beside Kepta's light-dim shape. "I need anything?"

"No. Not really."

He walked farther; the image walked, with smooth efficiency: *sequencing projectors,* he had decided once. *Projected from what? Fibers in the rug?* "This going to hurt much?" he asked finally.

"Yes," Kepta said.

They walked along, down the snaking corridor of gossamer-green humps and hillocks. The lights were all on, showing him the way.

"Haven't felt any push on this ship," he said. "We're inertial, aren't we?"

"Some ways off Endeavor, plus one plus thirty plus ten, one-tenth C. Make you feel better, knowing where you are?"

He nodded, relationships and directions flashing into shape. He felt familiar stars about him again. Home space. He drew a shuddering, long breath, pretended nonchalance. "Big nothing out here."

"It's a vacant spot. Where we're not disturbed."

VI

They walked side by side, he and Kepta, into that vast empty node where many halls converged—silent: his footfalls on the padded floor made no great sound. Rafe heard only the whisper of his clothing, his own deepened breaths. Kepta made no sound at all, except to talk to him from time to time down the winding hall:

"Tired?" Kepta asked.

"Does that matter? You pushed me along this way once, with the lights. What were you after, then?"

"Reactions," Kepta said.

He strode on a few more limping steps. "Like now?"

A few steps more. "No," Kepta said. "Now I know exactly what you'll do."

He looked at Kepta, but Kepta did not, seemingly, look his way.

"You're limited." Rafe asked him, the question flashing to his mind, "to one vantage point? To that shape? Those eyes?"

"No," Kepta said again.

"Physically—where are you?"

Silence.

"Makes you nervous? You scared, are you, to answer that?"

Silence still.

They came into the dark, warted heart of the huge meeting of corridors. Light came from home-corridor at their backs, a soft glow that lit the whole floor ahead in a dim gray succession of ripples and hummocks, stalagmites and lumpish stalactites afflicted with gossamer-shrouded warts and protuberances. There were no echoes. No sound. The carpet drank it up. "Can't afford lights here?" Rafe jibed at Kepta, trying to learn, by whatever questions Kepta would answer. "You don't like light, that it? Or don't you need it?"

Lights flared, illuminating a vast chamber, a craziness of lumps and hummocks and tunnels on a mammoth scale; lights died and left him in dark again, as suddenly.

Kepta was gone.

"Kepta?" He faced wildly about, flash-blinded, helpless, stumbling on the uneven floor. *"Kepta?"*

"First passage on your left," a voice said, close by him. The gold-glowing image resumed. "Just checking. I'm a little narrow-focused in this shape; a great deal of me is doing other things, and now and again I like to take a little look behind the eyes, so to say. That's right, this way. Not far now."

His heart pounded. He rubbed at his eyes trying to get his vision back, stumbling on the uneven floor, staying with Kepta in a winding course around the prominences. They skirted around a jutting protuberance of the wall and passed one black corridor opening. The next acquired dim light, showing gray and green no different than otherwhere.

"This way," Kepta said.

He matched Kepta's drifting pace. The way narrowed into a twisting gut, went from gossamer-green to bald glistening plastic in a green that deepened to livid unpleasantness.

Narrower still, and brighter-lit. "O God," Rafe said, and balked. Metal gleamed. Clusters of projections like insect limbs lined the chamber which unfurled from beyond the turning—some arms folded, some thrust out in partial extension, things to grip and bite, extensors armed with knives.

"Come on," Kepta said. "Come ahead. That's right. No sense running now."

"It's still there," Rafe Two said. They had tried the unseen barrier now and again, when one and the other of them grew restless in their dark confinement. He went back and sat down while Jillan and Paul had their own go at it, Paul with violence, which did no good, but it satisfied some need, and Rafe averted his face and rested his chin on his arm, knee tucked up, staring into the dark beyond the invisible wall.

Now and again there were sounds. The thing that wailed had become familiar, still dreadful when it came, but it seemed by now that it would have done something, attacked if it could or if it had the desire.

"Shut up," he told it when it came.

Paul and Jillan sat down again, Paul last; who cast himself down and hung his hands between his knees, to look up, again with a bleak, sullen stare.

He was being patient, was Paul, amnesiac, wiped of everything recent, even the remembrance that he was dead. They had had to tell him that all over again, and Paul had sat and listened, and objected. Perhaps he thought they were crazy; perhaps he believed it. Whatever Paul believed, he was quiet about it all.

Because Jillan was calm, Rafe thought; because he and Jillan accepted it and explained matters gently as they could. He detected the cracks in Paul's facade, the little signs of tension, the occasional sharp answer, the increasingly worried look on Paul's face when they failed to retaliate for his gibes. They were shielding him; Paul realized it. Jillan protected him—being merchanter-born, tough in spacer-ways, with a spacer's tolerance of distances, infinities, time and thinking inside-out. She was the stronger here. So was he.

Jillan and me, Rafe thought, *and Paul, on the other side, cut off from her. From me. He's trying so hard to keep himself together in Jillan's sight, up to her measure of a man—We joke; we seem to take it light; it's like salt in all his wounds.*

He got up, paced, for Paul's sake, to be human. Pushed at the wall.

"Give it up," Paul said.

He sat down again, slumped, elbows on knees.

So maybe it helped, giving Paul a way to seem calm and in control.

"Got any ideas?" he asked Paul then.

Paul was silent a long time. "Just thinking," Paul said, "that we don't eat, don't sleep, don't get tired—wonder how long it takes a mind to unravel, sitting still. Wonder if it's listening. Or if it's just gone off and forgotten us, this alien you met. Wonder if we're all crazy. Or you are. And we sit here glowing in the dark."

Rafe laughed. It was conscious effort. He remembered—a thing that turned him cold; a meeting Jillan had not known; that Paul assuredly had not; and for a moment he was the one pretending cheerfulness. It had hurt; it would happen again, he thought, for no reason, for nothing that made sense.

"Sooner or later," he began dutifully to answer Paul; but something caught his eye, a light far out in the dark.

"Something's out there," Jillan said, scrambling to her feet as he did. "Something's coming—"

It moved in that rapid way things could here. Paul got to his feet and Jillan held to him, steadying him by that contact.

It whipped up to the barrier, a human runner.

Paul.

Doppelganger's doppelganger. It stared, stark and wide-mouthed, glowing like themselves, and with one strangled cry of grief, it spun and ran away, diminished as rapidly as it had come.

"What was *that*?" asked Paul, remarkably calm, considering the horror in his eyes.

Rafe turned and looked at him, far from calm himself—considered this second Paul-shape that had materialized inside the barrier with him and Jillan.

Jillan too, he remembered—the arms that had gripped him with more than human strength—

He set his back to the phantom wall, facing both of them, their united, guarded stare.

The pain—O God, the pain!

Rafe screamed while he had breath, while he had the strength. But it was too deep and too long, too thorough, pinned him between breaths and held him dying there until air began the long slow leak back into his lungs. Then the cycle ran round again.

And over again.

"There," said Kepta's vast slow voice after all eternity. "There. That's over now." And there was dark a time.

"Try to move," it said.

Rafe moved; he would have done anything it told him, not to have the pain. He kept moving and thrust aching arms under him, took the strain of muscle-stretch across his aching ribs, his belly, trying constantly to find some position that did not hurt and discovering fresh agonies at every shift.

"Easy," Kepta said out of that vast haze of his senses, awareness of light, machines that hummed and moved, having him as a mote in their cold heart. A metal arm moved at his face, thrust a tube into his mouth with persistent accuracy, shot a dose of

tepid water down his throat. Other arms moved spiderlike about
him and closed about his arms, *click-click*. He was past all but
the vaguest fear. He let his limbs be moved because gentle as it
was he had resisted once and found no limit to its strength. *Click-
click*. It faced him about and held him upright as he sat on the
table.

"Over, then?" His voice was a ragged croak, his throat raw
from screaming. "Over?"

"All done," Kepta said, taking shape in front of him. "Rest a
bit."

He was willing; the spider arms stayed still, like a cradle behind him. He leaned his head back, his feet dangling off the edge
of the machinery. For a moment he blurred out again, head resting against the arms, heart still laboring, while the tears leaked
from his eyes and the sweat slicked his skin.

"Where is it?" he asked then, meaning the thing that he had
birthed. He had some proprietary curiosity; it had cost him so
much pain.

"Here," Kepta said, "here in the machine."

"You mean you'll give it a body."

"No," Kepta said, and rested a ghostly hand on a large hum-
mock that rose with several others to form the table, the base of
several of the arms. "It has one. In here. Do you want to know
how it works? Your template of a moment ago exists now. It will
never know more than you knew when it was made. Always
when I call it up it will be at the same moment."

Rafe shook his head and shut his eyes, feeling everything slide
into chaos, not wanting this.

"So I can always recover that point," Kepta said, "at need. A
point of knowledge—and ignorance."

Eyes slitted, till Kepta was a golden blur. "You still going to
let me go?"

"Oh, yes." Kepta moved among the machinery, through one
lowered metal arm. "You asked about bodies. This one—" Kepta
laid a hand on his own insubstantial chest. "You assume there's
some substance to it, somewhere. There's not. It's a pattern. You
want Jillan? I can call up that template. Or Paul. Or one of several of you."

Paul One ran, raced into the dark, sobbing at what he had seen: himself; himself possessing Jillan and Rafe and he-himself, watching helplessly from outside—

At last he found Rafe again, his own Rafe, beaconlike in the nowhereland, that shape that was Rafe and not, something blurred and larger, far larger.

"I know what you found," Rafe said. "I knew you would." And Rafe himself blurred further, into outlines vast and dark. "I knew it would hurt. Paul—"

"Was it me?" he asked. "Was that my real body?"

"No," it said. "Only another duplicate."

There was no more system of reference, nothing human left. It took him in its changing arms, took him to its heart, whispered to him in a voice still human though the rest of it was not.

"You don't have to be afraid. I won't hurt you, nothing will ever hurt you while I have you. You can't trust what you see, that's the first thing you have to learn. You want to be safe. But I can make you strong. You won't be afraid of anything. You want to know how this ship works? I'll tell you. Anything you want to know. That version you just saw? Nothing. Nothing. Another copy off your template. I have to tell you how that works, that next. The templates."

"I recorded you," Kepta said, waving a hand past the mounded protrusions beneath all the array of shining spider arms, "not just the outward form, but at every level, in every function and structure—everything. The template's as like you as if you'd been spun out in bits, down to the state and spin of your particles: that's how exact it is . . . all uncertainties made definite, particulate memory, frozen in the finest definition matter can achieve. We just—play it out again. Call it up in memory and let it integrate. The visible manifestation, the body—a very simple thing: just light, quite apart from the more complex patterns. An image conceived off the template and maintained by quite inelegant means: the computer knows its shape, that's all, and revises it moment by moment by the direction of the program; but that program that animates it—that's quite another thing."

"It reacts," Rafe said. "It *thinks*—"

"That's the elegance. It does."

"You've turned them to machines."

"No. Contained them in one. They react; they think; they think they move. They're programs, if you like, smart programs that can learn and change, that get input they interpret in the same way they always did, or they think they do, that eyes work and mouths make speech, and muscles move. The body—is merely light, for passing convenience. It changes in response to signals the programs give. It can't input. But on other levels, in the purest sense, the programs can input from each other, can imagine, tend to perceive what they expect—like smells and textures. Illusions, if you like. But they aren't. The programs aren't. They grow, and change, get experience, change their minds. They stay up and running until someone shuts them down."

Rafe shook his head. The words writhed past, heard, half-heard. He hung there in the spider arms, looked at the machines, the mocking image of himself. "One large memory," he said past unresponsive lips, "one hell of a large memory, that thing. Wouldn't it be?"

"Oh yes, quite large."

"Runs all the time."

Kepta lifted his head in a curious way, his own mannerism thrown back at him, half-mocking, half-wary.

"I threaten you," Rafe said, and found it funny, hanging there, naked, in the steel, unyielding hands. "Do I? Suppose I believe that's how you do it, suppose I believe it all—There's still the why of it. You want to tell me why? And you still want to tell me you're putting me out of here?"

"Why's not relevant. Say that I wanted the template. That's all. When I call it up and it talks to me, it won't know a thing of what we've said; won't know what it is. It'll be the you that walked in here of his own free will. That's the one I'll deal with. Why tell you anything? The template won't remember. You'd have to tell it what you've learned. And you'll be safe away from it."

"Why?" he asked again. "Why let me go?"

"I said. It's easy. —You're worried, aren't you? You're worried about your life, theirs—the whole species. That's why you don't really think I'll turn you out. You think of ships. Military. I understand this concept of yours, this collective of self defense. You think I've come to learn all I can; that I'm in advance of others who'll come to harm all your kind. No. I'm unique."

"Then come in. Come into some human Port and talk like you're civilized."

The mirror-image blinked. "You don't really want that."

"No," he said, thinking again, thinking at once of Endeavor, magnified a hundred-fold, *O God, some major port*—

"There'll just be yourself returning," it said. "The military will check records, put you together with the Endeavor business. You'll be answering a lot of questions. That's all right. Tell them anything you like. I'll be long gone from Paradise."

"Where? To do what?"

"You're worrying again."

"Are you afraid? Afraid of us?"

"*Responsibility.* You have this tendency—to make yourself the center, the focus. Jillan and Paul—you're responsible for them; if your species died, you'd be more responsible than I who killed them. An interesting concept, responsibility—and within your context, yes, you could become that focus. I could wipe out your kind, based on what you know. And on what you don't. You couldn't fight me. Your ships can't catch me; my weapons are beyond you; there's just no chance, if I were interested. I'm not. So you're not the center, are you? That's a great loss to you . . . that your kind will live on without your responsibility. Could it even be—that you're not responsible for other things? Or that your friends are not in your universe at all?"

"What becomes of them?"

"They're not your responsibility."

He flung himself to his feet. The arms prevented that.

"You're not necessary. You go to Paradise. You tell them what you like. Tell them everything you've seen. They'll be interested. Of course they will. You'll be famous of your kind—in certain ways. Very important. You'll certainly be the focus then. Won't you?"

Imagination filled it in—official disclaimers, the military swarming over him and his capsule like bees—*Hallucination,* they'd say, for general consumption. . . . "Damn you," he said to Kepta, shivering.

"Not my responsibility," Kepta said. "Not at all. I'll be gone. Nothing to fear from me; there never was. But you don't want to believe that. It takes something away from you." The spider-arms relaxed, the grip yielded. "Your clothes are there. I think you might be cold."

He moved, on his own, crawled off the sweating, plastic surface. Everywhere about him was the stench of his own fear. He tucked his clothing to him and held onto it. "I stink," he muttered at it. "I want a bath. I'm going back to *Lindy*, thanks."

Kepta would stop him, he thought; would move the arms again. But they all retracted with one massive snick of metal, clearing him a path.

"A machine could carry you," Kepta said.

"I'll walk."

It hurt. Every movement hurt, however slow. Every thought did, in this trap that he was in. He limped toward the exit from this place, the way he had come in. He cherished the pain, that it filled his mind like needful ballast, filled cracks and crevices and darknesses and took away the need to think. Tears ran down his face, and he could not have said whether they were true tears or only a welling up of too much fluid; he was beyond all analyses.

<> destroyed the Rafe-simulacrum that <> wore and expanded past its limits with relief. <> had already absorbed everything that surfaced in Rafe-mind, all the suppositions, all the facts, all the emotive feeling. <> felt a lingering distress.

There was a time of adjustment afterward, there must be, in which <>'s human experiences and <>'s own flowed past each other in comparison, and <> kept them all. <> was interested for various reasons, but one reason assumed priority, that <> was due for challenge—indeed, had, to a great extent provoked it, seeing opportunity.

More, there was additional use in Rafe-mind for </> had worn it. Ancient and unbending as </> was, </> had slipped into it, and this was worth interest. It was always well, under any circumstances, to know just what </> was about.

And if </> had found some congruency to </>self in Rafe-mind, then <> was interested.

"Is it pleasant?" <> taunted </> across the width of the ship.

</> had no answer, </> had taken a shape much more like </>'s own configurations, and the Paul-mind nested in it.

<> was thunderstruck.

"See," said <^> in an undertone of distress as <^> came slipping up to <>'s presence. "See, <^> said as much. So did ((())). Even ((())).

"Quiet," said <>, losing all amusement, and having searched the tag ends of Rafe-mind to account for the disaster, decided finally that Paul Gaines was, in this simulacrum, more than slightly warped.

Paul-mind, Rafe-mind informed <>, was *stationer*, and that meant a wealth of things. It meant a life style; it meant groups; and security, and comfort if one could get the value-items to exchange for it—which was one motivation for human ships moving constantly in transfer of materials from collection to consumption (but not the sole motive of those who ran those ships). This thread led to comprehensions. Paul-mind was not like Rafe. Paul Gaines wanted to be contained in something, in anything. Space frightened him; strangeness did; but what provided him comfort was never strange to Paul.

And there Paul sat, in </>'s heart, nested, protected and surviving.

<> was, to admit it, utterly chagrined.

Paul has other qualities, the Rafe-memories said. Rafe-mind called it bravery, and attached whole complexes of valuations to that word. Not group-survival over individual, though that was part of it. Not retaliation simply, though it might manifest in that; or equally well, by its negative. Not self-aggrandizement, either, though it could be that; or equally well self-denial. The term attached to valuations of person—the affirmation of some ideal species-type, <> judged.

Rafe-mind was not sure it itself possessed this quality; but it desired it. To evidence that it did possess it, Rafe tried not to be disturbed.

For that reason Rafe had walked the corridor to the lab, while paradoxically the remnant of Rafe-mind <> still retained, recognized this act for what it was, that Rafe might comply and intend at the same time to make violent resistance, the moment Rafe had the chance.

Rafe-mind called this second concept dignity.

<> thought of it as self-preservation, but remembered it was, perhaps, strategy, as well, that Rafe did this thing for all the group he perceived as his.

Responsibility.

And what group does Paul belong to? <> wondered, having information about the words Old Man, and ship, and an arrangement <> found disturbingly accusatory.

<> was Old Man too; <> had such a group. They were the passengers. Responsibility, Rafe would say again. <> felt no such thing. But to be the focus of loyalty, that appealed to <>.

</> would appropriate this Paul Gaines. There was no likelihood that </> would not, having no such thing as loyalty </>self.

Easier, <> thought, if Paul had met some segment of = = = =. Desire for containment, indeed. The Cannibal could have provided that, had <> not intervened.

"Mad," said <^>, nesting close to <>, which <> sometimes permitted. "Pity him, <>."

"Paul would find <^> quite disturbing," <> said. "So would all of them."

"<^> know that," <^> said. And, extraneously, as <^> often spoke: "<^> know bravery."

<^> had a certain skill, to dip into <>'s mind without leaving anything behind, not a unique talent, by any means. It was <>'s nature, and the ship's. "It is not—" <> said, and named a concept in <^>'s terms.

"It feels like that," <^> said. "<^> would have walked down that hall."

"Of course <^> would," <> said, unsurprised. "For somewhat skewed reasons. It is not—" and <> named that word again, which neither Rafe-mind nor Jillan-mind (which <> also had) possessed the biological reflexes to understand.

"Go," <> said to <^>, "and tell </> that </> need not skulk about. It's merely </>'s paranoid suppositions that <> would interfere."

"</> supposes that <> can't," <^> said. "</> said to tell <> so."

<> sent a pulse through the ship, violent enough to touch any sense. "So much for can't," <> said, and went off to keep a thing for which the Rafe-mind had no complete word, but *promise* was close enough.

Rafe Two sat, tucked up against the dark, invisible wall; and Jillan and Paul kept to their side of the containment. They stared at one another. That was all that was left to do, in the limbo they were in.

"I have to explain," Rafe had said, taking that position from some time ago, "what happened to me." He spoke quite calmly, quite rationally, thinking of his back against an interface that something might pierce very unexpectedly; his face toward—"I'm not sure what you are," he had said to them. "That Paul that came up to us, that's not the only double that exists. There was you too—Jillan. It got me. Strong, really strong. It took me to that place, that—" He did not like to remember it. "I don't know what it did; it hurt. Like the first time. Maybe it did some adjustment. Maybe—maybe it did something else." Suppositions about that had tormented him thus far; he did not fully trust himself. "I'm telling all of it, you see. I just don't know what it did to me. But it used you to get at me. Now I don't know what I'm locked up with. Just let's keep to our own sides of this place awhile."

There had been pain on Jillan's face. That was the worst.

"Well," she had said in a quiet tone, "I can pretty well guess it's you. That's something. And I can tell you it's me, but I guess you won't believe that."

"I'm not one of them," Paul had said next, and shifted uncomfortably, arms about his knees, while both of them looked at him. "I can swear to you I'm not. There was—there was, remember, this bar on Fargone where we used to meet. The man there had this bird, remember, this live bird—"

"Named Mickey," Jillan said.

"Lived on frozen fruit," Rafe had said himself, remembering the creature, the curiosity, the small reminder there were worlds, that Earth was real somewhere.

—Their captors would be interested in that; homeworld; center of origin. A chill went up Rafe's unprotected back.

"There's one double of you," he had said to Paul. "Maybe more of us. But just stay there. On your side. Please."

"He was a pretty thing," Jillan said at last, "that bird."

"He bit," Paul said.

"Don't blame him," Jillan said. "I'd bite too, being stared at." She hunched her shoulders, looked around, dropped the subject altogether.

"Wish I had a beer," Rafe said.

"Downer wine," said Paul. "You know I bet it got that last bottle."

"Couldn't have come through that spin."

"Bet it did. Bet Rafe's got it. They gave him everything."

"Can't share with him," Rafe said, playing the small game, talk-talk, anything to fill the silence; but he mourned the wine he could never touch.

Paul frowned, who had never seen what they described to him, the place where they walked through furniture and walls or his living self's offered hands.

And Paul's disbelief comforted him, one small confirmation that seemed least likely to be contrived.

But maybe it's smart enough to do that, Rafe thought, growing paranoid. *Maybe it's got all the twitches down.*

He did not know the alien's limits, that was all. He stared at his sister and his friend and could not believe in either of them.

And abruptly they were gone.

He leapt up.

In light, in a tunneled hall of nodes and gossamer-on carpet.

His living self lay there on the floor, in a nest of blankets and disordered clothes.

"Rafe," he said.

There was no response. The living body looked sorrowfully small, tight-curled among the blankets. He walked over and squatted down, immune to heat and cold himself, put out a hand— living habits were hard to break—to the sleeper's shoulder. "Rafe," he said, with great tenderness, because somehow, some-when, and not because they were identical, he had come to love his other self, to think of him as brother, and to have a little pride in himself—without modesty—because of this steady, loyal man. "Rafe, wake up. Come on. Come out of it."

The sleeper moved and groaned in pain.

It was a doppelganger—one of them at least. Rafe stared at it leaning above him with the light shining through its body, then struggled to sit up and heave his naked back against the wall.

"What do you want?" he said, in what of a voice the hoarse-ness left.

"You're hurt. It hurt you."

"Some." Rafe shut his eyes. The light wanted to fuzz. He

opened them again, discontent, for the ceiling light interfered and blurred out part of the doppelganger's form. They were only holograms, the alien had said. And other things he clamped his jaws upon.

The manner was not Kepta, he thought. Or it was Kepta playing still more bitter jokes, with that anguished, frightened look.

"I'm all right," he said to it, to him. "Just a little sore."

"What in God's name did it want? What did it do to you?"

"Just a look-over. A workout. I don't know. It hurt. That was incidental, I think it was. How are you?"

The doppelganger laughed, not a pleasant, happy laugh, but one of irony, all the answer it gave him.

"How's Jillan and Paul?" he asked it then. "Paul still not speaking to me?"

A shadow touched the eyes. "Paul's better now."

Better now. He drew an uneasy breath. *Which one are you?* "I really wish," he said, "you'd back off a bit. The light is in my eyes."

The doppelganger reached; he flinched, twitched back. "You're scared," it said. "Scared of me."

"Who are you?"

"Me. Rafe. It's used my shape with you. Has it?"

"Yes. It has. *Our* shape, friend. You know about that?"

"What did it do?"

"Its name is Kepta. He or she. I don't know." Rafe's voice cracked. "Maybe you could say."

The doppelganger shook its head solemnly, its eyes locked on his own. "It got me too. It used Jillan's shape. I've seen something using Paul's. And it hurt."

"It copied you." It made sense then, in a tangled skein of threads. "That was copy-making, friend. Now it's got three versions of me and you. Four, counting the original."

"Me; the one it made from me; you—"

"It got me," Rafe said. "That's how I know. Mine's four. I saw the machines—" The voice cracked again. His joints felt racked. "Plays havoc with the nerves. Goes all through your body. Copies everything."

"Why? For God's sake, what's it doing with us?"

"It wants different versions. You've grown." He thought now he knew which one it was; there was no way to be sure, only to guess. He guessed. "You're not me, not the way you were; I'm not that me either. It just took a new impression. That's all. It's going to let me go, it says."

"Let you go. Where?"

"Says Paradise."

"How'd it know that? How much does it know?"

"Like names and places?" He stared into the doppelganger's face, and thoughts came to him, knowing this self, its need to know—

—its own condition. To know what it was. The doppelganger had no idea, he suspected; no idea at all what he really was, or where.

"It's got access to everything," Rafe told it carefully. "It has my mannerisms; yours; my turns of speech; everything I know. Like names. It wants to know a star the way we name it. It's got a map in my head; it just overlays that on the charts it knows. So it knows Paradise, Fargone, knows everything—"

"Mickey."

"What Mickey?"

"The bird in that Fargone bar."

"I guess it does. I'd forgotten. I guess it could remember. Probably has better recall than I do."

"Jillan remembers it, really well."

"Meaning it's got us all."

"I don't know," the doppelganger said, hugging himself round the knees. "I don't *know*. What's it up to? You figure that?"

"It says it doesn't matter. Kepta. Kepta's what it calls itself. It says—" His voice gave way again. "—says it's got no military aims. That it could take our *species* out. The whole human race. Says it's not interested."

The doppelganger stared at him.

"I think," Rafe said, "maybe it could, near enough as wouldn't matter. Its tech is—way ahead. Got circuits, memory storage, stuff I can get around; it's mechanical, like that. But the power it throws around, the way its computers work—" He shut his eyes while he swallowed; it hurt. "I don't know comp's insides; you know that; we just run the things. But this ship's got tricks we don't. That's a fact. Doesn't even hurt to say. It runs through our heads all it likes, digs up everything it wants. Think of trying to defend our space from one of us who'd just inherited this whole ship and aimed it at humankind. If we wanted to—we could be real trouble, given what this has. And it is trouble. Knows every target. Every ship." He blinked. Tears spilled, a wetness at outer edge of his right eye. "Amazing what's not classified. Can't be, can it? Where worlds and stations are—any human knows the star names, and God help us, we know the charts. Any human knows how to run machines; so it knows what we've got. And what we don't have. That too."

"How many of it are there?"

"That's a real good question, isn't it? It says *I*. That's all I know."

"Easier if it were."

"Easier to *what*? Fight this thing?"

"Got nothing better to do," the doppelganger said. "Maybe it's going to do everything it said, let you go, just go its way and let human space alone. If it does, that's fine. If it doesn't—well, we're still here, aren't we? We'll fix it."

"*It can shut you down.*"

"So," the doppelganger said with a small, worried shrug. "There's several of us, aren't there?"

"One of us—" Rafe felt a new and spreading chill. "*Rafe, there's five of us.*"

"How, five?"

"Versions. Me. One before I waked. That made you, but it still exists. Naïve as it ever was. There's you; that's three. There's the version of you it just got. Four. There's the me it recorded, the stupid one that walked into that lab and lay down where it said, and let itself be recorded because it had no way to know—"

"No way to stop it either."

"But that's five. You see what the difference is. Mindsets. Number one's straight out of the wreck, shaken up and scared; two's me, who's been through everything; three's you,—we're oldest, seen the most. Four's you without this meeting; five's me who was willing to lie down in that machine and hoped I'd get out—It can take any branch of us it likes. Live in it. Watch it work. Twist it any way it likes."

"You mean it's not just a mask it wears," the doppelganger said, his brow knit up in worry, in far too little worry.

Rafe stared at him. *Tell him?* he wondered. *Tell him what he is?* He knew his own limits, how much truth he could bear. *Sorry, brother, you're repeatable. Jillan, Paul, them too.*

"Maybe it'll really let you go," the doppelganger said at last. "I hope it does."

"You're lying," Rafe said. "You need me."

The doppelganger shook his head. "No. I want you out of here. With all the rest that means. That it's not interested in us. That it *won't* attack."

"And what becomes of you, then? You don't die, man. You can't. What happens to you?" He wished at once he had never said it. He saw the fear it caused, the sudden freezing of mirror-Rafe's expression.

The doppelganger shrugged then. "That is a problem, isn't it?" He dropped down to sit flat against the floor, against the illusion of it—

—because he expects a floor, Rafe thought.

"But it's our problem," the doppelganger said. "Not yours. For one thing you can't very well tell it no. For another—let's just get you out of here, if we can. You can get hurt. Call it sympathy pains, if you like. Self-preservation. Something of the sort. Just take our surviving substance out of here, first chance you get. What's it going to do, walk into Paradise Station with you?"

"Capsule with a beeper."

The doppelganger frowned. "Chancy."

"Scares me too. But it was the best you could think of."

"Don't make jokes like that."

"Sorry. But it's true."

The doppelganger slumped, arms against his knees. "At least it's not going inside Paradise," he said.

"At least. There's that to be grateful for." He leaned back against the wall, tucked the blanket up about his arms. "You don't think you can trust Jillan—or Paul."

"I don't know which copy I'm dealing with," the doppelganger said in desperation. "It sent me here. Without warning. Rafe, it's got them both."

VII

There was no one. Where Paul had been in their confinement, was suddenly no one, in the time it took to blink, the way it had taken Rafe; and Jillan Murray lurched to her feet all in one wild motion, stifling the outcry—*no good, no good to yell.* The dark was absolute, featureless, soundless; she stood sense-deprived and still, bereft of everyone.

"Jillan," said a female voice. Her own doppelganger blinked into green-gold glow in front of her, naked flesh a little bony about the ribs.

"That you?" she said, all cold. "That you, self?"

"No," her own voice came back to her, from mirror-image lips.

Her knees wanted to shake. If she tried to run they would fall. "*My* turn, is it?"

It stood still, with a pensive, frowning look which slowly changed as if thought were going on behind the eyes and arrived at puzzlement. "It feels as if," it said, "you get some satisfaction. from my coming round to you."

"Huh." She laughed.

"Very bitter satisfaction. You were really afraid—of being discounted in favor of the men in this situation. It's a very confused feeling."

Her skin felt like sweat she could not shed. *This is crazy,* she thought. *Should I run?*

Strong, Rafe had said. And: *It got me. Got me*—in ways unspecified.

"Anger," the doppelganger said, "that comes through."

"That doesn't take mind-reading. Where am I? Where are we? Dammit, *why?*"

The doppelganger's head came up a bit, a centering of the eyes, her eyes, beneath an untidy fringe of bangs.

"Take a walk with me."

"Like hell."

It blinked. "You did ask for answers."

"You can tell me what I asked. Right here."

And Paul was there, behind the doppelganger, lying still and helpless on the dark immaterial floor. He vanished as quickly. "Creation and uncreation," the doppelganger said. "That's what you are. No more, no less."

She was shaking. Pockets, she thought extraneously, wanting somewhere to put her hands; her hands missed pockets, touched only naked skin. "So, well," she said, "is that trick supposed to mean something?"

"Not in terms you're used to thinking of. Life and death are valueless. You're here. Your body's long since gone. But you're still living. So was that. Now it's gone. Want it back again?"

It was. It vanished.

"Dead again," it said. "Or gone. However you define it."

She swung at the doppelganger.

She was on the floor, loose-jointed, with the memory of blinding pain, sound, shock that ached in the roots of her teeth; and it stood just out of reach. It squatted down, arms on knees.

"Doesn't it occur to you," it said, "that I could just turn you off?"

Jillan got an elbow under her amid her shivering, pushed up, sat, as far as half squared her with its eyes. She glared at it, and nothing occurred to her, nothing in clear focus, but a dim, small fear that if she hit it again she would get the same hard shock. She had done no damage to it. None.

It sat there, a long, long moment. "Your mind's different," it said. "Self-preservation . . . differently defined. I've seen you through Rafe's eyes. Your mind is shocked at his simplicity. So is Rafe-mind, to know you so thoroughly. Devastated."

"Shut up!"

"That's your strength," it said, this double of herself, this thing with shaggy, disordered hair and infinity in its eyes. "Rafe-mind wouldn't have attacked me bare-handed for anything but one of you. He's afraid to die. So are you. But you *have* died, haven't you? He's afraid because he's got so much to lose—you, and Paul—even his own double. He's full of fears like that. His universe is you and Paul, quite simply; and that ship he's lost. Himself, of course; but he's sure I'd retaliate on you. He can't conceive of the universe without him in it; can't conceive of your survival if he didn't exist. Responsibility for the whole universe. That kind of thinking's very remote in you. . . . Not that you don't care," it said, settling crosslegged to the floor. Just that you don't think in terms of being anything but alone. Not universal like Rafe; just solitary. The men take care of you; they look for nothing from you, so you think. You'd defend them if you got the chance. But you expect no chances, for you, or them. On the other hand—you've died once, you think; and that didn't impress you much. It didn't affect you. You've still got yourself; and that's your universe."

"Sure," she said. An icy worm crawled somewhere at her gut. "You got anything to do besides this? Let's see your face, why not?"

"You don't like me using this shape. Your brother's—your husband's; that you can tolerate. *This* bothers you."

"I hate your guts. Surprising?"

"And now you're scared. Something's got inside."

She was. She stared at the thing eye to eye and it had her own most determined look.

"Go to hell," she said.

"Your strategy is self-defense. Around that you arrange your priorities. I understand this."

It had made her angry. It had made her afraid. It had indeed gotten through. *Stupid,* she thought, *stupid to debate this thing.* That it had *her,* that it lived inside her head, made her afraid not to listen to it, and that was a trap. She shut that worry down, assumed its own crosslegged pose in mockery. "Suppose we see your face. The way you really are."

"Clever," it said.

"I shut you off, didn't I?"

It smiled, her own most wicked smile. "Shut me down cold," it said.

"That brain reacts—mirror image to mine."

"When it's on the same track. *Think of children.*"

Back in her lap. She went off her balance, confused.

"You don't like the idea," it said. "Rafe's upset you didn't live to have the kids he wanted so, he's upset and ashamed he's upset, and won't mention it to you because he thinks in the first place you're grieved at losing that chance and secondly that you'd think it affects his care for you. I know. I felt it quite distinctly."

"Thank him for me," she said hoarsely. "Spare him my opinions."

"You did. Spare him that, I mean. Your sex bears the young, with some pain; more than that—the time. You bear one at a time; there had to be several. It meant going to *Ajax*, being absent from everything you valued, for a long period of your lifespan; it meant inactivity; it meant kids' noise and helplessness, which you don't like; it meant pretending for years and years that you were happy when you weren't, because your misery would affect the men, and cause them pain, and affect the kids, and ruin all the rest of the years you had left to live. Everything Rafe's worked for—depends on you. And you hate it."

"Don't tell them that."

"This is the center where no one comes. Death can't affect it. This is the strategy: silence, and to strike from this place where nothing can come. This virtue. This anger that sustains you. You know your limits. You cherish no illusions. But I'm here."

"Welcome in," she said, staring through it. "Now there are two of us. You want a fight? I'll give you one."

"Yes," it said. "I know. But I would win. I have, before. I destroyed that version of you. It was no longer whole."

"Fine," she said: There was a knot in her throat that made talking painful. "That was kind of you."

"Humor," it said.

"Absolutely."

"I want your help," it said.

She looked at it, a sudden shortening of focus, a centering of hate. *"Do* you?"

"You don't fully understand," it said, "what these versions are. They're alive."

"That one was?" She moved her eyes where Paul had lain, unconscious on the floor. "You *killed* it? *You want my help?"*

"He. That version died in his sleep, without pain. He can die— infinitely often. No," the doppelganger said, lifting her hand. "That wasn't a threat. I'm explaining what you are. You have a certain integrity, right now. You're unique, much more flexible than the template I have in storage. You've learned. That version of Paul I twice destroyed—never waked after the wreck. The one I sent you to keep you content, that one was from the same template; and it came to consciousness with you all settled in your state.

You brought it—gently up to date; it's more stable as a consequence. Paul, you know, doesn't like shocks. He relies on you in these circumstances. He needs your flexibility. Your expertise as spacers, greater than his own. Oh, I know—you're lost. That's why the first Paul ran off. He leaned on you and you didn't provide the prop. So he leaned on himself. And he ran."

"O my God."

"No, indeed you didn't get the same Paul back. And you did, in one important sense. The one you have now is healthier. He still belongs to you. The other one, the one that ran, has diverged—considerably. You thanked me for destroying your damaged selves. But Paul's first copy was damaged too. It's not a Paul you'd understand. And a stray version of Rafe exists, that's gone way off. Rafe has his weaknesses. That's why I'm talking to you. The stable one. The one with the solid core. The only one it hasn't got. Yet."

"It. What—*it*?"

"This ship has a lot of passengers. One of them."

"And who are you?"

"Kepta. Kepta's what to call me."

"You're in charge?"

"Captain would be close. I'm going to copy you again. It's the best defense. That there'll be one version of you neither naive nor—if things go wrong—corrupt. It will hurt, Jillan. It's not my choice. It's just your nature."

It was gone.

And the pain began.

"</> knows," said = < + > = = <−> = =. "</> knows <>'re disarranged."

<> was not surprised at the Cannibal's report. <> stayed quiet now, digesting what <> had learned, while in the lab, with another part of <>'s mind, <> was quite busy.

"Move us," said <∧>, anxiously, from elsewhere in the ship. <∧> feared the Cannibal and stayed far away. "Move us from this place. Others of this species may come."

"No," <> said, "not yet."

<∧> raged and wept, fearful for <∧>self. <∧> was very old, and very fond of <∧>self, besides being slightly mad, and <∧> skulked off, with |||000||| slinking after in growing despair.

"</> knows what <> have done," <-> said again, turning back.

"</> knows," said another, unexpected voice. It was </>self, </> had ventured to the limits of </>'s security, that line across which <> did not go. This intrusion into <>'s affairs was purest insolence, demonstrating </>'s strength; but demonstrating impotence as well: </> had met a limit </> could not pass.

But </> brought a companion who had no such disabilities. <> saw this. "Paul," <> addressed Paul One, which hung back, twined with crippled Rafe-mind, the one that </> had worn. Paul had acquired new pieces, shadow-limbs, extensions in the dark, at least three arms, maybe four; and legs as well.

The Paul-mind said something, garbled like itself. ". . . . fear," came out. "jillan rafe bastard want come now . . ."

"Not very articulate," <> said. The template <> was making was complete. With deliberation <> released the subject, dismissed her out of reach and fronted </>'s vexation with insouciance.

Gentle, human arms were about her, light shone above her, and for a moment Jillan believed in both implicitly, having no wish to move at all, only to be, and not to think.

"Jillan," Paul's voice called. His fingers touched her face, brushed back a stubborn lock of hair—he often did that small thing, of mornings, to wake her up. Tears leaked between her lashes; but the pain was gone, just gone, as if it had never been, hard even to remember now. She opened her eyes and blinked at Paul's face, at two of Rafe's, one of the twins like Paul, dimmed by the lights; the other, Rafe's living self.

Her men, she thought, exhausted. All three of them safe, here among *Lindy*'s pathetic pieces. She sat up and held to Paul's shoulder, hung on it like a drifter to a hold in null, and gazed at both her brothers, the living and the one neither live nor dead.

"You all right?" Rafe asked, a rusty, painful sound.

"What happened to your voice?"

"Had a bad while," he said. "Over now. I'm not hurt. You?"

She nodded. Her mind felt adrift in fragments. There was too much, too much they did not know. She tightened her grip on Paul's bare shoulder and drew a deep and shaky breath. "I'm all right," she said. "You know somebody named Kepta?"

"Yes," said her living brother in that strained, hoarse voice. "I know him."

"Him." The mental shift made her think again. "Her. It. Whatever. Whatever it really is." She slid her hand down to Paul's and clenched its solidity. "I'm all right. You?"

"Fine," Paul said. "Fine," said Rafe, her Rafe, the one the light shone through. She felt a chill—*how be sure it's them, mine, not something else?*—as if the floor were falling away, the gossamer-carpet floor her body could not feel. She stared at them and froze a moment, then drew her limbs under her and sat apart, pulling her hand from Paul's, resting her forehead on her knee.

"Destroy all of them," [] said, one of ten of []kind, one of a chorus of voices, hundreds of outraged protests which <> ignored, occupied as <> was. Paul-mind had retreated, with </>, to that place where </> was firmly in charge.

It was too late to recover Paul One, <> knew. Paul One was quite, quite beyond any reason. More, he had gained a certain wariness, which indicated that his immunity against shutdown was increasing.

<> could not keep </> from the controls long. There would be distractions. <> knew.

"Aaaaiiiiiii!" ((())) wailed, irreverent of boundaries, passed <> and hid, pathetic in ((()))'s disturbance. But ((())) had never been particularly self-restrained before ((())) slipped from sanity. "Aiii," ((())) mourned, in short, painful sobs, "aiii, aiii."

"Accurate," said <>.

"Jillan," Rafe said, unable to touch her—he reached, that was all that he could do; and every movement hurt his sprains. "You're sure that you're all right?"

"Sure," she said in a hoarse small voice. "Rafe—how do you know it's me?"

A chill went over him. "Your asking makes it likely," he said after a moment. "Doesn't it? It's you. Question is—how far down the line?"

"You know, then."

"I know," he said.

She ran a hand through her hair, disturbing its disorder, blinked at him; at the ones insubstantial like herself. "Paul? Rafe?"

"What?" Rafe Two answered.

"You know—both of you—about the copies that exist—"

"I saw my double," Paul said. "Didn't all of us?"

"That question's always worth asking," she said to Paul. *"Didn't all of us?"* Her eyes came back to Rafe, haunted. "You know what dawns on me? That even I don't know which I am. It copied me. Which one left? Which stayed? It's all academic, isn't it? That copy's back there, and if it's awake, it's scared as I'd be. Doing everything I'd do, thinking every thought, because it is—me. I am there. And here. That's the way it works."

"For God's sake, Jillan—"

"Rafe, I talked—*talked*—I'm not even sure of that . . . to something that calls itself Kepta; it's in charge. There's more than one."

"You're sure of that."

"It said there were a lot of passengers. A lot. And, Paul—Paul, that copy of you we saw—one of them's got it. Got one of you, Rafe. This Kepta says they've gotten—damaged somehow. That they're maybe—dangerous."

"Jillan," Rafe Two said, sharp and brittle. "Jillan, save it. Our brother's not involved in this. He's leaving."

"Leaving?"

"Tell it to me," Rafe said to her, hearing things that made far too much sense. Jillan looked afraid, glancing from one to the other of them. Paul's face was stark with panic. "How—dangerous?"

"What's this about leaving?" Jillan asked him; and when he said nothing, looked at Rafe Two.

"It's given him a chance," Rafe Two said. "It'll take him to Paradise, a capsule of some kind, a signal—it'll drop him off."

"You believe that?" Jillan asked, looking round at him.

"What did Kepta say to you?" Rafe persisted in his turn.

"It's the best promise we've got," the doppelganger said in his, crouching there, hands loose between his knees. "It says it's moving on, going elsewhere. No more concern with the whole human race. Wants to drop off our living component, it does. Maybe before his food runs out. I don't know why. I don't care. I've told Rafe I'd just as soon he was out of here."

"Rafe," Rafe said, "mind your business. Jillan, what's going on?"

"Nothing," she said, tight and quick.

"Don't give me nothing. It's got—what, the first of Paul? The one that ran. And me. Which me?"

"I don't know." She shook her head, with panic in her eyes. "I've no idea."

"Early or late copy?"

"I don't know. It didn't tell me that."

"It's not your business," Rafe Two said. "You're leaving. You're getting off this ship."

"It's got to get there first." Rafe felt his heart beating double time, looked from one to the other of them, Jillan, Rafe—Paul, whose panic was all but tangible.

"You take any ticket out of here you've got," Jillan said. "Look—Rafe: you're only one of you. You understand? I'm not alone. Paul's not. You're still with us. You'll be with us—in duplicate."

"She's right," his doppelganger said, putting out his hand as if to touch his arm. "You're superfluous—aren't you? You take any way you can off this ship. We've already settled that."

Rafe sat still, staring at all of them, wiped his hand across his lip.

"He's right," Paul said from over by the wall, in a small and steady voice. "You're the one that's really at risk. Get out if you've got a choice. We want you to do that. We want to know you're safe."

The voice lingered. Paul's body was gone. All of them were, suddenly, as if they had never been. There was only the corridor, the remnants, the pieces of *Lindy*.

"That's not enough!" Rafe shouted, in his ruined whisper of a voice. He looked up at the warted, serpentine ceiling, the trail of lights and raised his fists at it. *"Kepta—"* His voice gave way, beyond audibility. "Kepta," he tried again "Kepta, send them back!"

There was a passing wail, loud, devastatingly loud. He clapped his hands over his ears until the worst of it had gone.

Then was silence, long silence. He sat down, aching, in the vacant chair at *Lindy*'s console. He passed his hands over controls, the few that worked, and looked at the starfield vid gave him.

He knew where he was now. He had confirmed Altair, and

Vega burning bright, the two great beacons of the dark near human space, virtually touching from this perspective. The myriad, myriad others, the few wan human stars. Sol . . . was out of field.

That way? he wondered. *Is that the direction it means to go? Is that what it's telling me?* He could see Paradise, a dim, common star, nothing much, the kind mankind preferred.

He switched on the com. "Kepta," he said, patiently, watching lights flicker, reckoning it might be heard. "Kepta, you want to talk to me?"

No answer.

He bowed his head on the console, looked up finally at the vid. Nothing changed. Inertial at 1/10 C. Drifting, after jump, in some place off human routes.

No one would find them. God help whoever did. God help the whole species if someone did.

He wiped at his eyes, his cheek resting against the metal console. To leave this place—to let it take Paul and Jillan on—

To let it have himself, in infinite series, erasing what it liked, keeping what it wanted until he was whatever Kepta chose—

"Kepta, talk to me."

And after a long while of silence: "Kepta, you want to discuss this?"

"I don't think," someone said behind him, "you'd recognize my voice on that radio."

He spun the chair about, wincing with sore ribs and joints, blinked at the dimming of the lights, at Jillan standing there.

"Don't do that." His hoarseness betrayed him, cracked in his disturbance.

"Come up behind you?" Kepta asked in Jillan's fair clear tones.

"Her."

"Use this shape, you mean? It was convenient. Most recent, even more than yours. I don't like to partition off more than I have to, or struggle with a mind too long out of date."

"You going—where? Vega, maybe? Somewhere near?"

"Might," Kepta said. "Might not."

"You won't say."

"I don't know," Kepta said. "I haven't decided that. Is that why you called me?"

"Jillan said—there was trouble on the ship."

"There may be."

"Look, are we going to Paradise?"

"I told you that we were."

"*What* trouble?"

"I don't see it concerns you."

"Dammit—I want to know."

Jillan's eyes looked up at him, with Jillan's innocence, beneath a fringe of disordered hair. "What difference can it make?"

"I'm not going. I'm not leaving this. I want to know."

"Not leaving the ship?"

"No more than you ever meant me to." His voice broke down. "You set this up. Didn't you?"

"No. But between this mind and your own—I figured that you'd stay."

He gazed at his sister's shape, untouchable, something it hurt even to curse "You always right?"

"No. That would be unbearable. Besides—we need only delay your trip. We can settle this thing, if you'll cooperate. Then I'll take you to Paradise. Or anywhere you like. We'll make it reciprocal. I get your wholehearted assistance. You name your destination. I'll take you there. Reward. We do share that concept."

"Paradise is good enough." His voice broke down, came out small and diminished, and he hated it. *Jillan,* his eyes kept telling him. The mind inside was half hers at least, knowing him with her thoroughness, memories shared from infancy, childhood, all their lives. "What do you want—another copy? That help?"

"It might. But taking it so soon might weaken you considerably. It might even kill you. And I won't."

"I don't mistake that for sentiment."

The Jillan-figure paused, its hazel transparent eyes quite earnest. "No," it said. "Disadvantage outweighs advantage. Transspecies, transactions can be explained like that, in motiveless simplicity. Advantage and disadvantage. Facts and acts. True reasons, trans-species, rarely make full sense. Even basic ones. Suffice it to say I can use this simulacrum; I just partition. It takes very little attention. On the other hand, if you tried my mind—it would be the other problem. You'd probably not wake up: large box, small content."

"Real modest."

"Factual. I'm complex." Kepta diminished in brightness. "You have your qualities. I don't say they're unique. The combination of them is. In all the universe, the snowflakes, grains of sand, chemical combinations, the DNA that makes up, for instance, Rafael Lewis Murray—" The voice faded too. "—not to mention his experience at any given moment—the chance of finding anything exactly duplicated is most remote. Haven't you seen that on this ship? Infinity is always in you, Rafael Murray, and the other way around. . . ."

It was gone, faded into silence.

It was Jillan he found in the dark, or who found him, starlike striding across the nowhere plain.

"Rafe," she said when she reached him, in that gentle tone that was very much her own.

But Rafe Two was wary, having landed without preface in this nowhere place, alone and unprepared.

"Jillan?" he asked of Jillan-shape, and knew, by the splitsecond it had hesitated to answer him, that it was not. "You want—what?" he asked. "What do you want from me?"

"You know that," Kepta said. "You know a lot of things by now. Your state's become valuable to me again."

Rafe-Mind, Paul One, all woven together, like the multiplicity of limbs: it moved in shambling misery back to the territory </> owned.

"I," it mourned, "I, I, I—" not knowing what that *I* meant until </> took the Rafe-mind up and relieved Paul of carrying it.

</> shuddered despite </>self as </> extended a portion of </>'s mind and straightened things. </> forced Rafe-mind to resume the configurations </> remembered, and went on rearranging.

Rafe screamed, and took in </>'s partitioned intrusion—grew quiet then, carrying on his reflexive functions, beginning to re-sort and gather on his own.

</> left him then, and Rafe at least went on functioning. Rafe-mind had new configurations, certain amputations, a certain dependency. "He's yours," </> said to Paul.

Paul felt of it and insinuated a portion of himself, imitating </> in this.

"Be careful," </> said, though pleased. "It will deform. Go in more gently this time."

Paul derived memories, sorted them and reconfigured himself. He had learned. </> taught him—many things. Self-defense was one. To enter another simulacrum was another.

He handled Rafe-mind this time with some skill: </>'s re-arrangements had slipped him past Rafe-mind's defenses in some regards, given him a new chance at others.

He looked about him with increasing confidence. He knew = = = = in = = = ='s various segments and knew that all such were dangerous, but he was stronger. He knew ((())), that ((())) was mad, and was unafraid of the sometime howling that streaked panic-stricken through the passages. He knew [] and <v>, <^> and |:|, which began—justifiably—to be afraid of him.

Paul, he still thought of himself. Paul One was something which adequately described him, since he was the inheritor, old-est and wisest of all Pauls. About destroying his other simulacrum he had no compunction whatsoever, no more than he had had in his former state for shed hair or the trimmings of his fingernails.

He sought both Rafes and Jillan with a different intent—re-membering how they had sought him out back on Fargone sta-tion, wanting his money, his brains, his back, and most of all his genes for the getting of other Murrays. He had let himself be used in every way there was, and that thought burned in him like acid.

He could still forgive. He could forgive it all, on his own terms, in their perpetual atonement. He would no longer take their orders, no more orders from Jillan and from Rafe, no more be-longing to them; but them to him, belonging the way this Rafe-mind did. It was afraid of him.

He stroked it, taking pleasure in its fear and dependency, as if it were the original.

His own template he meant to destroy, along with his dupli-cate. He would be unique. There would be no more duplicates to rival him. He had become a predator, and wanted, for practi-cal reasons, nothing in the universe exactly like himself.

He developed wishes very much like </> and was well satis-fied with that outlook. He knew most that happened elsewhere on the ship. </> spoke to him and kept him well informed.

He knew, for instance, that the living Rafe had just made a

mistake, in that territory too well defended for </> to breach as yet. He had let <> get a very dangerous template, one that trusted everything far too much. Paul ached to have that Rafe, in particular.

"Patience," </> said. "Not yet. </> promise you."

<>, across the ship, was shifting to another simulacrum, and Paul knew that too.

"Attack," Paul wished </>, constant on this theme, and [] was interested.

"Not yet," </> insisted.

"<>'s chosen you to use," [] said, prodding at him.

"And <>'s having trouble configuring it," </> reported, to Paul's keen satisfaction.

"It would fight," Paul said; and in an access of passion: "Take <> now. Now's a chance for us."

"Be patient," </> insisted still. "<> will get <>self into difficulty sooner or later. That's inevitable. Then all the rest will come to us. Won't they, Rafe?"

The simulacrum shivered, best substitute they had. "I'll come," it said, having difficulty distinguishing I from they, "I have to."

Paul was satisfied. Rafe's fear was sensual to him; gender had stopped mattering, along with other things, but sex was more important than it had ever been.

In that regard he shared one tendency with = = = =. He aspired to multiplicity. He was not large, not like </>. He knew his level and his limits, and had no designs on <>. Being born a stationer he had never thought about command. He aimed at simple competence, to function well within the whole—and he had his place all picked out, in something very large indeed, which understood all his appetites.

"I want to talk with you," Paul's voice said; and Paul blinked, suddenly without his companions, alone, in the dark, with this version of himself.

"Who are you?" he asked. He felt his nonexistent heart, another insanity—dead, his heart kept beating. It sped with fear; his skin felt the flush of adrenalin, and he faced this thing in a panic close to shock. "Which are you?"

"Kepta," his doppelganger said. "The others know me. You're quite safe. You want to sit down, Paul?"

He sat down where he was, in the vast and shapeless dark. He set his hands on his crossed ankles and stared at his mirrored shape which took up a pose very like his own.

"You're the hardest," the doppelganger said, "the most difficult to occupy. I ruined several of you with Rafe's memories; one with Jillan's. Two went to pieces of their own accord. Keep yourself calm. I assure you I won't hurt you."

"You will," Paul said, remembering what the others had been through. "Let's get that on the table, why don't we? You want me the way I am. You want a copy of me, a sane one; and it's going to hurt like hell. Can't we get on with that?"

"You've stabilized," it said, "considerably. You're quite complex of your type. Your mind goes off at tangents, travels quite rapidly compared to the others. You make fantasies of elaborate and deliberate sort. Not the most elaborate. There's an entity aboard—I could never say the name in frequencies you'd hear—who sits and modifies, nothing else. I'm not quite sure it's sane, but it's bothered no one yet."

"Cut it," Paul said. "Why should I talk to you at all?"

"I want to find out what I can. To learn anything that may have bearing on what you are. There's trouble, understand, and one of your versions is in the middle of it."

"Good."

"No. Not good at all. Not for your sake. Least of all for Jillan and Rafe."

"How?"

"Their freedom. Their existence, for that matter. That's at risk. Not to mention your own.   Stay calm. Keep calm."

His breath was short. He locked his arms about his knees, conscious of nakedness, of vulnerability, of rank, raw panic with this thing. "Nothing of me would ever hurt them."

"Yes. It would. You have more to your mind; you have—you'd call it—a darker side."

"Not against them."

"Especially against them."

"You read minds, do you?"

"Only this one. The one I'm in. It reacts to things I think. It's painful. Quite painful. I can feel this body's processes going wild. Give me help, Paul. It's going out on me."

He blinked, saw the rigid muscles, the evidence of stress in corded arms, saw it shiver—felt ashamed of its mirrored weakness.

It faded out, in black.

Dead? he wondered. He wiped at nonexistent sweat, at a blurring in his eyes. His heart was still going fit to burst.

Fear killed it. Mine.

It came back again, materialized sitting crosslegged in front of him.

"I had to make a new one," Kepta said. "You see what I mean."

"It just broke apart."

"It wasn't a small stress I put on it. Can we keep off that subject? I'd rather think of where you came from for the moment. Fargone. Please—don't panic. —Paul, do something."

"What?"

"Anything."

"Like get the hell out of here?"

"Keep talking."

"Where's the rest of us? What *is* this place?"

"A ship." The mirror-image looked more relaxed "That's where you are, you understand. I think Rafe and Jillan have told you some things. I want you to keep one fact very much in mind, keep thinking on it constantly, even at the worst."

"What's that?"

"Love. They love you, Paul, no matter how dangerous you are. Never lose that thought."

"Huh," he said, shook his head in embarrassment. "Murderer gone maudlin. You killed me, damn you; killed Jillan—"

"It's true; don't doubt that they love you, don't doubt it for a moment. It's very important. It's the most important thing, isn't it? It's your whole universe."

He felt heat in his face, utter shame.

"I know," it said with his mouth, looking steadily out of his eyes at him, with his squarish, stubborn face. "I'm absolutely sure what you're doing here. Love describes it, why you came, why you worked all those years with them at things that frighten you. To avoid Fargone mines. That was one reason: being afraid of the deep and dark, where your mother died—shot in riot. Riot. That leads places—"

"Shut up."

"But most of all—you want company. You want to give and get love. You think there's something inherently wrong in that. It's not a rational transaction. And you value rationality; your species does, yes, I know—while you, you operate from the gut; that's the word, isn't it? From the gut. You find this embarrassing?"

"Maybe," he said, because it was, because saying anything else was too complicated and even worse. He looked off into the dark, to evade its eyes and had to look back again.

"You rate Rafe and Jillan," it said, "higher than yourself. *Braver*, you would say, because their actions come more often from rationality. Rafe-mind thinks that's nonsense, but never mind—you rate them smarter too. That's difficult for me to judge, even having used all three of you. You've taken Rafe for your senior, though the age difference is small. It's not the real reason you have him for superior, though it's the one you prefer to use. You acknowledge the same superiority in Jillan, who's your age, and you've partitioned off a small resentment for this, much stronger toward Jillan, who evokes strongest feelings in you. Your gender is physically the stronger. Your emotional faculty equates strength of all kinds with fitness to mate. But many individuals are stronger and better of your species; you really rely on opportunity—a contradiction at the root of many insecurities."

"Every man has that."

"To Rafe—it's *ship*. In him, your kind of thinking is very short range: he'd only think that way on the docks. In specific. Not constantly measuring himself. He knows what would make, him fit to mate with fit mates—A ship. He's lost that now, and that hurt him; but he's too busy yet to think of that. He has other priorities. He knows his measure. He's got the universe to save . . . in his own self. And that comes first. While Jillan—"

"Leave her out of this."

"Why? Why leave her out? That's an important question. Isn't it?"

"Just don't."

"Don't consider her? She'd resent that, you know. Do you understand, she thinks like Rafe—about the ship. With it, she was merchanter. Free to take whatever mates she fancied. The one freedom she would have—outside the children. Outside childbearing. She was happy in that prospect. She looked forward to

it. But *ship* drives her, the way it drives Rafe. She went to you—
your money, your attachment—your friendship—"

"Stop it, dammit."

"—for Rafe's sake. For hers. *Responsibility.* It drives her in a
different way, to do unpleasant things. She feels quite powerless
in the most important regards. This marriage—this permanency—
took away the one reward she had reserved for herself. That too
she did. For the ship."

"O God."

"You resent her every competency. And Rafe's."

"No."

"At heart, you suspect your validity. You resented the thought
of the Murray name on all your offspring; you gave in on that.
You gave up your money to them. You rely on them for smallest decisions; and you need them—emotionally. You have no remote goals like theirs. Yours is very simple: to validate
yourself—continually. And to do this, you attached to those who
had no weakness in your eyes. You wanted a larger thing to belong to. In them, you found it. You have to understand that about
yourself. You do have to belong."

"I know," he said. There was nothing else to say to that, nothing at all.

"You've always doubted your importance. Your grandmother
was born in a lab and had a number tattooed on her hand. You
rarely saw your mother. She supported you by mine work. You're
not sure whether that was love or duty. She never said. She died
and left you a station share, which gave you the ability to live
in some comfort. But your species needs attachments of stronger
sort. Rafe was one. And Jillan. They were your shelter in youth.
They ran wild on the docks. You envied them—not their freedom, but their unity. And they made you a part of them. Adult
needs grew into that. For you—there were no other possibilities."

"Why don't we try for that copy you need?"

"No. Go on thinking on that point. It's a crucial one for you.
There's ambiguity there. You went into a very dangerous situation; mining, which you hate; in a very unsafe ship; left all your
comforts; exchanged all values you had for this one return, that
you give and get love from both of them. That seems an important point. Doesn't it?"

He drew a deep breath, feeling naked in more ways than physically. "Yes," he said.

"Vulnerability is upsetting to you."

"To anyone."

"Upset is itself a vulnerability."

"Is there some point to this?"

"Oh, yes. There is. I fell victim to that aspect of you myself. Your simulacra were all painful to me. And I avoided that upset. I drew an unwarranted conclusion, that you would not adapt. Rafe did warn me. Your survival should have warned me. Your runaway copy evaded every danger but one. That's quite a defense you have."

"Sure."

"There is aggression in you. There is—what you would call that dark side; secrets you keep partitioned. So you understand a little of what I do when I occupy a mind. I partition off those parts of me that would be incompatible. But you don't have as fine a control on that partitioning; Jillan *uses* hers; Rafe operates in simplicity: his secrets are all little ones, excepting one. Excepting one. But you—You deliberately disorganize yourself, destroying connections—like now, like this mind's trying to do, and I won't press it. Remember that one thing. Remember what I told you was important to remember. That's how the first Paul Gaines went wrong."

"What—went wrong?"

"Mad. From your viewpoint, he's quite mad. Pull out everything you hold behind those barriers and you'll know in what respect. I know you, Paul. There's no aspect of this mind I haven't been through, nothing I haven't handled. I've killed several of you doing it, at some cost to me."

"What do you want from me?"

"I want you to deal with Paul One. It's very likely that you're the only one that can both reach and affect him."

"You can't?" Wit started working again, and seized on that hint of limitation. *Learn something—bring it back to them—*

*—prove myself—*The truth of it jarred.

"I'll be—otherwise occupied. I know that I will be. And if you break down, Paul—if you do break down, it's very likely I'll have to wipe the templates out. That's death. For Rafe, and you, and Jillan. Real death, not a power-down. There are several worse things that could happen. Remote, but possible."

"What's that?"

"One, that you'd become his. The other Paul's. That he'd have all of you, and the templates, to do with as he pleases. That could happen—if I should go under. And it's possible I could. It's always possible. Believe me, destroying the templates against that event—would be charity."

He clenched hands that felt cold in the absence of all cold, swallowed against a knot that was not there. "And if you're lying, all the way—what then, Kepta?"

"You might take the chance and assume that I'm lying. But you've seen that first version of yourself. Did you like it? Did it look healthy?"

"No," he said. "No."

"Do you want to fight this thing? Or had you rather go now? Which will you choose? To get back, to go to sleep? I can arrange that. Or I can tell you what you have to do, to avoid catastrophe."

"What's that?" he asked. It did not seem himself asking, as if he watched from some great distance where he had gone for safety. "What am I supposed to do?"

"Understand it. Understand what that first version, what every version of you has behind every partition of its mind. Understand *yourself.* If there's one weakness it will find it; if there's one doubt, it's going to discover it. Think of those partitioned things. Think through all your mind until it has no seams, no joining-places, no contradictions at all. Did you know you enjoy giving pain? That you fear the dark? Do you know that Rafe uses you, even while he loves you? That you want Jillan to be less than she is? That you want to be feared?"

"That's a lie."

"Not a lie. It's the obverse, the wellspring of all the strengths you have. You come from a place, from Fargone; I remember. Hundreds of thousands of your kind are crowded together there. You exist in stress and refrain from every hostile thought and violence. You partition off these things. You live by active denial of them. That other Paul, that you ran—has no partitions. The moment you meet him—neither will you."

He stared into eyes the like of his, feeling ice lodged in his gut.

"Let's talk about sex, Paul."

"What about it?"

"Defensive," Kepta said. "You wish most of all you had clothes. That really bothers you."

"I haven't got the urge. Haven't. Won't." He felt a sweat break out that could not possibly exist. "I don't think I'm likely to."

"Rafe feels these reactions, but generalized and rarely in this place. Worry—fear—kinship—these suppress the drive."

"So does dying."

"Does it?" Kepta asked.

He stared at Kepta, recalling what it knew, what it remembered.

"The clothes," Kepta said, "the clothes. An inconvenience in the templates, but a very important protection to you. Jillan's bothered least. Rafe—inconvenienced. You're terrified. Aren't you, Paul?"

He said nothing, only looked it in the eyes.

"Physiology betrays you," Kepta said. "This body can react—in many ways. It will. You fear it will . . . and Rafe—has stopped being . . . *brother* . . ."

"Damn you."

". . . become—*rival*, in this dark aspect. In several senses. So has she."

"They're better," he said at last, between the two of them. "They're better than I am. Aren't they?"

"I can't judge."

"Can't you?"

"I won't be there. You will. In this—it's not better, Paul. It's what survives."

"It can't all rest on me. Dammit, give me—give me more than that. . . ."

Kepta rose, straightened, unfolding in midair so that he stood. He held out his hand. "I can't. Take my hand. I'll send you back to familiar referents . . . after I've made a copy. This is a valuable point with you, this moment. If you disintegrate hereafter, I might try—perhaps once more with you. Only perhaps. I won't risk the ship. You mustn't depend on anything but yourself. Remember what I told you is important."

He thought back, and another thought came, far colder. "You know my mind inside and out. More than lying—isn't it possible you know how to manipulate us? You know just what strings to pull, and when. You're not learning things from this. You're *moving* us—to do the things you want."

Kepta's brows lifted slowly; as slowly, the mouth assumed a grudging smile. "Of all of you—you're the first to challenge me on that. Of course I am. I see why the others value you, Paul Gaines. You do have surprises. And now you have a choice. Your hand . . . if you will."

He held it out, repulsed as Kepta's closed on his in a dry, temperatureless grip. Kepta's clasp was strong, like living metal, perilous in its potentiality.

"Don't close down," he said. "Let *go!*"—as the air around them dissolved and whirled in a blur of his own glowing limbs. *"No!"* he cried.

It let go.

Pain shot through him then.

It was worse than he had expected, and longer. Far longer.

"Kepta!" he cried, over and over again, "Jillan, Rafe! O God, God, God—!"

—thinking he was dying. He remembered death.

But he awoke in tranquility, in Rafe's nest of *Lindy*'s parts.

"You all right?" Rafe Two was leaning over him. Jillan wiped his brow and for a moment he lay there.

He stopped breathing for a moment, experimentally; started it up again, not for air: for the comfort of it.

"Paul, are you all right?"

He let Rafe help him sit, hugged Jillan to him, her head against his shoulder. There was light. Light all about him. He cherished it, looking about him. He saw Rafe One standing there, helpless-looking in his solidity.

"It got its copy," he said to them all. "That was what it wanted. A lot better than the last, I think."

No, he had screamed. He remembered that suddenly.

Remembered other things.

He had taken terror into the experience. That, along with his self-knowledge and self-disgust.

That was his backup. Flawed.

VIII

There was silence in the corridor, among *Lindy*'s pieces, the silence of waiting, when everything had been said, when the only needs were his own, and Rafe moved about those when he must, under the eyes of those whose remaining necessity was breathing, and that only because they could not forget to do it.

To eat, to drink—these things seemed cruel to do while they witnessed; to sleep—Rafe did sleep as he sat against the wall, a nodding of his head, a panicked look to see whether they were still there.

"All accounted for," said Rafe Two, who read all his body language with more skill than Jillan ever could. "None of us have been anywhere."—Meaning they were all intact, and as much themselves as they had been when he went to sleep.

"I'd think," said Jillan, "it could have gotten its business together by now."

"It's waiting for something else," Rafe said.

"What would it be waiting for?" asked Paul.

Rafe shrugged.

"You know something we don't?" asked Rafe Two.

He shrugged again, wiped his face, got up and went about his toilet—shaved, because he needed it.

"Not sorry to miss that." Rafe Two perched on the counter edge, transparent and only partly phasing with it. In the mirror, Jillan and Paul leaned against the console of *Lindy*'s dead panel, watching him with proprietary interest.

"I wish you wouldn't stare," he said.

"Sorry," Jillan said. "It's the only action going."

Rafe-nothing crept along in the dark, blind as he had become. At times he thought he wept; but maybe that was illusion like the dark, for his hands felt nothing when he touched his face.

He had seen horror. Some of it still lived inside, and consciousness came and went; but he had seen his chance and slipped away, crawling in the dark.

He had had many limbs. And few. Now he had no under-standing what shape was his. He only traveled as he could, as far as he could, and he supposed that limbs took him there.

Then something began to move beside him in the void, shadowy at first, with the outlines of some leggy, rippling beast. It brushed against him and the touch of it sent a shock through all his nerves.

He screamed. *"Aii! Aiii!"* it shrieked back at him, which so unnerved him he rolled aside from it and sat staring at this nest of coils and legs that swayed closer and closer, towering above him in black-glistening segments outlined in yellow light.

"Help," it cried, "help, help—" It was not himself which understood this, but one of those ruptured areas of his mind, one of those places that hung in painful ruin, like threads that went into the dark, into inside-out perspectives.

He stared at it, and it oozed from its heap and surrounded him with its coils. He heard it sobbing, felt the shock of its nibbling up these stray threads, and the tears ran on his face.

"Come, come, come," it wished him. He understood it through these threads. He recalled in horror what he was, and what pursued. "Get up and run," the worm-thing wailed. "It will take you. Run!"

He wished to run. He tried to. A murkish glow came about them and the worm-thing fled.

"No," said Paul's chill voice above him, and a firm grasp gathered him up again.

He wept, having again more than several limbs, being in pain, while that monstrous shape enfolded all of them, in a welter of disturbed perspective. It swallowed up the threads, and he was blind.

"Paul," he tried to say, "Paul, that isn't right."

"Rafael Murray," the tall man said, taking him by the hand, bending down to their level. "Jillan—"—taking hers, so they knew something bad would come: nothing good ever came of Welfare strangers, not especially official ones in expensive suits, and he wished this man away with the horror of foreknowledge. "There's been an accident," the man would say next. "Out in the belt—"

That was what Paul did to him for revenge. It used his memories, put him back in that, time until he had no more recollection of any worm-thing.

"No," the shining girl said, the star-jumper who had come to Fargone docks in her wealth and security. "No." And he could see in her eyes the long-hauler's prejudice against insystemers, that he would ever approach the likes of her and offer to sleepover with her, in this place longhaulers frequented and insystemers dared not come. She looked him up and down. She was all of, maybe, seventeen at most, unsure and offended in her inexperience. "Better get out of here," she said.

And he: "My name's Murray."

"There a ship that name?"

"There was, " he said, realizing it had been so small, so long ago, even spacers had forgotten. "Lindy was her name."

Dead ship. He saw the pity. "Buy me a drink," she said with fortitude. And maybe because she knew he had so little: "No, you have one on me."

"No thanks," he said. Desire had cooled in him. It was the first approach he had ever made to a woman of spacer-kind, after weeks of nerving himself. He guessed he might be her first, and even pitied her courage. She wanted her first with someone better. Someone memorable. She was good-hearted and would take him and never talk about it. Ever. The wound in both of them would live for years . . . whatever he did now. "No. Give it to someone else," he said. And he walked away.

‹/› was, at depth, dismayed at the near escape of Rafe-mind, ‹› detected it clear across the ship.

"Good for you," ‹› said the damaged Rafe-mind in a pulse transcending boundaries. *"Good for you,"* —in terms Rafe-mind might understand.

And a part of ‹›self, that portion which had several times participated in Rafe-mind—stirred.

"Good for me," it said.

And foreseeing crisis, ‹› raised a simulacrum, and pushed it to the light.

The pain stopped. Rafe caught his breath, lying on the floor among *Lindy*'s ruins—seeing himself in duplicate beside Jillan and Paul— "O God," he said, third of his kind, and gathering himself shakily to his feet, stood dazed in the shock of too many changes, far too fast.

"Damn you," his brighter image shouted, and he thought he was intended, that the outrage was aimed at him.

"Damn you," Rafe shouted at the walls, "—Kepta!"

"He's real," said Rafe Two. "Don't frighten him worse than he is."

Another duplication happened, another Jillan, another Paul, wide-eyed and terrified, who confronted their startled selves in voiceless shock.

"What are you up to?" Rafe screamed, himself, original, fists clenched. "Kepta—*They're not toys! They're alive, you hear me, Kepta? They don't just turn off. It's not a bloody game! Stop— stop it, hear?"*

There was riot among the passengers. *"Stop!"* <^> wailed. "Stop, stop, stop—"

<> did more than that. The pulse went through the ship in no uncertain strength.

Paul One flinched, dropped his tormenting of the Rafe-simulacrum and turned fierce attention toward the duplicates and the corridor <> protected.

"Diversions," said </>. "Don't regard them. <> means to lure you into reach."

"I know," Paul said, having gotten *I* back wider than it had been. *I* was wide as all the universe. *I* was unstoppable, having tendrils in Rafe-shape, and in his own; and extensions into </>. He pulled at another memory, warped it out of shape, and Rafe-mind writhed in agony.

</> gained another section of the ship by complete default, for = = = = realigned = = = = self: the Cannibal had ambitions, and <>'s indirection and </>'s aggressiveness advised = = = = which allegiance was, at the moment, the better choice.

<> sent out another pulse which resounded painfully through the ship.

But it did not deter desertions.

There was silence, dreadful silence, among *Lindy*'s ruin. Rafe recovered himself, wiped at his eyes, ashamed of the terror he had created. He was theirs, in common, their stability, the one thing impossible to counterfeit. He sensed their dependency. He sniffed, unheroically wiped his nose, sat down in the command chair and wiped his eyes again. None of them could touch him, none lay the least substance of a comforting finger on him, his sad-faced, devoted ghosts. They only waited in a half-ring about the console, two of everyone, even of himself.

I'm sorry," he said to them. "Really sorry." Another wipe at his eyes with the heel of his hand.

"That's all right," said one of his doppelgangers—he did not even know which one. They had a right to be ashamed, he thought; and upset; and they looked to be.

"Someone want to fill me in?" the other of his doppelgangers said. "I'm lost. I think several of us are. I think—" with a frightened glance at the one transparent as himself: "I was here; and talked to Rate—about leaving the ship. Then it got me—in the dark. Am I far off? How lost am I?"

"Hours," Rafe said, himself. "No farther."

"You're still hoarse."

"Yes, he said, looking at the two Jillans. He could not tell them apart. There was no difference. That, more than anything, hurt him. He wanted there to be a difference. He wanted one to be real, an original, his sister; and there were two, both hurting, both claiming the right to existence and to him.

"We're all right," said the leftmost Paul, who had the rightmost's steadying hand on his shoulder. The speaker's voice was thin. "We understand. I think we've got the drill down pat. It's just the shock. . . ."

"Dammit," said Rafe One. He stood up, holding out empty, helpless hands, to him, to the Jillan-newcomer. "I'm sorry. I'm sorry, hear."

"I know," said Rafe Three. "It's what he says—the shock of it. Waking up—finding we're not . . . what we were prepared to be."

"But we are," said one of the Jillans. The other's mouth was set hard; this one had Jillan's most brittle look, don't-touch-me, don't-pity-me. "It's what I said. We never know—we never know, after a copy's made—which one we are."

"Shut up," the other Jillan said.

"You don't need me," said Jillan (he was sure now) One. The chin firmed, the head lifted. "I'm not your *self.* Stop thinking of me that way."

"Sister," Rafe said, to comfort Jillan. Both faces looked his way, instinctively, and the horror overwhelmed him.

"I didn't plan—" Rafe Three said in his default. "I didn't plan to be superfluous. Wasn't that the word I just used of you? How many of us does it need, for God's sake?" He walked off from them, through *Lindy*'s console. Rafe winced, knowing the self-torment behind that move. "It could get real crowded here," Rafe Three said, recovering his humor, a desperate look back at all the surplus of them, a look upward as something went howling through the speakers overhead. "*Damn* that thing!" And then, with a futile reach at the com controls: "*Com light's on*—Rafe, Rafe—for God's sake, I can't touch it—"

Rafe moved, dived through the simulacrum, pushed the button; but the light went out under his hands and the sound was gone.

"Games," he said. "Dammit, it's playing games with us!"

"((()))!" <> shouted at the culprit, but ((())) ran, evaded a wandering segment of = = = = and kept screaming.

"Lonely," ((())) said when ((())) had stopped eventually. This was improvement of a kind. ((())) had acquired an opinion after eons of raving lunacy. ((())) peered from behind a weak barrier ((())) had erected and looked doubtfully at <>.

"Away!" <> raged at ((())). "Get out of here!"

((())) drew ((()))self up on all ((()))'s legs and dropped the barrier. "((())) remember," ((())) said, "*flesh—*"

And that word whispered through the ship with a multitude of connotations as ((())) fled.

<^> leapt out of ((()))'s path and shuddered, coming close to <>.

"Why haven't <^> deserted too?" <> wondered.

"Bravery," said <^>.

"I was the last it copied," Paul said, in the silence, in the devastation of them all. "I think—I think I know things. I think my double understands best what's going on. I was the last it took."

He walked over to the counter, settled on the edge in a parody of sitting, for it was hard to recall after a lifetime of having a body that it made little difference where it rested, except it put him near the one of them that could occupy a seat and make its fabric give. Rafe looked at him—bruised, shadow-eyed. Rafe Two stood godlike in his handsomeness; Three had a foredoomed look, brooding and quiet. And Jillan, his Jillan, was the image of her brothers, her face so much like theirs and so much more delicate, so doubly resolute, in both her shapes. His own doppelganger came to settle at his side—*so tired he looks,* Paul thought, shocked at himself. He drew an unneeded breath, straightened his shoulders, looked once and achingly at Jillan.

"Kepta and I," he said, "had a real frank talk. I don't know all it expects of me. I suspected it might lie, in several ways. Eventually I—had another impression. That Kepta's got a problem and he's scared. I don't know what he's up to now."

"Do you know more than I do?" his doppelganger asked him.

"No," he said. "More than that, no. God help us."

"God help us," it echoed. "Both."

"What's it want?" one of the Rafe-doubles asked. Three, Paul thought. "I wish someone could bring me up to date."

"There's one of me," Paul said quietly, "my first version, Kepta said. Said he's got some kind of enemy—Kepta has. And that other version of me is on that enemy's side and crazy as they come. Maybe I know how. But that's all I know—" he said to Rafe, slid a glance at Rafe Three. That Rafe was afraid—he saw it, and felt a dim, ugly affirmation of himself.

My darker side, he thought, because it gave him, deeply, secretly—satisfaction. *Rival.* He seized on that idea, refused to let it go until he had turned all sides of it to the light. *Because I'm not strong, and he is. And Jillan is.* He lifted his head and looked at the Original.

"Barriers," he said. "Barriers, Rafe. Jillan—I love you two, you and Rafe. That's the one thing I have to keep telling myself over and over. Kepta said I have to figure out why I love you. And now that I do try to figure it out it's very simple. I'm not a good man without that."

"That's nonsense," Jillan said.

"Oh, but it's not. Without someone to trust I'm not trustable myself. I work on reciprocities. You provide me—environment.

You're my morality. And if you fail me I'm worse than lost. You get my other side. Or it gets me. There's a part of me wants more than anything to be like you, independent. Capable. There's a part of me wants to prove you're not capable at all; wants to see you're like me, in need of props and braces. Wants to—affirm my own humanity, I guess, by proving you're like me—Don't say anything," he said to Jillan, because she began to protest the mandatory, affirming things. "You've never seen my insides. I think you needed me, all right. Needed my station credit, someone to work with you, another strong back; my—friendship. I believe that. I really do. You and Rafe. I don't think you really have the least idea what I wanted when I dragged a merchanter into marrying. It was that kind of thing. Affirmation. Environment. Something to define *me* and give me the props I need."

"You're not like that," Jillan said. *His* Jillan, the older one. "That isn't why I married you."

He looked at her, smiled sadly at loyalty reflected in both her versions. "But I am," he said. "That's what you got, Jillan-love. A bad man who's told you the truth for once, because he had to tell it to himself." He gathered himself to his feet and walked off from them, their eyes. Looked back again, having remembered suffering beside Jillan's and his own. "Kepta said a lot would rest on me; and knowing me," he said to Rafe Three, "Kepta judged I needed help. Maybe that's why you're here. I don't know. You're stronger than I am. I need you." And having admitted that: "I'm full of shadow-spots. He said you had only one secret. I won't ask you what that is."

"I have a thousand," said Rafe Three in uncomfortable charity. "Doesn't any human born?"

"You have one," Paul said.

"Damn that thing!" Jillan cried, leaping to her feet. "It's got no bloody right to mess with us!"

"And you," Paul said, staring at her directly, "*use* yours."

Her eyes fixed on him in sudden, white-edged shock. "He told you? He told you that?"

"Not what it was. Just how you work."

"What does it know about humanity?"

He listened to that. Secrets wielded like a shield, deflecting questions that could go through to the heart. He nodded, quite calm about it, armored in the truth. "Trust isn't the way you work.

You never trusted me with the truth. Maybe I couldn't have stood it. You always protected me."

"What's that supposed to mean? You're not making sense, Paul."

"You are. Making sense, I mean. To me. Don't change. I love you. Love me back. That's all I want. Does it cost too much?"

"No," she said, not understanding him. She would not, he thought, understand him; or believe truth when she heard it, though she was wise in other ways. And in the wickedness of his heart he found that he was in one way stronger, and wiser, and for once he had something to give away.

He smiled at her. Watched both her versions frown.

"Rafe," he said, looking back at the Original. "I figure when the stuff starts to go, hard, you know?—we'll be separate. Could be any minute. Maybe when we figure something essential Kepta wants he'll snatch us out of here. I want you to know—you're brother, father, mother to me. *She,* my real family—they made her mother in a lab; she and gran did the best they could with me. Ma wasn't any rebel like I told you. They shot her by accident. She just got in the way. That was the way she was. Like gran. Wrong place. Wrong time. That's all."

"Guessed she wasn't any rebel," Rafe said in the faintest, most diffident of voices. "They gave you that station share. They never would have, if she'd been on the rebel side. However young you were."

He nodded, head up, discovering the nakedness he had always suspected with them. "Couldn't impress you, could I?"

"Didn't have to," Rafe said. "Not that way. You're *family,* Paul."

"Family," he said back. Yes, you are. All the love and hate and everything that is. Everything that holds me together. I want you to know that."

He felt a hand slide past the hollow of his arm, his own Jillan's slim, smooth touch; her head pressed against him.

And beside the counter, the other two, the new-made set, not touching, nonparticipant and already alive, because they had chosen not to touch, because they had not consented to what he felt. He put his arm about his Jillan. At last his doppelganger did, for whatever his own thoughts were—put his about the other Jillan, who drew a deep, insubstantial breath for hers.

"It said," said that other Jillan, "that *two* of you went wrong."

"One of me," said Rafe.

"Or me," said Rafe Two, moving finally, to sit on the counter edge. "We don't really know which one."

"Does it make a difference?" Rafe one asked

"As to how far off it is," said Rafe Two, "as to how it adapts to the dark—it might."

The Original shook his head. "No. If it came from as early as I think it might—no difference, except in what it's been through."

"Isn't that always the difference?" Paul asked, discovering this in himself. "Events change us. Isn't that why we all exist? I'm not that other Paul. He's not me. We're all of us—very real."

"I feel that way," Rafe Three said with a small, desperate laugh. "I *feel* alive." And looking distractedly at Jillan: "You said that once."

So <> had made <>'s move. </> was not impressed.

"Mistake," </> said, and unleashed the entity </> had made, Paul-Rafe, while </> stalked larger quarry.

"See," <∧> wailed, knowing this, skipping along at <>'s side as they proceeded elsewhere in the ship. "<> have *lost*."

"Not yet," <> said.

<∧> remained. Puzzled; and angry. And frightened, that foremost, as <> and <∧> built barriers.

"This is retreat," <∧> said.

"Maneuver," said <>.

"It's late for that," said <∧>.

"Everything is late," <> said.

"<>," <> heard, a pulse that made <> wince. </> had gathered strength. "<> , </> am waiting for <> to cross the line."

Meanwhile, Paul One had moved, slipping through the corridors. = = = = went at Paul One's side, in all = = = ='s segments. Some of them shrieked in protest, but they all went, having no choice in this new alignment.

There was dark in the side-corridors of Fargone docks, the kind of deep twilight of betweentimes, between main and alterday, and someone stalked. Rafe ran, in starkest terror.

"Hey, miner-brat," security yelled and he ought to have turned

*and faced the man, but he had no pass to be across the lines at
this hour, a miner in spacer territory.*

*He rounded a corner, slid in among shipping canisters await-
ing the mover to pick them up. Their shadows passed and his
heart crashed against his ribs in regular, aching pulses.*

*They searched. If they caught him they hauled him in for ques-
tions; questions led to Welfare, and Welfare to assigned jobs. Forever.*

*"Please," they would ask of spacers, shyly on the docks, asked
them daily, nightly, in the shadows of twilight hours, "sir, got a
fetch-carry? Just a chit or two?"*

*Most had no job for them. Some trusted Jillan but not him.
Docksiders stole. Now and again one gave him a message to
run—payment at the other end. Sometimes he was cheated. Once
a white-haired woman offered him money and a bed and he took
the key she offered and went to that sleepover, humiliated when
he discovered what she had not wanted at all. Just charity, for
a starving kid trying to stay off Station Welfare lists.*

*He was humiliated more that he had been willing to sell him-
self, for what she gave away.*

*And he did not tell Jillan about that night. He did not tell it
even to Paul.*

"The time has come," <> said, and made two simulacra. "Wear
this," <> said to <^> of Jillan-shape. "<^>'ll find things in common with her."

"I don't know what to do," Paul said to Rafe's question. "I
don't—"

And there were two more of them: a fourth Rafe; a third Jillan standing there, in front of the EVA-pod that reflected them
and the hall askew in its warped faceplate.

A pair of them, with that deep-eyed stare. There was horror
in newcomer-Jillan's eyes.

"Kepta," Paul said, guessing.

And: "Kepta," said Rafe, getting to his feet as the rest of them
had, "dammit, let Jillan be!"

"Call him Marandu," Kepta said of the anxious Jillan-shape
beside him. "That was something like his name. *He* doesn't quite
describe him. But *she* doesn't do it either."

"More games."

"No," Kepta said. "Not now." Jillan/Marandu had hold of Rafe/Kepta's arm. Kepta shook off the grip and walked aside with a glance upward and about as if his sight went beyond the walls. "It's quiet out there now. It won't be for long. It's moving slowly, expecting traps."

"What are you here for?" asked Jillan One.

"You," Kepta said, and turned a glance at Paul; "It's time."

"Leave Jillan here," Paul said.

"Which one?" it asked him, and sent a chill through his blood. It faced him fully. "You choose. A set of you will stay here safe. A set of you will face it. Likely the encounter will ruin that set. Which?"

"*None* of them," Rafe said. "Leave them alone."

"*It* won't," Kepta said, and looked back at Paul. "I sent a full set here—to keep the promise; I brought them early so that they would have some contact with the oldest. Continuity. That's as much as I could give. Now it's time, and no time left. Four to stay and three to go. Shall I choose? Have you not discovered difference?"

"I'll go," Paul said. He cast a look at his doppelganger, poor bewildered self, standing there with its mouth open to say something. "No," it protested. "*No.* It's why I was born, isn't it?"

Then things seemed clear to him, clear as nothing but Jillan had ever been. "Take Jillan and Rafe of the new set," he said, "and me, of the old." He looked straight at his doppelganger as he said it, proud of himself for once. "I know what the score is."

And the dark closed about him.

"*No!*" he heard Rafe's hoarse shout pursuing them. He felt a hand seek his in the dark—Jillan's. Felt her press it hard. He trusted it was the latest one, as he had asked. "You did the right thing," Rafe Three said—unmistakably Rafe, clear-eyed and sensible, as if he had drawn his first free breath out of the bewilderment the others posed. "What now?" —for Rafe was not senior of this group.

They were gone, just gone, and there was silence after. Rafe stood helpless between Rafe Two and Jillan; and Paul's hours-younger self, his substitute, whose look at Jillan was apology and shame.

She just stared at that newborn Paul, with that dead cold face that was always Jillan's answer to painful truths.

"What's happening out there?" Rafe Two asked. "What's *happening?*"

"War," said that Paul, in a faint, thin voice. "Something like. That Paul that changed—it wants the rest of us. And he's got to stop it. Paul has to. The real one. The one I belong to. The one I *am.*"

"It can make more of us," Jillan said. "It can keep this thing going—indefinitely."

"It won't," Paul Three said, "It won't take the chance. It said it wouldn't risk the ship. Kepta's words."

"It—" Jillan said; and: "O *God!*" —her eyes directed toward the tunnel-length.

Rafe spun and looked, finding nothing but dark; and then the howling sound raced through the speakers, leaving them shivering in its wake.

</> made haste now, sending tendrils of </>self into essential controls. </> encountered elements of <>, which </> had expected, but <>'s holdouts were growing few. There had been major failures. <>'s resistance collapsed in some areas, continued irrationally in others.

Other passengers, such as |:|, declared neutrality and retreated to the peripheries.

Paul, meanwhile. . . . </> wielded Paul/Rafe like an extension of </>self.

The variant minds of the simulacra were the gateway, </> reckoned. <> had invested very much of <>self in the intruders, which had proved, in their own way, dangerous.

The passengers were mobilized, as they had not been in eons. There was vast discontent.

"<> has lost <>'s grip," </> whispered through the passages, everywhere. "<> has been disorganized. </> am taking over. Step aside. Neutrality is all </> ask—until matters are rectified."

"Home," said one of [], with the ferocity of desire. [] forgot that []'s war was very long ago, or that []'s species no longer

existed, and whose fault that was. But they were all, in some
ways, mad.

Kepta joined them, a Rafe-shape with infinity in its eyes. It
stood before them in the featureless dark, and Paul faced it in a
kind of numbness which said the worst was still coming; and
soon.

He was, for himself, he thought, remarkably unafraid; not
brave—just self-deprived of alternatives.

"It will be there," Kepta said, turning and pointing to the dark
that was like all other dark about them. "Distance here is a function of many things. It can arrive here very quickly when it
wants."

"What's it waiting for?"

"My extinction," Kepta said, "and that's become possible. You
must meet it on its own terms. You must stand together, by whatever means you can. You will know what to do when you see it,
or if you don't, you were bound to fail from the beginning, and
I will destroy you then. It will be a kindness. Trust me for that."

And it was gone, leaving them alone; but a star shone in the
dark, a murkish fitful thing. Rafe pointed to it; Paul had seen it
already.

"Is that it?" Rafe wondered.

"I suppose," said Paul, "that there's nothing else for it to be."

"Make it come to us," Jillan said. "Get it away from whatever allies it has."

"And what if its allies come with it?" Paul asked. "No. Come
on. Time—may not be on our side."

They advanced then. And it moved along their horizon, a baleful yellow light.

IX

They waited; that was what they were left to do, prisoners of the corridor, of *Lindy*'s scattered pieces, of Kepta's motives and the small remnant of former realities.

"I can't," Rafe Two mourned, having tried to will himself away into the dark where Paul had gone; and Rafe himself looked with pity on his doppelganger.

"That'll be Kepta's doing," Jillan said. She sat tucked up in a chair that phased with her imperfectly, near Paul, loyally near their relict Paul, whose face mirrored profoundest shame.

"I tried too," Paul Three said, in a hushed, aching tone, as if he were embarrassed even to admit the attempt. "Nothing. It's shut down, whatever faculty we had."

"You were outmaneuvered," Rafe said. "He's a little older than you."

"Not much," Jillan said to Paul on her own. "Hours. But a few choices older. He *knew*, that's what. He'd had time to figure it out; and he was way ahead of us. He got us all."

There was a glimmering of something in Paul Three's eyes. Resolve, Rafe thought. Gratitude. And something he had suddenly seen in that other Paul Gaines, the look of a man who knew absolutely what he was doing.

Rafe Two picked that up, perhaps. Perhaps envied it; their minds were very close. That Rafe got up and turned his back as if he could not bear that confidence.

Why not me? The thought broadcast itself from Rafe Two's every move and shift of shoulders. He walked away, partly down the corridor. *Why not choose me? I was best. Oldest. Strongest. Responsibility.*

"Don't," Rafe said. "Stay put."

"I am," Rafe Two said, facing him against the dark, with bitterness. "I can't blamed well get anywhere down the hall, can I?"

And then there was a Jillan-shape at his back, glowing in the dark.

"Rafe," Rafe said, and Rafe Two saw his face, their faces, if not what was at his back. Rafe Two acquired a frightened look and turned to see what had appeared behind him in the corridor.

The light retreated before them, continually retreated.

"I guess," Rafe said, not breathing hard, because they could not be out of breath, or tired, nor could what they pursued, "— I guess it's not willing to be caught."

"If that's the case," said Jillan, "we don't have a prayer of taking it."

"Unless it's willing to catch us," Paul said. "Maybe it's counted the odds and doesn't like three of us at once. *I'll* go forward. Maybe that will interest it."

"You can bet it will," Jillan said, and caught his arm. She was strong; strong as he: that was the law of this place; and he was going nowhere, not against her, not by any means against the two of them. Rafe stepped in his way and faced that distant light in his stead.

"You!" Rafe yelled at it. "Lost your nerve? Never had it in the first place?"

"That's one way," Paul said. "Let me tell you about that thing. It knows it's a coward. It lives with that real well. It knows all kinds of things about itself. That's its strength."

"You're wrong," Jillan said. "If it's you it's not a coward."

"Let's say it's prudent," he said. "Let's say—it knows how to survive. If we split up—it'll go for one of us. Me, I'm betting."

"Me," said Jillan. "I'm the one it doesn't have."

"It's scared of you," Paul said with a dangerous twinge of shame. "I really think it is."

"What's *that* mean?" Jillan asked.

"That. Just that. It is. Keep pressing at it." He walked farther with them. The light they pursued grew no brighter.

"Ever occur to you," Jillan asked then, "that we're being lured—ourselves?"

"Where's Kepta?" Rafe demanded of the uncounseling dark, the void about them. "Dammit, where is he? He could be more help. What's he expect of us?"

"Kepta's saving his own precious behind," Jillan said. "We're the delaying action. Don't you figure that?"

But they kept walking, kept trying, together, since he could not persuade them otherwise. "Think of something," Paul said. "That's *me* we're chasing. It knows every move I'd make. Think of something to surprise it."

"It knows us," Jillan said, a low enthusiastic voice. "Too bloody well. It's not taking the bait."

"Kepta?" Rafe Two asked, facing Jillan's shape that strode toward him; but even while he asked it he kept backing up until he was within *Lindy*'s limits, until he had Rafe beside him, and true-Jillan and Paul Three. There was something very wrong with that Jillan-shape, something very much different from Kepta in its silence, the curious unsteadiness of its walking.

"Kepta?" Rafe himself asked it, at his side, half-merged with him.

"Maranduuuu," it said, this puppetlike Jillan-shape, *"Marand-u,* I—"

"Stay back from us." Rafe Two held out a forbidding hand, making himself the barrier, remembering in a cold sweat that it could touch him, if not the original, that he could grapple with it if he had to—but he had wrestled Jillan-shape before when it was Kepta and he knew his chances against that strength. "Keep your distance. Jillan, Paul, get Rafe back. Get him back!"

"Safe," it said. Its hands were before it, a humanlike gesture that turned into one chillingly not, that tuck of both hands, against Jillan's naked breasts, like the paws of some animal. One hand gestured limply. "Safe. Kepta sent—" Eyes blinked, as if it were sorting rapidly. *"Me,"* it decided. "Me. Marandu. To defend you."

"Do your defending from there," Rafe Two said, hand still held out, as if that could stop it.

</> invaded another center of the ship, dislodging a few of the simpler passengers, who wept; and one complex, IIII, who sent out a strong warning pulse.

</> did not counter this, or attack. The entity was not capable of aggression, but of painful defense. </> offered IIII choices. In time IIII redefined the necessities of IIII's situation and wandered away.

That was the first layer of <>'s defense about the replication apparatus. It went altogether too quickly, tempting </> to imprudent advance on the chiefest prize: the inner circle, the computer's very heart.

So </> guessed where <> had centered <>self: </> would have done so. <> was there, wound about the replication apparatus and possessing every template there was. It was necessary to advance against that center sooner than </> had intended, and </> knew raw terror, approaching this place.

There were doomsday actions that <> could take.

"</> advise <> against such measures," </> said from a safe, distance to the core. "They are ultimately destructive. Surplus copies of——" (</> used a pronoun collective of the ship and passengers) "would complicate matters. Get out of there. Give up. </> promise </> will replicate <> when </> have won the ship, when things are secure."

And in <>'s infuriating silence:

"<>," </> said, "have </> not always kept the promises </> make?"

"Are not </> one that <> kept?" came the answer, faint and deceptively far away. "<> regenerated </> in our last such impasse. <> did as <> said. Give up," <> added, a hubris that astonished </>, "and <> will show </> this mercy one more time. The struggle is inconclusive again. There *is*," <> added further, "always another time."

</> laughed in outrage. "</> will amalgamate these newcomers with <> when </> copy <>, since <> are so defensive of them. </> will add <˄> and lump all </>y enemies together."

"Do this," <> whispered, no louder than the whisper of the stars against the ship-sensors, loud as the universe, "do this and regret it infinitely. Reciprocation, </>. Remember that. </> don't have the keys <> have. </> always have to resurrect <>. <>'ve changed the keys; <>'ve been doing it all through <>y waking. <> learned—from </>ur old trick."

This was likely truth. <> was fully capable of altering the ship. But </> disdained the warnings and pressed forward, urging </>'s other parts to advance as well.

Paul/Rafe was one. He was afraid, in aggregate. He trembled, constantly keeping his enemy in sight, but constantly assailed with doubts.

He was in space, the, stars about him, nothing for reference.
He looked about for Lindy, *but there was nothing there.*

So Rafe-mind fought him still, deep within his structure, having saved back some shred of itself for this. It fed Paul self-doubts.

Fargone station's deepest ways, and it was not Security after Rafe Murray this time; it was another kind of force.

No one freelance-smuggled with the likes of Icarus, *no one crossed the moneyed interests that ran what they liked past customs; and if they caught him, if they saw his face—*

So Paul fought back, and drove Rafe-mind into shuddering retreat.

Rafe made a mistake, a wrong turn in docks he had known all his life; but a stack of canisters against the wall became a maze, became a dead end, and cut off his retreat.

"Got you, you bastard, " said the first of the four that filled the aisle between the towering cans.

He did not defend himself. It was not wise to antagonize them further. He only flung up his hands and twisted to shield himself as best he could, let them beat him senseless in the hopes they would be content with that, private law privately enforced, the kind they might not want Fargone authority involved in.

They did a thorough job. They knew, from his lack of defense or outcry, that he would not be going to authorities to make complaint; that he had something to lose that way more than they could do to him. And in that frustration they took their time about it.

"Where's the other one?" they asked him over and over, knowing they had clawed him, but he had diverted them his way. He never answered them about Jillan, not a syllable.

That was not the kind of thing Paul had hoped for. The memory died, quickly; but Rafe-mind stayed intact, locked into that moment with deliberate focus, with a certain satisfaction, the same he had shown the smugglers from *Icarus.*

I, Paul kept thinking, until it was himself who had been betrayed and Rafe had done it. So he warped all such memories.

Rafe wept, believing it at last.

No police, he had thought, dragging himself away with a broken arm that, finally, had cost him and Jillan four months' savings for the meds. He evaded the police, passers-by, all help.

There were questions that way; there was Welfare always ready to take charge of them and assign them a station job or send them to the mines to pay for Welfare help, forever, no hope of ships, no way out of debt for all their hopeless lives. A broken arm, the other things they did—that was small coin for freedom; and he must not talk, never complain, no matter what they did.

"*I fell,*" he told the meds, three days after, when the arm got beyond their care, and Jillan made him go.

There were inconsistencies. At times he thought that Paul had helped them; at others it seemed that Paul was destitute as they, which he had not remembered.

Rich, always rich, Paul Gaines, superior to him, clean and crisp in his uniform, station militia, sometimes Security—

Was it Security, then? Was it the police and not Icarus *crew that had found him in the corridors that day and left him bruised and bleeding among the canisters for outbound ships?*

Welfare agents?

Paul?

Things muddled in his mind, defense collapsing.

"Paul," he murmured, and felt the invasion of his mind, the superfluity of limbs which worked against his will.

"They're there," Paul whispered to him. It seemed that he could see the folk of *Icarus* far across the dark. "There they are."

"Crazy," Rafe whispered back; and in a paroxysm of effort: "Paul—you *died*."

"Good," Paul said, quite satisfied with his state. "They're Icarids, Rafe. Aren't they? Let's go do something about them, why don't we?"

The legs moved.

"No," Rafe cried, "no, no, no."

And Paul enjoyed it. It was a weapon, Rafe's fear, and he had mastered it.

They were no nearer than they had ever been on that dark and starless plain, the horizonless void which felt like nothing to their feet. The glow moved steadily, changing angles as they did, as if some invisible line connected it and them.

"It's leading us," Rafe said, glancing aside as he said it; and Paul agreed the same heartfrozen moment that *something* turned up in their midst, all black segmented coils and legs glowing yellow, at their joints as if light escaped. It towered among them, in nodding blind movements of its head.

"Aaaiiii!" it wailed.

"Get *back*," Jillan cried, hauling at his arm. "Run, for God's sake, run! Paul! It can't catch us—"

It did. Shock numbed his nonexistent bones, ached in his joints as it roiled into him and out again. "Paul!" Jillan yelled; she and Rafe came back to distract it from him, darting this way and that.

"Help," came a strange multiple voice, choruslike, as it pursued their darting nuisance to it. "Help, help, help—"

"Look out!" Paul cried, for Jillan misjudged: he flung himself at it as Rafe did, as she screamed.

It hit like high voltage: the beast itself yelped and writhed aside. All of them screamed, and then was silence.

Paul froze . . . in the numbness after shock, the fear that Jillan and Rafe were likewise crippled—all these things applied. Most, it was the voice, the dreadful voice that wailed at them and stole wits with its frightfulness. "Help," it kept saying, and its forward end nodded up and down serpentlike, like something blind. It made a whistling sound. "Rafe? Rafe? *Fles-sh-sh.*"

"O God," Jillan, breathed, moving then, tugging backward at their arms. "Get back, hear me—*get back.* It's nothing we can handle, not this thing—"

"Lonely," it said, snuffling; it had the sound of a ventilation system, a periodic sibilance. "F-f-flesh-sh. Rafe—lonely."

"Don't!" Paul cried, for it had encircled them, leaving them nowhere left to run. And to nothing at all, to the betraying, lightless air: *"Kepta! Help!"*

"Can't," it said, snuffled, in its myriad of voices. "Name—can't—*Aaaallleee!"*

"It's that howler-thing!" Jillan cried.

"Aaaaaaee," it said. The head swayed back again and aimed toward the dark. "Came to this ship. We. Long time—long—Crazy, some. Rafe-mind ran."

"What, *ran*?" Rafe Three asked it.

"Fight," it said, blind head questing. "Fight." The voices entered unison. "—go with. Fought once. Paul—" The head nodded off toward the star, the glow along the horizon, that seemed nearer now.

"What are you?" Paul asked.

"Fought once," it said, which seemed the sum of its identity. It started off, in pursuit of the ebbing light.

Dead, Paul reminded himself. *You're already dead. Quit worrying. Time's short.* And he wished that death was all.

"Come on," he said to Jillan and Rafe Three, because he saw nothing else to do. He started walking in the wake of the looping creature, which humped and zigged its way through the dark like some great sea creature aswim in the murk, with graceful fluidity.

Rafe was by him; he never doubted his constancy; and Jillan at his other side, never faltering.

The star grew in their sight.

Worm came circling back to them when the will-o'-the-wisp they chased had begun to shine globular and planetlike in the dark.

"Paul," Worm named that light. "Rafe. Pain."

"Take us there," Rafe Two demanded, of that Jillan-shape that had come to them. "Take us there, you hear me? If you want your enemies fought, then, dammit, let us out of here!"

And the shadow-eyes turned from regarding the wall, came back to them, so full of secrets that a chill stirred all through Rafe's own all-too-substantial bones.

"You," Jillan yelled at Jillan-shape, "answer, will you? Why do you keep us here?"

"For his defense," it said; Jillan/Marandu in a far, soft voice. "For yours."

"Kepta cares," Rafe Two said in heaviest bitterness. "I'm sure."

"For his defense," it said again, making different sense than before.

"For *Kepta's*?" Rafe asked, himself. "Is that the game?"

"Game." The thing stood there with that infinity-look, god/goddesslike in stillness. "That's not what to call it. The ship is at risk. We're all at risk. There are always quarrels. Some would like to sleep. Some find that more comfortable. Time wears—on some. But we go on doing what we were set to do."

"What?" Rafe asked. He stood behind Rafe Two's shoulder, dodged round him, to the fore as if he were solid, out of courtesy. "*What* were you set to do? What are you up to?"

"Some passengers never ask," Marandu said. "There's one, for instance, completely without curiosity. It doesn't dream either. But it knows a lot of things. It can't dream because it can't forget. Different approaches to consciousness."

"Stop the nonsense," Jillan snapped at it. "You've got your fingers in my mind right now. You can guess what I'd ask; so answer it."

"Where the others are?" A blink. "But you *don't* know that. You think you're physical. So do they." It cast a disturbed look at Rafe. "You know. Kepta knows you know. You saw the apparatus. You ought to have told them."

A chill like ice came over him, foreknowledge of harm.

"What's it mean?" Rafe Two asked. "Rafe, what's it saying?"

"You don't have physical bodies," Rafe said. He turned his shoulder to the intruder, to look instead at them. "Patterns, Computerlike. Simulacra. You're not physical."

"What do you mean?" Jillan asked. "Make sense, Rafe."

"I'm making the best I know."

"We're *here*," Jillan said.

"Position in the ship," said Jillan/Marandu, "is simultaneous. You only control a small priority. Kepta's, mine—is virtually universal in the circuitry. Size—is illusory; distance is; all these things—are what you choose to manifest. What I choose—in your shape."

"You mean we're bloody *programs?*" Rafe Two cried, and with a wild, despairing look: "Rafe?"

"You're real," Rafe said. "You go on living, changing. You always knew that. Is a separate body so important?"

"Oh, damn," Rafe Two breathed, and shook his head. *"Dammit, twin."*

"Rafe," Paul said fretfully, stepping through the counter. *"He* doesn't know. Paul doesn't know . . . what he's up against out there. They don't know what they are. Marandu—whatever you call yourself—Send me to him. Now. While there's time."

There was doubt in Jillan/Marandu. It showed in the eyes, in the nervous clench of hands to the breast. Indecision.

"Where's Kepta?" Rafe asked, in sudden, horrid certainty. "Marandu, has Kepta—place?"

The head jerked in a faint—perhaps—negation.,

"What *is* Kepta, Marandu?"

"I," it said, flinching back, almost fading out. It looked afraid. "I'm one version."

"One?"

"One," it said.

It had grown from globe to legged shape to figure, still coasting along the formless horizon in the dark.

But the legs were many; the reverse-silhouette warned of deformity.

"Steady," Paul told his companions, told himself, for now he truly knew why he had come, that it was his monster; and that in one sense and perhaps both shapes he was to die here, again, and soon. He searched for Rafe's hand, Jillan's, hugged them close; and Worm lurched along beside him.

The light receded then.

"It's running away," Jillan said. "How can it get distance on us, when we can't catch it?"

"Now," said Worm in its multiplicity of voices. "*Fight.* Fight now."

"How?" Paul asked it. He had nerved himself, and now in default, the old weakness came back, the old insecurity, deadly as swallowed glass, and worked within his gut. He should not have taken the lead. He was not up to this. It outmaneuvered him—that easily.

Then he cast a look at Worm, one wild surmise. "Worm—how? How do *you* come and go?"

It knotted upon its coils like a wounded snake, convulsed, phased with them in one aching shock that hit the nerves and fled.

"O *God*," Rafe moaned, catching his balance where it had thrown him, as it had thrown them all. Jillan gasped and staggered on her feet, and Paul—Paul refused to think of ground or up or down, but absorbed the shock and shuddered.

Homeworld, he thought out of some source like old memories; remembered—a world like orange ice, with skies that melted and ran; with lightnings like faint glow constant in the clouds; and drifters, drifters with no color at all except the backflare of the clouds—*That you?* he whispered to Worm. *Was that you?* But whatever Worm had tried to say was gone.

The nodding head touched him, and now, with the whiskered,

chitin-armored head thrust up before him, it arched its body and presented to him the upper surface; five jewels shone atop its head, black and glistening, and he thought of eyes.

"Come," it whispered back, and its bristles quivered. "Passage."

There was difference in the dark, as if something dire had happened, and yet nothing had changed.

Except suddenly, to their left, a figure loomed distinct.

"O God," Jillan said. "It's *moved* us—" —meaning Worm; for they *were* where the enemy was.

Paul stood still, and Rafe did beside him, facing this nightmare, this many-limbed amalgam of themselves, a thing of legs and arms and faces. It turned slowly, presenting Paul-face to them, and it smiled with a gorgon look.

"The thing got you here," Paul One said. "I wonder if it can get you out. What do you think?"

And Rafe-face answered: "*Kill* it, Rafe, kill it, stop it, stop him—"

"Let me hold you," said Paul One, offering its arms; and Worm gibbered: "*No—*"

"What do we do?" Rafe asked, Rafe Three, tight and low, backing up until they made one line with Jillan. "Paul, did it tell you what to do?"

"Worm," Paul said, his gut liquid with fear. "Worm, get us out of here!"

They were elsewhere, at a little greater distance. They hugged one another in shock, trembling. Paul held Jillan; Rafe held them both; and Worm made a circle about them, looping and making small hisses of defiance or consternation.

Lost, Paul thought. *We're lost, we're helpless against that thing*.

And then he remembered Jillan, and took her gold-glowing face between his hands, making her look up at him. "It hasn't got you," he said. "It hasn't got *you*, Jillan. That monster's one short. We're one stronger. You're my difference."

"I can't do it, Paul. *Can't*."

You must meet it on its own terms, Kepta had said.

You will know what to do when you see it, or if you don't, you were bound to fail. . . .

"There's one way," he said to her, "one way we can meet it

all at once, the way it is, on its terms." Jillan looked so much afraid, for once in her life afraid. He wanted to cry for her; wanted to hit out at whatever threatened them, and instead he touched Jillan's face, reminding himself they both were dead and hopeless and illusion only. Rafe had more than he: a living self. And less, far less. "Want you to trust me," he said, "Jillan; want you to do with me—with me—what it's done to Rafe. Just slip inside; we're not that substantial: *it* did it. So can we."

There was already contact. She pressed herself against him then, harder and harder. "I can't, she said then. "I *can't*. You're solid to me."

He tried too, from his side. "Rafe," he said, extending his left arm, and Rafe came against them, held them tight with all his strength, but there was no merging.

"Won't work," Jillan said, "*won't*."—And he felt all too much the fool, trying the possible-impossible, the thing that Paul did, that Kepta did as a matter of course. Worm looped about them all, circled, wailing its distress. "Help," It cried. "Help, help—"
Worm.

"Worm—how do you do it? How do you pass through us? Show us, Worm!"

"Make," Worm said.

"What—make? Make what?"

It whipped through their substance with one narrowing of its legged coils. Rafe screamed, becoming part of it, and Jillan—

The pain reached him. His vision divided, became circular, different from his own, and he owned many legs—

—view of skies like running paint, lightnings, repeated shocks, the sound of thunders never ceasing—

Fargone swinging in ceaseless revolution; Lindy's *dingy boards; the oncoming toad-shaped craft and, the merchanter* John Liles—

Got to destruct, destruct, destruct—All those kids and lives—
A thousand of them, Rafe—

—self-abandonment—

It's dumping!—

Jillan's voice, reprieve, with his finger on the button, the red button that was a ship's last option—

Cool and calm: It's dumping, Paul—

We're here, Rafe said, calmer and calmer now.

We're—wherever we've gotten to. Take it easy, Paul; easy—

The pain had stopped. Worm eased from their body. Their hearing picked up multiple sound from somewhere, like wind rushing; there was—if they opened their eyes—too much sight, though the universe was black; and the knowledge ripped one way and the other like tides, memories viewed from one side and the other, shredded, revised.

—walkwalkwalk—

Some one of the multiple brain chose movement: Rafe, Paul thought; Paul tried to cooperate. There was progress of a kind.

Awkward trifaced thing maneuvering into Paul's way. There was humor in that self-image, even in extremity: that was Rafe-mind, steady and self-amused.

I love you, Paul thought to their amalgamated self over and over again, without reservation, without stint; and got it back, Rafe-flavored. He wanted Jillan too; felt her fear, her reserve against all their wants· it was all too absolute.

Me, she insisted, *me, myself, I, I, I*—even while she moved her limbs in unison with them. There was pain in that.

"We need you," Paul whispered, desperate. He *knew*, of a sudden, knew what privacy in Jillan this union threatened. She shielded them from her own weapons, from rage, from resentment, every violence.

"You're our defense, Jillan; Rafe's our solid core; me—I go for *him* when I can get at him. But I need what you've got—all of it, hear—no secrets, Jillan-love."

"No one needs all," Jillan flung back at them both. "But that was always what you asked."

It stung, it burned. It took them wrathfully inside itself and taught them privacy.

No one, thought Jillan-mind, with a ferocity that numbed, *no one can ask myself of me.*

Our shield, Paul whispered to Rafe, in the belly of this amalgam they had become. *Give way. Give up for now. Let Jillan have her way.*

There was outrage left: memories of Fargone docks, of Welfare and Security.

You asked it. That was Rafe, in self-defense.

I never asked. You made up your own mind what I should be. His arm was broken. He had never talked. He never would.

There was terror (Jillan now) *in the dark, hiding there, dodging a drunken spacer who had a yen for a fourteen-year-old, a kid without ship name to defend her—she eluded him, hurled invective at him; shook, afterward, for long, stomach-wracking minutes.*

Grandmother had a number (Paul-mind, in self-defense) *which all lab-born had.*

"*Why don't I?*" *he had asked, wanting to be like this tranquil model of his life. He touched the number, fascinated by it. He could see it forever, fading-purple against Gran's pale mine-bleached skin, against frail bones and the raised tracery of veins under silk-soft skin. It was one with the touch of Gran's hand, the softest thing he knew; but she had wielded blasters, shoved rock, had a mechanical leg from a rockfall in the deep. Her eyes, her wonderful eyes, black as all the pits, her mouth seamed and sere and very strong: the number brought back that moment.*

"*You don't want one,*" *his mother said, harshly, as harshly as she ever spoke to him. "Fool kid, you don't want one of those.*"

"*Your gran's lab-born,*" *a girl had said once, seven and cruel as seven came, the day his gran had died. "Made her in a tank. That's what they did. Bet they made a dozen.*"

He had cried at the funeral; his mother did, which reassured him of her humanity.

But perhaps, he thought even then, she was pretending.

"None of her damn business," Jillan-mind insisted of that seven-year-old, with a great and cleansing wrath; and Rafe was only sorry, gentler, in his way. "Stupid kid," he said. There was no doubt in them of humanity; the memory grew clean, purged; "She loved you," Rafe-mind said, confusing his own half-forgotten spacer mother with the daughter of lab-born gran. *He* knew; Jillan knew; there was no doubt at all in them, why a woman would work all her life and hardly see her son—to leave him station-share, the sum of all she had, her legacy. Merchanters knew, who had bought a ship with the sum of their own years.

They progressed; limbs began to work.

Rafe's suffering in this—a stray thought from Paul, shame, before the man who was so godlike perfect, feeling his horror at the shambling thing they had become.

Shut up, Jillan said, severe and lacking vanity, as she had killed it in herself years ago (too great a hazard, on the docks, to look better than one had to, to attract anything but, maybe, work. One had to look like business; and be business; and mean business; and she did.)

Use what you've got. (Rafe-mind, whose vanity was extreme, and touching, in its sensitivity).

You can't get pregnant, Jillan hurled at him, ultimate rationality; and caught his longing, his lifelong wish for some woman, for family—

Vanity serves some purposes, Rafe-mind thought, recalling it was his smoothness, his glib facility with words that got them what they had: he had bent and bent, so Jillan never had to—*A room in a sleepover, an old woman gave it to me—I took even that. Even that, for you—*

She felt the wound, shocked. Her anger diversified, became a vast warm thing that lapped them like a sea.

Mine, she thought of them, and saw Paul-shape ahead of them. Wailing went about them. Worm nudged their flanks, little jolts of pain too dim to matter.

"*Paul,*" Worm said, slithering about them, round and round; and the creature before them lingered, murkish in its light. Limbs came and went in it. The face changed constantly.

X

"You're a copy," Rafe said to Marandu/Jillan's faded image.

"Yes," Marandu said. The hands, drawn up to the breast, returned to human pose; Marandu/Jillan grew brighter and more definite, with that unblinking godlike stare.

"Computer-generated," Jillan said in self-despite.

"Or we are the computer," Marandu said, turning those too-wise eyes her way. That stare, once mad, acquired a fearsome sanity. "We're its soft-structure. Its enablement. We're alive individually and collectively. We've been running, and growing, for a hundred thousand years. That's shiptime. Much longer—in your referent. That we're partitioned as we are was accident. It's also kept us sane. It provides us motive. In a hundred thousand years, motive's a very important thing."

"And the enemy," said Paul. "The enemy: what is it?"

"It's Kepta, of course," Marandu said. "It's Kepta Three."

"Be careful," <> said to <>'s counterpart: </> had come very close now, to the center where <> had invested <>self. "You know what <> can do."

At this </> hesitated. "Fool," </> said. "Make another <> and watch it turn on <>. <u></u> did."

"It was <>y nature then," <> said. "Perhaps <>'ve grown."

"Only older," </> returned, gaining more of <>'s territory. </> extended a filament of </>self all about the center, advanced Paul-mind and = = = = in their attack. The passengers huddled far and afraid, in what recesses they could, excepting ((())), who had forgotten who had killed ((())), long ago; excepting entities like [], who ranged themselves with </>. "<>'ve grown older and less integrated, <>. Give up the center."

"</> are long outmoded," <> said in profoundest disgust. "<> learn; <> change. Come ahead and discover what <> have become."

</> shivered then, in the least small doubt </> circled and moved back.

"Attack," [] raged, the destroyer of []'s own world. *"Take it!"*

But </> delayed, delayed to think it through in Paul-mind. </> had fallen once before into that trap, <>'s mutability.

Therefore, </> used Paul—to learn what <> might have gained from <>'s latest acquisitions; to be certain this time that </>'s strength was equal to the contest. <> *collected* things of late. <> modified <>self in disturbing ways, and was not what <> had been.

</> circled farther back, with more and more agitation, sent out more and more of </>'s allies to scour the perimeters.

"</> want the strangers," </> said. "</> want everything in them."

Hunger was very like that </> felt; and self-doubt; and hate, that too. </> even felt these things in human terms, experimentally.

"This time," <> said, "<> fed </> a warped copy." And suddenly </> doubted whether </>'s theft had indeed been </>'s own idea or half so clever as </> had thought.

</> turned back.

"Where are </> going?" [] howled, ravening at </>'s back. "Coward!"

<> was far from confident. <> huddled in the control center, realizing a serious mistake. <> had, in a taunting lie, revealed too much of </>'s vulnerability; and </> went to solve that problem.

</> had realized the key to </>'s previous defeats.

"Call it a very long time ago," Marandu said, "a very long time ago . . . this ship set out from home. Trade, you might call it; but it's always a mistake to try to translate these things. Call us a probe. Or a sacrifice." The hands drew up again, knotted like prayer beneath the chin; the body drew up in midair and drew toward the floor, legs folding, fetal-like. "Go. Go . . . go. The—. . . . There is no word in this brain for that. But that was why. *Life*, you might say. To sample—everything. Exchange. Trade. Commerce . . . of a kind."

"Why?" Jillan insisted to it; "hush," Rafe said, afraid of losing that tenuous truth, of breaking whatever held it to them.

"No translation," Marandu said. "There's never translation of motives; only of acts."

"What happened?" asked Rafe.

A long pause. "An incident. A copy of me existed as precaution. When I died, when the crew did, when the ship was without orders, it activated me."

"Me?"

"I was Kepta then. Division came later."

"What happened then?"

"I kept going. I kept going. Kept transmitting, as long as seemed profitable." Marandu's female mouth jerked. The hands drew up. "Passage of time—negates all motives. Survival is still intact. So is curiosity." Jillan-shape flickered, brightened again and the eyes were set far, far distant. *"Difficulty—"* Marandu said in a voice that moved the lips but scarcely. Sweat glistened on its lip, on its brow beneath the ragged fringe of hair; the legs settled crosswise; hands came down on knees; the shape hovered in midair, naked, dim and glistening with perspiration.

"Marandu," Paul said.

"Difficulty," the voice hissed again.

"Where?" asked Jillan.

"Your duplicates."

"Send me to them," Rafe Two said. *"Let me help them!"*

The eyes which had rolled up came down again and centered. "Kepta is threatened," Marandu said. The sweat rolled in illusory beads. "The enemy has gained a vital point."

"Paul—" Paul said.

"Not yet," Marandu said. The hands were clenched. *"Not yet."*

Rafe clenched his own hands, stared at it in helplessness. "What's it doing? What's Kepta up to?"

"Holding what's essential."

"What's essential?" he flung back at it, but it answered nothing, only sat there, pale and drawn. *"Marandu, what's essential?"*

"Controls," Rafe Two said.

"The computer." Rafe turned, empty-handed, pushed himself off from the control panel and ran, ran in desperation down the hall.

"Rafe!" he heard—his doppelganger's voice.

"Rafe." Jillan's or Jillan/Marandu's; and a shape leapt into being beside him, a running ghost—Paul, racing along by him

in a confused blur of light. Jillan was there, or Marandu; and his doppelganger, half-merged with him.

"Where are you going?" Jillan cried.

"Controls," Rafe gasped, springing perilously from lump to hump of the uneven floor. "*That's* where it has to be, what it has to have—I've been there. I know—"

The knives, he was thinking as he ran, remembering that he was flesh, remembering the arms and blades in that center of the ship. *O God, the knives—*

Station dock; manifests—Lindy *got on toward her loading with* Rightwise *and a Fargone agent wanted to make a fuss, small, dim man with a notepad, a checklist, suspicions.*

"Where's your form B-6878?" he asked.

Rafe searched, desperately, through the sheaf of authorizations.

The clock ticked away, meaning money, each second that loader was engaged. Money and life. All their years had bought—

"Careful," Paul Two said, "careful—" for they had come very near that misshapen thing. Worm hovered round them, and Paul-shape shambled, sidling round them in a green-gold glow that spread along the horizon.

"—is there," Worm whistle-moaned at their backs. *"Danger-danger-danger!"*

"Look!" Rafe cried; and their conjoined, rotating sight discovered a new glow at the opposite side, a thing like Worm, but more horrible, whose white-glowing segments were interspersed with lumps and legged things. Some of them had mouths and others, eyes.

"Eater," Worm gibbered. "Can-Can-Cannibal."

"Come ahead," Paul-voice taunted them from the other side, a god-voice, Paul's deeper tones underlain with Rafe's.

"Fight," howled Worm, hovering behind them. "Coward," it sobbed to itself, over and over again, in half its voices.

Paul One flickered nearer and nearer, growing incrementally in their sight. He opened his/their arms. "Rafe," it said. "Jillan."

"Run," Rafe-voice screamed within it. "Run—!"

"Come on," Paul-mind challenged that shambling thing. He

stood firm. Jillan braced herself. "You've caught me; now take me in."

"Look out!" Worm cried; and it was Rafe-mind turned them quick enough: the Cannibal-horror rushed past them in flank attack as the amalgam struck from the other side.

"—an accident," the Welfare man said, "—in the belt. . . ."

"Shut up!" Jillan cried, had cried that day, before he could say the words. Eight years old—she knew, knew what Welfare came to say

But: "Brother," Rafe Three said, meaning his battered other self, that thing that hung in rags from the monster's side. "O brother—" with the stinging salt of tears.

And Paul: *"Listen to me—"* he told his twisted self, with sorrow that gathered up Jillan-mind and Rafe and all. "Oh, no. You've got it wrong, my friend."

Ugliness flowed back. His own darkness, like a wave: his desire to hurt—

—*Rafe wept and begged. He savored that, felt a thrill of sex*—

"That's me!" Paul said, accepting it, treading on his pride, stripping off all the coverings, revealing all the darks. "Don't be shocked, Jillan; I did warn you, I told you the best I knew—don't leave me, Rafe. Don't. O God, don't—break—"

Paul One writhed, sought Jillan-mind with its hate; sought Rafe. *Kill*, it raged. *Have you—all—all—all—*

It was too much; too strong, too mad. "No!" Rafe pulled them back, dodged aside, for the Cannibal loomed up: *"Back!"* Worm shrieked, and plunged between, tangled its black body, with that pale one.

"Worm!" Rafe cried, and Paul dodged again as Worm came flooding back from the Cannibal's assault. Worm's substance was in ribbons. It was missing legs in great patches all down its length; it limped and moaned. But the Cannibal ran, wounded too, ran until it met a thing which took shape out of the dark, a Devourer far larger than itself.

"Paul," that thing said, in a voice far too small and human for its size. Cannibal merged with it; it looped closer to gather Paul One's misshapenness against its glowing side.

"There," it said, contentedly; "there." And lifted up its face to them.

"*Rafe—*" Paul said. A shudder went through his/their flesh; he felt Jillan's horror: Rafe Three's own dismay.

It was vast. It kept lifting up and up, serpentlike, and the eyes of Rafe-face stared down at them. Beauty—it had that too, Rafe's gone to cold implacability. "I've won," it said; and Paul-Rafe wailed as it sank unwilling into the serpent's glowing side. "There's nothing more to fear."

"No!" Worm wailed. "No, no, no, no—"

"Hush," the whisper thundered. "*Worm*—worm, they call you. Do you know, Worm, what that is? For shame, Paul, to give him a name like that."

"Kepta?" Paul asked. "Is that you?"

"Yes," it said. "Of course I am. Come here."

They reached the great hall, the noded dark. Things gibbered as they ran, voices howled through the overhead, chittered, roared like winds where no winds existed. Rafe kept running, stumbling, fell flat and scrambled up without pause, holding his aching side.

His ghosts stayed with him. Perhaps Marandu was one: he could not tell. There was no light but their bodies, no guidance but their hands that reached impotently to help his weakness. "Where?" Rafe Two asked him, "where now, Rafe?"

"Hallway," he gasped, "third to the left of ours—"

"This way," Rafe Two said, at home in dark, or not truly needing eyes. Rafe gathered himself, sucked a pain-edged breath and ran, staggering with exhaustion.

A Jillan-image materialized in the dark ahead, blazing gold. "Stop!" she/it said. An arm uplifted in a gesture human as the image and as false.

Rafe Two slowed; Rafe ran, experienced nothing but a flare of light and image, stumbled his way on blind in the dark of the passage, reeling from wall to wall. A glow passed him, gave him fitful light, became Jillan before it faded out.

He sprawled, hard, in the shimmer of insubstantial arms that tried to save him; he clawed his way up, sobbing, and kept going. His ghosts were with him again, Jillan, all; they went about him, a glowing curtain, a cloud. He fell again, a third, a fourth time on the hummocks of the floor. He tasted blood, was blind, phosphenes dancing in his eyes.

"*Look out!*" Jillan cried and waved him off, her body out in

front of him. He reached out his hands, facing darkness beyond
her.

White, sudden light blazed from the ceiling nodes. It lit the
room of knives, arms that moved, snicked in unison toward him
all attentive, in the lumpish barren plastic of the center he had
sought.

"Kepta!" he shouted, backing, for things that gripped and
things that cut were still in drifting motion toward him, traveling in extension he had not guessed. "*Kepta!* Stop!"

They kept coming. More unfolded out of recesses of the wall.
"*Kepta!*"

Jillan-shape materialized there among the knives, flung up
arms, opened its mouth and yelled something a human throat did
not well stand.

Knives stopped then, frozen in mid-extension, a forest of metal,
perilous limbs in which Jillan-shape stood immaterial.

Rafe stood shivering, perceived a dance of light as his own
ghosts hovered round him as close as they could get, demolish-
ing themselves on his solidity and reforming.

"Tell Kepta I want to talk with him," Rafe said.

"Kepta won't," Marandu said. His female hands tucked up
again like paws. "Go *back*."

"Because I'm substance? Because I'm alive, with hands to
touch this place?"

"Substance," said Marandu among the knives, "is dealt with
here."

"Rafe," Paul pleaded with him. "Rafe—*stay alive*. Get out of
here."

"It's threatened," Rafe said. He was shivering. They could not
feel as much, but the shivers ran through his limbs. *O God. It's
going to hurt*—"I'm standing here, Kepta—hear me? I'm not moving. I'm not going to move."

"Kepta advises you," Marandu said—and Marandu's eyes were
far-focused, vague and full of dark—"advises you—"

The thing loomed up, serpentlike, seductive in its implacability, the serenity of Rafe-face become unassailable and vast.

"Lie," Worm cried, and writhed and looped its wounded coils
aside. "Lie, lie—"

"Are you lying?" (Paul).

"Examine me," it said, this thing with Kepta's name. It extruded a shape from its side, the agglomeration of Paul One. Paul One wailed, writhed as Worm had done. A glowing coil materialized and took it in again. "Come close. See me as I am."

"Go to hell," said Jillan Murray-Gaines, through the amalgam of their lips. "Or are you already in residence?"

"Humor," it said. "Hell. Yes." It laughed, gentle as a breath. "I appreciate the reference. So would the passengers. I'm Kepta. There are dozens of us. We create one another—in endless cycles." It slid closer, and it seemed dangerous to move at all now; but Rafe-mind did, veteran of the docks. They slipped backward together.

"Do you understand?" it asked again. (Another gliding move. Rafe-mind moved them back, but not far enough. It gained.) "Dangerous," it said, "to move without looking. Where's Cannibal? Where's Worm? Are you sure?"

"Don't look," Paul whispered, shivering in their heart. "Don't be tricked."

"You've been ill-advised," Rafe-voice urged, smooth, so very smooth. "Even death—can be remedied. Your copies are exact, down to the very spin of your particles. Your cellular information. Would you be reconstituted? I can do that much."

Paul caught the breath he did not have, felt limbs that were not real—instincts yearned after life and breath, after humanity—

"No," Rafe said. Just—*no*, unreasoning, suspicious. He was twelve again, dockside; the hand held out the coin, too large a coin for simple charity. . . . *No*—from Jillan-mind, brittle-hard, plotting how to run. *Nothing's free; not from this thing—*"

"Look out!" cried Paul

The serpent shape was quicker. Its vast body slammed down in front of them, turning about them, surrounding them with its coils.

"You just lost your chance," it said.

"Lost," Marandu whispered, fading. "They've failed."

"Let me go to them!" Paul cried. "Let me try!"

"Against a Kepta-form?" Marandu drew itself away, retreating in its dimness. And then it stopped, turned, gazing at them with Jillan's calm face. "Bravery. Yes. I know."

It shimmered out.

"Paul!" Rafe cried.,
Then all his ghosts were gone.
Marandu with them. And the lights went out.

Disaster. <> had felt it, not unanticipated. <> felt <^>'s fear.
It shivered through that portion of <^>self that remained partitioned outside Jillan-shape. There was irony in this: Jillan-mind
was darkly stubborn, and <^> was trapped in that fierceness.

</> discovered that too. Discovered other things.

"O God," Rafe Two murmured, arrived on that darkling plain.
"What *is* that thing?"

"The others called it Worm," Marandu said.

It came snuffling and limping toward them, tattered and missing legs among its segments. "Run," it called to them multi-voice;
and in other voices: "Fight."

Then they saw the other thing, a thousand times its size.

"My friends," it saluted them like thunder, rearing up to stare
down at them with Rafe's haggard face.

"Friends, hell," Jillan said.

"It will take you," Marandu said, a faint and fading voice.

"Damn you," Rafe yelled at Marandu, snatched to hold it by
the arm. "Don't leave us—"

Marandu steadied, grew brighter then. "I'm very old," it said,
as if that were some grounds for its desertion. "Oldest of all but
one."

"So fight it," Jillan said. "Where's your guts?"

And Paul: "Help us. We don't know what to do."

There was silence. The serpent-glow flowed closer. It had
Rafe's voice, a whisper that murmured like the sea, but spoke no
human tongue.

"Run! Fight!" Worm gibbered; but it did neither. Worm stayed,
limping aimless circles on missing legs. "Help! Help! Help!"

"Marandu!" Paul cried.

The slim Jillan-body shuddered, once. "I will take you in,"
Marandu said. "Partitioned—I can't—"

Jillan-shape broke apart in shimmer. A larger glow appeared,
folded about them, an order, a structure, a body vaster than their
own.

Worm was in it, snuffling.

Move, the impulse came, or something very like the command to legs and limbs.

"Go with it," Rafe tried to say, at least he willed himself to say. He could stretch very far if he wished: or that was Marandu's thought.

<> was dying. <> knew distress at that. The crew had already passed. "Ship," <> said, tried to say, "go home."

But Ship could not/would not hear. The Collective had betrayed <>, implanting instructions <> could not override.

<> died and remembered it when <> woke, with Ship long underway.

FIND. REPORT. <> obeyed, until <> had calculated that transmission scatter was too much, and the years too many, and nothing mattered any more but <>self.

<> traveled. It was all <> had left.

<> made <>self for company. <> sought other goals.

<> took on passengers.

He/they/she and Worm . . . participated in a body that had more limbs than they had collectively. They were old; and badly scared; and knew too much.

They/<^> were victims of <>self, helpless in their voyage. Passengers multiplied. <> took them in. <> changed and grew complex and made other selves.

<^> shuddered, gazing at </> in memory.

But one of <^>'s new-gained segments was of different mind.

Ship, he thought, with vast, vast desire. He was structure; Paul was complexity; and Jillan—Jillan was going at that thing, possessed for once of strength and size and a wrath stored up for years.

</> swooped and struck.

They/Marandu moved, lancing through the patterns of the ship, darting this way and that at transmission speed, being here and there with electron lunacy.

"Aiiiiieeee!" Worm wailed, and discovered <(((($\wedge$ them)))>self alive, to (((()))'s total startlememt. "Aiiii-ya!"

</> was in pursuit, was on them, through them.

"Hate you," one thing said, collectively; Cannibal was tangled with it and it lusted, that was all that filled its mind.

Fargone docks—

And They/Marandu/Worm; no-failure, not-now—beyond clear

thought, beyond reasoning, except that they were still alive, like Worm, who had been a pilot once, and hurled ((()))'s skill into their evasions in the patterns.

"Aiiiieeeiiiiii!" Worm cried, going to the attack.

A red world lay in Marandu's past, much loved betrayer—for that memory, Marandu fought. *"Lindy!"* Rafe yelled, and felt Jillan and Paul distinctly at his side. Their own focus was a little ship, a hope, pilot-skill and stubbornness . . . no world to love at all, only Fargone's hell.

"Aiiiieeeeeeyaaa!"

A wall loomed up at them, Rafe-face amid it, howling as they merged.

<> was amazed.

Bravery, <^> had said. It was.

<> moved, with that same electron-swiftness as </> took <^> in.

<> dived after, rummaged through almost-congruencies, started ripping things into order in </>'s distorted substance.

Merged—with <>'s own mad self; and <^>; and sucked up disordered bits of other things.

Worm—retreated, whimpering.

Cannibal fled, outclassed.

Only Paul One stood, howling rage at <>.

And two others of itself surrounded it, denying divisions.

Two more joined with Rafe-mind, such of it as remained. It clung to them.

One cast herself amid it all, discovering loyalties beyond herself. Her double chose another target.

<^> rode this last particle, straight to </>'s heart.

<<<∧/they + +>>> became <<∧they>>.

Became<<^>>.

Then <>.

A shock went through the ship, a long silence.

Something very old had passed.

The passengers began at last to move. Certain ones fled for different refuges, old alignments having become impolitic, unsafe.

Worm danced, quite solemnly, for ((())) had gained a name.

((())) had become like Kepta in this, even if ((())) was Worm. ((())) had regained sanity; and pride; and glared from ((()))'s five eyes at Cannibal, who found it safer to retreat.

[] fled, precipitate.

<*> shivered, in deep mourning for <^>; for <^> had remembered <^>'s savagery at the last, and become quite sane.

<> stretched throughout the ship-body, taking all territories, all systems.

Trishanamarandu-kepta came to fullest awareness, and looked about <>'s surroundings as <> had when <>'s voyage began.

And at what <> had retained within-the-shell. That too.

Rafe put out his hands in the dark. His fingers met the extended arms, hard metal, rigid. He tried to feel his way backward amid this maze. Razor steel sliced his back in more places than one. His questing hands met the same no matter where he turned.

"Kepta," he said aloud, quite calmly; "Kepta—" Patiently. "I want the light back, Kepta; at least give me the light."

Kepta might have lost; might have won; the blades might start to move of a sudden and dice him down to something disposable.

"I want the light!" he cried.

Light blazed. He jerked, hit his back and arm against the knives and froze at the sting of wounds. The glittering arms were starkly poised about him, a web of razor steel and claws.

Rafe-shape phased in. "I've won," it said.

"Who—won?"

"Kepta, Me."

"Which of you?"

"Ah. Marandu told you." Rafe/Kepta moved through the metal arms, through the razors, coming clear to view. "The original. Myself. The one who brought you here."

"Either of you could have done that."

"Either would be me. But both my copies are gone, dissipated."

"Keep away from me!" And—*Either would be me*—sank in. He stared at it, finding the razor points at his back more comforting than its presence.

"Anxious still? It's your doing, you know: all three of you.

Yourself, for instance—It never could quite break you down, not while Paul was there. Not while there was any vestige of him. That's your secret, your one secret. Responsibility. My double worked so hard keeping you alive. Mistake. And Paul: Paul One always trusted reason: and he couldn't withstand it when he met it face to face in Jillan; he couldn't bear that—or her solitude."

"Where are they? Are they all right?"

"Jillan, now," it said, inexorable. "Jillan was the crux. Marandu knew. She gave him—sanity. He was once very fierce—Marandu was, in certain causes. He'd forgotten all of them. And Worm— they called him Worm—he has affinity for you: nibbled up a bit of you, in your other form, as if he'd found one of his own missing bits."

"Kepta—where are they?"

Rafe/Kepta's face showed—it seemed—disappointment in him. A ghostly hand lifted, motioned to the center of the place, among the arms. "Come on, Rafe. Lie down. You'll sleep now. I'll keep my promise. We'll go to Paradise."

"Where are they?"

"I had to erase them, Rafe. I had no choice."

"You—" He dodged past the arms, the blades, half-blind.

Snick-snick—Arms moved in unison. Clamps seized his limbs and held, irresistible.

"Damaged," Kepta said. "They were irrevocably changed. What would you have wanted me to do?"

Rafe wept. He shut his eyes and turned his head; it was all the movement left him.

"I'll bring them back," Kepta said.

"Damn you—" He rolled back his head, heaved uselessly against the unflexing arms. The strength went out of him. Resistence did, and gathered itself up again.

"They'll be new again," Kepta said. "You understand. What happened to them—won't ever have happened—to *them*. The templates are clean of that. I do have charity." The arms clattered and retracted, *snick!* "You can harm them, far more than I ever could. Do you understand that?"

"No," he protested—everything.

"Not make them again?"

He wiped his eyes, hung there, his arms about the metal limb. It was cold. There was, for him, sensation; heat and cold; touch, taste; all the range of senses. "For what?" he asked. "What do you make them for in the first place?"

"Should I not?"

"You talk—" He caught his breath, caught his balance, straightened and walked over to sit on the smooth plastic bed amid the humps, the nodes, in the shining forest of the limbs, where it wanted him. "You talk about Paradise. Leaving me there. Forget that. I'm not leaving them to you, to make into what you want. Take me with them. Hear?"

"They'd object," Kepta said. "I know them very well."

"Damn you." He shuddered, lifted up his arm, flesh and bone. "You want to strip me down to what they are? Do that. At least I could touch them then."

"But you can. You already have. You're not thinking straight. Don't you know one Rafe-template's *you*? In every respect—he's you. You've already had your wish. He can touch them; be touched; touch *me*; do all the things you'd do. Dead, alive—that makes no difference. The only decisions are selfish ones."

He wiped his eyes a second time, bleak and blank and knowing insanest truth.

"Think about it," Kepta said. "There are choices."

"What am I leaving them to? Where are you taking them?"

"Vega, maybe; you mentioned that. Altair. They interest me. Places that have names—are so rare in the universe."

He looked at the doppelganger. His pulse picked up with hate. "Truth, Kepta. Once, the truth."

"Motives—"'

"—won't make sense. *Make* them make sense. I want to know."

"Say that I travel," Kepta said. "And they will."

"For *what*?"

"Don't we all," asked Kepta, "travel? Who asks why?"

"I do."

"That is worth asking, isn't it? We are kindred souls, Rafe Murray."

"Don't play games with me!"

"I know. There's pain. I never promised you there wouldn't be. I never promised them. Do you want them back? Now?"

He was paralyzed, yes and no and loneliness swollen tight within his throat. He shook his head, found nothing clear.

"No choice is permanent. Except your first one. Will you go to Paradise?"

"I don't know," he said hoarsely. It included all there was. "Can I talk to them?"

"You said it to me, didn't you—they're not toys."

He dropped his head into his hands. "Don't do this to me."

"I only asked for choice."

"What if I ask you to wipe them out here? Off this ship. Out of this. Would you do that?"

"No," Kepta said. "Their templates would exist. I'd use them. Eventually."

"Honesty."

"Would it be—what they would choose?"

He sat and shivered until it seemed Kepta must lose patience and go away; but Kepta stayed, waiting, waiting.

"I want to be with them," Rafe said at last, so softly his voice broke. "Make me one of them."

"You don't understand," Kepta said. "Even yet."

"But I do," Rafe said. He swung his feet up and lay down on the machinery, blinked at the lights, the metal glare of knives. "I won't go. I won't leave them. Wake us up together, Kepta."

For a long moment Kepta stood. The cold seeped in.

"Yes," Kepta said. "I know."

Vega shone.

"No human's ever been here," Rafe said, confronting that white, white glare, that dire A-class star that no human would find hospitable. He felt its wind, heard its voice spitting energy to the dark. Ship had invented sensors for them, human-range.

"*Look* at that," said Jillan; and passengers hovered near, delighted in the four human-shapes, in new senses, in mindsets both blithe and fierce.

"Let ((())) try!" said Worm, who looked through human eyes, and shrieked and fled.

" " " crept out of hiding, as many had, who had been long reclusive. The timid of the ship had appeared out of its deepest recesses, now that </> was gone.

"Look your fill," said <>. "There's time."

Paul just stared, arm in arm with Jillan-shape. Rafe and Rafe Two stood on either side. They kept their shapes, unlike some.

They kept to their own senses exclusively, quite stubborn on that point.

"We're human," Rafe insisted. "Thank you, no help, Kepta. We don't make part of any whole."

Perhaps, Rafe thought, for he could still see human space, perhaps Kepta had betrayed him after all. Perhaps he had waked back there too, in a capsule near a much smaller star.

He hoped that he had not. He dreaded its loneliness.

"It was crazy," Rafe Two had said when they had waked together in the dark. "Rafe, you didn't have to."

"Come on," he had said then, in that dark place where they waked. "Sure I had to. I'd miss you. Wouldn't I? Maybe I do, somewhere. At Paradise."

Shapes crept close to them, hovered near.

Worm snuggled close, ineffably content.

It was a small, very old ship that *Hammon* found adrift.

"Something . . . 24," the vid tech deciphered the pitted lettering. "The rest is gone."

"God," someone said, from elsewhere on the bridge. "That small a ship—How'd she get out here?"

"Drifted," *Hammon*'s captain said. "Out of some system."

And later, with the actinic glare of suit-lights lighting up the wrecked insides, hanging panels, bare conduits, tumbled and crumpled steel:

"It's a mess in here," the EVA-spec said. "They were hulled, half a hundred times. Dust chewed her all to bits."

"Crew?" asked *Hammon*'s com.

The spec worked carefully past jagged edges, turned spotlights and cameras on frozen bodies.

"Three of them," the vid tech said. "Poor souls."

"She's old," the spec reported. "Real old. Out this far—at the rate of drift—"

The spec shivered, adding up those years.

WAVE WITHOUT
A SHORE

I don't know how many readers have come to me after reading **Wave Without a Shore** asking where I went to university . . . readers absolutely convinced I'd had their particular professors, in their particular disciplines. Suffice it to say . . . the story indeed comes out of the year I spent teaching at the collegiate level.

Understand, I'd never had a writing course. The local college wanted me to teach one. I certainly can say my approach was a bit looser than the one in the story: I walked in, asked the students what they hoped to learn from me, since I simply wrote for a living, and had no concept what went on in a writing class. I had no idea at all what I was supposed to do with the enrolled students except turn some of them out able to sell and the rest at least still able to enjoy their hobby. "First, do no harm . . ." ought to apply to teachers as well as doctors.

This isn't necessarily the case with the principals in **Wave**.

What was my collegiate experience? Well, I'm a Latin major—most useful course of study I could think of—still true.

I had, among other snippets of course work, a session with the philosophers . . . Aristotle's my favorite, if you want to know. But we also studied the modern philosophers to see what it had all come to—and I did conclude that, while philosophy is the most dangerous art and the Queen of the Sciences, a little grounding in real world science and human behavior is indispensable. Certain modern chaps have taken old Aristotle too far into the woods of abstract reasoning.

Let me explain my own philosophy: it's Stoic, old, Roman, and stubborn. Our eyes, ears, nose and fingers are composed of sensors taking in signals from the visible and audible spectrum, and signals from chemical and temperature changes in our environment, all of which reach our nervous system, go to the brain, and meet a set of stored experiences that say, yes, it's daylight and it's not raining—and that touches a set of educational experiences that say the weather satellite predicted this very set of events. The one we're born with: the other, we can improve.

Second step: the "I" who receives all those stimuli forms an opinion and expresses the notion to another "I" whose independent sensors have registered much the same. "Fine day," I say. "A bit hot," you say. Each of us observes our environment our own way.

But being a Stoic, I can say, "I imagine I'm content with the temperature." And I am.

Being a Stoic, I can say, "I imagine I'm discontent with the daylight," and I can paint so vivid a night in my mind I can see the stars come out. This is very useful for a writer—but one should never use it in heavy traffic, or in front of strangers.

Being a Stoic, I can receive impulses that warn me, "That candle flame is going to burn my fingers if I touch it," but I can say, through experience, "Only if I'm too slow." And I can put it out with my fingers.

Being a Stoic, I can say, "I control my own perceptions. I am completely in charge of my own happiness. If I am unhappy, it is my own fault. So I can be happy if I can change the situation or change my own opinion." Both require energy. Both are a bit of work—but usually worth it.

As to whether it is worth it—that's my choice. So everything is my choice.

Others are also free to choose. I'm not in control of them.

There are, besides that, forces larger than I am. If I fall off a boat a thousand miles from shore I can't think I'm not drowning, though I suppose a positive thought would make the situation more pleasant. What I am responsible for, when outgunned, is my state of mind, and being able to say, "Well, this is an interesting phenomenon. I wonder how deep it is . . ." is a way of life for a writer who enjoys her craft.

But there are people who carry the art of positive thinking to an extreme.

To them . . . this book is dedicated.

I

Man is the measure of all things.
—Protagoras

Freedom was one of those places honest ships avoided, a pleasant world of a pleasant star, but lacking a station at which ships could dock, and by reason of its location on the limb's sparse edge, inconvenient for ships on fixed schedules.

A few outsiders came here, pirates who were afforded a shuttle landing, and who therefore restrained themselves from their habitual destructions, preferring to charge exorbitant prices selling what on Freedom were rare goods. There were occasional free merchants with similar larceny in mind, but there was also a strong likelihood of *meeting* one of Freedom's piratical clients in the neighborhood, and that prospect discouraged most merchants of any category. Freedom was moreover a poor world, in outsider reckoning. It had grain and preserved meats and vegetables. That attracted the pirates, who had no world at their disposal and needed such things; it did not attract much trade of other sorts.

There were inevitably the military ships, who came pursuing the pirates on one of the occasional campaigns for order, whenever the' pirates had gotten too daring and touched off a hunt, or when the powers which ran the Alliance decided it was time to hold a military exercise.

Freedom had no ships of its own, not since the original, which had once been intended as an orbiting station, but which had finally, through disuse and failure of its maintenance, broken up in a spectacular display over the Sunrise Sea. Freedom had assets, sunny skies over large land masses, abundant population both indigenous and human—a condition completely contrary to Science Bureau regulations, since they mingled without safeguards. There was in fact no place on all of Freedom where both human and ahnit could not in theory mingle unchecked and without expectation of violence, a condition superior to that of some worlds under Science Bureau management and control. Freedom possessed broad, moderately saline oceans, reasonable weather with rainfall in convenient places, an oxygen/nitrogen/carbon-dioxide atmosphere with replenishment by vegetation, a vegetation which incidentally furnished inhabitants a minimum of ordinary difficulties with natural poisons and allergens. Tides, under the benign influence of the large single moon, bathed white sand beaches and thundered majestically against basalt, jungled cliffs, sufficient to have inspired poetry in the deadest souls. Humanity thrived on Freedom, multiplying at a rate sufficient to give the main zone of settlement, on the curved, many-peninsulaed continent named Sartre, a very respectable shuttleport city, Kierkegaard, with industry and manufacture sufficient to supply the needs of the farmers who ploughed Sartre's fertile plains. Freedom was almost totally agricultural, virgin abundance well-suited to man (or ahnit), and its lack of trade was no handicap to the economy.

But even the pirates refused to go outside Kierkegaard's port area, and the occasional military personnel who paid official visits to the Residency and the First Citizen, went and returned as swiftly as possible, staying to modern Port Street, which tall firebush hedges screened from the rest of the town.

Curiously, Freedom was not a notorious world, not, like Gehenna II and some of the limb's other plague spots, a breeding ground of legends. Those who had visited Freedom had no wish to talk about it, indeed, tried to ignore it as thoroughly as ships avoided it in their courses.

It was not that it was a place where humanity failed, or where men lost their souls to the strangeness of aliens.

Freedom was a mutual failure.

Instructor Harfeld: *What is truth?*
Herrin: *Whatever is real, sir.*
Instructor Harfeld: *What is reality?*
Herrin: *Whatever the strongest thinks it is, sir.*
Instructor Harfeld: *Who is that, Herrin?*
Herrin: *Here? In this room?*
Instructor Harfeld: *Of us two, who is stronger?*
Herrin: *You're older.*
Instructor Harfeld. *Does that make me stronger?*
Herrin: *Right now it does.*

Herrin Law thrived on Freedom, young, well favored by nature, chance, and the powers which governed the world. "He's gifted," the instructional supervisor had visited the Law household to say one night: Herrin recalled the night with perfect clarity through the years, the amazing visit of a man all the way from the township of Camus, to their bare-boards farmhouse in Law's Valley, where he and his father and mother and sister had been gathered in their town best clothes to see this caller, who had come all the way out from the township to report the result of his first tests. "He'll be University material," the man—citizen Harfeld—had told his parents. His parents had cried a little after the visit, as if it were some kind of disaster; but during it, citizen Harfeld had patted him on the shoulder and congratulated him on a talent so rare that Camus could not possibly nurture it properly. . . . "He'll have the taped courses, to be sure," Harfeld had said, "up to appropriate level; there'll ·be a government stipend, all the best for such a special student. An educator searches a lifetime for such talents—rarely finds them." So Herrin had swelled up with a seven-year-old's vulnerable pride in himself and understood that he was something different from anyone else in the house, so he was already able to look at his parents' reaction from a certain distance of that specialness. His older sister looked on him differently, too, and seemed to shrink after that special night, casting furtive looks at him, jealousy and perhaps a little self doubt, which increased over the years, and cast her in a new role of second sibling despite their sequence of birth. She developed a whole new bearing after that night; and so did he.

He loved his family, from his slight distance. He was capable of being wounded when his parents petted his sister Perrin in a different way than they did him. He clung to the consciousness that he would be leaving and that in a way he had already left them; and Perrin because she was a walking wound, and she was the one who would stay with them into their old age. Perrin was duty. She tormented herself with her inferiority; she lost all confidence, and bestowed superiority on others who had her about them. Perrin was uncertainty and self-doubt; Perrin clung; and Herrin, after that night of the visitor, was simply separate, understanding the position his precocity enabled him to enjoy as virtual outsider. That this was the price of superiority, that the same height from which he looked down on others and analyzed their feelings, also obliged him to live removed from the run of humanity. He grew up extraordinarily handsome and more graceful than his agemates; grew up with a sensible reserve which made it possible for him to associate with agemates less mature and less self-assured than he. He was confident of his merit and basked in slightly lonely love, loved in return from that height at which he lived; and tolerated jealousy with the understanding that those less favored had to have *some* defenses. He was kind because no cruelty had ever shaken him from that plateau on which he lived, since that momentous visit. Love poured up to him, and he rained it down again.

III

Perrin: I hate *you.*
Herrin: Yes. I know.
Perrin: You want everything.
Herrin: Yes. I do.
Perrin: That's not fair. *What do* I *get?*
Herrin: Take what you want from me.
Perrin: How?
Herrin: Just do it. Be stronger. Take it.
Perrin: How?
Herrin: (Silence).

He felt pain when he parted with his family, seventeen and bound for University in Kierkegaard. They cried, even Perrin, but his parents cried because they were hurting at losing him and Perrin cried because. . . . Perrin's tears were more complex constructions, he thought, jouncing along in the leather seat of the Camus bus over the dirt roads, and eventually over the smoother road on the weekly Camus-Kierkegaard run. Perrin cried for herself, and that she saw a chance departing which had never been hers.

They would all be happier without him, he reckoned, leaning his head disconsolately against the window brace and watching the cultivated fields roll past the unwashed windows. He had been too strong for them, and despite all the tears of various quality shed at his parting—the wound would heal now; Perrin might blossom in her share of the sun, a belated, slightly twisted blossoming, to be sure, but it was possible now; and his parents could devote themselves to their more comfortable offspring and he—*he* could draw breath in a somewhat wider room. That reasoning did not entirely cure the loneliness, but he was used to separation in all its aspects. He did not, with the confidence he possessed, brood overmuch on other possibilities. He would not choose to be anyone but Herrin Law, eminently satisfied with his fortunes. He had seen Perrin, who was popular, and unlike Perrin, he understood the reason of her popularity, and he was too kind to explain it to her: he simply congratulated himself that he was *not* Perrin, or anyone else he had met in Law's Valley or in Camus, even citizen Harfeld, who, from his almost adult perspective, was considerably diminished, a rather sad man who sought out and encouraged an excellence which Harfeld himself was not competent to comprehend—a useful job, but a depressing one.

Herrin created. He had discovered in himself an aptitude for art; and while he pursued the literary and philosophical and musical studies the school of Caraus had promoted, his real joy was in form and substance. He worked in clay and in stone, finally settling on stone as his greatest love, work with old-fashioned chisel and more modern tools, with ambitions still greater than his young hands could yet achieve. He had, boarding that bus for Kierkegaard, left every item of his art behind as inadequate, incomplete, a provincial past to be forgotten along with every other taint of his upbringing.

If anything frightened him at this stage it was his own power, his own intellect, which was in steady ascension. He realized that he was dependent on such as Harfeld, educators of less than his ability, who yet possessed the experience he knew he lacked.

He knew that he could be warped, even destroyed, by inexpert guidance, like some machine of vast power which, set off balance, could destroy itself by its own force. He knew that he must analyze all the help that he was offered for fear of being misdirected; that he must, in essence, *train* those who were to help him in the proper handling of Herrin Alton Law, and that mere good intent or worldly wisdom in those about him was not sufficient, because most people were not capable of comprehending the logic on which he functioned or of comprehending the abilities which he felt latent within himself. This made him uneasy in going among strangers . . . not the strangeness itself, because he was perfectly confident that his own grasp of a situation was superior to that of others, and that, if anything, it would be a relief to be safe within the environment of the great University, where he could reasonably anticipate that his instructors might be more competent to direct him and that his companions—perhaps a few of them—might be strong enough to withstand his strength at full stretch. He was just generally cautious.

He feared . . . that Kierkegaard itself might be a disappointment, that perhaps nowhere in all Freedom was there a place of sufficient stretch for him and that somehow his self might still fray its edges at the limits of what Freedom could offer. He was young; he was not sure that the universe itself could contain him.

He got off the bus on hedge-rimmed Port Street, and walked the short distance to the University, which was, like the Residency near it, of sufficient magnificence compared to Camus to reassure him. He registered, received all the suitable authorizations in his papers, and settled into the very comfortable apartment the government allotted him.

IV

Senior Student: What do you see on the streets of Kierkegaard?

Herrin: What I wish, sir.

Senior Student: Are you aware of things you would not wish, Citizen Law?

Herrin: I am aware of everything I wish.

Senior Student: You're evading the question.

Herrin: I'm aware of everything I wish to be aware of. I do not, sir, evade the question.

Senior Student: That is a correct answer.

Master: How large is the universe?

Herrin: How long is a string?

Master: Should Freedom concern itself with space?

Herrin: The universe is irrelevant: the possibilities of Freedom are as infinite as the possibilities of all other locations in the universe.

Master: Should Freedom concern itself with Others?

Herrin: The only meaningful concern of man is man.

Kierkegaard was a city growing according to plan, now three hundred years old and acquiring some sense of time. There was of course the Residency of the First Citizen, Cade Jenks, descended from the original Planner of Kierkegaard. In that long, five-storied building the government was carried on, and the planners had their offices and facilities. There was the University, mirror image of the Residency and next to it on that section of Port Street which lay within the city limits. The rest of Port Street extended to the shuttleport, the mostly disused facility which interested Herrin only in theory. MAN, the inscription over the Residency's main entrance proclaimed, IS THE MEASURE OF ALL THINGS, and it was humanity which wanted attention, not—not whatever was outside. Freedom itself was on its way to what it might become, and it had no love of the outsiders who came intruding on its search. The port was, like those who came in through it, irrelevant.

There were ten streets in Kierkegaard itself, excluding Port Street, which everyone did. The central street at a right angle to Port Street, beyond an archway and footpath through the firebush hedge, was called Main. Two vertical streets ran on either side; there was a central east-west named Jenks with two laterals paralleling it, and a paved commons where Jenks and Main intersected: Jenks Square. Warehouses, manufactories, apartment houses, all production and residence fit, completely mingled, within the geometry of the City Plan; an apartment might stand next a mill or a manufactory next a warehouse. The port's near edge was the site of all small trade, in a daylight market. Of construction, there was great regularity: a company in Kierkegaard turned out building slabs, all concrete on a meter of the upper section and a meter of the lower, and covered with river pebbles on the middle; there was one completely without openings, one with a warehouse-size door; one with a double door; one with a single. There was one with a window, a meter square. Out of these the whole city of Kierkegaard was built, with such conformity that it seemed all one building. It was an eye-pleasing coherency. Only the port escaped it. It was a city without ornament or variance. The whole world lay at its vulnerable beginning. Its greatest minds were being brought from all regions of Sartre to assure the right beginning—and Herrin Law was part of the program. He surpassed his instructors; he gazed on the void regularity of Jenks Square with a proprietary eye and the sobering consideration that the artistic expression of a planet lay under his young and guiding hand, for he knew that the blankness in Kierkegaard which was meant to be filled with art was his arena, that *his* work which would one day stand there— he was sure it would—would influence the total of artists to come in Kierkegaard. He knew that if it were great, they must either imitate or react against what he chose to do, and that therefore he would, more than those in the halls of the Residency, shape the reality of Freedom.

His reality, imposed on a forming world.

His self, extended over all the globe of Freedom, because

there was talk now of going into the other hemisphere and the continent of Hesse. His work would go *there*, as well.

It was a thriving city, with vehicles coming in from all the Camus River plain, and going out again with raw materials converted into needed goods. It held thousands upon thousands of residents, who passed—afoot—in its streets. But Herrin did not form associations with the folk who came and went in the streets of Kierkegaard. The important ones he met at social gatherings at the University and the Residency; the unimportant went their ways in their own and limited realities, reminding him much of those he had associated with back in Camus Province. He brushed past them on his trips through the city, noticing with simple aesthetic satisfaction that the run of people in Kierkegaard were better dressed than those in Camus. That there was prosperity here, fit his sense of what Kierkegaard should become.

There were more Others, too, which one might expect: a great city was like a magnet for drawing things to it, and like a great machine for producing debris of broken parts. There were those who were mad, or defective. It was debated in University what to do with them. It was early in the history of Freedom, so it was deemed enough until the ethical dilemma was resolved, to allow the defectives to resolve their existence in their own reality, which existed principally at the shuttle-port, at night, and rarely in the city. They were the Unemployed, the invisibles; they were excluded and in abeyance. They were inconvenient, but not greatly so. They were not greatly . . . anything.

And more than these—the primary Others, midnight-robed, who stalked through the streets of Kierkegaard mostly by night, with their own purposes, in their separate reality. Herrin was almost trapped into staring, for they were a sight he had never seen; they avoided Camus. But he recovered himself and pretended he had not seen, which was the only courtesy that passed between human and ahnit. It was their *modus vivendi*, mutually practiced, separate realities, neither contaminating the other. Presumably the ahnit gained something in Kierkegaard, but a sane man did not speculate on something that was not human, not in aspect, not in manners, not in art or logic or in any other respect. They left humans alone. It would have better pleased humanity had the ahnit stayed out of human places altogether, but there had been ahnit on the lower course of the Camus obviously for a longer time than there had been humans, and it was a question of prior occupancy. Realities in Kierkegaard overlapped, perhaps, but a little schooling in the courtesies of the city made it possible to walk a street without remarking on the dark-robes. They had nothing at all to do with man, or man with them.

V

Master: What is man?
Herrin: Man is irrelevant. My own possibilities are as
infinite as the possibilities of all other beings.

Herrin *enjoyed* Kierkegaard.

"Living here," breathed Keye Lynn, who was one of Herrin's pleasant associations in the University, "living here is Art in itself. Imagine the effect. We're shaping ten thousand years."

He thought of this, lying in Keye's bed with Keye's body delightfully filling his arms, and experienced a cold moment when he thought that Keye was an influence on *him*. From that moment on he abandoned trust of anyone, suspecting that Keye, who knew herself less talented than he (they were both artists, Keye in ethics, a more abstract field than his), meant to use her art to warp him from his absolute course. It set him to thinking much more widely, analyzing all his associations past and present for possible taint, suddenly aware that there were people whose motivation might be to *use* him, knowing his brilliance; that they might, robbed of their own hope of consciously warping the future—lacking the personal scope or talent for that—yet might seek that effect by using him, who did have such scope and talent.

It set him back for a time. He lay staring at the ceiling in the determination to have that matter sorted out, and resumed his relations with Keye in a new understanding which he kept entirely to himself, that now that he was aware of the possibility, he could do that to others—seize them, warp them to suit himself, that he could sculpt more than stone.

He could widen his effect on the future by being quite selective in his relationships with others at the University. He could gain vast power in many fields by seeking out talents of great acuity but less scope.

Like Keye.

He was grateful to her for that thought. Like Perrin, Keye did not understand him, simply because his reach was wider. Keye would see only a part of Reality, and yet she was brilliant in ethics.

He sought others, became far more confident and outgoing than before.

But the loneliness was there, which Keye could not fill. He experimented with others, who might, by providing him new situations, confront him with new ethics, but his own Reality still encompassed them all, and his own ethic belittled theirs.

There remained Waden Jenks.

VI

Master: Does the end justify the means?
Herrin: What is justice?

"I should feel myself threatened," Waden Jenks said to him. Waden was an acquaintance of Herrin's twentieth year, when some of the graduates of the University were separated out and returned to provincial tasks, out in Camus and some of the remoter areas; or to preparatory work on the expedition which should set them on the way to planetary domination—but Herrin was not one of those so condemned. He was entering on the second phase of his University existence, not as instructor but as working artist. He had an apartment-studio in the University itself, and Keye was there as well, holding seminars in ethics, and Waden Jenks . . . remained. "I'm obviously of moderate talent," Waden proposed to Herrin over a beer in the Fellows' Hall. "I'm obviously here because I'm Cade Jenks's son, and it's my father's wish that *I* become First Citizen after him. I should properly feel threatened by all you brilliant students. No instructor would dare set me down; that's why I've gone on and poor Equeth, for instance, has been shipped out."

Waden was drunk, but cheerful in his self-estimate.

"Evidently you're exercising a subtler talent," Herrin judged. "Strength is a talent."

Waden chuckled. "So is flattery."

Herrin flushed. "By no means. I simply state a fact: strength and possession are primary talents, not necessarily creative but of great importance. If you were weak your father wouldn't throw you into the den of so many predators, would he? Or if he had, you'd have been pulled one way or the other by one of us and swallowed alive. After three years others have left and Waden Jenks remains at moral liberty with all his former strength; ergo, he has not been swallowed or diverted. *That* evidences a talent sufficient for survival. What matter whether you get marks by skill or by intimidation? Intimidation is the manifestation of your talent."

" 'Not necessarily creative.' "

"Perhaps your father intends, by thrusting you into this medium, to inspire you to creativity."

"You're remarkable. I say that freely." Waden leaned across the mug-circled table and jabbed his arm with a forefinger. "Do you know, Herrin, I *am* strong, stronger than my father, strong enough to say that and to know that he daren't take exception to it. I am intelligent, more than he, and again, I can say that. Frankly, most of University is beneath my abilities. *You* know. I think you do. You know what it is to live with wings cramped, knowing that you'll break all that's around you if you really extend them. You have few friends, and you dominate them. *I* am the same. I always have been. There's not an instructor you haven't terrified with your talent, not a student here who doesn't resent you—truth, even Keye—who doesn't subconsciously recognize what you're doing to him and yet find himself powerless to stop you. You're the rock against which most of the University sea crashes. Truth."

"You're talented, Waden Jenks, and you're constantly depre- cating your own abilities, which makes you a liar, a slave, or a coward."

"Which am I?"

"Liar," Herrin said with the arch of a brow. "Because subtlety is a part of your talent for control. You are yourself capable of flattery; you flatter me. And of being invisible as the invisibles themselves. You are hated, because you stay here and others don't know what your talent *is*. You're the one they've never devised a class to instruct, but you take the whole University for your classroom."

Waden smiled and sipped at his beer, gestured toward him with the mug and set it down between them. "It *is*. It was cre- ated by the First Citizen to be that, do you see?"

"To gather sufficient talents together to provide a classroom for the heir to the State."

"Exactly so."

Herrin was thoroughly amazed; the possibilities ran at foun- dation level of all assumptions in the University. "By gathering the greatest minds and talents in the world in one place, under one set of instructors, under the eye of the First Citizen himself—and by the shaping of those talents—"

"To shape the course of the world."

"And by observing and learning them, to *know* potential rivals—"

Waden's grin became wider and wider. "Most exactly. You don't disappoint me, Herrin. I thought you would understand when your suspicions were jogged. I am delighted."

"And I am in danger."

"A key to successful manipulation is the dispensing of information. Had you stumbled on this thought unobserved, who knows what actions you might take? I am in potential danger. Hence this conversation. Do you feel threatened?"

Herrin sat back. "So you thought that I was on the verge of discovering this for myself."

"You have been steadily approaching that point, yes. I shall surmise, Herrin, that right now you're more than threatened, you are offended."

"I reserve judgment."

"It's an observed fact, is it not, that when adults want privacy and peace they dismiss the infants to the nursery, shut the door on them; that there's a certain amount of juvenile development that has to take place on that basis."

"The University."

"My father knows the hazard I am to him. Knows my talent, although when he began this project he was willing to have seen me destroyed, had I been weak. Indeed, the University he created would have devoured me—had I been weak. Had I failed, he would have selected the most apt as his successor."

"Myself, perhaps."

Waden laughed, picked up the mug, gestured with it before drinking. "I have no doubt it would have been you, none. But do you know, the older I grew, the more my father was certain that eugenics in my case had paid off. Oh, there *are* failures, a dozen little bastards farmed out and totally useless . . . I'll never threaten them because there's no need. I could swallow them whole. No, the older I became, I'll wager, the more Cade Jenks realized the sensible course was to occupy me. Had he seen to my upbringing, I'd have devoured him. No, instead, he sent me to the nursery—to University, collected this entire den of raven-

ing and powerful intellects and set me out in it naked and un-
armed but by wit. Survival of the fittest."

"So he has no prejudice for or against your survival."

"None. None. He simply wants to keep me here as long as
possible, because on the day *I* emerge from this chrysalis, *his* existence is threatened. He knows that he can't keep power away
from me. For one thing because of our kinship and my access
to the Residency. He'll surrender his office, being pragmatic and
having a strong wish to live. Indeed, he's intelligent enough to
know that the world will benefit from the exchange, that the wisest course for him is to provide me the benefit of his experience
and to step quietly out of my way. But that's in the future. I'm
only beginning to do that other thing which the University makes
possible."

"To remove rivals?"

Waden shook his head. "I *have* no rivals. There's not a one
here I can't manipulate or intimidate beyond any possibility of
harm; I know the University. Those stupid enough to despise
me . . . are the most easily handled. Pride is useful only with those
whose opinion we value, is it not? I don't value theirs. No, I'm
gathering forces. Persons whose talents are not rival, but complementary to my own. You, for instance, an artist. Do you know,
Herrin, that you are the one person in University to whom I shall
admit these things frankly? You're the one mind, the one being
who *might* rival me, if our talents were not, as they are, complementary. You create. Your supposition is correct, that my talent is not creative; so I seek out one which is."

"No. On the contrary, you've simply delivered yourself to *my*
search, Waden Jenks."

Waden considered a moment, and his eyes danced. "Oh, marvelous! This conversation is worth all the years in this dreary
place. Do you know, for the first time I feel I'm talking *with*
someone, with a mind quick enough to answer me."

"And you wonder if you can manipulate it."

The grin became wider. "Absolutely. Ah, Herrin, Herrin, you're
a delight. As you're wondering can you use me, and which of
us is likely to survive. I have native advantages."

"Indeed you do. Which argue that I should go cautiously. Likewise there were contradictions in your arguments that suggest a
silent assumption."

"Were there?" Waden's smile was ingenuous.

"What do you suppose of me?"

"That you have ambitions. That they're artistic in foundation, as anything would be that passed through that intellect of yours; but that they may not be limited to the creation of superlative statues, the inner vision made exterior, no. You have a very strong reality, and the grasp of a generalist. So am I, a generalist of sorts. I know how to respect one."

"You are a superlative generalist. You do what I do, but having captured the vision internal to each field, you store it, against need. And you will have power, Waden, indeed I believe it. I know that my talent doesn't lie in political manipulation."

"No, indeed, your hubris surpasses mine."

"Philosophy argues that hubris doesn't exist."

"But it does. There are offenses against the State."

"I purpose nothing against the State."

"No, your ambition is far greater."

"Then you know what it is."

"I know. It's Reality itself, isn't it? To impose your internal vision on all of Freedom. Herrin's reality. Herrin's perceptions. I believe you when you say you were searching. That you plan to use me. And I you. We balance one another. If I let you loose, if I let you perceive these things in your own time, Herrin Law, you might ally with some lesser talent, and you would either steer that talent against me, or you would be warped out of your true possibility. I offer you more than any other could: to be at the top, to have full scope for your ambitions. That's the business of a good ruler— to see that the best and strongest function to the fullest. I shall give you what you want; and you'll provide me the security of knowing you aren't inspiring some secondary talent to rise against me. That's what to do with complementary talents, Herrin, give them scope."

Herrin sipped at his beer; his mouth was dry. "You recognize what I am and confess you mean to warp me to your purposes."

"What, so little confidence? From you; I'd expect you to say that you were satisfied to know that you could bend *me*. After all, I'll be the State. And shall I not be one of the subjects you mean to influence? Teach me art, Herrin. Isn't that what you want, after all? Here I reveal to you all my defenses and you refuse the entry."

"Oh, of course, I shall trust you immediately and implicitly."

Waden's brows lifted, and then he laughed. "Of course you will. That's the trouble with my field; every amateur feels entitled to practice my art, but who would have the temerity to walk into your studio and pick up a chisel, eh?"

"You have a sobering manner of expression, Waden Jenks."

"My art has the disadvantage that no one who sees it can trust the shape of it. I can lay hands on the beautiful marble flesh, and find the outlines."

"But if you believe it's flesh, you've been taken in."

Waden grinned, and then went sober, his brown eyes and thin face most serious. "I *like* talking to you. And that's a motive. There's a feeling of finding someone at home when I'm talking to you, Herrin. And that is *rare*. It's very rare. You know what I mean. Keye is possibly the third greatest mind and talent at the University, on all of Freedom, most probably, because previous graduates don't rival the two of us. Keye's mind is amazing. And yet, can you talk to her—except where it regards ethics? And even then, don't you see things which she would not be able to take into her reality?"

Herrin turned the mug in a circle, until the handle was facing his hand again, studying the amber and crystal patterns on the wooden table.

"Are you never lonely, Herrin? Even with Keye—are you never lonely?"

He looked into Waden's. eyes.

"I am," Waden said. "Loneliness on a scale you understand. Keye—has you. And me. Keye has two living minds greater than her own, two walls off which to reflect her thoughts. But our scope is more than hers. There are thoughts you think she can't comprehend, connections you perceive she can't grasp, because you have explained all the pieces of them, haven't you, and she still doesn't see? No one does. Not the *way* you do. But I guess them. I can talk to you, and you to me. Do you know what frightens me most in the world, Herrin? Not dying. Discovering that I'm solitary, that my mind is the greatest one, and that I'm damned to think things beyond expression, that I can never explain to any living being. Have you ever entertained such thoughts, Herrin?"

Herrin found nothing to say, not readily.

"I think you have, Herrin. And how do you answer them?"

"By crowds. By crowds. Three or four pitted against me—can entertain."

"But satisfy?"

"I have my art. You're right, that I can lay hands on it, that it gives . . . presence and substance. Yours, on the other hand, is far more solitary. Whoever sees it will not admire. They *fear*."

"Unless there were one to complement me. One who could take my art and put it in breathing marble and bronze, who could make me *monuments*, Herrin, who could provide something that would not be feared, but treasured, who would make my works visible. Complementary, Artist. I provide you subject and you provide me substance. And we *talk* to each other. We communicate, as neither of us can communicate with others, in our own language."

"How can there be trust?"

"That too, I leave you to discover. Solve my dilemmas, Artist. Lend me vision and I lend you power to spread that vision."

"You don't yet have that power."

"But shall."

"And is power shared?"

"Dionysus." Waden chuckled and drank deeply of his beer. "And Apollo. You are Dionysian and I Apollonian, urge and logic, creativity and rationality, chaos and order. We function in complement. Adopt your protégés. I have my own. We are opposite faces of one object; a balance of forces. Beware me, Dionysus, as I am wary of you. But cooperate we can—and must. The alternative is sterile solitude. We shall beget ideas upon each other. We shall contend without contending, by being."

"I reject your analogy. They're old gods, and we are both of us half and half. Our contending is potentially more direct."

"But the manifestation, the manifestation, Herrin, isn't that the important thing, because there's no way my Apollonian art can have dominance over your Dionysian one save by inspiration; and yours similarly with mine. Inspire me. I defy you to do more."

"When I defy *you* to do more, I fear you can."

"Then have you not, Herrin, met your master?"

"Then have you not met the thing you say you fear most?"

Waden stared at him a moment, then all his expression dissolved in humor and he poured more beer from the pitcher, poured for Herrin as well. "See, I'm your servant. I must be, because I have a need, and you are that need. Without Dionysus, I become stasis, and the world stops."

"We are both Dionysian, and drunk."

"Drunk, we are soberer than most will ever be. No, we are still in complement, because our opposite natures are on the expressive side, and our internal realities are therefore opposite. We are a doubled square of dark and light, complete pattern."

"Then, my complement, *give me Jenks Square.*"

"That is your ambition."

"That is a step toward it."

"But I'm only a student." Waden held outward his empty hands. "Who am I to give gifts?"

"Waden Jenks."

"That I am." His laugh at this was different, sober, conscious. "I shall give you the Square, Artist, and you will make me visible to all of time. Visible. You're right that I live like the invisibles, and I don't savor it. Give me substance. Whatever you need, that I'll give. . . . Ah, Herrin, respect me."

"Fear *me*, if I'm your outlet to the world; your substance flows through my hands."

"I've told you what I fear. What do you fear, Artist?"

Herrin frowned, and looked him in the eyes and grinned, lifting his glass. "Your art can't function until you know that, can it? You open your mind to me, that's one thing, but to open mine to you, ah, that's another."

"Marvelous. O Artist, I tell you I find no pleasure greater than this, to find a mind to answer mine, a recognition passing all other pleasures. I ask you no more questions. What you want— is possible. Indeed, you'll find it's possible. Begin your work in your mind; I'll give you the stone."

Herrin's heart beat very fast. He was drunk, perhaps, but only half with the beer. It was Waden's intoxication which infected him. He believed, and that night in his own bed, alone, for Keye had other business, he still believed, and began to build the plans he had already made—bigger, and finer, and more far-reaching.

He had his means. Waden Jenks frightened him, for he knew himself, how dangerous he was in his own power, and he believed that Waden Jenks was at least second to him, in a way that Keye could never be, for Keye was tunneled in on a very narrow reality and Waden Jenks—had scope. And intelligence.

And worked in different ways.

There was nowhere in the University or in the Residency that one was likely to discover the handiwork of Waden Jenks; Waden's work was silence, was subtlety, the warping of a purpose; was kinetic and impossible to freeze. Herrin thought of capturing this in stone, and began to despair.

More and more it became his obsessive concern, the thought that this Man, this potentiality against which all Freedom was measured, had an essence which defied him.

VII

Master: What is matter?
Herrin: Appearance.
Master: What is the validity of appearances?
Herrin: Whatever value I set on them.
Master: Are you not also a manifestation of the material
  universe?
Herrin: The universe is irrelevant.
Master: Are you then relevant,
Herrin: I am the only certainty.

He went out into Jenks Square and considered the foursquare blankness paved in all directions, stood on the bronze circle which marked the center of Kierkegaard and therefore of all civilization, and tried to envision Waden Jenks, turning on his heel to the bewilderment of those passersby who must recognize the somber Black of a Student, and therefore, a purpose which was higher than their own or a talent which exceeded theirs.

The conceit amused him. He laughed aloud, and spun, and finally in the spinning world about him, conceived the image of Waden Jenks, a frozen form of many dimensions, embracing all the square, an element, a structure inside which all the citizens of Kierkegaard must pass in their daily affairs. It would be a sculpture of monumental proportions, a Reality through which others' Realities must pass daily, until their courses were diverted by it and their minds were warped by it and it became like Waden Jenks himself, so subtle an influence it would distort minds and attitudes without the subjects' being aware, and impose terror on those who looked on the whole and recognized it for what it was.

He walked the ten streets of Kierkegaard, omitting his classes; he looked on the exterior of Kierkegaard, the beige and gray of the solid citizens, the workmen, the sellers, the manufacturers, the occasional midnight blue of one no one saw.

His reality. His visions. And Waden Jenks, captured in stone, apertures and textures and surfaces shifting as one passed *through* them.

He went back to his studio in the University, locked the door, stayed and sketched and planned, mad with the vision.

VIII

Master: What is more real, my reality or yours?
Herrin: Mine.
Master: How do you demonstrate that?
Herrin: I need not.

"Come out," Keye pleaded with him through the door, and to someone else, outside: "I think he's gone mad."

He laughed to himself and kept at work. "Call Waden," he said. "Call Waden here. This is for him."

And Waden came.

"Well," Waden said, "Artist?"

The clay lay before them, the three nested shells which he proposed. The central figure, lifelike, emerged out of a matrix of similar apertures and texture within the dome. He waited, anxious, enormously vulnerable.

Waden walked about the model on the studio table, bent, looked within it. A smile spread over his face and his eyes lighted.

"Everything," Herrin ventured, "and everyone . . . must flow through it. For all time to come in Kierkegaard."

"Amazing," Waden pronounced, and grinned and clapped him on the shoulder. "O Artist, amazing. Order the stone. Select your apprentices."

"What, *now?*"

Waden looked into his eyes, and a curious smile, a subtle smile, sent a slight chill into the air. "I shall move into the Residency soon."

And the week the stone began to arrive, moved by truck from the quarries, to be set in the Square and in the studio, First Citizen Cade Jenks died, of causes unspecified.

The coincidence occurred to Herrin, if to no other. Herrin went very soberly about his own business, matter of factly shut everything down for the three-day mourning and memorial, and very quietly resumed when the public ceremony was done. In fact the mourning was official and very little private, a condition more of uncertainty than of grief, mutterings and wonderings, what manner of person this son was who assumed—*assumed* the power of the State, but no one had an inclination to prevent the assumption. At least no one *heard* of anyone who did. There was no disturbance; the Residency remained as mute as ever, as inscrutable. Waden Jenks sat within it. Nothing else changed.

IX

Master. Is art reality?
Herrin: Art reflects reality.
Master: The reality of the artist or the reality of the
    subject?
Herrin: (Silence).

The work began in Jenks Square. The five hundred apprentices and laborers allotted to the work began to consider their plans. The voices rang in the dead silence of official mourning, echoed off buildings draped with black.

Herrin stood amid the square, now ringed with stone blocks on which the foundation shapes had been plotted, himself experiencing a drawing of his skin, a sense of the power of his beginning creation, which was Waden Jenks's self, Waden Jenk's reality, the first layer of stones, the first courses of all three shells and of the central pedestal. In his mind he saw what should stand there one day, and shivered.

Waden came on the morrow, no longer in Student's Black, walked about the ring of white stones and acknowledged the respects of the apprentices with grave nods of his head. Of a sudden, Herrin thought, Waden *looked* like power. There was nothing obvious; the gray brocade and conservative tailoring was nothing more than a very wealthy citizen might wear; but the eyes seemed to miss nothing, to linger, invasively.

"With so many hands," Waden said, "you should make rapid progress."

"The image," Herrin said, "is alive in my mind. With the excellent equipment, I can make it flow into the stone. I've apprentices sufficient to work in shifts; lights will keep the work going through the night. I reserve the central image for my own hand. *That* is the focus. In the flow of *that*, the whole begins."

"I must sit for it."

"I shall need you to sit for it, yes."

"Did I not promise, Herrin?"

"I think you went rather far in getting me the Square, First Citizen."

Waden chuckled. "My reasons were complex."

"Undoubtedly."

"Do you flatter yourself you had something to do with them?"

"Do you say I didn't?"

"Does it trouble you, Artist?"

"Ah, no." Herrin turned and regarded Waden with a cool eye. "I don't believe in karma, my friend. It's all one to me, whether you acquired your power by abdication or assassination. It doesn't intrude on my Reality. Mine lies in the future; yours is present. Mine is length and yours is breadth." He laid a hand on the block nearest, cool, fractured marble from the quarries up the Camus. "This is my medium. Practice your art, First Citizen, and don't take up the chisel."

"Now which of us deals in intangibles? This stone of yours— becomes *me*, Herrin Law; and my reality—isn't that the subject?"

"True, First Citizen."

"Then where is yours?"

Herrin smiled. "I'm content. The more you're visible, the more I'm there too, First Citizen."

"I was always Waden to you."

"You are whatever you want to be, aren't you? In a few weeks you'll begin to see things take shape here. Those amorphous heaps are the central pedestal, the median arch foundations, the three shells, all the first courses. The first five go into place and the carving begins."

Waden walked further, walked back again. "You'll come to the Residency," he said. "You'll live there what time you're not working."

Herrin lifted a brow. "In the Residency?"

"What, is your self-confidence lacking?"

"Not in the least. I'll accept it without comment."

"There's inferiority in the word accept."

"Possibly. I admit it."

"Now I suspect you of arrogance."

"There's inferiority in arrogance. It assumes one cares. I'm simply as I am. I'll come to the Residency. It seems adequate for my comfort."

"Pathetic games. You're my guest, my employee."

Herrin turned a cold smile on him. "I'm your immortality. Your interpreter."

"Mine. What other message goes out, Artist?"

"Black and white, an interlocked pattern, lovers inextricably entwined."

"Ah, I've discovered your reality."

"You are involved in it."

"Does it occur to you, Herrin, that I'm using you?"

"Yes," he said, leaving pregnant silence, staring into Waden's brown eyes. He smiled finally, as did Waden.

"If you *were* master," Waden said, "you wouldn't have to argue from silences. But you must."

"I don't contend in politics. I argued that from the beginning, and the power you have is not mine. Since you lend it to me, I accept it, and I shall doubtless enjoy it. But rival *me*. I defy you."

Waden chuckled. "Come to the Residency when it pleases you. We'll drink together."

"You'll sit for me, I'll need both holographs and sketches. You'll come to my studio for the holographs, where I have the equipment."

"When?"

"Tomorrow at ten."

"You realize I have other schedules."

"At ten."

Waden laughed. "I accept. As for you, come when you please." He walked a distance, looked back. "Bring Keye to the Residency, if it suits."

"She may be amused. I wouldn't venture to predict."

Waden nodded, turned, walked his way back toward the Residency, as everyone walked in Kierkegaard, except the incapacitated, the infant, and the drivers of trucks which carried things too large or too heavy for carrying by hand. Herrin turned a cold eye on the apprentices, who put themselves as coldly to work, knowing they could not daunt him, but each attempting to assert an independent reality. They were not accustomed to such handling as he gave them . . . well, but they took it.

He walked about, directing this and that team as he had previously. He found himself ill at ease, knowing the temper of Waden Jenks, knowing that Waden had touched perilously close to the heart of matters. Cade Jenks was dead, and this proved certain things about Waden which Herrin had suspected; but then, there had been in that father-son relationship no love, or pleasure, or respect.

He also had power, by reason of his position in the University and in Kierkegaard. The apprentices regarded *him* with fear, because he had authority to hire and dismiss any Student or laborer from the project. At a word from him even an Apprentice would be banished from University and disgraced, condemned to the provinces; or a worker sent among the invisible Unemployed. The Students coveted the chance at Jenks Square. The laborers coveted the government support. They worked with zeal, in consequence. The dread with which they regarded that possibility of dismissal and the pride they took in being assigned to the project were evident in their application.

He watched the stacks of stone arranged, which were already waist high, and eventually, toward dusk, he spoke to his chief apprentice, Leona Pace, and saw to it that due care would be taken in unloading the stone which was still coming in on trucks from the warehouses.

"I shall hold you accountable," he told her, "if any damage is done; and twice accountable if there is any weak stone set into the structure. Remember the weight this foundation must bear. If there is a flaw in any stone, however it came there, set it aside and hold it for my personal inspection. If you have doubt in any stone, set it aside. The supply of stone is endless; the State provides. Am I understood?"

"Master Law, without question."

He nodded, walked away, through the stone circles and to that apartment overlooking Jenks Square which belonged to Keye.

"I've been watching," she told him when he had, in front of the window looking down on the building, taken her in his arms and kissed her. Their relationship was by turns cool and by turns warm, and lately the latter.

"It looks like nothing at all as yet," he said, relieving her of any duty to flatter him. He let her lead him to the table. She had promised dinner, and dinner there was, with flowerlights drifting in bowls among the dishes, and incense in the air. Keye had a servant to provide such touches, while he had never bothered, tossing things aside when done with them, to live in a warren of

discarded stones and clothes piled according to washed and unwashed, cleanly—he was obsessive about cleanliness—but he
confined his art to stone, not house-holding,

This was not, however, to say that he failed to appreciate
beauty offered him. He sat down, gave the flowerlight nearest a
push which sent it drifting through the maze of the crystal serpentine bowl and smiled at her.

"That was Waden down there today."

"What, spying from the window? I thought you had classes."

"Canceled still. The official, dreary respect goes on. You've
been my sole entertainment—watching the trucks, considering
your plight."

"How, plight?"

"You understand me. Nothing escapes you; you take such pride
in it."

"Because I work for him?"

"No."

"You mean to drag this through dessert, I can see."

"I trust not. I've warned you, but you see only endurance. You
plan to outlast him, encompass him, and he . . . has his vanity.
There was a time you knew where you were going; now you
apply to Waden Jenks for a roadmap."

"I am not political."

"Where do you live?"

He frowned, patient with her games. "On Freedom, in Sartre,
in Kierkegaard, in the University, in specific—how fine shall I
dice it?"

"Until you smell the air and know you *are* political."

"I confess to it then, but I'm politically unconsenting. I live
in larger scope than Waden Jenks; our arenas are different."

"Yours embraces his. As *you* embrace that monument—shells
within shells—he won't laugh when he perceives that Reality."

"You are uncommonly keen this evening."

"Only talkative."

"He asked you to the Residency, as my companion."

"What, are *you* going?"

"I said yes."

"Well, I'll not. Those who become embraced by stones of another's shaping . . . take what shapes they dictate, don't they? I
have my own comforts. I'll watch. Come *here*, when you will;

I'll even give you the key. It may be a refuge more convenient than your own."

"I suspect you of unguessed talents. You think I've erred."

"Go if you like."

He smiled slowly. "I shall, and come, and take the key too. I thank you."

"I remind you I am fastidious in housekeeping."

There was a time when he looked into Keye's eyes and saw something reserved, and again not; he was never sure. Keye deserved regard. He had never caught her at humor, but sometimes, he suspected, at kindness. When he was with her sometimes he smelled earth and old boards, recalled a world quite different from the competition of the University and the fierce, cold Residency. Recalled that provincial reality where in their Self and for their pleasure, or perhaps because they were bound by primal instincts—his parents had surprised him with kind acts. He had treasured surprises of that nature, unpredictable in the main because there was no particular reason for them, and they were small—a favorite dish, something of the sort. Keye, he thought, had come from such a provincial origin, even farther up the river; Keye did some things which had nothing to do with the study and practice of creative ethics, simply because there were unrecognized patterns within her behavior.

Or doing such things pleased her, because the following of childhood patterns was in itself satisfying, and she played purposeful games watching others' reactions to them, which was within *her* art. Keye's field was, like his and unlike Waden's, creative, and at moments when he thought of that, he reckoned Keye as greater than Waden gave her credit for being.

"No," he said suddenly. "I'll not take the key. And you know my reasoning."

"What, you surrender to Waden's bending but not to mine?"

"I have wandered between both. My eyes are open."

"Pursue your liberty."

She mocked him now. "Waden has erred about you," he said. "Go to the Residency. Exert your influence there."

"At your suggestion? Or at Waden's either?" She lowered her lids like a curtain and looked up again smiling. "I am the only *free* individual in Kierkegaard. Go or stay. I am immovable from my Self. I'm the ethicist, and I am continually creating the ethic in my personal reality, which I am doing at this moment. Consider all my advice to you in that light."

He thought it humor for a moment. Then he knew otherwise. He rose, stared down at her in outrage and distress. She continued to smile. "There is a reason," he said, recovering his mental balance, "that you tell me this."

"I refuse comment, perhaps . . . but I don't give reasons. Part of my creativity lies in letting others shape themselves around their own guesswork. You are—what? Omnipotent? Waden's servant? Mine?"

For a second moment she had thrown him totally off his balance, and then he smiled and nodded. Let Keye think as she would. "Good evening," he said. "I prefer a little quietude this evening, and I think we're approaching one of our cooler periods. When you've resolved your personal dilemmas, or when you find it convenient . . . I'll hear you, but I'm tired this evening, Keye, indeed I am. First Waden, and then Waden again tomorrow. So if this is your humor, do without me."

"You exude destruction. Perhaps I want you clear of me."

"Power never comes from retreat, Keye."

She stared at him, wise and amused as Keye could look, perhaps agreeing, perhaps refuting him by her very silence. He sighed, denied all but a good dinner, and walked out the familiar door, down the clean pebblestone hall, the same as every other hall in Kierkegaard, and down the stairs which was like every other stairs, all a blank slate which waited this generation, and his talent, and students of his teaching.

I shall be here, he thought, after them all. It's my nature to take in inspiration, and upon that thought, he suffered such a narrowing of the heart, such an apprehension that he stopped in his tracks there in the stairwell and leaned against the pebbled wall, thinking a moment and cold with fright. An art which was necessarily dependent on inspiration arriving from external forces was—perhaps enslaved to those forces; and if it was, then he was. Keye could be right. It shook the assumption of a lifetime and demanded thinking.

He wandered out then, through the foyer and onto the street where the white electric glare lit small black figures against the white stone and the cranes wheezed and lifted their burdens like grotesque giants. He saw yet another course of stone going into place as a view which had been open in Kierkegaard all the years of his residence here became forever obstructed, imprisoned, cut off.

He built a snare for the eye; he did things until now unthought of; he discovered unconsidered and unfelt dimensions to his own work which verged on the chaotic.

An irrational force, a madness, a dark and Dionysian force. That was his work, which begun, acquired its own momentum which seized minds and impressed them with its own Reality.

Kierkegaard changed. It was begun. Keye and Waden had no power against it.

He laughed as he had laughed the sunny day he stood on that bronze circle marking the center of Kierkegaard and spun; but no one would ever stand there again, no foot in all of time to come would likely tread that spot, no one ever have that vantage which had inspired the work. Even if ten thousand years made a crumbled heap of all man had done on the site of Kierkegaard, a hill would stand there, of crumbled marble, of ruin, and memories. A city would have stood there, the heart of which was forever sucked in and warped and changed by his mind. The world would not be the same, since that heap of stone began to stand there, and never could be what it would have been had there been no Herrin Law.

But Waden Jenks had permitted the work, urged it.

The perplexities overcame him. He had interrupted the workers with his laughter, and now with his silence, They stood there, surely wondering who was there in the shadows. But then they began work again, no one investigating. There were madmen in Kierkegaard, the invisibles, who sometimes with sound or action intruded on the Reality of the city—who screamed, sometimes, or laughed, as if they made some attempt to be seen by the sane. Herrin drew breath, and walked quietly away from Keye's apartment building and through the peripheries of the work.

"Sir," apprentices murmured, recognizing him now, and offering him respect. He walked on, paying no attention to them, casting instead a critical eye to the stone which gleamed white in the darkness, sheened with the artificial lamps. No flaws were evident.

"Sir," said Leona Pace, who came to intercept him. "I thought you'd gone."

"Going," he said equably, and walked on.

He refused to be disturbed. The physical fact of the sculpture reassured him that all Keye's hopes to manipulate him and all Waden's confidence that he did so . . . were the necessary illusions of Keye Lynn and Waden Jenks. *This*, this stone, was real. He was not deluded into believing the substance was real; he discounted that. The *shaping* far more than the substance of the stone . . . that was the reality. And the shaping was his.

He walked . . . up the long extent of Main, through the narrow archway in the firebush hedge, onto Port Street, intending to go to the studio in the University, to apply his restlessness to his labors . . . but the Residency was before him and he stopped, stared up at the bleak pebblestone façade which was identical to that of the University, or a warehouse, or anything else.

This, too, I shall change, he thought, conceiving further ambitions, wondering which was the more important, to involve himself immediately in the Residency alterations or to intervene in the proposed new hemisphere programs.

MAN, said the plaque inset above the Residency entry, IS THE MEASURE OF ALL THINGS.

And he smiled, knowing how that was set forth to the masses of Freedom, and what the real truth was, for in University they taught another maxim: The strongest survives, the weaker serve, the weakest perish.

Who am I? the masses in the provincial schools were taught to ask.

The masses went on asking, diverted by the question and never really wanting the answer if they had known it. The sign was for them. They took pride in it. They saw the world in their own measure.

The Students at University learned a second question. *What is reality?* They doubted all previous questions.

And a very few attained to the Last Statement.

I.

He smiled somewhat cruelly at the sign, which to the masses promised control of their destinies.

Perhaps the mad, he thought, *have seen their conditions*. Inferiority was a bitter mouthful. The mad in Kierkegaard were one step ahead of the sane and subservient . . . because most of those out there limited their thoughts—lest they see what the mad had seen, that they were not in control of anything.

Must not think further—or go mad, lacking power, which, after all, makes life worth living.

And is there one, he wondered (the inevitable question), only one man, after all, for whom the whole species exists? But humanity had no existence, of course, save in the mind of the one man who warped all that was about himself.

Himself.

He was, after all, very comfortable this night. He had simply recovered his previous state, before Keye, which was solitude. He thought of the first night he had begun to realize his solitude, the first night he had begun to conceive of himself as *psychurgos* and not as child, the night the visitor had come to tell him he was different.

His parents. Perrin. In fact his thoughts had not tended that way twice in a day in a very long time. He would bring them to Kierkegaard when his great work was finished. They would be an excellent test of it. The anticipation of the effect on them excited him.

Accomplishment, he thought, did not diminish goals: it opened new ones. To reach back to Camus and to alter that place too . . . one of his apprentices, trained by the work here, would suffice to change Camus. And to change his parents' and sister's lives, by enveloping them in his influence, giving them prominence in Camus. . . .

He smiled, self-pleased, confident, and walked from the facade of the Residency and its power and its philosophy toward his own domain at the University. He never meant to let Waden come too close to him, as Keye had come, until she tried to maneuver him and discovered that she could not.

He whistled, walking along the walk beneath the streetlamps, disturbing the night because it was his to disturb.

A shadow confronted him, gangling, robed. He *saw* it because it startled him, coming out of that patch of shadow between the two buildings. Or perhaps it had been there all along and he had not perceived it. He had truly not seen one of the Others in—he had forgotten how long. He had learned how not to see them, out of politeness.

It stood there, a blob of midnight in the light of the streetlamp, and from within the hood seemed to stare at him, a question posed. His path was blocked. The ahnit made himself . . . itself? inconvenient to his progress.

He walked round it and curiously—for he was beyond such curiosity—he had a nagging impulse to look back, to see if it regarded his departing back, or if he should see it taking its own way.

Anathema.

It did not exist. He refused it existence. An inevitable question occurred to him, regarding his existence in its eyes.

His mind rebounded perversely to his analysis of the insane, who confronted a reality which swallowed them, and who thereafter, had to ignore all realities, or establish their own rules.

He laughed nervously, silently, because the night was no longer empty of threat to him. He went not to his studio, but to the Fellows' Hall in the University, and sat at that table which he and Waden had shared on a certain night, familiar scarred wood.

The University was created for Waden, and created Herrin Law, sculptor.

He drank his beer and sat alone, because he was a Master and there were no younger Students who dared approach or question him; because he was known to be powerful and most of good sense would not come to him uninvited, fearing the edge of his wit. His apprentices had spread his reputation of late and the self-knowing retreated from hazard.

He was alone. Solitary in his Universe, the only real point.

X

*Master Herrin Law: Does emotion originate from within
or without your reality?*
Apprentice: Within. There are no external events.
Master Law: Is the stimulus to emotion also internal?
Apprentice: Sir, no external events exist.
Master Law: Am I within your reality?
Apprentice: (Silence).
Master Law: That is a correct answer.

Waden Jenks tolerated the sitting, suffered in silence, because
to admit discomfort and then go on to bear it was to admit
he was constrained. Herrin prolonged the misery in self-contained
humor, took whatever shots might be minutely necessary, sketched
from several angles, after resetting the lighting with meticulous
care.

And Waden, perched on his uncushioned chair, sat rigidly obe-
dient.

"The lighting," Herrin said, "will be from a number of sources.
I take the seasons into account; apprentices are running the matter in the computer, so that the lighting will be exact from season to season, the sun hovering hour by hour in a series of what
appear to be design-based apertures. The play of—"

"Spare me. I'll see the finished effect. I trust your talent."

Herrin smiled, undisturbed. Darkened an area beneath the chin
and smiled the more.

"A little haste," said Waden. "I have appointments."

"Ah?"

"A ship in orbit. An ordinary thing."

"Ah."

"There is some hazard. This is McWilliams's *Singularity*."

Herrin lifted an eyebrow, nonplused.

"An irregular client, one of the more troublesome. I'd like
you to be there, Artist."

Both eyebrows. "Me? Where, at the port?"

"The Residency, my friend.",

"What, you want sketches?"

Waden smiled. "I find the opinion of the second mind of Freedom—an asset. You have an insight into character. I value your assessment. Observe the man and tell me what you'd surmise about him."

"Interesting. An interesting proposal. I bypass your naïve assumption. I'll come."

"Of course you will."

He stopped in midshadow, made it a reflective pause, studiously ignoring Waden, refusing at this moment to interpret him.

XI

Apprentice: Master Law, what is the function of Art in the State?

Master Law: The question holds an incorrect assumption.

Apprentice: What assumption, sir?

Master Law: That Art is in the State.

And on the morrow the shuttle was down and Camden McWilliams was in the Residency.

Herrin wore Student's Black; it was stark and sufficiently dramatic for confrontations. He sat in the corner of Waden's office, refusing to be amazed at the splendor of the decoration, much of the best of the University culled for the private ownership of the First Citizen. He knew the individual styles: the desk with the carved legs, definitely Genovese; the delicate chair which bore Waden's healthy weight, Martin's; the paintings, Disa Welby; the very rugs on the floor, work of Zad Pirela, meant as wall hangings, and here trod upon as carpet.

He was offended. Vastly offended. He observed, catalogued, refused to react. It was Waden's prerogative to treat such things with casual abuse, since Waden had the power to do so; he recovered his humor and smiled to himself, thinking that there was one work Waden could not swallow, but which engulfed him.

Meanwhile he sketched, idly, and looked up with cool disinterest when functionaries showed in captain Camden McWilliams.

A black man of outlandish dress, bright colors, a big man who assumed the space about him and who had probably given the functionaries difficulty. Waden greeted McWilliams coldly, and Herrin simply smiled and flipped the page of his sketchbook to begin again.

"McWilliams of the irregular merchanter *Singularity*," Waden Jenks said, failing to hold out his hand. "Herrin Law, Master of Arts."

"McWilliams," Herrin said cooly.

McWilliams took him in with a glance and frowned at Waden. "Wanted to see," he began without preamble, "what kind of authority we have here. You're old Jenks's son, are you?"

"You've been informed," Waden said. "Come the rest of the way to your point, McWilliams of *Singularity*."

"Just looking you over." McWilliams studiously spat on the Pirela carpet. "Figure the same policies apply."

"I follow old policies where pleasant and convenient to me. That I see you at all is more remarkable than you know, for reasons that you won't understand. Outsiders don't. You'll accept the same goods at the same rate and we'll accept no nonsense. Trade here is not necessary."

"We," said McWilliams, "have the ability to level this city."

"Good. I trust you also have the ability to harvest grain and to wait about while the new crop grows. Perhaps the military will assist with the next harvest."

McWilliams chuckled softly and spat a second time. "Good enough, Jenks. Go on about your business. We're loading at port. You know my face now and I know yours."

"Sufficient exchange, McWilliams."

"What's this—thing—in the city?"

"Thing, McWilliams?"

"This thing in the middle of town. Scan doesn't lie. What are you doing out there?"

"Art. A decorative program."

McWilliams's eyes rested coldly on him. "Nothing military, would it be?"

"Nothing military." For once Waden Jenks looked mildly surprised. "Take the tour, McWilliams. There's no restriction in Kierkegaard. Wander our streets as you will."

"*This* city? Hell, sooner."

"The driver will take you to the port." Waden made a temple of his hands and smiled past them. "A safe trip, McWilliams."

"Huh," McWilliams said, and turned and walked out.

Herrin filled in a line, shadowed an ear, languidly looked up into Waden's waiting eyes. "Barbarian," he judged. "Limited in formal debate but abundantly intelligent. *Can* he level the city?"

"Undoubtedly."

Herrin's insouciance failed him. For a moment he almost cred-

ited Waden with humor at his expense, and then revised his opinion.

"Freedom," said Waden Jenks, "navigates a black and perilous
sea, Herrin. And *I* guide it. And I see the directions of it. And I
shape things beyond this city, beyond Sartre, beyond Freedom itself. I am a power in wider affairs, and when they come calling . . .
I deal with them. This much you should see, when you portray
me, Herrin Law."

For a moment Herrin was taken aback, "My art will encompass you," he said. "And comprehend you in all senses of the
word. The man saw my work, did he not? From that great height,
he saw it."

"That pleases you."

"It's an intriguing thought."

"Their vision is considerably augmented to be able to do it.
Kierkegaard is a very small city, by what I know."

"We are at our beginning."

"Indeed. So am I. Freedom is my beginning, not my limit."

"We once talked of hubris."

"And discounted it. Shape your stones, Artist. My way is scope.
We talked about that too. You'll never see the posterity you work
toward. You'll only hope it exists . . . someday. But I'll see the
breadth I aim for."

"But not the duration."

The words came from his mouth unchecked, unthought, un-
cautious. For a moment Waden's smile looked deathly, and a very
real fear came into his eyes.

"You serve my interests. Go on. Pursue your logic.

"You'll carry my reputation with yours." Herrin followed the
argument like a beast to the kill, savoring the moment, hating the
role in which perpetual caution had cast him with this man. "Mutual advantage."

Waden smiled. That was always a good answer. It was effec-
tive, because he had then to wonder if Waden conceived of an answer. It was possible that Waden did; his wit was not easily
overcome.

And Herrin smiled, because it was a good answer for him to
return.

So henceforth alone, he thought firmly. *Each to his own inter-*

ests. He was linked to Waden in one way and severed from him irrevocably in another, because the war was in the open.

"You've seen," Waden said, "all that could interest you. I won't keep you from your important work."

Herrin slowly completed a line, shaded one, sealing the image of the foreigner in all his dark force. Flipped the notebook shut and rose, left without even an acknowledgment that there was anyone else in the room but himself.

Creative ethics, Keye called it.

But in fact the visit did shake him; and when he walked out under the sky, leaving the Residency, he could not but think of a vast machine orbiting over their heads, observing what passed in Kierkegaard from an unassailable height . . . that there was a force above them which had a certain power over their existence.

He did not look up, because of course there was nothing of it to be seen; and he shrugged off the feeling of it. Laughed softly, at the thought that Freedom ignored outside forces as they ignored the invisibles; that in effect he had just spent a time talking to an invisible.

The man had spat on the Pirela weavings, had spat to contemn Waden Jenks and all Freedom, and Waden had treated that affront as invisible too, but it did not remove the spittle from the priceless artwork.

That man, the thought kept insinuating itself into his peace of mind, that man despised the greatest political power on Freedom, and the work of one of Freedom's great artists, and walked out, because there had been nothing to do.

Waden Jenks might have had him killed on the spot. Might have, potentially. But that ship was still up there with the power to level Freedom. Camden McWilliams had refused the rare chance for a closer sight of Kierkegaard, from fear? from distrust? . . . or further contempt?

He refused to think more on such matters. The man was an invisible. Meditating on invisibles was unproductive. Invisibles had nothing to do with reality, having rejected their own.

The analogy was incomplete: the ship and Camden McWilliams possessed power.

Herrin shivered in the daylight and walked on the way that the outsider had rejected, into the town.

The work progressed. He reached the Square, where the eighth course of stone was being moved into place, and even while that work progressed, apprentices were at work on the lowermost courses, some mapping the places to cut, some actually cutting with rapid precision, so that already the three shells, the touch-points of the interior curtain-walls, and the foot of the central support, showed some indication of shaping, troughs, folds, incisions.

A further portion of the view which had existed on this site since the initial layout of Kierkegaard—was gone. He refused to look up toward Keye's apartment. She might be there, might be at the University. She would spend her evenings at least contemplating what went on below. The noise would intrude on her sleep, impossible for her to ignore. He wondered how she reasoned with that.

He walked round the structure, actually inside it with a palpable feeling of enclosure. The art of it began. Other walkers, ordinary citizens, had ventured into it cautiously, because it sat in the main intersection of Kierkegaard. They gawked about them in spite of their personal dignity, avoiding the ominous machinery, touching the stone in furtive curiosity. This *satisfied* him. He found himself immensely excited when he watched a stray child, more outward than her elders, stand with mouth open and then run the patterns of the curving walls until a stern parent collected her.

And for the second time, he saw one of the Others.

The workers saw nothing, nor did the walkers, who continued without attention to it, perfectly in command of their realities at least as regarded invisibles.

But Herrin saw it, midnight-robed, walking through the structure, lingering to examine it as the child had, walking the patterns.

And that did not satisfy him. He turned from the sight, trying to pretend to others that he had noticed nothing, and perhaps their own concentration on their own reality was so intense that they could not notice his action in connection with the apparition.

Suddenly he suffered a further vision. Having seen the one midnight robe, he saw others on the outskirts, standing there, outside one of the half-built gateways. Three figures. He was not aware whether he noticed them now because he had seen the one and the shock of the night encounter was still powerful, or perhaps it was in fact the Work which drew them, and they had never been there before.

He wiped them from his mind, turned to his own work, which

was the central column. Leona Pace was not at hand, presumably being off about some important business. He interrupted an apprentice to look at diagrams, found everything in order, bestowed no compliments. They were not expected to exercise their own inspirations, but to execute his, and they were all doing so with absolute precision: had any failed, that one would have been discharged with prejudice. He pushed the apprentice aside, made a minor change, sketching with black on the stone itself, and the apprentice obediently altered the computer-generated sheet which was the master plan.

So doing, he put himself back to work and put the external from his mind. He worked until suppertime, and involuntarily thought of Keye, looked from the incomplete hemisphere of the dome, and saw the warmth of her window light in the dusk. He recalled sweet scents and a meticulous order, and the servant's excellent taste, and suffered a spasm of regret for their continued separation. His mind flashed back to Law's Valley, and to other such warm comforts, now lost. He prepared to make his solitary way back to University, and left the work in the capable charge of Leona Pace, who had returned from the shipping terminal and her own selection of the stone, a zeal he silently approved. Pace looked shadowed, hungry, exhausted; she kept at the work nonetheless, for her reasons, probably having to do with insecurity in her subordinates. He did not blame her: Pace was extraordinary, and anyone of lesser ability had to be a frustration and a worry to her.

He valued Pace, might have made closer acquaintance with her, with the thought of filling some of that solitude; there were looks he received from her which hinted a desire for his approval, which might lead to dependency on it, which might in turn lead to a relationship different and more controllable than he had known.

But no, experience of Keye and Waden argued caution was in order. Pace was zealous. Ambitious. He was at the moment too weary to deal with someone of ability and possible labyrinthine motive. Such entanglements with apprentices were all potential hazard.

Dinner, he told himself, at the Fellows' Hall; he still wore his black, and he would be inconspicuous as Herrin Law could ever be. A solitary dinner. Solitary tea. Solitary bed.

XII

---

*Master Keye Lynn: How do the realities of Freedom
coexist?*
Master Law: They don't.
*Master Lynn: How do you reconcile the realities of
Freedom?*
Master Law: I don't.
*Master Lynn: How are lower degrees of intelligence able
to maintain their separate realities?*
*Master Law: They delude themselves, they're part of
mine.*

He departed the structure, where lights had come on, glaring
with their nightly brilliance, and walked along an increasingly deserted street past the ever-same buildings, taking no
thought for his safety,

The slight traffic of Main vanished entirely at the hedge of
Port Street. He passed through the arch of the firebushes, and
experienced ever so slight a fear, outraged by it as soon as he
had come out again into the deepening dusk of the street, out in
front of the Residency, in which rows of lights showed interior
life. He was not accustomed to fear. He was the most confident
of men; had every reason for confidence. Suddenly he took on
caution in harmless streets, as if there were something there which
nagged at his attention, an eroding of safety, a thing which appeared only in the corner of the eye, as the blanking color of the
Others and the invisibles had screened them from eyes which had
learned not to see that color and that robed shape. He had never
been so troubled, had never had such sick fantasies.

He was an Artist, and *saw* details which others could not see.
That was his art.

And did he then, in his skill, begin to lose that ability which
screened out madness and the irrational?

I, he insisted to himself, and looked to the Residency façade.

MAN IS THE MEASURE OF ALL THINGS. MAN. MAN . . . and nothing else.

I.

There was a rumbling. Shuttles had come and gone at the port many times in his life in Kierkegaard; no one heard them or deigned to pay them notice, except those whose business it was to deal with the fact. But in the dark, and the slight chill, the disturbance of the air could not be ignored. The thunderclouds gathered like a summer storm, and he lifted his eyes to the far end of Port Street, where a light rose in the sky. And because he was alone and had no shielding distraction he found himself looking up, and up, and up, following the moving light of the shuttle, against a sky utterly black near the glare of the port lights, and then sprinkled with stars as the light climbed higher.

He was not wont to look up at all. He knew vaguely that the stars were suns like their own and that such suns had planets like their own and that organization drew those worlds together into complexities of politics. Knew that there were renegade powers, like Camden McWilliams. But for the first time he saw how *many* stars there were.

It was like looking down from a height, realizing that number. For a moment his balance deserted him. The *I* became less than it had been, a reality valid on Freedom, in Freedom's context.

Scope. Waden's art reached for those points of light. His art—bound to Waden—would go out there. Waden called himself Apollonian, orderly, light-loving and logical, but what he perceived in that scattering of dust was disquietingly Dionysian, chaotic, dark, and random.

Why do they stay in order? he wondered of the stars; and recalled half-heard tapes of natural structure, and forces, and his own art, which had to do with the architecture of a dome, and of inner, chemical structures of stone, vision plummeting from macroscopic to microscopic in one dizzying contraction and out again. He realized that he was staring, that someone might see him and think him gone mad, but he had never been concerned for the opinions of lesser minds; had disturbed Jenks Square with equanimity, uncaring. Now he felt exposed, catching a glimpse of something, like the Others, which refused to fit.

I, he reminded himself, defying the stars, and lowered his eyes to the street and walked across it.

Why? The question echoed in his mind, unwelcome; along with *how far?* and *how wide?* and *how old?*

I.

The invisibles looked at Reality and flinched from it, retreating into madness. His art was to see, and to go on seeing. It occurred to him that something dangerous was happening, that he had started a chain of events which led precipitately somewhere, and there was no stopping it.

He heard Waden asserting an exterior reality as valid. The University had been founded for Waden.

And might not other things have served Waden Jenks?

If he were sane, he thought, he would back off from such questions, which kept demanding others and others until the perspectives went spiraling up and down from molecule to star and back again.

He kept walking, past the safe front of the University, ignoring the hunger which he had nursed past a neglected lunch, the faint savor of food in the air from all the houses in Kierkegaard. He followed the avenue, which was deserted, and came closer and closer to the port.

Fear was there. He knew that it was. Fear was what he pursued. He walked as far as the open gate in the wire fence which ran the circumference of the port area—fenced for what reason was not clear, for there were no guards, no one defending the access. There were lights, glaring in the night like the lights which he could see if he looked back, where the glow of the work in Jenks Square lit the darkness above the hedges and the tops of buildings. Lights glared in the area from which the shuttle itself might have lifted, a bare circle, of machinery fit with floodlamps all up and down its ugly and yet interesting height, like the cranes which labored to place the stone in Jenks Square.

And figures, robed, walked among booths garishly draped under the fieldside floods. He stared, recognizing them as Others, or invisibles, there for trade.

He knew that invisibles somehow pilfered by night in the port market, where citizens of Kierkegaard traded by day, disdaining any robed intruders out of their time, but there was no mention that *this* went on by night, organized, booths manned—if they *were* men—money changing hands from opened cashboxes. . . .

He walked farther, facing fear, because it was there, as he would have faced down Waden or Keye or anyone else fit to rival him. Fear ran the aisles, skipped along almost visibly in the rippling shadows of robes which should have been invisible to his trained perceptions; but it was night, and robes cast shadows, and shadows were everywhere, There was no one like himself, a citizen. Pilfered goods disappeared and no one cared to complain, because had the invisibles been a problem, something would have been done about it, the solution so often proposed and never, because they did not care for the untidiness, carried out.

To kill them all, some had argued in University, would remove a blight. And whoever proposed the solution stood self-consciously admitting that they existed.

And who knows how many there are? another had proposed. Or how we should track them all? They do no harm.

In point of fact, no one knew . . . how many there were, who had gone mad. No one knew how many ahnit there were, or how many robes here might conceal one or the other. The invisibles had stopped being human.

Perhaps they bred, making more invisibles. If so they were quiet about it, and perhaps the offspring, lacking proper care, died; no one asked. No one noticed. It was not good health to take overmuch thought in the matter.

As for ahnit, they were not even in basic question. They were a separate rationality. *The proper study of man is man,* the maxim ran.

Who had proposed such a thing, when their ancestors had been merchants, or at least merchants had been among their ancestors? Who had made the decisions, when they found this perfect world that was Freedom and laid down the Reality which existed here? A Jenks?

But once . . . all their ancestors had been up, out there, far away.

Once. . . .

He cancelled that reality, preferring to start time over again. It was his Reality, his option. He smiled self-confidently, walked up to a booth manned by an invisible and found the meat pastry there attractive. He gathered up two of the hot pies, not see-

ing the invisible who sat there watching him, and humorously
walked away, eating the invisible pie and quite pleased with the
taste of it. Men could pilfer under the same law as invisibles.
No one was going to ask him for payment. No one dared, because they did not want to be noticed.

Much more savory than what was served in the Fellows' Hall.
He recalled an old saying about stolen fruit and, finishing one
pie, sought a beer amongst the booths.

Quite a different reality, he thought, intrigued now that the
disturbance of the day had been settled—food was what he had
evidently needed to settle his stomach and his metaphysics. He
was fascinated by the swirl of no-color and no-substance against
the powerful glare of the port lights where the shuttle had gone
back to the invisible ship and its invisible threat. Quite, quite fas-
cinating, this walk through an invisible's dream of reality, where
madmen went about commerce and no-men stalked about on their
own inscrutable business.

There must be a certain economy to allow it to function. Sane
farmers grew crops, which invisibles pilfered, which in turn *he*
pilfered, and it all somehow balanced, because what was pilfered
was sold, turnabout day and night and his small consumption
merely fed the engine that was Kierkegaard and Sartre itself,
which fed this mass as well as the daylight trade.

And how did the ahnit fit in? Some of the goods in the
booths—the clothes—the robes which ahnit and men wore . . .
ahnit robes. Ahnit Jewelry. He paused and *took* a piece, turned
it in his hand, found it, with its convolute patterns, of passing
skill. He pinned it to his collar, laughing at the conceit. An economy which functioned on universal theft, with sales only among
like and like; founded on the principle that no one stole, just pilfered. He walked on, saw one of the University stamped hammers for sale, doubtless pilfered from Jenks Square, from *his*
work. Amazing. He declined to repossess it. It was a minor item
and heavy to be carrying about. Let them have it.

He found his drink in a brightly draped booth which passed
out an assortment of mugs. He appropriated what was destined
for another hand, right from under the invisible's reach, and
walked his way, consuming his second pie, tasting cool beer and
dazzled by amazements right and left.

When he had done he set the mug down, reckoning it would

be pilfered back along the circuitous route, likely back to the very same booth from which he had taken it. *Nothing* could get lost in the labyrinthine system. He had lived within it all his life and had never quite seen it so clearly delineated, so vividly exercised . . . for even in Law's Valley things had vanished, to turn up again in market in Camus, and it was not good form to question.

Kill the invisibles? He wondered. How would civilization survive if not for them? Where would be the humor in that?

Not to go searching the market for a lost plowshare? Not to have the confidence it would turn up again? No one ever hungered because of it. And a good many times were never missed, or were missed with gratitude, and discovered by another with pleasure, whenever some citizen bought it back again. This was somewhat like the country markets, indeed it was, and the few new-goods warehouses in town were dull by comparison. Only in Camus there had been just the Place, where goods tended to appear, and remain, and perhaps—he had never wondered—there was also this nighttime activity.

By day, simple citizens; by night, invisibles. The same merchandise.

A balance, indeed.

He had quite shed his fear and walked now in utter abandon.

An ahnit set itself in his path, and from within the hood a glitter of eyes regarded him with such directness that he forgot himself, and stopped, and then had to recover his self-possession and walk around the obstacle, instead of employing that graceful sidestep one used when the obstacle was expected. He was shaken. It was deliberate. It was very near aggression. The thought occurred to him that if a citizen should ever be found dead in Kierkegaard—and it happened—the inquiry did not extend beyond citizens and natural causes.

He kept going in his chosen path, which took him again to the gate, and to Port Street.

He looked back. For the first time in his adult life he committed such an indiscretion, and there was an ahnit there.

A shadow, a robed shadow on the street, beneath the lights by the gate. It had followed.

He had looked—and never meant to again—but this one time he had looked, simply to prove himself wrong. His apprehension had been correct, and thereafter, alone or in public, whenever beset with the temptation to yield to the urge to look behind him, whenever insecure in his own reality he would remember . . . once . . . there had been something there. He shivered. He hurried.

The University doors received him, solid wood, carved, safe and sturdy. They closed behind him and he walked down the corridors toward Fellows' Hall, hearing the slight boisterousness from it long before he reached it. He sought the familiar, the banal, desperately.

XIII

Student: Master Law, is friendship possible?

Master Law: What is friendship?

Second Student: We propose it's a sharing of realities.

Master Law: Do you also propose to step into the same river in the same instant and in the same place?

Student: Perhaps ... friendship is equivalency of realities.

Master Law: How do you establish that equivalency?

Student: If we were equal.

Master Law: In all respects?

Student: In the important ones. In the ones we consider important. Is that possible, sir?

Master Law: Have you not equally defined rivalry?

Second Student: If we agreed.

Master Law: If common reality is your reality, it exists, within that referent. It either of you exists, which is by no means certain.

He betook himself to bed in the studio, having a cot there for occasions of late work; it was his own familiar clutter and he had had a great many beers. He reckoned that the best cure for his troubles.

Overwork. He had overstrained himself, and his agitated brain was seeking occupation even when it reasonably had none, simply burning off adrenalin; that was the source of his bizarre fancies.

But when he sat on his cot and reviewed the sketches he had made in his sketchbook, he stopped on the last one he had done of Waden, knowing that another turn of the page was going to bring the nightmare back again.

He turned it, because he could not refrain. The image of Camden McWilliams was there, black and broad-shouldered and solid, refuting invisibility. He had sketched an invisible, and brought it home with him. And on his collar was another thing, which he had forgotten, until he saw the outsider again.

He pulled off the ahnit brooch and it lay chill in his palm. He was numbed by his evening's drinking. He sat there unsure what he ought to do with the thing, which was . . . fine. It was no-color, lapis, nothing very precious, but . . . fine. There was no destroying such a thing. It went against all his sensibilities.

He laid it atop the portrait of Camden McWilliams, who had spat on priceless art, canceling him from his thoughts. He lay down on his cot, with the light on, and stared about him at what had been real and solid and true for so many years, and finally the Reality reasserted itself. *He* reasserted it, and snugged into the warmth and slept a drunken sleep.

His head hurt in the morning, as expected; he had a bewildered recollection of himself and his wanderings, and with light pouring in the studio window and peace everywhere the series of encounters seemed entirely surreal and his fear somewhat amusing.

He shaved, washed, dressed, in spirits as ebullient as an aching head and slight embarrassment would allow.

Keye, he decided. The fact was that he missed Keye and therefore he indulged himself in such nonsense. If he had had Keye's apartment to go to he should never have been doing such incredible things—the market, the *port* market at night, of all things!—and making a spectacle of himself. He had fallen quite seriously. He had let Keye disturb him, that was it; she had gotten to him and he had wobbled from the blow. There was nothing for it but to reestablish himself with her, move back in on his own terms, ignore her attempts to manipulate him. It could only make him stronger. He had to school himself to withstand her undermining effects, and on the contrary to affect her. He was the superior, and anything else was unthinkable.

He dressed, and clipped the ahnit brooch to his collar, which no citizen of Kierkegaard would *dare* do, adorning himself with invisible jewelry made by invisibles and Others. It smacked of madness.

But so did dancing in the main square of Kierkegaard, and he had done that. And laughed there. And as for dread of what others might *think*, he was too powerful for that. If they thought they saw him wearing something which invisibles had made, then let them say so; it was a dilemma for them, a discomfort for all about him, a challenge. He wanted challenges this morning; he was, perhaps because of the headache, in an aggressive mood, and the humor of it vastly appealed to him.

He swung out the door of his studio, headed for the square, with a lightness in his step, skipping down the stairs.

He had met all there was to fear; had bested it; had come out of a bad dream, and headed for his work with enthusiasm.

XIV

Waden Jenks: Ah, Herrin, respect me.
Master Law: Fear me, if I'm your outlet to the world.
Your substance flows through my hands.
Waden Jenks: I've told you what I fear. What do you
fear, Artist?

"I'm back," he announced that evening at Keye's door. The servant let him in and Keye herself, about to sit down to a solitary supper, betrayed herself with a slight lifting of the brows.

"Oh. Should I be happy?"

"Be what you choose. I trust there's something in the pantry."

"See to it," Keye told the servant, waving her hand, and indicated the other chair. "So you're back. And how much else do you assume?"

"Oh, be yourself. I'd never interfere."

She dropped the smile, sat there looking as if something had gone down the wrong way, and stared at him a moment. He kept smiling, because if she threw him out he would have won, and if she let him stay he would have won.

He stayed.

If Keye noticed the brooch she said nothing, nor touched it, nor commented on the rift which had been between them. Keye was either on the retreat or, falsely self-assured, thought that she had won. He did not think the latter. "Have you," she asked, "moved to the Residency yet?"

He shrugged. "I'm waiting a moment of convenience. I've been too busy lately to consider an interruption."

"The work out there is going much faster than I would have believed."

"What, do I surprise you?"

"If you like."

"I'm satisfied with it."

He wondered for a moment about Keye. Meekness was not

her style, but possibly she was lonely, as he was. He admitted that much, having also admitted to himself that he could live in solitude if he chose. And Keye, who was superior to all but him and Waden, had to have come to similar decisions.

His reality, he concluded, was flexible enough to tolerate Keye. And to laugh at her pretensions.

XV

Master Law: How fine shall I dice it?

Master Lynn: Until you smell the air and know you are political.

Master Law: I confess to it then; but I'm politically unconsenting. I live in larger scope than Waden Jenks, our arenas are different.

Master Lynn: Yours embraces his. As you embrace that monument, shells within shells. He won't laugh when he perceives that Reality.

He looked out Keye's window at a night somewhat removed from that night, when the whole apartment was dark and the only light was coming in from the glaring floods outside. The noise went on, the grinding of cranes, the voices of workmen and the voices of apprentices giving orders, the occasional ring of hammer and chisel. The twelfth course was laid. What had been three rings from above, with the thick central pillar and the apparent random placement of additional touch-points to act as supports . . . began to show other curves. The inward curve of the dome began to be apparent, and the curve of the pillar which was headed to meet it in three levels. That slamming of pipe . . . the scaffolding was going into place, the supports which would hold the developing dome until the last courses could be laid, and their keystones settled. During the next several days, the cranes would work nonstop. The whole shell would be put up; lighting was being arranged interior to the shell as well as exterior. Apprentices with their computer printouts and their cutters would sit at the base of a surface completing their tasks in sculpture, while cranes swung the vast stones into place above them. The major perforations would be made only when the whole structure stood solid. Minor texturing proceeded.

He put on his clothes, disturbing Keye as little as possible: "Difficulty?" she lifted her head from the pillow to ask. "Restless," he said. "Make love?" she murmured politely. "No need," he said, and Keye snuggled contentedly into the sheets and pillows, having had what she wanted and as happy, he knew well enough, to have the bed to herself thereafter; Keye was an active sleeper. He finished his dressing, padded out and down the hall, down to the foyer and out, into the glare of the floods and the business of the workmen and apprentices.

"Is it stable?" he asked of the night supervisor, Carl Gytha. "Any difficulty?"

"None," Gytha assured him. "The engineers assure us so."

He nodded, pleased with himself, looked about him where now the bone-white marble formed the strong bend of an arch against the velvet sky and the staring eyes of the floods. While he watched, another block settled, homed by the seeker-sensor that told the crane operator it was coming down on target. It hovered. The sensor plate became aligned with its mate as it settled. Workmen hastened to strip off the paired sensors, free the fore and aft clamps, scrambling along the scaffolding. Liberated, the crane swung with ponderous grace and dipped its cable after the next block the master apprentice would designate. The clamps settled, embraced, seized, lifted.

That smoothly.

Block after block, through the night. The operation had smoothed itself into a precision and a pace which held without falter; shifts worked and rested in alternation, enjoyed food and warm drink, cups which sent curls of steam up into the air. Herrin savored the hot sweet liquid, fruited milk and sugar, which fueled the crews and, keeping them off stronger drink, kept their perception straight and their reflexes instant. They were bright-eyed and enthusiastic, pampered by the project, afforded whatever they reasonably desired while on the project and promised a bonus if it met deadline, and wherever Herrin walked there was a flurry of zeal and an offering of respect.

"I'm not great, sir," an older worker said to him, when he inquired the view of the man, who had been rigging scaffolding. "But this thing is real and it's going to go on standing here and I'll look at those stones and remember doing them."

That was to him a tremendous insight, first into the thinking of the less than brilliant, with whom he had had little association and less conversation; and secondly, into possibilities and levels of the sculpture's reality which he had himself hardly yet grasped. "Indeed," he said, sucking in his breath, stirred by the concept of others falling within this design of his making. "Do you know—what *is* your name?"

"John Ree, sir," said the worker, jamming uncertain hands into his pockets as if seeking refuge for them. He was a big man, graying and weathered from work out of doors. "Ree."

"John Ree. It occurs to me to make a great bronze plaque when all's done; to set the name of every hand that worked to rear this sculpture, the apprentices, the stonemasons, the crane operators, the runners, every single one . . . out before the north wall."

"Would be splendid, sir," Ree murmured, looking confused, and Herrin laughed, walked away with energy in his step.

Within the hour, before dawn, the word had traveled. Supervisor Carl Gytha had heard, and asked him. "Everyone," he confirmed, "every name," and watched Gytha's eyes grow round, for Gytha was competent and knew at least a degree of ambition within the University.

"Yes, sir," the supervisor said earnestly.

"Make a list; keep it absolutely accurate. Cross check with Leona Pace."

"Yes, *sir*."

"To the least. To the sweepers. *Everyone*."

"Yes, sir." Gytha went off. Herrin smiled after him, marvelously self-content. "Come *on*," he heard yelled from the top of the courses, workers exhorting each other. No different than had been . . . but was there yet a sudden keenness in the voice?

He sculpted lives, and intents. Promised John Ree a place in time along with Waden Jenks and Herrin Law. Created . . . in John Ree . . . a possibility which had never been there in his wildest fancies.

See, John Ree would say to his son or daughter, to his children's children, *see . . . there. There I am.*

I.

Ambition . . . for ten thousand years of that unremarkable worker's descendants. And what might it not do?

He felt a sudden lassitude, physical impact of half a night awake, as he considered creative energies expended, looked at the dawning which began to pale the glare of lamps, realized what sleep he had missed. But the brain was awake, seldom so much awake. He paced a time longer, finally knew that he was exhausted, and headed outward, through the developing maze of the shells, out into the pink daylight.

A row of dark figures stood there, robes flapping in the slight breeze. Eight, nine of them, all in a row vaguely artistic—an arc observing the arc of the dome itself, he realized; invisibles, all of them. Watching. He stopped, unease touching him like the touch of the wind, and on an impulse he turned and walked back through the maze to the *other* side, the other gateway, to the south.

There were more invisibles, and more than one row, not appearing to have any symmetry to their standing, but symmetrical all the same, because they were focused on the dome.

He refused the sight. He turned and retraced his steps, the way he had started in the first place. Workers called out to each other, still shouting instructions. He swept through the dome, out past the line of watchers, managing this time not to see them, except as shadows.

He made no particular haste, walking in the dawning up through the street, on which morning walkers were beginning to appear, ordinary citizens. *Safe*, the thought came to him, and why he should subconsciously reckon hazard he did not know. There had never been any hazard from invisibles. It was fancy, imagination, and he thought that he had purged fear of that.

He moved to the Residency that morning. It was a matter of packing up a sackful of clothing and personal items from the studio and appearing at the Residency entry desk in the main hall, casting himself on Waden's recommendation and the staff's invention. The room turned out to be extravagant, by his standards, with white woodwork and a wide, soft bed. It had a magnificent view of the Port Street walkway, the hedge, the grand expanse of Main beyond, and most important, the dome, the Work.

He was delighted, grandly pleased, stood smiling into the daylight which was streaming over distant Jenks Square.

He did not delude himself that Keye would come here. She had an almost superstitious fear of being inside this place. He grimed with amusement. So much for Keye's fears, and his twilight nightmares and watchers about the square.

So much for any assumption Keye might now make that she

had dissuaded him from this venture into the Residency. He had, he thought, delayed overlong on her account . . . or his own comfort. It was, after all, a mere change of address. And Keye's apartment was still accessible from the Square . . . when there was time. He foresaw a time of increasing preoccupation, when he would not indeed have time to have made the shift to the Residency, and he would not have Keye pouring her own opinions into his ear without also doing what he chose on the contrary tack. That Keye should know his independence . . . he had no vanity in that regard—in fact whatever she wanted to think was very well, and better if she deceived herself—but he would not be dissuaded by her, or oppose her for its own sake, which was likewise to move at her direction. It was simply a good morning to get around to the move, when he could do so without particular reason one way or the other.

He found it even more pleasant than he had thought.

The door opened uninvited. "Welcome," said Waden's voice from behind him.

He turned, raised brows. "Well. It's splendid hospitality, First Citizen."

"It's nothing too good for you, is it?

"Of course not."

Waden laughed softly. "Breakfast?"

"Gladly."

"You choose strange hours for moving."

"Convenient to my schedule."

Waden's eyes traveled over him minutely. "You worked all night? Zeal, Artist,"

"I enjoy my work."

"Doubtless you do."

Waden walked to the window, turned, wiped a finger across the brooch he wore on his collar, smiled quizzically. "Bizarre ornament."

Herrin smiled, said nothing, which brought a spark of amusement to Waden's eyes. Herrin laid a hand on Waden's back, turned him toward the door. "Fellows' Hall?"

Waden agreed. They walked together, ate together; Waden went back to his offices and his work; Herrin went back to his, in the studio, at peace with his reality. He gathered up his own cutter for the first time since the project began, selected his tools, went out to the Square on the nervous energy which had fired him since midway through the night.

The cranes groaned and ground their way about their business. Leona Pace came up with her checklist to see if there was anything that wanted doing; he refused her, waved off a question about the plaque and the proposal of the names to be engraved there.

"True," he said simply, and knelt down and began unwrapping his tools, his own, which were the finest available, before the pillar which would be the central sculpture. He was sure now. That had been the reason for the lack of sleep, the anxiety, the energy which had suffused him and dictated so many shiftings and changes and readjustments in recent days.

He focused himself now on his own phase of the work. The cranes hefted enormous weights which sailed like clouds overhead, any one of which, slipping, could have crushed him to grease, but he refused even the slight concern the possibility suggested.

He focused the beam, and began, oblivious to all else.

XVI

Student: Is there reality outside Freedom?
Master Law: I imagine that there is.

He dropped the cutter, finally—saw his hand was wobbling and jerked it away from the stone before disaster could happen. It fell, and he sank down where he was, dropped head into arms and arms onto knees and sat there, aware finally that he was getting wet, that rain was splashing onto his shoulders and beginning to slick all the exposed stonework. He was not cold yet, but he was going to be. His joints felt as if the tendons had all been cut and there was fire in his shoulders and his arms and his legs.

A plastic wrap fell about his shoulders. Leona Pace was there, her plump freckled face leaning down to look at him sideways. "All right, sir?"

He drew a breath, massaged his hands, nodded, looked up past Pace to the Shape which had begun in recent days to emerge from the stone, which had begun, with the beam-cutter's swift incisions, to *be* Waden Jenks. He sat there, with the rain slicking down his forehead and into his eyes, and stared at what he had done, numb already in the backside and with a grateful numbness creeping into his exposed hands.

Leona Pace followed his stare, looked down again. "It's amazing, sir."

"I should have rested." He tried for his feet, wrapping the plastic about him, and Pace made a timid effort to steady him; it gave him equilibrium. Other workers and apprentices had sheltered in the curve of an arch. The lights had come on as the clouds darkened. He turned full about, saw a dry spot under a curve and went to it, thinking Pace was following. But when he looked back she was walking away, her brown hair straggling as usual, her bearing matter-of-fact and lonely-looking.

He was spent, as from a round of sex. He felt the same melancholia as encounters with Keye tended to give him; he looked reflexively toward the window where Keye might be, and saw nothing because of the curve. The new reality was closing in. Permanent. Strangely he felt no more desire for Keye, for anyone, for anything.

And as after sex, it would return. He leaned against the stone, watching the sheen of water flow this way and that. It was the first time the work had stopped, the only circumstance which could delay it. He looked up at the sky, which was already showing signs of breaking sunlight. Such storms came and left again with suddenness in this season. The stone would dry within a short time when the rain had stopped.

The hot-drink cart made the rounds; an hour's rest became holiday. Laborers tucked up in plastics, drinking the steaming cups which splashed with raindrops, came from their shelters to stand and stare at the central sculpture, and Herrin, his own hands clasped about warm ceramic and his belly warmed by the drink, watched with vast satisfaction.

Laborers asked questions; apprentices swelled with importance and answered, pointing to the imaginary vault of the roof, the future placement of curtain-columns, and laborers explained to other laborers . . . Herrin watched the whole interchange and drank in the excitement which suffused the whole crew.

Pride. They were *proud* of what they were doing. They had come here diverse, and something strange had begun to happen to all of them in this shell, contained in this sculpture of his devising.

And then the Others came.

They filed in through the gateways and stood about, four at first and then more, midnight-robed. Ten, twelve, fifteen.

The workers *saw* them. The excitement which had been palpable before their coming tried to maintain itself, but there was an erosion, a silence, an unease. Men and women tried to maintain equilibrium, realities, *choice*. Herrin leaned against the stone and looked elsewhere, trying to ignore all of it, but they came from the other side as well.

"*Out!*" Leona Pace cried, shocking the almost-silence. Shocking every reality into focus.

She had *seen. Admitted* seeing. Her reality had slipped, and Herrin stood transfixed and helpless.

The same look was on Leona Pace—rigidity, panic. Suddenly she cast off the plastic mantle and left, running.

He kept staring at the hole where Pace had been when she passed the gateway; and the cold from the rain crept inward. He recovered after a breath, walked out casually among the workers and the invisibles, ignored what they should not see, and quietly dismissed them.

"The rain may continue," he said. "Things will have to dry. Secure the area and go home. Come back at your next regular shift."

Tools were put away against invisible pilferage; the cranes were shut down and locked; and one by one and several at a time, the workers and the apprentices drifted away.

"Andrew Phelps." He hailed the senior apprentice. "You have a responsibility next shift, to be here early, to keep accounts, to direct."

"Sir," the man said, youngish, dark and thin, his eyes still showing distress, which rapidly yielded to surprise. "Yes, sir."

So he replaced Leona Pace.

He had no illusions that she would return. It happened, he reasoned, because of the sculpture; for that moment, humans and Others had had a common focus, had gathered within the same Reality, and Leona Pace had been thrust into the center of it, responsible.

Had broken under the weight of it. Would not be back, either on the site or at the University or indeed, among sane citizens. No one would see her, just as they did not see other invisibles. Survival was for the strong-minded, and she had not been strong enough.

He drank himself numb after a moderate dinner at Fellows' Hall, walked through the slackening rain to the Residency, just barely able to steer himself to his room without faltering.

He slept and woke at the first light of another day, still lying where he had lain when he fell into bed; he bathed, assumed sober Student's Black and walked the distance to the Square; he set matter of factly to work and so did everyone else, wounds healed.

Leona Pace did not, of course, return. The cheerfulness of the crew did. Andrew Phelps was an energetic and intelligent supervisor, and that was sufficient. He did not care for the past day, revised time and his Reality and recommenced his carving with full attention to the moment.

The Shape emerged further under his hands. It was slow now, very slow. Above him, the cranes labored, and he worked in the shadow of scaffolding and stone which had sealed off the sky once and for all.

XVII

Apprentice: Which is superior, reason or creativity?
Master Law: Neither.

The scaffolding in days after was lowered again to permit work on the detailing of the triple shell, and there was solid stone overhead. There was no more sound from the cranes, which had filled the center of Kierkegaard with their groaning and grinding for what had begun to seem forever; their job was done. The crane operators took their leave, returning now and again as other jobs or simply the course of coming and going through Kierkegaard took them through the dome.

Most of the workers of other sorts were discharged with their bonuses, only a few kept for the labor of clearing away the dust and the fragments. It was work for the skilled apprentices now.

For weeks the dome remained dark except for the lights which shone inside it. And then the perforations of the innermost shell revealed the lacery which had been made by apprentices burrowing wormlike between the second and outermost shells, and light began to break upon the interior, flowing moment by moment in teardrops and shafts across the pavings and the curtain-pillars and upon the walls of the shells . . . and upon the central pillar, where the stonework became the uplifted countenance of Waden Jenks, which became first calm and then, as the hours passed and the light angles changed, shifted.

Watchers came. Citizens passed time watching and from time to time invisibles strayed through . . . few, and tolerable, a momentary chill, like the passing of a cloud; at times Herrin truly failed to notice, rapt at his work, until the shadow of a robe swept by. It was inconsequential. He paid far more attention to the shadowing of a brow, to the small indentation at the corner of the mouth, to the detailed modeling of illusory hair which swept to join the design itself. He worked and sometimes after work must straighten with caution, as if his bones had assumed permanently the position his muscles had held for hours, ignoring pain, ignoring warmth and cold, until sometimes one of the apprentices had to help him from the position in which he had frozen himself.

"It's beautiful," one said, who was steadying him on his feet, on the platform. Gentle hands, careful of him. "It's *beautiful*, sir."

He laughed softly, because it was the only word that would came to the man's tongue; *beautiful* was only one aspect of it. But he was pleased by the praise. He got down from the platform, which was a man's height from the ground, was steadied by another apprentice who waited below, with a group of others, and there was a pause among the workers, a small space of silence.

It struck him that this had been going on, that at times they did pause when he walked through, or when he was in difficulty, or when he began work or when he stopped.

"What are you doing?" he asked roughly. "Back to work." His back hurt still; he managed to straighten, and heads turned. He looked back and met the faces of the apprentices who had been helping him, eyes anxious and unflinching from his outburst. He shook off their further assistance and walked on, flexed aching hands and turned to look back at the Work, which was bathed in the play of light from the tri-level perforations of the dome.

He took in his own breath, held for the moment in contemplation.

Not finished yet. The central work was not finished. The outer shells were all but complete. Apprentice after apprentice had been sent off. Perhaps, he thought, he should acknowledge those departures, offer some tribute; he realized he was himself the object of a second silence, all the heads which had formerly turned to feign work turned back again.

"Good," he said simply, and turned and walked away.

It took him at least through dinner each night to get the knots out of his muscles. It was not just the hands and back; every joint in his body stiffened, every muscle, from the greater which held his arm steady to the tiny one of a toe which had been balancing him, rigidly, his whole body a brace for his hand which held the cutter, for hour after hour, without interruption. He had given up on lunch; often omitted breakfast because once awake he had not the patience to divert himself to eat; dinner was all there was left, and he had his plate of stew at Fellows' Hall, and a second and a drink which helped ease his aches and relax his muscles . . . not too much any longer. It had occurred to him that such a regime might ultimately affect his coordination and his health; he attempted moderation. He sat in Fellows' Hall at dinnertime, in Student's Black well dusted with white marble dust, and swallowed savory food which he did not fully taste because his mind was elsewhere, and drank cold beer which was more relief because of the temperature than because he tasted it. He saw little of where he was, perceived instead the dusting of marble, the cutting of the beam, the image itself, as if it were indelibly impressed on his retinas, persisting even here. He walked back to the Residency and without noticing the desk and the night guard on duty there, walked to his room and stripped off the dusty Black to bathe in hot water, to soak the aches out, to wrap himself in his robe against the chill and look a last time out the window. He gazed on the night-floods and the dome far beyond the tall hedge of Port Street, the lighted dome resting there as the bright heart of Kierkegaard. This he did always before going to bed . . . no reason, except that his thoughts went in that direction, and it was more real to him than the room was; more real than the Residency, than any other thing about him. He looked to know, to set his world in order, because it *was* there, and seeing it made the day worth the pain.

He looked his fill, and started for the bed, with his eyes and his mind full of the Work, seeing nothing about him, his thoughts occupied wholly with the alteration which he had to make tomorrow, which could only be made when the sun passed a certain mark, and he had to *see* in advance, and do the cutting then.

There was a knock at the door.

It took him a moment, to blink, to accept the intrusion. Waden. No one else ever disturbed him here. He knew no one else in the Residency . . . and in fact, no one else in the city ever called on him.

"Waden?" he invited the caller without even going that way; and the door opened.

It was, of course. Waden walked in, casual-suited, in the Student's Black he affected at some hours and on some days. "Sorry. Ill?"

"Tired." Herrin sat down in one of the chairs, reached to the convenient table to pour wine from a decanter, two glasses. Waden took his and sat down. "Social call?" Herrin asked, constrained to observe amenities.

"I haven't seen you in two weeks."

Herrin blinked, sipped, sat holding the glass. "That long?"

"I see . . ." Waden made a loose gesture toward the nighted window. "*That*. From my office upstairs. I get reports."

Games. Herrin refused to ask, to plead for reaction, which Waden would surely like, that being the old game between them. He simply raised his glass and took another slow sip.

"They talk," Waden said, "as if you're really doing something special out there."

"I am."

Waden smiled, "And on budget. Amazing."

"I told you what we'd need."

"I could wish for equal efficiency elsewhere . . . Am I keeping you from . . . someone?"

"No." Herrin almost laughed. "I'm afraid I'm quite dull lately. Preoccupied."

"Not seeing Keye?"

He shook his head '

"What, a falling out?"

"No time." He had not, in fact, realized that he had not seen Keye in the better part of two months. He had simply postponed events. Waden, Keye, whatever had been important before . . . waited. He was amazed, too, to realize that so much time elapsed, like someone disturbed from a long sleep. "I'm afraid I haven't been social at all. To try to hold the details in my memory . . . you understand . . . it shuts out everything else."

"Details."

"Perhaps you don't understand. Your art is different, First Citizen."

" 'Not creative.' I recall your judgment. I am capable of such concentration; I currently have nothing that demands it; the limits of Freedom do not exercise me."

Herrin raised a quizzical brow, drained his glass, added more. "I heard a shuttle land last week."

"Two weeks ago," Waden laughed, and chuckled. "You *are* enveloped, Artist. Are you really that far from consciousness? A shuttle, a considerable volume of trade, a fair deal of traffic on Port Street, and none of this reached you."

"It made no shortage of anything *I* needed."

"You *are* master of your reality," Waden mocked him. "And it's all made of stone."

"No," Herrin said softly, "*your* reality, First Citizen. You are my obsession."

"An interesting fancy."

"*Should* I have noticed?"

"What, the shuttle?"

"*Should* it have been of interest to me?"

Waden smiled and refilled his own glass. "A man who forgets his personal affairs would hardly think it of interest, no. It was a military landing, Artist. There's a campaign on. They were interested in *Singularity's* itinerary. I've opened negotiations with them. I happen to have years of McWilliams's past records, cargo, statistics on all the pirates. The military is very interested. But that's very far from you, isn't it?"

"What negotiations?" he was genuinely perplexed. Waden had come here for a reason, bursting with something pent up. He drew a deep breath and looked Waden in the eyes. "Let me venture a guess. Your ministers and your departments are beyond their depth and you have no confidence in them. This is no casual call."

"Your intelligence surpasses theirs."

"Of course it does; it surpasses *yours*, but of course you have no intention of admitting it. What have you gotten yourself into?"

For a moment there was a baleful look in Waden's brown eyes, and then humor. "Indulge your fancies. They're of no consequence. You're only moderately wrong, my Dionysus: rationality is always superior to impulsive acts, even creative ones. But no, I don't want your advice; I don't need it."

"What do you need?"

Waden laughed. "Nothing, of course. But possibly what I've always needed, a little less solitude. Already you relieve my mind. I've shaken the world, Artist, and you've not even felt the tremors; what marvelous concentration you have."

"Have you taken sides?"

"Ah. To the point and dead on. Negotiations: Freedom will always be commercially poor so long as it relies on piratical commerce. And I am too great for this world."

"What have you done?"

"What would you do, as Waden Jenks?"

"Build this world. You're about to swallow too much, First Citizen. Digest what you have already; what more do you need, what—?" He lifted a hand toward the roof and the unseen stars. "What is *that*? Distances that will add to the vacancy you already govern. Hesse is still uncolonized. Half this world is vacant. What need of more so soon? Your ambition is for *size*. And you will swallow until you burst."

Waden Jenks tended to laugh at his advice, to take it in humor. There was no humor in Waden now.

"I will jar your Reality, Artist. Come with me. Come. Let me show you figures."

Herrin sucked in his breath, vexed and bothered and inwardly disturbed already; arguments with Waden were not, at this stage, productive of anything good. "My Reality is what I'm doing out there, First Citizen. Don't interfere with my work. I have no time to be bothered with trivialities."

Waden's eyes grew darker, amazed, and then he burst out laughing. "With trivialities! O my Dionysus, I love you. There's all a universe out there. There's scale against which all your ambition is nothing; there are places you'll never reach, peoples who'll never hear of you and never care, and you're *nothing*. But you shut that out, no different from the citizen who sweeps the streets, who has all the Reality he can handle."

"No. You'll give it all to me. That's what you're for. You asked me what *I* would do. I'd build up this world and attract the commerce you say we have to have. You're looking for a quick means, because Waden Jenks has no duration, only breadth. You'll devour everything you can, First Citizen, and those same people beyond your reach will always gall you; but not me. Because someday . . . at some time however far away . . . someone who's known *my* work will get out there, and carry my reputation there, and in *time*, in time, First Citizen—when we're both gone—I'll get there. My way."

"Will you?" Waden's grin looked frozen for the moment, and Herrin, wine-warmed, felt a little impulse of caution. "A little time *giving* orders has improved your confidence, hasn't it? I neglect to mention your program would simply build an economy the pirates would delight to plunder. We have *one* commodity now which we have to sell: the pirates themselves, which will buy us what will save us great expense. But I did invite comment. Plan as you choose. You've taught me something?"

"What, I?"

"That duration itself is worth the risk; and that's my choice as well, Artist. By what I do . . . neither Freedom nor other worlds will go unshaken.

"Whom have you dealt with?"

"The trade . . . we can't get from merchants. But there's more than one way to get it, isn't there? The military wants a base in this sector; wants to build a station, to do for us what would take us generations. So I give them our cooperation. And Camden McWilliams ceases to annoy us."

"You've cut us off from the only commerce we get," Herrin exclaimed. "They'll desert you, this foreign military. They'll leave you once they've got what they want. They'll *change* things here, impose their own reality, never mind yours.

Waden shook his head.

"You're confident," Herrin said. "Do you really think you can handle them? It's *wide*, Waden."

"Does it daunt *you?* You talk about posterities. Does that length of time daunt you? And does it occur to you that what I do cannot be without effect in duration as well as breadth?"

"It occurs to me," he admitted.

"You never fail me," Waden said. "Whenever I'm in the least perplexed, you're the best reflection of my thoughts. My unfailing mirror. Arguing with you is like arguing with myself."

"You no longer have to flatter, First Citizen. Do you merely flex your unpracticed talents?"

"Oh, excellent. Still barbed. What of that masterwork of yours? Shall I come to see it?"

"Not yet. When it's done."

"What, afraid of my reaction?"

"When it's done."

"When will that be?"

Herrin shrugged. "Possibly a week."

"So soon?"

"Before deadline. I have had outstanding cooperation."

"I've heard you plan a tribute to the workers."

"Out of my account."

"No, no, the State will fund it."

"*Will* you? That's quite generous."

"A gesture seems in order. An inspiration to the city. I'm really impressed, Herrin, truly I am. I have administrators accustomed to such tasks of coordinating workers and supply who find less success. You have a certain talent there too, by no means minor."

"I should not care to exercise it. My sculpture is the important thing. I credit my choice of supervisors."

"One lost. Most unfortunate."

Herrin fidgeted and recrossed his ankles, feet extended before him. The reference was in total bad taste.

"An invisible."

"One supposes," Herrin said. "I'm sure I don't know."

"You're a disturbance," Waden said.

"Do I disturb you?"

Waden tossed off the rest of his drink, set the glass down, still smiling. "I shall expect to see this wonder of yours next week. Dare I?"

"Barring rain. I don't fancy working in the wet."

"Ah, you're admirably restrained. You're dying for me to see it, and probably a little apprehensive."

"Not in the least apprehensive."

"But anxious."

"I should imagine the same of you."

"True," Waden said. "True. I'll leave you to your rest. I see you were on the verge." He tapped the decanter with his fingernail "You ought not to indulge so much. I hate to see a great mind corrupted."

"Only on occasions. I've reformed since my Student days."

"Have you?" Waden rose, and Herrin did. Waden brushed his clothes into order. "A pleasant rest to you."

"Thank you."

Waden started out. Stopped, halfway to the door, looked back. "Keye's well. Thought I'd tell you."

"My regards to her."

Waden registered mild surprise. "Bastard! Did you know?"

"She is with you, then."

"Ah, she visits. Says you've gone strange."

Herrin shrugged. "A matter of indifference to me."

"Do you know, I think she prefers you."

"Again a matter of indifference. Beware of Keye."

"Do you think so?"

"Creative ethics, Waden. She'll create yours for you; doubtless she's doing so at the moment. But that's your problem."

"Ah, you are offended."

"I'm not offended." He folded his arms to take the weight off his shoulders. His eyes were growing heavy from the drink. "I'm far too weary to cope with Keye, and she'll drift back again. Or back and forth. I'm quite surprised you two haven't reached an arrangement long before this. Evidently she feels herself in one of her stronger periods; she avoided you once; now she avoids me. I've always thought you underestimated her." A thought came to him and he penetrated his lethargy with a more direct look. "Ah! you've talked to Keye about this—plan, this ambition of yours. And lo, Keye is *with* you."

"Worth considering."

"Indeed it is."

Waden gnawed his lip, laughed softly. Nodded. "Warning taken, Herrin. Warning assuredly taken."

He left. Herrin walked to the bed and sat down, utterly weary, disturbed in his concentration. He had not asked for disturbances. What had been contentment deserted him.

He tried to put it all from his mind, revise the time, wipe it all out and start over. He failed. He was muddled, vaguely and irrationally, knowing Keye was *not* sitting in her apartment over the Square waiting for his attention. He was hurt. Of course she would not wait. Of course there was no reason that she should. He would have had no objection had she taken a horde of others to her bed. She had done so, in fact, while taking him on convenient days.

But Waden. *Waden*, who rivaled him. He took that maneuver seriously. The three greatest minds in all Freedom . . . and always Keye had maintained at least neutrality, with the balance tipped toward him. Waden conceived ambition and the Ethicist went to him like iron to a magnet.

When *his* great work was almost complete.

That desertion hurt, and the news of it had to come when he was tired, when his maintenance of his reality could be shaken. There was a cure for that. He got up, walked to the table and poured his abandoned glass full of wine. He sat down and he drank, and when he could no longer navigate steadily, he headed for bed, to lie with the lights on because he was too muddled to turn them out, with a confusion of anger in him that was not going to accept things as they were and an exhaustion too great to think his way out of it.

He slept, more a plummet into oblivion than a sinking into rest. And he waked, leaden-limbed and with a blinding headache. He lay abed until he could no longer ignore the day, then rolled out gingerly, bathed, which diminished the headache and finally cured it.

Thinking . . . was in abeyance. He toweled off, dressed, held out his hands to see if they were steady, and they were.

Possibly, he thought—because his mind *was* most brilliant—the restlessness at night would get worse. He thought of what Waden feared—the same perspective, to have no one equal, anywhere. To be throwing out thoughts and ideas which no one could criticize because there was no one competent to comprehend.

Life without walls. With endless, endless outpouring of ideas, and nothing coming back, being at the center of everything, and radiating like a star . . . into void.

To be cursed with increasing intellect, and increasing comprehension of one's reality, and increasing grasp. . . .

You'll swallow, he recalled saying to Waden Jenks, *until you burst.*

That was not, he thought, what Waden feared. It was rather expansion . . . until expansion became attenuation, became dissipation . . . until Waden had never been.

A wave with no shore.

The thought began to occur to him as well. As it might have occurred to Keye. He had left Keye alone, without a shore to break the wave, and she had gone to Waden; as Waden went to him when Keye did not suffice.

And where now did Herrin Law go?

To deaden his mind every night because the thoughts were too vivid and the brain too powerful, so powerful that the only way to deal with it was to anesthetize it, to get null, for a few precious hours?

Until the machine tore itself apart?

The hands were steady at the moment. He had that confidence, at least.

XVIII

Waden Jenks: Your hubris surpasses mine.
Master Law: Philosophy argues that hubris doesn't exist.
Waden Jenks: But it does. There are offenses against the State.
Master Law: I purpose nothing against the State.
Waden Jenks: No, your ambition is far greater.

He decided on breakfast, to be kind to his abused body, to guard his health, food was a good cure for such moods. Well-being generally restored his confidence. He left for the University dining hall rather than order breakfast up from Residency kitchens, which could take far longer than it was worth, which was why he had given up on breakfasts, when he thought about it. He considered his physical condition, which was approaching excessive attrition; hours of physical labor on small intake and limited sleep. Food at regular hours had to help.

He was, in fact, stripped of resolve, of the energy which had sustained him thus far. He ate a far larger breakfast than he had ever been accustomed to since childhood, full of sugars and washed down with milk; he asked the kitchen to pack him a cold lunch, which he took with him in a paper bag; and he walked at a slow pace toward Jenks Square, letting breakfast settle.

He did, he concluded, feel better for all these measures of self-improvement. He walked along the street noticing his surroundings for the first time in weeks.

And invisibles were there.

He flinched from that realization. The first one he saw was where Second intersected Main, coming from a corner, and perhaps there had been others all along, but *after* this one there were others, farther down the street.

Another difficulty of a brain which could not be shut down. Perception. *He* saw them. And what should he ask of others who had been born in Kierkegaard? *Do* you *really see them?* They

were there, that was all. He had not put on the brooch this morning—hubris did not go with his mood—now he was desperately
glad that he had not. He no longer felt like challenging anything.

One cloaked, hooded figure had stopped, and he stopped. It
was Leona Pace.

He stood there perhaps half the beat of his heart, and flinched,
walked on past as he ought. The midnight robes, which blanked
both ahnit and invisible human from the view of the sane, veiled
a shoulder, a blankness.

Perhaps it was the shock he needed to jar him from his private misery, that sight of a reality fractured, a fine talent lost,
the waste, the utter waste of it. He did not look back.

The dome lay before him, the vision which made all other
things trivial. *This* was the thing, this beautiful object, on which
he had poured out all his energy for months, which had taken on
shape and life and form. To have it finished, to have it be what
it was meant to be . . . was worth the Leona Paces and the pain
of his own body. Was worth everything, to have this in existence,
shining in the morning, the sun sheening the stone with the illusion of dawn-color, with the interior now opened and hinting
at convolutions within. It glowed with interior light at the moment because they had not yet shut down the inside lights which
the night crews used, bright beads gleaming in the perforations.

He walked within, where steps and taps on stone echoed, where
voices spoke one to the other, hidden in the huge triple shell and
the curtain-walls and bent about by acoustics and the size of the
place. Some of the echo effect he had planned; some was serendip-
itous, but beautiful: the place rang like a bell with voices, purified sounds, refined them as it refined the light and cast it in
patterns. It took chaos and made symphony; glare and made
beauty.

The center, beyond the devolving curtain-pillars, held the scaffolding, the image, still shrouded in metal webbing.

And he stopped, for crews were gathered there, both crews,
and both supervisors, Gytha and Phelps; the apprentices, the workers, everyone . . . more coming in until there could be no one of
the active workers omitted, past or present.

"Done?" he asked. His own voice echoed unexpectedly in their
hush, which was broken only by the human stirring of a quiet
crowd. "Is it finished?"

Carl Gytha and Andrew Phelps brought their tablets, the daily and evening ritual, and another brought an armload of computer printout, the maps from which they had worked, all solemnly offered. He signed the tablets, looked about him at all of them, somewhat numb at the realization that for most of them there was nothing now to do.

"*Well* done," he said, because saying something seemed incumbent on him. "*Well* done."

There was a murmur of voices, as if this had somehow been what they wanted to hear. He was bewildered by this, more bewildered when apprentices and workers simply stood there . . . and finally Gytha and Phelps offered their hands, which he took, one after the other.

"Go," he said. "I've some finishing. I'll still need a small crew; Gytha, Phelps, you stay to assist. Pick a handful. The rest of you—it's *done*."

He winced at the applause, which multiplied and redoubled like madness in the acoustics of the dome. He nodded in embarrassment, not knowing what else to do, turned matter-of-factly to his platform and his tools, and took off his kit with his lunch and set that down; scrambled up with the agility of practice, and set himself to work.

Confusion persisted. People stayed to talk, and voices and steps echoed everywhere. This failed to distract him, rather calmed him, because it was the life he had planned for the Work, that the interior should live, that there should be people, and voices, and laughter and living things flowing through it.

Eventually the noise changed, from the familiar voices to the strange voices of citizens, but the tone of it was much the same. There was, occasionally, a soft whisper of wonder, the piercing voice of a child trying out the echoes; but the scaffolding wrapped the centermost piece, the heart of it, and his activity fascinated those who stood to watch him work. "Hush," his remaining assistants would say. "Hush, don't bother him." And: "That's Herrin Law. That's the Master." He ignored those voices and the others, much more rapt in the consideration of an angle, the waiting, the aching waiting, for the right moment, as the afternoon sun touched precisely the point of concern, and he had a very small time to make the precise stroke which would capture one

of the statue's changing expressions without destroying all the
rest of the delicate planes.

This day and the next and the next he labored, now with abrasive and polish, now smoothing out the tiniest rough spots. It
rained, and he worked, until Gytha came and wrapped a warm
cloak about him and got him off the platform; and others were
there, who had not been there, he thought, in days, wrapped in
their own rain gear and bringing raincoats with them. "I thought
he might need it," one said. "He doesn't take care of himself,"
said another, female.

He looked at them askance, huddled within Gytha's cloak. He
was offered warm drink, coddled and surrounded by dozens more
who had come, some with blankets and some with warm drink.
"Well," said one, "it's raining outside; we might as well share
the drink and wait."

And another: "*Look* at it," in a tone of awe, but he was looking toward the statue, not the storm. "Look at it," another echoed,
and despite the water which dripped in curtains through the apertures, a thousand tiny waterfalls, they moved to see.

Herrin watched them, drank and sat down where it was comfortable, warmed by their presence as much as any physical offering. John Ree was there, and Tib and Katya . . . he knew all
their names, every one. They were artists and stonemasons and
cranemen and runners, all sorts; and there was a strangeness about
them as they sat down and shared their drink and their raincoats
and sent their voices echoing through the curtain-walls.

It was the sculpture, Herrin thought suddenly. It was that which
had taken them in, seized them by the emotions, a reality more
powerful than theirs. He shivered, recalling the Others, and Leona
Pace, the day they had been trapped into seeing each other, because sane and invisible had had, here, a common focus.

The effect went on. It kept drawing them back. Those who
had been *in* the Work belonged to it; sane, prideful people began
to lose their realities as surely as the invisibles lost their own.
The Work did not let them go. He thought that he should warn
them. And then he tried to analyze his own impulse in that direction and suspected *that*.

These people frightened him. Perhaps they frightened each
other. He wanted to have things *done*, and it was all but finished.
He had to look elsewhere, to other things, to the rest of his re-

ality. And that was where the rest of them had failed. They could not make the break.

"I think," he confided to them, and voices fell silent and faces turned to him, "that we can take down the scaffolding tomorrow, all the lights, clean it and sweep it and prepare it . . . It's complete. It's finished. But—" Their watching faces haunted him. He groped for something less final, hating his weakness. "There'll be more projects. Others. Those of you who want will always have first priority when I choose crew; maybe here, maybe elsewhere. You're the best. We can do *more* than this."

"I want on," said John Ree. Voices tumbled over his, all asking. *Me, Master Law, Me.*

He nodded. "All who want." They were shameless as children. As if they were his. They stirred that kind of protective feeling in him, an embarrassment for their sakes where they had no shame. In fact they were comfortable about him, like an old garment; with them he could breathe easier, knowing things were going well without his watching, because they *were* good.

"We can get that scaffolding down," said John Ree, who was discharged and already had his pay.

Herrin nodded. "Everything but mine. There's still some polishing. That comes down . . . maybe in two days."

There were nods, tacit agreement. The drink passed; the rain splashed down. There were warmer places to sit than where they were and certainly drier, but there was laughter and good humor, people who had known each other for months discussing families and how they had gotten on and what they had done with their bonuses and whose baby was born and who had what at market and how here and there people should meet for lunch or dinner. Herrin listened, both included and excluded, taking interest in the whole bizarre situation.

Then the rain stopped and they went away again, taking their empty bottles and their tarps and wishing him well. Even some complete outsiders from the street who had sheltered here and stood amazed on the fringes of the group had gotten to talking, and bade each other farewell and in some instances invited each other to meet again on the streets as if they knew each other.

And quietly, a lingering echo, the wet tap of footsteps which had been behind the curtain-walls, in the outer shells; Herrin heard them, casually, because there was no reason not to. He

looked, and his skin drew, because he saw Others, whose midnight cloaks were wet, who did not depart, but stood there staring.

He cleared his throat, shrugged, turned to the scaffolding and
scrambled up again, taking up the polishing, which was tedious
work but mindless. He dried the area with a cloth from his pocket,
and took up the abrasive again, set to work, ignoring Gytha and
Phelps and the others who stirred about disassembling some of
the other scaffolding.

He worked until his shoulders ached, and became awake,
slowly, of the presence of a shadow at the foot of the scaffold.

He looked down, drawn by a horrid fascination, fighting his
own instincts, which knew, as from one night he had known, that
something would be there.

The invisible was looking up. It was Leona's face framed
within the midnight hood, her plump freckled face and her brown
hair and her stout shape within the cloak. There was longing in
her eyes, which looked up at the statue.

"Leona," he said, very, very softly, and frightened her and
himself. "Are you all right, Leona?"

She nodded, almost imperceptibly. There was a vast silence.
Perhaps Gytha and Phelps were looking this way. No, they could
not. It was like the wearing of the brooch—people would not see
it because they dared not see it, because it was not right to see.
And if people went on seeing . . .

There were solutions for the invisibles if people started seeing them. There was the Solution, which the State had always
avoided; and he knew it and surely Leona Pace knew it, and he
wished that he *could* look through her.

She turned and walked away. He found himself shivering as
if the wetness of the wood on which he was sitting had gotten
through the tarp, or the coldness of the stone traveled up his
hands into his heart. He thought that perhaps he should go home
for the day, rest, drive himself no further. But that was to admit
that something had happened. He looked at Gytha and Phelps,
when a clatter drew his attention: they were working away, and
probably they had *not* noticed.

Or they were stronger than he at the moment.

He shivered and steadied his hands enough to begin his polishing again. He felt everything slipping again, everything bal-

anced on a precipice and ready to tumble over the edge. What did the rest of his life promise if this was the beginning: brilliance, leading to madness?

There was a thunder in the sky that for the moment he attributed to the clouds and the rain, but it kept coming, and steadied, and he knew then what it was, that at the port a part of Waden's reality had come to earth. A part of his own, at some time to come. He had no time for it at the moment, did not want to think about it . . . yet. There was a cold spot where that knowledge rested, colder than the stone or the recent rain. He heard the shuttle come down and heard the noise stop. His mind kept running with the image, the prospect of Waden Jenks's offworld negotiations, the world irrevocably widening, the walls all abolished, and nothing to do but keep staring at the horizons and widening and widening forever.

He pursed his lips and dipped his cloth in the abrasive, concentrated on the curve he was smoothing, finger width by finger width.

Something stirred near him, a step. Suddenly someone reached up near him and took the hammer. *Leona*, he thought; he did not want to see. There was the impression of midnight cloth in the corner of his eye. Slowly the tool moved off the platform, and there was a crash, metal on stone; he looked, alarmed.

He stared within a blue hood at no human face, and at once his vision blanked and he caught for support against the statue itself. It went away, a shadow in his vision, and he stayed there with his heart beating against his ribs and the impression of what he had *almost* seen lingered in his vision, wide dark eyes, a dusky color like the cloth, and features . . . he did not want to see. Ever.

"Sir?" Carl Gytha asked, coming near the platform. "You all right, sir?"

He nodded, shrugged, put himself to work again.

Simple pilferage. He finished the place he had begun, calmly set himself at the next. It had gone long enough . . . he could work late, drive himself just a little longer. . . .

. . . get finished with this, once for all.

No, he reminded himself. He had tried that and nearly broken himself. "I'm folding up," he said. "Going back for the day."

"We'll stay," Gytha said, "by turns. Keep things from harm."

They came to help him down. He accepted the help, dusted

himself off and started the walk home, for a decent supper and a little rest.

They had seen, he persuaded himself. Even normal people *saw* as much as he had seen. They proved that, by offering to stay and protect things. He was not abnormal. Perhaps they had seen Leona Pace, too, and were too self-possessed to admit it. He had never been able to ask anyone. No one was able to ask anyone.

He walked as far as the hedge and through the archway. He stopped then and blinked in surprise at the entourage which had come down Port Street and pulled up in front of the Residency. There were vehicles and troops; men in no-color uniforms ... with weapons. He had never seen the like, not in such numbers. They filled four trucks; a fifth was vacant, with soldiers all over the frontage of the Residency, and some in the doorway; and now came transports with what might be dignitaries. Those were not Kierkegaard vehicles, they had come from offworld. From up there and out there, and something larger than an ordinary shuttle had landed to carry all of that.

His appetite deserted him. He walked across the street, between the trucks, startled as one of the Outsiders swung a gun in his direction.

"Got out of here," they told him in a strange accent. He gave them a foul look and walked on to the Residency steps, stared in outrage as one of those guarding the door barred his way with an extended arm.

"I live here," he said. "Get out of my way."

The soldier looked uncertain at that, and he pushed past in that moment, found more Outsiders in the halls inside. "*You*," said a soldier near the desk, but the regular secretary intervened. "He's Master Herrin Law."

"Master of what?" the offworlder asked.

Herrin turned a second foul look on him and the man declined further questions. "I want this lot clear of my room," he told the secretary.

"Sir," the secretary said meekly, caught between.

"I'll have supper in my room. Send the order."

"The First Citizen asked, if you should come in before midnight, sir, he's in his office, sir."

Herrin said nothing, paused for a third look at the offworlder, young and unrecommended by his manner, which would have had him eaten alive at University: from bluster he had gone to a perceptible flinching. "Not quality material," Herrin judged acidly, and walked off.

He was trembling in every muscle. Outraged.

Outsiders. Invisibles no less than Leona Pace. They were *here*, in the Residency, and Waden Jenks invited them in. He headed for the stairs, walked up the five flights of stairs and into a whole array of guards.

"Out of my way," he said, and walked through with the assumption they would not dare. One seized his arm and he glared at that man until the hand dropped.

"Excuse me, sir. Presence up here has to be cleared."

"You're incompetent and ignorant. Clear it."

"If you'll tell me who you are, sir."

"Get the First Citizen out here. Now."

The hand left his arm. The man backed off, blinked and backed a few paces to Waden's door, knocked on it. "Sir. *Sir.*"

The door opened; Herrin walked toward it and soldiers shifted in panic. A rifle barrel slammed into his arm. He kept going nonetheless, through the door before they stopped him. Waden was there, risen from his chair among others.

"Let him go," Waden said at once, and Herrin stalked in, shedding the soldiers like so many parasites. "What is this?" Herrin asked.

"Herrin Law," Waden said, gesturing to the others. "Colonel Martin Olsen, Military Mission."

Herrin failed to follow the hand, stared at Waden instead. "The halls are cluttered. Something struck me—I call your attention to the matter."

"Citizen Law," one of the Outsiders said, offering a hand. Herrin looked past the lot of them, smiled coldly, seeing Keye standing, in Student's Black, by the wall of the ell the room made.

"Keye, how pleasant to see you. I meant to come and call. Waden explained things. I owe you profound apologies for my desertion. You distressed me; I admit it freely. I've mended my ways, you see, moved into the Residency. Are you living here or just sleeping over?"

Keye's mouth quirked into a familiar smile. "Does it concern you?"

"Herrin."

He looked at Waden, read behind the slow smile which was less amused than Keye's.

"First Citizen," said the intrusive voice. "Would you explain?"

Waden ignored it too. "Point taken, Artist. But there is a certain reality operative here that *I* choose. I'll remind you of that."

"Construe it for me. I'll decide if I want to participate."

"Bear with me. Master Herrin Law, let me present Colonel Martin Olsen, with that understanding."

The hand was offered a second time. Herrin looked the stout gray-haired man up and down, finally reached and scarcely touched the offered fingers. The hand withdrew.

"Not an auspicious color," he commented of the midnight clothing.

"I agree," said Waden. "Herrin, don't be argumentative in this. A personal favor."

"There seems to have been a misunderstanding," said the colonel. "If there was some difficulty, we extend an apology."

"Second mistake," Herrin said, passing a glance past him on the way to Keye. "Are you going to wait for this or will you join me for dinner?"

"I have a commitment," she said. "Another time."

"I trust so," he said. "Waden, I reserve judgment on your Reality. What do you purpose for them?"

"Easier if you sit and join this."

"Another time." He glanced down and brushed marble dust and abrasive from his black-clad thigh. "I'm hungry; I find no prospect here."

"First Citizen," said the invisible voice, carefully modulated.

"He's a University Master," Waden said. "Colonel, I suggest you withdraw that escort of yours to the suggested perimeter immediately, and trust us for your security; the scope of this incident is wider than may appear to you."

"Go," the colonel said. Waved his hand. There was a hesitation. *"Out."* His forces began to melt away.

"I'm going to supper," Herrin said.

"Citizen Law," said the colonel. "We're anxious to have an understanding."

Herrin turned and walked to the door. "Keye, Waden," he paused to say, "good evening."

"Herrin," Waden warned him. "They will be confined to the port area."

"That is the appropriate place."

"There will be no intrusion."

"Good evening."

"Good evening, Herrin." Waden walked forward, set a hand on his shoulder, and pulled him into a gentle embrace with a pat on the arm, then let him go again. It was odd, without particular emotion, neither passionate nor personal; it was for the invisible, and Herrin suffered it with some humor, patted Waden's arm as well, exchanged a wryly amused look at Keye, and left, into a hall now deserted.

But he was disturbed at the prospect of Outsiders, and his heart was still beating quite rapidly. It was begun, Waden's work, Waden's art. He felt a residue of anger, and at the same time tried to reason it away . . . for whatever was begun in there, whatever—and at the moment he had no wish to divert himself with speculations—it meant a new policy and program which would widen more than Waden's reality: it was his own which was being expanded. Things which *he* had set in motion were simply coming into play and, he reasoned, perhaps it was as well, with his own Work almost finished, that another phase should begin unfolding. He was melancholy with a sense of anticlimax, that somehow he had expected more elation in his own accomplishment than he felt at the moment.

Keye occurred to him, a recollection of her quiet regard in that room, her understated presence . . . her silences, which warned him that whatever was underway, Keye never announced her programs, that she perhaps deluded herself of power, and might do things without warning.

What have I said to her? he wondered, but he had always been reticent. In his heart he had always known that Keye was apt to undertake such a maneuver. He had never spilled information to her which he did not ultimately destine for Waden's ears.

But he might have given her silent communications.

And she had deserted him at the moment when his own accomplishment was highest. She had never come to admire his work, not that he ever knew. She had watched it until the closing of the dome sealed it, but she had never seen the heart of it.

Had not, he supposed, wanted that influence upon her. Not yet. Perhaps she would never come; would always evade it. That evidenced a certain fear of his strength and talent. He decided so, more satisfied when he put it in that perspective. And Waden avoided it; in another kind of fear, he thought, fear of disappointment, perhaps——or the enjoyment of anticipation. He knew Waden, knew well enough Waden's unwillingness to be led; of course Waden was going to feign nonchalance at the last moment, was going to occupy himself with whatever he could and ignore him as long as he could.

He felt more and more confident. He smiled to himself as he walked down the stairs to his own apartment, a stairway now clear of strangers and invisibles.

That night he stood at the window to look out on the city and there was a darkness where before lights had shone over the dome. He missed the glow, and yet the darkness itself was a sign of completion. Generations to come might want to light the Square by night; but for his part, it belonged in the sun, which gave it essence. He turned his face from the window and paced, restless, his thoughts more toward the port than, this night, toward Jenks Square.

He took the brooch which had lain on the table, from beside the tray which the servants would take away, but no one had pilfered the brooch and he had not, in fact, expected that it would vanish. He ran his fingers over it, traced the smooth spirals of the design and the silky surface of the blue stones. Invisible, like the makers, like the mind which had shaped it and the hands which had handled it until his took it up.

And he went to the closet and clipped it to the collar of the Black he would wear tomorrow. The humor of it pleased him; he had had enough of invisible absurdities, because still the memory of that Outsider hand which had dared check him rankled. His arm felt bruised. So he chose his own absurdities. Let Waden comment. He dusted himself and stripped off his still dusty garments and tossed them into the corner, his old and own habits; the Residency had made him too meticulous, as Keye had wished to make him, observant of her amenities.

So let the servants pick it up if they liked. Servants *washed* the clothes. They could find them wherever they were dropped and he had no present desire to be agreeable to anyone. He began to weary of the Residency, this stifling place where Waden's guests came and went.

He thought of returning to the University. He thought even of Law's Valley and a visit to Camus Province, recalled that he had thought of summoning his family here for his great day, that on which the Work would be finished, but *that* . . . that indicated a desire for something, which he denied, and the mere thought of the logistics involved was tedium. He desired nothing; *needed* nothing. He found himself charged with a surfeit of energy, facing physical work on the morrow, but with nothing for his mind to do. He could not face bed, or sleep, and thought of Keye again, with vexation. He paced and thought even of dressing again and going out and walking the streets to burn off the energy.

He should have stayed in that conference. Waden's invisible might have been interesting. And if he had stayed, there would have been trouble, because he was in a mood for encounter, for debate, for anything to occupy his mind, and Waden and Keye *without* the visitor would have been the company he would have chosen. But he had sensed in Waden a protective attitude toward the intruder: Waden's Art . . . he did well, he decided, to have walked out, and not to have been there in his present state of energy.

He paced, and ended up at the table again, staring at the rest of the wine which had come with dinner, and reminding himself that he had decided not to take that route to sleep; that he was headed away from that very visible precipice. It damaged him. So did lying awake and rising early, and doing physical and mental labor on two hours' sleep a night.

With resentment, he uncapped the bottle, poured the glass full, set bottle and glass by the bedside.

He began to think where he was going next, what project he might have in mind; but the one he was finishing was still too vivid for him, refused to leave his thoughts and yet refused further elaborations. It became a pit out of which he could not climb, offering no broader perspectives, affording him no view of where he was going next.

The vision would come, he reckoned, lying abed and sipping at the wine and staring at the wall opposite, with the dark window at his left and nothing out there to dream about. It *would* come. As yet it did not.

XIX

Waden Jenks: Inspire me, I defy you to do more.
Master Law: When I defy you to do more, I fear you
can.
Waden Jenks: Then have you not, Herrin, met your
master?
Master Law: Then have you not met the thing you say
you fear most?

The finish came at night. The Work stood complete and it was all done—in the dark and with no admirers. The night was cold as nights in the season could be, with a beclouded moon and puddles of rain in the dome, water which had drifted through the perforations as a light mist that haloed the lamps.

Herrin had seen the finish near, so near, had pushed himself on after dark. "Light," he had asked of Carl Gytha and Andrew Phelps who remained with him; and John Ree, who was there for reasons unexplained; and some of the others who had decided to work the off shift of other jobs they had gotten since the project finished, or after classes they had joined after the finish of the project and nighttime strollers who had found a place to be and something going on ended up lending a hand with the carrying of this and that. *"Light,"* he would say, his back turned to all of this activity, and peevishly, for his arms ached and he had bitten through his lip from the sheer strain of holding his position to polish this place and the other. It did not occur to him to inquire whether holding that light was a strain; or it did, but he was having trouble reaching a spot at the moment and forgot to ask afterward. His own pain was by far enough, and he was beset with anxiety that he could not last, that they would face the anticlimax of giving up, and coming back at dawn to do the last work, all because *his* strength might give out. He worked, and gave impatient orders that kept the beam on the sculpture so that he could see what he was doing; he ran sore hands over the

surface which had become like glass, seeking any tiny imper-
fection.

"We'll *do* it," they said about him, and, "Quiet, don't rattle
that," and, "The foundry *has* it; we can get it. . . ." The plaque,
they meant: he had asked about that, in a lull for rest, and he
trusted they were doing something in the matter, because he had
shown them where it should go, had picked a paving-square which
could come out, out where the square began to be the Square,
and not Main. They had hammered the paving-square out during
the day, and prepared the matrix, not only to set the names in
bronze, but to seal the bronze to protect it from oxidation and
from time. He heard some activity outside, and ignored it, locked
in his own concentration on his own task.

He stopped finally and took the cup a worker thrust to his
lips, took it in his own aching hands, drank and drew breath.

"Get the scaffolding down now," he said, a mere hoarse whisper. "It's *done*."

"Yes, *sir*," said Carl Gytha, and patted his shoulder. "Yes, *sir*."
He swung his legs off the platform.

"It's *done*," someone said aloud, and the word passed and
echoed in the acoustics of the dome . . . *done* . . . *done* . . .
done . . . drowned by applause, a solemn and sober applause, from
a whole array of people who had no obligation to be there at all.
He slid down into steadying hands, and there was a rush to get
him a coat and to hand him his drink, as if he were their child
and fragile. "What about the plaque?" he asked, remembering
that.

"In, sir," said John Ree. "Got it set and setting, and not a bubble."

"Show me."

They did, held their breath collectively through his inspection
of it, which was exactly the size of one of the meter square
paving blocks. It was set in and true as John Ree had said. They
had lights on it to help dry the plastic. WADEN ASHLEN JENKS, the
plaque said, FIRST CITIZEN OF FREEDOM, BY THE ART OF MASTER
HERRIN ALTON LAW and . . . Leona Kyle Pace, Carl Ellis Gytha,
Andrew Lee Phelps, master apprentices . . . Lara Catherin An-
derssen, Myron Inders Andrews. . . .

The names went on, and on, and filled the surface of the
plaque, down to the foundry which had cast it.

Pace. That name was there, and how it had gotten there, whether they had used an old list and no one had wanted to *see* the name to take it off before they had given it to the foundry, or no one wanted to take it off at all, or both of those things . . . it was there, and an invisible was atop the whole list of workers and apprentices. He fingered the pin he wore, tempting the vision of those about him, and nodded slowly, and looked back past the encircling crowd of those who had gathered in the dark, where light still showed inside the dome and the scaffolding was coming down,

"Let's get it all done," he said, "so the sun comes up on it whole, and finished."

They moved, and all of them worked, carrying out the pieces of the scaffolding, worked even with polishing cloths and on hands and knees, cleaning up any hint of debris or stain, polishing away any mark the scaffolding itself might have made.

The lights went out, and there was only the night sky for illumination, a sky which had begun to be clear and full of stars. Those who walked here now shed echoes, and began to be hushed and careful. The sculpted face of Waden Jenks, gazing slightly upward, took on an illusory quality in the starlight, like something waiting for birth, biding, and lacking sharp edges.

Some went home to bed, a trickle which ebbed away the bystanders, and more went home nursing sore hands and exhaustion, probably to lie awake all night with aches and pains; but some stayed, and simply watched.

Herrin was one, for a time. He looked at what he had created, and listened, and it still seemed part of him, a moment he did not want to end. Gytha and Phelps were still there. He offered his hand to them finally and walked away, out through the silent gates of the dome and into the presence of Others, who had come as they often did, harming nothing.

The silence then was profound. He looked back, and stood there a time, and enjoyed the sight, the white marble dome in the starlight, the promise of the morning.

Keye's window . . . was dark.

Not at home, perhaps.

He looked aside then, and walked on up Main, occasionally flexing a shoulder, recalling that he had missed supper. He resented the human need to eat, to sleep; there was a sense of time weighing on him. The mind, which he had vowed not to anesthetize again, was still wide awake and promised to remain so, working on everything about it, alive and alert and taking no heed of a body which trembled with exhaustion and ached with cramps. He thought of the port, with Waden's guests; of Keye, with Waden; of Pace, whether *she* might have come this night and gone away unnoticed; of Gytha and Phelps; of dinner and what it was he could force his stomach to bear; of Outside and ambitions and stations and the other continent and what he should do with that and how the morning was going to be and whether it would rain; and how he could keep going if he were to go to bed without supper, whether he could force himself to have the patience for breakfast, and how long he could keep going if he skipped both—and whether Waden Jenks, in perverse humor, would not try to make little of the day and the moment and all that he had accomplished. All this poured through his mind in an endlessly recycling rush, robbing him of any hope of sleep.

He was alone on the street; it was that kind of hour, and a chill night, and sane citizens were not given to walking by night without a purpose. He passed the arch in the hedge which led onto Port Street and remarked with tired relief that there were no Outsiders about and no prospect of meeting any.

"Tell the First Citizen I expect him at the Square tomorrow morning," he told the night secretary. "Master Law," said the secretary, "the First Citizen has it in his appointments." That relieved his mind, and when he was about to walk away, "Master Law," the secretary said to him, "is it finished?"

The interest, the question itself pleased him. "Yes," he said, and walked away, suddenly possessed of an appetite.

He slept, on a moderately full stomach, in his own bed and without the wine.

And he wakened with the sense of a presence leaning over him, stared up startled into the face of Waden Jenks.

"Good morning, Artist. What a day to oversleep, eh?"

He blinked, gathering his wits, decided no one just wakened was capable of matching words with Waden, and rolled out of bed in silence, stalked off to the bath and showered and shaved while Waden waited.

"Hardly conversational," Waden complained from the other room.

"What shall I say?" He negotiated the razor past his moving lips. "People who break into rooms shouldn't expect coherent responses. What time is it?"

"Nine. I didn't want to go without you."

"Well, I wasn't sure I'd go. After all, *my* part's done."

"You're incredible."

"Meaning you don't believe me?"

"Meaning I don't."

Herrin smiled at the mirror, ducked his head, washed off and dried his face. He walked out where Waden was standing, searched the closet for clean clothes, nothing splendid, but rather his ordinary Student's Black. Waden was resplendent in gray, expensive, elegant; but he usually was.

"You know," Waden said, watching him, "that you could *have* better than that."

"I don't take care of things like that. I forget. I start to work and ruin clothes. I'm afraid I'll never achieve elegance." He pulled on trousers and pulled on his shirt and fastened the collar and the cuffs, sat down and put on socks and boots, all sober black.

"You really mean to wear that?"

"Of course I do."

"Incredible."

"I'm simply not ostentatious." He finished, stood up, and combed his hair in the room mirror . . . paused there, recalling the invisible brooch which was his private absurdity, his only ornament. He found Waden's presence intimidating in that regard, and for a moment entertained the thought that *this* day at least he should not play the joke.

No. On those terms he had to, or Waden did intimidate him. He hunted out the clothes he had dropped the night before, unclipped the brooch and stood up, smiled at Waden, clipping it to his collar. "I'm ready to go if you are. Will Keye come?"

"She's waiting outside."

"*That's* remarkable. She's always refused. Possibly a taste for the finished and not the inchoate."

"Do you suggest so?"

"Ah, I was speaking of art."

Waden smiled tautly. "Such deprecation isn't like you. *Are* you hesitant?"

"What, to offend you? Never. You thrive on it. But we're both finished now, while before, you'd achieved and I'd done nothing. *Something* stands out there now."

"Not to win Keye's attention."

Herrin laughed. "Hardly. Keye's attentions are to herself and always have been." He opened the door, stopped because there were Outsiders there. Blue-uniformed Outsiders.

"Something wrong?" Waden asked.

Half a heartbeat he hesitated, seeing the game and still finding it early in the morning for maneuvers like this. Invisibles. He wore a brooch. Waden Jenks had attendants. He stepped aside to let Waden out and closed the door. Keye was there, sitting in a chair a little distance down the hall, reading, legs crossed and nonchalant.

"Keye," he said, and she looked up, folded the book and tucked it into her pocket, rising with every evidence of delight in the day.

"Good morning," she said.

"Good morning." He looked back at Waden. The escort was still with them. He smiled, oblivious to it all, and the three of them and their invisible companions trooped down the several turns of the stairs to the main level and out, into the pleasant sunlight.

"The light is an advantage, he said.

"I should think," said Waden.

They walked across Port Street and the escort kept with them, dogging their steps. *Notice them*, Waden defied him; Herrin drew a deep breath and strode along briskly with Keye and Waden on either side of him, but in his heart he *was* disturbed, angered that Waden had found a way to anger him, a means which he had not anticipated to try to make this day less for him than it might be. Waden was Waden and there was no forgetting that. This troublesome fragment of his own reality existed to vex him—and that Waden took such pains to vex him—was in itself amusing.

Through the archway in the hedge and onto Main itself, the escort stayed; he heard them, a rustle and a crunching step on gravel and on paving. Looking down Main even from this far away he could see an unaccustomed gathering, where the dome filled the square at the heart of Kierkegaard.

His own people would be there, of course, and by the look of it, a good many citizens . . . an amazing number of citizens.

The street was virtually deserted until they reached the vicinity of the dome, and then some of the bystanders outside saw them, and the murmur went through the crowd like a breath of wind.

People moved for them, clearing them a path, and the main gateway of the dome emptied of people, as the crowd moved aside to let them pass; people flowed back again like air into a vacuum, with a little murmur of voices, but before them was quiet, such quiet that only the footfalls of those retreating echoed within the dome.

"Master Law," some whispered, and "Waden Jenks," said others; but Keye's name they did not whisper, because the ethicist was not so public; the whispers died, and left the echoes of their own steps, which slowed . . . even Herrin looked, as the others did.

Sun . . . entered here; shafts transfixed the dark and flowed over curtain-walls and marble folds, touched high surfaces and faded in low, touched the clustered heads of the crowd which hovered about the edges, the first ring, the second. . . .

And the third, where the central pillar formed itself out of the textured stone and dominated the eye. The face, sunlit, glowed, gazed into upward infinities; there was little of shadow on it. It seemed to have force in it, from inside the stone; it was hero and hope and a longing which drew at the throat and quickened the heart.

It was not Waden as he was; it was possibility. And for the first time Herrin himself saw it by daylight without the metal scaffolding which had shrouded it and let him see only a portion of it at a time. It lived, the best that Waden might be . . . and for a moment, looking on it, Waden's face took on that look, a beauty not ordinarily his; others, looking on it, had such a look—it was on Keye's face, but quickly became a frown, defensive and rejecting.

Herrin smiled, and drew in the breath he had only half taken. Smiled when Waden looked at him.

And Waden's face became Keye's, doubting. "It's remarkable, Artist."

"Walk the interior, *listen* to it, it has other dimensions, First Citizen."

Waden hesitated, then walked, walked in full circuit of the pillar, and looked at the work of the walls, let himself be drawn off into the stone curtains of the other supports and of the ring-walls. Herrin stood, and cast occasional looks at Keye, who once stared back at him, frowning uncertainly, and at the invisible escort, who had also entered here. He *knew* that they saw something remarkable, and for a moment had lost themselves in it. Waden walked temporarily unescorted; and if the escort was supposed to watch *him*, that failed too. Herrin looked beyond them, smiled in pleasure, because he saw members of his own crew, who grinned back at him.

Walking the circuit of the place, appreciating the folds and complications of it, took time. Herrin clasped his hands behind his back and waited, in the center and under everyone's eyes, until at last Waden Jenks finished his tour and came back.

Waden nodded. "Fine, very fine, Artist. But I expected that of you."

Herrin made a move of his hand toward the central pillar, the sculpted face, on which sun and time had now passed. Waden looked, for a moment surprised: the stone face had changed, acquired the smallest hint of a more somber look to come.

"It's different, isn't it?" Waden asked. The change was small and to the unfamiliar eye, deceptive. "It's *different*."

"It changes every moment that the sun touches it, with every season, every hour, with storm and morning and nightfall and every difference of the light . . . it changes. Yes."

Waden looked at it again, and at him, and reached and pressed his shoulder, standing beside him. "I chose you well. I chose you well, Artist."

"A matter of dispute, who chose whom. I don't grant you that point."

"But how do I see it? How does anyone see it, in its entirety?"

Herrin smiled. "It's for the city, First Citizen; for everyone who walks here and passes through it for years upon years, at varied hours in different seasons of his life, and for every person, different because of the schedule he keeps; different vision for anyone who cares to stand here for hours watching the changes progress. You're a moving target, Waden Jenks, a subject that won't hold still, and not the same to any two people. It's time itself I've sculpted into it, and the sun and the planet cooperate. Done in one season it had to be. It's unique, Waden Jenks."

Waden had not ceased to look at the face, which grew steadily more sober, the illusion of light within it in the process of dying now. And the living face began to take on anxiety. "What does it become? What are the changes going toward?"

"Come at another hour and see."

"I ask you, Artist. What does it become?"

"You've seen the Apollo; Dionysus is coming. It achieves that this afternoon."

"This thing could become an obsession; I'd have to sit hour after hour to know this thing in all its shapes."

"And, I suspect, season after season. Look at the time and the sun and the quality of the light, and wonder, First Citizen, what this face is. You don't live only in the Residency any more: you're here. In this form, in changing forms."

"Would I *like* all the faces?"

Herrin smiled guardedly. "No. In Dionysus . . . are moments you might not like. I've sculpted possibilities, First Citizen, potential as well as truth. Come and see."

Waden stared at him, and said nothing.

Whatever you see in it," Herrin said, "will change."

"I'm impressed with your talent," Waden said. "I accept the gift, in both its faces."

"No gift, First Citizen. You traded to get this, and you were right: it will give you duration. It's going to live; and when later ages think of the beginnings of Freedom, there'll be one image to dominate. This. All it has to do is survive, and all you have to do is protect it."

Waden sucked at his lips, as he had the habit of doing when pondering something. "Now time is my worry, is it?"

"It always was; it's your deadliest enemy."

The sober look stayed, and yielded to one of Waden's quizzical smiles. "And your ally?"

"My medium," Herrin said, and for a moment Waden's smile utterly froze.

"We remain," said Waden then, recovering the smile in all its brilliance, "complementary."

There was Keye, frowning; and the invisibles, who stood with their hands tucked into their belts looking at the place and at the crowd, and the crew, who watched them. On the fringes of the crowd were the pair no one else might see, midnight-hued and

tall and robed, skeletons at the feast—Herrin imagined wise and
unhuman eyes, baffled—and Waden's Outsiders watching them.

People did not make crowds in Kierkegaard; citizens were rational, cautious and conservative of their own Reality, avoided
masses in which they could lose their own Selves. People gathered *here*, in this shell. And suddenly, when he looked at them
in general and Waden did they began a polite applause, as people might, to express approval of something they had accepted
as real and true—something they desired.

Strangers applauded, and the sound went up into the triple
perforated dome, and echoed down again like rain. "Herrin . . ."
he heard amid it, *"Herrin,"* *"Herrin Law,"* as if his name had
become their possession too. *"Master Herrin Law."*

He smiled, sucked in the air as if sipping wine and nodded
his head in appreciation of the offering. More, he spread his arms,
seeing some of his chief apprentices near at hand, and invited
them. "Carl Gytha," he said, "Andrew Phelps. . . ." He went on
naming names, and the gathering applauded and faces grinned in
pleasure. "Were you one of them?" people asked each other, and
when one claimed to be, those standing next would all ask his
name and touch him. Theirs were names written in bronze; names
to last . . . and it was the only art which had come out of the
cloistered University into the streets of Kierkegaard.

"It's unprecedented," said Keye, gazing with analytical eye on
the chaos.

"Of course it is," said Herrin.

Waden laughed and squeezed his shoulder. *"You* are unprecedented, Artist; *now* it's unveiled, not before. That's the nature of
your art, isn't it? It's not stone you shape—time, yes, and Realities. You're dangerous, Artist. I always knew you were."

"Complementary powers, Waden Jenks." He lifted his arm toward the face, which had lost its inner glow, which began to
shadow with doubt, which led toward the other shadows of itself. *"That* . . . will be with generations to come. The weak will
emulate it; the strong will be obsessed by it—because it challenges them. You'll always be there. *Give me substance*, you
asked, and there you stand."

"I chose you well. Dispute what you will, I chose you well."
Waden grinned like a child, pulled him round and embraced him
in public, to the applause of all the crowd; and the doorways

were jammed with more people seeking to know what happened there. "Walk back with me, to the Residency. They'll give you no rest here; walk back with us and let's celebrate this thing."

Herrin hesitated; he had planned to stay, or to do something else; to talk to Gytha and Phelps, he supposed, but the crowd overwhelmed him. He nodded, agreeing, and walked with Waden, with Keye, with the escort of invisibles who suddenly organized themselves to stay with them.

At the first wall of the dome, Waden stopped and looked back, with awed reluctance, but Keye watched him, and Herrin watched him and Keye.

Then they parted the crowd and headed back the way they had come, changed, Herrin thought, as everyone who came inside that place must be changed.

No one followed them—no one would dare—but the invisibles stayed at their heels, silent as they had been from the beginning.

XX

Student: How does a person fit death into his reality, sir?

Master Law: Whose?

Student: How do you fit your own death into yours, sir?

Master Law: One has nothing to do with another.

Student: You deny the reality of death?

Master Law: (After reflection.) With all my reality.

It was a pleasant day, Waden in high spirits and prone to argue. "I find myself too tired for fine discussion," Herrin confessed.

"You've grown thin," Waden said. They sat at a table in Waden's rooms in the Residency, with exquisite tableware, Waden's ordinary set ... "*Eat* something, Herrin; you'll waste away."

"By my standards I have." Herrin leaned back, drinking tea and comfortable with a full belly. "A supper last night, a lunch today ... gluttony. I plan to increase my tolerance."

"You have to," said Keye, third in their threesome at table. "I know your habits, Herrin, and they're abominable."

He grinned pleasantly and briefly. "I fear the Residency is responsible. I find myself reluctant to bestir the whole array of kitchens and servants. It's easier in the University to go downstairs and trouble cook for sandwiches. I'll be leaving for awhile."

Waden shrugged. "Wherever you're comfortable?"

"You'll have new projects," said Keye.

He shrugged.

"What do you propose?" Waden asked.

He smiled. "I'll know when I find it."

"Ah, then you don't know."

"I suspect that I know but that it hasn't surfaced. Allow me my methods."

"You ... have no interest in exterior events?"

"What, yours?"

"Exterior events."

"*Are* there any?"

"Rhetorical question?"

"No. Inform me. What's happening with your Outsiders? Anything of interest?"

Waden shrugged and toyed with the handle of his cup, lips pursed. He looked up suddenly. "The station module is due to arrive. Past that point it begins to grow, a station, widening of the port. . . ."

"Irrevocably."

"*My* art, Herrin. Trust that I know what I'm doing."

Herrin smiled tautly.

"Ah," said Waden Jenks. "I see the thought passing. You say nothing; ergo you have very much to say. It's only on trivialities that you debate motivation. You think—using that creation out in the Square, to have some great part in *me*."

"I do. I'm very self-interested."

Waden smiled. "I'll never carry your argument for you. Only be sure I know what it is, even unspoken."

"I'd expect nothing less. So why should I bother? Mine's a nonverbal art form."

"Beware him," Keye said, chin on hand and smiling over her empty plate.

"Which of us?" asked Waden.

"Both of you."

"And you?" asked Herrin.

"I'm always wary," she said.

That had the feel of the old, the hungry days. Herrin laughed, set down his cup. "Surely," he said, "Waden, your appointments are waiting; and I'm due a rest. I'm going to walk off this excellent meal. And rest."

He tried. He left the upper hall of the Residency and walked downstairs, thought about going to his room and attempting a nap. He was tired enough to be very much tempted, but he also knew that the moment his head touched the pillow, he would begin thinking about what was in the Square or about something equally preoccupying, and he would lie awake miserable.

He walked outside, and onto the streets, and onto Main . . . alone this time. He stopped and looked at the crowd which still clustered about the dome, almost lost his taste for going there at all, ever. It gave him a sense of loss, that what had been his private possession now belonged to everyone and he could never get to it in private again.

The crew was dispersed . . . or if they were not, at least they would work together no more until he could conceive of some new idea.

But the Work had its power. It drew at him inexorably, and he strayed slowly in that unwanted direction.

"Master Law," they whispered where he passed. There was no anonymity.

"It's beautiful," some boy ventured to say to him, a breathless whisper in passing on the street, in fleeing his presence: a University Master did not converse with townsfolk, for their sakes, for their realities' sake—because theirs were so vulnerable; but someone interrupted that silence to offer opinion. The boy was not the last. There were others who called it beautiful; and some who said nothing, but just came close to him. "My father worked on it," said a freckled girl, as if that was supposed to mean something.

"Wait," he said, but she was embarrassed and ran away, and he never knew whose daughter it was.

He walked inside, and even now there were a great many people in the dome, in the outer rings. He walked into the sunlit inner chamber, where people gathered before the image.

It was the Dionysian face. A patch of sun fallen on the other side and at another angle had turned it into somber laughter, dark laughter, that expression of Waden's when he was genuinely amused.

It went on living; it possessed the chamber with a feeling which was, to one who knew Waden in that mood, not comfortable. Herrin deserted his own creation, and kept walking, shivering past shadows which had come to watch the watchers, invisibles.

Leona? he thought, turning back to see, but he could not be certain, and he kept walking, slowly, out of the dome and out of the Square, farther down Main.

People here recognized him too. The novelty of that passed and he tried simply to think in peace, disturbed and distressed that even the refuge of the streets was threatened.

On one level, he thought, he should be troubled that he could not stay there; on another, he knew why . . . that he was ready to shed that idea, to be done with it, and the persistence of it frightened him. It was Waden Jenks . . . it *was* powerful, and had to be dealt with, and now that he had created this phenomenon, he could not allow it to begin to warp *him*, and his art. Having created he had to be rid of it, erase it, get it out of his thoughts so that his mind could work.

But Waden, set in motion, was not a force easily canceled.

And what Waden did threatened him, because it came at him through his own art, and gave him no peace.

Perhaps it was the intrusion of Outsiders in Freedom which made it harder to settle himself again; an intrusion argued that events were at hand which might offer subject . . . and that bothered him, the thought that no matter what he began, something might then occur which would offer more tempting inspiration: *wait, wait,* a small voice counseled him. *Observe.*

But while he waited his mind was going to have nothing to work on, and that vacancy was acute misery; an adrenalin charge with nowhere to spend it, an ache that was physical. He could not sleep again with that vacancy in his intentions; could not; could not walk about perceiving things with his senses raw as an open wound, taking in everything about him, keeping him in the state he was in.

His course took him to the end of Main, where it became highway, and led to the Camus river. From that point he could see the river itself, which led inland and inward, back to the things he had been. He walked to the edge of it, where the highway verged it along a weed-grown bank, and the gravel thrown by wheels had made it unlovely . . . the scars of too much and too careless use; it could be better, but no one cared. He sat down there and tossed gravel in and watched the disturbance in the swift-flowing surface.

In one direction it became the Sunrise Sea, and led to the other continent of Hesse; and men were going there. Humanity on Freedom was spreading and discovering itself, and he had duty there.

In the other it was safety, Camus township, and Law's Valley.

I'd like to see them, he thought of his family, and then put it down to simple curiosity, one of those instinctual things which had outlived the usefulness it served.

He had outgrown them. It was like the crowds back there at the dome. Approbation was pleasant but it diverted. Probably they would applaud him back in Camus Township, but they would no more understand him than they ever had. It was not simply that there was no going home to what had been: there had never been anything there in the first place but his own desire for a little triumph, to be able to explain what he had done to those who had been there at his beginnings.

He laughed at himself and flung an entire handful of gravel, breaking up the surface into a cluster of pockmarks. He created the thing he wished existed, and it did, and he could look back on it—reckoning that his family did, at distance, perceive what he was, and that was the best they could do. They were, after all, no better than any others, and no less hazard: like Waden Jenks. Like Keye. He found pleasure in the crew because the crew adored him; they in fact adored the importance they gained through him. If they were really anything, truly able to rival him, they would suck him in and drink him down as readily as Waden Jenks would, given the chance.

Power was the thing. He had Waden worried; and in fact—in fact, he told himself—Waden ought to be worried about him, and about Keye, who was now feeding her own reality into Waden's ear. He comforted himself with the thought that of all humans alive who were not about to be taken in, Waden Jenks would not be—would in no wise let Keye have her way with him.

Creative ethics was Keye's field; indeed creative ethics, and Keye was busy at it. She chose Waden either because, being political herself, she comprehended him best and rejected Art, or because she knew Herrin Law and saw she was getting nowhere with him.

Keye's art had to have political power to function—as Keye saw it. *He* saw an ethic in his art which Keye had never seen.

Therefore he was greater. And sure of it.

A second handful of gravel, which startled a fish and disturbed the reality of a very small life. He smiled at the conceit. The fish knew as much of Herrin Law as most did, and it was better off that way.

He stripped some of the weeds and plaited them; his fingers

were sore from the abrasive and from the work, but he could do it as dexterously as he had on the grassy hillside overlooking his home.

His own bed would be a comfort, porridge cooking when he got up, the scrape of wooden chairs on wooden floor and the smells of everyone and everything he knew woven together and harmonious like the braid of grass.

Herrin, his mother would say, *time to get up. Did you hear?* his father would say. *He can go on and sleep;* that would be Perrin. *I get his bowl.*

He smiled, laughed a breath and stared into the water.

Trucks passed in one direction and the other, never slowed, but roared past on their own business; it was not the day for either bus, which wandered opposite directions of a loop somewhere in the outermost reaches of the Camus valley, linking village to village and all with Kierkegaard.

The river came from the high valleys, from places he had known. It was, even with the truck traffic, a pleasant place to sit.

It was the cold that moved him finally, the shift of wind which accompanied a line of clouds marching on the city, which ruffled the water and bent the weeds and persuaded him it was time to walk back. The sun was sinking. He thought of the dome, where the disquieting image would have settled toward peace. He wanted to see it, but he was drained, and it was cold, and he wanted only to go unrecognized and to stay private in his thoughts. He had achieved at least a measure of tranquility, and found he ached in his bones and that his feet and backside were cold.

He angled off toward the east, avoiding the straight of Main and Jenks Square. It happened to be the direction of the port, and his palate remembered meat pies. There, in the gathering twilight, existed a place where he could walk unremarked. All the way to the port's south gateway he thought of the pies and the strange and peaceful market.

But there was a silence when he had gotten to the wire fence and the open south gate. It was almost dark; he stood there bewildered, staring at the closed booths and wondering if he had lost track of things. He walked where there had been the smell of things good to eat and the busy commerce of invisibles . . . and there was nothing. There were occasional invisibles, robed forms which melded with the shadows and the booths and the dark, between the shops and the fence, but it was all dead; the few shapes which moved here were like insects over the corpse of the life which had existed here.

The port itself . . . lived. He looked out where a machine sat in the port, stranger than any he had ever seen, a gray monster attempting nonchalance on the soil of Freedom, where lights glared and motors whined. It was gulping down supply drums; and those drums were about to be lifted off Freedom, to something which, if he looked up, would not be visible, the size and the nature of which he did not clearly picture to himself, although he had seen pictures of ships.

Waden's. All of this belonged to Waden, and indirectly, therefore, to him, and yet he had never imagined it, or *had*, in the sense that he had conceived at least of the possibility in comprehending Waden Jenks, in that statue in Jenks Square. Like the sculpture in the Square, it took on independent life, surprising him, disquieting him.

His mind flinched back to the escort which had come with Waden, the unwelcome visitants who had walked within the dome at Jenks Square. More of them would come. His Work was great, and all those who came to Freedom's station and to Freedom itself would be drawn to it. He thought of Camden McWilliams and the Pirela weavings, and felt a slight insecurity, the apprehension of a destructive, not a creative, force, which had begun to disturb him even then. He remembered the face and the form which were safely shut in that sketchbook he had not touched after that day, that dark and overlarge figure which had occupied Waden Jenks's office as that ship occupied the port, radiating things Outside, a figment of Waden Jenks's private ambitions, which now began to have many faces.

That was what had begun to nag at him, that was the disturbance which had made these strangers unbearable to him . . . that unfinished portrait and the whole concept behind it, that . . . presence . . . in the untouched sketchbook, which was not a part of Freedom's reality, and was; and was his; and was not. It was in there, imprisoned in the leaves, reminding him of the same thing the machine out there told him—that within the ambition of Waden Jenks, and therefore within his own, was the like of Camden McWilliams and the foreign colonel who wanted him . . .

what, dead? Was that what became of enemies in the Outside? It was all full of uncertainties, things half-formed.

That was what kept at him. *Open the book,* it said, that unfinished sketch, wanting him to do something with it, interpret it, bring it the rest of the way into view of all the rest of these people, for Waden and for Keye and for the city, make them see what he saw, make their vision . . .

. . . Outward.

As his kept leading him. *Look,* look at the potential in this individual; consider the perspective of his being; look at the hazard; and the possibility; look.

See him, this invisible, this Outsider,

He wiped his mouth, which had gone dry, stared at the inspiration which was trying, combined with what sat out there in the floodlights, to rear up inside him and claim his undivided attention.

His own reality suddenly discarded the whole project of the expedition to Hesse as irrelevant—an expedition to a place which would be as rude and bare of need for art as Law's Valley; the prospect stifled him. This, on the other hand, *this* argued for seizing an opportunity before Waden Jenks could have it all his way, before Keye could work upon Waden or anyone else. Make them see *his* visions instead. . . .

Camden McWilliams. Waden had betrayed the man to his hunters, had traded that man and that information for what Waden wanted, which was the station Freedom had never had since the colony ship broke up. A second chance. And from that second chance, that station which would bring the military to Freedom— a chance to extend the grasp of Waden Jenks. To take the minds of their leaders, to divert them for his purposes . . . all these things.

Camden McWilliams, whatever else he was and whatever potential he had, became the commodity in this trade, which was being made now, for good or for ill for Freedom. That brooding black figure stayed central in his thoughts, the solitary image, dark, like the Outside; unknown, like the Outside.

He started walking toward the University, toward the studio. The port, the street, the stairs passed in a blur of other thoughts, of visions which began like fevered dreams to tumble one over the other. He forgot about supper, remembered it when he was already in the University building, and from one direction there was a soft noise of the Fellows' Hall, and in the other the stairs, and the studio.

He had no appetite for food now, not with the other hunger.

He took the stairs, the way to the studio which he had visited only infrequently of late. He walked into the studio and turned on the light. Everything was disordered as he had left it, dusty with neglect. He kicked papers this way and that, kicked some old rags aside—they were for wiping his hands from the clay. He remembered where he had left the sketchbook on the table by the bed, sat down on the rumpled sheets—no servants ever gained access here; they had never been permitted. He knew the place and the page, and opened it to that series dark with shading out of which the Outsider face stared. He had caught the expressions, the frowns, the menace, the poses of the powerful body. It was all there; he remembered.

He laid the book down and made the pages stay open, cleared a working surface on the second of the modeling tables—the first one still held models for the dome—and opened the vat by the tableside, scooped out large handfuls of wet clay, flung them onto the surface, lidded the vat and straightened, his hands already at it. He should stop, should change to his working garments—there was already clay on his black clothes—but the vision was there, now. He worked, feverish in his application, blinded by what he saw it should become if he could only get it in time.

It became. He watched it happen and loathed what he was creating, but it went on becoming, a face, features contracted as if it stared into something unapprehended, a force, which itself radiated and got nothing back. There was despair within it; there was—hate. It was citizen Harfeld's look, and his sister Perrin's; it was that of Leona Pace, that hunger which never filled itself, which stared at lost things and never-had things and ached and got nothing back.

XXI

Waden Jenks: You've taught me something.
Master Law: What, I?
Waden Jenks: That duration itself is worth the risk; and
*   that's my choice as well, Artist.*

He stopped, when his shoulders had stiffened and his arms ached from the extension and his hands hurt from working the clay. He looked at it; he had not the strength to work to completion at one sitting. That would take days and months to do as he had done the other, but the concept wanted out of him, refusing patience, promising months of effort if he lacked the stamina to go on now, in hours, to finish what vision he had. It sat rough and half-born, the essence of it there. He touched the wet clay, brushed at it tentatively and finally surrendered, dropped his hand and folded his arms on the table and rested his head on them and slept where he sat, fitfully, until he gained the strength to walk over and fall into the unmade bed—to waken finally with hands and arms painfully dry and caked thick with clay, to open his eyes and stare across the room at the creature on the table as if it were some new lover that had come into the room last night and stayed for morning. He had feared it was a dream which might fade out of reach; but it was there, and demanded, unfinished as it was, an attention he presently could not give it.

He washed, stiff-muscled and shivering in the unheated studio; dressed, because he had not taken all his clothes away to the Residency, against some time that he would want this place. He paused time and time again to stare at what he had done in the fit of last night, and it no more let him go than before, except that he had spent all his vision and was drained for the time. He knew better than to lay hands on it now, when nothing would come out true, when his hands and his eye would betray him and warp what he remembered. The vision was retreated into the distance and hands alone could not produce it or impatience force it. It was waiting. It would come back and gather force and break out in him again when he had rested. He had only to think about it and wait.

Never—he was sure—never exactly as it had been last night; those impulses, once faded, could not be recovered. He mourned over that, and paused in his intention to go downstairs to breakfast, just to look toward that disturbing face.

He laughed then at his own doubt. It had more in it than the work he had just finished, more of potential. It could be greater than what was in Jenks Square. It could become . . . far greater. He suffered another impulse to work on it, which was not an impulse he ought to follow. After breakfast; after rest; then.

People approached the door; classes were starting, he reckoned. It was daybreak; maybe someone was starting early.

The door opened. It was Waden.

"Well," Herrin said, because Waden's visits to University were normally limited to the dining hall. Outsiders were with him. Evidently that was going to be a permanent attachment. "*I* was headed downstairs."

"You've been working." Waden walked to the table, touched the clay, walked around it. Frowned and touched it again. "That's what you're doing next."

"It's far from finished."

"McWilliams. He's not like that. He's a narrow, narrow man. You make him a god."

"I've only borrowed his features. It's not McWilliams; just the shell of him."

"This is *good*."

"Of course it is."

"Did you have this in mind all along?"

"Started it last night. . . . Do you have a point, Waden? Come down to breakfast with me."

"I don't want you to do any more statues."

Herrin stood still and looked at him. "Am I to take you seriously?"

"Absolutely."

"First Citizen, you're given to bizarre humor, but this—whatever it demonstrates—is not for discussion at breakfast."

"It has rational explanation, Herrin. I'm sure you even understand it."

He thought about it. The best thing to do, he thought, was to walk out the door on the spot and give Waden's absurdity the treatment it deserved; but the doorway was occupied: invisibles stood there, Waden's escort, large men with foreign weapons. And he did see them and Waden knew that he saw them.

"You were useful," Waden said, "in creating what you did. Art's the more valuable while it's unique. If you go on creating such things, you'll eventually overshadow it. I'm telling you . . . there'll not be another. You've created something unique. *Protect it*, you said; *time is your enemy*, you said; and I believe you, Herrin."

He was cold inside and out. It was very difficult to relax and laugh, but he did so. "I recall what your art is; but do you fancy years of Keye alone? You need me more than ever, First Citizen. Look at your allies and imagine dialogue with them."

"I know," Waden said. "I agree with you on all of that. I don't want to lose you. You've accomplished a great deal. You're a powerful force; you've swallowed up Kierkegaard itself; you have people doing strange things and Kierkegaard will never be the same. But, Herrin, you've done as much as I want you to do. As much as I *want* you to do. Enjoy everything you have. Bask in your success. *Know* that you've warped a great many things about your influence, and that you'll have your duration. *Look*, they'll say for ages to come, *look* at the work of Herrin Law; he only made one, and laid down his tools and stopped, because it was a masterwork, and it was perfect. Quit while your reputation is whole. Stop at this apex of your career, and you'll challenge ages to come with what you've done; you'll have accomplished everything you ever said you wanted. *Paint*, if it suits you. Painting's not the same kind of art; your sketches are brilliant. Be rich. Teach others. Continue here as a Master. Do anything in the world you like. You want comfort—have it. You want influence—I'll give you control of the whole University. Just don't do another sculpture."

"At your asking."

"I ask this," Waden said quietly, "I *plead* with you—which I have never done with anyone and never shall again."

"Meaning that you're threatened; meaning that my art has to give way to yours, and you mean I should admit that."

"Mine is the more important, Herrin. My art guides and governs, but yours is Dionysian and dangerous. It provokes emotion; it gathers irrational responses about it; it touches and it moves, like energy itself. While your energy serves me I use it, but you've done enough. It's time to stop, Herrin, because if you go further you put yourself in conflict with me. You threaten order. And you threaten other things. I asked you to lend me duration; and now I have to be sure you don't lend it to anyone else. Like that—" He gestured toward the sculpture. *"That*, a man hunted by agencies friendly to us—"

"Your reality's becoming bent indeed if you care in the least what *they* think. If you had power you'd tell them what to think. But aren't you losing your grip on it—that the best you can do is come here and tell me *not* to create, that your reality can't withstand me and what I do? Are you that fragile, Waden Jenks? I never thought so until now."

"You misunderstand. The power is not illusory. It is *real*, Artist, and it can be used. I've told you what I want and don't want, and the fact that I can tell you is at issue here, do you see that? All you have to do is admit that I can. And think about it. And take the rational course. Leave off making statues. That's all I ask."

Herrin shook his head. "Really an excellent piece of your art, Waden. Consummate skill. I *am* intimidated. But I exist, I do what I do, and it's not to be changed."

"I understand. You won't give in, reckoning this is a bluff, that at any moment I'll let you know you've been taken." Waden reached to the table beside him, took up dried clay in his fingers and crumbled it. Suddenly he grasped the table edge and upended it.

Herrin exclaimed in shock and grabbed for it; but it fell; the head hit the floor and distorted itself and he grabbed for Waden, seized up a handful of impeccable suit and headed Waden for the wall.

The Outsiders grabbed him from behind, hauled him back while he was still too shocked at the touch itself; and at the destruction; and at Waden Jenks.

"I'm very serious," Waden said. "Believe me that you *won't* go on working as you please, and I know what it is to you— admit it, admit that after all, you don't control what happens, and ask me, just ask me for what I've offered you, on my terms . . . because those are the terms you'll get. Those are the terms you have to live with. It's my world. I can make it comfortable for you—or harsh; and all you have to do to save yourself a great deal of grief is to admit that truth, and follow orders, which is all you've ever really done. Only now you have to see it and to deal with that fact. Admit it. When you can—you're quite safe."

"I'm not about to." Herrin tried to shake himself loose. It was going to take losing the rest of his composure and still he entertained the suspicion it was all farce. "We'll talk about this later. Rationally."

"No. There's no talk left. I just ask you whether you're willing to be reasonable in this. That's all."

"Oh, well, I agree."

"You're lying of course, I know. Humor me, you think, try eventually to move me. No. I'm leaving now, Herrin. I've borrowed these troops from the port; they don't have the reluctance in some regards anyone else in Kierkegaard would have. Others wouldn't lay a hand on you, but they will. They'll see to it that you can't use that talent of yours again. You see, I also deal with the material as well as the mind; and by the material—on the mind. I don't want him killed—understand me well—I just want it assured he won't make any more statues. Physically. Herrin, I don't want it this way."

"Then you've already lost control."

"It's not a game, Herrin; not a debate: I'm leaving. And if you ask me and I know you've come to my Reality, Herrin, you can get out of this." Waden walked to the door, waited, looked back. "Herrin?"

He shook his head, suddenly made up his mind and jerked loose, headed for Waden in the intent of getting to him, the head, the center of it; a hand grasped his arm, dragging at him and he spun, elbowed for a belly and rammed his free hand for a throat, but they hauled at his arms again. There was no one in the doorway; the door closed, in fact leaving him with them, and a blow slammed into his midsection in the instant he looked.

He threw his whole body into it, rammed his feet into one of them, twisted with manic force and threw one of them over, came down on that one and rammed a freed forearm into his face. A blow dazed him, sent his vision red and black, and he tried to heave himself to his feet, met a body and heaved his weight into it. The body and a table went over, and they went on hitting him, over and over again, until his balance left him and he hit the floor on hip and shoulder. "Don't kill him," one reminded the others. "Don't risk killing him." One trod on his arm, and a boot came down on his hand, smashed down on it repeatedly. He tried to protect himself, but they had him, rolled him on his face and smashed the other hand. He had not, to his knowledge, made a sound—did then, cried out from the pain and lost all his organization to resist the blows that came at him and the blurred figures which swarmed over him. He curled up when they had let him go. Even that instinctual move came hard, muscles twitching without coordination, some paralyzed. One of them kicked him in the belly and he could not prevent it.

They walked away then. He lay aching on the concrete floor and heard the door open and close. He moved his arms and tried to move his legs and to lift his head. His stomach started heaving, dry heaves that racked torn muscles from chest to groin. He tried to push his right hand against the floor and there was both pain and numbness. He saw the hand in front of him distorted beyond human form, hauled the left arm from under his ribs and went sick with the pain as wrist and fingers ground under him, that hand distorted like the other. He moaned to himself, tried again and again to roll onto his elbow to get an arm under him while his stomach spasmed. He collapsed, tried it again, finally sat up and tucked his wounded hands under his arms, rocking and grimacing against the pain that washed over him in blurring waves.

He saw himself finally. He saw himself sitting in a room where enemies could come back and find him, to hurt him further or simply to stare. He saw himself faced with the need to go outside, a Master of the University, who had to go maimed into public view and face the people who had feared him and the people who had relied on him for their own realities, and the students he had taught and most of all Waden Jenks and Keye Lynn. He shuddered, swallowed down another spasm and could not stop shivering. He tried to get up, finally made it, still doubled over, and reached the wall to lean on.

Had to go out. There was nowhere to go and nowhere to stay. He hurt, and he could not straighten, could not even change the clothes which were smeared with clay and dust and blood. He tried, ineffectually, to straighten the studio . . . gathered up the sketchbook which had been stepped on, clenching his teeth against the waves of sickness. Tried. There was no saving the clay; it was ruined, and he did not want to look at it. He managed finally to stand with his back against the wall, though it hurt, managed to catch his breath.

Waden's reality. They came now, the Outsiders, whenever they would; and wherever they would . . . Waden's doing. Waden had meant this—always meant this.

His eyes stung; he wept, and pushed from the wall to the doorway, managed finally with his ruined hand to reach the latch and to open it.

No one saw him, down the hall and down the stairs. They looked at first, but he flinched and they flinched from seeing him.

He fell on the steps outside. It was a moment before he could recover from the impact, and some had started toward him, but when he looked up at them and they looked at him, they pretended they had been going somewhere else, because he had fallen from more than the height of the steps, and he knew it and they knew it. It was a matter outside their realities. He gathered himself up finally, and leaned against the wall for a time until he could walk.

He did so, then, because he ached and walking seemed to make the ache less, or it distracted him, or it was the only reality he had left, simple motion to evidence life. He was no longer sure.

XXII

Waden Jenks: Freedom is my beginning, not my limit.
Master Law: We once talked of hubris.
Waden Jenks: And discounted it.

He kept walking, a slow, a public process . . . incredible how long it took just to go the length of the building unsupported; or to try the next distance. He went the opposite way from the Residency, which was along Port Street, and necessarily toward the port, because there was no way off Port Street in this direction but that wire gate at the end. There were some students walking, three, four meetings to endure; but they passed without evidencing that they saw. He walked bent, because of the pain, and when he would reach a place where there was a surface to lean on he would rest. He was not, at present, rational, and knew it, but standing still hurt, and he was too ashamed to sit down. He had no idea where he was going, only where he refused to go, which was to Waden Jenks, or to the center of Kierkegaard where people could see him, or the University where he had to face people he had taught and people he had directed.

The port gateway was ahead; he did not want that either, but when he stopped, swaying on his feet and subconsciously reckoning how long he could stand without falling and how much strength he had . . . he conceived of himself wandering mindlessly back and forth, back and forth on Port Street between the Residency and the University until he dropped, too dazed to do otherwise.

He went for the port. Passed the vacant gateway, walked along the edge by the fence, leaning on it when he had to, shoulder against the wooden posts and wire, scuffling through the debris the wind gathered there, among the empty drums and stacked cargo bins. The stacks were the only privacy he had found. He dropped to his knees and leaned against the wire and curled up, trying to will the pain away, winced from the sight of his hands, which were knotted and swollen, at once so deadened and so bone-deep with pain that he could not let them hang down. He kept them tucked up, so that the blood did not throb in them so much. He rocked because motion comforted, even when he lacked the strength to walk.

It got worse. And worse. The numbness of the injuries wore off, and he sat still finally, in a haze of pain; the only comfort was the chill of the concrete and he stretched out on it three quarters on his face, simply trying to last through it.

He was thirsty; that, most of all. His lips were cracked and his tongue stuck to his mouth. He thought of places he could get a drink, one by one realized they involved witnesses. There was the river itself if he could walk that far, but he could not, at present. Once there had been the port market, but he was not sure it was open; what had been going on out here at the port, what had been going on in general, he had no clear picture because until now he had not wanted to know. He wished he could think. He was, he knew on one level, functioning on animal instinct; and it was keeping him going when perhaps he was going to wake up from this and wish he had not survived it. He had no idea what else to do but what he had done.

Waden perhaps expected him to come back, to plead for shelter; he reckoned that he could still do that. A sting of anger welled up in his eyes, but he had no tears. Keye . . . was with Waden. And there was no one else. Shivers began, convulsive and painful, which jerked muscles against damaged joints, and for a long time he lay as still as he could with as little thought as he could, only counting the intervals and trying to calculate whether the spasms were increasing or decreasing.

After that came a blur of time and misery. He heard machinery, once jolted awake in the apprehension that the moving of drums might crush him, because the booming and shifting of the loaders came nearer and nearer. Then it stopped, and there was nothing for a long time, but cold. The sky clouded, and the warmth of the sun diminished, even that. He laughed at that final calamity, in which the whole universe conspired.

And he wept.

Finally, because a feverish strength had come back to him, and because the paving itself had begun to hurt his joints, he worked at getting to his feet again. Walked, following the fence which divided the port from Kierkegaard. Far across the pavement, diminished by distance, the alien machines conducted their business; and somewhere across the port, Outsiders settled into residence behind new fences. He saw the market, a scattering of small buildings and stalls, and his pulse quickened with hope, because some looked open, at least a few of them. He staggered in that direction, tried to straighten and walk normally, but he could not keep his steps from weaving.

Outsiders were among the shoppers, trading among the booths, strangers in no-color uniform; and citizens staunchly pretended not to see them while they were robbed of whatever the Outsiders wanted to carry off.

"*Look* at them," Herrin raged when an Outsider simply walked away from a merchant with a silver bracelet. "*See* them; they're *here.*" But no one did; no one seemed to see him, standing out from the market on the pavement, filthy and disheveled. Only some of the Outsiders looked his way, and he went cold under those stares, hesitating to come in at all until they had decided to go about their business.

There were booths where food was sold, and drink; Outsiders clustered there, and some owners must have left, because some booths were wholly Outsider, with an Outsider tending grill and tapping the beer and passing it out as fast as it could come.

Citizens crowded together at one booth . . . where a harried woman tried to keep up with demand, where mugs were snatched as soon as they could be poured, and Herrin thrust his way into the crowd which melted about him, tried to get to his pocket where he had a little money, but his hands could not bear the pain. "I have money," he said to the woman at the counter. "I *have* money," because he was not an invisible, who could pilfer what he wanted. "If someone could get it from my pocket. . . ." But she paid no attention to him, just mopped at the crumbs on the counter and took an order from someone else. She set the mug on the counter, amber and frothing and wet, and he reached for it in desperation, with a hand that could not hold it; the owner did not stop him. "I want my beer!" the man shouted at the owner as if she had failed to deliver his order; and Herrin got his other arm to the counter, braced the mug between his wrists and got it to his lips. The cold liquid eased his mouth and throat. He found space about him; the crowd had simply melted aside and

come at the booth from another angle, while he stood hunched
and drinking with huge, bitter swallows, all the while feeling the
heavy wet glass sliding from his awkward grip on it.

"Master Law," a female voice said, and someone touched him
gently on the arm. He looked round into Leona Pace's eyes, a
face surrounded by chestnut hair and a blue hood.

"Get away from me!" He dropped the mug, and it broke. He
lurched away and stumbled, recovered and kept going. She did
not follow. He fled, until he came to the corner of a building
and leaned there, and suddenly found himself face to face with
Outsiders.

He turned and ran, darted into another aisle, bent with pain
and uncontrolled. Walkers evaded his touch, even when he stumbled and sprawled; he lay on the concrete and they simply walked
around him.

One did not. He saw blue robes sink into a puddle of cloth,
felt a touch. *Leona*, he thought, willing finally to surrender, because he knew where he was, and what he had become. He levered himself up to look into the face that looked at him, and saw
blue skin like leather, wet and large black eyes, a nose—if it was
a nose—that curved toward something like a mouth. A hand was
on his shoulder; he began to shudder as it moved to touch his
back. It spread the midnight blue cloak, which smelled of wild
grass and country herbs and something dry and old; it enveloped
him. He stared into a face . . . nothing at all human, with that
hypnotized compulsion with which he looked at a model, the liquid black of the vast eyes, at midnight blue skin which took alien,
symmetrical folds about down-arching nose and pursed, small
mouth. The teeth were small and square, inverted lips parted upon
them as if it might speak. His arm shuddered under him and he
feared falling, being helpless with this thing, whose cloak was
about him. *Go away*, he almost said, and bit it back; he did not
see this thing, refused to see it.

Its arm across his back tightened and it pulled him over face-
up; he resisted and stopped resisting in panic. He did not see it,
refused this reality, and the other arm slid beneath his legs as it
gathered him to its breast beneath the cloak. Panic assailed him,
fear of being dropped in his pain—no one had handled him that
way, ever, in my memory; in infancy, surely, but that was not in
his memory—was not *there*, and did not happen. It was strong;

he had never comprehended ahnit as strong. It rose with him
without apparent effort, hugged his stiff body against it the more
tightly and snugged the cloak about him, enveloping him in its
scent, its color, its reality. He was aware of its powerful strides,
of the sound of sane citizens it passed, of conversations which
passed without interruption by a reality which was not theirs.

Help me, he might cry to them; but there was nothing there
when they should look, nothing that they would want to see, only
something which had been Herrin Law being swept away by
something which had nothing to do with humans.

There was no pity, not for what they did not perceive.

There was no fighting this thing, for even by fighting he lost.
He tried not to feel what was happening, nor to perceive anything about him; he retreated into his own mind, rebuilding the
reality he chose, as he chose, which ignored the pain, which denied that anything extraordinary had happened this morning, insisted that in fact he might continue to be in his bed, to sleep as
late as he chose. That if he chose to open his eyes—in his imagination he did—he would see the clay bust of Camden
McWilliams sitting on the table as it had been, where it would
go on sitting until he chose to do something with it.

His reality, as he chose to have it.

He imagined the clay under his undamaged hands, imagined
it malleable again and the face, the most perfect work he had
ever done (but he would do others) gazing into infinity with a
look of desire.

He felt the arms about him. He had gone limp within them,
yielded to the motion; it had nestled him more comfortably, and
there was dark cloth between him and the daylight, a woven fabric which scarcely admitted the declining sun; there was alien
perfume in his nostrils; there was midnight cloth against his cheek,
which rested on a bony breast as hard as the arms which enfolded him.

No, he thought to himself, trying to rebuild that warm bed in
the studio. When he was aware, his hands hurt, and his ribs did,
and the pain throbbed in rhythm with his heart and the movement of what carried him. He made no move. Horror occurred
to him, that perhaps it took him away to commit some further
pain on him, or to feed on . . . he knew nothing of ahnit, or what
they did, and there was no rationality between human and ahnit.

There is no relevancy, he insisted to himself. It and Herrin Law were not co-relevant; and what it in its reality chanced to do to Herrin Law were overlapping but unrelated events.

He could choose not to feel it; but his self-control was frayed already by the pain. And he was not strong enough to prevent it, had not even the use of his hands.

Here was an external event; he had met one or his mind had betrayed him and conjured one. It had taken him up, and the three greatest minds on Freedom, he and Waden Jenks and Keye Lynn . . . had not planned this. Only he might have caused it. He had shaped his reality; and the shape of it suddenly argued that he had not been wise.

Or that something was more powerful, which was a possibility that undid all other assumptions.

Muscles glided, even, long steps; arms shifted him for comfort, adjusted again when the position hurt his ribs and he flinched. The pain eased and it kept walking. He heard nothing more of the human voices of the port, heard rather the whisper of grass, and his heart beat the harder for realizing that they had passed beyond help and hope of intervention. The pain had ebbed and exhaustion had passed and his betraying senses were threatening to stay focused, to keep him all too aware of detail he had no wish to comprehend.

It's not here, he tried to tell himself, testing the power of his mind; but sense told him that it was striding down a steep slope; that he heard water moving and smelled it . . . they had come to the river. It might fall, or might drop him, or even fling him in, and he could not catch himself. His hands throbbed, shot pain through his marrow—it shifted its grip, was going to drop him. . . .

He stiffened and slipped, tried to catch at its shoulder and could not, his hand paralyzed; but it caught him itself and slowly, a shadow between him and the sinking sun, its cloak still tenting him, eased him to the ground. He hurled his body frantically aside, to get away, but it knelt astride him and pressed his shoulder down, keeping him from going anywhere. He twisted his head. They were beside the water, on the riverbank. He looked dazedly at the brown current, staring in that direction and trying to think, muddled with pain and longing for the water; he had hurt his hand trying to use it. The pain was starting up again, headed for misery.

The ahnit got off him, a tentative release; he stayed still, not looking at it, reasoning that if he treated it as humans always did, it might treat him as ahnit always did and simply go away.

It moved into his unfocused vision, a mere shadow, and dipped water; it *was* only a shadow—he had achieved that much. But then the shadow moved closer and obscured all his view, like dark haze in the twilight; it leaned above him and laid a cold wet hand on his brow, so that he flinched. It bathed his face with light touches of leathery thin fingers. It leaned aside and dipped up more water and repeated the process. *Let it*, Herrin thought, and tried to stare through it.

Then it picked up his hand, and he flinched and cried out from the pain. It did not let go, but eased its grip. He stared into the midnight face, the wct dark eyes. Tried, with tiny movements, to indicate he wanted to pull his hand back; even that hurt.

"You see me," it said.

It was a rumbling, nasal voice. A rock might have spoken. It chilled him and he ceased even to reason; he jerked from it and hurt himself. Quickly it let him go.

"You see me," it said again.

He stared at it, unable to unfocus it. It reached to his collar, touched the brooch he wore there, forgotten. "You see this, you see me."

And when be had almost succeeded in unfocusing again, it unpinned the brooch that he had handled daily, that he had worn in defiance of others, thinking it a vast joke. It was no-color, like the ahnit.

"See it," said the ahnit, "see me."

He could not deny it.

"I have a name," said the ahnit. "Ask it."

"I see you," he said. It was hard to say. It was suicide. He gave up hope. The ahnit uncloaked itself, unclasping the brooch at its own throat, and baring an elongate, naked head, and a robed body which hinted at unhuman structure; it spread the cloak over him, bestowing oblivion, spreading warmth over his chilled body,

"Go away," he asked it.

It stayed, a shadow in the almost dark, solid, undeniable.

"Do they all begin this way?" he asked of it.

"They?" it echoed.

"All the others who see you."

"No others."

"Leona Pace."

"They don't see. They look *at* us, but they don't see."

It had the flavor of proposition. Like a Master, it riddled him and waited response, conscious or unconscious of the irony. He searched his reason for the next Statement and suddenly found one. "My reality and yours have no meaning for each other."

"They talk about reality. They say they lose theirs and they're no longer sane."

"They obviously talk to you."

"A few words. Then no more. They try to go back; and they live between us and you. They just talk to themselves."

"From that you know how to talk to us."

"Ah. But we've *listened* for years."

"Among us." The prospect chilled. No one had known the ahnit *could* speak; or wanted to know; or cared. Humans chattered on; and ahnit—invisible—listened, going everywhere, because no one could see them. He shook his head, trying to do what the others had done, retreating to a safer oblivion; but he had been in the port, had tried to function as an invisible, and it had not saved him from shame.

Or from this.

"We've waited," said the ahnit.

It was Statement again. "For what?" he asked, playing the game Masters had played with him and he had played with Students in his turn. He became Student again. "For what, ahnit?"

"I don't know the word," it admitted. "I've never heard it." It made a sound, a guttural and hiss. "That's our word."

"That's *your* reality; it has nothing to do with mine."

"But you see me."

It was an answer. He turned it over in his mind, trying to get the better of it. Perhaps it was the pain that muddled him; perhaps there was no answer. He wanted it to let him go . . . *wanted* something, if the words would not have choked him on his own pride. The fact was there even if he kept it inside. Had always been there. He had denied it before. Tried to cancel it.

Truth was not cancelable, if there was something that could coerce him; and he had no wish to live in a world that was not of his making . . . in which Waden Jenks and his Outsiders, and now an ahnit limited his reach, and crippled him, and sat down in front of him to watch him suffer.

"What do you want?" he challenged it, on the chance it would reveal a dependency.

"You've done that already," it said, and destroyed his hope. "Do you want a drink, Herrin Law?"

It was not innocent. He looked into the approximate place of its eyes in the dark, in its dark face, and found his mouth dry and logic on the side of its reality; it *knew* what it did and how it answered him. He defied it and rolled onto his belly, crawled to the water's edge and used his broken hands to dip up the icy water, drank, muddying his sleeves and paining his hands, then awkwardly tried to get himself back to a dry spot, lay there with his head spinning, feeling feverish.

Patiently it tucked the cloak about him again, silent statement.

"Why did you bring me here?" he asked. Curiosity was always his enemy; he recognized that. It led him places better avoided.

"I rest here," it said.

Worse, and worse places. "Where, then?"

A dark, robed arm lifted, toward the west and the hills, up-river. The road ran past those hills, but there were no farms there; were no humans there.

I'll die first, he thought, but in this and in everything he had diminished confidence. "Why?" he asked.

"Where would you go?" it asked him.

He thought, shook his head and squeezed his eyes shut, pressing out tears of frustration. He looked at it again.

"I'll take you into the hills," it said. "There are means I can find there, to heal your hurts."

An end of pain, perhaps; it worked on him with that, as Waden Jenks might, and perhaps as pitilessly. "Do what you like," he said with desperate humor. "I permit it."

The ahnit relaxed its mouth and small, square teeth glinted. "Mostly," it said, "humans are insane." Herrin's heart beat shatteringly hard when he heard that, for what it implied of realities, and this reality was devastatingly strong. "Who broke your hands, Herrin Law?"

He was trembling. "Outsiders. At Waden Jenks's orders."

"Why?"

"So there would be no more statues."

"You disturbed them, didn't you?"

He rolled his eyes to keep the burning from becoming tears, but what he saw was stars and that black distance made him smaller still. "It seems," he said, carefully controlling his voice, "that raw power has its moment."

"Where would you go?" it asked. "Where do you want to go? What is there?"

He shook his head, still refusing to blink. There was nowhere. Wherever he was, what had happened to him remained.

Carefully it slipped its arms beneath him and gathered him up, wrapped as he was in its cloak. It folded him against its bony chest and he made no resistance. It walked, and chose its own way, a sure and constant movement.

XXIII

Student: *What if Others existed?*
Master Law: *Have they relevancy?*
Student: *Not to man.*
Master Law: *What if man were* their *dream?*
Student: *Sir?*
Master Law: *How would you know?*
Student: *(Silence.)*

There was a long time that he shut his eyes and yielded to the motion, and passed more and more deeply into insensibility, jolted out of it occasionally when some stitch of pain grew sharp. Then he would twist his body to ease it, faint and febrile effort, and the ahnit would shift him in its arms, seldom so much as breaking stride. Most of all he could not bear to have his hands dangle free, with the blood swelling in them, with the least brush at the swollen skin turned to agony. He turned to keep them tucked crossed on his chest and thus secure from further hurt. He trusted the steadiness of the arms which held him and the thin legs which strode almost constantly uphill. It was all dark to him. He was lost, without orientation; the river lay behind them—there was no memory of crossing the only bridge but his memory was full of gaps and he could not remember what direction they had been facing when the ahnit had pointed toward the hills. *Across* the river, he had thought; and up the river; but then he had not remembered the bridge, and he trusted nothing that he remembered.

They climbed and the climb grew steeper and steeper. Grass whispered. The breeze would have been cold if not for the ahnit's own warmth. *We shall stop soon*, he thought, reckoning that it had him now within its own country, and that it would be content.

But it kept going, and he had time for renewed fear, that it was, after all, mad, and that he was utterly lost, not knowing back from forward. In time exhaustion claimed him again and he had another dark space.

He wakened falling, and flailed wildly, hit his hand on an arm and cried out with surprised misery. His back touched earth gently, and the ahnit's strong arms let him the rest of the way down, knelt above him to touch his face and bend above him. "Rest," it said.

He slept, and wakened with the sun in his face. Waked alone, and with nothing but grass and hills about him and a rising panic at solitude. He levered himself up, squeezing tears of pain from his eyes, broken ribs aching, and his hands . . . at every change in elevation of his head he came close to passing out. Standing up was a calculated risk. He took it, swayed on his braced legs and tried to see where he was, but there were hills in all directions.

"Ahnit!" he called out, panicked and thirsty and lost. He wandered a few steps in pain, felt a pressure in his bladder and, crippled as he was, had difficulty even attending that necessity. It frightened him, in a shamed and inexpressible way, that even the privacy of his body was threatened. His knees were shaking under him. He made it back to the place where he had slept and sank down, hands tucked upward on his chest, eyes squeezed shut in misery.

There was sun for a while, and finally a whispering in the grass. He looked toward it, vaguely apprehensive, and an ahnit came striding down the hill, cloakless. By that, it was the one which had left him here: it came to him and knelt down, regarded him with wet black eyes and small, pursed mouth, midnight-skinned. It reached beneath its robes and brought out a ball of matted grasses, contained in some inner pocket; it spread it and revealed a loathsome mass of gray-green pulp. "For your hands," it said.

He was apprehensive of it, but suffered it to take the cloak on which he sat and to shred strips from it . . . finally let it take his right hand and with its three-fingered hand—two proper fingers and opposing member—begin to spread the pungent substance over it. The touch was like ice; it comforted, numbed. "Lie down," it advised him. "Lie still. Take some of it in your mouth and you will feel less."

It offered a bit to his tongue; he took it, mouth at once numbed.

In a moment more it dizzied him, and he tried to settle back. It helped him. It took his numb hand then and bound it, and while it hurt, it was a distant hurt and promised ease. "The swelling will go," it promised him. "Then I shall try to straighten the bones. And then too I will be very careful."

He drew easier breaths, drifting between here and there. It tended the other hand and probed his whole body for injury. "Ribs," he said, and with its cautious touches it exposed the bruises and salved them and bound them tightly, holding him in its arms when it had done, for the numbness had spread from his mouth to his fingertips and his toes. He breathed as well as he could, eyes shut, out of most of the pain that he had thought would never stop. Only his mouth was a misery, numb and dry; he tried to moisten his lips over and over and it seemed only worse.

It let him back then, and pillowed his head. "Rest," it seemed to whisper. He was aware of the day's warmth, of sweat trickling on him, of a lassitude too great to be borne. The sweat stopped finally, and the torment of his mouth grew worse.

"Water?" a far, alien voice asked him, rousing him enough to focus on its dark face and liquid eyes. "I can give it from my mouth to yours if you permit."

The thought made his throat contract. He shut his eyes wearily and considered the incongruency of their mutual existence, finding their situation absurd and his fastidiousness merely a shred of the old Herrin Law, before he had begun to see invisibles and lost himself. The ahnit in his silence delicately bent to his lips, pressed his jaw open, and moisture hit the back of his throat with the faint taste of the numbing medicine. He choked and swallowed, and it let him go, letting his head back again. His stomach heaved, and the ahnit held him down with a hand on his shoulder. The spasm ceased and the pain which had shot through his ribs at the convulsion ebbed. The taste lingered. He moistened his lips and found some vague relief, suffered a flash of image, himself staring vacant-eyed at a too-bright sky because he was too drugged to care. The ahnit sat between him and the sun and shaded his face.

"It hurts less," he said thickly.

And eventually, when thirst had dried his lips again: "My mouth is dry." He did not want another such experience; but misery had its bearable limit. It leaned above him again, pressed its lips to his and this time brought up a gentle trickle that did not choke him. It drew back then, but from time to time gave him more, until he protested it was enough. It kept holding him all the same; and it spoke its own language, softly, nasals and hisses, in what seemed kindly tones. He rested, finally abandoned to its gentleness, too numb to rationalize it or puzzle it, only accepting what was going to be because of what had been.

Far later in the day the ahnit took up his hand and unwrapped it. "It will hurt now," it said, and it was promising to, little prickles of feeling. The color—he focused enough to look at it—was green and livid and horrible, but the swelling was diminished. The ahnit probed it, and offered him more of the drug; he took it and settled back, trying to gather himself for the rest of it, resolved not to let the pain get through to him.

It did, and though he held out through the first tentative tug and the palpable grate of bone against bone, the subsequent splinting with knots to hold it, he moaned drunkenly on the next, and it grew worse. The ahnit ignored him, working steadily, paused when it had finished the one hand to mop the sweat from his face.

Then it started the other hand and he screamed shamelessly, sobbed and still failed to dissuade it from its work. He did not faint; it was not his good fortune. *If it were my reality*, he told himself in delirium, *I would not have it hurt.* It seemed to him grossly unfair that it did; and once: *"Waden!"* he cried out in his desperation, not knowing why he called that name, but that he was miserably, wretchedly alone. Not Keye. Waden. He sank then into a torpor in which the pain was less. He rested, occasionally disturbed by the ahnit, who held him, who from time to time gave fluid into his mouth, and kept him warm in what had begun to be night.

He was finally conscious enough to move his arm, to look at his right hand, which was swathed in fine bandage, fingers slightly curved in the splints. He was aware of the warmth of the ahnit which held his head in its robed lap, which—when he tilted his head back—rested asleep, its large eyes closed, lower lid meeting upper midway, which gave it a strange look from this nether, nightbound perspective,

The eyes opened, regarded him with wet blackness.

"I'm awake, " Herrin said hoarsely, meaning from the drug. "Does it hurt?"

"Not much."

Its paired fingers brushed his face. "Then I shall leave you a while."

He did not want it to go; he feared being left here, in the dark, but there was no reason he knew to stop it. It eased him to the ground and arranged the cloak about him, then rose and stalked away so wearily and unlike itself he could see the drain of its strength.

He lay and stared at the horizon, avoiding the sky, which made him dizzy when he looked into its starry depth; he looked toward that horizon because he judged that when the ahnit came back it would come from that direction, and he had no strength to do much else than lie where he was. All resolve had left him. Breathing itself, against the bound ribs, was a calculated effort, and the hands stopped hurting only when he found the precise angle at which he could rest them on his chest, fingers higher than his elbows. His world had gotten to that small size, only bearable on those terms.

XXIV

Waden Jenks: Does it occur to you, Herrin, that I'm using you?
Master Law: Yes.
Waden Jenks: If you were master, you wouldn't have to argue from silences. But you must.

He was on his feet when it returned, when the sun was just showing its first edge, when he had decided to climb the sunward slope to see what there was to see. Of what he expected to see—the river, the city—there was no view, just more hills; but a shadow moved, and that was the ahnit, which stopped when it seemed to have caught sight of him, and then came on, more wearily than before.

It said nothing to him; it simply stopped on the hillcrest where it met him and rummaged in the folds of its robes, offered something. He started to reach for it and the pain of moving his hand reminded him. "Food," it said, and offered a piece to his lips. He took it, and found it to be dried and vegetable; he chewed on it while the ahnit started downslope and he followed very carefully, aching and exhausted.

It sat down when it had gotten to the nest it had made in the grass; it was breathing hard. When he sat down near it, it offered another piece of vegetable to him, and he took it, guiding it with bandaged fingers. "Better," it said to him.

"Yes," he said. The pain had been enough to fill his mind; and then the absence of it. Now he discovered that both states had their limit, that the mind which was Herrin Law was going to work again; he had had his chance for oblivion and chosen otherwise, and now—now oblivion was not so easy. The sun was coming, and day, and he was alive because of that same stubbornness which had robbed him of rest and sleep in Kierkegaard . . . which, drugged, had wakened again, incorrigi-

ble. It saw ahnit, and existed here, robbed of its body's wholeness; it just kept going, and that frightened him.

"More?" the ahnit asked, offering another piece to his lips.
He used his hand entirely this time, though it hurt. "Why do you
do this?" he asked the ahnit. There it was again, the curiosity
which was his own worst enemy, wanting understanding which
another, saner, would have fled. The ahnit, wiser, gave him no
reason.

"What's your name?" he asked it finally, for it was too real
not to have one.

"Sbi." It was, to his ears, hiss more than word.

"Sbi," he echoed it. "Why, Sbi?"

"Because you see me."

"Before," he said. "Sbi, did you—meet me before? Was it
you?"

"I've met you before. I've been everywhere . . . in the University, in the Residency."

He shivered, hands tucked to his chest.

"Why," it asked, "are you blind to us?"

"I? I'm not. I see you very well. I'd be happier if I didn't."

"We exist," Sbi said.

"I know," he said. "I know that." It left him nothing else to
know.

"Do you want water?"

He thought about it; he did, but undrugged he was too fastidious.

"It disturbs you," Sbi said.

"All right," he said, and Sbi touched his chin to steady him,
leaned forward and spat just a little fluid into his mouth. Herrin
shuddered at it, and swallowed that and his nausea.

"I simply store it," Sbi said, and hawked and swallowed.

"An appalling function."

"Our nature," said Sbi.

Herrin stared at Sbi bleakly. "Your reality. I'd not choose it."

Sbi made a sound which might be anything. "Mad," it said.
"*Look*, at the sunrise. Can you or I make it last?"

"Material reality. *Man* counts where I'm concerned, and we
can't agree."

"You've made things so complicated out of things so simple.
There is the sun."

In a single flowing movement Sbi rose and walked to the hill-side, stood there with hands slightly outward and face turned to the sky . . . sat down then, and ignored him entirely, seeming rapt in thoughts.

"Sbi," Herrin said finally, and Sbi looked over a shoulder at him. "What do you intend?"

"When can you walk, Master Law? I've spent too much to carry you."

"I can walk until I have to stop," he said. "A while."

"Don't harm yourself."

"What *am* I to you?"

"Something precious."

"Why?"

Sbi stood up again. "Will you walk now?"

He considered the pain of it, and nerved himself, took the cloak in his hand and used his legs more than the ribs getting up. He used his splinted hands to put the cloak to his shoulders, and Sbi helped him. The act depressed him. He bowed his head and clumsily pulled the hood up, no different finally from other invisibles; safe—no one but Sbi would see him—even in the city no one would see him. He supposed that was where they might go.

But they walked slowly, and something of directional sense, the sun being at his back, argued that they were bound only into more hills.

I shall be further lost, he thought. He did not wholly mind, because while in one sense he was dead, he was still able to see and to feel, and the mind which sometimes frightened him with its persistence of life began to yield to its besetting fault, which was at once his talent and his curse.

"You don't care," he prodded at Sbi on short breaths, "to go back to the plain. Where are you leading?"

"Where I wish."

He accepted that. It was an answer.

"See the hills," said Sbi. "Smell the wind. I do. Do not you?"

"Yes," he said. What the ahnit asked frightened him. "How much else?"

"Tell me when you know."

It took the pose of Master. His face heated, and for a little time he thought, on the knife edge of his limited breaths and the weakness of his legs in matching strides with the ahnit. "I will tell you," he said, "when I know."

He walked, with the sun beating down on him, with the gold of the grasses and the sometime gold of flowers, and it occurred to him both that it was beautiful; and that humans did not come here—ever.

He looked to the horizon, where the hills went on and on, and it occurred to him that Freedom was full of places where humans had never been.

He thought of the port, where Kierkegaard played its dangerous games with Outsiders, and Waden sought to embrace the world; there were things Waden himself did not see, choosing his own reality, in Kierkegaard, and outward.

I could make it visible, he thought, and at once remembered: *I could have. Once.*

He stopped on the next hillside, out of breath, stood there a moment. "I'm not through," he said, when Sbi offered to help him sit down.

"Rest," said Sbi. "Time is nothing."

He started walking again, hurting and stubborn, and Sbi walked with him, until he was limping and his ribs were afire. "Stop," Sbi said, this time with force, and he did so, got down, which jarred his ribs and brought tears to his eyes. He stretched out on his back, resting with his hands where they were comfortable, on his chest, and Sbi leaned over him and stroked his brow, a strange sensation and comfortingly gentle.

"Why are you blind to us?" it whispered to him.

It had asked before. "Do you play at Master?"

"Why are you blind to us?"

"Because—" he said finally, after thinking, and this time with all earnestness, "because if we shed our ways on each other . . . what becomes of us and you, Sbi? How do we choose realities?"

"I don't," said Sbi softly.

He rolled his eyes despairingly skyward and shut them because of the sun. "You don't care," he said. "Your whole existence is of only minor concern to you."

"There was a time humans saw their way to come here to Freedom; there was a time you were so wise you could do that; and there was a time you saw us, before my years. But you took your river and built your cities and stopped seeing us; you stopped seeing each other. Why are you blind to each other, Herrin Law?"

He shook his head slowly, not liking where that question led.

"Why did they cripple you?"

"Because I saw." He lost his breath and tried to get it back, with a stinging in his eyes. He felt cold all the way to the marrow. "We're wrong, aren't we, Sbi?"

"What do you think, Master Law?"

"I don't know," he said, and blinked at the sun, which could not drive the cold away. "I don't know. Where are we going, Sbi? Where are you taking me?"

"Where you'll see more than you have."

He shivered, nodded finally, accepting the threat. Sbi slid a thin arm under his shoulders and supported him as if the cold were in the air, resting with arms about him and sleeves giving him still more warmth.

And finally he found his breath easier again and knew he had strength for more traveling. "When you're ready," he said quietly to Sbi, "I am."

Sbi's three-fingered hand feathered his cheek. "Are you so anxious?"

"I won't like it, will I?"

"I might carry you a distance."

"No," he said, and began to struggle, with Sbi's careful help, to sit, and then to stand up. He was lightheaded. It took Sbi's assistance to steady him.

Perhaps, he thought, there was much of Waden in Sbi, to persuade, to create belief—to prove, at the last, and cruelly, that he was twice taken in. Perhaps Sbi also had a Talent, and perhaps Sbi was coldblooded in his waiting, since he had learned to reason with a human Master. Waden Jenks had disturbed a long stability between man and ahnit; and he had had no small part in it.

Perhaps there was a place that Sbi would turn as Waden had.

He pursued it, to know. It was all the courage he had left.

And late, after hours of sometime walking and walking again, when the sun had gotten to the west and turned shades of gold, they crossed the final hill.

He had been ready to stop. His side hurt, and tears blurred. "I'll carry you a little distance," Sbi had offered, but he hated the thought of helplessness and kept walking, wondering deep in his muddled thoughts why of a sudden Sbi was so anxious to keep going.

Then he passed one hill and looked on the base of another mostly cut away; on a gold, pale figure which stood in a niche beneath the hill. There had been no prior hint that such existed, no prelude nor preface for it, in paths of worn places or adjacent structure. "Is that it?" Herrin asked. "Is that where we're going?"

"Come," said Sbi.

Herrin started downslope, and his knees threatened to give with him and throw him into a fall he could not afford; he hesitated, and Sbi took his arm and steadied him, descended with him, sideways steps down the slick, dusty grass until they were in the trough of the hills, until he could look close at hand at the figure sculpted there, in the recess of living stone.

It was ahnit. It was not one figure but an embrace of figures, a flowing line, a spiral . . . he moved still closer and saw ahnit faces simplified to a line which he would never have guessed, ideal of line and curve in a harmony his human eye would never have discovered, for it did not, as he would have done, try to find human traits, but made them . . . grandly other, grandly what they were. They shed tranquility, and tenderness, and, in that embrace, that spiral of figures, the taller extended a robed arm, part of the spiral, but beckoning the eye into that curve, in the flow of drapery and the touch of opposing hands. It was old; on one side the wind had blurred the details, but the feeling remained.

Herrin reached to touch it, remembered the bandages in the motion itself, and with regret, not feeling the stone, stroked it like a lover's skin. He looked up at alien form, at something so beautiful, and not his, and loss swelled up in his throat and his eyes. "Oh, Sbi," he said, "Did you have to show me this?"

There was silence; he looked back. Sbi had joined hands on breast and bowed, but straightened then and looked at him, head tilted. "You made such a thing too," said Sbi. "For all the years the city was plain and people walked without meeting . . . but you found something else."

"I *created* something else."

"No," said Sbi. "Don't you know yet what you did? It was always there. It was always real. Your skill found it."

It offended him. He was acutely conscious of the presence

above him, the alien pedestal on which he rested his hand. "So where does it exist to be found?"

Sbi folded upright hands to brow, indicating something inward, a graceful gesture.

"Then I created it," said Herrin. "It wasn't there before."

"No," said Sbi. "You only shaped the stone. You made nothing that was not before. There is one maker; but an artist only finds."

"A god, you mean. You're talking about an external event. A prime cause. You believe in that."

Sbi made a humming sound. "You believe in Herrin Law. Is that more reasonable?"

Herrin shook his head confusedly, suspecting the ahnit mocked him. And the work above him oppressed him with its power. He looked up at it, shook his head hopelessly. "Who made this?" he asked.

"Long ago," said Sbi. "Long dead. The name is lost. Few come here now, so close to your kind; the place goes untended and the grass grows. If humans came here, they couldn't see it; not minds, not eyes. But you see us."

"We share a reality," Herrin said. "That's what you saw . . . that this . . . is in common. What I made, and this."

"What you found in the stone," said Sbi. "What you found in Waden Jenks."

"I was mistaken about Waden Jenks," he said bitterly.

"Perhaps not," said Sbi.

Pain welled up in him the more strongly. He shook his head a second time and walked back from the statue, the entwined figures which beckoned his eyes into the heart of them. He made a helpless gesture, shook his head a third time, seeing things in the statue he had not seen before, the delicate work of the hands which touched, the faces which looked one almost into the other, suggesting a motion caught in intent, not completion.

"It's triangular," he said. "There should be a third. It's missing."

"No," said Sbi. "It's here."

His skin contracted. "Myself. The one who sees."

"Whoever sees," Sbi said. "You stand in the heart of them. You've become their child."

"Child." He looked at the faces, the embracing gesture, and

the contraction became a shiver. They were alien. And not. "It's *good*," he said. And in despair: "I might have attained to this. Sbi, I would have. But it's better than mine. Old as it is . . . whatever it is . . . better. Before the wind got to it. . . ."

"It was a strong thought," said Sbi, "and it will take very long to fade away entirely."

"You just leave it here to be destroyed. Alone. For no one to see."

"Humans have this land now. Only a few of us remain to watch. You walk past such things and don't see them; you don't see them."

"What do you see? Sbi, when you look at this, do you see things I don't?"

"Perhaps," said Sbi. "Perhaps not. We're alone in our discoveries. It's only such things as this that bind you and me together, by making us see what we thought we alone had found."

He went back, aware of the trap set up for the eye, and was drawn in all the same, into gentleness like Sbi's. He flexed at his hand and had no movement, reached out again to touch the stone, the shaping of a dead and three-fingered hand. He passed his fingers over the stone and felt very little of it but pain.

"Better than I," he said.

"At seeing us. But looking on it has reached something in you. It *finds*, Herrin Law."

He looked aside, his knees aching and unsteady, went back to the hillside and dropped down. He absorbed the pain dully, holding his breath, settled, holding his side with his arm, looking away from the statue which dominated the place. His eyes shed moisture, passionlessly; he hurt and he was tired and empty until he looked back at the statue which still beckoned.

Sbi had come; Sbi sat down by him. He thought of thirst and hunger when Sbi was there, needs which had begun to be obsessive with him, because he was unbearably empty, and the tremors had come back.

I shall die, he thought with a certain fatigued remoteness; and remoteness failed him. He wept, wiped his eyes with a bandaged hand, simply sat there, and Sbi edged close and patted his knee. He flinched. "I can't take from you anymore," he said. "Sbi, it . . . upsets me. I can't do it. And I'm not sure I can walk anymore. Are we done? Is this the place? If you leave me here I'm going to die."

Sbi said nothing. In time Sbi got up and walked away and Herrin watched him go, saying nothing, only despairing. There was only the statue then, aged, anomalous in the sea of hills and grass, giving no indication it had ever borne relationship to anything understandable. It offered love. It was only stone. He had sent Sbi away and Sbi had simply gone. The sun sank and the wind grew cold, and he listened to it in the grass and watched the change of light on the stone.

And then, at dark, a stronger whispering, and Sbi was back.

Herrin sat still, the wind cold on the tears on his face, and still did not hope, because whatever Sbi intended, Sbi's care of him was not sufficient to keep him alive, a simple mistake, a lack of comprehension.

Sbi came, squatted down, knees shoulder high as usual, held forth a small dead animal. "I have killed," said Sbi in a voice quivering and faint. "Herrin Law, I have killed a thing. Can you eat this?"

He considered the small furry animal, and looked from that to the distress in Sbi's eyes, sensing that the ahnit had done something on his behalf it would not, otherwise, have done. It looked, if ahnit could shed tears, as if it would. "Sbi, if we can get a fire, I'll try."

"I can make one," Sbi said, and set the little body down, stroked it as if in apology.

"It's not," Herrin asked in apprehension, "something of value to you."

"It was alive," said Sbi, ripping up grasses and digging a bare spot. "I don't wish to talk about it."

Sbi worked, furiously, hands shaking in an agitation Herrin had never seen in the ahnit . . . went off again for a prolonged time and came back again with sticks. Herrin watched in bewilderment as Sbi coaxed warmth, smoke, and then fire out of twirling wood, and then, comprehending, bestirred himself to push grass over for Sbi to add. Fire crackled in the night, a tiny tongue of brightness in the cleared circle.

"In this place," Sbi mourned, and rose. "Eat. Please, when you are done, bury it, I don't want to watch."

Sbi fled. Herrin touched the small creature it had left, edged the limp, furry body close to the flames and suffered qualms himself, not knowing what to do with it but to push it into the fire and char it into edibility.

Oh, Sbi, he thought, trying not to inhale the stench or to think about what he was doing. Sbi had probably found a place remote from the smell and the memory. He swallowed the tautness in his throat and looked past the smoke to the statue under the moon, that mimed love. *Sbi.*

XXV

Waden Jenks: The University becomes your problem. We take the Outsiders in, and you instruct them. You'll have your ambition, Keye. The University; and through it the Outsiders who come here.

Master Lynn: The shaping of ten thousand years and more . . . of all time. Quite enough for me. Unlike Herrin, I don't meddle with the present. I don't make his mistake.

Waden Jenks: I regret him.

Master Lynn: Need him? I think not.

Waden Jenks: No. I regret him. That's different.

Master Lynn: (Silence.)

Herrin buried the remains, such as his crippled hands could not handle, and the skin and bones. He had a small store of meat, which he had stripped with his teeth—his fingers could not do it—and which he dried over the coals and hoped to keep. He felt sick in one sense, but better with something in his belly. The tremors had stopped. He dug with his booted heel and dumped the pitiful scraps into the pit, then smoothed the earth with the edge of his hand, soiling the bandage, which already was soiled, with grease. "Sbi," he called, and after a time, "Sbi!"

Sbi returned, pausing before the statue in an attitude of —offering, Herrin thought, watching the gesture. Tribute, perhaps, to a forgotten artist; or to a god who believed ahnit into reality.

Eventually Sbi came to him and sank down again.

"I'm all right," Herrin said. "Maybe I can walk now."

Sbi moved close to him and put a rangy arm about him. "No. Rest."

"For what, Sbi? Where do we go? To your own kind? Or is this where we stay?"

Sbi said nothing for a moment. "No. You tell me where you want to go."

"Sbi, why are you doing this?"

"Tell me where you want to go."

"Back to the city? Is that what you want me to say?"

"Tell me where you *want* to go."

He rested against Sbi and thought a while. "The river, higher up the river. There's a town called Camus. There's a valley, up in the hills; a farm. I'd like to go there, Sbi."

"I know Camus," Sbi said.

"There," said Herrin.

"You came from this place."

"You know a great deal about me."

"Remember how long I've observed."

"I came from that valley. Yes. I want to go back there."

"All right," Sbi said.

No argument, no discussion. "You want something," Herrin surmised. "Is this it?"

"Go where you wish. I'll help you."

"Why?"

Sbi said nothing. But he had not expected answers from Sbi.

XXVI

*Waden Jenks: I informed you on Camden McWilliams; if
    you're not having success, don't look to others.*
Col. Olsen: The information was accurate beyond doubt?
*Waden Jenks: Colonel, what you doubt is at your
    discretion.*
Col. Olsen: Reasoning with you people is impossible.
*Waden Jenks: You asked for information; I gave you
    precise past patterns. You see the whole situation. You
    complain to me about your lack of success. Hardly
    reasonable.*

The pain grew less. There was a morning, a dewy, otherwise
unpleasant morning when clothing was sodden, when the bandages were somewhat looser, and Sbi so carefully began to adjust the splinting, substituting slim green wands.

"They bend," Herrin said, and clamped his lips against the
pain as he tried to flex his right hand. "Sbi, they move."

"Yes," said Sbi, although the movement was more a tremor
than voluntary. Sbi avowed to have seen it, and kept to his wrapping. "Try, whenever you think of it, try to bend the hands."

"Not much hope, is there?" Herrin asked. "There'll not be
anything close to full use of them."

"Bend them when you can."

He nodded, sat patiently while Sbi worked on his bands.
Winced sometimes, because the pain was very much still there
when some jar set it off again. Sbi chewed a bit of grass . . . in-
congruous to watch it disappear upward from stem to bearded
head and vanish; Sbi did not much eat the stems, but chewed on
them from time to time. Herrin had a bit of meat tucked away,
but would not eat it in front of Sbi, and a handful of fire-parched
grain which at least gave him no stomachache as the raw grain
did.

"Here," said Sbi, leaning forward, touched him mouth to mouth and transferred a quick burst of sugary fluid, moisture without which he could not survive. Sbi had developed a deftness about the process which he greatly appreciated, so matter-of-factly performed it failed to bother him as it might.

"It doesn't hurt much," Herrin said, trying the newly bandaged hands. "That's good, Sbi. That's good."

"I hoped so," Sbi said. Sbi plucked another heavy-headed bit of grass and stuck it in his mouth. "Come, are you ready?"

With that they broke their camp, no more than picking themselves up off the ground. They did not use fire often. Sbi had no particular use for it . . . *it crumbles*, Sbi objected of parched grain; and: *There's always something*, to the question what ahnit ate when there was no grain ripe. Not animals, Herrin reckoned, never that; he tried this and that as they walked . . . and more than once Sbi stopped him before he picked some plant. "Deadly," Sbi would say, or: "You won't like that; very bitter."

"Don't you ever eat in the city?" Herrin wondered once.

"I fancy beer," said Sbi, "and cake."

Herrin thought of both and suffered. Of a sudden he thought of porridge, and cold mornings and warm beds; of sights and scents and sounds which came back together and had to do with home.

And that afternoon they came to the Camus valley, overlooking the town he remembered.

"It's there," he exclaimed; "it's *there*, Sbi."

And he started down the hill, tired as he was, remembering where a road was which led to home.

XXVII

John Ree: They say he's in the city. One of the invisibles.

Andrew Phelps: (looking about) We shouldn't talk about this.

John Ree: I'll tell you. we've hunted. Apprentice Phelps, I've hunted.

Andrew Phelps: Among them?

John Ree: Wherever he might be. Wherever.

The house was there, as he recalled, bare boards one with the color of the earth, a corrugated plastic roof . . . they did not even get the building slabs they had down in Camus. The windows were lighted in the evening. There was no better time to come home.

Herrin stopped on the hillside, in the midst of a step, and looked back at Sbi, who had stopped on the hillcrest. Ungainly, alien, robes flapping in the slight breeze; Sbi just stood, whether sad or otherwise Herrin could not tell. And then he thought of the midnight cloth he himself wore, the cloak, the bandages, which he had taken on him like a brand, which no one put off once on.

He shed the cloak and took it back, held it in his hands toward Sbi, there in the wind, on the hill. "Good-bye," he said, which curiously had more of pain in it than leaving that brown board farmhouse had had for him long ago, because there was so much of Sbi he had missed and never seen and there was so much Sbi had done that made no sense and now never might. He thought Sbi looked sad, but with Sbi's face that was no certainty. "Good-bye," he said a second time, and left the cloak in Sbi's hands and walked back down the hill.

Faster and faster.

He was tattered and worn, his Student's Black dusty and seam-split at the arm; his face was unshaven and his hair hung in dusty threads; the bandages remained on his hands—he could not have borne the pain without them—but the color was obscured by grease and dirt. Home . . . and cleanliness, and food, and most of all, to be what he had been. He almost ran as he approached the lighted windows and the door. *"Hello!"* he called, to make them listen, "Hello!" He reached the wooden door and hit it with his elbow, and listened in agonized excitement as chairs moved inside, as familiar furniture scraped on a familiar wooden floor and steps crossed to the door.

"Who's there?" It was his father's voice.

"It's Herrin," he cried. "Father, it's Herrin, home."

The door opened, a rattling of the latch, swung inward. His father was in the doorway, his mother beyond, both grayed and older than he remembered; he crossed the threshold, opened his arms although they had never had the habit of touching him, and if they embraced him it would hurt him—he would bear the pain of his ribs to ease that ache inside.

"What happened?" his father asked, looking frightened. "Where did you come from?"

"I'd like a drink. Something to eat."

They looked at him in evident disturbance. He stood still, letting them sort it out slowly, trying to remember as he had always remembered, that they thought differently and less deeply than he. After a moment his mother drew back a chair at the table in front of the door and joined his father who was busy in the small kitchen at the left of the table, virtually one room with the bedroom on the right.

It was small; it was poor; there was so little here that had changed over the years, except there was a new rug on the floor, and it was far newer and brighter than anything else in the room. Dishes rattled comfortingly. Even the feel of the chair was right, the table under his elbows what he remembered it felt like. There was the place on the other side of the door where his bed had stood. A plow leaned there now, probably waiting sharpening. Perrin's bed was still there, beyond theirs. It *smelled* right, the whole house, as it had always smelled; there was something about the spices they cooked with, that no one in the Residency kitchens and no one in University had the knack of. Food had always tasted better here.

His parents brought him a sandwich and a cup of tea, steaming hot, set it down in front of him. He took half the sandwich up in dust-crusted, bandaged hands and bit into it with a bliss that ran through his body, choked that bite down and handled the tea the same, a delicate sip of purest steaming liquid out of old, familiar dishes; for a moment he felt Sbi's lips and shuddered, and felt the old china again.

He ate, tears welling up from his eyes, because it was chill outside and warm inside, and the inside of him was coming to match it, filled with food and comfort. He could not eat all of it, could not possibly. And that seemed bliss beyond compare, to know that he need not be hungry, or thirsty.

Only then, his belly full to hurting, he began to notice the silence and their eyes, which waited for him, as they had waited in years long before, knowing that reasoning with him was not easy or often possible, on their level. The world had changed; they had not. He looked back at them, frightened by that old silence.

"What happened?" his father asked a second time. They were still waiting for that precise question. "Where did you come from?"

"Kierkegaard. I walked."

Silence. They stared at his face, not his hands, fixedly at his face, without expression on their own beyond a residual fear.

"I've come home," he said.

They said nothing to that.

"Why did you walk?" his mother asked.

"I've quit the University. Mother, there are Outsiders there. The First Citizen is bringing them in. I can't stay there. I don't want to stay there the way things are getting to be."

Fear. He still picked that up in the expressions. And something else, a deeper reserve.

"I need a bath," he said.

Without a word his mother nodded toward the back of the house where the bathroom was, where an old pump produced water with slow patience.

"I'm going to stay," he said.

"Heard you're a great artist, a University Master," his father said.

"Was," he said. "I quit."

There were nods, nothing of warmth, nothing of comfort in his presence.

"I've stopped all that. I don't belong to the University. I have nothing to do with it any longer. I want to stay here, to farm."

Nothing. Their faces were like a wall, shutting him out.

"Perrin's moved out," he asked, "has she?"

Silence.

"Is she here, then?"

"Perrin's dead," his mother said. It hit him in the stomach. Fantasies collapsed, a structure of new beginnings he had imagined with Perrin, an intent to do otherwise than he had done, a half-formed longing to enjoy a closeness he had thrown away without ever knowing it.

"What happened?" he asked.

"She couldn't be you. She killed herself the year you left. Everyone talked about you. Everyone was proud of you. Even when you were gone she had no place for herself. Except here. And that wasn't good enough."

He sat motionless.

"She left a note," his father said. "She said she had never had anything important. It was all for you, for University."

His eyes stung. He stared across the room at the wall while his parents quietly, together, rose from the table and took the dishes back to the kitchen. The tears slipped and slid down his face. He was not sure why, because he did not particularly feel them, more than that stinging and a leaden spot in his stomach which might as likely be the sandwich on an abused digestion, far more food than he should have eaten all at once.

"You're important," his mother said, drying her hands by the counter. "We heard all the way in Camus about that big statue, about how you're the most important man in the University. You can't want to live in Camus."

"I'm not that, anymore." He held up his bandaged hands. "*I had an accident*. It's all right to say something about it. I can't work anymore, not like that. I've come home to do a different kind of work."

There was dead silence. His parents stood there and stared bleakly at him. After a moment his father shrugged and walked over to the fireside where evening coals were left. "You'll make something important here in Camus . . . better you should go down to the town and work there. There's nothing up here for you."

"You're not listening to me."

"Mind like yours . . . I suppose you've come out here to start a whole new branch of the University. A whole new way. But that's nothing to us."

"Perrin was ours," his mother said. "Perrin was ours. We understood Perrin and she understood us. She wanted so much she didn't have. It wasn't fair. Perrin was *ours*. Nothing was fair with her. She hated Camus after you'd gone. Talked about Kierkegaard. Wanted to come to University. Couldn't. She wasn't talented like you. That was the way of everything, wasn't it? You're going to start to work in Camus now. What are you going to build there?"

"They're wrong," he said. He stammered on the words. "Everything, everything is *wrong*. They broke my hands, you hear me? I've *walked* to this house from Kierkegaard. They've brought in Outsiders from off the planet and they're doing things that are going to change everything and no one sees it. Do you know, these Outsiders pilfer, too? Right off the tables in the market, they walk away and people pretend they don't see because that's what they're supposed to do, and they play the game, but it's a hole to nowhere . . . those goods don't turn up in market again, they don't come back to Kierkegaard, not even to this *world*. It goes out from here. We've opened the door on something that isn't small enough for us. We *think* we know what's real and we don't. It's all a structure that's operable only if we all believe it."

They moved, his mother drying her hands which were already dry, and his father walking back to the kitchen counter as if he had business there.

"They're wrong," Herrin said again. "I've been through the system and I've taught in the system and I know the structure of the whole thing and it's wrong."

"Long wet autumn," his father said to his mother. "I think we've got to expect a cold winter."

"Father," Herrin said. "Mother?"

"Leaves have gone dark," his mother said. She looked through to the wall, still wiping her hands on the towel. "I think it's time to pull some of those tubers, take a look at them."

"Might."

"Can't afford a ground freeze. Could come any morning." She seemed to shrink, a slight shiver.

"Mother?"

There was no answer. They started putting away the dishes. Herrin sat, hands on the table, with the sandwich lying undigestible in his belly. He sat and watched in silence as they began stirring about the evening routine, the complaints about the quality of the wood for keeping the fire at night; the reminder about the kitchen fire and the old argument about the temperature in the room, something played for him, and in his absence. He watched, hungry for the sights and the sounds, nonparticipant. He rose finally when they were about to go to bed and searched out a towel and filled it with food, got a bottle for water and filled it from the kitchen tub; while they settled into bed he entered the bath, pawed through things until he found a razor, and soap, and he searched the closet for clean clothes, but his father was smaller than he and there was nothing of his own left. Just Perrin's things, still hanging there. He closed the door and snatched up the things he had pilfered, hastened past his parents' bed in the main room and out through the door.

He left it open, ran, stumbling and blind with tears. "Sbi," he called out, but he had said good-bye to the ahnit, had turned Sbi away. "Sbi," he wept, and ran up the hill clutching the bundles in his arms.

A shadow met him just the other side, Sbi's tall shape, Sbi's scent, Sbi's enfolding arms, which took him in, gently comforting. He wept, long; Sbi sat down with him on the grassy hillside and simply held him.

"They stopped seeing me," he said.

"Yes," said Sbi. "I feared so."

He drew another breath, wiped nose and eyes with the back of his bandaged hand, blinked in the grit it left. "I pilfered things I could use."

"Good," said Sbi.

"I want to leave this place," he said.

"Yes," said Sbi, and rose, keeping an arm about him to help him. Something warm settled about his shoulders, the cloak Sbi had kept waiting for him. "Where shall we go now?"

He shook his head. "I don't know. I don't know."

Sbi picked up the bundles of toweling, and laid an arm again about his shoulders. "Come. Out of the wind at least."

He came, settled where Sbi wished, a place still not out of Law's Valley, nor far enough from the house for his liking; but rocks sheltered it from the wind and he could sit down next Sbi and curl up with knees and elbows inside the midnight cloak.

There was dew the next morning too, but at least they were not hungry as well as cold and wet. Herrin breakfasted on parched grain and a bit of cheese . . . he offered a bit of bread to Sbi, but Sbi would not take it, for whatever reason. And he drank from the jar, the merest sip, which Sbi watched silently.

They packed up then. The house would have been visible, he thought, if he climbed the hill; he could have looked down on his father and mother's house by daylight . . . had he just walked up the rise. He would not. Sbi wove grass braids with great dexterity and bound up the bundles he had to carry. "Here," said Sbi. "We might go to Camus and pilfer a basket, but until we do. . . ."

"Not Camus," Herrin said. He leaned against the rock and hitched the grass rope to his shoulder, a weight on his hand for the instant, which hurt despite the splints.

"Where?" Sbi asked again.

He shook his head. "I don't care." He looked up, looked at Sbi's face, recalling that last night he had deserted Sbi. Sbi had waited. Dismissed, had simply sat down outside the house and waited last night. His own predictability disturbed him. All that he did assumed the nature of a pattern of Sbi's choosing. Sbi's reality.

"What do you want?" he asked of Sbi again. "You stay with me . . . why?"

No answer. He looked at the morning-lit face, the black, wet eyes, and found the morning bitter cold.

"Do what you like this time," he told Sbi. "Go to your own kind; I'll come with you, if that's what you ultimately want."

Sbi's lips pursed in one of those unreadable expressions. "That would be a far walk, Master Law."

"Where are your kind? Where do you live? What do you do with your lives?"

Silence.

"Sbi, what do you want from me?"

Again silence, which was like what his mother and father had done to him, and he did not find it comfortable. But Sbi put out an arm and embraced him very gently, beginning to walk from where they had camped. "I'll tell you," said Sbi, "that there are very few of us now. You brought us disease. Disease went where humans never have, into the far hills. We died in great numbers; but you never saw. It was a significant fact to us; but it wasn't real to you. We used to live in the hills, but we yielded up this valley. We were in awe of you . . . once. But I am educated in your University; and you never saw me. *That's* why we came, to learn the things you know."

He walked, not looking at Sbi, finding Sbi's embracing arm a heavier and heavier weight as they descended the hill. "What will you do with those things you know?"

Silence.

"Sbi, is that it? That you stay with me . . . because you think I can teach you something? Is that what you want from me?"

"No," Sbi said.

"What then?"

Silence. They walked the level ground now, making their way across the fields in the direction Sbi chose, back the way they had come into the pocket valley. Herrin thought, tried to reason, kept turning back to the thought of ahnit *in* the University, invisible in the halls. In the Residency. In the dome in the Square, where others had started seeing them.

Sbi embraced him still, keeping him warm, keeping him close. So Waden had done to him, lulling his suspicions, using his weakness to bypass his reason. That Sbi was doing so seemed only reasonable. There would be a time that Sbi had extracted all the use possible from him, but for the moment it was a convenient source of help. The difficult thing, he decided, was knowing when to pull away, when to elude such users before they had their chance to harm him.

But he did not know where to go.

The size of what Sbi wanted, he reckoned, had to be measured in terms of the discomfort Sbi was willing to tolerate to get it; and what Sbi wanted had to do with his own will, his own consent, or something beyond the physical, because anything other than that, Sbi could do.

He tried to reason around an alien mind, and there was no

reason; he tried to reason what he himself wanted, which was formless. Mostly he was not afraid of the world when he was with Sbi; he was only afraid of Sbi, and that limited things to a visible, bearable quantity.

That day, Sbi led him out of the valley and again into the hills. Sbi stopped whenever he grew tired, and comforted him and kept him warm, which was the limit of what he asked. It was limbo, and Sbi seemed patient with it.

He slept that night in Sbi's arms, his belly comforted with pilfered food, his misery somewhat less than it had been; he thought again and again, half-sleeping, what pains Sbi had taken with him, and what inconvenience Sbi suffered, and he wondered.

Sbi hated him, possibly, for what he had made the ahnit do, in taking that small life.

But then the ahnit was not capable of killing him and he did not easily imagine that Sbi meant to do something *to* him.

To do something *with* him, undoubtedly. Whatever use he had left in him that appealed to an alien mind. He thought of his own work in the heart of Kierkegaard, and of the lonely pair of figures in the hills which Sbi had so wanted him to see, and neither made sense.

Sbi's hand massaged his back, over tense muscles. "Pain, Master Law?"

"No." The voice had startled him. He had not known the ahnit was awake. It disturbed him and he tried to relax, while Sbi's hand massaged a spot which was particularly tense.

"You haven't slept much."

"Nor have you."

"I don't sleep as much as you."

"Oh," he said, and shut his eyes again and accepted the comfort, tired and puzzled at once.

"Master Law," said Sbi, "why did they cripple you?"

He stiffened all over. It was the Statement again; it was never, to Sbi's satisfaction, answered.

"I don't know, Sbi. What is it that I don't see?"

Silence.

"And how could you know?" he asked. "You weren't there. You don't *know* Waden Jenks. How am I missing the answer?"

Silence.

"Waden—couldn't bear a rival. He warned me so."

"Why?"

"Why what?"

"Either. Why warn you?"

He thought about it. "It wasn't rational, was it?"

Silence.

It lay at the center of what he did not want to think about. He lay still, staring into the dark. "Sbi. Where do you want me to go? What do you want?"

Silence.

"Whatever you want," he said, "I'll do it. I don't see anything else. I don't see anywhere else. You don't make sense to me. I don't know why you're out here or why you bother or what you want. What is it?"

Silence.

"Sbi."

More silence. He grew distraught. Sbi patted him gently, as if trying to soothe him to sleep.

"Let me alone." He scrambled up, pushing with his hands, which hurt him, and stalked off close to striking at something, his bound ribs not giving him air enough. He stopped, staring out across the plains and finding nothing on the horizon but grass and night-bound sky, and stars, which belonged to strangers, the vast Outside, which went on and on, challenging illusions.

Suddenly he was afraid. He looked back, half expecting to find Sbi gone, or near him. Sbi simply waited.

And that did not wholly comfort him either.

XXVIII

Master Lynn: Where were you?
Waden Jenks: Where I chose. Is that your concern?
Master Lynn: You were out there again. In the Square.
Consider your appearance. You pay homage to that
thing. Your curiosity has you, not you it.
Waden Jenks: I find its counsel superior.
Master Lynn: He was your enemy. Do you consider that?
Waden Jenks: Are you my friend?
Master Lynn: Is anyone, Waden Jenks?

There was no particular direction. Sbi walked east, this day, and sat down after a time, munching a grass stem, and seemed content to sit. Herrin lay down full length on his back and stared at the clouds drifting, fleecy white and far, with such a weight on his mind that it seemed apt to break.

"Sbi," he said at last, "teach me."

"Teach you what, Master Law?"

"My name is Herrin."

"Herrin. Teach you what?"

"What reality is."

"What do you see?"

"Sky."

"What do you feel?"

"Pain, Sbi."

"Both are real."

"Whose reality?"

"Everyone's."

"What," he snorted, having finally discovered Sbi's depth, "*everyone's* forever and however far? That's hardly reasonable."

"Throughout all the universe."

"You're mad."

Silence.

"How can external events be real to you, Sbi?"

"I feel them."

It angered him. In frustration he slammed his hand against the ground and rolled a defiant look at Sbi, with tears of pain blurring his eyes. "You tell me you felt that."

"Yes. All the universe did."

Sbi proposed an insanity. He retreated from it, simply stared at the clouds.

"I've taught you," said Sbi, "all I know."

"You mean that I'm not able to perceive it."

"Where shall we go, Herrin?"

He bit down on his lip, thought, trying to draw connections through the maze of Sbi's logic. He gave up. "How long are you prepared to sit here, Sbi?"

"Is this where you wish to be, then?"

"What does it matter what I want?"

Silence.

"Sbi, I was wrong. I've spent my life being wrong. What can I do about it?"

Silence. For the first time he understood that answer. He turned on his side and looked at Sbi, who sat chewing on another grass stem. His heart was beating harder. "What were you waiting for all those years in the city? For me? For someone who could see you?"

"Yes.

"And what difference does it make whether I see you?"

Silence.

"It makes a great deal of difference, doesn't it, Sbi?"

"What do you think?"

"That it makes everything wrong. That the whole world is crazy and I'm sane. Where does that leave me, Sbi?"

"Invisible. Like me."

He found breathing difficult, not alone from the bandage. He pushed himself up on his elbow. "You had to let me go back to my own house to find that out."

"I had no idea what would happen. Reality is not in my control. Nor are you."

"You'll wander all over Sartre taking care of me if that's what I decide, is that so?"

"I will stay with you, yes. And keep you from harm if I can."

"Why?"

Sbi sucked in the grain-bearing head and chewed it. "Because I want to. Because when you struck your hand I had the pain, Herrin."

"I could ask you; I could ask you question after question and when I got close to what I really want to know you'd say nothing."

"The important questions are for you to answer. It is, after all, your world that's in jeopardy; mine is long past that."

"Why were you among us?"

"If someone had destroyed your world, would you not have an interest in those who had done so?"

"They *did*. And I don't want to go back. I don't want to see them again or be seen."

Sbi simply stared at him.

There was no relief for the silence, none. He sat up with his bandaged hands in his lap and contemplated them, flexed his hands slightly against the splints and bit his lip at the pain which won him no great degree of movement.

"Who broke your hands, Herrin Law?"

He shut his eyes, weary of the repeated question.

"Why?" Sbi asked inevitably.

He shook his head slowly, drew a breath which suddenly stopped in his throat. His eyes unfocused. He thought to Fellows' Hall, a certain evening, and a conceit which had gripped them both, him and Waden. "I'd begun to see *you*. I'd begun to see things the way they were; and Waden was never dull. I think he saw too, Sbi. I think he did. He *does*. Sbi, I'm going back."

"Yes," said Sbi.

He had reached for the bundles of toweling and grass rope which were all his possessions; and suddenly he caught Sbi's expression, and Sbi's tone, and it was not the same as when he had proposed going to the valley. Then there had been disappointment, vague reluctance. Now it was different.

"You've pushed me to this," he said, wrapping his arms about the bundles and staring at Sbi. "Sbi, have I guessed enough of what you want? Or do you go on the way you have?"

"I don't know that you're right," Sbi said. "But your logic seems irrefutable save by Waden Jenks. I will tell you what I want, Herrin. I have found it: a human who can see. I'll tell you what I've waited for all these years as you say . . . to learn what that human will do, when he sees. But one thing frightens me: what those who don't see will do to him."

"They won't be *able* to see me," he said, disliking Sbi's proposition. But he thought about it. "There are the Outsiders, aren't there? And they see."

"To my observation—yes."

He sank down off his heels and frowned with the pain and with the fear the pain set in him. He stared straight before him and thought about it for a long while."

"Now it's hiding," he said finally.

"How, hiding?"

"Before, I was surviving. Now it's hiding, staying up here in the hills. Now I don't go back because I'm afraid. Or if I don't go back I *am* afraid." He rolled a glance at Sbi. "You're good; you've had the better of me. You set it all up. Located the best of us . . . studied how to intervene. You had your best chance when I came out of the University and worked in the open. Then you could get to me. Accosted me in the dark that night, on Port Street. That *was* you. Drove Leona Pace over the edge. Came back to plague me. Worked at me—constantly."

"Yes," said Sbi.

"Now I should go back to the city. Now I should take on Waden Jenks and finish drawing him into this."

"Yes.

"Why, Sbi?"

"Our survival."

"Reasonable," he said, trying at least to admire the artistry of it.

"What are you going to do?"

He shook his head. "Surrender Freedom to your manipulation? That's what you've set me up to do, isn't it? Me, and Waden Jenks; one of us set against the other . . . myself, taken out of influence; and on the other hand given the chance to change the world. I'm one of the invisibles. It occurs to me that murder is possible for one of us. That I can push Waden over the edge . . . I can do that, because I've nothing to lose, have I? Or I can sit here in the hills and know that the greatest thing I ever did fitted your purpose."

"All that humans have done is bent around us, Herrin Law. The way you live, the pains you take to ignore us, the insanity which claims some of you . . . are these things spontaneous? Were you ever—reasonable?"

He stared at the horizon, colder and colder. "No," he said.

"Herrin. I'll go *with* you. I'm concerned for you."

He thought of the statue in the hills; of a small dead creature in Sbi's hands; of Sbi's hands caressing what Sbi had killed.

Of his parents going about their business not seeing him.

He rested his face against the back of his hand, wiped at the left eye. "So, well, tell me this, Sbi, what do you expect to happen?"

"I don't know. But it will be of human choosing, and my choosing, both, my friend. Both at once. Is it not reasonable?"

It was, as Sbi said, reasonable. "I've taught students," Herrin said. "I thought I knew, and thought I saw, and I taught. For them, I'm going back, and Waden . . . I don't know about Waden." He struggled to his feet, started to bend for his belongings again, but Sbi anticipated him and caught them up.

"It's not far," Sbi said.

He had guessed that too, that Sbi had brought him generally in the direction Sbi wanted him to go.

XXIX

Waden Jenks: Do you know what frightens me most in the world, Herrin? Not dying. Discovering—that I'm solitary; that my mind is the greatest one, and that I'm damned to think things beyond expression, that I can never explain to any living being. Have you ever entertained such thoughts, Herrin?

Master Law: (Silence.)

Waden Jenks: I think you have, Herrin. And how do you answer them?

Colonel Olsen: The module's come through; the station begins its construction. Now there's a matter of the other agreements. Of supply. My aides will draw up a list of requirements.

Waden Jenks: Of no interest to me. Consult appropriate departments in the Residency.

Colonel Olsen: We find no cooperation in these departments of yours.

Waden Jenks: You intrude, colonel, we have our ways. You persist in coming in person. Use the liaisons we are training in University, that's their purpose, after all.

Colonel Olsen: Nothing you've given us has been of value; not your information; not your promises of cooperation.

Waden Jenks: Yet you remain; you and I both know you are obtaining something you desire: a base. Supplies have become important to you. Let's then admit that you want them badly and that it's a matter for my personal attention; let's adjust the price accordingly. Let's talk about agreements that keep your bureaus from disturbing us. From setting foot here.

Colonel Olsen: We have policies. . . .

Waden Jenks. They don't get you what you want.

A ship passed in the night sky, a shuttle, headed offworld. Herrin watched it go, from the hills above Kierkegaard. He looked down on the city, with its dimly lighted streets, with the bright glare of the port like a bleeding wound. He felt Sbi's presence at his elbow without needing to look. "Do you know what that was, Sbi?"

"One of the shuttles. I know. You taught us about other worlds."

"Does it occur to you that we two don't control everything?"

"Ah, Herrin, I understand more than that."

"What more, Master Sbi?"

"That somewhere among those points of light stand others who misapprehend their limits; that somewhere at this moment someone is in pain; that somewhere a life has begun; that somewhere one has ended; I feel them all tonight."

"I'm trying to feel them."

"Somewhere," said Sbi, "is someone else wrestling with dilemma. Somewhere is someone wondering the value of life itself. The universe is always asking questions."

"Somewhere," said Herrin, "someone is scared."

"Beside you, Herrin Law."

He turned and looked at the ahnit, who almost blended with the night, a shadow among shadows. A strange impulse possessed him, a melancholy; he opened his arms and embraced Sbi's alien shape, gently, because contact hurt. He had done so in his life with his parents, with his sister when they were both small; with Keye when he made love; with Waden when Waden had a public gesture to make; with the workers when they helped him from the scaffolding . . . only those times in his life had someone touched him; and with Sbi again it was different. Sbi embraced him very gently, and he stepped back and looked at Sbi sadly. "I don't see you have any need to go down there."

"Probably you don't see," Sbi said. "In some things you're very complicated. Why did you go to your old house, Herrin Law, and to those people?"

"I don't know."

"A Master does something and confesses not to know why?"

"I wanted shelter. It didn't quite work out, did it?" Heat came to his face. "I've made that mistake several times; it brought me here. Possibly it's got hold of me again. Why else am I going down there? Stubbornness. I have some perverse desire to try it again, to talk to people I knew, to shake them till they see. I'm sure the Outsiders will see. I'm sure those who did this to me will." He thought a moment. "I'm mad, aren't I? Invisibles are. So why should you go?"

"Why did you go to your old house, and to those people?"

"Not satisfied with my answer?"

"No."

He folded his arms across his ribs and stared at all the lights. "Well, it doesn't make sense."

And after a moment: "Why go, Sbi? Answer *my* questions."

"But this is what I've lived my life for."

"What, 'this'? What *this?*"

Sbi rested a hand on his shoulder. "That you give me back my faith. That I see our destroyers have the capacity to create. For one who believes in the whole universe, to one who doesn't . . . how can I explain?"

Herrin looked up at the sky above the city.

"We've become part of it again," Sbi said.

"And if we all die, Sbi? Somewhere in your universe, somewhere out there—is there some world dying tonight?"

"Do you feel so?"

"O Sbi." He shivered, and shook his head. And started down the slope, losing sight of the city among the hills.

Sbi overtook him, a soft pacing beside him in the grass, company in the dark.

"I don't think," Sbi said, "that the port market is likely to be open. The Outsiders were unfriendly to it. And without it—invisibles will go hungry; and some will pilfer in-town and some will trade for what those pilfer; and some who are ahnit will have gone away."

"Best they should," he said glumly. He considered what he should do, what there was to say . . . to Waden Jenks.

Try reason again? He had no doubt that Waden could kill him. Likely there were Outsiders about who would never let him close enough to say anything at all. They walked among the hills a long while, back and forth among the troughs and through the sweet-smelling grass. He savored the time finally, for what it was, because of the grass and the smell and the sounds and the hills and the sky. And Sbi's presence. That too.

Then he rounded the shoulder of a hill and had a limited view of the city again, faint jewels against the dark.

And some of them were red.

"Sbi?—Sbi, what do you make of that?"

"The port," Sbi said.

"It's not fire. It's not that." The lights flashed. There was a whole cluster of them. The unwonted sight disturbed him. It was an Outsider phenomenon. He recalled the shuttles which had lifted, more activity than Freedom had ever had from Outsiders. He thought of Waden, and increasingly he was afraid—for Waden, for Keye, for all of them down there who had started to disturb more than they knew how to see.

"Let *me* go to explore this thing," Sbi said. "I know where to go, how to move and when to move. Let me go ask questions. Some of us will have seen this thing close at hand."

"No," he said at once, and started off again, hurrying. "No, we're both going. I have a place to go, too, and questions to ask, and I know where to ask them."

"A ship," said Sbi. "Herrin Law, look, see it."

Something was lifting from the port. He began to laugh, a breath of relief. "A launch, that's all. Maybe it looks like that from up here."

"No," said Sbi. "I've seen, and it doesn't."

The ship climbed, shot off with blinking lights.

And exploded.

"Sbi!"

"I see," the ahnit said.

The flower died in the heavens. Suddenly there were bursts on land, flares which curled up silent, firelit smoke that traced toward the city.

Herrin began to run, downhill. "Wait," Sbi called to him, hastening after. Herrin ran, slid, slowed when his ribs shot pain through him and shortened his breath . . . he walked then, because that was all he could do, and the bursts of fire continued, stitching their way through Kierkegaard.

"Waden's Outsiders," he mourned to Sbi. "Waden's ambitions . . ."

XXX

Colonel Olsen: (by com) That's Singularity. *You'll be gratified to know, First Citizen, that we've finally found McWilliams and his lot. So much for your information.*

Waden Jenks: (by com) Do something.

Colonel Olsen: Oh, we got him, First Citizen. That's a certainty. Only how many others are there?

Waden Jenks: (Silence).

Colonel Olsen: First Citizen, what damage to landing facilities?

Waden Jenks: (Silence.)

There were fires, in the grass, a wall of fire which swept away to the sea, a curtain of red and orange two stories high that made black skeletons of trees and bushes and glared eerily in the water of the Camus.

There were fugitives, who straggled away from the city along the Camus-Kierkegaard road, and crossed the bridge over the fire-lit waters. Some were terribly burned, in shock; some, perhaps mad, had flung themselves into the river and drifted there, dark pinwheels in the red current.

"Stop," Sbi pleaded, catching gently at Herrin's cloak. "Stop and consider."

Herrin did not, but wove his way across the concrete bridge of the Camus, past scarecrow figures headed away, past a cloaked figure who reached out hands and caught at his companion, telling Sbi something in urgent booms and hisses. Herrin delayed, wanting Sbi if Sbi wanted to stay with him—saw Sbi accept the other's cloak and fling it on, bid the other some manner of farewell, but the other ahnit, naked of the cloak, stood staring as Sbi came away to go with him. "It's bad in the city," Sbi said. "Some of the buildings are afire."

He had reckoned so. He thought of his work, vulnerable in

the center of the city, and hastened along the paved highway. It occurred to him that another burst of fire could come down on them at any time. He looked up as they walked and saw nothing but the smoke, the stars obscured.

Breath failed him finally, where the road bent from the riverside, where the buildings began and he could see the city streetlights dark as they had never been, and fire. He saw the dome, distant from him, outlined against burning, and stood there, trying to get his wind. There were no fugitives here. He could see figures beyond, but those who were running for the highway had already run. Here, from this perspective up Main from the highway, there was only himself and Sbi, Sbi a reliable, comforting presence.

"Herrin," Sbi said quietly. "Herrin, were they weapons and not some accident?"

"I think they were." He drew a deep and painful breath. "Waden said . . . of a certain man . . . that he could level the city. It's not so bad as leveled, Sbi, but it's all gone wrong; and whatever I could do—it's too late. Waden's new allies haven't helped. And I don't think my people will want this reality."

"They'll *see*."

"They'll go mad. They'll not survive this."

"I thought," said Sbi, "that ahnit had learned all the bitter things humans had to teach. I had not imagined this."

"Come on. Come on, Sbi, or go back. This can't be what you waited so long to find. Maybe I'd better go from here on my own."

"No," said Sbi, and stayed with him.

He walked slowly in the dark streets, deserted streets, with pebblestone and concrete buildings, faces all alike, eyeless black windows, open doors likewise black. Ahead of them a wall of flame burned in the city, outlining the dome and everything beyond. "It's the hedge," Herrin realized suddenly. "The hedge is burning, up by the Residency, the University. . . ."

So was a building close to them, somewhere near First and Main, beyond, the dome, a steady spiral of firelit smoke. A warehouse, perhaps, or something more tragic: apartments were everywhere.

The dome was before them. Fire showed through the perforations here and there like tears of light. There was, even here, a wound, a fall of broken stone where the outermost shell of the dome was damaged. Herrin saw it and ached, walking across the paving and up to the entry and within.

People huddled here, citizens, invisibles . . . there was no telling in the deep shadow; the dome had become a shelter. Children wept, setting off bell-like echoes, a cacophony of mourning and sad voices. Herrin walked through, and Sbi with him, past the outer, triple shell and the curtain-walls, into the central dome, where the face of Waden Jenks survived untouched. Fire provided the light through the perforations now, dim and baleful, and cast the features into torment.

Herrin shut his eyes from the sight, looked back at Sbi's hooded form, saw beyond him dark masses of refugees. His own workers would be among them. If anyone would have come here, they would have come, as they always had. Fearfully he lifted his clumsy hands, pushed back his hood, knowing well the enormity of what he was doing; but they had seen far worse tonight than an invisible's face.

"Gytha," he called out, setting off sharp echoes which shocked much of the other echo into silence. "Phelps?" And because he committed other unthinkable things: "Pace? Are you here?"

Master Law, some voice said, somewhere in the dome. There was a flood of echoes, other voices whispering it, and one calling it out . . . "Master Law!"

People came to him, some that he knew, some that he did not, and suddenly he panicked, because in the dark there was no color, and he had deceived them. They came, and near him Sbi stood, still hooded. Someone tried to take his hand, and he flinched and saved himself, looked into Carl Gytha's tear-streaked face and flung his arms about him, which hurt too. He could not make himself heard if he tried: the whole dome rang with voices. *Master Law!* the shout went up, and people surged in until they pressed on him and Gytha and someone thrust at the crowd trying to clear him room.

"Let me out," he pleaded of Gytha, of Sbi, of anyone who could hear him. He shouted into the noise and could hardly hear himself. "Let me out!" The whole place was mad and Waden Jenks's firelit face presided over it in rigid horror.

Perhaps Gytha understood. A tide started in the press which surged toward the other side of the dome, which swept him along

with Gytha's arm to protect him . . . or Sbi's . . . in the confusion
he was no longer sure. The crush compressed his ribs, threatened
his hands, and he would have fallen but for an arm which encircled his waist and pulled him.

They broke forth into the air, a spill of the crowd like a wound
bleeding forth onto the firelit paving. He had a momentary view
of the distant, dying fires of the hedge, of ancient shrubbery gone
skeletal and black as winter twigs.

"Sir," someone was saying to him, but he shook his head
dazedly, finding even breathing hard. The crowd was pouring out
after him, threatening to surround him here as well. Panic took
him and he pushed at someone with his arm, saw Gytha's anxious look directed to the outpouring crowd.

And there in shadow, a taller, hooded figure, which unhooded
itself and stood with naked head facing the crowd, which wa-
vered, which slowed. Sbi turned and purposefully came and took
him by the arm, drew him away in the moment's shock, even
away from Gytha, even from those he would have wanted to see.
He yielded to Sbi's encircling arm, walking farther up Main, slipping into what fitful shadows there were from the light of the
burning, where Second Street offered them shelter.

Herrin stopped there, sank down on the doorstep of a dark
and open doorway, his arm locked across his aching side.

"You are hurt?" Sbi asked him, touched his face with two gentle fingers, wiped sweat from him.

"Drink?" Herrin asked, for shock threatened him and somewhere—he could not even remember where—he had lost the bundles of his belongings, everything. Sbi bent and touched his lips,
transferred a mouthful of sweetish fluid to him, caressed his brow
in drawing away and regarded him with great black eyes, pursed
mouth bearing an expression of ahnit sorrow.

"Sit," Sbi wished him. "O Herrin, sit still."

"Waden," he said. "He and Keye . . . won't know what to do.
Can't know what to do. I have to go to the Residency, Sbi, and
talk to them . . . if I can help there—I have to."

He tried to get up. Sbi did not help him at first, until he had
almost made it and almost fallen, and then Sbi's arm encircled
him. A dark runner passed them, slowed, looked back and ran
on, quick steps fading. Soon there were others, straggling after.
Sbi's arm tightened protectively. "I don't trust this, Herrin."

"Come on. Come on. Let's get back to Main, into the light."

"Your species frightens me."

"Come." He walked, insisting, anxious himself until they were back on the main line of the city, with the smoldering hedge in front of them and the fire from the burning buildings still lighting the smoke which hung over the city like a reddened ceiling, casting light to all that was below it. It all looked wrong; and then he realized that he had never seen the buildings on Port Street without the façades lit. Only a few windows showed light on the Residency's uppermost floor. He could not see the University clearly, but they had emergency power over there too, as they did at the port, and it was all dark, as far as he could see.

He was afraid . . . on all sides, afraid. More runners passed them, one screaming: he thought it screamed his name, and flinched. Back at the dome they were still shouting, still in uproar, and the echoes made it like the voice of some vast single beast.

They left the concrete for the berm, which was powdered black with the burning of the hedge. Smoke obscured their vision. Fires still crackled, knee-high flames in a line down the remnant of the hedge on either side as they passed what was left of the archway and crossed onto Port Street, in front of the Residency.

The whole west end was a shambles, the roof of the fifth level caved in, making rubble of that level and the next, where he had had his rooms . . . and cracking walls beneath. The east wing, the source of the lights, stayed apparently intact, but the cracks ran there too.

I would have died here, he thought dazedly, reckoning where his rooms were. He crossed the street with Sbi close beside him. No one prevented them, no one appeared on the street or on the outside steps. The doors gaped dark and open, showing only a little light from somewhere up the interior stairs when they walked in. The desk at the entry was deserted, dusted with fallen cement and there was rubble on the floor.

"Waden?" he called aloud, and his voice echoed terrifyingly in the empty halls. Something moved, scurried, ran, stopped running in some new hiding. The skin prickled on his nape, and he felt the touch of Sbi's hand at his arm as if Sbi too were insecure. He started up the stairs, careful in the shadows and the lit-

ter of rubble. Sbi imprudently put a hand on the wooden railing and it tottered and creaked.

They came into the uppermost hall, where light showed on the right and wind from the ruined west wing came skirling in with a stinging breath of smoke. "Waden?" Herrin called again, fearing to surprise whatever guards Waden Jenks might have about him. He trod the hall carefully, toward that closed door where Waden's office was.

He called again. Something moved inside. He heard a voice, used his bandaged hand to press the latch and pushed it open.

Keye met them. She had been sitting opposite the door in the long room, and rose, and her hands came up to shield her face. She cried out: *Keye* . . . cried aloud, and Herrin reached out a hand to prevent her dissolution. "Keye," he said, but she darted— for him, he thought for the instant—and then slid past him, past Sbi, for the dark hall, out, out of his presence and the sight of him. He looked back again to the room, dazed and of half a mind to go after Keye, to stop her if he could and reason with her if there was any reason. But there was movement in the doorway beyond the ell, and Waden was there, his face quickly taking on that look that Keye's had had.

"Waden," Herrin said, before he could do what Keye had done. "What happened?"

Waden only stared at him, in frozen stillness.

"The Outsiders," Herrin said. "Waden, you see me. You see I'm not alone; you always have, haven't you? Wake up and see what's going on, Waden. The city's afire; your Outsiders have run mad. It was a lie. From the beginning, everything University set up—was a lie."

"Your reality," Waden said from dry lips. "This is your reality, Herrin Law."

He blinked, caught up in that fancy automatically, for one mind-wrenching instant that made all the walls shimmer, that rearranged everything and sent it inside out. "No," he said, and reached his clumsy hand for Sbi, for a blue cloak, drawing the ahnit forward, into Waden's full view. "Real as I am, Waden; real as you are, as the fire is real. You can't cancel it."

"It's yours," Waden said bleakly. "I would not have imagined this. I failed to kill you, and you did this."

"You're mad," Herrin said. "*I* did this? I did nothing of it. It was your doing, from the first time you brought them here. What ship attacked us? Was it *Singularity*? Or your own allies?"

"Whatever you imagine," Waden said. It was a lost voice, a lost look in his eyes, which spilled tears. "I should have had them finish you; I *needed* you. That should have warned me where control was . . . really. O Herrin, your revenge is excessive. Remake it. Revise it."

It was an ugly thing to see, a hurtful thing. He closed his eyes to it and looked again, saw Waden still standing there, hands open, face vulnerable. "I wish I could, Waden. But you see—" He sought, half humorous, some logic to devastate logic, to break through to Waden Jenks. "—I let it go. The reality I imagined was a reality that would become universal, that would exist on its own in time and space . . . that I myself could no longer interrupt, *that's* what I imagined. And now the world has to take its course under those terms. Sbi exists. We'll all see each other. We'll listen to the ahnit and see them. We'll not do things the way they were; we'll not teach dialectic to shut down minds; we'll not *be* what we were. And I can't stop it. That's what I imagined."

Waden's eyes were terrible. Not vacant but following that speculation, gazing into possibilities. "What do you imagine that *I'll* do?"

"I imagine . . . that you'll do things that are natural to this reality. Whatever they are. I can't stop it. You can't. We have no more control, Waden. Nor do the ahnit. We share this world and it comes down to that. It has its own momentum and it can't be canceled."

Waden turned away, fending himself from the door frame, walked back into the dark.

"Waden," Herrin objected.

"You created paradox." Waden's voice came back out of the dark. "And you abdicated. You've done this, Herrin Law, you've done this."

Herrin started forward, to go in, but Sbi's arm intervened. "No," Sbi said. "No, don't go in there. Come with me. Please, come away from this place. *Now.*"

Herrin shivered, and stopped, lost in his own paradox.

"Come," Sbi insisted, and drew him away, out the hall be-

yond the ell, into the corridor outside. He remembered Keye then
and looked to all the shadows, half expecting her to be there.

Sbi drew him farther, toward the stairs, and down them, where
the wind skirled in with the taint of smoke.

He hurried, wakened by the shock of the wind, hastened to
be quit of the place and Waden's fancies, his reasoning which
threatened to swallow up all the things he thought he knew, down
and down the rubble-littered stairs, deeper and deeper into the
dark. His breath came short. Sbi gripped his arm to keep him
steady and kept his pace.

Something started in the dark; a running shape pelted from
the floor below to the staircase and down again.

"Keye!" he shouted, making echoes. "Wait for me! Listen to
me!"

The steps retreated, defying his control, racing away into their
own reality.

And wood splintered, and crashed down in hideous echoes.

"Keye!"

He ran, almost fell himself at the turn where the railing had
broken, where it hung now, swinging in the almost dark, and a
black-clad body sprawled on the steps below.

Sbi made to protest his haste, but he caught his balance against
the wall and made the last turn down, dropped to his knees to
try to lift Keye from where she had fallen on her belly, touched
her shoulders and realized his hands had no strength to lift . . .
and that lifting might kill her. He patted her shoulder helplessly,
leaned to see her side-turned face, at once overwhelmed to realize life in the eyes and a breath beneath his hand.

"Keye. It's Herrin, Keye."

"No, it isn't," the answer came. Her lips hardly moved and
the sound was no more than a whisper. "I cancel all your realities. And my own. And my own. And all the world."

The lips stopped moving and the breath sighed out. In an instant more the body diminished, a looseness very different from
sleep.

He drew his hand back, recoiled slowly. He had never seen
death happen. It seemed to take something of himself away too.

But the universe stayed.

Because, he wondered, he had indeed abdicated it? Because

there was paradox, and he had made it? He knelt there, fixed in the thought, and Sbi gathered him to his feet and drew him away.

"Herrin," Sbi said when they were outside, on the steps and in the wind. Sbi hugged him tightly, till the ribs hurt, and set him against the wall and touched his face. "Herrin. Don't lose me. Listen to me."

"I hear you," he said. It was hard to speak, to pull his reason back from that logic that tried to claim it. He focused on Sbi's dark eyes, on Sbi's expressions which he had *learned* to read, and which he had never understood; on a remote monument which had stood before man had come to Freedom.

He looked up, above the door.

Man, said the inscription, *is the measure of all things.*

"No," he said.

There was a lightening in the east, down the ruins of Port Street, and it showed the University intact at least from this perspective. And the city . . . always before, the hedge had separated the Residency and the Outsiders from the city. A view was open now which had never been there before.

It was not fire in the east, but the sun coming up. He gazed at it in fixation, thinking that the world had turned, and that the greater forces in the Universe existed, as the star came up visible over the curve of the world with no one able to affect it.

There was argument which might prevail against that reasoning; he refused to pursue it, only staring toward the daylight as toward a goal that had to be won. "It's there," he said to Sbi. It was a horrid dawn, smoke-fouled and revealing ugliness, but it was the light, and it was coming.

XXXI

Herrin Law: Why go, Sbi? Answer my questions.
Sbi: But this is what I've lived my life for.
Herrin Law: What, "this" What this?
Sbi: That you give me back my faith. That I see our
  destroyers have the capacity to create. For one who
  believes in the whole universe—to one who
  doesn't . . . how can I explain? . . . We've become part
  of it again.

The sun kept coming, making real the cindered hedge, the building which still poured a twisting column of black smoke, but a wind had come with the dawn, and began to sweep away what had hung there. They walked into the long expanse of Main together, cloaked but unhooded, both of them. There was debris left from the night, paper, scraps of clothing, wisps of cindery stuff like pieces of the night left over, which blew lightly along the pavement and collected in the gutters and against the lee side of buildings.

And there were some who lay dead. Herrin stopped by each, to know whether this man, this woman, this boy or girl was in fact dead, or lay in shock, or unconscious, or helpless with injury. *He* had lain helpless once and only Sbi had seen him. But he and Sbi this time found none to help.

They saw the living, too, furtive shapes which flitted from building to building, shadow to shadow in the dawn, some cloaked and some in the plain clothes of citizens who had once—before the night—been sanely blind.

There were ahnit, a few, who glided among the shadows, and one who came out from a vacant doorway and, seeing Sbi, spoke a few quiet hisses and clicks. Sbi answered. That one slowly unhooded and walked away down the steps and around the corner and on through the streets.

"Tlhai," Sbi said. "Tlhai says some of us have stayed. That

C. J. Cherryh

some have taken the injured away. That some have gone away, but may be back. We have the habit of this city. I think they'll come."

Herrin looked about him, at two or three of the human fugitives who had stood to stare in the shadows, but when he looked they ran away, and others came, and did the same.

"Stop," he called to them. They did so, some of them, three or four, some distance down intersecting Second Street. They looked at him, and seemed likely to run away. But when he walked a few paces on down Main, showing no intent to force his presence on them, they drew a few paces closer.

Others came, and still others. They looked from the windows, and peered out from dark doorways. . . . They crept down steps into the daylight, their clothes stained with soot and dirt, their persons disheveled. Sbi drew closer to him, touched a hand to his back. He turned half about and saw more of them from another direction.

His heart beat in panic. He tried not to show it, but when another glance back the way they had come showed them now surrounded, he despaired of himself and of Sbi. He had felt violence, which was in Kierkegaard, like seeing invisibles; such things did not happen . . . visibly. But there was no retreat out of this reality.

"Come," he said to Sbi. Up against invisibles, one just . . . walked, quietly past. He headed the way they had been going, which must take him through some of them, and they showed no disposition to back away.

They did not stop him. They all turned to keep their eyes on him but they offered no harm. "Master Law," one said. "Master Law," others murmured, and at his back he felt others following.

More gathered. He looked aside, and back, and faced a throng of solemn faces, expectant faces, haggard with desires and fears and every sort of need.

"The city still exists," he said, meaning that Kierkegaard still had people, still had needs and life of its own, but he saw the faces which drank that in desperately and realized what he had said to them, saw hope struggling there. They wanted to hear him. Perhaps, he thought, to them he was all they could find of the authority that had defined what was. A University Master. That was what they had found. They waited for reason and the only reason he knew on their terms was paradox, that had swallowed Waden Jenks.

He could, he thought, destroy them. They came for answers and he could tell them lies.

"I've no answers for you," he said and saw that hope painfully wounded. "But—" He reached for something, anything to give them, because the need was so unbearably intense in that place, all about him, stifling breath. "—I know other things. I've seen a place . . . not so far from here . . . where other things exist. Where I've seen what's old. There's a place in the hills where a statue stands, all alone, but it goes on existing in the middle of all that grass and the bare hills. It goes on saying what someone created it to say, all by itself. I've seen it. It has to do with love, and it's out there all alone with no one to see it. Listen to me," he said, but there was no need to say: the crowd grew, in utter silence, with eyes fixed painfully fast on him. He needed no loud voice. "We were just born. All of us. We were new, this morning. We've gotten through the night and the sun's up even though we doubted it. Ahnit are here, and we are, and maybe Outsiders will come back. I think there'll not be another attack; there was a man named McWilliams who had cause for what he did . . . I think it was he, but there are other Outsiders, and likely they've done for him. There's not been another attack, so someone out there either went away or couldn't do it again. Go out in the city. Find everyone who *can* see, and tell them the sun's come up. And it's all right to see."

The silence hung there. He walked away through it, his hand resting on Sbi's shoulder, and people moved aside for them. Some flitted away; some followed still.

"Master Law," said a man. It was Andrew Phelps. Herrin's heart wrenched, recalling the mob, but Phelps's look was sane, and anxious. "They said you were hurt," Phelps said.

He reached out his bandaged hand, very carefully, and Phelps only let it rest on his, not closing on it. "It hurt," he said. "But it's not so much, Phelps. They thought it was, but I don't. Can you find the others? Can you bring them? There's more than statues to make here. There's so much to *do*, Phelps."

Andrew Phelps stood there, his mouth trembling, and looking as he used to when he had gotten some new instruction . . . a moment to take it in, and then an eagerness. "To *do*, Master Law?"

Herrin nodded. "Sir," Phelps said, and gently gave back his hand, and hesitated a moment before he hastened off.

"Master Law!" they began to shout from house to house, and people came and did nothing more than touch him. He flinched at first, and then understood himself as a reality they wanted to test; some touched Sbi as well, and fled in dismay. The touches became more and more, until it seemed everyone who met them on the street wanted to lay hands on them, and Herrin grew afraid, because even little jolts could cause him pain, and one of them might try to take hold of him too violently. Hysteria swirled about him.

"Sbi," he said. "Sbi, stay close to me."

"They chase their own fears," Sbi said. "Ah, Herrin, I'm afraid for you."

They had come to the dome itself, where others poured out, and more gathered from other streets. They pressed in, each pushing the others, until one did seize him, embraced him, sobbing; and another did, and they hurt him, for all that Sbi tried to fend them off: they were as anxious to touch Sbi as well. *"No!"* Herrin shouted, and somehow and by someone he found himself shielded, was taken by yet another pair of arms, but gently this time, protecting him, and a second pair, while people he knew were suddenly between him and the crowd, making a ring about him and giving him and Sbi a place to stand.

Gytha was there, and John Ree. And more and more of them. There was Andrew Phelps, shouldering his way through the quietened crowd. From another quarter a blue-robed figure pressed forward, hood flung back from brown hair and broad, freckled face. Herrin saw her, held out his hand fearing someone would stop her. "Leona Pace," others of the workers murmured, and hands went out to pat her shoulders as she passed. "Apprentice Pace," others whispered, because the name was one set in bronze, ahead of all the others. Herrin put his arm about her, looked into a plain face, radiant through tears. Others cheered her. There were others who unhooded. Here and there in the crowd someone recognized someone lost and found again. There were names cried out, and tears shed. Some hunted those they remembered. "Mari," a man called out forlornly. "Mari, are you there, too?" Whether an invisible named Mari heard, Herrin did not learn, the noise of the crowd was too great, the press too insistent.

"Be still," he called out, close to exhaustion, and others tried to pass the word, a confusion of shouting until finally the noise was subdued.

"Ask them to sit down," Sbi said. It was inspiration. He did so, and uncertainly the word passed and people settled where they were on the pavement, disheveled and exhausted, many holding onto one another. Herrin still stood, and Sbi, and Gytha and Phelps and Pace.

He talked to them, in a silence finally so profound he need not shout. He said much that he had said before. "Don't be afraid," he told them, "Not of the ahnit, not of Outsiders, not of anything. Clean up your homes, clean up the streets, share with anyone who needs food or help. If anyone lacks shelter . . . there are rooms in the University; there's shelter there. See everything. *Do* something when something needs doing. That's all."

He was very tired. He thought if he did not get away soon he would fall down where he stood, senseless. His vision kept going gray and the sunlight blurred. He put out a hand for Sbi's help, and Sbi put an arm about him. So did someone else, and the others cleared a way for him, parting the crowd, which stayed seated, all but the narrow aisle dislodged. There was a murmuring, and finally others gained their feet, a wave spreading from that disruption, but they did not rush in on him.

They found him a place to rest, on the steps of a building. People brought blankets, and food and drink, and he sat there with Sbi and Leona Pace and Gytha and some of the others, but most of the workers were out cleaning up the Square, out investigating shelter in the University, wherever he sent them. Some went to the port to order the market opened.

He slept a time, cradled in Sbi's safe arms, and, on the edge of sleep, knew that people walked soft-footed up to be sure that he was all right. Those with him hushed them and sent them away.

But finally there was a thunder in the heavens, and cries filled the streets. Herrin waked and looked up. "Something's landed," Carl Gytha said. "Master Law, we have to get you out of here."

"No," he said after thinking about it. "No. They can come if they like." He laid his head down again against Sbi, and shut his eyes.

And in time the visitors came, blue-clad, walking with rifles down the center of Main. People began to come there, anxiously, betraying him by trying to protect him. He was aware of it all, still resting but with eyes open.

"Come *on*," Leona Pace pleaded with him. "Please. They'll hold them."

"No. I have no anonymity anymore. They'll have been to the Residency. They'll talk to citizens. They'll hunt the city for me, and that's no good." He stood up, brushed off their protesting hands, even Sbi's, whose advice he valued, and walked down the steps and onto the street, parting the crowd to walk out to the Outsiders.

The colonel was one, resplendent with black plastic and weapons, like the rest of them. They had lifted the weapons when he came forward, lifted them again, because his companions had insisted on following him, and standing with him, and the crowd gathered uncertainly behind.

"Master Law," the colonel said, seeming doubtful. They had met only once, and perhaps he was much changed.

"Colonel. What do you want here?"

The colonel lifted a hand, pointed back toward the Residency. "I don't make sense of the First Citizen, Master Law. He's alone. He refused to see us. Only he said something about *your* controlling things. That this was your doing."

Herrin regarded him sadly. "So you come to me for answers?"

"Do you have control in this city?"

"We're restoring order. Ask me, if you will ask things. I have the responsibility."

"We deal with you?"

"For convenience's sake, I think you might. I can deal with you."

The colonel frowned. "I'm not here to play logical games. I want order."

"No. Go back to the port. This is Kierkegaard. We invite you to come back this evening. I'll talk with you. There are so many things I want to learn, colonel."

The colonel looked uneasily beyond his shoulder, where Sbi stood.

"I am also," said Sbi, "curious. I shall be with Master Law."

"This evening," Herrin said.

The colonel hesitated, and then nodded, started to offer his hand and Herrin held up his, refusing the gesture with his bandages. The colonel stopped in consternation and looked confused for the moment. "Sir," the colonel said. "Where shall I find you this evening?"

"The University. Come there. You need no guns, colonel. There's no need."

"Sir," said the colonel, and, motioning to his companions, turned and walked back the way they had come.

A murmuring broke out around them. Herrin turned, saw the street jammed with people shoulder to shoulder, as far as he could see to the dome and all along the fronts of buildings. He was dazed by the sight and the relative silence with which they had come, lifted a hand to tell them it was all right.

They simply stood, not offering to disperse.

"Please," he said, "go on. Go tend things that need doing."

There was no panic rush this time. Some did as he said; some moved necessarily in his direction, but gave him a great deal of room, watching him the while. A few put out hands in his direction as if they would like to touch, or as if the gesture itself meant something.

He went to the University that night, and Sbi went, and another of the ahnit. There was Pace and Phelps, but Gytha stayed outside in view of the crowd. He had put on blue robes himself, as many did, and stood on the steps to keep matters calm.

"Come and go as you like," Herrin told the colonel. "Enter University. We honor all agreements that benefit us both, but we won't have weapons in the streets."

"What about the First Citizen?"

"He doesn't want to come out," Herrin said quietly. He had tried; himself, he had tried, but Waden stayed to his own refuge. "Someday, perhaps." They had buried Keye, with the rest of the dead that day, all in one sad grave. "We welcome visitors, colonel. But while you may have your port compound, once across that line, you're on our soil and in our State, and while we'll be hospitable, we'll issue the invitations. We take responsibility for ourselves, and for those who come here."

The colonel said nothing for a moment. Perhaps he remembered walking through that vast, quiet crowd outside.

"So," said Sbi, "do we—issue the invitations."

"That puts the matter," the colonel said, "in a special category. If there's native government."

"Oh," said Sbi, "there is."

The colonel did not stay long, even on the world itself. Outsiders came and went, silently building their station and dealing in trade.

There was a time that Herrin found it possible to walk the streets again unescorted. "Master Law," they would hail him there, and touch his sleeve very gently, with great reverence. He talked to them in the streets, and sometimes sat down on a step where half a hundred would gather to listen to him reason with them. Sometimes Sbi gathered crowds mixed of ahnit and human, or they reasoned together. Perhaps they did not all understand, but Herrin tried, at least, to use the simplest of things.

There was a path worn to the statue in the hills, and there were always humans and ahnit thereabouts; it was the tradition to walk, even when it became possible to use transport.

His parents came on the bus from Camus, and came sorrowfully and begged his pardon. He forgave them, even understanding that they came because he was visible again, and people asked them about him, and they could no longer pretend him away. Sbi and Leona Pace, Gytha and Phelps and John Ree . . . they knew him much better, and loved him, and so it was only a little painful to regret that his parents did not.

Harfeld died; Herrin was sorry: he would have gone to Camus to be with the old man, who had evidently wanted that, but it was too late when he heard the man was gone.

And finally Waden Jenks came, from his dark refuge in the Residency, thin and blinking in the sun, and brought by ahnit, who had finally persuaded him out. "Waden," Herrin said, and offered him an embrace, which Waden accepted, and looked in his eyes.

"It's not so bad, your reality," Waden confessed. "I've seen it . . . from the windows. I thought I would come out today."

"Good," Herrin said, laid a hand on his shoulder—the hands healed, but never quite straight—and walked with him along the street, with Sbi and the other ahnit who had brought him out. He let Waden choose the way he would walk, but knew where Waden would go, ultimately.

And Waden stood in the dome, tears running down his face

while he looked at the hero-image the morning sun made of him. There were others there, surprised by sudden visitors, but the silence was very deep.

"There are years to come," Herrin said. "There's need of you, Waden."

Waden looked at him, nodded slowly.

Herrin left him there, walked away with Sbi and the others, trusting that Waden would follow, in his own time.

PRECURSOR
by C.J. Cherryh

The Riveting Sequel to the *Foreigner* Series

The *Foreigner* novels introduced readers to the epic story of a lost human colony struggling to survive on the hostile world of the alien *atevi*. Now, in the beginning of a bold new trilogy, both human and *atevi* return to space to rebuild and rearm the ancient human space station and starship, and to make a desperate attempt to defend their shared planet from outside attack.

☐ **Hardcover Edition** 0-88677-836-0—$23.95
☐ **Paperback Edition** 0-88677-910-3—$6.99

Be sure to read the first three books in this action-packed series:

☐ **FOREIGNER** 0-88677-637-1—$6.99
☐ **INVADER** 0-88677-687-2—$6.99
☐ **INHERITOR** 0-88677-728-3—$6.99

Prices slightly higher in Canada   **DAW: 123**

Payable in U.S. funds only. No cash/COD accepted. Postage & handling: U.S./CAN. $2.75 for one book, $1.00 for each additional, not to exceed $6.75; Int'l $5.00 for one book, $1.00 each additional. We accept Visa, Amex, MC ($10.00 min.), checks ($15.00 fee for returned checks) and money orders. Call 800-788-6262 or 201-933-9292, fax 201-896-8569; refer to ad #123.

Penguin Putnam Inc.   **Bill my:** ☐Visa ☐MasterCard ☐Amex_____(expires)
P.O. Box 12289, Dept. B   Card#_____
Newark, NJ 07101-5289

Please allow 4-6 weeks for delivery.   Signature_____
Foreign and Canadian delivery 6-8 weeks.

Bill to:

Name_____

Address_____City_____

State/ZIP_____

Daytime Phone #_____

Ship to:

Name_____ Book Total $_____

Address_____ Applicable Sales Tax $_____

City_____ Postage & Handling $_____

State/Zip_____ Total Amount Due $_____

This offer subject to change without notice.

C.J. CHERRYH

Classic Series in New Omnibus Editions!

☐ THE DREAMING TREE
Journey to a transitional time in the world, as the dawn of mortal man
brings about the downfall of elven magic. But there remains one final
place untouched by human hands—the small forest of Ealdwood, in
which dwells Arafel the Sidhe. *Contains the complete duology* The
Dreamstone *and* The Tree of Swords and Jewels.
0-888677-782-8 $6.99

☐ THE FADED SUN TRILOGY
They were the mri—tall, secretive mercenary soldiers of almost un-
imaginable ability. But now, in the aftermath of war, the mri face extinction. It will be up to three individuals to retrace their galaxy-wide path
back through the millennia to reclaim the ancient world that gave them
life . . . *Contains the complete novels* Kesrith, Shon'jir, *and* Kutath.
0-88677-836-0 $6.99

☐ THE MORGAINE SAGA
Scattered through the galaxy are the time/space Gates of a vanished
alien race. They must be found and destroyed in order to preserve
the integrity of the universe. This is the task of the mysterious traveler
Morgaine . . . but will she have the power to follow her quest to its
conclusion—to the Ultimate Gate or the end of time itself? *Contains
the complete* Gate of Ivrel, Well of Shiuan, *and* Fires of Azeroth.
0-88677-877-8 $6.99

Prices slightly higher in Canada   **DAW: 121**

Payable in U.S. funds only. No cash/COD accepted. Postage & handling: U.S./CAN. $2.75 for one
book, $1.00 for each additional, not to exceed $6.75; Int'l $5.00 for one book, $1.00 each additional.
We accept Visa, Amex, MC ($10.00 min.), checks ($15.00 fee for returned checks) and money
orders. Call 800-788-6262 or 201-933-9292, fax 201-896-8569; refer to ad #121.

Penguin Putnam Inc.   **Bill my:** ☐Visa ☐MasterCard ☐Amex_____ (expires)
P.O. Box 12289, Dept. B   Card#_____
Newark, NJ 07101-5289

Please allow 4-6 weeks for delivery.   Signature_____
Foreign and Canadian delivery 6-8 weeks.

Bill to:

Name_____

Address_____City_____

State/ZIP_____

Daytime Phone #_____

Ship to:

Name_____ Book Total $_____

Address_____ Applicable Sales Tax $_____

City_____ Postage & Handling $_____

State/Zip_____ Total Amount Due $_____

This offer subject to change without notice.